ALSO BY JAMES D MCCALLISTER

NOVELS

King's Highway

Fellow Traveler

Let the Glory Pass Away

Dogs of Parsons Hollow

Dixiana

Dixiana Darling (2019)

Reconstruction of the Fables (2020)

Mansion of High Ghosts (2021)

Wando (2023)

STORIES

The Year They Canceled Christmas

Fables of the Reconstruction (2020)

The Night I Prayed to Elvis (2021)

DOWN IN
Dixiana

OMNIBUS EDITION

PART 1:
CRACKERBOX PALACE

PART 2:
THE PARTNERS

PART 3:
DOCTRINE AND RITUAL

JAMES D. MCCALLISTER

MHP
Mind Harvest Press
COLUMBIA, SC

Mind Harvest Press
PO Box 50552
Columbia SC 29250-0552
www.mindharvestpress.com
www.jamesdmccallister.com

CONTENTS

DOWN IN DIXIANA PART ONE: CRACKERBOX PALACE

DOWN IN DIXIANA PART TWO: THE PARTNERS

DOWN IN DIXIANA PART THREE: DOCTRINE AND RITUAL

PART ONE

Crackerbox Palace

Most civilized people are out of touch with reality because they confuse the world as it is with the world as they think about it, talk about it, and describe it. For on the one hand, there is the real world. And on the other, a whole system of symbols about that world which we have in our mind. These are very, very useful symbols, all civilization depends on them, but like all good things they have their disadvantages. And the principal disadvantage of symbols is that we confuse them with reality. Just as we confuse money with actual wealth, and our names about ourselves, our ideas of ourselves, our images of ourselves, with ourselves.

— ALAN WATTS

ROY AND BECKY L

Snorting, pissed, impatient; a state of grace for you, the bossman, Roy E. Pettus.

Fury is your fuel, as is the greasy, Southern breakfast you just shoveled into your gaping maw courtesy of your ancient but no less industrious grandmother. As your hands white-knuckle the steering wheel of your grandfather's Ford F-150 you belch bacon, a buttery, smoky backwash mitigated by your grandmother's mass market coffee sloshing in a travel mug. Sitting at the highway waiting to turn out from the long driveway framed by ancient crepe myrtles almost as tall as the trees of the pine barrens that stretch dense in either direction, all you can think: You ain't got time for this, in the parlance of Edgewater County, SC.

"When, when, *when*. I'm in a fudging hurry, you yokels."

You've been sitting here ready to pull out of the dirt driveway by the fallen END STATE MAINTENANCE sign onto River Ridge Road, waiting for not one, not two, but six passing vehicles, an unusual occurrence, including some tattooed beardo on a hog with ape hangers. Not as uncommon as once might have been, all this traffic, but houses are getting built in the woods to the north.

More.

People.

That's all y'all mother-fudging need.

Bad attitude. People equals customers. And for what you have in mind, the transformation of The Dixiana and all of downtown Tillman Falls, you're gonna need folks ready to empty some wallets.

After a month of being back home in Edgewater County while dealing with your wife's detox and your grandfather's estate, your simmering anger reminds how much you need to try some of this meditation your semi-cousin Button Sykes keeps yammering about in her stilted diction. Button's laid this whole rap on you about breathing, presence, stillness. Talked about a mantra. Talked about goin' *ohm,* over and over and over again, a sound that she explained to you was actually spelled AUM.

A vibration in your throat.

A silence in your mind.

A peace in your heart.

All sounds fancy enough. Maybe when you find some more time. Maybe when you figure out how to relax enough to meditate.

Relax, too, with more of that weed of hers, stuffed in the pocket vape you've started carrying around with you. A grown man. A town father. No one must know.

And last, perhaps you'll chill out once you get all this trash along the highway picked up.

Your anger swells like a presence in the truck cab. Your vision blurs. A moiré pattern of wavy lines fills the blue Carolina sky. Littering—it boggles the mind.

Breathe. Deep. Pay attention to each breath. In through the nose, out through pursed lips. Slow. Every breath its own little life—beginning, middle, end. It's Button's voice in your head. You could swear the girl's a psychic cell phone tower.

You give the pay-attention breathing a try. You pay such close attention that you don't even notice the cars finally passing, and you snap out of this hippie-dippy shit and get'r in gear, beau.

But wait—it kinda worked. You feel better.

Eh. All a bunch of BS. Silly as hell, Button, with her Eastern platitudes and new-age nonsense.

Or maybe not. Feeling better would not come unwelcome to you. You'll work on the meditation. For now, taking a hit or two off that vape ought to do the trick.

❋

As for the meditation program, Button explained to you that any little phrase or series of sounds, as she reckoned, could be used to get into a place of stillness, this trance that's like going to the brain spa. The two of you, power walking around the concrete snake of a trail by the river, a mile down from the fishing bluff where you scattered your granddaddy's ashes. You told her that you were missing your walks around the paved trail on Sedge Island; she offered you a solution. An answer for everything, Button.

Seemingly.

"Don't think too much. About it."

"How can you decide something if you don't think about it?"

"Get out of. Your own way. Let the mantra come to you."

"Sounds random."

"Some things. Can't be forced."

"I'm a doer, though. My motto's 'if it don't fit, force it'."

Waving you off. "Getting into the flow. Can't be 'forced.' But if you wish? An affirmation. Call it that. A high ideal, let's say. Allow oneself to feel the meaning behind the words. Hold that feeling in silent attention."

"But if you're not 'active' in the sense of doing—of getting somewhere—how do you hold a feeling?"

Despite claiming to be a regular power-walker, you thought she seemed winded. "When you. Pay attention. In the right way—without paying attention. Without giving everything a name. A concrescence of consciousness."

"A con—*concruh*—a do what, now?"

"A state of—um—high novelty. Within an already complex system."

"And concrete—whatever it is, that's achieved how?"

"It's not achieved. Look for coincidences. Occurrences. Synchronicity. Positive feedback from the universe."

"Just don't look too hard?"

Smiling. "Exactly, yo. Like one of those optical illusion posters. They used to sell. At Spencer's. In the mall. Most of all, stay in the moment. And if you do it right, you'll find the moment never ends."

All you know of synchronicity is the Police song from your youth. It would be stuck in your head for the rest of the day, that guitar hook. Maddening. Not the mantra you were looking for.

Later that afternoon, and against your better judgement, you broke out the laptop and logged into Facebook. It all seemed like kid stuff, this social media —all bullcrud time-wasting foolishness; in other words, your principal nemesis in life. Not to mention one of the sources of evidence about your wife's infidelity. A kinda-sorta sore spot. Needless to say.

But Button, her words ring in your head and you're paying attention to this'n that, looking for connections and patterns and syncs, signs and wonders; and the first story in your feed happened to be a YouTube video one of your Island buddies shared, just the tonic to get that earworm out of your brain: good old Buffett doing a live version of his tune, the steel drum intro of 'The Weather is Here, Wish You Were Beautiful.' You cranked it up. A happy little ditty like you'd hear on speakers at the bars and restaurants on the island.

A stinging reminder of happier times, sitting in your grandmother's house in front of the Macbook. It spoke volumes to you, that song—its otherwise innocuous lyrics holding for you now what felt like ancient and indelible truths, like an occulted text filled with subtext and twilight language that had heretofore gone right past your distracted ass. You and Creedence, tipsy and full of yourselves, dancing around to it on the Bayfront top-shelf yacht club balcony, the hot Atlantic wind blowing against your faces and bodies, her white dress flowing, the world at your feet—you, a chubby but no less helio-centric hero of a twice-told tale, a legend, both myth and myth-maker bundled into one attractive and monied package, and on your arm, a raven-haired goddess both sexy and sweet. Back before the truth of your fraudulent marriage had slapped you in the face like you imagined her lover's nuts slapping against her pale buttocks.

Ouch.

OUCH.

Remembering the debacle of reading Creedence's messages to her lover, you snapped shut the laptop in a cold, dreamlike rush of oh-no. Stumbled over to the master to change out of your damp workout stuff. Fiddled with your exercise iPod, a ten-year-old 160g model that still worked. Jamming the earbuds in, spinning the menu and hitting a Genius mix, the first song to come up?

Yeah—you guessed it. No way, right? The album version of 'The Weather is Here, Wish You Were Beautiful.' You flashed on Button's cherubic, freckled face, an eyebrow arched in recognition.

Sometimes aloud, sometimes in silence, you sang the line over and over for the rest of the day. A mantra. Doing it all wrong, probably. But the end result, all that mattered.

Relaxed. *Boo-yow.*

◉①✻

GARBAGE ALONG THE ROADSIDE, IN THE DITCH, STREWN COLORFUL AND constellation-like from the turn off all the way to the curve of the highway. Trash the likes of which you've never seen, even in an ignorant backwater like Edgewater County, where rednecks have made a generational tradition of throwing crap out of their pickup trucks. And here you sit, stoned, neither picking it up nor arranging for someone else to do so.

Burning up fossil fuels like a dope.

Trying to breathe.

You ought to know how to do that by now without being told by Button Sykes.

Enough. Get going, boy.

The garbage, receding in the rearview along with Reynolds Pettus Road, named after your grandfather in the manner all dirt roads here in the sparse, deep countryside were designated after the 9-1-1 system came into use, when the patriarchs of these patches of farmland north of Tillman Falls along the river found themselves memorialized in reflective street-sign green. You bask in the honorific glow a family street-naming conveys to the world.

Gracious sakes alive, though—the way these freaks treated their roadsides. Animals lived out here who would throw trash like this. Only last week you walked the drive and the dirt road all the way to the highway, stooping over and picking up crap with a grabber or your gloved hands. Enough exercise that you turned down Button's invitation for a walk. She'd sounded so disappointed.

More trash than ought to be, statistically speaking and all. Too much.

More than from random rednecks chucking chicken-finger wrappers out of their windows.

A deliberate effort.

A voice whispers, this time your own intuition: it's that asshole Jezmund Rembert. Or one of his thugs.

Of course. The local gangsters, they hate you for what you did to their precious Confederate chicken mural on the side of The Dixiana. So much so that death threats—yeah—have been left on the voice mail at the honkytonk. Trudy, already pissed at you about the mural, having puppies over the whole deal. Says, you don't know who you're messing with. Says, you ought to be scared for your life. You're not sure she means from the gangsters, or from her and her Sasquatch-sized biker husband.

You know full well what you're dealing with—a county full of bumpkins. In any case, too effing bad. For all of them.

Steaming. You're gonna get that sheriff on the horn, have him bring a gang over. Get this crap policed up, as they say.

The rumbling of the truck engine under your nuts, a mysterious cycling up of the RPMs for a second. Yep. A sign. An indicator of your rightness, your power.

But at a four-way stop sign you catch whiff of a burning rubber smell; a puff of oily smoke wafting up from the grill, not a grill full of burgers and dogs, but the F-150. A reminder that you need to get this heap looked at, but only by someone you trust. You don't yet have 'your' mechanic here in Edgewater County. But you will.

Or not—maybe you won't be here long enough to need any of them around this podunk backwater. Your future, it's unwritten. If you're predestined for anything, it's that you are making this up as you go along.

◍◉✳

POWERFUL AND AUTHORIAL YOU MIGHT BE, BUT NEEDLESS TO SAY THE ROLLING OF the mural hasn't made you a popular fixture around town, and with more than

Rembert's a-hole nincompoops. Blistering letters in the *Edgewater Advocate*; nasty messages on various voice mails; a graffiti tagging incident—BURN IN HELL, PETTUS—that necessitated more rolling of white paint.

Crass and crude. 'Hell'? That the best you can do? Far as you're concerned, you already reside there.

To the credit of your detractors, it must seem bad enough, you suppose, that after giving exactly two shits about Tillman Falls for the last thirty years you decide to up and ROLL back on in here like you own the joint, hardy har. But more than that, you literally took from the townspeople one of their little shrines. That's how it'd been put to you, and in a variety of ways.

Like this trash. A message.

Uncle Burnie still cussed a blue streak whenever he saw you. And that Rembert criminal, you've heard he'd still like to 'whip your ass' over it. Tough guy.

You would see about all that. Wouldn't you, though.

Maybe right now. Swing by Pike's, where you've been told the movers and shakers congregate like flies on shit, the next generation of the same crowd that used to meet in the upstairs private area at The Dixiana. Before your time—by the age when your granddaddy had had you swabbing the urinals, the days when the redneck gangsters hung out there had ended. For whatever reason.

A confrontation?

At this hour?

Better to let the biscuits and pig-sausage digest first.

Thoughtful, you reach down and scratch at your ankle above the newish pair of Crocs you sport instead of your Tevas or Keens. Your rough heels, dry and cracked. Nasty. Back home—on Sedge Island, rather, not the house back at the end of the dirt drive—Creedence always kept lotion by the bed. You'd rub it on your feet, elbows too, which tended to get ashy. They smelled first class, her fancypants, top-shelf emollients and creams. Felt good. They'd better, for what she paid. You never once yanked it using that lotion. Not at those prices.

The thought of Creedence's lotion opens a chasm of grief. More conscious breathing assuages the sting, but only just-so.

Maybe later you'll call and check on her. Yeah. After figuring out how best to deal with this trash crisis. You're overdue for a chat with Sheriff Oakley. Time to plant your flag with the LEOs in town. Get to a lodge meeting. Let them know who's in charge, now.

Oh—but only after your visit with the lovely Rebecca LaFreniere, and a tour of her arts facility now in your beloved old Palmetto Grande movie theater. Get that out of the way, then call Oakley. Becky L, she makes your antennae wiggle. As well as a few other body parts. But this, only a courtesy visit. Despite your wife's high crimes and misdemeanors, you won't be doing any hooking up, not for some time. Unlike her, you're better than that. You have scruples. Don't ya.

◎①❋

S TANDING IN THE PRESENCE OF THE OLD MOVIE THEATER FAÇADE SMACKS YOU upside the head, a marvelous and bittersweet sensation. You are like a weed having grown through the cracks in the sidewalks, born into this dirt, but all you can think is that you'd love to take a pressure-washer to the concrete, blast it into a pristine state.

Hell—why not think bigly? Jackhammer every sidewalk into pulverized dust rolling down every street and pour new cement. Inlay the crosswalks with pavers; new lamps with hanging baskets; make this place not merely as new, but reimagined in every detail. Knock down every building but this old movie theater.

Anticipating the outcry from members of the ELMS and other hysterics, maybe keep the hundred year-old courthouse across the way at 123 Congress Street, with its stately oaks and Classical Revival architecture, one of ten in the state designed by William Augustus Edwards. Even that halfway attractive legacy structure, with its columns, arched windows and rain-streaked brick-work, stood profaned and loomed over by the blankly impersonal glass munic-ipal building, a shiny, modern, bluish ice cube looking as though it may melt on a hot Edgewater County summer day—hotter than Hades in the South Carolina midlands—and flood the whole of downtown.

Wash it all away. Clean. The virgin SimCity grid, waiting for trees and water features. For growth.

Goosebump city.

But this, the movie theater, worth keeping. This, the true center of your upbringing, your cultural awareness. A center of gravity; a window to the greater universe beyond the bypass.

Not your granddaddy's honkytonk.

Nuh-uh. Not for a minute.

You've no sentiment for The Dixiana.

At all.

Thinking of svelte and sophisticated Becky L, a different sort of blade thrums and stiffens along your leg, shorter and stubbier than the proverbial 'black blade' primed to slay subordinates and petitioners alike. Becky, a little shorter rather than taller than you. Brunette, intelligent, monied. Stylish hair-cuts, contemporary business suits, killer heels and perfect pedicures. Viva-cious. A vibration of bright energy. A vision for the preservation of the movie house, and the promotion of the arts.

Powerful, you would be together.

All too soon for that, though. A month into your marriage falling apart, with your wife getting out of the dry-out clinic any day, leaves little justification for such revenge tomcatting, which is all a hookup with LaFreniere would represent. Especially ill-advised in a small town like Tillman Falls. Only an idiot poops where he chows down.

◉◎✳

YOU CALLED BECKY THE DAY BEFORE TO TALK DOWNTOWN POLITICS, AND SHE suggested it was time for the tour of the arts center she'd promised.

You had other *schtuff* on your mind, like:

This last-will-and-testament mandate about a street festival in your grandfather's memory, another problem left in your lap, but also the big thoughts about your big plan to become a big-time Edgewater County developer.

As for the festival, you doubted a competent team could be cobbled together from local talent to handle the actual event. From Becky you only wanted guidance on maneuvering, or manipulating, if you will, power centers like the ELMS. And to feel her out on creating synergy. How to get traction on streetscaping, which had to be part of the deal if you were going to stake part of your fortune knocking down and putting up buildings.

That would need tenants.

In a sour, but supposedly recovering, national economy.

The PTB will be kissing your feet. When they all find out. What you have in mind.

At least the locals the new reactors over at the Sugeree River Station going for them. Jobs jobs jobs, in the short term, anyway. Multi-billion dollar build-out, years long. Good time to spruce up downtown.

The real reason you're here today: not to flirt. Not to reminisce about movies. No. To find out whose palms needed greasing.

Which egos needed fluffing.

About the unknown unknowns of navigating Tillman Falls politics.

You know how such matters go, mainly that information is worth more, oftentimes, than the capital you'll be able to acquire without batting an eye.

◉◎✳

BUT BEING HERE ON THE SIDEWALK IN FRONT OF THE THEATER—UNDER THE marquee you used to change standing on Mr. Sortwell's shaky wooden stepladder, a task performed on Thursday night as the last show unspooled, the sound of your grandfather's thumping honkytonk, muted, from two blocks away—you're awash in remembering the feel of those chunky plastic letters; the damage to your cuticles and hands from the tight metal clamps that held them to the runners. Letters like you see on the marquee now—FINE ARTS CENTER—but a different shade, midnight blue, from the ones you'd clipped onto the marquee, a deep purple that when backlit appeared cough-drop red.

A rush of niggling, nettlesome memories. Being here now, your soul feeling turgid and thick, you suffer the hot-cold remembrance of sitting in a damp puddle—in what passed in your adolescent mind for love—and half-trying to watch *Gremlins* while plotting a way into Chesnee's heart. It's as though it had happened five minutes ago rather than thirty-odd years in the past:

After one of the big scenes where Gizmo did something cute and the house, packed, exploded in laughter, a deep breath, and making your move: reaching over, finally, and holding Chesnee's hand.

A staggering moment: *she returned the gesture.*

Held your hand right back.

Squeezed! Snuggled over closer to you! Whispered, "I sure do think you're cute."

"Me too," you stammered, every molecule in your body vibrating in a state of arousal.

True: merely holding Chesnee's sweaty palm had made your 14 year-old dick so hard it started leaking grease, a tickling trickle that left a wet splotch on the front of your shorts. On the walk out of the theater with the credits rolling, you'd yanked out the shirttail of your red Izod shirt to cover the evidence.

But not even getting a tongue kiss out of it all.

Ever.

Unrequited.

"You can't walk me all the way home." She'd stopped in front of the courthouse, pulled you over behind one of the plaza oaks named for a variety of historic Edgewater County figures. "My daddy. He don't want me dating no one yet."

How you'd tingled at the thought that you'd been on a date with this beauty, whom you'd observed from afar in school since you were eleven, had dreamt of and masturbated over, had imagined making love for the first time in your life with her. Your first great love; how you had ached. And now rebuffed.

"Can't we go to another movie? Next week?"

"I wouldn't mind seeing *Gremlins* again. That sure was funny."

"And scary." You understood movies so much better than most everyone. "It was supposed to be scary, too."

She had just smiled.

In truth, you hadn't much cared for it. Not only had this silly, cartoonish *Gremlins* movie replaced *Indiana Jones and the Temple of Doom*, which nobody but you seemed to like, but now Mr. Sortwell had *Karate Kid* booked for next week, which he said had killed in a special early screening he'd seen at the National Association of Theater Owners convention that spring.

Then again, how could you really know what you thought? You'd barely watched *Gremlins*. All you'd known was the pliant pink hand of Chesnee Campobello, that she'd had to wipe off on her own jeans after letting your palm sweat all over hers.

"That'd be cool. We'll have to hurry," explaining the whole *Karate Kid* booking. Loving the fact that you had the inside dope on what Norrie Sortwell had going on at the Palmetto Grande. Feeling grownup and wise. "We could go again tomorrow, in fact."

"But Roy Earl—it's—I can't."

"What, sit through *Gremlins* again? Me neither. But we could—"

"I can't go to any more movies with you. At all."

"Why?" Your voice had broken like when Mama Runelle kept you from activities you wanted to pursue she deemed as too dangerous. How you wanted to blurt to Chesnee, *but I think I love you*. Instead, only another strangulated and piteous, *"But why?"*

In that Edgewater County patois that you still despise. "I just *c'ain't*."

You begged for a further explanation.

She shook her head.

Got your courage up. Expressed love for her.

"Naw. I just c'ain't." As you both walked along she held herself, closed off and nowhere close to the intimacy she'd projected inside the darkened theater. "Daddy went to the hospital one time? Cause he was drinking too much? And so he can't stand booze now."

On the verge of blubbering. "But—but—booze? I don't get it."

"I like you. You're cute. And all. But if he found out I was messing around with you? He'd whip my butt. And your'n, too."

Frustrated beyond all reason. "I don't understand."

"Because of your granddaddy's honkytonk," she stage whispered.

Epiphanic understanding coursed through your body. "Because of The Dixiana?"

"Duh."

The syllable, hanging in the air with portentous finality.

"Now you got to stay here and let me walk by myself the rest of the way home."

Stunned into silence, Chelsea left you there on the plaza with a wet spot on your shorts and a fog of bewildering resentment about your station in life. About your family. And especially that cruddy Dixiana.

You'd never yanked it over her again.

Never fantasized.

Not once.

Wait wait wait—not Chelsea. *Chesnee.* Chelsea is your fucking wife's name. Chelsea Colette Rucker-Pettus, whom you call Creedence. Soon to be ex-wife; soon as her ass is out of rehab this week, and you can speak in a rational and sober manner about how to proceed on splitting up. Because, yeah—that's where your head's at, bay-bee. Cheating lousy drunk.

Done. With her. Like you were done with Chesnee in the summer of 1984, with her own form of disloyalty.

Quit mixing up your heartbreaks, champ.

As for Chesnee, now there was some ancient butthurt not worth wasting energy over. Her you lost all because of The Dixiana, not something wrong with Roy E. Pettus.

In your granddaddy's defense, though, The Dix was far from the worst place around. Look at Rusty's Railroad Track Inn, or the Pot O'Gold, one of those juke joints out in the sticks, or The Hollow Bone, a ramshackle, rundown barbecue joint way out past the airfield. Maybe Chesnee's own drunk daddy had spent time on those downmarket stools watching NASCAR. Feckless nitwits, every drunk, every redneck. Everybody but you and the way you think.

Which is: Now you're on Mr. Campobello's side about the booze. Look what it'd wrought in your own adult life.

The manifestation of your anger known as the Black Blade, thrumming. Wanting to lay waste to it all—The Dixiana, Creedence, your whole life. Burn it down into ashes, let the wind blow it all away. Wanting to see that two-story decrepit old den of inequity collapse into its own footprint at the speed of gravity, as though you'd radioed in for the airstrike, a silverjet slicing through the brilliant blue sky and unleashing a ghastly inferno of greasy orange flaming death and destruction within which the whole block would be right-eously obliterated down to the molecules, scattered and smothered on the blackened grill of your holy, ordained, and inspired retribution.

Gone forever, your hurt and disappointment.

For eternity.

Plus one.

◉◉❋

Shaking off that darkness, standing in the sunshine waiting for Becky L, you seek a different vibration. Changing the tone. Changing the level of thought. An idea Button's put in your head. If the old vibration is making trouble, seek a new one—because it's all your own creation, after all. All of this reality.

And, you attract that which you're thinking about; evil begetting evil, with positivity attracting more of its own ilk.

Maybe.

That Button, way out there.

She takes you for long walks out at a lovely paved trail the county put in next to the river that's one day supposed to become a leg of the Palmetto Trail that will span across the Sugeree River on a repurposed rail bridge on the other side of the old mill. Should offer a great view of the nuke plant plumes downstream.

Oh, boy—Button and her no-nukes stuff. Don't get her started. It's the only time she seems to be able to complete a thought without pausing, standing in the center of the thousand-foot old iron rail bridge now over a hundred years old, with the bases of the original bridge's pilings visible beneath the green, flowing waters of the river, the bridge the Confederates had burned to keep Sherman's army from crossing:

"Fukushima's just the beginning—it could be argued it was Chernobyl—of what'll become a continual series of nuclear power plant disasters, and these will wipe all life off the face of this planet. A slow, but exponential, Extinction Level Event."

"C'mon, they're safe, the reactors—"

"They are all going to fail. And these nutcases are building more—right here in Edgewater County."

"But the jobs—"

"Every engineering project has a shelf life. In the case of nuclear power plants, it's about 30 years."

"That's why they're building new—"

"Now, how many NPP's are well past this shelf life, getting extended operating licenses all over the world and running high plutonium MOX fuel that no plant was ever designed to run? New replacement parts that are no good, in NPP's all over the world, yet no one is spending a dime to replace? No one goes to prison for falsifying nuclear component documents, or lying during nuclear plant inspections. No one."

"Yeah, but is there proof of that, or is it just fake news—"

"It's too late. You, me, every child alive on this planet and quite a few to come, are fucked. Japan is fucked. North America is fucked. Europe next, then the rest of the world. There's enriched uranium and plutonium in the oceans. In the rain. In our food, in the air we breathe."

"That can't be true. Otherwise everyone would have cancer, everyone would be—"

"Worst part is the psychopaths that run this shitshow knew this would happen, and they did it anyway. They sacrificed their own future generations for short-term profits. That's what psychopaths do, and we didn't stop them."

Even though you don't have children, this is a gut punch. "What can we do?"

She laughed. "Things are not going to get better—ever. *There is no cleaning up global nuclear contamination at growing exponential levels.* The cumulative All-Life-On-Earth's DNA is melting. We're the last of Homo Somewhat-Normal-DNA. We are all going to watch the children die—it kills the kids first—while we all get sick and die early ourselves."

You don't know how to respond to any of this. "How do you know all this? How can you be so sure?"

She muttered some foolishness about the Tao, and how the Master who admits that she knows nothing is closer to the truth than the one who claims ultimate knowledge. "But I do know this much: Printing money to infinity isn't going to stop what what's already occurring."

You had talked and talked while walking the three mile trail and back again. By the end she seemed beat, really winded, and clutching her side.

On the island you were used to walking eight or ten miles, as you said with pride. "Walked ya into a side stitch, did I?"

"Something." She smiled and squeezed her half-Vietnamese eyes, sweat running down apple cheeks. "Like that."

"Mind if we lighten the subject matter? Before I lose my wind, too?"

"Sure. How's this: What're you gonna do?"

"About—?"

"About the old honkytonk."

"This why you got me out here?"

"No. But it's the—um—million-dollar question."

You chuckled, low and rueful. "A little subtext there, eh?"

Punctuated by Button's trademark *ums* and *uhs*: "None that. I'm aware of. Merely a way of. Depicting the importance of. What's on. Everyone's mind."

"Uncle Burnie's probably the main one. Ain't he?"

Button, stretching her calf by pushing against a tree with her stubby leg extended behind her. "One of many."

"All in good time. You'll know when I know. Now let's go get a milkshake or something."

Button, clutching her ribs, tried to smile. She needed to warm up more. Like you'd had to back at the start of your Sedge Island walking campaign, before you'd gotten into shape. You'd suggest some exercise tips. Now that you've lost fifteen pounds off a still-extant food gut, you're a TOTAL EXPERT on this fitness crud. Yeah, you are.

WAITING ON THE WARM TILLMAN FALLS SIDEWALK AND MAKING FRESH SWEAT, YOU consider how there could be veracity to what Button said about mindset and attitude, which she ought to try with regard to all the nuclear scare-talk. Like you mentioned, she's way out there, man. But true enough that you need to make a new vibration concerning The Dixiana. That's for sure.

Since you own it now.

Stunning. Unbelievable, this mess left in your lap.

Hated it then; hate it now.

A purity of hate.

Especially after what happened with Chesnee. Before, that nasty place had represented old people and cigarette smoke and the worst music anyone could imagine being forced to endure, but had now cost you your first girlfriend.

The Palmetto Grande, however, remained close to your heart. Never sat in those seats again, though, the ones where you'd held Chesnee Campobello's hand. The next week you'd seen her walking down the hall at Byrnes High with a football player, a Junior. At least it hadn't been one of the Waugh twins. At least.

You watch as a van—JIFFY Comfort Specialists—rounds the green and heads east out of town, tools and ladders rattling over a street in dire need of resurfacing. The modern iteration of Dickie Giuffrida's granddad's HVAC service trade is an ongoing, multigenerational affair: yep, good old bullying Dickie, another of your nemeses, now running the family business.

The asshole. Never a kind word as a kid. You don't forget crap pulled on you by the Dickies of the world. His granddad and your granddad may've been friends and peers, but that didn't stop him from torturing you on the baseball diamond during your misbegotten little league days. Now that's a story you'd rather not relive any more than the heartbreak of any number of women.

Oh, but you shove all this troublesome reminiscence out of your mind: Standing here underneath the old marquee, you're swept away into happy memories. The movies allowed you escape, a portal into other realities far afield of Edgewater County. And would all throughout your adolescence.

The Dixiana, however, represented reality in all its most distasteful manifestation. How ordinary and colorless, this stupid honkytonk. Served the same sort of wastrels who turned out for the Clint Eastwood movies, and left cups of tobacco juice and beer cans and full baby diapers on the already sticky bacteriological soup that was the auditorium floor, as you'd discovered after you started working at the theater. That particular season after Chesnee's heartbreaking rejection, the Eastwood had been *Pale Rider*, the first western he'd done in years. Yokels had come out in droves.

Of course, you'd come to find out that the shitkicker crowd who populated The Dixiana on most any afternoon and evening were the same louche hayseeds who plopped down for movies. Tillman Falls, then or now, ain't big enough a town for it to be any other way.

◎ⓘ✳

SPEAKING OF SHITKICKERS, YOU SNORT AT THE SIGHT OF HOWDY SHULL perambulatin' 'round the corner from The Dixiana, having walked down from his and his sister's haunted mansion a few blocks behind the cemetery in Whaley Way, not far from Button's equally rundown house, which having once been your Uncle Burnie's—nice, everything always updated and painted to a T —has shocked you in its ramshackle and cluttered decrepitude.

Howdy, approaching and muttering to himself in his impenetrable Old South Carolina brogue.

You call out as he crosses the alley and hits the block with the Grande. "Hey, jackleg. Keep your distance."

"Numerous authorities have written on the subject of ever-burning lamps." Howdy, stinking to high heaven, which you can smell with him still yards away. "W. Wynn Westcott estimates the number of writers who have given the subject consideration as more than a hundred-fifty, and H. P. Blavatsky at a hundred-seventy-three."

What nonsecular—non sequitur, you always get those mixed up— nonsense. You suffer a propensity for impatience toward the more eccentric characters in neighborhoods where you own businesses: "Your very existence lowers the value of my property. Keep moving."

Damn if the elderly miscreant doesn't stop right in front of you and start blowing sour-breath fumes like a rusty tailpipe. "Only a few maintained that the lamps would burn forever, but many were willing to concede that they might remain alight for several centuries without replenishment of the fuel. Some considered the so-called perpetual lights as mere artifices of the crafty pagan priests, while a great many, admitting that the lamps actually burned, also made the sweeping assertion that the Devil himself was using this osten- sible miracle to ensnare the credulous, and thereby lead their souls..." He stag- ger-steps, seems tired, short on fuel. "Into perdition."

Dude, obviously nuts. Needs help. Your attitude softens. "Them's some right fancy lamps, pard."

All but out of breath: "Many of these—ever-burning lamps were found to be—the devices of devils."

Despite the rote recitation of all this, like Howdy has no idea what he's saying, your dimpled skin crawls. "Sounds like some real Linda Blair crap."

"You have any gas?"

"Only from my grandmother's breakfast. What for?"

"If you knew, you'd know."

"Duh-uh, pal. That's real Rumsfeldian. Now skedaddle before you get a ride out of downtown in one of Oakley's prowlers."

Howdy, with his ridiculous, wide-stepping gait, continues on down the street. "A perpetual flame, because the devil set them there, maliciously intending thereby to obtain fresh credence for a false worship."

Wafting BO in his wake—and yeah, with notes of gasoline—Howdy leaves you thinking that this blight on the community ought to be removed. You've got to be a hard-ass about grifters and beggars and scruffy cats hanging around in decent townships like Tillman Falls. Particularly when you're a town father, and all. No other choice.

◎①✳

YOU FIND THAT THE PALMETTO GRANDE, FROM A BRASS PLAQUE YOU'VE NOTICED near the box office booth, has been designated an historic site as part of some tourism hoodoo called the Heritage Corridor Discovery Route comprised of various antique buildings. Now, this old grindhouse might not boast an appearance by the Man in Black and June Carter whilst Bob Dylan sat on a tour bus outside and probably wrote three songs, as many as the Cashes had sung at The Dixiana, but what this old theater could say for itself—to you, anyway —were possession of all the dreams, and nightmares, of the most glorious fantasies that'd carried you away on celluloid, pillowy waves of happiness. Away from Tillman Falls, like the bus that'd carried the music legends cruising through the town back in your long ago toddlerhood.

Rabbit loved to tell that story, about the time the tour bus with those famous cats pulled up. You'd been a baby at the time. That'd been the honky-tonk's true peak, had meant more than any appearances by the Marshall Tucker Band or old Hawg Hickens, the only halfway significant country singer to have come out of The Dixiana and Edgewater County. But even back in the day, you hadn't put much stock in any of that music stardom BS your folks went on and on about at supper every night. From his TV show you remem-bered, barely, Johnny Cash seemed old like your people and their music, and by the time you were an adolescent and begun to dig rock music, Bob Dylan had gone on some dang fool Christian side-trip as equally musty and stodgy and countrified as the music Granddaddy Rabbit played at his honkytonk.

Who cared about any of that when there were movies?

The Palmetto Grande, in your blood in more ways than one: it would be your first real job. But the fear you felt when telling your grandfather you didn't want to work for him anymore! How the awful times spent working at that wretched stinkhole of your Pa-paw's honkytonk were torture, but you couldn't say that to him. Finally you'd blurted, I want to get a job somewhere else, and he had only replied that it was a good idea. That a boy should get a taste of different flavors of life.

"Hell, I was a farmer in North Dakota for six years," Rabbit would always say. "Taught me a lot. Taught me how to be alone." As if to say, you will one day be alone. Go out and learn how to do something besides what I do. Work you can do on your own.

Good advice.

You cultivated friendship not with Pa-paw and his crusty old buddies, no; instead it was to Mr. Sortwell and his movie theater you turned, which after reading the plaque you agree possesses actual and genuine historical value. The enterprise dates back almost to World War I, when cinema had taken on its current feature-length storytelling form. Wasn't called the Grande, but Chaplin, Gish, Valentino, Chaney, Fairbanks, they all flickered ghostly on its screen.

This hadn't even been the first theater, you learned. The first had opened up in 1907, but had burned down before the war in the Common Street fire of '14. Fires had struck along the main drag in both McBreeley's Crossing and the later Breeleyville and later still Tillman Falls quite a number of tragic times, except in a rich Southern fit of irony when Sherman's passing troops had been thwarted.

Of course, no fire compared to the Sunbury School event, the memorial to which you sometimes went with Mama Runelle and Letty Glasscock, who would lay flowers—she'd lost her mother and sisters in the fire. Grim, sad, et cetera, but again, well before your time. Outside of your personal experience.

No more real than the movies.

Not even as real, really.

When you really think about it.

From a young age, pubescent pudgy and shy, you managed to linger in the lobby, finding the voice to talk about what you'd seen. Eventually Sortwell let you hang out in the office, and sometimes he'd relent and bow to your begging to order an extra one-sheet of a particular title to burnish your modest lobby poster collection. You still have them put away in the storage shed in Charleston where you chucked a shit-ton of business paperwork and personal crap from your early years while you lived in the smallish downtown condo there on the peninsula, a two-year sojourn; a whim of Creedence's, your time in the holy city. But now that you own a badass big old marsh mansion, you keep meaning to go and retrieve those boxes and crates and whatnot; you imagine those posters, creased and folded in the old manner they used to ship them to the theaters, might turn to fusty dust.

How one summer you mustered the courage to ask him if you could work, but of course Mr. Sortwell, duly charmed by your pluck, said no. "Get back to me when you're a little close to voting age, pal, or shaving, or some other notable milestone," in his unfamiliar, Yankee accent. "Little closer to high school. Something."

"Nobody knows more about movies than I do." At eleven you're saying this. "Nobody."

He scowled and sucked back snot, spat into a yellowed handkerchief like all the grown man seemed to carry. After checking to see if he'd fished out anything of note, he put it away. "C'mon, kid. There's somebody here that knows more than you. Yeah. In this little burg. Hell—there's one sitting across from you," there in his office so cluttered with mysterious papers and publicity stills and lobby cards, all achingly collectible, but to him so unremarkable— disposable, even. "So imagine in all the little burgs everywhere—and the big towns too, boy. Movies used to be the only thing we had to talk about, besides baseball." Leaning back with his loafers on the desk, he slicked his hair, which sat up high like a rockabilly singer, and on a hard pot-gut under a knit two-button golf shirt, plaid, he rested knobby old man's fingers, knuckles swollen with arthritis. "Think how many hepcats out there in the world know more about movies than you, Daddy-o."

"Still: I seen about every one that ever played here."

"*Ever?*"

"Well."

His eyes went all shiny. "So maybe you do know a lot."

Your heart, pounding through your chest in a different way than it would with Chesnee a few years later in that same movie house. "So can I come work for you?"

"A couple more summers. And then we'll talk."

Whining. "My Pa-paw says I got to work at The Dixiana soon."

Whistling. "Your granddad's a real SOB. But a job's a job. Be glad ya got one."

"But there's so much—excitement here."

"Kid," leaning back and lighting up a smoke from the pack of Camels in his shirt pocket. "When you're a grownup, it's about the money. Not the movies. Not the freaking excitement, whatever that means. Like your granddad's place: on a certain level, it ain't about the music. Even if it used to be, believe me, it ain't about nothing but the money."

"I don't know about that."

"Oh, yeah?"

Prophetic: "Seems to me like it's more about the beer."

He busted a gut. "You're a riot, kid. Just wait till you get grown up, find out what responsibility feels like. Then you'll need a beer. Believe you me."

No job. But at least no working at the honkytonk either, which Mee-maw forbade until you were at least twelve. Next year. Gulp.

In the meantime, you lived at the Grande anyway, there in the summer of *The Shining.* And *The Empire Strikes Back,* for god sakes. And *The Blues Brothers,* which you had loved except for the 'Rawhide' scene, which had seemed so close to the truth of your life half-lived inside your granddaddy's honkytonk that, instead of laughing? You only felt self consciousness. Embarrassment. A way of life for the fat kid back then—eating in front of people. The picking of sports teams. Gym class. Nightmare stuff. Nowadays? All those little sons of guns are fatty fats. Back then, felt like you were the only one. The class pic in front of the elementary school bears it out.

Worse, right as the "Rawhide" sequence began, some wit—you knew it was Harlem Waugh—hollered out, "That ain't Bob's, that's that shithole The Dixiana!" Many had laughed, haw haw haw, and how one of them—did it matter which?—had thrown popcorn at the back of your head.

How you'd sat stiff as a statue, hating the rest of the movie, which otherwise you'd have loved. Ackroyd and Belushi were your favorites, at least for a year or two, so much so that you thought *1941* was great, during their cultural hot streak before Belushi ended up a drug casualty. Not that "Rawhide" scene, though. A different sort of spoiler from what in modern times they warned readers about seeing in reviews on the internet.

Out on the street afterwards, everyone jabbering and mimicking the Blues Brothers, the Waugh boys had followed you and Dobbs, calling out the F-taunt and forging a complete and thorough enough humiliation that its sense-memory remains vivid in your mind's eye, as though it were still happening; as though all time were one time, which sounds more like Button Sykes than you.

But this, an exception to the generally wonderful memories to come throughout your teens. Young love, if unrequited. Working at a job you enjoyed, once you made the move and Sortwell brought you on board. Being treated with respect by Norrie Sortwell, a non-family adult. Maybe the first adult to do so—the others in your life, so cloying and smothering and worrying over you as though you were more fragile than others:

Mee-maw, don't let your fat ass Roy Earl grow up to be a cowboy. Too dangerous.

She'd always been scared of her own shadow, and of yours; when you told your Mee-maw you were going to work at the theater, she'd cursed you. Said you didn't know your butt from a hole in the ground, and you couldn't understand why it was such a big freaking deal, man. You never understood. You were fifteen going on five to her. Always.

Still.

So, working for Norrie Sortwell at fifteen, finally, felt so much like freedom. Freedom, and only a block away. You couldn't beat it; couldn't even buy it. You know this now more than you knew it then, but working over here at this movie palace unspooling the products of the Hollywood dream factory had felt pretty darned special.

As for getting a job, you didn't wait for It to happen. You asked; you went for it. And got it, but only for the mastery of remarkable patience. And from this and other experiences you learned how to do this—how to get what you wanted. How to make your own reality. The Palmetto Grande, you would only later understand, would be the first iteration of this power, of intense wanting resulting in manifestation through positive thought and action. You and Button have discussed this. At length. She helped explain an idea that you'd always felt but could never articulate. Special lady, your quasi-cousin.

◎◉✳

Yours, a childhood and adolescence filled by movies. Whose wasn't.

Specific early memories: Vomiting up peas and carrots and rice from Lucinda's meat-and-three buffet during a matinee of the Disney rerelease of *The Jungle Book*, Mama Runelle cooing and dragging you up the aisle to the bathroom. Falling asleep in any number of them, including *The Eiger Sanction*, which seemed dull for a Clint Eastwood, and started with some guy who wasn't Clint getting his throat cut, the fake blood from which made your head dizzy, and it had Eastwood as some art professor, which seemed all wrong. Bond picture of the season, *The Man With the Golden Gun*, not as good as the ones you had seen on TV with Sean Connery; and as an aside, how you loved loved loved and lived for those 007 movies to come on the *ABC Friday* or *Sunday Night Movie*. *Godzilla* pictures, the mutant lizard versus any number of Toho latex creatures, including silly ones like the Smog Monster. Mr. Sortwell ran such fare on Saturday mornings, along with programmers, as he called them, like *The Computer Wore Tennis Shoes* and other kid movies.

But as established, your granddaddy and your Mee-maw took you to all kinds of movies, and the one that scarred you the most, at the age of seven? Yep. *Jaws*. That'd been opening night, a Friday, and the whole town seemed to buzz, everyone lined up around the block, and how you had the Fear of Being Eaten driven into you on more than an innate level. Mama Runelle only covered your eyes near the end, during Captain Quint's awful, bloody, screaming death; and you remember your Mee-maw with the paperback novel she'd gotten at the IGA that next Monday, and how she wouldn't let you read it. Told you it wasn't as good anyway.

But the best of the best in this movie house? Oh. How you remember Karen Black trying to pilot that giant crippled plane in *Airport 1975*, the title of which felt like a forward-leaning arrow, a signpost to the future: when it came out it had still been 1974. And how, oh, how much you'd wanted Karen Black, the gorgeous woman with the most beautiful big eyes you had ever seen, to be able to land that wounded, gape-faced jumbo passenger aircraft—you didn't want Charlton Heston riding that zip-line down from the jet helicopter to save her.

You'd already fallen in love with her.

You wanted Karen Black for your own.

Movies. Powerful psychological effects. Almost like magic.

By the time you got to college you had become more interested in reading, a would-be English major planning to be a writer, a journalist, a poet. You had written for the yearbook and the school paper, though. Your friends like Billy and Libby, however, they also loved the movies, so much so that they studied them. Maybe they had had the right idea.

So, you read. Kept to yourself. While they all had relationships. And you kept Karen Black. Kept her close. Titillated by thoughts of Karen Black's vulnerable, bloodied bare feet in *Trilogy of Terror*. You wondered what your grandparents thought, you cutting her picture out of magazines and from different places and making a collage on the door of the narrow closet in the old house sitting in the high weeds you've got to see about getting cut back. Rabbit had obviously long ago ceased keeping the old yard landscaped.

Not as long ago as when you put away all your old Karen Black memorabilia in a plastic bin, still here, you reckoned, in one of the numerous and generous storage areas in the Victorian. The house you built them. And soon to be yours—how long would your ninety-year-old Mee-maw manage to hang in there?

◉①❋

AS YOU PACE AROUND AWASH IN BOTH MEMORIES AS WELL AS CONCERNS REGARDING the future, Becky LaFreniere, head cocked and mouth agape, comes bustling out of the door by the old box office. "Roy Pettus—I know you haven't been standing in this hot sun very long?"

"Seems a thousand centuries," you hear your voice saying. "Maybe always."

"Gracious. Why didn't you come on in?"

"My mind, it wanders. Memory lane." You extend your arms to the heavens in a V. "Used to clamp the letters on this marquee every Thursday night."

"We all have a soft spot about this old barn."

"First movie? That you can remember?"

"*Grease*. I was four and half. You?"

"*Jungle Book*. I puked in the lobby."

"Nice." Such warm and attractive laughter. "Poor Norrie Sortwell."

"True that. I used to work here, you know."

"So you keep telling me."

"Like I said—I'm a little scatterbrained."

She smiles with sympathy. Says, so, when are you flying that *airplane* of yours again, that silly question with its inflection of wonder, and you fend it off, reminiscing instead about the movie theater. Now you only associate pain with flying the Piper—coming here for your Pa-paw's death; zooming back for Creedence's hospitalization; and so ready to get away again that you flew back instead of driving. Only this time, the F-150, already waiting at the airfield. Hobby piloting, now the last activity on your mind.

"If Rabbit bitched about me working here in high school instead of his bar, he had only himself to blame—they got me hooked on movies. One thing, though: I grew so sick of the snacks that I never drink cokes or eat popcorn."

"Get out of here—never?"

"Nope."

"You must still drink cold drinks, though," canting her head sideways and dropping her mouth open in what seemed to be her schtick—a look of genuine, if exaggerated, disbelief. "I love a cold, ice-cold, Dr. Pepper."

"Used to drink way too much Mountain Dew when I was kid. Still recovering."

"You switched to coffee," noting the stainless steel travel mug in your hand. "Not good for you, either."

"Yes. Or, no. I agree, is what I'm saying. Coffee trade, now, that's my lifeblood, though. I can't be too down on it." Hinting, now. "Coffee's still part of the future. Everyone's future. Corn syrup? The past."

"Fascinating. I'll have to keep that in mind tomorrow morning," she says, demure and smiling. Radiant, even, in her skepticism.

Her gaze is pulled over your shoulder, however, a little faraway, and you detect flirtation and longing, or perhaps that's only ego. Rebecca's beautiful and fit and vivacious. You would make a formidable team. That's your real deal, not sexual attraction. Better and cleaner that way. Where can we go together, not what can we do. That part's gravy.

"But, gosh," stepping back and admiring the marquee again. "Did I love the crushed ice that we poured over, the little round pea-sized kind? The summer I started, Mr. Sortwell put in this new pellet ice maker. I must've chewed the enamel off my teeth with that ice, standing behind the concession stand."

Of course she knows that pellet ice. Loves it too, she says. "Crunch-crunch."

What chemistry. Even as you wish to romance your fellow town powerbroker, you file away the notion.

Mostly.

◉◐✹

IN THE LOBBY, THE BOUQUET AND ATMOSPHERE HITS YOU DIFFERENT NOW; MORE like the remnants of a fresh build-out than hot popcorn. Fifteen seasons since its renovation, you are told, the space has further benefited from a capital campaign conducted by the ELMS to finance new, better quality carpet and a coat of paint throughout all public areas and passageways.

You can dig it.

What had been a deep storage closet full of old theater equipment and where large surplus bags of popcorn were kept in advance of busy weekends, has been converted into small meeting rooms where she says a number of local musicians and other artists give one-on-one salons and lessons. The old balcony upstairs, unused since the days of segregation—in your day it'd been shuttered and dusty, but being a Sortwell insider meant you could go up and watch movies anytime you wanted—is now a space for workshops and meetings. All pretty god-durn upmarket for this quaint burg, but this thought you keep to yourself. "You should be proud."

Blushing, she asks about 'Miss Runelle' and how your grandmother is faring, as well as you; and in a terribly direct manner as a kind of stinger to the personal inquiries, about the future of The Dixiana.

Coy. "We're chipping away at our lists."

Her head cock again. Waiting. Expectant eyebrows doing all the work. She wants to know. About the building. About the mural-wall. The sign. The future. Whole bit.

You get this anticipatory vibe—it's how you roll. You don't mind. She doesn't have to say any of it. You are of similar worlds. Neighborhood advocates. Being in small business in a community, if only nonprofit in her case, makes one a busybody about the activities of fellow stakeholders.

You divulge that plans, ideas and options are in the offing, sure; that you'll let everyone know when you know. That type-deal.

"But it's like this," musing and expansive. "Whatever I'm gonna do, I'm thinking that what this town needs is a fresh approach to community organizing and leadership."

A frost descends. "Meaning what?"

You describe a vision of founding a new merchant's association. "Maybe the team we put together for the Rabbit festival, that's the core of the new group. Which kind of hangs around afterwards, and codifies itself, and becomes a 501c/6, let's say, that can then act with impun—"

"Roy, no offense? But gracious, I don't really see the necessity of duplicating such a group here in town. Besides the Chamber of Commerce, the ELMS, of which you of course know I'm a member, well—there's much to be said for um respecting traditional corridors of influence."

Whoa—Becky L has transformed into Rebecca LaFreniere, old Edgewater money, holding the line on you and your dilettantish foolishness. You see now that maybe you aren't peers. Not yet, anyway.

"It's not a competition."

"A duplication of effort." Becky, dry. "It won't fly."

Grudging. "I see the effort more as forging new partnerships."

A fake smile. "A discussion to be continued in another venue. Yes?"

"Oh, my—yes." A hint of Daniel Plainview. "I have nothing but time."

She relaxes. "I'm just saying—mechanisms are already in place."

"Let's finish our tour."

"Yes. Let's do that."

Hah. You'd see what they all thought once the demo of the Dix began. And what you'd put in its place. Then they'll listen to anything you have to say. Inwardly, you make a Mister Burns-style finger tent and fib a little lie: "I'm only spitballing, anyway. I'm here to learn more than lead."

"Sounds like a healthy attitude."

◉①❊

A TRAIL OF ICE CRYSTALS PLUMING IN HER JET EXHAUST, REBECCA FILLS YOU IN ON the path taken to arrive at the healthy state of the PGAC—the Palmetto Grande Arts Center—as the facility is now known. Public-private money, grants at the state and federal level. Grants grants grants, as she says, the pursuit of which eating up much of her time, not to mention programming of the various events —community theater, live music, a children's arts camp in the summer, and so on. The facility's availability for private functions completes the formula for success in keeping the enterprise solvent here in the ongoing "Bush Economic Crisis," as she puts it with a knowing laugh, one that withers at your own *Hrm* response.

"Bush ain't been in charge for years now."

"Economic decisions take time to come into effect."

"Yeah—I'm still waiting for it to 'trickle down'."

"You seem to have done all right for yourself."

"True story. But nobody trickled anything into my pockets."

"I suppose you came by your entrepreneurship honestly."

"Said a mouthful there. No doubt."

But in truth, you despise politics almost as much as sports. Want no part of such conversations, except in how they impact your businesses on the local level. Another point on which you and Button have found agreement—politics, sports, entertainment, all of it blatant mind control. How her face lit up when you said what a ridiculous waste of time watching TV was. Like she'd fallen in love with you.

If only. In her own way, Button, a little hottie.

In an offhand, calculated fake-musing manner, one designed to provoke lefties like Becky L: "But I tell ya, I wish old W'd been a better president. He seemed like such a nice fella—hell, he even left some money behind in the old Dixiana, didn't he."

"Only yards away from where we now stand."

Ten years ago, W, a country music fan, toured Fort Jackson and had photo ops with troops about to deploy to Iraq, requesting that his entire thirty-vehicle entourage drive him all the way to downtown Tillman Falls and The Dixiana to get barbecue baskets for lunch later on Air Force One, scheduled to wing him along to another photo op at another army base at fifty grand an operating hour. The story of the presidential down home Carolina barbecue side-trip had run all over world media through about one and a half news cycles, and included a standup interview from your grandfather, who'd literally spat tobacco while on camera and answered the reporter's question about the president's visit—did they talk about the Iraq war—by responding, "We didn't talk about nothing but football and barbecue," Rabbit had said. "Seemed like he had the weight of the world on his shoulders. I feel for him."

The reporter had pressed: "So what did the President say about the barbecue?"

"Said he thought mustard-based sauce like ours was 'a uniquely Carolinian flavor of sauce to have,' whatever that meant. Tipped real good. That's how you know somebody's got a decent soul." A shining moment in Dixiana lore. Your Pa-paw told you after all that free advertising they had sold out of Dixiana T-shirts, an idea Burnie gave him back in the 80s that he said finally paid off.

Musing on legacy: "Still trying to figure out what it is everyone says Georgie-Porgie 'lied' about exactly."

She blanches. "Maybe we shouldn't talk politics."

Don't be too hard on her, a voice says. She's adrift in a red sea around here, none of which you subscribe to either, except maybe the idea of fewer taxes on wealth like you now possess. That you can get behind, but it's still all boring as shit and all fake and exhausting nonsense. They'd get the money out of you one way or another.

Still, you can't help it: "I sure was sorry I missed him when he dropped by to visit the honkytonk that time. Yeah—a visit. Like when he and Vice sat down with the 9/11 committee. Thank god we had 'em in office to protect us when Saddam attacked."

Becky L's pale countenance, now pink. "That 'visit' was an extravagant waste of taxpayer money."

"I dunno. Just seemed like a plain old feller you could have a beer with, watch the Redtails beat Foothills State, talk about the weather. And yeah, eat a barbecue basket."

But as for tweaking Becky L, you love pulling this stuff. You've an Obama version you lay on your hanger buddies, old rich guys, all Republicans, of course. Tell them about how happy you were the time the then-Illinois Senator and his wife had been in Charleston, had stopped into the tourist trap Spotted Banana™, a 2008 campaign-era photo op for TV. You hadn't been there, but your manager had said the future president seemed to know how to use the cameras and the attention of all the people. You always claim to the hanger guys, however, that you were in fact there, and had kissed both Barack and Michelle on the cheek. How you believed in hope and change, and had prospered in the Obama years.

In that partially falsified anecdote you go on to say how much you'd enjoy hanging out with the President, who seemed like "a regular guy." How'd it be a lark to enjoy hang time with a smart, articulate dude like that constitutional scholar. The hanger boys all hoot and deride you for it. Not a clue that you're playing them.

In truth you find it all risible: the partisanship, the sputtering, rhetorical puffing and huffing. The media forces everyone on either of two sides of the same fence, making them think each group has the One True Answer. They don't; it's all a game. Divide and conquer.

And yet; and yet; you and Creedence, both tearful with relief when Obozo got elected. So glad to be rid of Bush. You had worried his ass would keep on until they got us in a war like your grandfather and uncle had gone off to fight. The world would not survive another one of those.

◉①❋

In the auditorium, all new curtains and seats and railings and whatnot, you're desperate and wishing for some semblance of the old theater to be there, and but for the railing on the re-carpeted stairs to the balcony, it's all so different that you get flustered and ruinously disappointed. The familiar, gauche, ochre curtains, now gone. The walls look too pale. Seems too big. But that's why you paint with light colors. This place isn't only for movies anymore. It's not even for that, mostly.

All different.

No longer reeks of stale popcorn and dried soda syrup.

Your beloved Grande—here, but not.

Until your eyes come to rest on the last two rows of seats closest to the back wall. Where you and Chesnee Campobello sat on your misbegotten date.

You approach the rows, quivering with glee. The seats seem reupholstered, but the metal hinges still squeak in a comforting and familiar manner when you sit and grip the armrests, on which your elbows rubbed for hours at a time. In a flash you taste the twang of the yellow popcorn seasoning at the back of your teeth. The redolence of Chesnee's hair products, floral-sweet, a maddening olfactory enhancement wafting ghostly as the *Gremlins* flickered on the screen and your hand crept—no, slithered from the damp sweat—toward hers.

Your head grows hot. Water springs to your eyes.

Becky L notices with concern you being in the grip of this moist-eyed reverie. "Are you all right?"

Stroking the fabric and metal of the old movie theater seats: "These are originals—*you kept these the same.*"

With a hand on your arm, she explains that these two row were bolted into the concrete in such a lasting manner it would have added too much to the seat replacement budget. "Cheaper to re-foam, re-cover, paint the metal and hit the hinges with a li'l WD-40."

Breathy and high. "Used to build things to last. Didn't they."

"Roy—what's wrong?"

"I used to sit back here," trying to catch your emotional breath. "Went on my first date. Saw my favorite movies. All that junk."

"I'm a sentimental old sap, too," looking faraway. "Dates. Relationships."

Well now, that makes your antennae wiggle. "Look, I'm glad everything's so nice now. But relieved these seats are still here."

Before it gets any sappier you head back to her office and announce how impressed you are with what she's accomplished, essentially a black-box theater facility easily converted for a variety of uses including film programming. The new seats in the auditorium, except for those storied last rows, can even be removed and the space converted into an open floor plan with partitions for art exhibitions.

"Damn fine community-building machine you got here."

"A wonderful way of putting it. I should write that down. But as for the community, I recognized that I had a responsibility. My family name's on the courthouse square, after all."

"That it is. Respect." You decide this tour's gone on long enough. That it's time to get on with it. "It's clear I'm really gonna need your wisdom. Like, politically, and all."

Beaming with pride, she agrees and nods, self-effacing rather than boastful. "If I'm civic-minded and active, it's always in the service of the larger goal, which goes beyond Tillman Falls—it's the arts. The arts remain my bedrock passion, with education not far behind. Who knows the ultimate end of the seeds our programs plant in the minds of children?"

"No way to tell."

"Do you have children?"

"Nope."

"Nor do I. By choice, if I may ask?"

"Nope. Her insides, they were a rocky place."

"Oh, my word!"

But you're kidding, as you explain; a line from some dumb movie. "By choice."

"I've never married." Rueful, but smiling. "Never say never. Perhaps one day I'll adopt. So many orphans needs homes."

"My wife and I, we've discussed it." Hah—maybe adopting a rescue kitty from the pound. But it sounds good and worthwhile to say. "Big decision, though."

"I've a busy schedule."

"True dat, sister."

She seems to brace herself, takes a breath. Has been waiting to say this. "I'd be remiss if I didn't point out that, as a *preservation*-minded *legacy* citizen of this county, I appreciate that what happened with the mural occurred in a moment of stark emotion, and I suspect one of catharsis for you. But before you make any *further* decisions about the future of that notable tavern, I'll love to take the opportunity to impress upon you how important I feel The Dixiana could be in its own way, as a piece of Edgewater County *history* here along the Discovery Corridor. Oh—well."

A finger held to your lips, and yet: you remain smiling and warm and gentle, your eyes crinkling. "Time enough for all that later. Speaking of catharsis and emotion, this visit today? It's for me," in your deepest, most serious tone. "So if we can let it be only that, I would appreciate it very much. I'm taking a mental health afternoon. And all that sounds like work talk. Too-soon work talk. I've suffered a terrific shock. Still reeling, even after a few weeks."

Becky L's a strong-willed leadership bossman type, too, but she also seems mortified by the possibility of having breached etiquette and propriety regarding the loss of your grandfather. "I'm so terribly sorry." Her smile, more forced than flirtatious. "Another time."

"But one thing's for sure. Whatever happens over there on that corner, the mural's gone for good. My friend, the Reverend Nixon, certainly liked what I did. How it seemed in the bold spirit of the old civil rights days. How it had allowed him to clarify his platform for the future of the town. Focus on other issues."

"What about those other issues," her jaw hardening and clenching.

"The name change stuff?" NEW FALLS CITY. Bumper stickers. Blue yard signs accompanying the red Nixon ones. The election, a foregone conclusion, so Nixon, in the market instead for political capital. Putting the money into the pet issue. Astute. "Sounds fancy enough."

She nods, vigorous. "Thoughts?"

"Why not? Still feels a bit nineteenth century around here. Long as new signage doesn't break the Parks budget, or anything heinous like that."

Rebecca LaFreniere, family going back here to the time of slave-owning and landholding and whose bloodline has seen no fewer than two and probably all three such changes of name for the township, lets out a breath like the Frost Queen. "A majority of the ELMS, Roy Earl—well. High heels are dug in hard, if I may resort to a sexist expression."

"It's more than that, isn't it?"

She bites her lip. Says, what do you mean.

"How about the other power center in town? What do they think?"

"The new municipal complex? What of it?"

You tell her, no, not that ugly silver cube poking up unnaturally to the east of downtown. "I'm talking bout Thurmond Pike's back room. You realize that bunch used to meet upstairs at The Dixiana, back in the day."

"Sounds like you know as much as I do about that little boy's club."

"You got to understand something: I ain't been around for a long time. I don't know what the situation is, right? Not even at my own place."

Frost queen again. "If there's another power center in Edgewater County, I'm sure those players will make their views known to you. As I have."

Stark. Frank. You can dig it. Tell her so.

On the way out you offer your own politician's smile—toothy and fake—and stride down the block toward the green. Bye-bye to Becky consists of miming the phone to the ear and calling out to her, "Again: good job in my old movie theater. Keep doing what you're doing."

The Dixiana sign, paint-peeling and half-broken, hangs anchoring the curved corner of the honkytonk. Oh, how you're gonna tear this place apart—brick by brick, down to the motes of irritating dust. If that doesn't demonstrate who now wields power in whatever they decide to call this crappy little town, nothing will.

CREEDENCE

Dear Devin:

I feel as though there's way too much to catch up on, but since you are not reading this and never will, I guess I can get away with skipping some of the details. No easy way to say it: I got myself into the same durn trouble you did. Let the bottle get inside me as much as I got inside it. Crawled down in there, Devin. Like you did. Enough to land me in the hospital. And rehab.

I feel like I have a new family here, even after only three weeks. A few days to get off 'the sauce,' and boy getting through the shakes and DTs wasn't like anything I could have expected. I remember one time you told me how nasty it was, getting straight after a long bender. I get it. I kept seeing these cartoon faces zooming at me. And when I closed my eyes, kitty-cat faces. That was the worst. How I felt like I'd let my pets all down! It was considerable, my shame. I probably don't have to explain to you, another cat person.

I will tell you this much: I was so sick getting off alcohol I'm glad I didn't do it on my own, and so are the people here in the hospital, at least after it come out how much I had been drinking.

Yeah. It was more than I had let on in these letters, or to Roy, to Estes, anyone else. I figured no one even cared enough to notice, so it didn't matter.

But like my counselor says, they know. They know, even if they don't want to know. They can smell it on you. 'You remember when you were sitting in your bedroom smoking dope, back when you were a teenager? And you thought they couldn't smell it over the musk incense cones? Booze is the same way. It's coming out of you.'

And I said, it comes out of you in all kinds of ways, and it was the first thing I said aloud in our group meeting. Everybody nodded their heads like they got it, but not even I knew what I meant. Not even me.

I tell you what, I sat up straight when he said how journaling is a super way to get all your crud dealt with, because you need to make notes and lists and figure out stuff besides the fact you were drinking yourself to death. I said, like, I don't journal, but I write letters to my brother who's been missing for so long and he never will see?

And the counselor, whose name is Russ Wetherell and has tattoos and some missing teeth and says he was a biker and doper for a long ass time, till he almost died but finally got straight with the man upstairs and all sorts of other stuff, says, girl, you already been journaling. "You tell him all your secrets, don't you!"

He was looking right through me, Devin. I said, of course I do. Because he'll never read it. I get it, Russ said. So you're on your way with your journals, and then he turned those dark pretty eyes on someone else in the group.

But at first? I thought Russ's eyes were on me like for another reason, especially because he would speak with me in private, give me encouragement and little pointers. I went to hug him and held on too long, I guess, because he said, whoa. "No hookups in rehab — it's too much of an illusion. Like Stockholm Syndrome." Which I had to look up. But I got it. Two people putting all their fucked up mess in the same box does not equal good order.

Putting things in good order. That makes me think of Roy Earl. But Roy, he's barely talking to me anymore.

Sometimes I feel lost without my vodka. Now I got nothing to cover up my guilt over Estes. And losing his job. And putting everyone in a pinch. And doing all this mess right when Rabbit was dying, but that wasn't no more my fault than you running off again the last time, when you had seemed so much better. I said back then I figured Mama dying had done that to you, but mercy it was such a shock I'm surprised I didn't run off with you. I didn't even know she was sick. Not really. That's how freaking dense I am.

When I told Russ about you, how I couldn't get why you had gone and done your mess all over again to us, he shrugged and said 'That's what drunks do, sister. That's the shit we pull.'

Unless you find it in yourself not to pull shit. Wouldn't that be nice!

We were better back then, ten years ago. For a while. Weren't we? All of a sudden, it was like I had got rid of Dusty, had lost my baby, you came back, mama died, and I went right on with things, hooking up with sweet Roy Pettus like, without missing a beat. I was so glad to be rid of Dusty, and of Mama, I think. Mama smothered me all those years. She kept me from growing up like I should've. When she died, it was like my life could begin at last.

Oh, I can't stand to admit such a thing, but I'm trying to be truthful to myself and everyone else now. That's part of all this recovery. Truthfulness.

Ok: So was Roy Earl — mothering me. There, I said it. Not like mama. Way different, but still the same.

And so? I started acting out like a teenager,

trying to show him who could be their own person. He treated me like such a baby, got mad over so much dumb little stuff. You know how I always loved sandwiches for breakfast? With tater chips? That would drive him up the wall. 'Nobody eats lunch food for breakfast. It's stupid.' Blah blah. Like, really yelling at me over it. Wouldn't most people think it was cute? Not Roy. Oh, no.

Of course you remember Mama and how she used to carry on about me wanting sandwiches and chips and macaroni and stuff like that for breakfast. The truth is that the first time I asked for a sandwich instead of cereal or pop-tarts or bacon & eggs she hit the roof. I could see how it got to her. So I done it again. And again. Till having lunch for breakfast didn't have the same power anymore. But by then, a routine.

Her and Roy both, getting mad at me all the time, and over the silliest stuff. In his case, the cats the cats the cats. You know, we keep one group apart from the other in the house, and we were on our way out to eat one night, and Sparkle, my sneaky tuxedo shorthair girl, darted into the hallway from the family room and ran down into our bedroom, hid under the bed the way they do. She goes right to the middle, that rascal, looking out with her big pretty green peepers.

Well, Roy goes and has a freaking fit. I mean, hollering and running from one side of the bed to the other trying to 'flush it out,' he kept saying, while I was screaming at him to stop, stop, you're scaring my baby. He threw himself around the room, falling on the floor and lunging under the bed, shouting about being late. His voice was breaking like he was gonna cry. We got choice fuckin' reservations, he kept screaming. Choice reservations? What does that even mean?

That butthole. He almost scared my sweet kitty to death. All we had to do was wait a few minutes, and she'd come sneaking out. Like always. He acted like it was the crisis of the century. A little inconvenience. He scared the cat that night. And me too.

He didn't never raise a hand to me, though, Devin. That much I want to make clear. Not like sorry ass Dusty did. But Roy, he still scared me. The way everything must be just-so, or it's the end of the damn world.

Oh, Devin! How stupid does all that sound?

Still. Why was I spreading my legs for some boy who worked for him? What was that supposed to fix? Lord have mercy. Strange being on the other side of delusion. That's what drinking and drugging will get you, though.

I wish you were here. I would love to know what mama and daddy told you about sex. I was taught I should not do it. "Don't you go spreading your legs and letting them boys come up inside you." That's all mama said when she caught me playing around one night. Did I ever tell you that? I used to mess around in the bathtub (well, I still do, and I know guys do too of course), and one night I had forgot to lock the door. She walked in and caught me. Had herself a hissy fit.

She got in my face before I could even get my panties pulled up. "If you're starting that already, you'll be fucking boys before we know it, Colette." I think that was the only time I ever heard her use such a word. "Don't you let Dusty put his peterpiper inside you and come up. You mess with that thing until he messes in your hand instead!" That method worked for a good long time, but Dusty pouted and whined until I let him put it inside, and I wanted to feel it too.

What did she expect me to do my whole life? That's no way to tell a daughter about sex. Made me feel like it ought to stay secret, how it was filthy and awful. And you know what? I ain't ever been able to conceive a baby and bring it to term. Spontaneous abortion—three times now. I am unclean, somehow. I am unworthy, my body and I, to make a baby.

Maybe I didn't get free of her when she died.

Hell, it's been ten years now. I still can't come without a bunch of rigmarole, except in my secret bathtub when I'm super relaxed. I did come hard with Estes once or twice, because only because it was secret and nasty. Which makes me feel so awful now I could die.

Or drink.

Or both. But I'm not gonna.

You know when I had my moment of clarity? The day Roy woke up and said he'd had a kitty-cat worry dream like I get. He said he dreamed the kitties had gotten loose out of the house and were darting everywhere, and he was running in this big circle waving his arms, trying to get them back inside. I don't never let my kitties out, but then you remember all that about me. He said his arms stretched out in the dream like Plastic Man, he wanted the kitties back inside so bad. That made me cry, it was so sweet.

But anyway, I thought my face would burn itself off, laying there hungover and guilty. Here he was worrying over my kitties, our kitties I mean, and I was to meet Estes later that afternoon. Before he was to report to work. For my husband.

I knew in my heart it had to end. But later, after I started drinking (which was always about five stupid seconds after Roy left to fly his stupid plane or check on that dumb-ass coffee shop he never needed to open), it didn't matter what I did or who I hurt.

Now it matters.

I hope I can fix me. More than I already fixed it far as the drinking goes. I got to figure out a way to fix it with my husband. If I can. That's where I'm at.

Or maybe I don't want that.

Shit. It is a puzzle.

Russ says journaling and inventory is key. 'It ain't gonna be pretty, but you gotta do it.' So I have to face up to the truth, and ask myself how many childhoods do I have to live through before I grow up, finally? And that ain't coming from any counselor or drug rehab talk or AA or any of that. It's coming from me.

That's enough for tonight. I'm going to say my prayers, get in some reading, and think about sleeping and relaxing and staying in the middle of it all. And knowing there's another day tomorrow to do it all again, and that each day comes one after another, but you don't have to think about anything but the one at hand. "Worrying is a misuse of your imagination." Somebody posted that on Facebook.

Goodnight, lost brother of mine. Wherever you are. Now that my cheeks are all wet and red, it's off to bed. Love you. More work tomorrow, more sessions, but I'm out soon, which in a way scares me worse than I have let on to anyone. Another day, another page. I got so much to fix. So much. All starting with me, though, and so that's what happens first. Me. If I'm fixable. I'm not sure everybody is. You're living (haha) proof of that, buster!

Love,

Creedence

ROY, GOOCH, AND DOBBS

Done with Becky L, you see Trudy's faded red Taurus outside The Dixiana. Think, naw. C'ain't go there. She glares at you with ill-disguised disgust, tinged with a pathetic, pleading hopefulness about the future of the honkytonk. An unsettling mix of contorted facial muscles.

Instead, you visit the comedy team of Wimmel and Vandegrift, both pleased and effervescent at seeing you tromp up the narrow stairs to the second-floor offices of the *Advocate*, situated above Cecil Waugh's body art empire. On the way over you thought about courthouse square, in which the fountain needs a good scrubbing, and to whom you should direct your complaints about the groundskeeping. Whose tree needed a good shaking. Mural aside, you have not begun to ripple their pond around here—but you will.

Yours is not only a backslapping, friendly check-in, but intended to give a personal and official statement regarding the quote-unquote desecration of the mural, put the issue to rest and lower everyone's hackles. Now that you have shown with the move of rolling the mural how big thy dick, time to build bridges instead of burning them. You have a town to remake into a better and more worthy version of itself.

Your version.

Before you even get in the door good: "How'd you like that special section we did on Reynolds?" Gaston asks. "Last Sunday?"

A month ago. Poor Gooch. He's asked you that ten times. "That was really kind."

Dobbs clears his throat. "Little farther back than last week. It's late October."

"Oh, that's right—I just get mixed up on my days, sometimes."

"Gooch, don't you worry." You're cheerful, aw-shucks. "I can't remember what I did five minutes ago."

"Must be going around. Y'all ain't funning with me, are you?"

Dobbs, serious as a judge. "No, sir."

Gooch, squinting at his iPhone calendar, stabbing at the touchscreen with a shaking, knobby finger. "Well, I be dog—October already? Mercy."

"Hard to believe that granddaddy's been dead for a month now." Grief wells up from your nuts. "Dang."

Gooch goes bugeyed: "Do what, now—?"

"You know." Dobbs, gentle. "Mr. Rabbit passed away."

Gooch relaxes at recovering the memory that Rabbit Pettus has died. Nods to you with sympathy. "Town's never gonna be the same without him."

A refreshed travel coffee mug in hand, you plop down across from your wheelchair-bound childhood friend tucked into his corner workstation, an open area wherein he may navigate with ease. As you speak, the journalists both take notes. You observe Gooch shifting in his chair, wincing as though stuck with a pin.

As to your terrible perfidy re: the mural: You begin an oration about how much Rabbit loved the town and his honkytonk. Fought and beat the Nazis. Loved Redtails basketball and football—who don't? You declaim all this in deliberate downhome phrasing designed to play to the readership of the paper; in the parlance of your childhood. You speak their language, or at least slip into the patois with relative ease.

"But most of all Rabbit Pettus was his own man, a self-made mane, as everybody already knows. And the rub for the naysayers on this issue, the niggling nabobs, is that he himself had already expressed similar sentiments about the mural as I hold, mainly being that the occasional complaint or controversy over the antiquated rebel flag element made the peeling, faded relic more trouble than it was worth. I won't lie and tell y'all I'm carrying out some deathbed wish of his. Nor will I deny that, as a Southeastern Redtails fan from the time I could walk, the act of wiping the General Reb mascot from the historical record—as I chose in the heat of an emotional moment to do—feels almost like another death in the family." You try not to snicker at this blatant falsehood. "But maybe I am, in a sense, responding to his wishes. Wishes not exactly expressed to any particular degree or specificity, no; but nonetheless in the spirit of what he thought regarding the mural's future. About having a 'final say' in such matters. At least near as I can reckon from what I read in this here paper of y'all's."

"You never discussed the mural?" Dobbs, suspicious. "Not once?"

"We never talked much about the honkytonk. Or the future."

Mr. Wimmel, as you still think of the aging newspaperman, leans forward, whispers. "You know. Just as an aside. Reynolds, your granddaddy didn't... you know. He—well. What you said. Earlier. Yeah. That's—that's what he— how he put it—he–to the—others. At the ELMS meeting."

You and Dobbs exchange a look of concern. "How he put what? About him not wanting to mess around with the preservation of the mural—?"

"The mural!" Gooch, delighted and relieved. "Yes. Yes. Yes. He said that to me only two days ago, Roy. The day he—passed away. And I'm so sorry. Again. What an enormous loss. My mind's still not right."

You wait, looking at him. He goes back to his screen, typing away. "Gooch?"

He sits staring, absorbed in whatever he's typed. "Yes, what's that?"

"What'd he say?"

"Who?"

"My granddaddy."

"Your granddaddy."

"Yep."

"Oh—about what?" His eyes, wide. "The—mural?"

You say, yeah yeah, ask him if he's all right. He tells you he took a fall the day before, had spent a few hours in the hospital. That he hadn't been sleeping right. All while avoiding eye contact with either of you, and touching his face, and repeating statements, all tells of the liar trying to fabricate a fiction to some degree.

"Anyway, yeah. Old Reynolds. He didn't want to mess with that mural. No sir. So, I don't know. It's not for me to say. Made for good copy now and then. And letters. Pro and con. Letters letters letters. He said it had a particular meaning."

"What did? The mural itself?"

"Letting it fade away, as he had." Gooch, confiding: "You know there was some hoodoo surrounding the mural."

Enough already. "Nonsense."

"No. It's true."

"I'd've heard of it." You must get this interview back on track, make the most of having the press as your willing mouthpiece. "Thing is, getting rid of that divisive, provincial, race-baiting rooster was on my mind from a very young age. In any case, to make The Dixiana—or whatever takes its place— into America's Honkytonk," hoping they could hear the capital letters, "instead of merely South Carolina's Honkytonk, stuck in a version of the past few modern people are keen on keeping alive, seemed a worthy move to make. Mired in the mud of what used to be, instead of what is? No. General Reb, as a symbol, says little about what my granddaddy's joint is, or was. Or who I am.

What twenty-first century Tillman Falls needs to be. It had to freaking go. It's my wall. End of story."

That statement settles in the air like flatulence, or the way cigarette smoke used to drift around in all the newspaper offices of the land. The barber shop downstairs. Everywhere, until people got a clue about smoking.

"Dobbs, good sir? Any other questions for Mr. Pettus?"

You note Dobbs's professionalism and happy demeanor. He's like a different person from the initial years after Devin's explosive head-on car accident had shattered both their lives, albeit in different ways. For the longest time Dobbs had sat in his wheelchair depressed and hopeless, stuck here in Edgewater County, his legs gone, his future forestalled. But alive, unlike Devin's girlfriend. Poor Libby. At least she hadn't suffered. Not like the survivors. Devin and Dobbs, like two sides of a coin—one tarnished, one shining and fresh. A relief.

Dobbs, saying he'd get a story written up for next week's paper, if they deemed your statement about the mural to be newsworthy, which he punctuated with a sly wink.

Spectacular. Getting your list whittled. "Lunch?"

Dobbs, patting his round belly. "You can bet on it—fact, I'm thinking about going over to Manny's. You game?"

Gripping your own expanding gut. "I got a wicked gurgle going here."

"Excellent. How about you, Gooch?"

No response. Wimmel, a pair of earbuds now jammed into his half-moon old man's ears, lost in clicking and surfing.

You ask what's the story with this Manny's on the Green. Not that you don't already know; you've asked around. Multiple interviews, myriad viewpoints to get at the truest sense of how things are.

Dobbs informs about Manny and his folks being Katrina refugees who ended up here because of his wife's family history in the area, had liked it and stayed to recreate what he'd had in New Orleans—a restaurant and music club.

"Another honkytonk, eh?"

"More of a juke joint—that's what your granddaddy, rest his soul, called it at first. But he liked Manny. Said he had good business sense."

"I gotta meet this guy. Let's go get fooded."

Dobbs tosses a pencil at Gooch's head, but he waves off the distraction. He's squint-eyed and scrolling through an article on Buzzfeed: *Orgies, Rumors, and Other Lurid Revelations From The Golden Age Of Gay Hollywood*.

"I guess we can eat without him—he's a grown man. Most of the time."

"You guys get along?"

"I do most everything now." Whispering, bidding you to lean down to his level. "Remind me to tell you about his little 'fall'."

You note that Gooch, no spring chicken, ought to have retired by now, but like Rabbit, you supposed these stubborn old Edgewater County goats didn't have the sense to know when to make the down payment on a golf cart and factor in the marina fees. "This rag down to twice a week?"

Dobbs, grave. "Soon to be a weekly."

"Hm." That can't be good. But why say it—a dying breed, this dead-tree media. "Less work, I guess."

"One way to look at it. But the idea of me carrying on without him—it's hard to imagine. We stay busy with other projects—keeping the blog updated alone takes time every few hours, really, to keep up with the breaking news cycle. We also print another weekly, the *Lake Country Dockside Reader*, which recycles content from the Wednesday paper and adds in comics and puzzles, a human interest feature, usually arts or sports related. In the spring we also put out a slick, the *Edgewater County Visitor's Guide*. That's distributed in rest stop brochure racks from the mountains to the sea."

"Dang. You need to hire some help. Interns. Something like that."

"We'll be fine. All in the works. It's just so sad. Seeing him decline." Dobbs, his voice tight, cough cough, and eyes moist. "But look, I'm dying to hear how my babygirl Creedence is doing—where is she, anyway? And what about Rabbit's memorial? Everyone's eager to know when you plan to reschedule."

"Questions questions," your stomach rumbling. "Off the record, we're going to put on a street festival in his honor. Music festival. Multiple stages. I've had a vision type-deal. Maybe by next spring. If I can pull it off. That's the memorial."

"Fantastic. Can't wait to hear more."

"I've already said too much. All off the record, please."

You gather yourselves, but first you get Gooch's attention.

Fumbling his browser closed, he wrenches around and scowls; you mime eating and rubbing the belly, but he declines by pointing to a pack of Nekot cookies and a twenty-ounce Coke sweating in the Indian summer humidity.

You can dig it. You often work through lunch. Why waste time, right? More to be done. Always more to be done.

◉①✳

AFTER WATCHING DOBBS RIDE HIS SPECIAL LIFT DOWN THE OLD STAIRCASE AND sliding with deft familiarity into his personal wheelchair parked on the landing, out on the sidewalk comes an apology, his strong right hand gripping your wrist.

"Putting that on the paper's website—about your granddaddy's private memorial being public? A stupid mistake. On my colleague's part. Don't you know."

You hoped no need to till that scorched earth again. "Truth be told, I don't remember what I told Gooch that night. Maybe it was me all mixed up. My mind, it was an awful mess. Still is."

He releases your hand. "Let's go eat. Old buddy-row." Warmth. Decades of friendship, with great joy on your part that Dobbs seems so happy with his life. If only Devin were here to round out the trifecta of friends. If only. On the walk over the restaurant, cutting across the green and by the obelisk at its center, you get around to telling Dobbs that you and Creedence had Devin declared dead, but only after a round of expensive private investigation turned up less than a whisper—Devin had become like vapor. Lost. "God knows what happened to him."

Dobbs, nodding, all the blood drained from his face. "At least him and Libby, they're together again."

"At least."

MANNY THEODORE AND ROY PETTUS

"Here come that cripple-ass reporter!" Ahmad, hollering and busting through the kitchen doors, banging them hard against the wall like Manny done told him not to do.

"Him and the Alzheimer's muh-fuh?"

"Naw. Him and another'n."

"Another wheelchair brother?"

"Naw. The one, he walking all right."

"So what the problem, champ? We ain't got a clean two-top for they asses?"

Ahmad, stretching out his skinny arms, his grungy apron needing a good bleaching. "You told me to always keep an eye out for they newspaper asses. Cause you don't never know when there's free advertising to get outta them."

Manny go, aw shit: Ahmad right. "Word."

"Why you got to always bust balls and shit?"

"Cause when the bossman can't bust balls, he might as well not be—"

"Ain't the boss of jack," all under his breath. "Bet."

Staring down across the steam trays full of barbecue and veggies and baked-brown, stringy mac and cheese. Manny got wrote up in Southern Living for it. No shit. Framed on the wall. "Act like you got some sense."

"I'm acting, bossman," doing a bug-eyed shuffle. "Don't you worry. Acting good as you."

"What that supposed to mean?"

"Ain't mean nothing."

"Everything mean something, dog."

Ahmad shrug like, whatever.

He lucky—Manny still want to slap him over hitting that door so hard, or any number of other offenses, but with all they got going on? Hell. He ain't going to start nothing today. Lunch is popping. Peoples's eating and digging it and the cash register ringing. Manny need Ahmad ass to cook and get on with it, and damn if they ain't a catering gig tonight, the County Archives fundraiser over in the old movie theater.

How he move them trays over there? Roll across the green?

Shit no—a long haul on them bumpy walkways. He gonna load the van and drive over. And he need Ahmad for that, too.

"We still got to load that catering order, take it round to the Fine Arts Center." Ahmad, like he reading Manny mind. "Don't forget that."

"I ain't gonna forget."

"I know you ain't."

Ahmad, peeking under the stove vent, glaring across the kitchen.

Manny still thinking. "We might could roll it over if we went over the walkway past the statue stead of going round on the outside—sidewalk all crooked and broke up from them oak tree roots, though. Courthouse side worse."

"Yo, word—we taking it in the van, bro. Ain't rolling no shits over yonder. F'real?"

"Yeah. I reckon so."

Ahmad wash his hands and go to poke at the collard greens which ought to be done by now, and good on that cause people eat they way through Manny greens. Nobody collard greens taste like his, and he'd be damn before he told anyone the secret: nothing but a teaspoon of Liquid Smoke per quart of greens. He make up some shit before he tell folks that kind of simple truth. It not always complicated. In fact, if you know where the bumps and cracks are, you can roll your durn food cart down the most crooked of pathways.

"Fish special in." Kachina, a sweet little server who don't look much older than Manny own babygirl, bangs in and back out the door after grabbing a stack of clean plates. She trained right. "She say she want it extra crispy."

"Ten-four."

Ahmad work the line as two more special orders for oven-fried flounder come back. Ain't nothing but fried fish with apricot jam, but the breading got secret spices—Old Bay all it is—that rock everybody world, and take a few extra minutes to serve up.

Manny's cook get his fish frying and turn to check on the big oven. "Fresh tray of mac and cheese coming up in five, four, one-two-three; next tray going in. Order hup. Order hup," and slinging two prior menu orders for meatloaf now ready under the heat lamps. Ahmad, always be-bopping along to a tune in his thick head, cause Manny don't let no one wear no headphones, not in the kitchen. That a safety thing, there. That ain't no control shit, like Neecie always trying to pull on his ass. He tell them what to do for the good of all their fat asses, like making them wear the right shoes with some rubber on the sole. Shit like that, it ain't rocket surgery. Lord, but people need a Manny in the world to point it out, though! Bet, as Ahmad would say.

Manny listen as him and the prep cooks call to one another, the two old women, Idahlia and Old Neecie, working in tandem. They got them a musicality, like when Manny ass hit that stage after he loosen up his embouchure and soak a reed. Start warm and slow on his tenor before rocking that high, shiny soprano. He do it without thinking, the way them women can work that line. Muscle memory, after a few decades at it.

The boys he got swinging these days—a white dude on bass, no shit, and a few different cats cycling through on the kit; an associate music professor from the university up in Greenville who come down twice a month and set up an electric keyboard—lay way way back on some chill, slow piano blues, deep r&b cuts. Manny and them get toked up, way in the back behind the building where the grease trap sits. Manny ass make sure Lillyanne ain't here on them nights. He catch babygirl burning trees at her age, it gonna be apocalypse now.

Neecie—young Neecie—sometimes take a notion, get up and do a standard like Billy Holiday or whatever she feel like. Mostly Manny doing his smooth jazz thang though.

For now. Manny, he talking to Jasper Glasscock about moving the open mic over from the honkytonk to the hep room in town. Manny say, you bring me in shitkickers with folding money, I let you do open mic twice a week, many times as you want. That the way folks make a living now. Mix and match gigs, put a headstash together. Bring in country music to Manny's? Shit. For all his ass know, that honkytonk gonna close up, that what he bet. Bet anything on it. Manny need to capitalize on the vacuum.

◐◉❋

MANNY WAVE AT THE WHEELCHAIR REPORTER AND HIS BOY, KEEP AN EYE ON THE steam table set up in front of the stage for the lunch buffet, already thinking bout breaking that shit down. Getting the stage set for tonight. Warming up this afternoon. Ain't usually but a few tables there, some cats at the bar. People, they ain't coming out for Manny's music. Not like they done back home. His home. This place Neecie home. It all right though. It making a living.

But music, that why he got in this club ownership bidness. Not to sling barbecue.

"About time for another tray of pudding." He call for it to Old Neecie, who waddle on her cankles, take out the old tray and roll back a fresh one, a big mess of that crap everybody like so damn much.

Manny, he too nice sometimes, agreeing in the lease to keeping 'Oreo

Pudding' on the menu, like it some gourmet shit. Ain't nothing but yeller vaniller pudding with them double stuff Oreos broke up in it. People try they asses to hold onto more stupid crap than a righteous sax– and cocksman like Manny can feature, yo. Small town B-S, there. He play along. He don't care. Pudding. Folks crazy in some ways.

Manny go over after the wheelchair man get settled—Dobb Vandasmit, or whatever the hell it be. Some weird ass name like white people round here would throw at you. Not Becky. Becky sweet. Becky LaFreniere sound like she be at home back in the Quarter where Manny ass wish he was.

Sometimes. Ain't as humid here. But close.

As for the beefy whiteboy rolling in with Dobb, the bro rocking a salmon-colored polo shirt and khakis and these old Tevas like he come in from up yonder at the river. Sandals and slacks—another'n, as Ahmad say. Manny think, I wonder how they fuck with one of them in that chair. How that shit work. Hell, Manny can't see how it work between two normal muh-fucken brothers getting in on, much less a mixed couple of gayboys like this—one broke in half, the other all upright. He ain't want to know.

"Well well now." Manny greet them in his restauranteur voice, not much different from what he use on stage introducing the band, and with that shiteating grin he put on for customers, especially for muh-fuckers like this newspaper boy who can get the restaurant name in print for free.

Manny offer his hand to Dobb V's gay salmon boy. "Mr. Vandsmchidts, who this? You got a new reporter at the paper?"

"I'm no newspaperman—Roy Pettus." He say this with a little smile playing round his lips. Hold out his hand.

"Manny T, they call me round the hacienda."

"Looks like you and me's gonna be fellow merchants here on the green."

"Wait—you Rabbit Pettus grandbaby. Ain't ya."

Roy Pettus say, shit yes he is.

"So I guess you got yourself a Dixiana, now."

"That I do, my friend."

"Man, I'm sure as heck sorry. A good man, that Rabbit Pettus." Manny feel a warm wave of sincere gratitude, all gooey inside like when he getting his dick suck—he mean this shit. "He make us feel at home here."

"My Pa-paw had respect for another solid small biz guy like himself. Like I do. Say—you mind?"

Manny watch as Roy Pettus extend his hand all graceful and shit to the empty seat by the window, 'join us' he saying with one eyebrow arched like old Dr. Spock. Manny think, ok. He go slide past Dobb Vandershits in his chair, sit his ass down.

What he notice most already is how Roy Pettus be like, he the boss here in Manny place, too. He the boss everywhere he plant his flag. Manny don't take no offense—he like that, too. Like when you the headliner in a club: it ain't your home stage, but you the act, you the shit, and you do load-in like you own that room. Manny bet Roy Pettus take his ass in everywhere and act that way. Man, that how a muh-fucker get successful—you rock that shit. You own it. You look around and make eye contact and stay all chill. Like you don't care.

Look at him. Manny hold his eyes for a minute—he don't look away. That playful smile. Like, I got one up on you. That what money do for a man. He know shit you don't, at least it seem that way when you ain't got money.

"What?" he finally ask.

"Nothing, man. I'm digging the vibe." Smooth as silk. "That's all."

"Me, too," he say. "I'm good that way with people—I grok vibes."

"You do what, now?" Manny bust out laughing. "'Grok'?"

"I can dig what somebody's up to. My antennae's tuned to an open wavelength."

"You a psychic, then."

"Not exactly. It's from working with the public all these years."

Manny and Roy Pettus bump fists. "Heard that."

A server bring iced tea, made so sweet by them old women back there you can bout durn near pour it over your hotcakes on Sunday morning. Roy Pettus and Dobb, he roll over there and they fix plates. Wheelchair nigga do it all the time. Manny like the way he get around so good without nobody much helping him. Gay or not—and Manny, he don't much give a rip—Manny admire both these muh-fuckas.

As his boys eat up eat up eat 'em up good, Manny, chatting and happy right alongside his customers. He relaxed like he done got worked over by one of them Beaudock girls he go to some afternoons when he horny as shit. This before he started doing Becky L, of course, screwing her every which way but Sunday. The way that sweet sugar pussy grip onto his prick and squeeze it, that wasn't nothing you could pay money and get. Not when she looking Manny ass in the eyes and grinding and going oh-baby.

Looking with love. Not sex-love, but love-love.

Shit.

Manny think he gonna lose his mind sometimes when Becky L pull that. Especially the first time, back in the winter when they first hook up while Neecie and some of them other ELMS gone off on a tour of a buncha historical societies over in Georgia, when Becky L had a conflict and stay behind to run some shit at the art center. Stupid, Manny know. But it happen.

And Becky L, she say the same thing. "But it's happened now, consequences be damned," as she say the other day with a sorta finality that make Manny blood run like ice.

What a brotherman to do? He love his wife and shit. Word.

But Neecie pussy, it wrecked back when she have Lillyanne. It have a different quality after they push out a baby. It one of them things. It don't mean you don't love they ass. You just want some tight pussy is all, now and then. What you want?

Roy Pettus spill barbecue sauce on his pink-ass shirt and let loose with a cuss—"Mollywhopper!"—Manny ain't never heard. It make his ass laugh, watching Roy Pettus turn so pissed he start making up words. Manny get how it is. He got T-shirts that mean a lot. His ass wear a bib to keep from dripping stains on his skins. When the levees broke, Manny lost a shit-ton of phat shirts. He ain't forgot that shit, either.

◉◐❋

OVER SERVINGS OF THE FAMOUS PUDDING, ROY PETTUS SAY HE WANT TO TALK TO Manny about some specific idear he got. Manny say right-on, but Roy ain't sure he ought to, not with the naughty, nosy newspaperman forking hash and rice into his beak and taking notes with his ears. Which is how he put it word for word, and Manny bust a gut. Roy Pettus, his ass funny as shit. A good-old-bubba-boy, but more sophisticated. He from here, but he ain't from here no more. If that make sense.

"Any news would have to wait for next week's edition anyway—we're put to bed for this week."

"In any case, consider 'off the record' my middle name. No leaks. My PR people will handle the roll-out."

Manny don't know what up with put to bed—that some kind of cock-sucking double talk? Now he ain't know what the deal is with Roy Pettus. Maybe he so warm and nice cause he gay after all.

"You married?" Manny ask real quick.

"I am." Roy Pettus, down and troubled. "Separated, right now. But yeah."

"Sorry, champ. Manny need to keep his mouth shut."

"We're—it might still work out." Dobb and Roy Pettus glance hard and fast at each other. "I should've told you before."

Dobbs real upset by this news. "We can talk later."

"It's—she's developed issues. Similar to Devin."

He all aghast and shit: "Excuse me? For heaven's sake—" "Settle down. She's got a social drinking problem due to boredom. A touch of affluenza. Sure. But she ain't putting it away like old Ruck."

"Still. Bless her soul."

"Yeah." But Roy Pettus, he burnt inside about some shit. Ain't no doubt. Man's eyes go hard as marbles about whatever between him and the old lady.

Preach, Manny think about his own troubles. Amen. Manny curious as all get-out bout Roy Pettus woman named Creedench and this old Ruck boy and whatnot, but he more interested in what Roy Pettus got in mind for that honkytonk of his. What he gonna do, leaving off the part bout his thought it needing sprucing up and maybe what them muh-fuckers in marketing call re-branding, or some shit. Manny don't say none of that—you don't push with Roy Pettus. You let him set the pace.

Which he do. "Hm. Again, I don't know how much I should... oh, screw it. I'm breaking it to the staff later."

Manny wonder what all this be. Sit forward, waiting.

And then his mind blown by what Roy Pettus say, which he ain't expect at all. And he halfway like it too, as do Dobb Vander-smidgen, rocking and rolling back and forth in his wheelchair and saying, now he and Button won't have to go hang out in Columbia at the hip places there—they're gonna get their own coffee shop in Tillman Falls.

More: Roy Pettus say he developing that whole block.

Well, I be dog, Manny think. Don't sound half bad. Long as he keep live music—what they got in coffee shops? That folkie shit? But whatever. That Manny vision for Tillman Falls right there, yo. Music City, SC. Promote that shit the way Pike Bait & Pawn do, billboards up and down the highway. Get muh-fuhs to drive off the interstate, take a chance on the way to the beaches, leave behind some of that vacation money. Small-town southern charm; all them antique shops back on the block over beyond the art center to comple-ment down-home roots music and authentic food—here, and across the street at the honkytonk. Music out on the green. Festivals. Manny and Neecie see some big lunch pops then, boy. Ahmad be baking trays of mac and cheese till his narrow ass croak.

"You look troubled." Roy Pettus seem that way his-self. "Your sunny smile, it faltered."

Manny shrug. Say, ain't-nothing.

"I'm no psychic, but I see something simmering in those wise eyes. Tell me, Manny: What's the flaw in my thinking." His voice changes. Sounds more like he from around here. "Look, I ain't no tenderfoot, but every master's got his blind spot. I can take it, beau. Tell me what I'm missing."

"I say what on my mind. In my own time, though."

He pleased as shit with Manny. Wrinkle his nose. "I like you, m'friend. Tell me about showbiz."

Manny, riffing about his musical rap sheet while keeping his eye on the steam table and buffet, and the knot of elderly black women dipping and yakking it up and happy, all on their second plates and Manny hope them plump hens don't waddle back for a third—that group coming in twice a week like to put him out of business. All them Reverend Nixon Jesus muh-fuhs got beaucoup bucks. Barrels. That what Becky tell him, though not in them words. Ain't nobody got to say it aloud—that church they built over yonder say it all. The crystal cathedral, broadcasting live every Sunday. Now that showbiz, Manny think.

"But truth be told, I kinda like that old honkytonk." Manny, trying to sound all bright and happy. "It almost like we got a little *music city* going here, between us. It ain't never gonna be like N'awlins, where my ass from. But with my place, we getting some decent acts coming through. R&B, jazz, even rock bands. My thinking, if you want to hear it—well."

Roy Pettus lean forward like he do want to hear this rap of Manny's, but he troubled now, like he don't like where this going.

Manny, flapping his gums how if The Dixiana could be re-branded—fuck it, he think, he sound all uptown and shit, like he on Madison Avenue—and could be fixed up and all? Refurbish that beautiful old sign, and your ass say it that way, too, which make his eyes melt and look all sad, y'all could have a durn tourist attraction. "All them old pictures, the stories. Paint yourself a different mural on the side, with some guitars this time instead of no flags waving."

"You're kidding."

"I think it sounds wonderful." Dobb V, wiping Oreo pudding off his mouth. "How lovely—The Dixiana forever."

Manny, going right-on. "Man, y'all already got people coming in from out of town for Jasper Glasscock open mic. What if it rock all weekend long, too? I mean—country music, shit yeah. But y'all getting them rock bands in from Columbia, from Greenville, Charlotte. Them old-timey mofos, wit the long beards and washtub basses and shit. Man. What about that? Music City, South Cackalackie. Not that I don't like your—what you call your coffee shop idear? Hell, do it around the corner, up yonder by the courthouse."

Roy Pettus say 'third-wave coffee,' which he explain is all artisimal and uptown—or upmarket, that how he say it—has been decided, sorry, et cetera; and it gonna bring in all sort of dollars on its own. But as to live music, he don't know, he don't know, he don't know.

"Maybe poetry readings. After growing up around it, I never wanted to mess with any band nonsense. Too much bullshit. Egos. If you don't mind me saying. As a non-musician, and all."

Manny say, no no. He been all round this world. He know what Roy Pettus mean. "Running a joint? It all nothing but rigmarole—they ain't no doubt bout that part. But the music, it in my blood."

Manny say he'll tell Roy Pettus bout his daddy blowing the bone in the big jazz bands, including Preservation Hall for a goodly stretch, one of these afternoons. "But man, it your place now. You got to do what your business sense tell you right for you. I'm thinking about what right for me, and what right for the town. It ain't got much identity, ya dig?"

"In deed-a-ly dood-a-ly."

Whatever that mean. "Between my place and yours, and Cecil Waugh's side, and the PGAC, maybe it could. Easton across the river annexed and getting new subdivision construction, and bedroom commuter types from over in the lake country—man, I don't know. We could get it going on. Just need a little gas on the fire."

"Have no fear. Coffee will bring them off the highway quicker than some fusty old honkytonk. Let's take the 'sin' out of synergy, so I don't gotta own a tavern catering to a rotating cast of inebriates."

"I'm just trying to think how to exploit what we got. For the good of my business. All synergistic and shit, sure. Ya got me on that."

"An honest man."

"Yo. I own up to that part."

Roy Pettus get it. "Hell of a speech. But I don't know. Coffee. I wonder if the train hasn't left the station."

"The Dixiana, it got a vibe and a history you c'ain't deny. That a hook your ass can market. All I'm saying, champ."

Manny notice Ahmad looking out from the kitchen. His bro-in-law send out Idahlia to check over what left after that last run on the buffet. One of them fat shits drop a whole chicken leg, leave it laying on the floor.

"I reckon I got to get back to work—we got catering today, too. Work me like a old gray mule in there."

"And then you play?"

"Not tonight. A few nights a week, though. Them some long-ass days."

Roy Pettus nod and press his lips together. "Small business ownership, it ain't for slackers."

"Hell no it ain't."

"Gumption is a key tenet of membership in the merchant class."

Manny laugh and stretch and scratch at his tight T-shirt. Today he got on a vintage heat transfer of Chico and the Man on a yellow and red ringer Neecie snag off eBay, nice and new like somebody kept in a plastic bag for forty-ass years.

"Here's what: I'm gonna give 'Music City' a fair mulling. Respect?"

"Respect."

Dobb V been listening close. "Manny's got insight, I think. But a good coffee shop? I'd be in heaven."

"Roy Earl?" Manny give a chuckle. "That a good Edgewater County name right there, y'all."

Them cheeks flash pink as his polo shirt. "Only Dobbs gets to use that. Roy, or the Royster. That type-deal. For everyone else."

Manny say he feel him. Say he'll be Roy Pettus to him, and nothing else. "That sound good, champ?"

Roy P, he belch o-k at that. Good on him. For every belch, a dollar in Manny pocket.

Wiping his hands with a branded Manny's on the Green moist towelette, Royster go, "Look here—the chicken. Is it organic?"

"The fried chicken?"

"Yessir." He go all guilty and shit. "I've gotten used to organic free range."

"That shit orgasmic. I don't know about no organic. Ain't it all organic?"

"Never mind."

Manny compliment Roy Pettus for rolling paint on that durn confederate rooster over yonder. "That was a part of my idear anyway, to get rid of that thang. That keep away more people than it bring in. Just sayin'."

Roy Pettus beaming and satisfied, like he been waiting a long-ass time to roll that mural. "My ever-loving pleasure. Overdue is an understatement."

Manny excuse himself. Help replace steam trays and then seat motherfuckers from the power plant in they short sleeve shirts and ties and khaki pants, two of them fat as hogs, and Manny holler that Ahmad better get to prepping mac and cheeses for tomorrow lunch as well as that catering order, and mercy but it don't stop. Yeah, Manny think. He play tonight after all. Call the fellas. That his happy place, onstage. That worth all this bullcrud. He ready to turn this part over to Neecie ass, but she too busy being one of them ELMS.

Oh, lord: what she gonna say to Becky, though. He keep putting it out of his mind—that only way he not shitting himself. He just wanna play music. Or maybe get his ass out of town before she cut his prick off, snip snip.

Shit; fuck it.

He go and make that mac and cheese himself; it take his mind off this tired worry-wart bullshit. Until a sexy-ass text Becky L send get him stirred up. Manny don't know how he gonna break it off. But he got to. Somehow.

ROY

As Manny's fine-ass southern-fried comfort food transforms your gut into a roiling, greasy sea, you linger to sip tea and watch the restaurant ease down from a lunch pop. Dobbs, whom you promise to fill in later regarding Creedence, wheels back to work while you watch the proprietor small-talking the last of the diners and directing his kitchen with stern efficiency, all of which gives you a chubby.

Smiling with admiration, you get caught up on email and Facebook. Staring at the blue light from the screen, skimming and skipping along the surface of random internet content, memes, gifs, cartoons, ads, occasional MSM news—stocks on the move upward, yay, but world war breaking out in Ukraine any time now. Oh, good.

Manny sits down again and asks about your life, your success. How you got so fat.

"Just good old-fashioned hard work."

"Word. But I like to hear how people pull it off. You got your own plane, dog."

The plane; the plane. You hold no truck with this fluffing. No, you say, nothing special; you tell him it's only a Piper, and you didn't even buy it new.

You get to the meat. That's what he wants. "Rewind twenty years: I thought with the coffee shop I bought and renovated next to the campus—my campus, where I'd lived since leaving here—I'd found my little pigeonhole. My happy. I loved college. Loved being in the college ghetto. And I don't mean anything racial by 'ghetto,' yo. Not in that. You know. Context."

"None taken." Manny snorts and laughs, sucking on a toothpick.

Blushing. "Anyhoo. Thought about opening a kiosk out at one of the malls next—that'd been my big plan. Woo-hoo. Reaching for the sky. Little did I know." Remembering the proper order of the story—after a while, you find it all rolls into one. "So then this cat who owned the yogurt shop half a block away, he says, he says, Roy, looky here, you ever wanted to get into yogurt? And I said, not as such. But smoothies—smoothies were breaking big. And this second business, it'd be right across the street. I could see the building from the front tables at the Carolina Beanery."

Manny tells you he remembers that smoothie craze shit. "All-a sudden, you had a smoothie joint on every corner. And now it come back round again, too."

"Right on. And I had a mess of good promotional ideas." You pull out one of your old SBFC cards. "See that cartoon banana? I painted those on the walls. Put them in the ads. T-shirt. Stickers. Koozies."

"Look like, I dunno. Mr. Peanut."

"Hey—nothing new under the sun."

You talk about how successful you became, the amusing TV commercial in which you acted out all the parts Eddie Murphy-style, printed the cute little anthropomorphized bananas on T-shirts and banners and posters and stickers, and how the re-branded smoothie joint in the college neighborhood thrived, especially after being kick-started by a reporter on the business beat who saw you supervising the new signage installation, interviewed you, wrote a glowing article.

Yeah; you also slipped him fifty bucks to 'polish up the prose,' sure. Make thy own luck, as they say.

"A couple years go by. Big success. Then, corporate rep from guess where calls? Yep—the local mall. And she's all like, we got a hole in our food court, beau, right between a Puddingford's Old Timey Gelateria and a high-volume Cracker Barrel Express."

Manny cackles. "Not a hole in ya food court. C'ain't have that."

"Hell no you can't. They'll, they'll think the mall's going under!" Big laughter from you, too. "And so, we—meaning me—went over and had ourselves a looky-look. It'd been an Orange Julius, so the build-out wasn't gonna be nothing. Most expensive part of our operation are the industrial blenders, worth every penny. And of course you run into shit like signage. Fucking brutal how much they ask to hang a freaking shingle with your logo on it."

"Them sign boys surely do. I looked into all that shit after the storm, when we was gonna stay. Build it all back out—new signage the least of it. Be part of the revival folks was talking about putting on. Before we give in and decide to get out."

"Hard to leave? That was your home."

"Took me a while to get used to this place. Tell you what."

"Can only imagine."

"Better here for my babygirl. Less trouble for her to get into. Ya know ya know."

With no frame of reference regarding children and such responsibility, you continue about how that next Christmas the mall's corporate office called and yet another chirpy rep said, hey, why don't you put a Spotted Banana Fruitshake Company™ (after opening the first mall stand, you trademarked the name and the dancing bananas) in 'the palace,' as the young woman called the new mall on the beltway outside Charlotte, and you'd said, without missing a beat, I'll drive up there today.

You took a tour of the entire dazzling property, gazed upon the shimmering tile floors and conditioned, scented air of the mall, buzzy and busy, and you declared, yeah, boy. A cup with a straw in every freaking hand. Your trademarked logo and product should prosper there among myriad food court choices, a grand oval at the center of the mall that included a cathedral-like skylight and a full-sized merry-go-round and the ringing cacophony of the diners at the small tables. Happy children running free. Strollers. Purchases in bags. Deliveries. Background music. Banners and messages and meaning, but most of all?

Money.

You hauled ass on the freeway back to Columbia, blazing through Edgewater County without stopping to see your grandparents sitting in their decrepit old house you wished you could afford to replace for them. Your mind, racing at seeing this smoothie stand turn into an honest-to-god franchise. You pictured the logo, back-lit, on storefronts and mall façades and in plazas and emblazoned across multiple advertising platforms, promotional items, uniforms, uniforms that would feature a different colored polo shirt for staff, assistant manager and GM, red, blue and gold and featuring insignia embroidered upon the left breast. Minimum wage payroll. High margins, even with your healthy ingredients, but because of that, an easily attained bump. The prestige of the Spotted Banana smoothie, worth an extra fifty cents. The Starbucks model.

You spent that night putting together a business plan going WAY beyond simply one additional store. In the morning you got on the horn with various suppliers in the Greater Charlotte metropolitan area, population two million and growing.

Yeah. That's where you'd gone in your head—go big, or not at all. All in. Some stupid saying.

How far could you take it? That was the question, as you tell Manny.

You have him on the edge of the seat. Leaning forward, face framed by a throwback thick ring of receding afro, damn if this dude doesn't have some muscles under his vintage Freddie Prinz T-shirt. Ignoring questions from his staff, waiting to hear more, dude has bitten his toothpick clean in half.

"But I also said, hold on. I didn't much cotton to the corporate atmosphere in the malls, the edicts and orders regarding when you had to open and close. How you do this and that; you don't do this, no no, not ever. And CAM fees—Jesus, what a racket and a ripoff. I got into this entrepreneur crud because I didn't want to work for anybody."

"I can dig it."

"So from there, I opened Charlotte #2, but this time, in the university village to the north like the first SBFC, on an outparcel near a busy intersection that also got major-league traffic during NASCAR and outdoor concert season —both venues are right up the highway, and visitors funnel through from the interstate. Location; check. Twenty-thousand all stoned on their way to see Dave Matthews; a hundred-thousand rednecks and their families on the way to spend a whole weekend watching Dick Trickle burn up gas going in a circle. Big-ass success."

"Where you go next?"

"Charleston. Not only into university areas, but tourist traps. Right off the Market where the cruise ships dock. Just took off. Biggest numbers yet."

"Where you'd get the scratch? Loans?"

"At first I had plenty of credit, and used it, and took all sorts of risks that could've backfired. But they didn't. And I had cash—man, by then I'd been running a decent trade for almost ten years, and hadn't spent hardly a cent on anything for myself, or my new wife. I kept putting it back into the company. Investing—I managed solid growth all through the dot-com shit by going with strong traditional blue-chips, steady performers, slow growth. We didn't live nothing—anything like we do—did," you correct, your stomach burning with acid from all the barbecue, "after I sold out to ConParAgCorp. And then we could live wherever she wanted to."

"Sedge Island, eh? That some tony shit there."

"Wasn't my first choice."

"You done it for your old lady."

You nod. "Like a chump."

"Naw, brother—a champ. That's how you think of that. Sometimes you got to do one for them—they mama to your babies. I didn't want to bring my ass here. I had to be told to do it. I'm glad she did, now. I think," he says, and a darkness passes through him that's visible in the deepened lines of his forehead, and you say to yourself, oh, boy. Manny's got some heavy trip going on, too.

"Even if she's—unfaithful? With some asshole?"

"Ah." Manny, making a pained face of male solidarity. "Yo. Well."

"Yo. Is right."

"I know it hurt."

"The little fu—fudging little crapdoodles. Both liars."

"It was a friend of your'n?"

"Worse—an employee."

"Yowza."

How it twists you inside to verbalize the truth, and you wonder if you'll ever get over her duplicity—at least when someone died, they were gone and you could move on. Dissolving a marriage, with this you have no experience. "A little hard to forgive."

Manny grims up and says, shit yeah. Hard to deal with the idea of a 'muh-fuh' in his parlance parking the ride in your old lady's garage. "Ain't gonna fly."

On this unsettled note, you explain that your story must for now remain 'to be continued,' and you get your ass out of there, go to call and see about the circumstances of your wife's release from treatment.

Decide you're going to tell her it's over, definitive; decide to decree that soon as she's signed out of rehab she may come home, but only long enough to get her crap the eff out of the house. That you're gonna freaking sell it out from under her cheating, whoring, freckled redneck Edgewater County ass. That'll get her, that last part—can't stand the thought of being an ordinary redneck homegirl.

And afterwards? It'll all feel better, and you'll start on your business plan for converting The Dixiana into the crown jewel of your burgeoning new empire, the Carolina Beanery Tillman Falls. Anchoring a mixed-use building—a temple built amid the decrepitude of what was, one modeled on the heavens and ruled by a benevolent high priest presiding over a new, rising city of the sun—its storefront stature heralding the advent of an incipient Edgewater County golden era will shimmer with self-possession and success.

You.

Your vision.

Your stamp on all things Edgewater.

Not for you—for them.

Before you call Creedence to impugn whatever psychological equilibrium she might have achieved you're buzzed by Button, to whom you'd rather talk anyway, and decide to go to the honkytonk to meet her and lay out your vision for the future. Now that, you think, feels like a plan worth pursuing. Positive energy needed, and nothing these days fills you with pep more than the idea of gutting the honkytonk, as well as hanging out with Button. She calms you. Little hippie's got it going on.

If only you could figure out how to monetize it, you'd get into the Button

Sykes business, bottling and selling her calm and wisdom. You'd make a fortune. Another one. Money, starting to pile up. It's as though you attract money-energy through your attitude about it. Or some crazy notion.

BUTTON

M id-afternoon, bright sunlight cut sideways into the honkytonk from the front windows. Button, since working there, realizing how much a bar's no place for natural light, except maybe the brand of beer.

She regarded the Pennsylvania hex, a mandala-like circle painted on wood, a flower within a star with a series of circles representing the lunar cycle, hanging shaded and shadowed over the empty stage. It was said Rabbit Pettus had learned powwow back in his West Virginia mountain childhood, could heal sickness with incantations and such, but Button had never gotten him to own up to it, to share spells and secrets. He'd laughed like it was all a joke. Said the hex above the stage had always been there and didn't hold any deeper meaning.

"I'm probably one of the few. Who would understand. Could dig it. The hex stuff."

"Shit, girl—Mama Runelle picked up that thing at a craft show. Ain't no magic about it."

His eyes said otherwise—a glimmer of recognition that spoke volumes. She let it go. Power is in part derived from secrecy. She got it.

Button, a keyholder, rued and grieved the loss of Mr. Rabbit while she waited in The Dixiana for Roy Earl, and while doing so she practiced conscious breathing, and focused on activating her heart chakra. She visualized a brilliant green light, crystalline, emanating from within her chest. Button both received and projected this energy, this glowing warmth of love and assurance, a divine feedback loop.

The walks out at the river trail had been quite beneficial, this much she could already tell about Roy E. Pettus. Slipping meditation tips in on him. Breathing. Mantras. Chakras. Consciousness. Shaking off the shackles of the matrix of artificial realities imposed upon the one true natural reality through the abstraction of symbol and language. And the like. Subtle, on that last point. Button knew to awaken someone gradually.

Or so she had been made to understand.

Button, unsure she'd awakened anyone yet. Maybe Roy Earl Pettus would be the first. A challenging project, as bound up in money and power as he seemed to be.

Looking over her list of Phish concert recordings chosen for this week's listening on her phone—

12/31/91 Worcester, MA
7/5/94 Ottawa, ON
10/21/95 Lincoln, NB
7/22/97 Raleigh, NC
8/1/98 East Troy, WI
7/31/99 Naeba, Japan
2/20/03 Rosemont, IL

—Button smiled with anticipation, especially for the 97 and 98. She had attended both with Heather, the music on those fraught with special memories. But all groovable. It was Phish. The worst show was still more interesting than most popular music.

Like any thoughtful phan, she had to plan her listening—phistening?—with such diligence. Otherwise, too many choices, thousands of concerts going back thirty years. You could browse the Phish archives on internet streaming sites for hours trying to find just the right show to play. Same with the Grateful Dead, at nearly a thousand more concerts than Phish! Better to have it pre-researched and structured. Reviews to contrast the fat jams with the flat shows, of which there weren't many until the last few tours before Button hit bottom. In any case, her playlists—phishlists—served as assistance for the decision-addled, distracted music lover.

Dizzy. Surreality, a wrinkle of déjà vu on top of vertigo. The spirit of Rabbit Pettus, brushing by her arm like the tickling surprise of unseen cat's whiskers on a cool bare ankle. Vision doubled, she went all tingly and braced herself to keep from falling, reminiscent of sucking on a nitrous balloon and skirting with unconsciousness. What—was she passing out?

A flash memory of dancing in the rain with Heather at a show in Raleigh, a massive thunderstorm rolling through as the band played 'Runaway Jim' while blue lightning popped from the thunderheads, so real it might be happening again—a simultaneity, an overlay, an alternate reality, or else all that's ever happened has always been happening and happens still now. Right now—rain sluicing down her body, the cotton dress clinging to her flesh; the vision of Heather's full and feminine body underneath her soaked T-shirt, as though she'd stepped barefoot out of a painting by the old masters. "I want to live this way forever," Heather had declaimed to the thunderous, desultory skies pouring forth. Pupils open and dark, mad laughter, thick hair weighted with the dew of heaven and hanging around a face shimmering with life-energy—a goddess descended. Button had whirled round, yes yes yes, forever, a cry, an edict, an exultation of intent.

And still, a flicker of that intention from a single glowing tea-light candle on an altar in an Edgewater County woman's bedroom, and driving all Button did and thought and believed. Hope—hope had taken her this far.

A few years back, she'd felt no such hope watching the DVD of that Raleigh show the band had released—it made her weep as hard as the storm had raged. She took the disc the next day to the used record store in Columbia, traded it for credit she'd yet to redeem.

Not much of a reality to the passage of time. Only a particular perception. Call PKD. She was halfway through the *Exegesis*, a PDF she'd been paging through day-by-day for the last six months. Orthogonal time had been Dick's big idea, the past and the future at right angles and coexisting; heady bullshit.

Button, checking the fleshy heel of her hand for the small 'A' she'd drawn in blue ink. Smudged, but intact. Awake—not dreaming. "I'm gonna dream about my hands tonight," she reminded herself, though it hadn't happened yet. She examined her palms. "I'm definitely gonna dream. About my hands. Tonight."

She'd been working on lucid dreaming for a couple of months. Thinking: much to learn in the dreamworld. Information. If for no other reason Heather Ponderview often dwelt in the dreams, and to have a lucid experience might make for a fun nocturnal consciousness journey. If Button couldn't be with the woman in reality, she'd be with her in the night, on the astral plane, or wherever dreams occurred. Lucid dreaming, allowing one to manipulate the reality of those dreams, consciously so. And boy, did Button want to manipulate Heather's reality... *oof*.

But lately Agatha of Aberdeen had been showing up in dreams, dancing in her flames of heartbreak and anguish. Agatha would seem to appear out of nowhere, incongruous with the other events. She wanted to stop and question the wraith. Perhaps mastering lucid dreaming would afford such an opportunity.

She freshened up her A with the indigo-black ink from a gel pen she carried. Checked the digital clock behind the bar by the register, all but obscured by postcards and band bumper stickers and old work notices everywhere, beer prices and menu items chalked over and changed on the old board by the back brick wall near the swinging doors of the kitchen. Read the menu board. Looked away. Read it again. Checked the A. Not a dream. If you did this stuff enough during the day, eventually your subconscious would try it, and when it did, you'd realize in the dream you were dreaming, and could become active in the unfolding. Touch your dream-girl again. That kinda stuff.

Button, glad for time's illusory nature. Hard to swallow not seeing the love of one's life for so long, at least in a linear sense.

An incantation: "Heather. Hands. Dream. Tonight."

Despite her work so far with Roy, her ego-mind worried the meeting he'd called would prove contentious, until castigating herself that worry represented nothing more than a misuse of the most powerful tool in the consciousness woodshed: imagination. Walfredo, her future self, sent a smidgen of reassuring warmth to spread through her midsection and remind her all was as it should be, and that whatever happened would be okay.

◉◉✳

ROY CAME SHUFFLING INTO THE BAR WITH A BEDRAGGLED AND UNHAPPY SLUMP TO his posture, no spring to his step, and she knew he needed to be engaged on a pleasant and human level. She beamed and hugged him tight, went to pour them both unsweetened iced teas. Roy, gesturing to the corner high-backed stools at the bar. Many important conversations held at that spot over the decades, as Trudy has said with such awe and pride at her bar being so crucial to the town's lifeblood. Here now, another such moment.

Cheerful and encouraging, Button let her new boss direct the ebb and flow of the conversation. His body language stiff and voice frostily formal and almost unlike his normal accent—a warning sign of a possible psychotic break, truth be told—he dove right into his plans, the all important plans for the future of The Dixiana, which as he explained to Button would be no future at all. Not in this form, anyway.

She welcomed this openness if not the news itself. "You're really gonna. Shut it down?"

Damn straight, he all but shouted with his chest puffed out.

Cringing at his near-outburst. "Aw. Crap."

"Let's not pretend it's a surprise."

"It's not. It's just—a shame."

Folding his arms, relaxing into his role as prime mover of this particular reality. "Far from it, m'dear. This block's gonna transform—like magic—into the premiere modern, green, multi-use redevelopment in Edgewater County. It'll change everything about downtown. The dynamic. The spunk. The spirit of Tillman Falls, which feels downright stiff and stale and in need of a poking with a stick to see if it's still got any blood left moving in it. I'm talking bike lanes and green space and livability. I'm talking an Apple store. Southeastern University will want to put a satellite campus here. People will live here again. Really live."

"They live here now." Her own family home lay only six blocks away, situated amidst other columned and ornate Greek revival houses of the legacy, monied section of old Tillman Falls, quite a few designated as historic in various registries of such matters kept locally and beyond. "Don't they?"

He waved her off, guzzling tea and crunching ice. Button stopped herself from castigating him about it. Nothing worse for the enamel.

"I've already got in mind the idea of starting from the dirt and building a couple more floors up. Put in four to six condo units on top of retail-slash-restaurant. Probably four. Loft-style. Upscale. Downtown living."

"And below?"

"The Carolina Beanery Tillman Falls will anchor. We're bringing the boho college coffee shop atmosphere back here to the green. Maybe another, smaller retail space or two. A nice boutique. An independent bookstore. Anything but antiques and tattoos."

"Bringing the 'boho' back? *Here*?"

He drummed his fingers. "Mm. You've got a point. There's no 'back' regarding what I have in mind. Change has already come—look at Cecil Waugh's place. Manny's. Imagine them being in business here back in the day. You can't. But you know what I mean."

"An act of destruction. Designed to usher in. A new epoch."

"A groovy way to look at it—I'm envisioning a golden age for Tillman Falls. We'll make a ritual out of the process. Do it with total reverence and respect and so on."

"Revitalization. From the ashes of what came before."

"You make it sound like the towers falling again. No. A seed in the fertile southern ground. Who knows what other development we'll attract—there's a shit-ton of money on the table, y'all."

"Who is 'y'all'? And—where's the table?"

"The royal—the rhetorical—okay," he broke off with a chuckle. "Some of this is above my pay grade, as old Rabbit might put it, and there're pieces of the puzzle that'll have to fall into place for it all to work out. Long story long, I sell coffee. And here in the EC, we're gonna sell a li'l mountain of it. Gallons. Oceans—an ocean, Button, of fine-roasted, fair trade coffee underneath my sandaled feet." Roy, his face slack and glazed with ambition. "And you'll be bobbing on the surface right alongside me."

"Me?"

"You."

"In what. Sense?"

"You, Button Sykes, are gonna be my GM. You, you. Wonderful You."

Her? Her. "Um—what about Trudy?"

Silence. Staring. A minuscule head shake. "Nope."

"She's put in. So many years."

A forced, fake smile. "Trudy don't—doesn't—know how to run a coffee shop. An artisanal coffee concern. She's—she's a Pirkle."

"Samuelson. Pirkle's her maiden name."

"Whatever."

"Trudy's smart enough."

"Be that as it may."

After hesitating, Button explained that whatever else Trudy might be—and inside Button thinks of her as she thinks of Roy Earl or anyone else, as a fellow spirit and node of spatially-specific, physicalized consciousness happening to reside inside the meat-shell that everyone calls Trudy—she meant a great deal to Mr. Rabbit. And with all due respect, Roy had an obligation to Trudy. "We all do. Which leads me to say. Thank you for your vote. Of theoretical. Confidence in me."

"You've earned it."

"How? I've only worked at The Dixiana for. A couple. Of years."

"By being cool. By—you know. Being down. Being hip. You went to college." He held up his hands like 'nough said. Then added: "Oh—and you're a jamband fan. You dig the Dead."

"More of a Phish-head. But guilty."

"Still, a free thinker. Intelligent. Curious. We'll get you up to speed on the Dead."

Roy expounded upon his rock concert experiences, making seeing the Grateful Dead twice sound like he had been 'on tour' for decades; asked Button about her own path to getting into the heady scene.

"Like most folks. I got turned on to it. For all the wonders of Phish tour? It caused me some problems, too. Well—not 'it.' But I fell into. Some bad habits. Ya know ya know."

Roy said, "That happens sometimes when we love things too much, maybe," an introspective and poetic aside that hit her spiritual sweet spot. "The things we cherish cause us problems. Yep yep."

❁❁❁

After the healing San Diego sojourn of the early 2000s with Heather and her fungible family in Ocean Beach, Button made the journey back home to South Carolina for a putative 'visit' that turned permanent.

Yeah. Permanence. Edgewater County 4-ever.

She didn't fully believe this reality until years later, after her father had died his painful and horrible death from the additional disease manifestation, and Thim had left Button holding the bag on the remaining family members. Her father's illness—how it had dominated her life for so long. Perhaps it still did.

Oh, sure, they fixed that bout of lymphoma, his little Agent Orange souvenir, as he called it. What a noncrisis—a full recovery. The second cancer? More of a battle than he faced in the war. Throat, spreading to the esophagus and beyond; lesions on the liver. A rough one. Painful. But not over fast—the cancer drama consumed his final three years of meatspace existence.

Worst of it for her dad had been the treatment, not the disease; the surgeries, poison pills and IVs which left him with an even ruddier complexion than before, and a sensitivity to heat, a problem with excessive sweating, but the lord knew, as Buddy said, he'd sweated his ass off in Vietnam, and this after sweating his ass off all his life spent living in South Carolina. Would sweat as much as necessary if it meant he could live long enough to see his girls grow up. Have their own babies. That, always his big thing. Didn't get his wish. The babies part, anyway. The growing up aspect, that also up to debate, at least from his viewpoint. And especially about Button.

Could she blame him? Not a world beater. Not much of anything. Until she became a nursemaid to a dying man, a duty she had fulfilled with grace and as little resentment as she could.

◉①✳

FOLLOWING THE BLESSED EVENT THAT'D BEEN HER FATHER'S RELEASE FROM HIS suffering, Button's mother Tinky collapsed like a skyscraper wired for demolition. Had been driven to the edge of madness by the horrifying effects of the cancer—before beginning intensive radiation, they'd removed all Buddy Sykes's teeth, sure to drop out anyway. Twin tattoos on either side of his neck like a pair of gun sights. The swelling that came, of his throat and face and his tongue, finally, protruding and rendering him unable to eat, speak. His eyes, glassy and imploring, but no less clear and blue. The stuff of horror-movie makeup.

The scratchy notes he'd written to communicate his thoughts and needs were kept archived in a Ziploc freezer-bag inside a plastic storage container. It also contained scraps of a writing life forever stuck in first gear, always more dream about rather than manifested into any meaningful work. A novel, an unfinished screenplay, poems, journals, the short scripts from college that had shown so much promise—supposedly—had been tucked away for several years. Button, like, brutal honesty moment? She only dabbled at creative endeavors, making nothing of all the stabs at purporting to write. But not dwelling on her lack of culmination as a failure. A necessary step on the path. No dwelling. More efficacious to get blazed or vaped, medicinal only, and get in a now-centered power walk. Direct return on energetic investment.

Two days after the funeral, Thim returned to Washington where she worked as an aide to then-Third District U. S. Representative Sandra Three-Rivers (R, SC), a one-sixteenth Native American former news anchor who exploited her 'tribal' heritage the same way casinos got opened, and about to launch her winning run for the governorship of the great state of South Carolina. As Button prepared a home-cooked meal for her heartbroken mother and grandparents, Tinky became ill—violent, sudden, epic. Had ended up later taking her to the hospital where she lay raving in Vietnamese and dry-heaving.

They began injecting Button's mom with various chemicals to control nausea and dehydration. A crapshoot with modest results.

"I think it's psychosomatic," Button said to a puzzled internist poring over inconclusive test results and leaning toward a diagnosis of a mystery virus or bacteria.

"What makes you say that?"

"Our dad—rather, my father—died a few days ago. He'd been ill a long time."

"I suppose that could be in play. Our emotions are powerful." The young attending physician, a resident, whispered with with a wink, "That's right. We can make ourselves sick. If we're not careful."

The doctor held Button's gaze, and she remembered perceiving a shimmery cast ripple over his face, another in a series of moments of mystical and crystalline clarity in this period she chalked up to having ceased smoking herb for the duration of her father's decline.

The kind-eyed doctor said they'd admit Tinky overnight, keep working on controlling the nausea. Button, saying she'd stay with her mother. She didn't want to go back to the house with her grandfather, who'd been drinking nonstop since his son passed away. How he refused to look at Buddy dying in that bedroom, hunched over because the tumor had grown so large it pressed against nerves and made it so her father could no longer lie down onto his bed, only sit slumped in his threadbare, stained T-shirt and PJ bottoms. With yellow mucus dripping from his protruding tongue, scratching out notes and receiving morphine and waiting to die, finally his eyelids began to swell, and the notes became all-but illegible. Including the one begging Button to give him all the morphine at once.

Plenty of drugs in the house to do the job. No one had missed a Xanax or two Button had taken from her mother's prescription. A passing fancy. Not a new habit. An extra banishing ceremony to rid her body of the wicked spirit engendered by the corporate pharmaceutical substance. A profanity against both sobriety and the spirit-path. Button had pretended to not understand the suicide note. Ignored it. Her dad had passed on his own that next weekend. And here she was.

Her mother's puking episode? Dramatic, yeah; a problem, but nothing compared to what Button had seen with her dad. In the hospital her mother thrashed, moaning and retching for most of the night, producing occasional bile recalling all too well her late husband's body expelling its own toxins. Button, supporting her mom's forehead over the plastic pan, wiping her mouth, comforting, clucking, cooing. Serving. Her part to play. It was fine. A new challenge. Took her mind off the complicated father grief.

At last Tinky settled down and stopped vomiting, the cocktail of meds sending her into a fugue state of hallucination and ir-reality. She pointed to the white board on the wall of the hospital room with the nurses' names and other info, demanding, "Change channel—change channel—I no like this! No! I no like this! Change channel." As for the actual flickering TV, she kept referring to it as the fireplace, for Button to put on another log—she cold, she cold. Then no, she hot, she hot; change channel; she cold; she hot.

At last, with the cable news cycle and propaganda glimmering like tawdry fetish porn across their hollow-eyed, late-night sickbed faces, she sat crumpled and chilled, watching her mother ease into a twitchy unconsciousness. Sometime before dawn Button realized she might be in shock from it all, but kept the conclusion to herself. Too much on her plate to wallow in PTSD.

◎◉✳

BEFORE TINKY PASSED INTO DRUGGED UNCONSCIOUSNESS, BUTTON WATCHED AS HER mother's face, in the wake of her fading nausea, transformed into a tight, pinched caul of concentration. The diminutive Asian wife and mother got onto her knees in the middle of the hospital bed, tangling her saline IV. Button sprang to her feet, at the ready in case the plump woman who had grown up a Vietnamese peasant rolled off onto the floor.

Bent over as though kneeling in prayer, Tinky began 'working' with her chubby fingers on a project, an invisible one, nestled amidst her tangled and damp sheets. Her fingers knotted and hands grasped.

"What're you doing there, Mama?"

"I work on this. I fix. I fix this."

Button got it—sewing. The trade her mother had learned once Buddy had gotten them settled in Edgewater County: Tinky, getting work as a seamstress at the hosiery mill, the manufacturing concern one of the last holdouts from the mid-century, linthead glory days of the county before all that work went overseas. The equivalent labor manifested as the loading and unloading of transport trucks over at the superstore distribution center, containers full of clothing sewn half a world away and shipped across the ocean. Quite antithetical to growing the cotton on nearby land, picking and processing and milling it into a commodity all in the same location.

Tinky, working through her pregnancy with Thim and then Button, too. Had worked after their birth, letting the grandparents care for the girls. Worked until the last day of the mill's operation, when its business of making pantyhose and stockings and knee-highs had been off-shored, and the factory shut by its corporate owner. Button, not sure she'd ever worn pantyhose a day in her life.

The mill closed when Button had been four, and since losing her job Tinky had run the house and worried over the girls and their behavior and where-abouts, a cloying and suffocating motherfucker of a mother-daughter relation-ship, one that'd driven Button away as much as her father's strict codes of conduct and thought.

Still, there she sat, Button watching as her drugged mother pantomimed the motions of sewing late into the Southern night. At least the woman had ceased vomiting, which had been the main goal.

Once Tinky finished her phantom sewing project and lay back down, Button crawled onto the extended hospital lounge chair made for such overnight stays by loved ones and covered herself with a thin blanket. After a time her mother at last lapsed into a full, snoring sleep, rest that eluded the daughter among the beeping machines and soft-shoed nurses drifting in and out of the room like curious spirits.

The next morning her mother had improved. Had no memory of vomiting or ending up in the hospital and began to panic anew, waving her hands around and asking for her hairbrush and about whether the two house cats had been properly fed. Button assured they had, and would soon take her mother home.

Tinky seemed to remember all that had gone on before. Her husband dying, the funeral. The reality of right now. Or so Button assumed from a flickering glance of her mother's dark eyes outside at the morning sun. Her occluded, medicated pupils skittered over to the date on the white board. She commented on the day. Button had said, yes: one more Saturday night.

Home they went. New routines. Cleaning up, cleaning out. Medical junk. Closets. Drawers. Her grandmother helped, dying a year later of a heart attack while out gardening in the back yard, such a sweet and easy death. Her grand-father, alive and kicking, another issue. Another charge to keep. Button, for the next few years, put her nose to the grindstone, set to the task at hand.

◎◐❋

AMID CLEARING OUT ALL THE MEDICAL EQUIPMENT FROM THE LAST PERIOD OF managing her father's illness, all the breathing and feeding apparatus, tubes and machines and cleaning supplies, rags and spray bottles of disinfectant, Button steadied the swelling of her shell-shocked, lovesick heart enough to courage-up and call Heather. Years since San Diego, and much longer since college, and their brief love affair.

Checking in, said hey there, how's the weather, how about the news about Phish resurrecting themselves from rock and roll heaven; my dad died after a nightmare bout with terminal neck and thoracic cancer.

Trembling at the sound of Heather's purring, loving voice, Button's mind reeled at the news her great love had been spending time at the family estate in North Carolina.

Wait—*what*?

Yep. That close. Dealing, it seemed, with her own problems re: eldercare. That time of life for us, as she said when comparing Button's own travails to hers.

Heather's proximity, a major thrill. But Button, unable to get away long enough from her duties to drive even three hours into the North Carolina mountains.

Could she?

Would Heather want her?

"A new chapter?" Button said, trying to keep her voice from breaking and from blubbering: *Oh, god, have I loved you so. Fifteen years. Don't you understand? I never stopped. And to the day I die, I will die loving you, and wishing one wish above all, and it is this; it is that I would one day die in your arms, Heather Ponderview. Dying in your arms, with you reading Rilke and holding me close and bearing me to Heaven. My fondest wish.*

But none of those words tumbled out. "Wow. Maybe we could. Hang out. Sometime."

"Dude, how fun would that be? It's amazing this cycle of ours," Heather said. "We really are like sisters."

"You mean so much to me," Button's heart aching and but striving for nonchalance. Polish up the Oscar. "A true friend."

"Once things settle down, let's go on one of our old hikes. Wouldn't that be amazing? After all this time?"

Button agreed it would.

"I'm so sorry about your father. No words."

"No," Button said, choking back the grief thus far assuaged by relief that her father's suffering had ended. "No easy way to describe it."

"How about these words: In a better place?"

"They'll have to do."

But by the time her mother's inability to care for herself had become apparent, and then her grandmother died and her granddaddy Burnie went off the rails and starting drinking sunup to sundown, Button settled into a life of care-giving that left little time for hiking trips, Phish shows, or seeing Heather. Dutifully, the daughter served; at least being sentenced to purgatory—er, a life in Edgewater County—meant she could write, finally. Try to make sense of the path that'd led her here.

Write she did, though no drafts ever got put into submission shape. The one short novel, MIRIAM MULLINS, had been her relative triumph, all fifty-five thousand words. Maybe she'd dust it off someday. Let someone critique it. No one had. Perhaps that person would be Heather, who would read the work and see the metaphors and think, oh, wow, Button's unrequited, she's pining for me, she is my person and I am hers, and it is way past time to do something about it, yo.

Heather; Button's person, her one true spiritual partner and companion. They used to talk about being able to read one another's thoughts and feelings, even from hundreds or thousands of miles away. Button still believed they did, and could feel Heather; was it reciprocal? One day she would have to break down and freaking ask the girl. Before Button Sykes went nuts.

◉◉✳

THAT TIME WOULD BE THE PHISH SHOW THE NEXT SUMMER IN CHARLOTTE, WHEN Button enlisted Thim to take charge for a weekend so she could have a break from all the toil and tragedy of the last few years. Thim, nonetheless crabby and ill-at-ease; much disorder upon Button's return. She supposed her brief contact with Heather had been worth disrupting everyone's routine. Maybe.

The two oldschool heads danced and laughed in the crowded general admission pit down in front of the band, but of course didn't do any drugs. Phish played well, Trey coming offstage after a raging first set with a look of pure joy on his face, bowing with prayerful hands, a smile as genuine as a gentle sunrise. Button turned and beamed love to the 18,000 rapturous fans, opening her heart to them all, to Trey and the band and crew and merch vendors. Thank you. Thank you. Thank you for coming back.

Thank you for making it possible for me to be here.

With her.

Again.

Were miracles possible?

"Man," Button to Heather, "it's so freaking hot down here."

"Let's head to the lawn."

Pushing through the wooks and dirt surfers filling up the concrete walkways inside the ConParAgPro Concert Amphitheater Button noted, "Trey looks like he's really high on this thing again."

"Instead of the pills and powders."

"Like me."

Heather squeezed her eyes, grabbed Button by the hand and went skipping up toward the lawn, dresses flowing in their wake, the light of day a smudgy purplish twilight behind heaving gray back-lit cumulus clouds on the horizon beyond the rise of the lawn filled with Phish acolytes in various stages of blissful abandon. One cloud appeared to Button like the giant stone head in *Zardoz* that came down out of the sky and vomited guns. She wondered if she weren't getting a contact trip going.

The jammy second set found them twirling under the stars in the back corner of the lawn, where sight lines were poor and the grass less populated, more real estate on which to boogie. Heather and Button had spun in the flowing cotton hippie sundresses they'd bought in the lot from a traveling vendor, all the while nervous about seeing her old posse after almost ten years and what she'd do or say. She'd seen no familiar faces, only in a generic sense, the aging fanbase comprised of mostly college-educated middle class white people pushing forty. Phish kids from 90s tour, now become weekend warriors with toddlers running around the minivans in the vending village outside, homes and careers waiting back home, spouses either along for the ride as partners in Phish, or else putting up with the obsession. A long way from the lot life draped in dreadlocks and bouncing around a stinky RV full of dirty feet and concealed stashes.

Phish laid down a freaking sick second set, the Velvet Underground's 'Rock & Roll' jammed out to twenty melodic and blissful minutes. Rarities, bustouts, all played with spunk and aplomb. Heather and Button sweated and did the herky-jerky boneless noodle dance to 'Twist,' and during a gorgeous thirty-minute 'Harry Hood' they held one another and swayed like lovers, their hearts intertwined and emitting a soft white-green glow of synesthesia that vibrated a frequency decoding as HEATHER, BUTTON, REUNITED IN LOVE.

Heather herself would not recognize this blazing hot instance of culmination and truth, as Button soon understood. In the moment, as she pressed her sweaty body into Heather's, trying to pull her inside, it had seemed mutual. At the 'Hood' peak, kissing Heather wet-lipped on the mouth, which she returned with an ephemeral, darting tongue, a soft, damp echo of faded glory.

The warmth pulsed on. They stood looking into each other's eyes. A flash of darkness in Heather's; Button, feeling a vibration, fleeting, of what she could only classify as mysterious guilt.

Button's great love, her face changing from cautious back to affectionate. Pulling her close and whispering, "My sweet sister. I'm so glad you're here. A return echo of happy times."

"I've missed you for so long," Button said, her words throttled with unrequited desire.

"I always wanted a sister. And here, I got one."

I get it, I get it, Button had thought, air leaking out of her balloon with a piffle of disappointment. Sisters don't make love. Another version of the just-friends speech from Foothills.

Devotion to a dream. A fairy tale, untenable, unrealistic. And the result of Button's feverish impetuous kiss? Not hearing from Heather again for a long time after the Charlotte show. D'oh.

◎①❋

THAT NEXT FALL, BUTTON STARTED RUNNING FRONT OF HOUSE AT THE DIXIANA and writing during her windows of free time, and when not piddling with a Heather novel, working on consciousness research and spiritual exploration through various practices and rituals. Myriad. Rabbit hole time. Chapel perilous.

Running sound, a task for which she'd received university training—fifteen years later, Button had become a working media artist, her college degree's putative bonafides at last put to professional use. She'd grown to love the mini-mum-wage, part-time job—low stakes and low drama, except from some younger bands who drove up from Columbia or down from Charlotte, all full of themselves at the idea of reinventing the wheel of traditional music forms and doing so onstage at the legendary Dixiana.

Button ran a clean board, a tight ship, and had to put up with all manner of guff for being a short, boyish Asian woman instead of the typical soundman. She killed them with kindness and competence. Forestalled problems before they occurred. The way of the Master.

◎①❋

THE DIXIANA. THAT ROY EARL PETTUS NOW SEEMED DETERMINED TO TEAR DOWN.

We'll have to see about that, Button thought. Another crusade, perhaps?

She understood she'd get nowhere with her nuclear protest on the town green, scheduled to begin next week after a final council session and the filing of the proper permits, all matters Jasper helped her prepare. She had already gotten her gear, the various safety accouterments required by the fire marshall to place an EZ-Up tent in a public space like this, the sort of statute that covered street festivals—the tent had to be secured by weights in case of wind-storms, terrorism or other disruptive events like civil unrest.

She hoped no one would put up any last-minute opposition. Mayor Hampton didn't think it would happen. Didn't see how there'd be any harm—he knew her efforts wouldn't matter anyway. That she was only making a point. He could dig it. He called her tent "a sacred expression of second amendment rights," which she took in the spirit intended, as well as his tag, "bless her heart," which in Southern parlance carries a peculiarly gentle yet scathing assessment of one's abilities and intentions.

What about The Dixiana as another cause, if the no-nukes angle was such an apparent waste and a wank? Forget the mural—on that issue she came down on Roy's side. No need to bring a version back, not if he didn't want art on his building. But the business itself deserved preservation—this dump, as Roy seemed to regard it, existed as a genuine and fading piece of Americana, vital and worth saving. Not simply a honkytonk or shitkicker bar or whatever people thought of it—Button herself had helped changed that by getting the rock and blues bands booked.

The damned place had given her life meaning. She couldn't simply see it shuttered, not out of convenience to the rich schlub who'd inherited the joint, which she knew how he saw The Dixiana: a massive inconvenience. Its energetic signature held so much more power than any one person's misguided, capitalistic, ego-driven sense of 'ownership,' a vast illusion under which the Roy Pettuses of the world operated. One way or another, everyone rented.

She'd have to have a grownup convo with him soon. She knew he still saw her as a chubby little weirdo of a subordinate child-figure, but Button, now anything but a kid. He'd listen to her had accumulated wisdom. She'd found out stuff. Some secrets.

Oh, yeah.

The secret of secrets.

How to shape reality.

No one must know such truth about the person practicing magic and forging reality. You couldn't allow laypeople to see the workings, that you were pursuing alchemy, because then the processes wouldn't culminate with the appropriate efficacy. That'd been among the first lessons in her ongoing initiation, which had come to her in a tangential fashion, the way truth paths often revealed themselves—in secret, lurking in the gloomy half-light of dusk, on the threshold between HERE and THERE.

So in silence and secrecy she utilized the magic and made the reality, and would do so again. Roy Earl would never know—again, no one could. But as in the Tao, the Master makes magic happen all the time, taking no credit, merely stepping back and letting the recipients believe, Why, how marvelous! We did it ourselves.

Magic—magic would save The Dixiana.

Button filled herself with positive, selfless intent—with love, pure and white-hot and nonspecific to any one person, for once—and engaged her heart, mind and spirit in what most people called prayer: prayer that Roy Pettus would see the clear and true path for the stakeholders in his grandfather's tavern. Even the ones who'd died were still here, munching spiritual popcorn and waiting to see how it would all come out. She projected this energy toward him across the surface of the bar top, sticky to the touch no matter how many times one cleaned. A shimmering strand of purple fire, reaching toward his midsection. Making an energetic connection. Beaming goodness at him as he talked about such prosaic materialist foolishness like burying the power lines and putting decorative pavers in the crosswalks and fine-detailing the landscaping and such.

He'd come around. She could sense he possessed a yearning, awakening spirit. In any case, Roy had become her charge to keep, now, as much as her blood family for whom she cared. A spiritual seeker. Who, whether he yet realized it, had come to her for help.

◎◐❋

ROY BLEW OUT HIS LIPS. BUTTON HAD BEEN TALKING FOR QUITE A WHILE—SHE'D intended to tell him about Phish Summer Tour 1998, and all the other personal crap had come out instead. Mostly about her dad dying. She'd needed to talk it all out with someone.

"Sorry about your pop. Hell of a nasty story. Makes me glad Granddaddy went as quick as he did."

"It was. Rough. But Dad seemed to take his death. With dignity. His luck. Of the draw."

"Sounded like a waking nightmare."

"It was. But it's over. For him; for me."

"Over." A cloud across his features. "Like for old Rabbit."

"And for everybody left behind. In a sense. A Dixiana death for real and forever, now?"

Roy went *Hrm*. Tapped his fingers. Messed around with his pint glass now emptied of iced tea. "Maybe I should talk it through with the key players. And not like last time."

"Yes! I mean, no. Not like that."

"I call that act—my anger—the Black Blade."

"What?"

"What you saw in here before. The—impatience I showed. The disrespect."

Button expressed her desire to never again see that side of him. Roy, agreeing. "I've been trying to put that fire out."

"Don't put out the fire." Button, emphatic, rising to grab the pitcher of tea to refill their glasses. Her back and side ached, making her wince. "Just learn how to wield it. Properly."

"Use it right."

"Use it for good," she corrected. "Not harm."

Roy, nodding and sipping the tea. "Might be time to assemble the troops again. No. Wait." Roy Pettus cooled his jets. "It can wait. I should mull it all over. Before I make some big pronouncement."

"You have. All the time. In the world."

"It's true." A sheepish, playful smile. "You got a line on more of that vape type-deal?"

"I didn't bring any."

Downhearted self-consciousness. "Raincheck?"

"Sure. In the meantime. We could talk about. Other ways to chill out."

"Like what?"

That's when Button said, let's do an easy meditation together, Roy Pettus. To which he replied with mild hesitation, okay.

"But my mind, it's too busy right now to meditate."

"Not true."

"Naw—I'm different."

Big smile. "Sure you are."

Button discussed meditation techniques, the chakras, grounding oneself, quieting the mind, developing abilities of super-focused intensive concentration, stilling the enervating frisson of the yearning, striving human soul. Roy said, God knew cultivating a little quiet me-time couldn't hurt.

Button, satisfied with the work she managed with him. That's how you made the goals and deadlines, as her college writing mentor Brenda LaRose had taught—a li'l bit here, a li'l bit there, every day until it's everyday.

She asked Roy if he'd been working on a meditation practice and he said yes; that he'd acquired a mantra and that meditation, while difficult and nettlesome and trying, in a sense, did seem to help. She advised him to make sure to more vibrate his mantra than saying it, but demonstrating the technique made her cough and feel another in a series of sore throat episodes coming on. If viral in nature, she hoped she wouldn't give it to Roy, or anyone else. Not the kind of vibe she wanted to spread.

CHRISTY, NEWBIE & HOWDY

Since dumping Christy's Daddy's body in the Sugeree River all had worked out right good, except that Christy and Newbie had disagreements about how to manage the day-to-day living in the trailer.

The only people who came looking for Christy's Daddy in the last month had been two beefalo son of a guns. They worked for Jez Rembert, a name Christy knew well. One thug, fat and black and mean, and the other white and muscular and mean, both with hard eyes set into lumpy faces that held no pity beneath their little fancy hats all of Rembert's boys wore, showed up announcing how Christy's Daddy owed money.

Back and forth: "Five grand."

"Yeah. Five large."

"And our boss wants to know where it's at, fatboy."

"And he ain't playin' none, neither."

"Which means we ain't neither, beau." Staring at Newbie sitting over on the couch, the white henchman said, "Got that, half-pint?"

Newbie's voiced cracked. "I ain't never even seen Christy's Daddy!"

"Yeah, he ain't been home in a durn month." Christy, simmering, but keeping his voice low in case he needed to use the LOUD ordering voice on these tiny-eyed enforcers. "He's supposed to be paying rent, too."

The black dude cracked his knuckles. "You saying he skipped town? Owing Jez Rembert five large?"

"Why you got to lie to us like that?" The white one ripped off a sharp fart. "Don't you know we'll beat you blind?"

The other one waved his fedora around. "Dude. That was raw."

"Trying to show them we ain't fucken around."

"By ripping off a hot poot?"

"Cool it, cool it." The thug, self-conscious, adjusted his own hat. "They got the message."

Christy, adamant. "Ain't seen my Daddy since the middle of September. Maybe even Labor Day."

Newbie affirmed Christy's truthtelling, but them a-holes slapped Newbie around anyway, and Christy too, till he hollered and cried for them to stop.

Christy, heaving and high-whining and covering his face with his forearms: "The truth is I killed him."

The black dude said, "F'real?"

Christy lowered his arms, wheezed out the words. "I killed him and drug him into the river. He ain't coming back. *There ain't never gonna be no money.*"

Newbie went pale as vanilla soft-serve ice cream. His red, swelling nose made him look like a clown. "We ain't seen his Daddy, but we also sure ain't done nothing like that!"

"Y'all better get some kinda story straight here."

Christy started crying like he swore he never would again, going *hi-hi-hi* like when his Daddy would beat him. Beat him like these men now did.

"I got a straight story for ya." The lumbering black man fussed with his little hat, getting it back in place just-so. "His ass ain't iced nobody."

The other thug, spitting brown tobacco juice onto the pile of dirty dishes. "Yep. Ain't nothing but a big fat crybaby."

Christy's tears dried up. He glared at the sink where the bully spat. He had been on Newbie about getting them dishes washed, and now more mess. "Did too kill him. Done it right over on that couch."

The men looked at the stained plaid upholstery of the old sofa. "What—did you sit on him, butterball?"

Christy shrugged. "Pretty much."

Newbie started cussing and saying again how wasn't a word of it true. Both evil henchmen busted out laughing. The white one slapped Newbie's face, hard. "Y'all retards quit making up shit."

After they left saying, we gonna get that money out of Christy's Daddy one way or another, and when he shows back up, you can tell him so, and no more stories, boys, because this is serious, Christy and Newbie started arguing about telling the truth.

"You're always s'posed to be honest."

Newbie, freaking the eff out. "You gonna go tell the po-lice, then? They'll give us both lethal injection, bro. Murder one." Newbie made the *Law & Order* sound effect. "*Dum-dum.*"

"No—the po-po ain't the ones looking for my Daddy."

"And if they do come around?"

Christy said, lord, but I wish you'd wash up them dishes; it's your turn. Bickering back and forth some more. Cussing and fighting.

Wasn't arguing like with Christy's Daddy, though. Not that bad. Mostly Christy staying on Newbie to pick up after himself, leaving pieces of himself lying around. Setting down his hat and keys and wallet all willy-nilly.

"A place for everything and everything in that place," Christy kept trying to get across. He had read a blog post about being organized, about How to Not Lose Things by always keeping them in the same place so's you don't have to hunt. It was basic shit, as Christy told Newbie, who also wanted to smoke inside the trailer, and that wasn't happening no more, either.

"That second hand smoke shit's bullshit," Newbie had hollered. "It ain't gonna hurt you unless you suck it yourself right out of the cigarette."

Christy, whining and saying, but smoke is smoke.

Newbie had wanted to go and get himself some spice or real weed to smoke, too. This was one night when he took a wild hair, as he kept putting it. Nuh-uh is all Christy had to say to that. Look where drugs, smoked or otherwise, got his Daddy.

In the river.

He told this to Newbie as his way of saying it was his trailer and his rules. Christy had a different voice from the whining one for that kind of talk, and looming over Newbie with one big hand on his shoulder, his roommate scrunched his face like he was about to mess himself.

"Okay, Christy. I won't go score no reefer."

"Or smoke cigarettes in here, or in your bedroom." Squeezing Newbie's shoulder. Hard. "Understood?"

Newbie went ow-ow, all right-all right. "You got more rules than you know what to do with. Like being in school again. I wanna do what I want to."

"Life ain't like that."

"Shit it ain't."

Whining, feeling defeated. "It just smells nicer. That's all."

After cleaning the sink Christy made supper, boiling water and cooking macaroni noodles and cutting up vegetables. He had snipped a pasta salad recipe out of the paper he bought at the Gas Chief when he had hung out again hoping to see Aisha after she got done with her home schooling. But Aisha's mother said, no, she is not here today and will not be coming. She is not feeling well. It sounded like a lie.

Failing to connect with Aisha made Christy sad and frustrated. He had thought after getting rid of his Daddy, all would go right for him. Maybe it still would.

One thing he had going for him: Christy, he quit going to school altogether. What for?

At this news his grandmother said, well Christy! in that disappointed tone of hers, but also told him, if you want to drop out of school then you drop out, but you will get a job somewhere.

Christy said he googled about ways to get his GED, and maybe afterward he would think about looking into how someone went about getting a part-time job, or going to Tri-County Technical College, and saying all that made her seem proud of him.

It wasn't nothing but bullshit. The idears weren't, but Christy, he ain't done nothing about them. Too busy picking up after Newbie, for one.

Christy felt naughty about fibbing to his granny, but something about what old Howdy Shull had been saying made Christy think the idea of going to school, and doing all that people were taught to do, wasn't nothing but bull-crud. Just a feeling he'd gotten lately.

Of course, most folks considered Howdy insane or weird or whatever, but Christy, heck, he thought Howdy had a lot to say. Deep idears that give Christy goosepimples and made his nuts draw up and make him do a little dance, and made him think so hard he's had a tough time going to sleep at night, especially on nights he don't drink no whiskey. So much so he's trying to always drink whiskey, much as they could afford to buy it on what Christy's granny gives him. That, along with Newbie's sad wages from washing dishes at the Applebee's over by the interstate. Christy told Newbie he ought to get a job building the new nuke reactors at the SRS plant, but Newbie said, shit, he ain't got no skills like that, beau. He didn't much like working at Applebee's, but it was something. Newbie liked to party too much to go without money. For long.

Howdy, though? The more Christy and Newbie ran across him, it was obvious he had stuff going on that wasn't good. Howdy had a secret place, at the old mill where he passed much time. That's why he had them drop him there that first time, on the day him and Newbie took and laid Daddy's body to rest in the river.

Another day when they gave him a ride over there, what Howdy showed Christy and Newbie back in a corner of the mill building felt strange and unsettling. Christy never wanted to go back.

It stunk of musty decay, and just—weirdness. Like black magic going on, or having gone on in the past. Howdy Shull, walking in a circle with a dingy, greasy gallon milk jug sloshing with gasoline, before a kind of altar he seemed to've set up. Howdy, engaged in the occult. Having himself mystical experiences. Or some such crapola.

THAT ONE AFTERNOON, NEWBIE ASKED HOWDY TO SHOW THEM WHAT HE HAD going on in the old abandoned mill building. After they parked the truck in the woods, Howdy led them through a jagged, rusty hole in the fencing, concealed within an overgrown of shrubs and river trees all gray and gnarled and dead-looking. They'd followed him around by the old loading dock, where the roof had rotted and water trickled in, puddled from overnight rain showers. It seemed to be raining inside the building, way back in the dingy shadows, the sound echoing and spooky. Christy got the shivers at the thought of rain falling inside the mill while the sun shined overhead. It seemed like a dream.

Mumbling and babbling, Howdy took them through a broken door at the rear of the dusty abandoned factory and down a concrete stairwell. Light the color of Grey Poupon mustard filtered in best it could through the high row of windows along the basement ceiling, which near as Christy could tell was about ground level outside. Damp, this corner of the mill built into the mud near the river. Scary down in here.

Christy, watching as Howdy prepared a greasy, black-streaked gallon jug by pouring into it what they found out was gas; gas Howdy carried with him in the Canada Dry bottle. Huffing. Christy, like, getting it. Had seen his Daddy rocking inhalants. Not good.

Howdy: Squeezing the jug under his nose and mouth; breathing in the fumes; eyes rolling back in his head.

And walking.

In a circle.

Chanting to himself.

Howdy's pacing had pounded a perfect flat circle in the dusty, trash and leaf-strewn floor of the old warehouse; a smooth, gray dirt ring before a set of spray-painted symbols on an old pallet propped up against the wall of the deserted mill basement.

The symbols, like two crosses with hooks, appeared downright Satanic.

On either side of the symbol, somebody had spray-painted, in different paint and at a much later time, the words 'chapel perilous.'

Sounded to Christy like a place of devil worship. Or occult shit. Both. All of it he'd been reading about, the rituals and spells and symbols and such, swirling around in his mind.

And Howdy, the more Christy watched and listened, seemed to worship those symbols.

What was most obvious: from the shear volume of crud, somebody more than Howdy Shull had been partying down in this basement throughout the long period of the mill's disuse. Graffiti covered every wall and part of the floor. Layers of brown leaves and beer cans and newspaper ad flyers and shriveled rubbers. Christy, not able to imagine making love down here. Christy, unable to picture this idea well in any context. But here? Really?!

Christy and Newbie had been drinking most of the afternoon before going out driving and finding Howdy walking along doing his rap. Newbie, off for the day from his dish sink at Applebee's. They had time to kill together—too much. Not much else in Edgewater County but get your drink on. Not living in a lousy trailer park called Mayfield Acres with no real jobs that mattered, and nothing for kicks except to play flight simulator and mess around on the net while Newbie looked at TV and drank Bud Light and squirted clear piss into the stained, cracked toilet he wouldn't clean no matter how much Christy whined and pleaded and ordered.

Christy: he wondered if he wasn't no better off with Newbie than he'd been with his drunk dead Daddy.

Worse, in the mill basement Howdy Shull's deal now became clear: he had weird shit going on, much worse in Christy's opinion than drinking and drugging.

◉①✳

ON THE DRIVE BEFORE THEY PICKED UP HOWDY—NEWBIE PERSUADED CHRISTY TO go out riding and get more beer, that he had gotten bored and wanted to get out of the trailer, which at times still smelled like the funk from Christy's Daddy's body—they went through town. Newbie, flipping off The Dixiana as they passed. He cussed Roy E. Pettus from here down to Columbia and back. Said he heard Pettus was a dick-sucking f-word.

Christy, telling Newbie not to use such language. That words held ungodly power. To wound. To hurt. Unnecessarily. Like when his Daddy called him fat-face. Christy, not able to help his weight any more than a gay person could being gay. Dumbass Newbie was the one they should've shoved into that Special Ed class.

"Was you in Special Ed?" Christy's nasal whine wheezed. "Cause you sure sound like it."

Newbie, stuck on a riff. "You go and suck a dick."

"I wish you'd make me."

Once out of town on the winding, narrow road toward the river, they encountered Howdy. Newbie of course pulled over, which Christy had not whined against. At that moment, Christy, he still maintained interest and respect for Howdy. He seemed like a person who, despite his outward appearance of being downtrodden, held great knowledge and wisdom about the world, and reality.

Howdy's talks about the pyramids and the great ages and Atlantean warriors driving out the Lemurians who formed the high civilizations like Egypt and Sumer, which blossomed out of nowhere from heretofore primitive peoples with the sudden ability to design and construct enormous 'megalithic' structures, if one subscribed to what Howdy referred to as the 'dunderheaded archaeological orthodoxy'; and that the cornerstone religious leaders, evil, patriarchally oriented men, Howdy emphasized, had subsumed the great mother and scrubbed clean the mysteries and myths those Lemurians brought with them from Atlantis, leaving us with a ten-thousand year journey to world serfdom. All of us. The five great tribes all mixed and subjugated together under the rule of dark artists and sorcerers, as Howdy insisted in his bizarre, offhand manner, as though speaking neither to Christy nor Newbie but other entities, unseen, in the truck or side of the road which he strode along with his two-liter bottle of gas.

On the drive to the mill Howdy spoke at length of an ancient race of Lemurians who still lived among us, but secreted inside a majestic city far beneath Mt. Shasta, a refuge constructed before the great cataclysm that'd swept away the glorious earlier incarnations of the civilization of man. Now that all sounded crazier than hell, which Newbie said aloud, but Christy, out of respect, had only thought.

But Christy, later on he googled mad links correlating with what Howdy described. Had stayed awake until first light reading up on the pyramids, and energy systems and water and magnetism and Mt. Shasta and Bigfoot, who as it turns out is another whole race like the Lemurians, and who still live in the deep woods, but being a peaceful brand of evolved humanoid bipeds they simply don't much wish to interact with our style of human being. As with the Lemurians chilling under the mountain, the Bigfeet know how to hide, and hide well.

Magicking. Esoteric knowledge. Wisdom.

Wisdom; knowledge kept in hiding. Rituals, conducted in silence.

Christy, unable to put his finger on why the importance. Of silence.

Mind=blown. Much left to google.

But then Howdy turned out to be a gas huffer, and after some time spent in the mill basement with the town weirdo, Christy wasn't sure anymore about any of his mess—and this despite all the support materials for Howdy's discourses found on online.

Most especially after Newbie joined in, huffing gas with a dude who, the more Christy thought about it, was certainly himself crazy and maybe ought to be considered a frenemy. A NARP—not a real person. Christy wanted to beat it before Howdy's NARPiness infected him, too.

Like his Daddy's deal did.

See? Get it? Right??

Newbie's attitude, though? YOLO. Giving it a go, that gas. Christy, understanding the desire for a new adventure. Somewhat.

Mostly whining and worried, though. He'd only recently started feeling settled inside, after being done with his Daddy good and permanent and all.

Christy, he'd had a turning point. No going back to the crazy of before, not with all he had seen from his Daddy and that bunch of no-goods and druggies traipsing in and out of the trailer.

Drinking whiskey was another matter—that was okay. You saw on the TV and in movies how powerful people drank whiskey out of glasses and were gentlemen. Drugging and huffing? Nobody got powerful that way. Christy would stick with his whiskey, which made him feel strong and confident. Straightened out his thoughts. Felt good settling into his belly—cold and bracing, but afterwards? Warm and relaxed. Christy didn't think he'd ever been relaxed a day in his life, not until he experienced the cleansing effects of whiskey. Couldn't be bad.

◉⊕❋

"Squeeze it slow, take a deep breath—the Yogic breath." Howdy, advising Newbie on how best to huff the gas; Newbie, who sat cross-legged just outside of Howdy's dusty circle before the strange altar. Howdy had arranged all manner of the garbage in front of the cross symbols, little rows and shapes and circles made of beer cans and pieces of paper and broken glass. He had his own bottle, his two-liter Canada Dry, out of which he poured gas into the milk jug for Newbie.

Newbie, huffing. He swayed on his feet, eyes crossing and going WHOA.

"Sit down, sit down," Christie whined. He made himself sound like the 007 villain in the Red Box DVD they had rented from outside the Walgreen's the night before. "Sit down before you fall down, Mr. Bond."

Newbie, snapping to. Like waking up. "Dang. That mess'll get you white-girl wasted, bro."

"*Sit down*." This is more in Christy's ordering voice, which he has to use on Newbie more often than not. "You could hurt yourself."

"You want a hit?"

Christy's all like, HELL no.

Meanwhile Howdy shuffled in his circle, chanting low and weird in his old man's gravelly Southern voice. He huffed and chanted and huffed some more. Christy, watching as Howdy's shoes, heavy-soled leather ones like you would wear with a nice pair of pants or a suit, kicked up fine puffs of gray dust.

The ugly mottled sunlight fell in dingy streaks across the hooked cross. A soft voice seeming to whisper in his ear: *Ha-ha-ha, why don't you strike a match?*

A woman's voice. Sexy. Weird. Christy's forearms stippled with chicken skin. "Who said that?"

Howdy came to a stop, sudden. He peered around, slow and attentive. "Who's there? Is it you? My lost love?"

The basement, deserted but for them. No ghosts moving about. Not even rats or bugs. A dead tomb.

"Could you be there, love?"

Nothing.

Newbie, wary and pie-eyed. "Howdy. The gas, it can't be good for us. For you."

Howdy relaxed his posture, took a step into his circle. "You realize I'm an Atlantean soul, don't you, son? I incarnated again in this cycle. A marvelous time, but one of transition. I returned to help you all. As a seer of visions. A magician. And a channeler. But it only works with the gas," shaking his finger and beginning to again march. "My works are done for, with, and by the grace of the gas."

Christy, shaking his head and scowling and like, ready to get the eff out. Go home. Get another Red Box DVD. Drink whiskey. Chillax with the flight simulator.

"Newbie," an order. "I wanna bounce."

"Naw, bro. Hold on." Newbie, squatting down and huffing some more, went into his own trance: a little rat-faced sidekick cartoon character, he seemed to Christy, with the whites of his eyes rolling up. Newbie said UH and let the jug fall over, spilling some gas.

That got Howdy out of his circular goose-step. "Hey-ho, there. You made a mess on the floor? With the sacred juice?"

"See?" Christy, hands on hips. "Messy, just like at home."

"Kiss my ass."

"Heresy." Howdy brandished an admonishing, spastic finger over Newbie. "Thou hast profaned the temple. With thine wastrel ways."

Newbie struggled to his feet. "Pro—what?"

Howdy, gesturing and mumbling in one of his chants, walking the circle and taking gentle, patient huffs on the Canada Dry bottle, the plastic crackling with each squeeze. The whole cobwebby, mildewy place stunk of petroleum, now. Stunk worse, anyway.

"Christy—this is whack in here."

"No duh. We're all gonna smell like we work at the filling station." Christy got up to go. "Later, Howdy. We got—stuff to do."

Howdy, talking now about biblical stuff instead of the Lemurians. About the book of Revelations in the Bible being code for the same cyclical cata-strophe myths that accompanied all religions, and how:

"...the four *horses* represent each of the four *cardinal* months or start of the seasons. The *riders* symbolize the four *fixed* months of the season. Together these are the four horsemen. The four beasts also stand for the four Ages of man called Veda Yugas. The Satya Yuga is man's Golden age. Tetra Yuga the

Silver age. Dvapar Yuga the Bronze age, and Kali Yuga the Dark age—a time of terrible and pernicious density. The densest time. Of all time."

This made Newbie mad. He called from the concrete steps leading out of the basement: "You better not be calling us dense, Howdy."

"Yeah," Christy agreed.

Howdy ignored them, walking his circle and huffing.

"Christopher, my stomach's queasy. I need to get a ginger ale for reals, yo."

"Told ya."

They left Howdy in the dim basement spouting his mixed up Yuga foolishness. It seemed like Christy had already heard this rap, a Howdy rerun or greatest hit. At least he had continuity going with his malarkey. Christy didn't know why he'd thought Howdy Shull might have wisdom to offer. Not on inhalants. Christy had seen his Daddy burn out every last one of his brain cells doing crap like that. Forget it.

◎◉❋

As for Christy and money, he said to Newbie how he wanted to work for money and all? But knew at fifteen it would be hard to get on at some place he didn't want to eat nor entertain the thought of working, like at one of the burger joints near the Applebee's? Trying to explain himself? Best he could?

"C'mon, beau. You ain't too good to flip burgers. You got to get some grease under them fingerprints." Newbie, saying this on the way to drop Christy off at the Gas Chief so's he could play video games and wait to see if Aisha came around. "That's everybody's first job."

"Ain't working at no burger joint."

"My first job was at good old Mickey D's. The one that used to be on the bypass before they built up the Chilton exit? That's how oldschool I am, Christopher."

"Ain't gonna work at no Mickey D's."

"Suit yourself. S'good honest work, is all. You can move up fast."

"Why didn't you, then?"

"After a while I couldn't stand the way them little onions smelled. We used to dump a big bag into a tray, spray them with water out of the sink. Whole kitchen would stink like them onions. And your fingers, too. Like I had them little dry, fake onions all under my nails. Nasty. Plus, I got let go by Mr. Lawler after they seen me on the security cam borrowing a case of quarter-pounder patties. I didn't have the first clue they'd tucked that camera up yonder in the corner by the freezer."

"You stole a box of hamburger patties?" Christy's stomach rumbled. "How many?"

"Dang, I dunno, like forty-eight or some shit. My mama was still alive then. That woman could eat a mess of meat. She was big."

"Big like me?"

"What? Not even, bro." Newbie's eyes went all teary. "I sure miss her, still."

They had much in common, him and Newbie. Both orphans. But they weren't brothers. That much for sure. Face it, Christy still didn't know how much he should trust Newbie. Trust his often dumb-ass judgement. Maybe Howdy's time of density rap rang true. Lucky for Newbie he's got Christy around being smart for them both.

⊛⊙❋

After another morning spent arguing over straightening up the trailer, it came time for Newbie to get his complaining ass over to work.

As the orange and yellow plastic sign of the Gas Chief appeared around the curve near where the two-lane road changed to four, Christy mumbled of his hopes for Aisha's attention. Newbie's like, she's cute but you ain't got no business messing with some little sand N-word.

Christy cussed and smacked Newbie so hard on the arm he almost lost control, swerving into the other lane and back again right as a full-speed SUV careened around the bend, screeching its tires and laying down on the horn.

Jamming on the brakes and sending Christy forward against the seatbelt so that it cut into his shoulder—Christy could fill up a seatbelt as it was—Newbie damn near overshot the Gas Chief.

Newbie throws the truck into park by the ancient payphone box sitting surrounded by weeds and tattooed by graffiti. "You like to broke my durn arm, Christopher."

"Don't call Aisha no N-word. You hear me?"

"It's what she is."

Christy rears back and hisses like one of the mangy tomcats skulking around their run-down, sandy trailer park. A sensation like scalding, bubbling hot lava expands in his stomach. His eyes bulge big as a *Simpsons* character. "Take it back."

"Ain't gonna—it's the durn truth."

Modifying a threat he'd heard his Daddy once use, Christy deploys a harsh devil voice, stabs a shaking finger right into Newbie's pinched face: "Take it back or you'll never eat my pasta salad with them teeth again."

Newbie's all, dang, bro. But he takes it back. Rubs his bicep where Christy smacked him. "I'm supposed to clean the trailer, and scrub them Applebee's rib platters, with a broke arm?"

"I'd take it back if I could. Like you took it back. Deal?"

"Whatever. Now get out. I'm gonna be late."

As Christy rolls out of the Newbie's truck he informs him he'll walk home, if Aisha doesn't finally ask him to come have dinner at her folks's house. This, a persistent fantasy keeping Christy awake at night: visions of laughing and sitting around the table, saying funny lines to each other like the families on TV shows—the sitcoms, not the dramas about cops finding out who killed who and how they done it.

Christy, unworried by such matters; didn't think none about his Daddy being found one day by the po-po. The river they put him into runs deep. Christy's Daddy is gone for good. But if they did find him? Won't the cops think it's somebody like the thugs who came looking? Christy, in a flash realizing that if the question, or body, ever came up, he's got himself a perfect alibi—two drug-dealing bullies wearing little Blues Brothers hats came around threatening Christy's Daddy's life. All he needed was to switch up the timeline a bit. Dope.

◉⊕❊

THE VISIT TO THE GAS CHIEF DIDN'T GO WELL, NOT AT ALL. NOT ONLY DID AISHA fail to appear, but her father was not there either, only the gray-faced, dumpy woman that Christy knew as Aisha's mom. If her Daddy had not liked him very much, Aisha's mom much less so.

In fact, after only an hour she asks Christy to leave, but he still has plenty of quarters left for the Galaga. He's pwning it today despite its foggy, semi-opaque screen—an old, old game, much more than the ones Christy played at Myrtle Beach one time when he and his Daddy went down to Horry County on an errand. They hadn't gone to the beach to play games or even see the ocean, no; it'd been some of Christy's Daddy's mess. His meth-mess. At least Christy got to visit the arcade on Ocean Boulevard and catch glimmers of the sunlight on the water out of the corner of his eye.

If only Christy could get across how good he was compared to his Daddy. How pure his intentions for Aisha. A boyfriend and girlfriend is all. Nothing nasty.

He knows his voice sounds thin and whiny because he made it so: "I sure wish you'd let me stay and play longer."

"No, no, no." The woman, shaking an ashy finger, her accent sharp to Christy's ears. "You are finished playing now." She had said her name was 'Ruth' but it did not seem to Christy to be her real name. Did they have women named Ruth where the family came from? The man, too, said his name was Paul, giving Christy the same feeling. NARPs, again.

"Ain't done with my quarters yet," sounding like *corters* in his high, pretty-please voice. "*Quarters.*"

"You are loitering. We're not—allowing this. This loitering."

"I'm waiting."

"Loitering. Go—you go," with sharp nods toward the door.

Christy, flustered, whines high and mean. The lava burbles up his gut and into the crown of his head, a sick hot throbbing there.

The woman's eyes bug out, her brown arms tight across her big stomach and bosom. Working her dark lips in silence.

A white-haired man in a knock-engined, rusting Cadillac from the 1980s pulls up at the pumps outside.

"See? I'm making busy with customers."

"Aisha."

"No."

Christy cusses and goes out slamming the glass door on the old gas station, which Christy's Daddy told him used to be a Gulf back in the 1970s. All he has next is a long walk to the same old nothing, the flight simulator back at the trailer, look at the TV or read crap on 'teh internets', which they snagged from an unsecured wifi router in the trailer park.

Or: He could grab lunch at Applebee's, get it at Newbie's discount. It was where they took a good many meals, which eat up more than little barbecue ribs: it ate up the money.

Christy, outside remembering how the Gas Chief, and the idea of robbing it, started the whole mess with what happened to his Daddy. He wished he could tell the old Arabian crone how much he done—a ritual killing, a sacrifice—to keep her family whole and safe. How this *earned* Christy access to Aisha, yo; Aisha, who smiled at him once and would no doubt accept and take him into her life as friends and perhaps more, if only Christy's given the chance to show off his sweet and high-voiced side; his smart side. As before, though, robbing the store won't get him anywhere but further away from Aisha, not that it's workable, anyway. Money, a real problem.

Christy, wishing he'd get on with it and turn sixteen. Things will change, then. He even considered going for Newbie's old job at The Dixiana. Christy, he likes housekeeping. How bad can it be cleaning the old honkytonk?

Outside the light looks softer than it has all summer, and the wind feels cool—fall is here, finally. He asks the old man if he'll give him a ride across town. The man looks him over and says if Christy don't step away from his vehicle, he's liable to finally put his concealed carry permit to good use.

◎①✿

Sweating his way down the Columbia Highway toward downtown Tillman Falls, where he decided to go instead of the Applebee's and the freeway offramp fast food row, Christy came upon who-else but Howdy Shull, walking along and swinging his arm and talking his talk to the air over his left shoulder. He clutches his soda bottle, now empty. Awesome.

Christy, cautious. "What it be, dog?"

Howdy's eyes are blood-red, his voice scratchier than usual—he's been huffing. "The solution to today's problems requires an approach which is ruthlessly candid. With no agonizing over religious, moral or cultural values."

"Why you keep on talking about all your mess? Don't none of it make sense."

"You have qualified for this project because of your ability to look at human society with cold objectivity, and yet analyze and discuss your observations and conclusions with others of similar intellectual capacity without the loss of discretion or humility. These virtues, exercise them in your own best interest."

Christy bites, asks what kind of project Howdy means.

He makes hard eye contact. Grabs Christy by the arm and propels them toward town, the opposite direction Howdy had been going. "Let"s get you briefed, get the backstory out of the way: In the interest of future world order, peace and tranquility, it was at the highest levels of elite shadow leadership, mind you, that a council of sages conspired to wage a quiet war against the American public. Their ultimate aim, of permanently shifting the natural and social energy—wealth, don't you understand—of the undisciplined and irresponsible sea of many—the great unwashed; that's what they call you—into the hands of those same self-disciplined, responsible, and worthy few elite buggers, it's all but come to fruition."

Christy has no clue. "I c'ain't follow you, Howdy."

"It's by design. They are magicians. Black magicians. Only one way to both fight and infiltrate and maintain the balance, and that's white magic. As such, we'll be wise to entertain a course of study in ancient hermeticism."

Life with his dope-addled Daddy taught Christy to make normal conversation with someone like Howdy, try to pull them onto a thread of rationality rather than gobbledygook. He also feels uncomfortable with Howdy's racial magic talk. Typical old person. "You don't know of no one hiring, do you?"

Howdy claps Christy on the shoulder several times.

"Knowledge is power."

"Knowledge is power—is that a company?"

"The company you keep," Howdy replies.

They march along with Christy's big thighs rubbing together. Despite the autumn air sweat still trickled down his big-boy black jeans he wears all the time. Christy, exhausted by Howdy's words all mixing into a stew of incomprehensible foolishness. By the time they walk the two miles to downtown, all he wants is to get away from Howdy Shull.

Easy enough to do. Christy, sitting down heavy on a bench on the town green near the honkytonk, sweat running down his back. Howdy Shull went on walking down Congress Street out of sight, heading along the tree-canopied avenue toward the old mansions on Whaley Way.

Christy worries the quarters in his pocket. He wonders if they got video games inside the redneck honkytonk. He's always been curious about The Dixiana, but since it's the kind of place his Daddy used to go, Christy didn't ponder too much about what went on inside. After getting thrown out of the Gas Chief and enduring Howdy's crazy spewing, Christy wanted his mind to clear itself out, so he sat for a spell and tried to think about nothing, which seemed to help settle his feelings. For once.

Only after the odd couple of a ruddy ginger fat man in a seersucker suit and a super-cute Asian girl with crazy wild dreadlocks come walking around, gesturing and talking about some tent she plans to set up, does Christy finally get on his way, loping off on his long, lonesome highway to nowhere. It's fine; always more cleaning to do at the trailer. He'd rather go and talk to the girl—any girl—but maybe after grabbing a shower. Being close to Howdy had probably made him stink to high heaven.

ROY AND THE STAKEHOLDERS

You stand alongside Button watching with impatience as a pair of vehicles pull into the angled spaces along the green in front of Ben Tillman, perched handsome and diminutive upon his red granite pedestal: Jasper's dented Accord, Trudy's red Taurus.

Fridge, dropped off by his sketchball, gangbanging teenage son, a rangy, skinny version of Fridge with cornrows and bandana like an extra from a prison-yard scene. Dude would make your well-tended customer base back home at the CBSI likely clinch tight their Hermes handjobs.

Handjobs? *What?*

Handbags. Hermes handbags, you dork.

Bro: you are one hot mess. And ragging on Fridge's kid's appearance makes you sound racist and classist. Cool out.

Oh, how these humans will plead and bleat at the earthshaking news about the approaching final disposition of this decrepit, paperboard, crackerbox palace. But T-S, as you'll explain. It's as you've always done when feckless and recalcitrant employees whine about a necessary if painful adjustment to every-one's lives for the maintenance of profit margins. They stand fortunate you've allowed the business to go on, even if you made them give up on the nonexis-tent lunch trade, start opening at four instead of eleven in the *ay-yeem.*

As you always say, look: you didn't make the rules of capitalism, but you're a smart player, and until the paradigm changes—when folks give each other the necessities of comfort and life in a sharing economy rather than selling via fiat currency to fuel a profit-driven one; gonna happen any time now, you're quite sure—these are the cards we must play. And the game is profit, which The Dixiana in its present form doesn't much produce.

A potential problem: you can see that psycho thyroid case Samson glowering from inside the passenger seat of Trudy's eyelash-adorned sedan, as the creep had during the misbegotten event on River Ridge Road, when the multitudes of irritating well-wishers tried to intrude on a most personal moment with your grandfather's ashes. A wild card. It irritated and rankled that she brought him with her. Threats regarding the fate of the mural had come to you secondhand from Trudy's husband, as well as from the Rembert crew in the form of the garbage strewn around your driveway. A proposal by the ELMS to find funding for the mural to be recreated but in a modern, PC-approved version produced by Columbia's internationally known painter and muralist Blue Sky also came your way, all of which landed upon a disinterested set of eardrums. Your eardrums.

Screw both the threats and the offers. Yeah: You'll pick an appealing color for the side of your coffee shop. Won't you. In due time.

After the gutting; during the build-out, however grand a shape it may take. That's when you'll make final exterior color selections. Way way way down the road. Murals, not on your radar.

CBSI had been easy to palette-select—located at the beach? It's pastels. But here, it'll take discernment and research. A tasteful homage to the Christmas-y reds and greens of the old neon sign, maybe?

The sign's shadow falls as the sun drops on its westward trek behind the rusting hunk of scrap iron, the icon soon following the joint's stalwart, long-lived proprietor into whatever form honkytonk afterlife takes. The thought of taking it down gives you a tingle. Wicked, like that of the Black Blade.

Along with a welling in your gut—grief for your Pa-paw. It hits when you don't expect it. You've read that these unpleasant flashes will continue.

Or, a generous spirit seems to whisper, you could see about donating the sign to the county archives. History, and all. Get the ELMS to pay for a truck to carry it down the street.

Or, sell it for scrap. Old metal signs like this have to be full of sellable pieces-parts suitable for conversion back into raw material. Nothing made like that anymore. Probably weighs a ton. You will hire a photographer, a pro, to take shots and preserve the memories for anyone who'll care, which won't include your ass. Drag it down, haul it off before anyone can investigate.

Like how you came, thief-in-the-night, to whitewash into non-meaning their precious wall of symbols. The act made your dick a foot long and thick as a brick. Still does.

"How's everyone today?" You greet them on the sidewalk with good cheer and bonhomie. "The light—it really looks like fall, doesn't it."

"Don't feel like fall." Fridge, sweat dripping. "Hot as *hale* to me."

Button, agreeing with a smile. "The air—its. Getting more. Clear. The haze —the summer haze. Is going, finally."

"Exact-a-mundo. I almost wanna meet out here."

"Been a hot one to me." Jasper's lavender polo shirt hangs sweat-stained, and spindly, white stick-legs jut out of khaki golf shorts a couple sizes small for his round foodbelly, worn topsiders on his longfellow feet, a pink cast to his winded features. "Rather we meet inside. If we could."

You were five effing seconds from saying so, and the blade along your thigh awakens, close like a lover's leg next to yours in bed. "Yes, Jasper. Let's do that. *That's a good idea of yours.*"

As you hold open the door they file in but for Trudy, fumbling with her Virginia Slims. You haven't made eye contact; anytime you're in her presence, she looks haggard and strained. Having Button call about the meeting probably sent the message you intended.

Nice and easy does it: "Hey—I need to tell you something."

The frequency of her anticipation shifts, and the squinted, pissy eyes soften: she thinks you're about to make up for the yelling. For the Black Blade. With tenderness Trudy asks, "Aw, what is it, sugar."

"It's that you might as well not light that cancer-stick. As established, no more smoking inside."

Shock. "*We ain't open yet.*"

"Even when we're closed."

"What a crock."

"The rule—the law, rather—protects the health of both employees and customers. All the time."

A standoff. Trudy, gripping her lighter and an unlit Virginia Slims Menthol 100.

"You can smoke once we're finished. Smoke the whole pack, far as I'm concerned."

"Why don't you go screw yourself."

"I called you in today as a gesture. It's time for bygones, not more drama."

"Awesome, dude." She lights the cig, blows smoke. "I'll just stand out here and burn one, then. Won't I."

You glance askance into the middle distance across the green. "Trudy?"

"Yeah?"

"I don't want this to turn into another slugfest. Do you?"

"I couldn't think of nothing no more fun."

"Right—the sarcasm. Maybe if we dialed that back, it'd help the general energy."

"Eff you. Naw, naw," she says, laughing all cruel and sassy. "Just a good old girl funnin' with ya. Go on in. Let me put my cigarette case back in the car. That all right, sugar?"

Sure, you tell her. Good on your cigarette stashing. Giving her a big smile but thinking, to the moon, Alice. You're this close, lady. You and your cigarette-sucking, gangly, sexy old redneck self.

◉⊕✻

AS PREDICTED, THE ASSEMBLED FACES SAG UPON HEARING YOUR GRIM BUT necessary news, worst of all Button's, whom you believed would be your ally.

"But, I thought. You were. Gonna take some time—"

"Sorry, but: it's been decided."

"When did you decide this?"

"Not an 'I was for it before I was against it' type-deal. I just reconsidered. After the others got here. Just now."

A caustic and verbose atmosphere develops, and suddenly neither you nor Button can get in a word.

Trudy, of course, is the hottest. "I knew the second you had her call me instead of doing it yourself something was up. Hell, it's not like I didn't know what was coming when I drove around that corner and seen how you took and desecrated the mural."

"We ain't gonna fight that battle again. It's over. Forever."

Her voice shakes as she tries to constrain a volcanic eruption: "You can't throw us all away. You can't just—change the way things is."

"The heck I can't."

"But Roy," Jasper says all slow and contemplative. "You let us go on for a whole month now. Like everything was gonna be fine."

"Yeah," Fridge says. "I got to think about my boy's college coming up. He got scholarships simmering, but I wanna be able to give him spending money next year. What I'm supposed to tell him? My hours already cut as it is. Mr. Roy Earl, I sure wish you'd—"

Your hand shoots into the air like the egghead student always with the right answer. This odd motion disarms and silences them.

Smiling and nonchalant, you reiterate how everyone's welcome to put in résumés to secure their place in line for employment at the coming Carolina Beanery Tillman Falls, or Carolina Beanery Edgewater, as you aren't quite locked on the name yet. "That simple. Nobody's losing their job, per se."

"But what if you don't hire us back?"

Fridge's question displays a fragility that makes your heart clench with pity. As such, you ignore it.

"Full disclosure: I consider you all stakeholders. So in that spirit, let me share my vision for the transition into this new endeavor. I'll be hiring a PR firm, probably Feebee Elmendorf in Columbia, to help us make a big splash even before we get the doors open—articles, social media, whole bit. She's a genius, a PR firebrand. I worked with her when I led the Downtown Business Alliance board as its president, for *two consecutive* terms, and stepping down only because we moved to Charleston." You flash a pair of Nixonesque peace signs. "We'll consult with her on the best name."

Silence. Four people whose body language appears in various shades of pissed-off. Trudy sniffles and blows her nose.

"And you know what else? We'll put ourselves a kick-ass press release out about the closing of this old barn. Have a few more of your, oh, what do you call them," waving a limp, offhand set of wriggling fingers in Jasper's direction. "Your little music concerts. Promote it all. We'll have ourselves one hell of a going away party."

"Don't you mean a 'little' going away party?" Jasper asks, glowering with ill-concealed displeasure.

Ignoring this, you continue in rally-the-troops mode. "I know it's sad, it's new; it's frightening. But only if we let ourselves become frightened. Change is opportunity, so along with all the change, there's going to be plenty of opportunity. Now, as for future employment with the company, having had experience as a barista will be a big plus. Can't lie to y'all about that part. But again: as legacy members of The Dixiana family, you'll all be given due consideration."

Fridge asks, "What kinda menu you got in mind?"

"Sandwiches and sides, the occasional salad. Poached infusions on the weekend. Locally sourced ingredients. Pastries and desserts from whoever does the quality work around town. If there is anybody."

"What about broasted chicken?"

"Not just no, Fridge, but hell-no on all that factory farmed meat. Vegan options. No more fried freaking chicken."

"We ain't gonna broast no more chicken?"

"Afraid not."

"What kinda sides?" Fridge, despondent. "Taters? Slaw?"

Your demon-eyes flare sidelong at him. "More like marinated olives or fresh fruit. Do yourself—and me, hint hint—a big favor by pulling up the CBSI website, which you'll find updated to include current specials. We rotate through a series of seasonal, featured sandwiches, most of which we'll offer here, at least initially. That'll give all of you an idea of what the decor and menu will be like. But we're way ahead of ourselves, really. Baby steps."

Jasper, barely audible: "Dang."

"Now, too, don't forget that we're going to make this our own, here in the old hometown. Not gonna copy ourselves, even though we're copying ourselves—our shit on Sedge Island stinks, and all? But we'll want to put our own stamp on the menu."

Nodding, you pace the length of the bar as everyone shifts around in their creaky old wooden chairs out of which you'd soon be making a bonfire back in the field by the cemetery. "This Beanery will be much much much much more like my original place over in Columbia. Kind of a college hangout type-deal. Maybe those of you who decide to stay on, we'll ride down there one day to the Old Market. Get ourselves lunch, look around, soak it up, soak it in. I want to get back to the basics—my roots—with this venture. I'm willing to take on as many of you who wish to come, too. That's what this meeting's about, folks. Deciding our future together."

"Roots?" Jasper, sipping a longneck Bud that you said you'd be glad to comp him—this time—but only if Trudy wrote it down on the inventory control sheet you've made them start using, speaks up in his molasses drawl. "Ain't The Dixiana your roots, son?"

Heat, along your thigh. Quelled. Deep breath. "Look—of course. But life is about change, guys. Change in your pocket, and change all around."

You go behind the bar, pour yourself a soda water, gurgle, get choked, cough for half a minute, continue in a breathy, strangled tone. "I'm sure we can factor in a nice little performance corner where Jasper can put on acoustic music, poetry readings, storytelling groups, writer's workshops. This is gonna be more like a library than some juke-joint full of hicks and rednecks and drunks and cigarette-sucking Edgewater County trailer trash," eyeing Trudy, who's freshly incensed at the connotation. "Gonna be a class joint all the way."

"Why the hell you staring at me?"

"So then, Jasper is my entertainment coordinator. And since that's an informal position, you may assume that, once we gut this wretched, broken-down palace and execute our build-out and get our coffee dripping and our gourmet sandwiches grilled, you'll schedule and book a rotating series of events," breathing heavy through your nostrils and nodding, "as described here today."

"Events?"

"Acoustic guitar. Poetry readings. Writer's workshops. Did I stutter?"

"I heard you. But acoustic-only ain't gonna make for much of an open mic night. We get lots of electric acts, especially the cats who come over from that very college town you want us to go look at, and—"

"Jasper?"

"Yessir?"

"Don't make me repeat myself. Maybe all that amplified music's damaged your hearing. Eh?"

The energy now beyond toxic, you endure various complaints and gripes and questions, though none from Trudy.

Even Button's love-light has dimmed. "Guess that means. Um. I won't bother. Applying. To run sound."

A bloom of happy warmth in your belly. "Might as well go ahead and use this opportunity to announce that Button, here, is not only my first-hire, but she'll serve as GM of the newest Carolina Beanery."

Trudy explodes out of her chair, knocking it onto the scuffed wooden floor. "What did you call me here for today—to make it all worse? *How much more are you gonna hurt me,*" rushing out the door into a flash of harsh sunlight reflected off the windshield of your Pa-paw's F-150 like a blinding, yellow-white laser.

"As much as you hurt me, you heartless bitch." Your heart pounds in your ears. "*More,* if I can. You wounding redneck skank. You—you—you little piece of chicken!" You fling your tumbler of soda water across the bar, but it doesn't break, only thumps to the floor. A limp toss—a Reecie Cup throw if you ever saw one.

It's because you're weak, on the verge of involuntary tears. Desperate to hold it all back, your vulnerability remaining unseen.

"I'm trying to imagine what on earth Miss Trudy did to hurt you so," Jasper says as the bells on the door jingle into silence. "You ain't even lived around here for thirty-something years."

You start to answer, but stop: the sunlight from outside the glass door darkens. But it's not a cloud—an enormous shape has blocked out the light:

Samson has come for you.

He wraps his cane against the glass. Muffled. "You get your chubby white ass outside, boy, before I come in yonder and yank you out."

Button, Fridge, and Jasper exchange looks of worry, but you only chuckle and wave away their concern. "Hang on a sec. Hold that thought. Et cetera. Let me go straighten out this refugee from some biker bar, and afterward, the real people can get on with the important and pressing business of their lives."

BY THE TIME THE HEAVY CANE CONNECTS WITH YOUR SHOULDER YOU'VE ALREADY discovered that your discussion, framed on either side by an aggressive, massive and protective Samson defending an unhinged Trudy, has not gone well; assault, however, wasn't on your list of possible eventualities. That much you know.

Searing, instant, white-hot—your anger, not the pain in your shoulder, which flares but much duller. "You dad-blamed son of a gun—"

Samson, a mountain of hard redneck fat half a head taller than you, roars with raw, sour beer breath and again brandishes the cane: a thunderstruck instance of force, a blinding flash as it cracks against your cranium.

Gooey all over, a high whine fills your ears and a pulsing red-white-purple light consumes your vision; you go down hard. The sidewalk feels hot and gritty against your face.

You gray out for a moment.

Their voices echoing like you're down in a trashcan, Button and Jasper and Trudy converge, pushing Samson away. Trudy bends over you—you'd have expected Button, who seemed so nurturing a spirit.

As though chanting: "Are you all right, are you all right—?"

Your words come thick: "I hit my head. On the sidewalk."

"I'm sorry—we're sorry. Please don't sue us. *Please don't sue us.*"

Stop it, you say. Stop this foolishness. "Help me up."

You get yourself to a sitting position and wipe grit off your face and feel stunned not by pain in your head, but in your shoulder. Sitting on the curb, your blurry vision finds Samson and Jasper in the middle of the street having themselves a somber talk, and you recover your bossman voice: "You white-trash maniac—you broke my goddamn shoulder."

Samson cusses and lunges in your direction. Jasper holds him back.

"Yeah—you realize Mr. Glasscock is my local attorney. Not to mention the sharks I keep back home at Verbrick, Adger and Hagood."

Trudy goes whiter than a freshly bleached Klansman's hood. "We barely got anything, Roy Earl—I mean, Roy. Please."

"Trudy: shut the eff up." Snapping at her makes you wince at the shearing, staggering pain. And, yeah; no fucking promises on that lawsuit, sister. But aloud you say only, "Someone run me over to the doc-in-the-box. I need to get this shoulder looked at."

"We can't pay for no doctors. We can't—"

"I have insurance, damn you."

"Oh—yeah. I guess you do."

Whoa. You actually cursed. You must be in real pain.

Button and Jasper walk Samson back across the street toward Trudy's car. They put him on a bench, the one closest to Pitchfork Ben.

Button sits with Samson, who remains agitated. As Jasper checks on you, you watch her and your assailant. She speaks to him in unheard whispers.

Well, dang—you watch him visibly calm, an unsettled lake of fire coming to placid rest. He's nodding. You can see him wiping tears from his eyes, covering his face. Button, comforting him.

"Jasper? I think my shoulder's sprained. "

"I see that—you're standing crooked. And you hit your head, beau. Let's get an ambulance."

"Shoot, no. It's only a fucking sprain."

Jasper, insisting: "I'd give you a ride, but it's a liability thing. Better to let the ambulance company carry the risk of transporting a grievous injury." Without waiting he calls 9-1-1, which you protest, but without vigor.

Trudy stands holding herself tight, shaking and smoking and trying not to cry. She's a wreck. You ask her to help you onto the bench in front of the honkytonk where your Pa-paw and Uncle Burnie would always sit, and as she does you offer comfort and reassurance that nobody's being sued.

"I got plenty of bread already. And emotions—they're running high," a grunting and painful admission. Striking your head on the pavement has given perspective. You stand outside yourself, seeing the drama you've been playing out with everyone, but in this case specifically with Trudy Pirkle. How you conspire to injure her for no good reason and to no good end. "I couldn't bring myself to sue someone I love."

Can hardly make the words come. "You sure got a funny way of showing how much you love me."

A warm glow spreads inside, different from the heat of the Blade. "It's suddenly important to say how I'm sorry for everything." You wince, hoping it looks close to a smile. "Hey—I should get knocked on my head more often."

Trudy crumbles and cries, but for only one or two heaves. "Thank you for that, sugar. Every time you open your mouth, it's like you kick me in the stomach."

"It's because that's what I was trying to do."

She asks why.

"Because you broke my heart, girl." This comes out as a thin hiss, accompanied by the full brunt of spiritual and emotional pain, a pernicious, cold roiling in your gut that makes the shoulder injury seem like nothing. "Broke it into pieces."

"You're not still thinking about that."

"Not till I came home. And saw you again."

A long pause. "Ancient history. We were drunk."

"True; but listen—I was just a kid."

"We both was."

"Think how it would play nowadays. They put women in prison for seducing underage boys."

This moment hangs. Her face, a mask of shame and confusion broken by lines and wrinkles from decades of smoking. An ambulance's wail, approaching. "I need another cig," is all she can manage.

"On that happy note, let me go yap at your husband for a sec."

"Don't fuss at him. Please. He's not well. He's—an alcoholic."

You shake your head. "It's coolio. It's chill."

Holding your arm across your stomach to keep from moving the shoulder, you hobble over and sit beside the red-eyed, wary Samson. You apologize to him, too. Saying, no hard feelings, no charges, no nothing. Moreover, that Trudy, and all of them, will have a job for a while yet. That your plans within plans will take time to come to fruition.

"Shit, beau. You been so mean about it, though."

"I realize this—but maybe it wasn't the real me."

Button, watching it all, wide-eyed. Smiling. Her hands pressed together in that 'namaste' thing you've noticed she always says instead of hello or see-ya.

"I brought this on," you explain. "I created all this. Myself."

Button all but dances a jig. Composes herself. Goes to check on Trudy.

Pain has given you clarity and wiped away the sense of urgency you've carried throughout the last month. But despite your shoulder injury and your head still buzzing from the impact with the concrete, you feel at peace and with a sense matters will go on as they have, at least for a while. Not for you, and not for your still-bereaved grandmother and hospitalized wife, but for The Dixiana? Sure. Why not. Beyond needing to get the arm in a sling, and maybe eventually seeing your wife again, no goals, no desires. Well—some desires. Ya know.

◉①❋

YOU LEAN ON THE DECK OF THE AMBULANCE JOKING AND DECLAIMING THE silliness of all this activity over a sprained shoulder. One of the EMTs, an overweight young woman sweating in the October sunshine, says it sounds more like a sprain masquerading as a broken clavicle.

Asked what precipitated this injury, you reply, "I tripped on the curb and went down like a sack of potatoes."

"It happens."

At the county hospital a tall, strong-framed female doctor, not a Southerner, bustles back through the curtain into the exam room in the ER full of African-American and Latino mothers with children suffering runny noses. It's not what you anticipated from an ER, which you associate more from the action-packed TV show than having been admitted to one. You expected more gunshots and stab wounds than poor kids coughing and sniffling.

"Mr. Pettus," she announces in a bright, brusque northeastern accent, maybe upstate New York, "it seems you've broken your clavicle! That's your collarbone."

As downtrodden as Piglet on the blustery day: "Oh, bother. Really?"

"That's right!" She's bright-eyed and cheerful, not unlike a newscaster, but never once looks at you because she's preoccupied entering data into a computer terminal jutting out from the wall on a swivel. "It's a clean break, though. You're most fortunate. This kind of injury often requires surgery—screws, pins, and so on. I don't see you needing that."

"Tremendous. And I mean that totally as it sounds. No snark."

"I understand." She swivels her screen and shows you the results of your X-ray—a thin separation in a bone close to your shoulder joint. A fracture. "See?"

You express your relief at such good fortune. "Next steps, doc."

Pulls back the screen. "I recommend arranging to see a doctor at Northeast Richland Orthopedic. Their offices are down near the lake country." Still without eyeballing you in the least, her keys clattering and mouse-toe clicking. "Do you need help arranging to see a specialist?"

"No. It's really broken?" You have a hard time accepting this reality. "No kidding."

"Like you saw, it's a fine break, and serious enough to warrant seeing a specialist."

She hands you a packet of pills that probably cost fifty bucks apiece, a mild pain reliever, she says, to get you through the night, and fixes you with a thin mesh sling, navy blue. A card with the name of the clinic, an address, a logo. "Stay still tonight! Try to get rest. I'm sure the specialist will prescribe a regimen of pain meds."

"How much are those two pills gonna cost me?"

She laughs, cheerful. At last looks into your eyes. "Not my department, my friend."

"A hundred bucks, I'll bet." Wincing, the pain redoubling now that you know it's more than a sprain. "I've never had a broken bone."

"Never?" Now she's already halfway out the mesh curtain. "Can't say that anymore."

"Nope. Reckon not."

Another challenge—that's your only real and measurable reaction to this unexpected occurrence. Some physical pain instead of all the psychic stress you've endured, it occurs to you, might feel like a vacation. Here's hoping broken bones heal faster than hearts.

MANNY AND DOBB V

Another day, another dollah dollah bill, y'all.

Manny hear about some shit that go down over at The Dix yesterday, but he can't make head or tail outta it. Ain't nobody gonna attack a bossman like Roy Pettus. Not if they know what good. If he like Manny, he bring lawyers and judges down on their asses.

No telling what true about it, though. Pics, or it ain't happen. People blow they BS way way out of whack. Stories gets twisted. Manny heard there was an ambulance. He try to get the scoop later, mosey over and ask Trudy Pirkle.

Ahmad and the help done breaking down the steam trays and cleaning up for siesta when Dobb V come rolling up to the door, right as Manny go to lock that muh-fucka and get out for a while—nice timing, yo.

Manny open the door. Dobb want to know could he put a to-go plate together.

"Aw, dog—we done broke down."

"Well, dang it all. Wanted to take it to Gooch."

"How old Gooch doing?"

Sad little smile. "Well, he's fine. A little housebound these days."

Manny think real quick: wait, he need to keep the newspaperman on his side. He want that free advertising. Ought to get Dobb to do an article about Manny's days on the road, from the chitlin circuit to some damn fine rooms. He never had his own band, not till he and Neecie go into business together and open a joint. Still, wild-ass stories he got. Couldn't print half that shit in a newspaper, though.

He ain't sure if it matter anymore if his ass get free advertising in that paper. Ain't nothing but shriveled-up old white crackers reading it, old black folks, too, ain't many of which coming to spend dollar one in his crib. Not to hear the music, anyway. Sunday brunch and dinner after church? Different story. Biggest day of the week. Hard to work with a head on after a big Saturday night jamming. All Manny know.

"Ain't no thang. I'll get Ahmad to bring you out a plate. What old Gooch like?"

"Mac and cheese, greens. What about protein? Probably not barbecue."

"We had slow-cook chops today. Them things melt in ya mouth."

"Chops sound perfect. You're all right, Manny T."

Manny say, we try. Our asses try.

Manny holler at Ahmad what need doing, and that skinny ass turkey start to give lip, honking his honk over the dishwasher groaning and rushing hot water all around.

"Why don't your ass do it your own self?"

Manny think if he get the chance one day, he gonna make Ahmad life miserable for real for real. For now he make that slashing motion at his throat and roll his eyes back like Blacula and say, do it do it do it muh-fucka.

"Nice management style," Dobb V say all smart-ass. "They must send you flowers at the end of the week."

Manny laugh it off. "Only way to get it done right is to stay on their asses. You can always hire a crew to work a gig, but if it ain't done right, might as well've done it your own self."

Dobb V say he hear Manny, note how he got some of that going since Gooch ain't been feeling well.

Having to write and publish a newspaper. It all Greek to Manny. Except for the advertising. That much he know.

"Take his recent piece about Rev. Nixon's campaign for council. Just between us, it needed so much work—well." Dobb V, leaning over in his chair and resting his chin on one hand. "About Nixon's call to change the name of the city—what does Manny's on the Green have to say about that plank of the Reverend's platform?"

"About New Jack City? Aw."

Dobb V nod all expectant, put his hands in his lap real quick like his ass ready to type. "New Falls City, actually, is the proposal."

"Right on, right on. But I ain't going on no record or nothing. I stay out of that political shit. You hit up my old lady. She the one getting mixed up in all that."

Manny let himself think about how much her civic do-gooding mean to Neecie—getting to be one of them ELMS and all. Manny kept telling her, they ain't nothing but bone-throwing. Token shit. So they asses look like right-now, but he say in they hearts he bet them women the same southern muh-fuckas they always was. Rich old snatches. That dusty Old South money, it still keep black assholes like Manny and his people in they places. Ask Paula Deen bout all that. That wedding, she got them brothers in tuxedos cause it all look so quaint to have us doing the serving? Shi-it. Bitch got a strange-ass idea about inclusion.

Like them ELMS do about Neecie. But ya can't tell her none of that. She still too happy about being in the club.

Becky L. She the progressive one who make it happen, yo. Get your mind round this shit. Sponsor Neecie into the ELMS; go and fuck the woman's husband raw behind everybody back. God-dog, y'all.

Worse? Fall in love with his ass.

Worser? Make his ass fall in love with hers.

They talked through all that shit, Manny and long-tall Sally. She felt bad about the deception, yo. Don't care. Her ass love him no less.

Neecie and Becky. Manny try not to think about what them two must've said to each other by now. He don't wanna know. No, he don't.

Except, yeah. He kinda do.

Dobb V, his face go like, aw-shit. "I'd hoped to get a reaction from you. As a stakeholder in the town—?"

"She straight-up own the business too, so best get with Neecie on what she think."

"Manny."

Manny go, whut.

"You're passing the buck on me."

"She the one—mixed up in—oh, hell. I'll tell truth. Why not?"

His eyes, shining and eager. Produce a pen and a flip notebook out of his satchel, poof, his work shit appear like magic. "So the question is, how do you feel about changing the name of Tillman Falls."

"I think it stupid."

"The name change? Or the new name itself?"

"Whatever. Both."

"On the record?"

Manny think, oh-well, pull up a chair right as Ahmad holler 'order up.' Manny holler back, well bring it out, dog, and his brother-in-law do, all bugeyed and poking out his lips like he too good to work, plopping down the styrofoam box without waiting for no thank-you from nobody.

"Appreciate it," the newspaperman call after Ahmad, and give him a smile that make Manny say, Dobb V for real over here in this chair. He not let it get him down. That smile not from no cripple. That smile from somebody who all right with himself. With God, too, Manny think.

And maybe his ass ought to get that way too.

Problem is he like hell outta that girl. Manny like hanging round her. It a different world now—muh-fucka like him get to go around with a white woman, everybody be all copacetic and shit. Go to the grocery store and squeeze avocados together, ain't nobody bat an eye. Even here in South Cackalack. Their asses once had riots and shootings over the lunch counters back in the day. Lillyanne tell Manny all about it. She learn it from the internet.

Well, he been thinking, maybe Manny ought to divorce Neecie. Lillyanne, she'd understand. Kids today? Shit. She lucky Manny ain't gone before now. Becky L ain't the first, yo. They'd share muh-fucken custody. That how that work. He don't know what they do about Manny's on the Green—it in both their names. Work it out, Manny reckon.

Shit, why all this running through his head? Crazy.

Manny hear what he say from faraway as he give his interview. How he don't give a rip about no Pitchfork Ben sticking black folks a hundred years ago. How that shit in the past, and muh-fuckas need to get over they tender asses about it.

But the main point is how Manny done built his ass a good trade in Historic Downtown Tillman Falls, he say in a deep voice like Eddie Murphy making fun of white people.

"But also, it literally different world from back then." Manny debate saying the next bit. Lower his voice. "If a brother like me—I mean, all hypothetical and shit—can go be-bopping down Congress Street with a white girl on his arm and not get beat up? Shit done changed about all it's going to, ya know ya know."

"No reminders of South Carolina history needed. I understand the feeling. But, plenty of work left to do in the world."

"You got that right. More'n anybody gonna do just changing the names of shit. Hearts and minds got to change."

Dobb V nod and make a pile of notes in his little pad, scribbling away. Puffing Manny chest out, he say all definitive he can't get behind no New Jack City or whatever their asses want to call it. "That's right. My ass done spent beaucoup bucks on all our shit that says 'Tillman Falls,' and I declare I ain't behind everybody having to print new stationary and business cards and shit. Or, what I'm saying is, I don't support this proposal from the Reverend. Can't feature it. Hope it don't pass, or however all that work."

"That's terrific. That's—awesome. I should get this plate over to Gooch's house, but first—what if I told you Mauldin Saugus has endorsed the proposal to change the name?"

"Who?"

Dobb V look shocked, explain how Mauldin Saugus is the district's representative in congress—the United States House of Representatives, he say all smarmy—and who happens to be African-American and from next door in Beauchamp County; a leader and spokesperson for many hundreds of thousands of citizens. "He has quite a machine. Can deliver votes. And so on."

Manny remember now. Call the congressman by a nickname he heard somebody use. "I don't care what Naughty Sawdust say, or whatever his name is. I like Tillman Falls. Sound all nice and quaint. What you call it—nonthreatening. I say, keep that shit. Ain't broke, don't fix it. That all I got to say."

"Word for word," flipping shut his notebook. Dobb V get that warm smile again. "Against the name change—but you do support the Reverend's campaign for the new council seat."

Manny feel all reassured inside. "Ain't sure I trust no Reverend. They ain't supposed to be in gub-mint. Is they?"

Dobb V shrug. "Suppose it's up to the voters."

"Well, still. He can run for dog catcher, mayor, prince of the city—I ain't give two shits either way. Long as he on the side of small business and all."

"You've been such a help today. Here—"

He go to get out his wallet, but Manny say nuh-uh, he done close out the register. Gooch's food on him, today. Manny T, he know how to give back to his community. "You tell him that plate come from the heart."

"I shouldn't accept."

"I insist, brotherman."

When he go to shake Dobb V stuff a ten-spot into Manny hand. "Aw, dog."

"Too late. Put it in Lillyanne's college fund."

"Right on. You all right."

Manny feeling good—he think now like Dobb V his best friend. Shit yeah, Manny a stakeholder. His ass got this idea for making this place—Tillman Falls, SC—into Music City. Now change the name to that, if ya wanna call it anything. That's what he should-a said. Oh, well.

Furtha-more? Manny seen Roy Pettus and his antennas all working around at that Music City branding idea. He a sharp operator, Roy Pettus. His ass ought to run. Made a shit-ton of scratch. He grasp the secret, whatever that shit is. N-word like the preacher—hell, most all them politicians—ain't none know how to run a business. Maybe that what wrong with the economy. Folks in charge ain't led no real lives.

⊗◐✳

Next morning, like a mind-reader, Neecie call his ass out on the Becky love shit. After they ain't said word-one for two weeks. Like it blown over at home.

"You think I don't see you moping around here?" Neecie, swishing in her robe and getting ready to go into Columbia on some mysterious errand she ain't got time to explain. "Your ass acting like you in love. *In love with that disloyal bitch,*" and now she let the curtain up and show you the hurt. You ain't heard her voice sound pitiful like that since her mama died, and before that, when she come running during Katrina and saying, the water ain't stopping. Oh, Manny, it going higher. What we gonna do.

Like they was gonna die—the whole city, dying.

And now, like Manny ass done killed something inside his Neecie.

But damn, she right. Her ass right.

Shit, though. He feel it for that girl. He think about her, try to hold her face in his mind. Not only her pussy. Like he love her spirit inside. That what he digging on. She make him look in her eyes when he come, and when she do, on top and holding him down, it like a cosmic experience, like back when Manny tripping and shit. When she takes a notion, Neecie still fuck him good with that big old sloppy mama pussy. But she don't care about looking into his eyes no more. And he don't worry about gazing into hers. It all just to come, the way it seem to him. Not enough.

"You better be careful with all your ass-suming. Cause you know what they say."

"This ain't right, doing me like this. Them is my people—Becky was *my* friend."

"I told ya it over. I don't know what else my ass can do." Manny know it nothing but bullshit. That nothing was over yet. But how else you get through it and get on? Necessary fibbing to restore order. That the way he see it.

"You pitiful, Manny."

"Your ass got to get over yourself."

"You go and get that restaurant open. And I'll be back later on today to pick up Lillyanne from school."

"She can ride the bus to the green like she always do."

"The fuck she can. She do what I want her to do."

Manny hold up his hands, go to put on his shirt, the blue Miles Davis one with the *Jack Johnson* album cover. He pull it on over his tight muscles and hustle that dick, and even though he hear Neecie slam that door out front like she mean it, he say, he say to himself, she get over this like she did all the others. It all cause it a white girl this time, too.

Who she seem to know Manny ass done fall in love with.

Shit.

He try to change the subject. "So old Dobb V come rolling over from the paper yesterday."

She like, yeah, and so mutha-fuckin' what?

"I told him what I thought about Nixon and his New Jack City shit. That I wasn't done with it. Think it stupid."

Neecie, having already heard you go around saying how much you don't give a shit, turn into devil woman. Say, oh holy shit, your ass better not have made a statement to the press in the name of this business we both share. And now Manny realize what having his fat go from frying pan into fire feels like. And brotherman, lemme tell ya: shit ain't good.

ROY, DR. KIP, COUSIN CARLA MAE, DALE AND DJ

No better way to start a new day in Edgewater County than dealing with a sprained—check; broken—shoulder. Samson, lucky he and his cane aren't in Sheriff Oakley's pokey awaiting bail.

Loopy from the pain meds, you awake from the cat dream out of a surrealistic sojourn, a rough night—your shoulder, it's difficult to manage with any sense of comfort. Hell, it's the side on which you like to curl up, fetal. That's when you get your best REM sleep.

But the dream—yeah. Your deep sleep has come from the painkiller they prescribed you. Last night you gobbled the pills and went to lie down, at first rolling onto your favorite side and shrieking in pain. Tried to psych yourself out. Said, you will not roll onto this side like you do every night of your life. Said it like your mantra.

Many hours later, you awakened flat on your back and absent any notable discomfort. Physically, that is:

In the dream you're trying to find a way into the Sedge Island Marshside mansion. You have anxiety. It's because you know you will catch them in the act. The house seems situated in the parking lot of the plaza next to the CBSI. There aren't enough live oaks; too much sunlight.

You take a long dream-time getting into the house. You search and search for the door, but can't find an entrance anywhere. Only catching glimpses of what you presume to be the shapes and movements of your wife and her lover, eventually you are at the front door and it's there like it ought to be, but you don't so much open it as pass through.

Inside you are greeted by a mad, impossible vision: one of the gray striped tabbies (there are three that all look alike, and which you cannot keep straight to save your life), lolling in the foyer. But here, a cat the size of a lion; a creature out of fabulist myth. An enormous Maine Coon, fluffy tail flicking and slapping the floor, reverberating like the subwoofer during one of those superhero movies in which buildings collapse into piles of pulverized dust during the final battle. Each flick of the tail like a mini-earthquake, your dream-feet leave the tiled floor.

More than an unnaturally large house cat, it lay not only with a pendulous belly, but as it rolled toward you an elephantine brown phallus, sickeningly human and leaking yellow discharge, flopped with a wet, slapping sound.

Terrified and disgusted, you tried to lurch away. Your feet, slipping and sticking on the tiles, stuck in dream-mud. You called for Creedence to hurry and clean up this cat mess. The sound of your dream-voice came out strangulated; yeah, you know the sensation. A mouth, but no scream.

Discharge. Yuck.

Like after the last stray she'd brought home—last one, I swear this time— had given birth. Oh, yeah, it'd already been pregnant. Had had three kittens. The gray tabbies. Young. You'll be scooping this tabby shit for fifteen years, as you'd thought. Awesome.

How you pled for her to have the kitties aborted. Knew the vet would do it. But no. Tears and rage and shock at the suggestion.

Horror.

Resentment.

Your own wife.

Little jibes and stabbing suggestions of perfidy, ever since. About the precious tabbies. "And you wanted to kill them." Not a dream.

◉◍❋

LYING IN BED WITH A FULL BLADDER BUT NO DESIRE TO JOSTLE THE SHOULDER, IT strikes you:

Why hadn't she chosen to screw Dr. Kip Epperton, DVM?

Wouldn't they have plenty to talk about?

To find in common?

Besides, you like Dr. Kip—hell, he's a medical professional, and at least more of a peer to a successful entrepreneur like you than some punk-ass barista with plugs in his ears. Hell, redux—Kip Epperton's not only a feline healthcare provider but a small business owner, and a prosperous one too, especially when factoring in the enormous expenditures Creedence and her island ilk contribute in keeping their pets healthy and alive. He's got a sign out front on the bulletin board that reads 'Dr. Kip Wants Your Toys, Games, and Other Pop Culture Items from the 50s, 60s, 70s' in Comic Sans font. Hip dude.

Probably into *Trek*. Angular, thin and with a good jawline, on any given Halloween the vet would make for a solid Spock.

Did that part matter to her—the success? You guessed not. Plenty of money, your wife supplied with a generous account. It's technically her household-running cash, mad money with which she may do what she pleases.

What else did she need/want from that literal little fucker Estes?

Or from you, for that matter?

What more could you do than make the awesomeness happen?

Once, you talked to the vet about Chelsea Colette 'Creedence' Rucker-Pettus behind her back, in this case consulting less as a veterinarian than a priest or psychiatrist. It'd been when you'd had to rush over an injured cat. Not one of the house pets but a stray, god help you, that she'd eagle-eyed on the side of the road crumpled from an obvious automobile strike. Alive but broken and bleeding. Horrors.

You transported the animal, blood running from its mouth, to the vet. You both stood in the exam room. Creedence, gripping herself with anguish as you listened to Dr. Kip explain with grace and gentle patience that the Unnamed 'tuxedo' shorthair male's injuries were too grave to repair. That if it were Dr. Kip's pet, he'd put it down, and with haste.

She nodded. "Of course."

You sighed with relief—one less to come home. Sure, you had room for another ten on top of the nine she'd collected. But Christ, the rigmarole. The odor. The feeding.

After Dr. Kip helped the tuxedo kitty across the rainbow bridge, Creedence asked for a moment to say goodbye to the cat she'd known for all of fifteen minutes. Wait—no, no, as she'd explained; he wasn't a stranger. She recognized this sweet poor boy from around the dumpster behind the Whole Foods. Had her eye on him for a while, bless his heart, as she told the men with her voice breaking and water flooding down freckled cheeks. She'd already decided on a name, Creedence added, which she tried to say aloud but couldn't through her sobbing. You supposed it had been a minor miracle she hadn't brought this one home already.

But if she had, he'd be alive now.

You understood her grief. You're not a monster. But you already have too many kitty-cat souls under your care.

The vet made eye contact and gestured with a subtle elbow to your ribs. You left Creedence with the body while the doc took you into his office, paneled and book-lined and adorned by awards and certificates. Comfortably credentialed, he'd been a professional vet for 26 years, it looked from the original degree. A leather couch on which you sat. Classy, reassuring, a hidden respite and oasis from the fluids and grief of the vet trade, a safe space you apprehend as needed for the doctor himself, as well as for such occasional side counseling:

You both could hear Creedence wailing back in Exam Room 2, the larger one—the close-quartered Exam Room 1 and Exam Room 3 both felt like coffins. "Dude. What am I gonna do with her?"

Dr. Kip Epperton explained to you that the cat fixation—there, I said it, he joked, winking and covering his mouth, exaggerating the gesture like a naughty mime—had much to do with the fact that the couple produced no human children. "Kid substitutes. That's what you're working with."

"We tried. A couple of miscarriages."

Dr. Kip apologized; you shrugged and smiled.

"Well, you get this syndrome—we hesitate to call it hoarding, but it does go that far. Child-substituting, what with all the empty nesters on the island. I see it a great deal. In your case, not exactly empty-nest, but—"

"But of course it is. Empty is empty."

"You're much younger than the folks I'm talking about."

Musing. "Maybe we should adopt. I've suggested adopting. Right?"

Surprised. "Oh. Really, now."

"Why not?"

"Mrs. Pettus already works with several of the cat rescue groups, one here on the island and one on the mainland—no shortage of adoptees awaiting their fur-ever homes."

"NO," you had exploded. "Not another cat, doc."

"Oh, I understand. Sure, adopting a child's a noble act. Wonderful idea. And, hey—sorry about Unnamed Tuxedo Male."

"It's a shame. But it's over."

◉①❋

OVER THE NEXT COUPLE OF MONTHS TWO MORE STRAYS JOINED THE PETTUS CREW, along with a third that had 'come up and started eating' with the other two she would feed in the backyard. This practice went against homeowners association covenants, a violation that made you so angry and embarrassed you could not see straight. But you let her get away with it.

Didn't you?

And how were you repaid for such indulgence? With more cats.

You scooped feces from litter boxes, at first. Then came the housekeeper, Averah, who also seemed to detest the activity of cleaning after the cats, the daily vomit and sputum and hairball expulsions. And with all the crunchy, gray, corporate sand underfoot, it's like you live on Tidy Cat Island rather than Sedge.

The beautiful downstairs bathroom had become little more than a giant litter box, principally the lovely bathtub on which you'd both commented during the tour with the realtor as being large enough for two. Everyone's eyebrows wiggling, warm chuckles and a squeeze around your wife's waist; what a bathroom. Now it served as the repository of a pair of uncovered shit and piss receptacles, an inexorable filling of the drain by tiny, super-absorbent rocks.

At the time, though: "This is our dream place, isn't it," she'd said in awe.

"It sure is."

You hadn't felt it, not at all, but saw how much the house seemed to speak to her, so you said, of course, angel. A creampuff. With a garden tub now good for nothing but temp storage of feline feces filled with fungus and parasites.

Your own fault; she'd pulled that tub deal in plain sight, but you hadn't visited the rec room level in weeks and weeks, not after you'd gotten busy with the new Beanery. You discovered the tub boxes only after a trying day with health inspectors, when you came home with a stiff neck and thought, shit, I could use a soak. Found the trays placed within the tub. Litter underfoot. The sharp, acrid ammonia odor from the dried piss in every nook and cranny, the tiles, the grout. Already.

You stood gape-mouthed and exhausted, sick to your stomach. But you didn't challenge her on the tub. You couldn't face the emotional bullying to come. "You're so selfish," as she always hurls at you when you complain about the cats seeming to come first.

Later, as you arrived at the luxury downstairs bath off the rec room during the housekeeper walkthrough, Averah asked, "These boxes. They stay in nice tub?"

"Afraid they do."

"Por qué?"

"Good question."

Creedence jumped in: "They feel more private in the tub. Plus, I'd rather it all go in there than on the floor somewhere."

The maid's face, a mixture of disapproval and bewilderment. "I see."

Five minutes in, and the housekeeper knew the deal. An ally; a comrade in outrage. Creedence had turned in a huff and gone upstairs.

There on Sedge Island, cashed out at forty-five, your own plane, bad-ass house, all the security anyone might hope for, it's like, yeah: dreams come true, sure. But standing with the cat litter under your sport sandals in your hollow home, you detected an amorphous sense of lack undergirding the whole enterprise. Surely not—look at the money we're talking. Lack? Get real.

❀

Another bad dream sequence: The day you went into her office-nook and leaned on the computer desk, and the monitor woke up, and you saw her Facebook account and email wide open. How you took a deep breath and thought about how little you'd seen of her in the last couple of months. How Sharolyn had told you that 'your woman been hanging around the Beanery an awful lot,' with your GM fretting that if you did not feel confident in her abilities to run the coffee shop without being babysat by your spouse, maybe you needed a more trustworthy manager; and you said, "Sharolyn, girl, you know me as a straight shooter. If I was gonna QC you with a secret shopper, I sure wouldn't use Creed." Neither of you realized the truth yet.

The images from the security cam would confirm the situation for you, not that you needed to have any more confirmation than what they'd written in the messages and emails through which you scrolled, your gut punched and nuts drawn up and boiling with anger and tears. Tears only of rage, you affirmed. Not sorrow.

A crime here. Not a tragedy.

Injustice.

Irredeemable.

And those security tapes, yeah; standing hunched over in the office, fast-forwarding. Seeing the arrival of Estes and the departure of Sharolyn. Watching Creedence arrive, order a coffee and sit reading at a table. Observing her and Estes chatting. Leaning over your wife. Pointing at her book. Touching her face.

Creedence, taking his hand. Holding it against her cheek.

And later, on the secret office cam that at the same moment also recorded you viewing the on-camera betrayal by your wife with an Assistant GM fifteen years your junior, staggering shock as you saw them clutching with passion at one another. Tongues swirling. Hands all over, unbridled, until realizing they should skedaddle. Nobody knew about this hidden office cam, concealed in a fake smoke detector, but you.

Why did she need that little a-hole? Indian men sport some of the smallest average penises on the planet, a factoid gleaned from a listicle that rolled through your Facebook newsfeed one morning only days after discovering the affair. Didn't add up.

It strikes you: You're the one who ought to collect cats. You're the neglected, brokenhearted, unfulfilled spouse.

◉①❋

You finally realize as you emerge from your narcotic shoulder coma and shuffle into your grandmother's kitchen for coffee that you're free—not so much from Creedence, but from other concerns, such as what you will make of the rest of your life. None of your choices feel right. So here in Edgewater

County, then, a chance to examine matters and set yourself on the correct path.

Truth: If it meant staying here for a time, and for Creedence behaving responsibly on her own, unsupervised, in order for y'all to reunite—if such a reunion is meant to be; the likelihood of this notion changes like the shifting wind—perhaps this hometown trial but a small price to grow spiritually. It's an idea that's gotten lodged in your noggin thanks to Button Sykes, with whom you enjoy such a warm relationship.

No pain, no gain.

Happy all the time. That's success. That's the goal. Which you accomplish through acquiring game pieces, benchmarks, milestones. Money.

Spirituality, my foot. You've never given it a thought. On a long walk down on the nice river trail with Button, she listened to you blather about only being concerned with what the senses could perceive. Called you a shortsighted materialist.

Of course that's what you are—matter is the whole matter. The rest is fantasy. The stuff of Harry Potter. Bullshit, in other words.

Button seems to think you ought to wake up. That you can't take it with you. Heard that one before.

Ha. You need not worry. Unlike everybody else, you have no plans to die nor any heirs to whom you may leave money or real estate. So, no death, at least not until you spend every last penny. In your case, anyway, this is the ultimate aspiration. Otherwise, the wealth goes to the state. And the state, with spendthrift pols of both modern political stripes running roughshod over sound economic policy, has not earned the honorific of inheriting your fortune.

Still coming down from the weird dream, you decide to get out of the house. Adjusting the sling, you make up an excuse to Mama Runelle, who sits frail and quiet, worried to death about the shoulder you 'sprained,' a gentle fib to spare her concerns.

"You better be careful driving that durn truck with a hurt shoulder. You're liable to run off that damn river road."

"Not I, said he." You raise your good arm and tap your left temple. "The pitching arm might be toast, but the mind remains sharp."

Your grandmother curses. Gives you a list of items to pick up, including a pack of her cigarettes. Why the heck not, right? About to be eighty-nine, soon. Maybe older, for all you know. Not like you've ever examined your grandmother's papers.

◉◍❀

At the Gas Chief filling up the F-150, you run into your cousin Mervin's wife Carla Mae, not seen since the night of Rabbit's death. She's driving the twins, Dale and DJ, to their whatever appointment. She greets you with a hug and stands with fists upon a substantial set of hips, Capri pants bulging at the seams with pink flesh, chubby manicured toes splayed atop cheap flip-flops.

While you both ding-ding-ding your tanks full of gasoline, Carla Mae asks first about your arm in the sling, followed by Mama Runelle, and last, the dog. "How's that big sweet Rico doing without his pappy? It's just so sad."

You give her the report, but based only on hearsay from your grandmother —you barely speak to the dog, only long enough to dump kibble into the huge, disgusting metal bowl by the gate. "He's a fine fine animal. I'm sure."

"Dr. Macelhaney, our vet? He says a Newfoundland like that won't live much longer than ten years. Normally." She sounds smarmy and self-satisfied at revealing the extent of her esoteric canine knowledge. "If that."

Idiot. "Rico's a Great Pyrenees, not a Newfoundland."

She wrinkles her nose and smiles in pity at your foolishness, pish-poshes you. "Shit—them ain't nothing but a white Newfoundland. Now, I know my dog breeds, and it ain't no separate one. I dunno who come up with 'Great Pyrenees.' I reckon that's supposed to sound all la-ti-da."

Troubled by this ignorance, you get a singularly exquisite tingle down the side of your leg: the blessed Blade, at your command. You vibe her with displeasure.

Grunting out a monosyllabic dissent, you replace the hose and turn attention to the twin boys immersed in their tablets.

"Well now, fellas. What's shaking today."

"Computer camp," Dale/DJ says, annoyed.

"Which at this rate we're gonna be late for," Dale/DJ asserts.

Casual, leaning against the cool tru-coating of Carla Mae's SUV. "Don't y'all get enough computers without going to camp for it? These fellas need to be out doing little kid stuff."

"Mama?" The other twin, eyebrows flatlining across his smooth forehead. "Who the freak is this freak?"

"*Darling*, this is Roy Earl. He's like your uncle."

The kid—Dale? DJ? Did it matter?—squints at you. "Oh. Right."

"How could you forget Uncle Roy Earl? Gosh, maybe they need their eyes checked," joshing and cheery and trying anew to connect. "But seriously. You guys should play baseball. Or go camping. Or—do you fish?" What bullshit. You haven't been fishing in decades. "You guys wanna go fishing sometime?"

"*Mama—*"

Carla Mae, in a practiced bit of suburban ballet, replaces her pump and wrenches the gas cap closed and whirls to snap off her receipt all in one graceful motion. "Roy, these boys is all scheduled out. Maybe we'll play baseball next year, though. What do you think about that, DJ?"

In utter disbelief: "I'd sooner cut my dick off."

"Son! Language!"

Dale snorts, derisive. "Aw. Mama's having one of her little control moments."

DJ glances up from his tablet. Makes hard eye contact, but only for a brief second, during which it's like *The Omen 5: Damien's Revenge.* "Moments only pass to make room for more moments."

Totally creeped out. "Is that a movie line? *Where do I know that from?*"

The kid's finger, tracing unseen icons. "Dunno."

"I can't heads or tails out of what they're talking about half the time, them little smart-butts. They're working on some role-playing game together. And I don't mean playing—they're making it up themselves, the little geniuses. It's the durn-dest thing."

"Color me impressed."

Furtive, she cuts her eyes at her boys and motions for you to accompany. "Little angels? Mama's got to run inside real quick to tinkle."

"What else is new," Dale says with fatigue verging upon utter despair. "You've got the bladder of a gnat."

"See what I mean? They don't even talk like they're from around here. Geniuses."

"I'm glad you called me over here," you begin at the entrance to the gas station. "I wanted to thank you for the food you brought over. And the card. Mama Runelle appreciated all that."

"Wasn't nothing. It's what you do."

She holds open the door, but you indicate that right here's fine. "What's on your mind?"

"I know it ought to be the man doing the asking. But-anyway. Here goes."

You feel an inner, descending frost: Your ass is about to be hit up. "Go on."

"We wanna move into the house—the old house."

Dumbfounded. "What old house?"

As she explains, your grandparents's old house. Twenty yards away from the Victorian. Where you now live.

Who was she kidding? Cue Twilight Zone theme. "That's a good one. Your idea."

"I know! Wouldn't it be awesome? I would so like to raise my boys in the house where Uncle Rabbit and Aunt Runelle lived. I mean, we'll pay *rent* on it and all," laughing with demure, phony self-consciousness. "I ain't asking for no handouts."

"Here. Let me ponder on it." You pause two seconds. Maybe three. "No."

"Oh, just like that?"

You bet—you say no in an automatic fashion, often with a sarcastic edge, as you'd adapted when dealing with reps like print and radio ad salesmen, especially so when you opened Carolina Beanery Sedge Island in the midst of the

2010s. Traditional advertising? That's what these tenacious, slick, arrogant chumps were still trying to sell? You laughed them out of there. You? You're paying a PR major half rates and signing off on a college-credit internship in exchange for her building social media engagement. Facebook posts. Instagram pics of sandwiches and pastries. Do all this meta-tagging, SEOs and other arcane nonsense, yadda yadda, deliver clicks and hits, but all to generate meatspace traffic and disposable steaming lattes in grateful, thirsty hands. Custies displaying emailed coupons on smart phone screens. Reviews and likes and shares. You chortle in the faces of those haggard, old media ad reps now. You decline deals that can never benefit you like they might once have in the analog days. Gotta be stern and steadfast with your dismissal, too, otherwise they keep pushing. Cold fact.

You explain a version of all this. "That's a negatory. Roger and out."

Blinking, confused. "Meaning what?"

"That, not only do I not know the final disposition of the estate—my grandmother still being alive is a big part of that uncertainty, hello?—but besides, I can guarantee these houses won't become rental property. Even for *family*," saying it with forced warmth that belies the insincere snark simmering in your black, beating heart. You don't give a rip. You da boss.

"'Your' property? Mama Runelle once said you'd never live here again anyway."

"Five little words."

She waited.

"Be that as it may."

"I ain't following."

Pitying her, you explain in direct language how you don't give a flying freak what your grandmother said or says; she's ancient, elderly, and not in complete control of her faculties; and with you being the bossman now, you will decide these matters in due time. How you'll be living on the property for an indefinite interim. That it's ridiculous to even consider her proposal; that you have other plans, a mild fib.

"But Roy Earl." She starts to blubber. "We gonna lose our house soon."

"Foreclosure?"

Uh-huh, all sniffly. "We ain't got nowhere else to go."

You don't know what to say. "—"

She rests her clammy palm on your arm, a gesture of desperation and quite unlike the cougars at the supermarket or in the Beanery, who find you charismatic and slap your forearm and want that power-walking, monied bod of yours; ooh, want it so bad. No—Carla Mae, your cousin by marriage, looms desperate with a different brand of desire.

Her other hand, extended, says help-me.

Your resistance, faltering.

Family.

The horn from her Expedition sounds. She cusses at the boys, both gesturing with urgency to be on with their journey. No wonder they're in such trouble—without enough income, payments on a beast like that would drown anyone. Well, not you, but ordinary wage-earners like your cousin and his wife. Not to mention the nearly hundred bucks in gas you watched the woman drop on filling it up. They probably live in some McMansion over in Chilton. Cul-de-sac city over there. Always was. Devin and Creedence had grown up in Pine Haven, one of the first from back in the 70s.

"Look—after I deal with other stuff, I'll help you figure out a solution."

"You will?"

As noncommittal as possible: "You bet."

She hugs you. "Thank you so much, Roy Earl."

"Look—it's just 'Roy' now. No Roy Earl."

"Do what?"

"Never mind."

The heat of the Black Blade finds itself replaced by a pulsing blue shimmer, like Luke Skywalker's first lightsaber exploding into life in the initial space opera that played for so long at the Palmetto Grande and had, for a time, seemed the apotheosis of everything meaningful about American culture, the culture of your world, of the entire world, far as you could tell. The sky-blue glow is like the one Button told you to visualize during meditation while you focus on your throat chakra, charging it up in service of using your words only for good, and never to wound. Difficult for you. But getting better.

You reach over and touch Carla Mae on the face, give her a hug. "Don't worry, I got resources. I'll be glad to help."

"Thank you, thank you, I'm sorry, thank you." Her gratitude, genuine.

"But I don't know about living in the house."

"Oh."

"Just yet. Let me think on it." You hand her your CBSI card, textured linen with raised print, a tremendous business card that screams MONEY. "Email or Facebook me. Good enough for today?"

She says it is. More thanking. Enough already.

You've always thought of Mervin as redneck caricature and unworthy of consideration, but here, his wife, his progeny—fellow human beings—present themselves in need. Distant blood, but even the farthest person away is, in the end, not that far. Still, before you throw down a rope ladder made of your money, you'll investigate what got them into the hole .

Besides, you lived a good boyhood in that old house, which you can suddenly imagine letting them move into, even if you end up staying in the Victorian for a spell. A lovely childhood back in those woods, down in the pecan orchard and the glade by the river. Dale and DJ might have been unpleasant modern little automatons, but perhaps wandering the Pettus backland would make their spirits soar the way yours once did, when Pa-paw and Mee-maw had fed and warmed and given you all the succor a chubby Edgewater County grandbaby could have been privileged enough to experience.

Make a difference in the lives of kids—was that the answer? At this rate, you'll never have your own. A meaningful way to serve. You'll run the idea by Button, see if it pegs her woo-woo meters.

And if Carla Mae and Mervin were living next to your grandmother... you could leave. Off the hook.

Now you're vibrating at a lucky frequency again, with a typical Roy E. Pettus glow of good fortune, though it's tempered by nagging guilt. As it should be—'twas ever thus, even in times like now when you have no clue over what to feel guilty. How you roll.

Speaking of guilt, probably next on your checklist is a conversation with the old lady. See how she fared in the clinic; what's next. Good times.

BUTTON AND A DOCTOR

After a quick walk-around, as Roy would put it, with Mayor Hampton regarding the imminent appearance of her protest tent on the town green, Button paid a visit to the first-care doctor to see about this persistent tender throat.

She didn't believe in Western medicine; but a fit of paranoia propelled her to the doctor's office. Peace of mind, or some such rationalization.

Her Q'i had gotten jammed up. That's all.

Walfredo, her spirit guide from the future, had already sent 'his' typical warm reassurance, but despite mental discipline and various practices esoteric and otherwise, Button remained troubled, cautious and anticipatory.

A constant scratchy throat-tickle. A persnickety persistent stitch in her side. The endless throat-ache stemmed not even by ceasing inhaled ingestion of the kind bud. She made a batch of butter and from that cookies, but misjudging the dosage. The cookies, potent. She ate two and passed out for ten hours, a comatose interval in which she'd lain oblivious to her mother calling from downstairs. Tinky, calling for Button so often that the sound disappeared into the background like crickets at night, or a low hum she could more feel than hear.

The hum in question she knew well; still in tune with her space. Her place. The resonant frequency of Gaia herself.

After watching a new Bill Hicks documentary, suffering a wave of fresh anxiety. The pancreatic cancer. The pains in his side, first cropping up on the Australian tour.

Stop it.

The occasional nosebleeds were another concern, like when she'd been with Mayor Hampton on the green discussing the setup for her No Nukes tent. Again, not a protest, only an 'information clearinghouse' about the dangers— or rather possible concerns, she clarified—over the production of nuclear power. Perhaps other environmental issues as well. "But not political. Not taking either side."

"Button I tell ya, folks my age remember hiding under desks and all that mess back when the Russkies was gonna hammer us with atomic bombs. And because of that, I can remember asking my daddy about the Sugeree Station, and was it safe. He told me it was; and I believe him still. My daddy never lied to me once, not far as I could tell."

"Nor did mine."

"God rest his soul. Wish he'd lived to see this."

"Me too."

"But them new reactors, it ain't like bombs. It's giving us more power, and light, and—" He sighed, heavy. "And, it's a done deal. They put on the biggest concrete pour in the history of South Carolina over yonder last week."

"Did they, now?" She felt her nose running. Wiping, she noticed a little blood on her finger. "I understood from the NRC permitting process. That shovels. Weren't breaking ground. Until the spring."

"For once, the government got out of the way. The pour's gonna be the lead story in tomorrow's *Columbia Record*. Just gave a statement on it."

She had retained a shred of irrational maybe-we-can-still-stop-this-travesty. "Can't say I'm happy. To hear this news."

"It's good news. The jobs that's coming to this county over the next ten years ain't even begun yet. But they will, and folks's gonna prosper from it. Families putting food on the table. Paychecks buying cars and houses. So I don't know what could be wrong with that. Or what you hope to accomplish."

"The spread of knowledge."

"So your knowledge is better than everyone else's?"

"Not fighting an epistemological battle here. But look, I know. The train, it's left—left the—left the—"

"*The train's left the station?*" he said in a rush, the way folks do when impatient with her stumbling speech patterns. "True-that, as the young'uns say."

"As it has. For my little project."

Only last week she'd gotten her five minutes before council to make the case. Peppered with questions and skepticism, she maintained a low voice of reason as she ran a few slides with various statistics regarding the half-life of radioactive isotopes. In the end they accepted her arguments about free speech, but on a narrow 5-4 vote.

"It ain't gonna be no Occupy Tillman Falls, or nothing like that," the Mayor reiterated on their visit to the green. "Next thing you know we'd have the preachers preaching, and Howdy Shull walking in a circle, and every hippie screwball from here to Greenville waving banners and signs. That ain't the vision I got for old downtown, young lady."

"No camping out; no crowds. I only want. To continue a longstanding American tradition. Of pamphleteering."

She noted a big blonde kid with a sickly aura, snot-green instead of love-green, sitting on a bench near the obsidian war obelisk. Obese. Bad skin. Sunken eyes. A downturned mouth. He needed spiritual help. But you can't walk over to a stranger and deliver such an assessment, however accurate. Besides, her service work already voluminous, perhaps even burdensome.

Mayor Hampton shook her hand and cocked his other thumb to the honky-tonk. "Sure hope your new boss at The Dixiana keeps it all just like it's always been. Other than the mural, of course. I wa'n't in favor of keeping it neither. Not a good look."

"Nope." Button added, hard to say what the future holds for the old barn, and did so with her throat burning and her side aching. She glanced at the blood from her nose drying around her fingernail and thought, what is going on inside me?

◉①❀

AGAINST EVERY PRINCIPAL OF HIGHER CONSCIOUSNESS AND ENERGY MANAGEMENT in her body, mind and spirit, she decided to visit the doc-in-the-box over in Chilton. Button said she had no insurance and filled in only the the minimum of personal data on the forms. Data equaled energy—hell, everything equaled energy—and Button felt it prudent to manage hers the way you'd manage money or thought or any other form. Carefully attended to, with all due attention.

"You know what this is." The doc leaned into her inflection on the 'know,' which gave Button goose pimples as she cringed away from the physician's onion breath there in the exam room.

"I do?"

"But I bet you're gonna be surprised when I say it."

"If I know, what am I? Paying you for?"

"Want to guess?"

"Sure. Cancer."

Dr. Dahlonega, dark-haired with purple pits under trowel-grade eye makeup teeming with toxins and chemicals, laughed with a soothing, reas-suring sense of abject dismissal. "Far from it, my dear. You shouldn't even say such an awful word. Many factors contribute to our manifestation of disease."

The exam over, Button sat in a hard, cold chair while the Doctor clattered a keyboard with fury, clicking and typing what seemed a terrific amount of data-entry for a person coming off the street with a mere scratchy throat.

"Now." The doctor, pushing the arm holding the monitor screen out of the way. "Ms. Sykes: You eat spicy food?"

"Sometimes Thai. But not Thai-hot."

Nodding, certain and grave. "But the little spice tray—yes?"

"Never. Maybe some extra chopped peanuts."

"Tea? Coffee?"

"No, not anymore. But I once did. Tons of coffee. Wait—you mean Thai coffee? With the cream?"

"Coffee-coffee. What about sodas? Colas, Pepsis and such?"

"Never." Button got a stab of panic at the thought of pouring those poisons down her throat. "Not a drop."

"*Hrm.*"

Where was this leading?

What did this croaker think was wrong?

Plus, who was this person to judge—what did *the doctor* eat and drink? From her chubby physique, it seemed nothing healthy. Button, always fascinated by overweight health care personnel; on her way to Columbia to hook up with her weed dealer she'd always see nurses in scrubs clustered outside the hospital satellite office smoking and sucking on soda fountain drinks the size of small buckets. One would think they'd know better. Being in the business and all.

Button had read an article called 'How Doctors Prefer to Die.' How smart ones eschewed the treatment they doled out to patients with diseases like, say, cancer. She came across it while scrolling Twitter looking for tidbits posted by Heather Ponderview, liking the tweets by clicking the heart icon, fleeting moments of connection with Button's forever faraway love, and with whom she had still only emailed in brief bursts. Heather, keeping it all at arm's length.

Button had experienced such a cancer case, in which every procedure and drug had been tried, even as they had only made her father suffer more in pursuit of 'buying more time'. During the ordeal she had wondered if the oncologists, surgeons and other specialists would put themselves through it all. Or one of their own children, a spouse, or a parent. Button, wondering then, validated now. The universe, sending her to articles and ideas as she needed them.

The internet, dude. Changing consciousness. Like Kubrick's monolith in 2001. A catalyst.

"Mission control calling Ms. Sykes," Dr. Dahlonega said, concerned rather than jovial. "You went away, there."

A sense of presence returned. "Sorry. What did you ask?"

"About soda pop. Spicy dishes."

"Yeah, no—I eat clean. Nuts. Berries. Whole grains. Vegetables and fruits. Vegan. Conscious eating."

"Well, that's safer than unconscious eating."

"Where's this heading, doc?"

"These symptoms have to do with your GI tract. This is acid reflux."

"But—I don't get heartburn. And, from what?"

"Combinations of foods. Stress. Coffee. Also, when you lie down at night, these juices can creep up," doing a finger dance along her sternum, "and cause all sorts of problems."

Button had suffered many stresses, but never manifesting as digestive tract issues. Anxiety attacks? Sleeplessness? Check. Not indigestion. She said so.

"Be that as it may, in my experience reflux is the likely cause of the scratchy throat. And the nosebleeds, too." She wrote a prescription. "We have many effective remedies, now."

"Not that interested in pills."

The doctor seemed not to hear, saying she would prescribe a heftier dose of a common brand name Button recognized. "However, as you don't have insurance," with serious disapproval, "I recommend you try the OTC version first. See if you don't have improvement. And drink water. Don't drink coffee and tea and soda, but do take the meds. If you don't improve, or your symptoms worsen, we can send you to a gastroenterologist."

The doctor made a series of further keystrokes into Button's medical records and clicked the mouse. "But try this, and see if you aren't better soon," she concluded with a reassuring smile.

Acid reflux? Maybe. More like lysergic acid, in Button's case. Not that she'd had any lately. Probably did enough on Phish tour to last her through a few lifetimes of psychedelic exploration.

Forget those pills.

Button wrote Heather a long and heartfelt 'I miss you best friend' email; Heather, replying to say she'd enrolled in a course on herbalism, in the science and magic of the plants. When she learned more, she'd advise regarding a solution that didn't involve pharmies.

Assuming—and one should never assume—the diagnosis here is correct.

Again, she knew all this to be a matter of the Q'i, and with the right course of herbs and meditative techniques, she'd banish these scratchy throats and nosebleeds. Get on with her life, which thanks to her newfound friendship with Roy Pettus seemed to have taken an interesting turn.

A good guy, Roy. She felt they were destined to be together—she had things to teach him. He did for her as well. We are all each other's teachers here in soul school, as it's been said. How *not* to behave seemed his most obvious contribution to the spiritual conversation, what with him and his Black Blade laying psychological waste. The anger and control issues, grief management, marital difficulties, and the like—*don't handle it like me*, his every action seemed to say.

We bring these trials upon ourselves, though, as she'd tried to suggest using gentle, nonspecific words. Most of what happens to us we create. Or maybe all of it, because who really knows? We're all in our reality bubbles, but how much of what we perceive is quantifiably objective reality, or our own version of it?

In her doc's reality, gut acid caused sore throats and dripping nostril blood. If Button went with that interpretation, would taking the pill work? Wouldn't a placebo do just as well?

Mind.

Body.

Energy.

Q'i.

Before she made any decisions about pursuing the recommended treatment for her nettlesome issues, Button would consult a book on Chinese medical philosophy called *The Web Without a Weaver*. Meditate, make dinner for the family. Get her grandfather the rest of the way drunk so he'd pass out and perhaps drop the body, an outcome she was sorry to have conjured in her mind while still believing it would be best for all involved.

◉⊕✳

Later, standing over the salad she'd prepared and watching the three bright red drops of blood go *plop-plop-plop* out of her left nostril onto the cutting board, she experienced a worrisome welling of urgency going beyond the physician's pills or consulting sacred texts or her friend Heather's herbal knowledge.

Releasing the anxiety, Button served dinner to her chattering mother and bleary-eyed, depressed ninety-year-old grandfather, who smoked and drank and lived on. How mysterious the workings of the web, she thought. How little they—we—truly know. But a web it is—the air, the earth, the water, the light, the life.

The water—speaking of urgency, she'd read on an alternative news site she trusted how the Japanese electric company hides from the world how much radioactive water may seep into the Pacific Ocean from Fukushima. Tons. Every day. 'Forty years to clean up,' they said, poisonous material that'd last for thousands of years. In the meantime? Radioactive isotopes flowing into the font of all life on the planet, the briny deep. Gotcha.

Roy Pettus had been duly amused about her pamphleteering, her passing mention of which had been dismissed by him, and everyone, as a quixotic quest with no tangible, possible outcome worth investing the time. She didn't argue the point. Button, she understood futile. She also knew sometimes one must act. And efforts beget consequences—ripples throughout the continuum of possible realities here in the multiverse from every decision, every thought, every physical action taken. Who could predict what a tidbit of knowledge from one of her little pamphlets might seed in the minds of readers.

Roy—so much work ahead. Once she got him to dial his vibration from rage, anger and destruction into peaceful and loving, he radiated a certain level of wisdom and insight he hadn't fully grown into yet. That he possessed, but didn't know how to wield. Certainly not as well as his mythical 'black blade,' which was all about control through fear.

Nobody had any control. Ask the people in Japan, those nearest the Fukushima prefecture, who'll develop the cancers—hell, had already done so. Thyroid cases already skyrocketing in the Pacific Northwest, too. Not that you'd ever see it reported in the mainstream news, which Button avoided at all costs, anyway. The starfish, washing up mottled and dying. Phytoplankton diminishing. The oceanic environment, soon unfit to support the food chain— to foster and feed the biosphere. Madness.

Ask her mother about human insanity, she who'd seen fire dropped from the sky on the surrounding jungle and her village, and men with hard faces sweeping through, shouting and killing; what were the modern cancer rates in Vietnam, soaked through with American-made dioxin? Ask Button's grandfather, who had served a hero in WW2 by dropping bombs on Pacific Islands.

Her grandpa—what a difference seventy years makes in a human. A war hero with no control over his drinking. Could barely control his own bowels. Adult diapers, now always on the grocery list. Time marches on.

Inner mastery. That's what Button sought to achieve in her time there in Edgewater County. Not in purgatory, as she realized more every day, but right where she was meant to be, and getting where she needed in the consciousness game, because it was the only game being played, especially when one shakes off the physical form and the transition occurs.

Button didn't want to deal with all this material-realm stuff again. She'd had enough of soul school, felt ready to graduate; she'd learned the essential lesson: to serve with selflessness. Being a lightworker to those in need. Roy Pettus seemed the final piece, somehow. Clearing her wheel of karma.

Final? Listen to her. As though anything ever truly ended. No endings—a universe of spinning circles.

Ten years to build the new reactors? Hah. Who knew what sort of earthbound reality would exist after another decade of solar spins. Tiny in the cosmic sense of time, but also forever. At least in between imaginary past and unknowable future lay a gulf of right-now, a platform on which to manifest love and light.

But 'right now' Button's throat hurt, and her side stitched, and she doubted the doctor's assessment but went by the pharmacy to get the pills anyway, as well to see old high school acquaintance Jouquoya 'Jackie' Moulton, who would make her feel loved from afar, if only for a few minutes. Button had money she'd saved from not buying weed. The household accounts were funded from her father's long career of working and saving, not to mention her mother's and grandfather's entitlement checks. But that money-energy was for their upkeep. These pills were about her, and so she should pay.

The light behind the pharmacist's smile shimmered around her face as Button approached through the colorful aisles of the CVS in the Chilton commercial strip at the end of the bypass. "You picking up for your grand-daddy again, sweetie?"

"Not this time. For me, for once."

The smile dimmed. "What's wrong? You feeling puny?"

The empathy Jackie projected filled Button with love like warm, humid breath inside a party balloon. "Just some reflux. No big whoop."

"Oh—good. I mean, I'm sorry, sweetie. Let's see what you got." She clicked and clattered. "We got a generic for this. Save you a mess of money."

"Won't say no to that."

When Jackie brought back the pills, Button sensed a different urgency—a longing to feel full again.

Love, she thought, would heal her stomach and throat faster than meds. Button knew this as much as anything. So she generated love, a pulsing glow that spread throughout her body. And in her stumbling, fragmented manner of speaking, asked Jackie Moulton if she'd consider going on a date.

ROY AND MERV PETTUS

For the second time in a week you find yourself accosted out on the graying, stained, chipped sidewalk you can't wait to see jackhammered into pulverized clouds of dust. Worse, only minutes after getting off the phone with your wife, out of rehab and back home with the kitties. You could hear the disappointment in her voice when you said, goody for you. See you when I see you. Click.

And piling on, Trudy, prepping the bar and playing the damn Wurlitzer, a Conway Twitty, 'This Time I've Hurt Her More Than She Loves Me' and keeping her back turned. You had come outside to get away from the song and her energy when your cousin came marching toward you all red-faced.

Merv Pettus, indignant as hell. "You and your'n never did give two shits about this side of the family."

"How can you say that? C'mon, beau."

His redneck yodel, as you think of it, echoes across the green. "Ain't hard at all. Not after hearing how you treated my sweet little wife at the Gas Chief."

Carla Mae told him about your negative attitude about the old house, sure, but you guess she left out the pledge made at the end to come up with an alternative.

"Lower your voice, dude. I don't negotiate in the street."

Spitting. "Reckon you ain't doing nothing but carrying on the durn tradition."

"Why don't you go kiss a duck?"

"I'm liable to do more'n kiss it, son."

Simmering. Your injured shoulder, throbbing. The sling, hanging over a bar stool inside.

Red veil; black blade.

But remembering a Button speech about detaching from strong emotions. Viewing them from afar rather than hot-wallowing, immersed and awash. Not reacting.

Deep breath.

You suggest to your cousin, whom you hardly know, to "relax, pal." To watch himself.

Detachment? Barely. A quivering edge to your voice. Rage-monkey, at your command, sire.

You note Cecil Waugh standing watchful in front of the piercing salon portion of the Head Trauma body art empire. Cecil, meaty, tattooed arms akimbo, squints with curiosity over the shouting. Like a good merchant should. An old childhood nemesis, you've avoided him but for passing condolences and pleasantries. Here, he's already started drifting over this way a little. Seeing what's what on his street. Good man.

Merv continues huffing and puffing and throwing aggressive gestures in your direction."You and that stuck-up grandmama and asshole granddaddy. All of you's the same."

Unleashing the almost-full bossman power you've cultivated through the years, your affable voice deepens and concretizes into a strident and dangerous throat vibration quite apart from sweet angel Button's gentle meditation mantras. "Stop shouting and stand still, son. *And I mean now.* Not five seconds from now."

Still gesticulating and cussing up a storm, he comes rolling back over in his ball-cap, ragged, greasy jeans and a garish, ridiculous T-shirt emblazoned with a manic-eyed, bright yellow Tweety Bird. You stare at the cartoon character and think, how can a grown man, or anyone, go around dressed in such childish iconography. You could see it if Warner Brothers were paying a royalty. If you owned Tweety Bird. Otherwise? Working for the man with no return, wearing their logos. Such wisdom about the economics of signs and symbols had come to you in a rush one day in high school when you saw a girl donned in sportswear from the new line of Coca-Cola fashions now available. Why, you thought all afternoon, would you pay to wear a Coke shirt? No. Not unless you were getting paid, like Michael Jackson doing a Pepsi commercial. It made you think people were stupid, or at least allowing themselves to be fleeced for no good reason, when you saw them wearing corporate logos on their body. Dale Earnhardt or Dick Trickle? They were getting fat checks. Tweety Bird ain't paying jack to no broke-ass Mervin Pettus. That much you know.

As you watch Merv deflate, you remind yourself to talk iconography with

Button, maybe the next time y'all got high together—the wearing of images like cartoon characters and other pop cultural signifiers, if not tattooing oneself with them. You've already discussed the Dead and Phish, how the fans ascribe almost religious allegiance and dogma to the music and the scene surrounding the bands. The fellowship, the gathering, the dance of the tribes; acolytes adorned by icons. You hope you'll soon see Button again, and not only because of the good pot she shares, an activity to which you've taken like a mallard slip-sliding into the Sugeree River.

Oh… how you totally dig Button.

But only as a friend, as you still struggle to accept. At the moment you need a friend more than a lover; this, the essential hard truth coming to you *about* Button Sykes. And it is good, your relationship as it stands. Right. The way you feel the rightness of the burgeoning friendship with Manny T, too.

Your little local support group.

"Cousin," he emphasizes. "Hear me out on this."

"It's pointless. But go ahead."

"You can't do this to us," a plaintive, cracking bleat by which you remain unmoved. "I got my little ones to think about."

You've a vague memory of him being an install tech for Jiffy's Heating & Cooling, or whatever they call it these days. "You still pulling duct for Dickie Giuffrida?"

"Nope."

"What happened there?"

"They named that son of a bitch right—he's a fucking dick. A *little* dick."

You tell him you get it; like Cecil Waugh, Dickie, never your favorite person. "What are you doing about support the family? Your boys?"

"Use your imagination about what all goes into raising kids."

"That's true. No clue what it's like to have kids."

"See—you ain't got young'uns. So you don't know shit about responsibility. And having to look them in the face and say, daddy's cousin won't let us live in a free house."

Faraway, you remember the miscarriages. "We tried. It never took."

"Guess somebody was shooting blanks, eh?"

You snap back into irritated reality. "Look, pal—no kids, whatever. But I've got cats. A dozen. Hell, a baker's dozen, for all I know. But more than that, I have employees. At one time a couple hundred under the supervision and ownership of the Spotted Banana partners. Not 'ownership' as in body, of course—not like we used to do it here in Edgewater County back before the Civil War. But definitely my flock. Tending to them, I did. And now, brother, it comes to me that I must tend to thee?"

"What, is that some bible mess?" Sour and dismissive: "What's that got to do with anything."

"It's Ezekiel 25:17. And, lo, have I come from the island to now have these sad wretches here at The Dixiana on my watch, too; and it is them, yea, whom I must serve first, the shepherd to the flock. But please, tell me again how I don't know about having responsibility. And what it takes out of a person when others look to him with needy eyes—the hopeful, the hungry." You breathe, tell yourself that's all a bit florid. "It's a heavy enough burden on the spine, being a small business owner. Backbone of the country's economy. If we're talking 'responsibility.'"

You close your eyes, press on with a proclamation you expect he will receive without further quibbling. "Now: get over this idea I owe you based on our tenuous blood connection. The essential nature of my hard-earned largesse includes no obligation towards bailing anyone out of whatever freaking mess they've gotten themselves into. I saw that freaking hunk of plastic she was driving. Nobody in your position needs to be driving a tank like that. I bet the payments on it are as much as this mortgage you can't afford anymore."

"It's for keeping my wife and boys safe."

"That's marketing nonsense. You mush-minded, pick-pocketed consumer. I'm talking personal economic responsibility. Which you as the head of the family aren't currently offering."

"I'm-a look for a job again, soon as my unemployment runs out."

You let loose with a stream of invective most unlike you, uncompromising in your disapproval. "You lazy fuck. Get your fucking ass off the couch and get a god-damn job."

"Beau. That's harsh."

"Just telling you how it is."

"You got to let us live in that house. I ain't taking no for an answer. It's like, this shit's meant to be. Besides, I'll fix it up. Roll paint. All that shit women always want done. I'm-a have to, beau."

"Meant-to-be that you're supposed to squat in my grandparents' old house? No can do. I'm living out there for now."

"We ain't gonna bother no one."

"I know you ain't."

"What kinda people you think we is?"

"Forget it."

"What about the young'uns?"

"You should've figured out how to balance a checkbook before you started to reproduce."

"Damn—you're one cold-hearted S-O-B, Roy Earl. Beats all I ever seen."

"That's business. Sorry, not-sorry." Exasperation. "Don't you get it? I'm not running a survivalist compound. I've earned the right to live where I want, and alone. And not next door to you, asshole. Any more clear?"

"'Crystal'," making the bunny ears.

"Look—you want some money? That it? A couple grand to get moved into an apartment or a rental house? How about in the old mill neighborhood? Rents are cheap enough. Aren't they?"

Mervin's face turns red as General Reb's feathers once appeared on the beloved mural. "You saying we ought to go and live with the colored po-folks? That what I'm hearing here?"

Oh, my. Has he gone and given you the golden ticket now. "On that offensive note, we can call off this pointless discussion. Anyone who'd throw around deplorable, racist rhetoric's worth neither my time nor my considera—"

Faster than you thought the fat ass could move, a blurring motion and a hot, heavy blaze of red fire thumps against your right eye. You've been smacked in the face like you observed out here on Saturday nights— if you saw it once, you saw it a hundred times. Rednecks, drinking and fighting and going home to make new little drunken buffoons. The Dixiana still being in business offered living proof of this sacred cycle of life.

But you think none of that until later, not until you recover from the overwhelming, staggering pain from the blow not to your eye, but rather the impact of your hurt shoulder against the brick wall. Down on the sidewalk; again.

☉①❋

ONCE YOU SIT UP, SQUINTING YOUR BLINDED EYE AND GRIPPING YOUR SCREAMING shoulder, you do so in time to hear heavy, approaching footfalls and shouting; as well, a second set of thudding footsteps hurtling your way across the green: Cecil Waugh and Manny T, both rushing to your aid from different directions.

By the time you get your senses back, wide-shouldered Cecil has crushed a squalling, hollering Merv against the front window, your squirming cousin's right arm twisted behind.

Manny, out of breath after a farther sprint than Cecil, curses and hollers. "Who messing with my boy all up in here? Who aiming to get his ass whipped?"

"Let me go," Merv shouts. "Somebody call the cops on these mofos!"

Manny, his face tight with anger, down on a knee and helping you back to your feet. "Who this jackleg assaulted you? *Assaulted*," he booms out toward the courthouse plaza two blocks away. "*Where my goddamn lawyer at?*"

You order Cecil to let Merv go, which he does, albeit with reluctance. "He's my cousin."

An awkward standoff. Everyone's body language remains coiled with expectation. Cecil, glowering at Merv. "I seen you hit a fellow merchant, pal. Not gonna fly."

"This asshole told me to go live—"

Your cousin pulls up short—he notices Manny's muscles bulging under his taught Funkadelic T-shirt, the shouting afro chick from the 'Maggot Brain' album artwork; Manny, the second of two big men, both looking pissed enough to put Merv's red rooster, whiteboy dick into the dirt.

Manny's tough, a streetwise cat. You dig his ass so much. A working musician who lived for years on the road, dude smoked and shot heroin, banged more babes than he can remember, dealt with gangsters, but most of all, bro ended up becoming a successful entrepreneur. And here, hauling ass across the town common like you'd have done for a fellow business owner in distress. Manny is all-right. Cecil and Manny both.

In this moment of pain—your head throbs as Manny helps you fully to your feet—it occurs to you that these two will sit on the board of the merchant's association you'll lead to break the ELMS stranglehold over the ways and means of the town. Just because those crones all outlived their town father husbands didn't give them say over squat, in your view. A side project designed to keep the energy stirring.

Special dispensation for Becky L, of course, and her healthy stewardship of the preserved and magical Palmetto Grande, which you glimpse before lunging with your good shoulder at Merv and thumping him in the chest, right in Tweety Bird's stupid, oversized, leering cartoon eyes. Merv swings at you again, and it's a scuffle complete with shouting. Your benefactors pull you off each other.

"Tell my man what you were gonna say, tough guy." You sputter, breathless and furious at Merv for laying hands upon you. "Tell Manny 'who' I told you to go live with."

"All I was about to say was that you ain't nothing, big bossman. That your shit don't stink."

"Aw-ight now, muh-fucka. This my man here you trash-talking."

"Why don't you go fuck yourself, boy?" Mervin shoves at Manny, catching the restaurateur off balance and almost knocking him off his clean Converse All-Stars.

"Hey, dude—?"

As your cousin turns around Cecil, in a lightning-graceful move like a ballet dancer, plants the toe of his Doc Marten underneath Merv Pettus's right eye, after which Merv collapses. Two seconds elapse. You put that on slo-mo instant replay in a Youtube video, and it's a million clicks.

Whoa.

Your cousin, down on his knees, bursts into burbling boyish tears. "He-he-he broke my goddurn cheekbone."

Cecil's shaved head has gone bright pink. "Looks to me more like you stumbled over a crack in the sidewalk, dipshit."

Manny, standing between you and your cousin. "Ready to call this off, champ? Before me and Cecil Waugh decide to finish this?"

"*He broke my face.* I'm calling the law on you assholes."

You see where this is heading. As with Samson, you'll handle this in your own way without involving Oakley, whom you don't fully own yet. "Cuz, we are the law in this town now. Now, everybody get outta here."

"Maybe I ain't done with him."

"I call this contest of wills a draw." You shake Cecil's hand. "Karate?"

"Taekwondo—used to teach it, before I got into the body art trade."

Ignoring the pain in your shoulder, you face your cousin, help him to his feet. "We're leaving this here on the street. Is that understood? As for your family's living situation, my offer to give you financial assistance stands—not only is it the second such offer, but made in front of these witnesses, and after what went down just now. That good enough to get me out of this and back to my afternoon checklist?"

Still wound up and hurting, he cups his cheek and calls bullshit on you and your friends and appeals to a higher power for a pox to fall upon all your houses, cries victim and weeps for justice to be done.

After you again remind him who threw the first punch, as well to reveal that you've installed a security camera in the Dixiana sign which recorded this scene—a useful untruth—Mervin goes all quiet and meek, nods, mumbles an apology and splits.

This entitlement business is blowing your mind. Family, indeed.

What was family?

You? You've always felt shortchanged.

And as the energy of the encounter settles, you realize Mervin isn't all wrong about the two sides of the family. Your granddaddy and his brother, Mervin's grandfather, had for whatever reason never been the best of friends, and y'all hadn't had too much to do with them. Still, so what his granddaddy Rut Pettus had worked in the mill and managed to retire right before it closed, only to piss away his retirement on gambling and booze and who knew what, and had left a legacy of two generations of similar assholes also pissing it all away? That's your grandmother's assessment of that strain of Edgewater County Pettus. But you aren't in the business of bailing out nitwits who can't fend for themselves. Besides, you have quite enough unfinished personal business on your hands as it is. Christ, though. You offered him a couple grand. You wouldn't even notice it being gone.

"Your ass okay, bossman?"

You lie to Manny and say, shoot-yeah. "Thanks, dude."

"I got your back. You ain't got to worry about squat long as Manny around."

"Back at you, beau. I should probably get this arm in its sling, though."

"Why you ain't wearing it?"

"I dunno. Made me feel vulnerable, I guess. Imperfect."

"C'ain't have that."

You go to shake, but the act of doing so makes your shoulder twinge and you wince, which he notices and comments upon. You say, forget it, Jake. It's Tillman Falls.

Manny seems worked up, sure, but distracted. Glancing forlorn down the street toward the old movie theater.

Of course he is; you've heard tell of a scandalous dalliance between Manny T and Becky L. Lucky bastard. You don't give a crap about anyone except Creedence, really, and maybe not even her anymore. But Becky L, you could still see it happening. If not for your man Manny. As with Button, however, you will find satisfaction from Becky's friendship and collegiality alone.

Besides, in a political sense she represents the fulcrum on which your civic plans lay—you'll be passing no plans by some shriveled-up old committee of southern gentry for approval, not about your grandfather's memorial music festival nor your façade and building plans nor what you aim to ultimately achieve, which is give them all a town about which they may be justifiably proud. You'll make your own committee, with its own rules and rituals, and it will approve your own festival; think of Dick Cheney running the Bush Jr. veep search only to pick himself for the role. In any case, Becky L's peerage and assistance much more important than sex. That you will leave to Manny. Lucky dude.

Or crazy asshole, more like it. Small town. He must get off on the risk.

"You got some of that sweet tea of Neecie's brewed up?"

"Is my dingus dangling? Shit yeah, brotherman."

"Then let's drink some. I need to wash down a pain pill. And talk about the future."

Manny's spell, broken. His eyes shine. "All right, bossman. Come on over and sit a spell. Let all this violence dissipate. What you got in mind for this future of ours?"

"That's what I want you to help me figure out."

Manny says ain't no thang, and you go drink tea and nurse your eye and your shoulder and end up listening to him more than doing the talking, which was your plan all along. Some of his ideas about Music City, South Carolina, sound kinda cool. When you let yourself forget your own plans, which will supplant his, but only when the time comes. If you can keep from getting your ass knocked onto the sidewalk long enough.

CREEDENCE AND SHAROLYN

Never had Creedence been so happy to see her babies. Long story short.

Maggie Passanant had been at the house when the cab dropped off the homeowner, fresh and squeaky-sober from the clinic; they had bonded with immediacy as the petsitter described the condition and behavior of the beloved brood.

"I had a hard time learning their names, sorry. But the tortie-girl was so sweet and loving, and the young gray tabbies, such a hoot." The older kitties, she said, all seemed fine. "You'll find everything in good order."

"My husband hired you, so I don't have any doubts."

"Yeah—he seems to know what he wants."

Creedence, stopping herself from saying, if only that were true, you and I might not be standing here. "Lucky him," is the best she could muster.

After giving the petsitter a hundred-dollar tip and retrieving the house key, she stood with arms crossed and watched Maggie say fare-thee-well to her clients. "I hope to see you all again one day soon. Don't hesitate to call when y'all go out of town and stuff."

"We will."

Alone at last, Creedence fell to her knees in the kitchen, hot tears dripping from her eyes and onto the coats of her fur-babies, all swirling around and meowing and swishing their tails with happiness at her return. The clarity and brightness of the light illuminated every detail; Creedence, feeling as though she were seeing her home for the first time in a hundred years, not twenty-eight days.

◉◉✳

MAKING AMENDS.

Was it quite time yet? The steps were the steps, but she knew one person to whom she should apologize right away, and that was Roy's manager Sharolyn. What a scene Creedence had caused. She had vague memories of the business with the money, and the cop; worse were the flashes she retained of starting up with Estes in the office at the CBSI.

She got out of the BMW, which had been sitting for a month and almost didn't turn over. So strange to be driving. The light, the trees, the islanders on their bikes and in their workout gear on the walking paths; streaks in the sky from the jets and gulls; the moss draping down from gnarled tree limbs. Everything had a crispness and clarity. Getting cleaned up was like having a gossamer shawl pulled from in front of the drunk's eyes. The world, so brilliant and alive.

Glancing at the smoky half-globe of the security cam up in the corner of the coffee shop dining area, she shuddered at the possibility of Roy watching footage of her with her lover. Prayed he had not reviewed the images. She still had a thought all of it could be swept under the rug.

Mid-afternoon, quiet. A couple of new faces working the counter, one of which swirled the water in perfect little circles over the grounds, slow-dripping a coffee for an elderly man in tennis whites who leaned scrolling through his phone.

"Is the manager in today?" Creedence asked.

The young woman pouring the water called over her shoulder for Sharolyn. "You here for the interview?"

"Interview?"

"They're hiring an assistant GM."

"Are they, now." Creedence chewed on her bottom lip, got a stab of adrenalized panic at a crazy idea that popped into her head. "No, I'm not. I'm the owner's wife."

"Oh, jesus. Why didn't you say so."

Sharolyn, eyes puffy and with the tail of her Carolina Beanery polo shirt pulled out of one side of her khakis, appeared from the office door, the small room where Estes had first kissed the wife's owner. "Oh—Mrs. Creedence. You're here."

"Looks that way."

"Are you—how are—I mean, I'm so glad to see you."

She came around the counter, thanking the gentleman who had taken the first sip of his Ethiopian and praised its full-bodied flavor suffused with notes of floral and fruit. Sharolyn and Creedence hugged one another.

"I'm so sorry. You must think I'm crazy."

"Don't be, hon. Life is full of messes and mess-ups. We all take the fall at some point." She pulled Creedence away from the listening ears of the curious, youthful baristas watching them. "When I was a teenager, I got mixed up with a bunch of potheads. My boyfriend was dealing. I'm lucky I didn't get all messed up."

"You turned out all right."

Sharolyn gripped her by the forearm. "I know it'll be the same for you."

They got caught up; Sharolyn said she hoped Roy would return soon, and maybe things could get back to normal. "I been working my butt off."

"Estes," Creedence said, her stomach going cold with shame, "isn't here anymore."

Sharolyn arched an eyebrow. "Here's how your husband would put it —'that's a negatory,'" lowering her voice. The women shared a rueful chuckle.

"I can't imagine what you must think."

"Here's what I think: I just want to keep this good job, do my best for y'all. That's all I care about."

Creedence smiled, her throat closing with emotion. If only Roy would be so kind and understanding. She hadn't yet called him to say she had been released, her moon-cycle of rehab at its end, but with an endless series of meetings ahead to keep from tipping over the edge again. "I know you're doing a good job. Roy praises you to the high heavens. But it sounds like you need help around here."

Sharolyn rolled her eyes. "It's under control. Mostly. But Roy got me trying to find somebody to—to replace—"

"That's what I wanted to say. Don't schedule any more interviews."

"But what about the position? Can't lie to you, girl. I'm having a hard time keeping up the pace."

"That's the thing. I think I know someone who'd be right for this." A wave of self-consciousness and shame. "Who you can trust."

"Don't keep me in suspense."

Creedence, fumbling in her purse for a pen. Taking a deep breath. "I'd like to fill out that application, if I could."

PART TWO

The Partners

Money is a very interesting philosophical idea in that we have all of humanity agreeing on this system. So even though we may radically disagree on some things—like let's say the U.S. government and Al Qaeda—they both respect money. So it's remarkable how we have this universal respect for this very esoteric virtual construct.

— RAY KURZWEIL

GOOCH

Spending more time at home, a godsend. Now that the election season had ended, retirement had taken hold in Gooch's mind and daily routine.

At least he had a routine. All of it—his life, memories, ambition, dreams—slipping away.

When he realized this.

Not that new news wouldn't come along soon. With a firebrand like Nixon now on council, and tempers flaring over integration and civil rights issues, who knew what grand political drama was to develop. The change of the town's name, for all Bill knew. Mayor Hampton, still on the sucker-hunt about his big idea, the water tower naming rights.

Scintillating. Wake me when it's over.

For now? Getting work and research done on the novel.

He opened a volume published by Southeastern University Press containing personal letters and excerpts of the Journal of Rev. Gervase Fulthroppe, one of the most complete records of pre-Revolutionary War life in the area now known as Edgewater County.

An Anglican missionary to the Kennesaw District and living in what was then called Rocky Creek Hill, Fulthroppe served from 1760 to 1766 as an itinerant representative of the Church of England. A busy man, he ministered both religion and as legal authority to an area bordered by the great western pine forest on one side and the burbling, stony Sugeree River to the East, giving him responsibility over forty congregations across forty square miles of barely settled, rustic Carolina country.

His journals, Gooch found with a chuckle, depicted an Edgewater County in some ways little changed:

As rude or more so than Savages, the backcountry Carolina Settlers herein dwell in Log Cabbins not much better than hovels, living and eating little better than the Hogs running aloose. Upon arrival with my man Denis, over a fortnight passed before acquiring suitable accommodations in the form of a parsonage in need of shoring and a roofer's nail. Among the people around, of abandon'd morals—Profligacy—Ignorance—Void of Manners and Education—it has yet to materialize a craftsman of sufficient truck worth hiring. The majority of my goods have yet to arrive via Charles Town, and not expected for an unknown elapse.

Worse, among Many other misfortunes and difficulties, my servant quit the District without word nor warning, leaving me for want of the most basic of services. As a Congregation is built, and from my perpetual travels around the district, which will be steady and regular with over forty settlements to serve, likeminded and worthy companions will make themselves Known. Already it has been my Occasion to preach before an Audience of various degrees, Countries, Complexions and Denominations, baptiz'd several Negroes and Mullatoos—such a pack I have never met with. Neither of one Church or other or of any denomination, not having ever seen a Minister, nor read Scripture. A mix'd Medley of Persons, the country contains ten times the Number of Persons expected, so many it is beyond my Apprehension. All very poor and extremely ignorant—Yet desirous of the Knowledge of Christ.

Beset by Itinerant Teachers, Preachers and Imposters from New England and Pennsylvania—Baptists, New Lights, Presbyterians, and a hundred other Sects, including the Weberites to the South in Saxe-Gotha, site of thrice-murdered acolytes and Heretical idolatry so Craven the militia called out to restore Order—the spiritual case of the Settlers here is truly pitiable. One day they might hear this System of Doctrine, and the next day, another…and among the Various Plans of Religion, they are at Loss as to which to adapt, and consequently are without any Religion at all. As well, mad tales propagate superstition, with talk of Chimerical creatures like skunk-apes and winged men from the Savages being spoken in hushed whispers. Hence, their many Vices—gross Licentiousness, Wantonness, Lasciviousness, Rudeness, Lewdness and Profligate Intoxication make the Savages, at many times better clothed, housed and comported, seem like the Civilized among these Settlers. My tenure here is likely further fraught with challenges the Nature of which will be difficult to Anticipate.

WHY WASTE TIME WITH ALL THIS? NO WAY WAS GOOCH WRITING A BOOK ABOUT colonial times. Couldn't imagine it, couldn't write it, who would read it? The Weberite Heresy incident the Anglican mentioned, the story of a cult-like leader involving sex and murder, offered juicy material, but way too much trouble to write it with any authenticity. He'd be buried in histories and biographies from now until doomsday. He closed the Fulthroppe letters and yawned.

With research becoming oppressive, Gooch tended to spend time on how-to-get-published websites. How to get an agent, how to write, how to come up with characters and whatnot. Books, articles, blog posts, podcasts, webinars, all that jazz, and all for a price. What Bill Wimmel wanted simply was to write without all the rigmarole.

What he had skimmed on those sites, though, had filled up his head with notions of high concept, of serial killers or paranormal teenaged lovers or perhaps both; of genres and plotlines and characterization and POV and backstory, how to weave it in.

One crucial fact Gooch had learned? He needed himself a through-line on which to hang all his Edgewater County history. A logline for the damn thing. A specific conflict. Not only a historical romance, but more.

A problem—that scalawag Cort Beauchamp, as Gooch kept remembering and forgetting again, had covered this territory already with his stupid and accomplished *Diary of Anna Dixon*. Released with fanfare during the book festival down in Columbia, it had put the author on *Midday Carolina* on WKNO and in a featured slot on the Litchfield Books Authors Luncheon roster, above the fold in what still passed for the arts and entertainment section of the Columbia Record, and as toast of Charleston's hoity-toity arts community and in the rest of the state to boot. Edgewater County's novelist of renown, back on the bestseller list, if only for a hot minute.

That son of a bitch—stealing Gooch's thunder before the rain clouds had even darkened. Or some such horseshit metaphor.

◑◐✳

Stories could still be told. Lord, could they. Covering the ins and outs of local graft and corruption and organized crime alone could make for a soap opera full of high drama and comedy, too.

What about a good old-fashioned perennial, the murder mystery?

Ideas.

Edgewater County's own Coy Wando offered a rich and lurid homegrown source, at least as depicted in Jasper Glasscock's interview book he published way back in the 90s. The truthiness regarding many of the murders to which Coy Wando confessed had never been proven, not to the authorities nor to an old reporter named Gooch: tales of picking up drifters and hitchhikers in the Pee Dee of South Carolina and taking them into the blackwater swamps. Torturing, maiming, sexually abusing and finally killing them, he said, by drowning, but by then, most all his victims lay grateful to die. Concealing the bodies in the brackish mud of remote cypress bogs accessed by logging roads. Victims never to be found.

To hear him tell it.

Whatever Wando had perpetrated, and they only knew for sure about the three little girls for which he went to the chair, most everyone found the killer's additional claims, whether about other murders or a secret society in Edgewater County and elsewhere that controlled the course of history—a fact Gooch knew well but also knew to keep to himself—to be horse-hockey of the first order. Killers liked to brag. Sick bastard.

What gripped local observers and fired their imaginations had been the most outlandish of his assertions, a boast of having caused the deaths of the Tragedy of '77 high school kids, during that terrible May weekend before graduation when all six popular and talented seniors drowned in the river under mysterious circumstances. Long after the fact, and completely tangential to the murders for which he was convicted, Wando asserted to have come upon the group of teens partying upriver in the woods. Forced them all at gunpoint to fling themselves off the steep bluffs there along the river in the upper part of the county. Tender heads and bodies bashing against rocks, as he'd told his interviewer. Bodies washing downriver and appearing in the canal, one by one. By the time the fourth body bobbed up, a power plant worker at the locks had suffered a nervous breakdown. A high point of Wando's life, watching the community grieve over those teenagers, the best and brightest. It gave him such a charge, as though feeding off dark energy, he told Jasper. Watched the news reports with a big bowl of popcorn, giggling the whole time. So he said.

Thing was…Wando's confession matched the condition of the bodies well enough, battered in the rapids leading down to the canal and the dam. The story, duly described in the local press by a youngish reporter, Bill Wimmel, who'd returned home from Atlanta earlier that year, had made the wires. The kids all registered high blood alcohol levels. The dried up former falls visible divulged the Sugeree's rocky course, and with it the obvious peril inherent in falling or jumping into the river from the high granite bluffs to the north of the county near Parsons Hollow.

But still. All six?

Why the seniors plunged into the Sugeree and died remained a mystery; absent a note, there'd be no reason to believe the rumors that ran rampant about occult rituals gone wrong, suicide pacts, combinations of the two.

Nothing Wando 'confessed' made his story the true version, either. He loved attention too much. After what he did to those three little girls, for whom justice would later come by frying the killer like a skillet of sausage patties, maybe Wando thought he needed to augment his legend by leeching onto the enigmatic Tragedy of '77, a capstone upon the execrable monument of his macabre, myriad claims of murderous depravity. Who knew? His behavior, though, typical of caught serial killers. Padding the stats. Easier to sleep at night thinking so, anyway.

The great irony came in Coy's claim not to have done the crime for which he sat condemned. That had been his point in telling Jasper the whole story—the 'final truth' as Wando termed it. "Y'all got me finally, yeah. Pat yourselves on the back. But I never done nothing to them little girls." And spinning a wild tale of having been framed by a wicked lodge in Edgewater County, who met and conducted blood sacrifices and rituals and manipulated the secrets of magic and reality. All a pile of rich, wormy manure, the fluff of conspiracy websites. Sure, Coy. Keep spinning yarn.

Bill stopped himself from getting Jasper's book, *Wando: A Last Confession*, down off the shelf to revisit the killer's account of having encountered the teens in the woods that day in May 1977. Whether true or otherwise, it remained a gripping, vicious and lurid account of torture and murder, reported in a spare and straightforward style that had warmed the journalist's heart. Not exactly light reading, nor an uplifting source of inspiration, except perhaps toward crafting a fictionalized version of the entire ghastly affair.

Only after quite a few further moments of rumination did Gooch remember how he'd helped Jasper edit the manuscript, which included an effusive thanks in the author's note to "longtime Edgewater journalist William Wimmel." No wonder the style and language seemed so appealing.

ON HIS WAY TO THE BOOKSHELF, GOOCH FORGOT WHY HE WAS GOING.

Went back to his notes. The best hook Gooch had come up with so far was a different story from town mythology, a singular image that kept popping up in his mind, a vision: a white clapboard church, broken from its foundation and floating away during the great flood of '18, back in the pre-dam days of the original mill and the mill village near the old falls. The gullywasher also swept away many other structures. Had foundered the mill, which put everybody out of work for many months. A true disaster.

But most poetically, God had further forsaken the town by floating its principal church away into destruction, splintered on what were the lower falls a few miles downriver, the track of which now lies under Lake Hollings below the nuclear station. Accounts in the *Advocate* of the day, the *Tillman Tribune*, told of hearing the church's bell ringing, forlorn and haunting, as the structure drifted away into the falling rain of the continuing deluge. The waters swollen beyond reason, the church sanctuary and steeple dashed into matchsticks on the rocky falls, now forever vanished by the diversion into the placid blue of the manmade reservoir that shimmered where once existed entire communities.

Gooch, fighting off a wave of stippled chill-bumps on his tingling, pale arms. What a novelistic image and symbol—the church on the river.

Or was it the towns vanished under the lake?

Maybe too much poetry. Getting it all mixed up.

"All right, forget it. Too obvious a symbol."

Bill, flustered, talked to himself in his cluttered study of boxes and papers and books. A musty smell, and ready for a good spring cleaning—spring would be soon, yes? Except that it was late October, according to the calendar. Still, he needed to get the windows open to air out this damned mausoleum, his Craftsman cottage tucked into an overgrown lot at the far end of Whaley Way, where such several blocks of such houses had been built in the early twentieth century. His area represented a more middle class inclination than the ostentatious antebellum palaces built the gentry of their time closer to downtown.

Gooch's memory from moment to moment might be going, but his grasp of Edgewater County history going back to antiquity and beyond remained sharp as ever. What were other defining events in the life and history of the county? Beauchamp had covered the burning of the bridge and Sherman's troops skirting by on the other side of the river and leaving the town intact.

The burning—of the bridge? No, Gooch. It's covered.

Burning.

Now what was he forgetting? He would have to work on this. Click around. Go to the archives. Drop in and check on Dobbs. See how his protégé was holding up.

❀

BILL WIMMEL SUFFERED A SPELL OF LUCIDITY AND PRESENCE, A FRIGHTENING condition. Remembered, now, how damn old his ass had gotten. Seventy, or thereabouts.

And how time seemed to go faster, ever faster, and waking up at odd times and getting confused, like on the night he'd zipped up his nuts. An itchy, burning ridge of scar tissue, intent on jogging his tired memory about how foolish he could be.

How confused.

Burning.

He snapped his fingers, sat up straight:

The Depression-era Sunbury School Fire, another grim area milestone. The death toll, nearly eighty. Children, men, women, in two cases entire families. So many victims that, in the days before modern technology could make possible the accurate identification of remains, the bodies needed to be quickly buried, anonymous and tangled and charred beyond recognition, in a mass grave behind the tiny Mount Nebo church still hosting congregations near what had been the school property. A more public monument, a large granite rectangle with a now-weathered brass plate inscribed with several columns' worth of names, sat beside a turnout along a nearby highway.

Besides linking the tragedy to many of the county's prominent families of the day, it also possessed other poignant and coincidental elements—it'd been during the graduation ceremony at what was to be the school's last day in operation; the town coroner himself, whose daughter attended and was performing in the musical skit being staged as part of the ceremony, was counted as a victim of the conflagration and stampede begun after an oil lamp ignited the curtains draped all around the second-floor performance space. Packed with students and loved ones. Bodies, piling into the narrow stairwell. Babies thrown from windows. Shrieking and crying.

A tragedy of such scale hit the wires and went global in a time when it took a big story indeed to make such an impression. The first time Edgewater County ever enjoyed such notoriety, if horrific in nature. One could at least consider the lives saved in the decades since thanks to a new standard of building codes influenced by this notorious clusterfuck, as someone of Dobbs Vandegrift's age might put it. A positive outcome, such as could be had from such a nightmare.

Now here, a homegrown source to mine for narrative drama: Sunbury School Fire. Mass grave. Entire families.

Chill-bumps; receding.

Furious, his knobby arthritic knuckles flying—oh lord, a lifetime of typing! —he worked until he had a few dozen grafs, a couple-thousand words. Bill went back to the browser and cut and pasted into his document various links and clippings to the master file for what he planned as his first novel of his retirement, which for this experienced writer would be anything but indolent. He wrote; wrote some more. And felt vitality, like a grown man again, one whose voice mattered.

After an hour spent roughing out a story with the Sunbury School Fire as its central event by somehow keeping his mind focused on this singular task and thought, Bill struggled out of his writer's trance, a warm berth different from the cooling mud-bog of his confused fugue states. Didn't feel that way now, thank goodness.

Shaking off a dazed sense of having done meaningful work, he called Dobbs and checked on the weekend edition; all was in good order. Gooch asked if he needed to do a last interview with Roosevelt Nixon before the county elections. He would be glad to see the perplexing NIXON signs come down.

"Probably all set on that, good buddy," Dobbs said, cheerful. "Since the election was last week."

Wait—he's right. The election? Over. It was November. Mumbling an apology, Gooch snapped the October page off his desk calendar and crumbled it into a ball. He flung it into the wire wastebasket, where it bounced out and rolled all the way back to the toes of his slippers.

How could he forget after the surprise campaign waged by Rutledge Newborn IV, a late entrant into the race? Alas, the callow Newborn's feint made few inroads into Nixon's substantial lead, and this despite Edgewater County name recognition on the level of LaFreniere, Westmoreland, Sunbury and Hampton. In the 1940s Newborn's grandfather had served as a three-term mayor, and a great uncle's championship football coaching had been worth a longstanding honorific in the form of the high school's Newborn Stadium.

Both Burnham Sykes and Rabbit Pettus had played ball for Coach Newborn, a town legend. That had been Burnie's contribution to the special section the Advocate published about Rabbit—a memory not of their many years together as fellow downtown merchants, but a football game in which they played as teammates, an initiation that forged a lifelong friendship. Burnie had wept like a baby as he struggled to describe two lanky young Southern gentleman striving alongside one another until achieving victory on the field, and indeed, later in life. Best part of the special section, Gooch felt.

As for Newborn the lessor, as Gooch thought of the forty years-young man, his run had been funded by mysterious, right-leaning interests from outside the county, or so he'd sniffed out on the grapevine and gleaned from Dobbs and his online column. Good reporting these days on the internet. Gooch burned with jealousy at the vigor and technological savvy young folks had.

For instance: "Here's a juicy tidbit I glommed onto," Dobbs confided during their phone call. "But for goodness sake, not a whisper to anyone, boss."

"Did Newborn pull some shenanigans? A high heel drop in the Nixon campaign?"

"Not about the election, silly man. Which we know is over. Right?"

"Correct. Just testing you."

"Get this: Roy Earl Pettus let slip he's not tearing down The Dixiana after all."

Gooch scrambled to remember anything about what Dobbs said. Roy Earl —Rabbit's grandson, yes—demolishing The Dixiana? And now changing his mind? News to Gooch. "Good. I couldn't imagine it being torn down."

"Instead, he's thinking of restoring it to a state of former glory."

"Former glory?" Gooch chortled. "Now when on earth might that've been?"

"Good question. But, he seems to have developed a newfound nostalgia for the place."

"Wouldn't've thunk it possible. Not the way he rolled the mural with such a vengeance."

"I doubt Roy'll restore that particular aspect."

"Would make certain folks happy if he did."

"And many more wouldn't take it so well."

"Doubtless. What prompted all this?"

"He said he tripped and hit his head on the sidewalk. Gave him a moment of clarity."

"Well—if that doesn't beat all." Maybe a blow to the head would do Gooch Wimmel some good.

His words tumbling unbridled from out of left field, Gooch asked Dobbs if he thought Coy Wando had really killed the Tragedy of '77 kids.

Dobbs mused it'd be a better bet to ask Jasper Glasscock. "All I can tell you is everyone's mama and daddy got squirrelly and clingy after that happened. But even still, nothing like today's world. We rode our bikes around. Had untold hours of unsupervised time. I remember camping overnight with Roy and Devin down by the river. Folks would probably never let their children do that now. But, no—no Coy Wando insight for you. Sorry."

After Dobbs pledged to bring him a care package, usually food and dry goods, they rang off.

See, the only part of passing on the paper to someone of Dobbs's generation that gave Bill pause is that they weren't near as interested in history as they ought to be. Only right now. Gimme gimme gimme. They knew not where they'd been, even less about where they were headed.

But listen to you, he thought. Nor knew the would-be novelist his destination.

Would an antebellum version of Coy Wando could enliven the plot of his historical novel? It sounded preposterous. Times were different back then. More elegant and civilized. Well—the brutality of slavery and lack of indoor plumbing aside.

The novel wasn't about such aspects of Southern life, Bill decided. What more to say about the miserable degradations of slavery? He certainly didn't feel he had anything to add, not from a far remove approaching two centuries.

Perhaps the killer could serve as a metaphor for the institution. A killer of slaves. Valuable slaves. More of a property crime, then, in the eyes of the callous and wealthy planters and owners? An allegory about the underlying inhumanity of capitalism?

"'This murderer must be stopped!' thundered the portly plantation boss

Alfred LaFreniere." Gooch, calling out to the overburdened bookshelves of his study. "'The scalawag's costing us a fortune in good workers.'"

Money and murder. He didn't need a self-help writing textbook to know what interested readers. He knew it from publishing a newspaper. Forget hifa-lutin literary woo-woo. A good story is what they want.

A quick web crawl for 'antebellum serial killer' came up with a doozy: Lavinia Fisher, a female murderer, no less, from only a hundred-fifty miles away in Charleston. She and her husband, the story went, operated a hotel called the Six Mile Wayfarer House, an inn from which guests disappeared, but only after being robbed.

Eh. Like Hitchcock's *Psycho.*

Hitchcock's *Psycho, but* in antebellum times.

Wait—now here, a logline. But still, it seemed too straightforward. gave Gooch a big fat *meh* feeling.

The scribe drummed his fingers and moved off the idea of killers and murder and mysteries. But tragedy—a personal tragedy. Now, that would really anchor his novel.

He remembered a story from a few weeks ago, which after he pulled the clipping discovered had occurred several years in the past, not weeks. In this tragedy, a young couple had crashed in the boy's SUV on the bridge, the late 90s model Ford Explorer ramming through the concrete guardrail and tumbling 80 feet down to the rocky, half dry river below. Both had died on impact. It'd been a troubled relationship, as someone told the authorities.

The bridge—now here, a handy metaphor. He mused upon a storyline:

A returning soldier from the War of Northern Aggression would rebuild Edgewater County and reclaim the love of his life from the man to whom she now cleaves, the action revolving around the reconstruction of the bridge burned to keep Sherman's troops from crossing the Sugeree and ransacking the township and the fancy houses on Whaley Way. The heartrending kicker: Once the protagonist regains his great love, they're killed in a carriage accident while leaving on their honeymoon across the newly constructed bridge.

Tragic romance. That'd be the ticket. Gooch would sell a million copies, get rich in his old age. Get the hell out of this town. He'd go back to being a younger iteration of himself, the one who left and went to Atlanta, but this Gooch would not return to the nest. Maybe he would do so again—the leaving part, that is. A man could write a book anywhere.

◉①❋

ONLY WHEN HE WENT TO TAKE A PEE AND CHECK THE BANDAGE ON HIS SCROTUM, the zipper injury still trying to get itself healed, did Gooch notice the copy of Cortland Beauchamp's Reconstruction-era tragic romance novel sitting on the back of the toilet. In a rush, he remembered that its plot line included all the elements Gooch had thought up! It all came back to him from the pages of the same book he'd been reading, day by day, as he tried to force out one of his lumpy, recalcitrant bowel movements.

Hot blood flooded to his cheeks. *You old fool. You'll never write a bestseller by stealing somebody else's logline.*

He sighed and dribbled urine, no longer pinkish now that his severe infection had cleared up, apparently on its own, since he couldn't remember being treated for it. He fretted that he'd never complete a manuscript of any length—Gooch didn't remember one second to the next what day/month/year it was.

Bill cried out in fury, flung the Beauchamp trade paperback into a bathroom wastebasket already overflowing with snotty tissues and old toilet paper tubes. He altered the aim of his small, hairy dick, felt his bladder opening up like it hadn't in ages, and sprayed a veritable torrent onto the damned book of his that some fool already managed to author as their own life's work.

Everyone needed to find their own story. Gooch's? It was barely there anymore to tell. If it'd ever been. Welcome to retirement.

BUTTON AND CHRISTY BEAUDOCK

Of all the problems Button faced during October while leafleting on the green, including her bad throat and achy ribs—or did the pain originate deeper?—the most troublesome element became the pustulant, looming presence of Christy Beaudock.

Bless his heart.

Christy. Who most unnerved her, more than Howdy Shull ever had. Oh, but Howdy kept showing up too with his raps. Howdy, Edgar Cayce-style, seemed to channel some real heady shit. Lengthy, detailed discourses. Impressive for an old whatever-he-was. On some days Howdy said nothing, kept walking on through town. A relief.

But she'd take a hundred Howdys, and even a thousand church deacons like Cole Breedlove all snippy and pissy and pious in her face, before Christy's seething vibration of need. Poor boy. On first meeting she'd thought, here, a gentle spirit.

No. Christy's vibration: toxic. Wound much tighter than his soft, childlike features and laconic comportment might suggest. His slight smile more a rictus of hidden stress and unease.

Button's intuition, preternatural and super-attuned, but this kid, she didn't know. Did-not-know, yo. And felt inadequate for not-knowing. But feeling better, because as any good Taoist will tell you, not-knowing leads to a deeper knowledge, one of those epistemological paradox dealies.

But Christy, he desired, and desired in some amorphous 'worst' way. What he wanted, she knew not. Could not read him to save her life. A touch frightening. Such as she knew fear, which was hardly at all. His vibration, though. Invasive.

Button intuits all this more than knows; yet suspects (bordering on being pretty sure) that Christy's got weird juju going. Bad energy. Recent, if not present, darkness. A possessiveness consumes him. Threatens to suck her in. He comes to her in dreams over the last few days. His eyes, blazing and sanguineous. Button, not suffering nightmares since she was a tyke.

Weird. Her lucid dreaming still not taking hold. Looking at her hands, drawing the A in blue gel ink, saying, I will look at these hands tonight in my dreams instead of Christy's demon-haunted eyes.

"What's his story?" she asked Newbie one afternoon on the sidewalk outside The Dixiana.

"Christy? He just dropped outta high school. Gonna get a job this summer when he's sixteen."

"That's not what I mean. Why'd he drop out?"

"Why not," Newbie said. "YOLO, yo."

"Check."

"He's got to go to work. His daddy duh—run off on him last month, around Labor Day. Ain't been back."

"That's terrible."

"Yeah. He ain't but fifteen. I'm helping him by paying half rent and keeping house and all."

"That's kind, Newbie."

"He's alright. I reckon."

"*Hrm.* What's he into?"

"Nothing. He can't stand drugs or nothing. His daddy—well, I didn't even know the guy. Don't want to bad-talk nobody who's, who I don't know."

"Gotcha."

Before leaving the house for the next day's leafletting, Button performed a full-on banishing ceremony including an invocation to the father of gods found in a text called *The Black Pullet, or The Hen with the Golden Eggs*. An esoteric grimoire, the book depicts the science of magical talismans and rings, the art of necromancy and the Kabbalah, for conjuring the aerial and infernal spirits, sylphs, undines, and gnomes, discovering treasures, gaining power, unmasking evil spells and sorceries. That type of grimoire.

Immortal, eternal, ineffable, and Sacred Father of all things, who is carried on the chariot rolling without cease, of the worlds which rotate always. Ruler of the Etheric Plain where Your throne of power is exalted and from whose heights Thy formidable eyes discover everything and Your beautiful and saintly ears hear everything.

Oh, Universal Father! Oh, Unique One! Oh, Father of blissful mortals and immortals! You have particularly created the powers which are marvelously like Your

eternal thought and Your adorable essence. You have established them superior to the
angels who announce Your wishes to the world.

Finally, You have created us sovereigns over the elements. Our continued exertion is
to praise You and to adore Your desires. We burn with the desire to be possessed of You.

Oh, Father! Oh, Mother, the most tender of Mothers! Oh, admirable exemplar of
tender sentiment! Oh, Son, the flower of all Sons! Oh, mould of all our shapes! Well
beloved Spirit, soul, harmony, and number of all things, we adore You.

And closing her sacred circle, pocketing a totem, slipping a golden ring upon her finger, blowing out candles and feeling gratitude.

As well she meditates with the Tarot cards with the question in mind of shedding light on Christy Beaudock's relationship to Button. Pulls a single card, the three of swords—a pulsing, crowned heart pieced to the hilt by three shafts of honed, razor-sharp steel, while in the background sluices rain angling down from a pillowy gray cloud deck. A card indicating upheaval, sorrow, disharmony, severance, misfortune, bad news, loss of a lover, separation, heartache. The three of swords suggests you are gonna have something to cry about. Oh boy.

◉ ⓘ ❊

THE PITCH SHE'D MADE TO COUNCIL: HER GOAL ONLY TO EDUCATE THE LOCAL populace about the realities of nuclear power, waste, the Fukushima radioactivity sluicing daily into the Pacific Ocean, and the connectedness of it all; how the population of the E-C lived literally in the shadow of nuclear threat in their daily lives, soon multiplied by the new reactors; how handling this dangerous and filthy crap don't appear sustainable, yo; and let's not get into worries about the radiation leeching into the groundwater, the air, the plants, the people. Here, a flow of information, from which citizens could make decisions about how, and where, best to live their lives.

She'd reassured the council body during a lengthy executive session, having to quell squirrelly nerves despite the Mayor cajoling behind-the-scenes and pre-quelling enough to move to a vote on the proposal to exercise free speech amongst the monuments to the war dead of Edgewater County, they who'd given those precious and irreplaceable lives for such rights as speech. All she had in mind, she asserted, was getting through to one fellow traveler. A modest goal. Getting across to one other person still constituted changing the world.

A dollop of reverse-psychology completed her presentation. "But also to show the world that a Saigon-cinnamon half-breed, a weirdo with dreadlocks," with a self-deprecating and warm laugh, one that every council member gave back as she swept her eyes along their faces and spoke, her words flowing freer and easier than normal, "can still make a fool of herself, and waste everyone's time. With all her. hippie-dippy nonsense."

"Well, now, free speech is not nonsense." The elderly Mousam 'Sammy' Beanhopper, nodding and supportive, made a dry clicking sound between almost every word. He'd been the original African-American member of council for twenty-nine years now, his election following the rural back country annexation near Easton before the first suburban housing developments were built on that side of the freeway in the late 80s. "You go and give out your little brochures, young woman. The day we can't tolerate a free reign of voices, the *vox populi*, it's called, we might as well take down that blessed stars and stripes. Long as she ain't cursing or nothing. It ain't no gangsta rap, is it?"

"It's not music at all. Pamphlets. No speeches. No bullhorns or loud-speakers."

The rest of council, especially the garrulous and avuncular Mayor, talked it through and added a bunch of provisos and no-nos: Button couldn't sell any merchandise, not unless she applied for a vendor's permit, which had been passed to keep people from setting up temporary roadside flea markets in turnouts and old filling stations, those unsightly, movable yard sales Button knew were necessary for poor people to make some scratch, but that the monied and represented of Tillman Falls found distasteful. Button assured the chamber of elders she intended no commerce, that she remained employed by Roy Pettus of The Dixiana, who supported her idea and had pledged to fund the EZ-UP and printing costs. Again they sat relieved and impressed, declaiming with trust and admiration over the character of Mr. Pettus, successful as he was, or so the subtext seemed. A buzzy recitation regarding the plane he flies back and forth to his various business meetings and wealthy-guy obligations. His plans for the The Dixiana and having said to them all how he's now a key stakeholder in the present and future of the town, and so Button having Mr. Pettus in her corner made for a strong factor in her favor. A capitalistic Superman, swooping out of the sky, Roy E. Pettus. A god among mortals.

How people worshipped money. It was something to watch unfold.

◉◑✸

Roy gave her a generous paid-out from his own pocket, peeling off bills from a money clip fat enough to choke a donkey. She'd driven down to Dentsville to the Office Depot and hooked herself up with a new laser printer, color toner and decent glossy card stock and and all manner of goodies. Stayed up a few days and nights making brochures, not only about the nuke issues but other pressing environmental concerns. The decline of pollinating insect populations. The gyres of plastic waste spinning in the oceans. A beginner's overview of conscious breathing, eating, meditation, the chakras. If she had this bully pulpit, she'd push out what she could.

While she still could.

Why did she think time fell short? Throat felt better these days, at least. But still under the weather half the time. Winded, now, after those walks with Roy. Winded and urgent about Heather, who remained standoffish, not answering emails or texts for many hours and sometimes days, and then in a manner terse and odd. A little manic. Hot-cold. Button felt on an emotional yo-yo.

Making the pamphlets took her mind off the aches and pains and low energy and Heather. Here, the text on one postcard-sized handout had been composed to alert the reader to the dangers of eating Pacific-caught fish, the text stolen from a blog post she'd found:

SEAFOOD LOVERS ACROSS THE WORLD!!!

The 'levels' of radiation in the seafood you are eating now and in the future certainly contain Fukushima radiation but will be considered 'safe' by government scientists. Let's boil it down quickly: Scientists say the only safe level of radiation is zero. YET, governments set 'limits' for radiation in food well above zero. These limits actually increase every decade or so. If you love nuclear power and nuclear weapons complexes, then you should accept these limits as well as the fact that a fraction of our cancer epidemic is blamed on nuclear emissions. If you *don't* want people (or yourself) to die of cancer to preserve nuclear power and nuclear weapons, then you should heed the scientific consensus conclusion that the safe level of radiation is zero becquerels of anything. Unless you are a nuclear nut, please protect your own health and regulate your genetic stability for the sake of your children, grandchildren, etc...

By NOT EATING SEAFOOD OR CONSUMING ANYTHING MADE IN THE SEA.

And yet, wild-caught seafood ought to be the healthier alternative.

At least you could eat farm-raised salmon, right?

Frankenfish? And what did fish farmers feed their stocks?

No good seafood choices anymore. Or with any complex protein like meat. Not with the environmental contamination so pervasive. Button, a vegan for quite a long while—a dozen years. More. A veteran. If she got taken out—by cancer, let's say—it wouldn't be from a thoughtlessly consumed diet of factory-farmed meat and GMO corporate fake-food.

◉◉✸

DEACON BREEDLOVE HAD BEEN ONE OF HER FIRST VISITORS, RAPPING THAT PITYING, saccharine small talk fundies deign to make with dreadlocked, new age sinners like Button.

Ha—if only he knew about all her occulted proclivities. Like the hot hubba-dubba she enjoyed with Jouquoya the other night:

Yowsa.

Long overdue, the sensation of resting her face within a warm, downy cleft. Fingertips caressing and exploring. Hot breath against her neck. Skin, soft and pliant. Soft moaning.

Except... it could never be as meaningful as with Heather. But as the hippies had harmonized: Love the one you're with.

Cole, in a houndstooth sport-coated and with a turkey wattle and shiny blue eyes under a too-big brow, loomed over her table spooning and slurping a cup of Oreo pudding carried over from Manny's buffet. His words came thick and sugary sweet. "I think this's a quite a little to-do you got here, Ms. Sykes. Ain't it, though."

"I consider. What I'm doing. As service."

Dumbfounded, he waited gape-mouthed, pulverized bits of Oreo speckled across his expanse of teeth.

"Community service. You've heard the term. Good works."

"These are your 'good works'? These pamphlets full of all this mess? Gracious." He set down his pudding cup, a dribble running off the handle of the spoon onto her stack of color-coded Fukushima radiation impact zone maps. "Sounds like a bunch of conspiracy hoo-hah, if you ask me. If the truth be told. I ain't ever even heard of no Fuh-*fuk*-fukishima," mispronouncing in a manner that caused his cheeks to flush scarlet. "Sounds made up. To me. Anyway, I can't believe council voted 'aye' to all this. Mayor Hampton ought to have his head examined—somebody needs to run against the old fart next time."

"Now that. Sounds like. Something fun. For you to do. Cole."

"Hah—feel like I ought to get back over yonder to the other corner and do my granddaddy's old service. That's what."

For many years, every Friday night street preachers would stand outside The Dixiana shouting pious admonishment to the thirsty patrons coming and going, hollering with holy fervor over the thumping of the tic-tac bass lines and the fiddle ripping from the musicians onstage, everyone either laughing them off or often offering angry or derisive rebuttal. To hear Rabbit and Jasper tell it, those men of God who so beset the customers and performers with their awful haranguing were such a part of the routine they became invisible; that they were wasting their time. Good works lay in the eye of the beholder, Button supposed.

"Look. They did vote 'aye.' And so. Here I am. Doing my service. And yeah

—Roy told me all about those days. Guess. Your grandfather wasn't. Able to run old Rabbit off the green. Was he."

Snorting, disdainful at Button's insult, he tossed the half-eaten pudding into the wire wastebasket near the tent.

"Hey. You wasted that."

He wiped his mouth with a handkerchief. "I had all I wanted—I was full."

"Food is sacred, Cole. You shouldn't. Waste it."

"Pish posh."

"No, this is important. Wasting food. It's a sacrilege."

"Maybe you should dig it out of there and finish it yourself, then." He pitied Button. "Haven't you heard the good news? The Lord will always provide to his believers. More, and more. The righteous will always be fed. Have you no fear of that."

"I do believe the Lord provides."

"Do you? I've never seen you in church one day in your life, Button Sykes."

"I've been to church. I pray. In my own way." Scoffing, his prissy strut carried him across the street toward the old courthouse. Over his shoulder: "Don't waste no prayers on Cole Breedlove. You need not worry; ye can bank thy God-fearing soul that Cole will receive as much pudding and custard as he desires—forever."

Sheesh. "Namaste, dude."

She straightened and cleaned her flyers where he'd soiled them. Felt anguish for the followers of the monotheistic religions, a horribly satanic trick designed to isolate individuals from the great spirit, not unite them with it. Make 'it' a separate and unreachable entity except through initiation and dogma rather than as the inclusive life-force that the truest idea of God portended, a singularity, a point of emanation engaged in the active act and permeating the ALL. Not a suitable discussion for a believer in white-robed cloud-men, like Breedlove. Difficult to persuade that belief is only a particular thought one has practiced with, indeed, faith and repetition. Perhaps to a fault.

The conditioned mind of a Cole Breedlove would be awakened from his doctrinaire slumber by someone other than Button Sykes. Her issues transcended his, and furthermore, live and let live, who was she to say, and so on.

❂❂❂

HADN'T TAKEN LONG AFTER GETTING HER E-Z UP ON A PRIME PARCEL WITH GOOD visibility to appreciate how little occurred on a daily basis in downtown Tillman Falls. She only got decent action on the weekend, when Head Trauma had business, and the antiquing 'crowds' came through hitting the side streets where once thriving and vital businesses plied their trades, like her grandfather's original appliance store. Which turned into someone else's furniture store. Which later become a rent-all place, one that had long moved over to the Chilton freeway-exit commercial corridor.

But on Thursday, Friday and Saturday nights, downtown showed life. Manny's packed them in at lunch and dinner, Becky L had a production of *West* Side Story going at the PGAC, and The Dixiana booked bands out of Columbia and other places; the honkytonk's kitchen staff continuing producing burgers, chicken baskets, and hot dogs, with a happy Trudy Pirkle out front pouring beer and calling the tune during Jasper's open mic night:

"Play 'Country Music' for me, sugar," she could be counted upon to holler from behind the bar near the end of the evening.

"Not sure I remember that one," he'd reply with a theatrical wink, looking off into the distance. Of course he knew it. It was Jasper's open mic anthem, and if enough regulars were in attendance they'd surely accompany him on its joyful, ringing chorus:

> *Well I was just a young boy, I was listening to rock 'n roll*
> *Never had an idea, I was way beyond control,*
> *Till I heard that music that's when I saw the light,*
> *I knew those folks in Texas man,*
> *they damn sure had it right*

> *Play me some music mister, play me a song*
> *Country music sure enough will help a body move along.*
> *Play me some music mister, play me a song*
> *One I know the words to, so I can sing along*

Button enjoyed steady work running sound, felt a sense of empowerment the way Trudy did behind the bar. No pamphleteering in the evenings. Luckily Thim agreed to help pay for an adult care custodian to help care for Button's mom and granddad, who had quit drinking at the bar. Said he could not stand to be there, not now that Roy had rolled the mural and Rabbit was dead.

Now, hanging out and shooting the shit with Newbie Harrell, Howdy Shull —not that you talked to him like a normal human—and this weird Christy kid, she guessed that could be called getting 'action' in her free speech zone. Except, Christy's vibration kept her sense of danger pegged to eleven, which coupled with the turning of the Three of Swords made for a big fat flashing warning sign. About what, she drew only a blank.

Or maybe Button held prejudice in her heart: Beaudock, an Edgewater County name carrying little good will—a lowlife crime family, as her grandfather still said of them. Hanging with Newbie didn't portend too sharp a knife in Christy's own drawer, though. That much for certain. Button, doing her best to limit judgement or comparison. Failing, often. Spiritually evolved as she might be, a flawed human shell remained.

Glad, in a way, Roy offered Newbie his custodial job back, since the act indicated growth and spiritual reconciliation on the bossman's part. Newbie's energy, however, and his own judgement and good sense, could manifest in problematic and troublesome ways. For one, he grabbed at Button on two different occasions when alone at the honkytonk with him in the mid-afternoon, the second of which literally trying to plant one on her.

She had demurred with gentle force. Newbie, blinking, leaning in again and Button having to yell to set him straight, which felt awful but necessary. And having him out here, now, with the weather turning cooler and grayer, and her throat itchy and side hurting, left her unsettled and annoyed. Neither were in keeping with her mission or her vibration, which typically buzzed high and wide and encompassing.

Winter. Winter would give her an excuse to give up on this enterprise. No one cared. Enervated almost from the moment she began leafletting, she started getting stoned again on the drive over in the Baja each day. But being high only made her more bored and self-conscious sitting slumped in her camp chair, allowed mind-worms to burrow in and replicate, like how to reconcile her affection for Jouquoya with her tenacious, unrequited yearning for Heather Ponderview. While she still had time.

◉◉✺

RIGHT; WORK. THE DIXIANA, FOR NOW AT LEAST, LIVED AND BREATHED.

At least Roy had had the decency to allow the staff to continue on as they had when Rabbit was alive, including Trudy. Till his grandson figured out what he wanted to do. Jasper Glasscock, a happy boy at this turn of events. His open mic nights well attended. The bands they booked, bringing people from all around. The Dixiana, enjoying a rocking renaissance.

Button had been nudging Roy on their walks. She admitted this. Doing powerful work with him. Giving him talks about meditation. Spirit. Soul work. The higher mind. But also nudging him in a direct and focused fashion. Firing up the old pineal gland, activating the living crap out of that chakra and beaming the signal to him to not tear down the building. She understood that he only wanted to go so far because rolling over the old mural had been so cathartic. Repair, she kept beaming to him. Refresh. Whether present or otherwise, she'd picture his face, his eyes open and meeting hers, and project at him the idea, the notion, the nudge:

Rebuild. Don't destroy.

Her pine cone, throbbing. The crackle of electricity across her crown.

More hippie dippy bullshit. She didn't even know why it mattered. Perhaps

The Dixiana offered itself not only as a honkytonk, but a state of mind worth preserving. Some aspects, anyway. Sounded like a good tag line for Manny's Music City idea. Or the water tower, the naming rights of which Roy joked might be worth getting, if The Dixiana were to live on after all:

That's right. After talking it out with Manny, Roy announced one morning at the turn-around of the riverside walking trail about a gutting and remaking of the old honkytonk, but no longer into his third-wave hipster coffee shop. No; he suddenly wanted to reconstruct The Dixiana from the inside out, from scratch—but without changing a single detail.

"So that it's—new, but old?"

"You got it. It's the approach I took with the coffee shops, especially the CBSI. The old record albums, books on shelves built to look as though made out of cinderblocks and two-by-fours, couches—the college dorm room of coffee shops. Capturing a moment. Well now, The Dixiana also captured its moment. We will perpetuate this moment. But in a controlled and exacting fashion, down to the last detail."

"That sounds. Interesting."

"And when we reopen? We will make our presence known. We'll do a shit-ton of social media engagement. Get to booking name touring talent. A PR blitz so expansive it might even go viral."

"We will?"

"You betcha. We have trademark applications in the works for the name, the neon sign logo, even Rabbit's mandala above the stage."

"You do?" Button, a rush of adrenaline. Rabbit's powerful symbol, that hex of his own design with its six-pointed creator stars, might soon wield even more power. He believed it a vital part of the energetic protection over the enterprise and its extended family, as were the hexes on the Pettus houses, with their more traditional and familiar floral designs. Roy knew not the subtleties of using symbols.

Or did he:

"Plaster the logo on every blamed tchotchke you can imagine—and give most of it away, except stuff like the new high thread-count T-shirts we're gonna churn out in, say, seven colors and maybe three body styles. Upon reopening, step it up with the rock bands. Go seven nights a week. Run shuttles from Charlotte and Columbia. Hook up every visitor's bureau in the region with brochures. A billboard campaign to match Thurmond Pike's—well, maybe not match. But show a respectable effort. 'The Dixiana—Now and Forever.' I'll work with Feebee on the tag line. And later? Who knows. A franchise. House of Blues is dead and moldy. How about a slew of Dixianas? Every one of them an exact copy. What would my Pa-paw think about that?" Roy seemed joyful at the prospect. A different man from before. "Charleston, Myrtle Beach,

Greenville, hell, why not Sedge Island. And then onto the rest of the freaking world."

At least his megalomania now had more to do with growth than fire-bombing all reality into base matter and crushing it beneath the rubber soles of his sport sandals. "All this from getting smacked around?" Teasing and testing. "From a fractured shoulder?"

His expression fixed and glazed over with the majesty of his vision, he ignored her and continued in an incantatory cadence: "It'll be exactly the same, sure, but we'll rebuild with a bigger stage and floor area. We'll tear out the old insurance office on the corner for a new green room. We'll make Manny's dream of Music City come true. We'll spare no expense. We're gonna make old Rabbit proud. We will be welcomed into heaven as partners and kings, one day, for our service to this ideal. For our veneration of the forebears."

"This is quite." She cleared her throat. "A profound statement."

At last he came out of his trance. His aura blazed bright. "I feel it more than know it."

Immense, her pleasure. "New, but old."

He held his arms wide. "And the community as a whole will reap the spoils. It is here said today, and will be so then." A proclamation.

There it was. 'Rebuild' had taken hold in his mind.

He'd develop and improve, while preserving the essence of what he sought to 'bring up to code,' as he kept putting his plan to refurb the whole place, while maintaining a scrupulous continuity and authenticity. More to his mind-set, he could see it becoming a truly profitable business enterprise again, one that'd spark new growth and financial health in the town at large.

Button knew this plan, of which she heartily approved, might still be destined to culminate in a manner likely to bear only modest fruit. But all she had learned was to get out of the way of another person who might be making a mistake. One never knew when the universe had sent the situation they were facing to teach a necessary soul-growth lesson—that's when you needed to step aside and let it all unfold.

But then, that's the way to treat every moment of everyday life. Let events happen. Give out your leaflets. And feel that making conversation with three charming town eccentrics, four if you counted Roy Earl Pettus, counted as service to the universe. Hah. Right. That is the drama here; that is the scene, the metaphor. Like on Phish tour, here, a confluence of misfit energy.

I get it, she said to the big U. I get it. A tribe to which she had to play savior. Her burden. Every shaman has one.

⚭

CHATTING IN BED THE OTHER NIGHT THIS IDEA OF TRIBES HAD COME UP, WHAT

Button had experienced in both her college media arts world as well as on Phish tour.

Jouquoya couldn't get it at all—she'd never heard of the Grateful Dead or Phish, or what hippies were about, the whole vagabond trip, lives lived in iconoclastic, non-mainstream fashions, even in some brave cases off the grid and (mostly) out of the matrix. Except, of course, when burning up fossil fuels chasing some jamband across the country and back.

Who knew how many miles Button herself had accrued.

She attempted to describe this world lying curled up next to the large and warm body of Jouquoya, a towel damp beneath in the aftermath of Button's third orgasm, stifled and muffled by her forearm so as not to wake up the rest of the household. Miraculous, the attention her friend and new lover paid, the flood of literal release deft ministrations had engendered. Now, lying bunched against the smooth small of her lover's broad back, Button felt as though drifting and dreaming.

Was this only a happy lucid dream?

Squinting in the darkness at the heel of her hand.

The blue A drawn in gel ink.

Awake.

Oh, how she'd hoped Jouquoya could have provided a more private location for their tryst. But no, shit no, GF, she'd said; don't nobody in my family know about me. And the way I am. That her grandmother would try to whip that woman-love out of her. Drum her out of her own tribe.

So yeah, they'd had to come hook up here, with both Tinky and Granddad medicated and wheezing in deep slumber, while Button enjoyed the communion and release of sex for the first time in so long.

"That kinda happened to me, out on the road."

"What did, sugar?" Jouquoya, humming and stroking Button's stomach. "Somebody eat your pussy good as me?"

"I wish. No, kicked out of the tribe."

She sat up on one elbow. "F'real?"

"Not really. I didn't get drummed out on Phish tour. Just left behind. Like trash."

"Still dunno why y'alls doing going to see the same durn band play every night."

"It's its own thing."

"How you get mixed up in it?"

In the course of describing her path to becoming a tourhead, Button ended up talking mostly about college. About working on the Disney movies, but eliding the relationship with the Durango sisters as well as Heather Ponderview. The group scriptwriting projects. Making the student film, from her own script. How the media artists bonded, had their own tribal stuff, a commitment to art, or maybe on the level of what they called the below-the-line crew, to an excellence at the work of pulling all the cables and loading the film magazines and adjusting the lights and recording the sound—yeah, like running the sound in a club. You had a tribal thing going with other front of house crew you met, like when the band brought their own board and she took a subsidiary role to their working sound guy.

"You made your own movies?" Wonder in her voice, Jouquoya stroked Button's dreads, their damp flesh sticking together. *"And you got a DVD?"*

"A VHS somewhere. This was right before DVDs came out. I've never bothered to get them digitized. A big so-what type-deal. A short documentary, about Otilya Duckett—you would dig that."

"A tape, yo. Oldschool. I know we got a VCR in a closet. You need to get it up on YouTube."

"Yeah. No. I don't think so."

"I wanna see your movie, girl. You could use your phone now to make another one, if you wanted."

Button, mulling. "Maybe. Sometime."

Mohammed's Radio, her student film, had come from a short script of Button's that had won the advanced scriptwriting class competition the previous semester. Brenda LaRose, a teacher who didn't seem all that much older than her students—of similar build and body type as Button, attractive, sweet, but not a soul sistah in the sapphic sense—had said it was one of the best scripts written in any of her classes. Button shot it with a bulky video setup and did the editing on three-quarter inch tape, a laborious process.

"Her praise. It made me feel like I was on my way. And making the film the next semester. But seeing the finished cut felt weird. Like seeing one of my dreams. Come to life."

"I ain't never thought of it that way. When you go and make a movie."

"Yeah—somebody dreams up the movie, the script. And then puts the camera. In the right spot. And gets the picture. And arranges all the pictures. And tells the story. And it's a dream, unfolding on a wall. That sucks you in. If it's done right. It's weird."

"I want to see your films."

"I don't know. Which box the tape's in." Up in the attic, no less. Hot. Turned to goo. Button, unable to say that part. "A *Do the Right Thing* ripoff. S'all it was. Same basic story—kid plays his boombox too loud, and gets it broken."

Jouquoya said, that only makes me want to see it more. How she reveres *Do the Right Thing*.

"To me, my movie's nothing but a reminder. That I not only had nothing original to say. But that I did nothing. With my degree."

"Aw, that don't matter none. Movie jobs got be hard to get."

"It wasn't that. I didn't even try. I got all—messed up. For no good reason. You don't know. The whole story."

"Not yet I don't," soft and whispery. "But we don't need to talk right now."

"Can you stay? For a while?"

"I can stay a bit longer. For reals."

Button, her tongue finding Jouquoya's, a tingling bloom of heat again forming between them. Button, sliding her foot up the leg and a hand up the other thigh, and Jouquoya sighing and making a puddle in Button's cupping palm. And indeed, nothing more needed saying. With words, anyway.

◉①✳

THE WARMTH AND SATISFACTION OF THE SEXING BED SEEMED A LONG WAY OFF WHILE leafletting on the green, facing her peanut gallery. Interesting, though, this trend: this had been the most engaged Button had ever seen Howdy Shull.

As the hulking, silent boy named Christy stood watching with his hidden eyes, Howdy rapped, punctuated by occasional guffaws and a 'man, that's crazy' from Newbie. Shull had been on a long, complicated digression regarding fiat currency and the fractional reserve banking system to a tangent regarding the various assassinations of Presidents who happened to challenge, or even hint about challenging, the banking status quo of their respective eras.

"And those who did speak up after the fact, these Presidents, they did not in fact live very long. Consider this quote from Woodrow Wilson, born not forty miles *from where we stand*," his stentorian voice deepening and booming out across the green, scattering pigeons with the cadence and tremulous power of an impassioned preacher. "Woodrow Wilson had this to say: 'Since I entered politics, I have chiefly had men's views confided to me privately. Some of the biggest men in the U.S., in the field of commerce and manufacturing, are afraid of somebody, are afraid of something. They know that there is a power somewhere so organized, so subtle, so watchful, so interlocked, so complete, so pervasive, that they had better not speak above their breath when they speak in condemnation of it.' And months later, Woodrow Wilson, dead."

"Now look here," Newbie said. "Wasn't he old by then? Maybe the motherfucker just died."

"There are dark rumors that suggest, suggest—rumors, facts, rumors, what have you—that Col. Edward House, a functionary of the Illuminati of which Wilson spoke, was the President's handler. And that he could, would, could have administered an injection to Wilson, one designed to simulate the pneumonia that killed this President born *not forty miles from where we stand here today*." Howdy made his point up on one leg, gesturing with his free hand— the other held his ever present Canada Dry two-liter—like a plane taking off, trying to get back to the right place in the narrative, snapping his fingers. "Forty miles. Woodrow Wilson."

"Illuminati," said Christy, finally, in his breathy voice. "They rock."

"Who that?" Newbie, his mouth hanging open. "A metal band?"

"You guys like music?" Button interjected. "We play music over at The Dixiana all the time. Don't we, Newbie."

"Sure do. It ain't no Illuminati, though."

"Or Phish," Button says. "Except sometimes when. No one's around."

Christy asked who is Phish; Button explained about their music best she could, which is mainly that, if she has to explain, it's not quite understandable.

Christy, huffing and pouting, like she doesn't want to tell him, for some reason.

Newbie, spitting tobacco juice onto the sidewalk, a brown *splat* like a Rorschach inkblot. "That stuff you play? That shit's weird."

"Out of context. I suppose. It probably is." Button. Pondering whether talking Roy into bringing Newbie back had been a good idea. Little energetic tendrils of uncertainty, tickling at her ganglia. Not like her to be uncertain or confused.

Maybe about Heather. But otherwise...

Now, Christy? Button watches clouds of bewilderment cross the kid's wide face. Flashes of anger and resentment. Button, wondering if Christy, like Roy, hasn't been sent for guidance.

Leafletting, guidance, care-taking of the old folks—Button, carrying a load. Maybe somebody would come along to guide her, for a change.

◉◉❋

HERE, A BAD BRITISH ACCENT FROM BEHIND HER. "WHAT'S ALL THIS, THEN. A sodding flash mob?"

Roy Pettus, beaming at Button. His gaze hardened, one of examination and skepticism, as it fell upon Newbie and Christie, at whom he peered from his modest stature almost a foot below the enormous teenager. Both shuffled their feet, intimidated. Roy, with his blazing energetic sphere of influence like static electricity, had that effect.

Back in his own voice: "I thought this t'weren't gonna be no Occupy Edgewater County."

"No chance. Just my fan club. Meet Christy." Button presented her new friend. "He's a pal. Of Newbie's."

Roy went *uh-huh* under his breath. Fixed his eyes on Newbie, for whom he did not care, and yet, as with Trudy, had allowed to remain in the Dixiana family fold. Unlike with the bar manager, however, Button knew Roy only brought back Newbie because Button said he was okay; he could use a break;

that he didn't have much going for him in life except swabbing out the tavern's restrooms and kitchen floors and cleaning the toilets and cutting the grass in the back field, which Roy paid to have cleaned of all the junk. She had not argued, do it because your Grandfather thought someone should do it for Newbie; she well understood the remaining residual magnetized energy regarding Roy's relationship with his elder, and so she knew to tread with delicacy and precision about matters like that of employment decisions. She'd done more pushing with her mind than suggesting in words what Roy ought to do, anyway. Seemed to work.

"Well, any friend of Newbie Harrell's a pal of mine, too." A little sarcastic, Roy extended his hand to Christy, who didn't seem to want to shake. "Or maybe not."

Roy, such a strong vibration. It'd been terrible the day after Rabbit died when he'd yelled at them all. A waking nightmare. At least he seemed to know this. Or had glimmers of awareness. Besides being an overbearing blowhard and verbal bully he could also glow with good will, infectious, attractive, loving, playful, but even that came overwhelming, a touch manic. Roy, whether he realized it, a deep channeler—if not quite a master—of energy.

Button hoped that her friend and sort-of cousin would continue to move to a place of humility, would learn that to govern, one must place themselves below the people and not above. That the belief they were doing it themselves will move and empower them, not forced into compliance with the leader's reality. It isn't a trick; it's an exchange of energy.

Many discussions ahead.

Hope there's time to have them all.

Huh? Where does this crap keep coming from?

Not Walfredo, Walfredo's voice said. A touch wry. Even sarcastic.

Uh-oh.

Pesky little thoughts. Almost time for afternoon meditation. She clutched her five-inch wedge of clear quartz crystal she'd been using to clear and adjust her Q'i. If she could rid herself of the hangers-on, the peanut gallery, the stooges, that would help. Walfredo—and all her magicking and nonsense—offered only pie-eyed New Age horseshit, anyway. She wished for the bliss of a Phish show, a few hours of noodle dancing. And maybe a mild pain reliever for this aching back.

◉①✸

As Roy bantered with the two young men, Newbie's vibration and body language bespoke mistrust and dislike of his new boss, who had killed him and resurrected him and now seemed all friendly-like for no discernible reason. Newbie, too suspicious to appreciate the volatile Roy E. Pettus in a lighthearted state of mind.

Button, realizing that the boss had vaped some cannabis she'd given him—yes. This accounted for his brightness, his lavender aura.

A miracle plant. The godflower.

"Newb, I got to say, you been keeping that old dump looking sharp. And all that dust and stuff I complained about—all you guys, really. Looks so much better."

Newbie said, well, we all know how important it is to please you, Mr. Pettus.

"Call me Roy, dude. It ain't like that."

Newbie, sticking out his lip. "Coulda fooled me."

This troubled Roy. "C'mon, bro. Bygones, dude. Bygones."

"Do what?"

"I'm trying to say, sorry I came down on everyone so hard."

"You already told me that the other day," Newbie said. "It don't matter."

"Well—I'm telling your ass again. And yours, Button."

"Hah. You're telling. My ass? Hah."

"You know what I mean."

At Roy's appearance Howdy had bolted stiff-armed, striding over by Manny's to take the east highway out of town. Probably going all the way out to the walking trail, maybe covering the 'forty miles' as he kept emphasizing.

Walking.

The walking dude.

Where she ought to be, walking in the woods somewhere instead of this fool's errand here on the green.

"So." Roy regarded Christy, who remained silent and taciturn throughout this stranger's badinage and joshing. "You're a real firecracker over here. Really, ace. You into standup comedy? That hair of yours, and the manner, the bubbly exterior." Roy tapped Christy on the breast of his bulky jacket. "I bet you're a big Rip Taylor fan."

Christy laughed. A little. But also frowned. "Who's Rip Taylor?"

Newbie, sour and dismissive. "Bro, I ain't never heard of him, and I watch Comedy Central all the durn time."

Button herself didn't have a clue who Roy referenced either, and only half listened as her friend told a ridiculously detailed remembrance of seeing a Mike Douglas variety show one afternoon—she didn't know who Mike Douglas was, either; like, the Gordon Gekko actor?—what he called a 'novelty episode' in which they'd taken the format out of the studio and put it on live from some beachfront in Florida, and Rip Taylor had been a surprise guest, all of which he described with unconscious and building excitement. Roy, in actual mimicry of Taylor, running around Button's EZ-Up and demonstrating the flamboyant prop comic's standard routine, which sounded indeed like running and throwing confetti and screaming bad puns and wringing laughs out of what seemed his own self-effacement and exuberant humiliation. The kind of comedian a kid like Roy, she mused, would have enjoyed.

Especially Roy Pettus.

But she didn't know why, exactly.

"And thing was? They had dug this pit." Giggling, pulling himself together. "And they—they filled it with water. Knowing Rip Taylor would race around on the sand doing his crazyman act. And when he finally falls into the pit, everyone was laughing so hard, no one more that Rip himself, who was way into the spirit of the the bit. John Davidson, standing in a Speed-o. They had him out in the surf, shivering on a Jet-ski, a hip new toy back then."

Roy collected himself. His gaze drifted around at the green and the sky above, which in the last few minutes had clouded over. "But it was cloudy. Yeah. Like this. They had taken the show out to do a beach segment, but got a cloudy day. I remember Davidson, he was freezing and complaining, but still had to ride the Jet-ski in his trunks. They were all disappointed, but keeping their game faces on. But Rip Taylor—man. He came on there and gave a thousand percent, leaving everyone crapping themselves with amusement. I was sitting right there on my grandmother's rug, in front of that old console TV I made them get rid of a few years ago. Laughing so much I might puke. Jesus—"

He caught himself. Sucked wind. Tried to smile, but seemed pained.

Button fretted—his energy, darkening. Nostalgia, a dangerous road for a wounded soul like his.

"That was forty years ago. More. And, Rip Taylor's dead. God help me."

Newbie, wiseacre: "No wonder I ain't heard of him."

"We could go and look it up on YouTube," Christy said, shy. "We could watch it. So you wouldn't have to tell it." Christy, all frowning and serious. Making sure Roy understood. "It can be seen."

Button watched with intrigue as Roy Pettus appeared on the verge of tears, she suspected, of gratitude rather than sorrow. "Over in the office?"

Christy seemed to hesitate. "In yonder?"

"Sure—why not?"

Button, waving from inside the EZ-Up. "Hey. Roy."

"Yes'm?"

"Look it up. On your phone."

Roy, perplexed at first. When the light went on, his aura brightened even further. "I got a supercomputer right here in my pocket."

Both Newbie's and Christy's eyes lit up. "That's the latest one, the skinnier one," Newbie said with awe. "Did you wait in line on the first day? Man, I wish I could do that sometime."

"Heck no, I ordered online. I don't give a flying fudge factory about being first. I just want the supercomputer part." Squinting at the glowing screen. "Not that an old codger like me knows how to use the damn thing."

"Man, I sure am glad I come back to work at the old Dix." Newbie, his face scrunched up with the effort of trying to keep from saying what he'd said.

Roy, sliding his finger on his phone. Without looking at Newbie: "Yeah, well, it could always go wrong again, pal."

Button saw Newbie look crushed, then angry; Christy, his face clouded and lips protruding like a disappointed toddler.

"Law of. The jungle," Button said, but none of them seemed to hear. "Right, Roy?"

"Excuse me?"

"Survival of the fittest. The fittest monkeys. Survived and turned into us. Humanity, I mean."

"Damn freaking straight." Pleased, he went back to his device. "Siri? Find me some Rip Taylor on YouTube."

Siri: "*Searching for Rip Taylor on YouTube.*"

Seconds later: "She found it. *I got some Rip right here,*" shouting with excitement. "Let me turn it up—we need one of them Bluetooth speaker jobs."

All stood silent and huddled, watching on the tiny screen as a dead comedian ran around and threw confetti and made them all chuckle despite themselves.

As Button's side ached and she tasted bile in the back of her throat, she couldn't help observing Roy's inability to contain a level of disappointment he felt in not being able to access the exact Mike Douglas show he'd described: the one, the one, the one on the beach, a need bordering on RAGING DESIRE for validation of these memories of this random daytime TV variety show from forty years ago, as inconsequential a piece of human art as could be conceived. That it still unspooled in the ether, Button thought, was possible. But really, how much access to data will be enough for future generations?

Ultimate access to all data?

Was it possible?

To what end?

Didn't we already have it, though? Wasn't finding this digital bit of the late Rip Taylor's residual energy enough? This YouTube video, and Roy's memories? What would it take for him, or for anyone coming along later—access to all the data there ever had been—to satisfy the energetic hunger for information now stoked in us all?

How much knowledge will be enough?

But as she'd read in the Scott translation of the *Corpus Hermeticum*: *If you do not make yourself equal to God, you cannot apprehend God. Like is known by like. Leap clear of all that is corporeal and make yourself to a like expanse with a greatness beyond all measure. Rise above all time and become eternal.*

Thus, she reasoned, the nature of the great work. Man as God. And so, no way to answer the question of how much will be enough. Just enough to seem like man knows what God knows.

C'mon, she thought. As it stood, they had all the Rip Taylor anyone would ever need.

◉ⓘ✳

Roy's routine was to swing by, make sure everyone felt good about their jobs—what a nice change from the Black Blade of Wrath. Rarely did he stay at the bar longer than five minutes, but tonight he lingered to watch the musicians tune up and socialize, the good-ol' boys and hipsters from Columbia commingling with bonhomie and cheerful repartee. The musician's tribe.

Earlier, he helped her break down the EZ-Up. Reveled in the task, the work of loading it and her table into Piper, her faithful Subaru Baja.

"I look around here, can't help trying to imagine more."

Button, musing how it seemed to her the idea of 'imagination' rested at the root of all that'd ever been built or achieved. "Visualize what you want it to be. And it will be. Unless the intention. In your heart. Isn't true."

Roy, wonderstruck. "'We make our own reality.' That's what that means?"

A shrug and a smile to compete with the stitch in her side. "Along those lines."

His face relaxed in a manner mostly unseen since his return to Tillman Falls. Button herself imagined Roy getting to a place wherein he understood we're all co-creators of this reality, and all had a shared responsibility to harmonize rather than dominate. And crucially, to let go; to not-know.

A man stood onstage with a guitar. His microphone fed back. She potted down the input on her soundboard. And tried not to worry. The sore throat, back with a vengeance. All the standing around in the damp weather outside. That's all it was. Another reason to pull the plug on the pamphleteering, work on a Heather visit, and try to get on without quite so much dire urgency and concern over a perfectly prosaic set of aches and pains and fatigue and weight loss.

ROY AND CECIL WAUGH

I f there's one thing a man needs after having his mind blown by a gal like Button Sykes, with all her talk about needing to get to a post-money societal construct, and about decalcifying third eyes, and activating chakras and transcending ordinary consciousness, it's a good solid haircut, a close buzz. Your tennis ball look. Yeah.

No fuss, no muss. Besides, these walks you're taking with Button, you work up a sweat. It's still so weird being down along that part of the river. You had played with your friends back there when it was all still wooded.

Sitting in the chair at Head Trauma you're buzzed by a heavy, middle-aged woman in a sea-foam green barber's smock, full sleeve tattoos down her arms, facial piercings and an ice-pink, spiky mohawk. Despite her modern appearance, she makes the same sort of town small talk you're supposed to get in the barber's chair or at the hair salon; unlike at Mr. Halsey's, however, there's a modicum of flirting, and for this you'll give Lenza a solid, meaty, juicy tip.

Your face in the mirror looks round. Kinky hair grown out, chunks of fuzz tumbling all down your rounded shoulders as she sweeps the electric razor. Creedence, always wanting you to grow it out. Looked stupid when you tried, though—too wavy and stiff. How you'd envied your rich college bud Billy Steeple, with his thick mahogany colored mane of hair like freaking Fabio. When your wiry hair grew out, in only made you look like potato-faced Larry Fine. Like now; now, more than ever: a thinning spot, right in front. You've kept it cut short so long before this grow-out you didn't realize the hair loss. Not even a good-looking widow's peak. Super.

"We all sure loved your granddaddy. What will you do with The Dixiana?"

Blunt. "*God*—whatever I *feel* like."

"That don't sound fun."

"Nah, only kidding. That's from some dumb movie. We're gonna spruce it up."

"They ever catch who rolled paint on that mural?"

"Nope. Darn vandals."

"Man, I tell ya. That thing was there fifty-some years. Did you know that?"

Was she serious? "That's what I always heard."

Boom, you're done. Outside you go to caress your freshened pate, but raising your hand makes your shoulder twinge and hurt deep as a sonofabitch, all down into your soul, almost. It's a damnable, deep and burning pain you hope will soon ebb away. Eventually. In the meantime, Samson and Mervin Pettus could both eff themselves.

◉◉✻

BEFORE YOU STROLL BACK TO THE DIXIANA, THE BOSSMAN OF HIS BLOCK, YOUR hated childhood nemesis Cecil Waugh, arrives with a mature manner that's cordial, an incongruity alongside the memories you suffer of his hateful and roguish youthful behavior.

In no particular hurry, you commit to a modicum of small talk on the sidewalk. Sure thing, 'pal.' Despite his defense of you during the Mervin assault, you retain long-engrained feelings of distrust. This tattooed oaf once made your life a living hell.

But now?

A member of the fraternity—the merchant class.

A stakeholder.

A peer.

The modern Cecil displays a kind and disarming manner, and you end up shooting the shit with your old enemy for a half-hour. You muse about the relative economic health of the area, how the town could benefit from a good solid mixed-use redevelopment opportunity, should anyone want to pursue it.

"You know what somebody ought to do?"

Cecil leans in. "Tell me, Roy."

Build a huge old folks complex, you say, centered on the old mill building by the river. "Hell, the original township was down that way, along the river."

"I never knew that."

"Yep. And now, with the baby boomers hitting retirement by the thousands every day, an investor could make bank on a retirement village. Build a walkable town center out of the shell of the mill. Buy up every property for a mile in any direction—it wouldn't take that much capital, ya know ya know, not in that part of the county. Tear down every blessed mill shack, work with the

DOT on resetting some roads. Build a few rings of condo, patio, single-family and town-homes, top-shelf street and decorative lighting, choice landscaping, fast wi-fi, a new country club, a Sheriff's substation—hell, a new bridge over the Sugeree to connect with an interstate exit built just for this development. Roy E. Pettus's 'Milltown by the River,' let's call it—a project designed to give Del Webb's Sun City near Sedge Island an acute case of penis envy."

"Damn. It's all I can do to keep up with my own industry standards. I just don't got that kinda mind."

"Just a mental exercise. Like a game."

Sizing you up, he whistles into the wind. "Take a lotta scratch to pull that off."

"Yeah—more than I got."

"Heard that." And a fist bump. "But nobody ever got anywhere without thinking big."

You both ease onto a decorative bench you note needs painting, if not replacement. The sun blazes behind the obelisk at the center of the green. A billboard looming above the trees heading out of town extols the DUI-specializing law practice of Kenly & Pretlow, a phone number emblazoned in yellow cartoon numerals visible to motorists sober and otherwise.

Two business dudes, two peers. No one could've seen this coming, thirty or forty years ago. You pretty much say so.

Cecil turns pink. "No. We weren't friends back then."

"Not exactly."

You seize the opportunity. Cecil, a major player. Look at the investment in retail square feet he has on this block. So you lay on him your idea of a merchant's association to complement—you stop yourself rom saying 'supplant'—the existing power structures, like the Chamber of Commerce and the ELMS.

In response to your proposal about a new advocacy group, and exploiting the town history and The Dixiana and Manny's idea about Music City, to turn this place around from its downmarket trajectory of the last few decades, Cecil says, wow; that by God he'd serve on any council, body, or 'away team' Roy Earl Pettus put together. This little speech seems less an endorsement of your business and urban development acumen than what feels like a gesture of genuine faith and friendship.

"You always seemed so smart and all. I shoulda known you'd be who you are."

"I seemed smart? But you were a senior, and I was just a—"

"Naw. I thought you were a sharp kid. And you are." A rueful admission. "Why do you suppose me and Harlem picked on you so much...?"

"Don't know. Boys will be boys?"

"We were jealous."

"Bullcorn."

"True story. You were Rabbit Pettus's kid. He was a town father. Ours was just a drunk."

Forgiveness wells in your heart for all Cecil's boyhood transgressions. If there's one thing you cannot stand, it's a drunk.

But one detail stands out, grabs your attention. "'Away team'? As in a landing party from the U.S.S. Enterprise? That's the NCC 1701-D Enterprise, by the way."

Cecil's flush deepens. Sheepish, he talks up his fandom of all things *Star Trek*, both TOS and TNG and the feature films, not so much the J. J. Abrams reboot series. His enjoyment of the franchise goes so far he says he named his kids Sulu and Uhura.

"Hardy har."

"No, seriously. They freaking hate me for it."

"Well... they'd hate you for something."

"You got kids?"

"Nah. Just cats."

"Ah."

You have often seen how fast your childless ass loses cred with parents when you start that kind of talk, offering purported wisdom regarding children. Your shoulder twinges and flares. "Dude, listen: I am into *Trek*. I wasn't back in the day. But I discovered it later."

"I was an original fan. Some of my earliest memories are seeing Nimoy's face on a little black & white set, and the animated series on Saturday morning. I fantasized about beaming out of here, or settling for a shuttle craft swooping down to pick me up."

He shows you a variety of Trek insignia and spaceship scenes within the Ray Bradbury-worthy panels and patterns of colorful artwork adorning his muscular arms, bare against the chill of a cool morning. "We could've had all kinds of stuff to talk about. If I had been into it then."

"Too bad. I coulda used another Trekker friend."

This feels sad to Cecil, or so you can tell from eyes gone hooded.

Button spends time on your walks out by the river talking consciousness and vibrations and auras and attuning the old insect antennae, so much that you've begun paying attention to other people's energy. Exploring in the moment how it affects yours—and seeing how you affect them. Generating a vibration of affection and gratitude whenever you see Trudy, for instance, the polar opposite of the resentment bestowed upon her when you'd first returned.

Button even got you to literally—like; literally, dude—hug a tree out there on the trail. Press your tender shoulder into the wood, she said. "Close your eyes, and meditate on the thought of this marvelous, complex being's energy becoming available to you. Healing energy. Wise, old energy."

You did it, but became self-conscious. But later, had to admit that the injury felt the best it had since Samson's caning. She goaded you into asking the tree for its help in fixing your injured clavicle. And it had worked.

Bullcrud.

And yet, you feel better.

In any case you remain thankful to Button, to whom you've grown close, and at whom you gaze, occupying her pop-up tent over on the green and with her fan club of the three doofuses, as you think of the oddballs she has attracted. Newbie seems like a garden variety dumbass, Howdy Shull's crazy and restless, but the kid, the big blonde kid, you don't know his story at all. And you wonder. Two tons of weird, that teenager. Not to be mean. Maybe he's on the autistic spectrum. Didn't smell good, though. Mildewy. Unclean. Greasy skin, blackheads, pimples. Newbie should pick up the garden hose and wash the stink off his friend.

But forget all that: Cecil has impressed the living mud out of you.

You tell him so, explaining that not only are you in agreement about friendship and the ideas for the future of the town, but you're extra pleased and surprised to see a progressive and hip small business concern right here on the green like tattooing and piercing, because who'd a thunk it; Cecil says, well, they always let your granddaddy have his honkytonk, and in a time when a lot of little conservative towns made sure such trade was kept under wraps. Under the radar, as a pilot would put it.

"What the bluehairs would call decorum, it don't pay no tax rolls. Not these days. Nobody blinked an eye when I said, I'm gonna rent these two empty spaces and turn this side of downtown into body-art row."

"In times like these, when the job creator comes calling, you let them create."

"They won't say no to such investment. That's for sure." He lowered his gruff big-boy's growl, sounding more like the old adolescent bullying Cecil. "They don't say no to under-the-table offerings, neither. Or the right people don't, anyway."

You slap your thigh. "No sir, them rascals don't."

You recall with disgust the venality of many municipal officials with whom you've dealt during the years of your entrepreneurship, in particular while as president of the old Downtown Business Alliance, back in the days when you had time for such civic minded foolishness. Once done playing that role, you wanted a good long shower. Said, I'll never do neighborhood politics again.

But you will. A turning of the wheel of fate. You are a business owner in this town, a legacy one. And will enjoy all the say in matters you deserve; all the influence money will buy.

Cecil chews on his lower lip. "So listen: My daddy always said The Dixiana was a front."

"A front?"

"I was just wondering."

"It might've been. You're talking about the VIP rooms upstairs, right?"

"I reckon. I never knew nothing about it. Just telling you what he said."

"It's barbecue and hot dogs and honkytonkin', beau. Far as I ever knew. But in the old days, I've heard tell it was a real center of power."

"The VIP rooms, you mean."

A shrug. "You tell me. That was before my time."

Thoughts of power centers make your wheels turn, and in a way you're not sure you desire. The Dixiana might stay around after all? But if you are to remain in Edgewater County, stuff is gonna change, dudes and dudettes. Now that Button has empowered you with her co-creating reality talk, you toy with the idea of creating for them all a new reality indeed, one that'll stick like peanut butter to everybody's ribs. Stick, and stay stuck. This, your gift to them. Your Better Way.

Sitting beside you looking like some kind of musclebound bouncer—or worse, an aging strong-arm goon working for Jez Rembert—Cecil tells you the best piece of business advice he ever got, what had started him down this path. It had come from a barber who cut heads at Carolina Military Institute in Charleston. Cecil had gone there to play ball, at least until he dropped out, he said, over the hazing and abuse.

"I had it in my head the team got a free ride. Nope."

"Like skating through the classes?"

"And the other stuff, too. But this barber, his name was Stecchini, like a pasta dish on a menu, said, 'Kid, I got into this business for one reason: you learn to cut heads, you got yourself a marketable skill no matter where you go in the entire world. Job security. Don't pass it up'."

"I'd buy that for a dollar."

"Right. So—not that it matters, but I left campus not only over getting razzed by a bunch of dickheads on some power trip. I also hurt my knee. My football days ended all in one afternoon. Roy Earl—it was the first scrimmage, beau."

"Damn."

"No way I was gonna put myself through all the military crap if I couldn't play football. It wasn't a week after that haircut I came home. Got my knee fixed." He held out his hands. "And here we is."

"I hear ya. Dang."

"A god-durn scrimmage. Your life can change in a minute."

"Don't I know it."

You tell him, well, he had plenty of epic games in high school, which you don't know at all, but assume can get away with saying. You had hated football until you got to Southeastern, and in a fit of school spirit your burgeoning love of all things Redtails had swept over you. Still hadn't made you feel affection for the mural on The Dixiana back home.

"I sure did. Me and Harlem both did. But it didn't turn into nothing."

"Unlike a different sort of Head Trauma, which is thriving."

"And I'm personally happy, too. That's the main thing. I got a good trade going. Maybe if I hadn't blown out my knee that day? Who knows. I'd have gone into a career army track, if I'd stayed at CMI."

"Probably."

"I would've graduated right in time for Desert Storm. And god only knows where I'd be now."

"It might've all led to this same end."

"Doubt it. I'd've been a different person after serving in the military. Being at CMI, even as short a time as it was, made me realize it wasn't for me."

"The discipline?"

"I didn't think much about the possibility of having to shoot people one day."

"Heard that."

You feel solidarity with your old nemesis that you ask the one question that's been on your mind about this salon-tattoo-piercing endeavor. "Ever thought about franchising this puppy? You could make a shit-ton of money in a college neighborhood like the Old Market..."

"It's been talked about."

"Good on that."

"But you know, it was kind of a gold rush with body art. Lot of competition. Must be four or five salons there already."

"Maybe so, beau. Maybe so."

Listen to your patois, your phrasing. *I have returned to walk among them; I am one.*

In the past, the old Halsey's Barber and Shave and Miss Rachel's Hair and Beauty Salon had been twin centers of social interaction in the town, where the ELMS and all the other old ladies like Letty and Flora Mae Harkin and Mama Runelle herself went, in her case usually on Wednesdays. Often in the summer you'd ride into town with her and hang around the green, wander, sit in front of The Dixiana with your granddaddy and Uncle Burnie, which Mama Runelle didn't want you doing too often, not with it being a place of alcohol purveyance. She had a conniption when you turned twelve and Rabbit started you doing what would one day be Newbie's job. Bawled over her grandbaby going off to work, your smothering grandmother did.

Thing was: Granddaddy might have run a honkytonk, but your grandmother never allowed a drop of booze in that ramshackle house crammed with music memorabilia and records and pictures of Mee-maw in her singer outfit, the ruffles and skirts showing her knees, the sparkling white cowboy hat that still hung off her big dresser in their bedroom, the classic movie star gloss of her soft-focus, 'Dixiana Darling' B&W headshot.

Childhood—the hair salon, and Mr. Halsey's, and Cecil giving you a wedgie out on the field during the horrible first official little league game, which you'd forever resent no matter the level of his adult business acumen. The years, falling away...

◉⊕✸

RIGHT, SEE: YOUR HISTORY WITH CECIL WAUGH GOES FARTHER BACK THAN HIGH school, such as during that awful season of your eleventh year playing Dixie Youth League baseball.

In a humiliating scene at Mr. Halsey's barbershop, the team's Coach had suggested to Rabbit and Uncle Burnie that you sign up to help 'get some of that baby fat off'n you.' The old men, including that cigarette-sucking, yellowed, cadaverous old fart Halsey himself, had agreed with vigor and aplomb.

Worst part? They were right. You needed exercise.

"Put him out on the baseball diamond with the coach," to murmuring and assent. "That'll make a man out of him."

Sherm Wrightson, looking duly burdened, yet willing. With several returning players, Gray-Peel would field a strong team, all agreed, with room to expand the bench for a few new players. Including you.

A horrifying thought.

Gray-Peele was what everyone called the last operating textile mill in the county, the name of a corporation that bought it and the smaller hosiery mill, the one that closed the next year and would presage the sale of the Gray-Peele corporate parent a few years later during senior year. They moved operations overseas to Vietnam, of all places. And while you heard Gray-Peele coming out of everyone's mouth forever, from your earliest days of your grandparents talking about the mill's owners, the words resonated now as they sounded then:

Grape Eel.

Hey, as you remember thinking: The Gray-Peele Grape Eels. That's what the name of your baseball team ought to've been. You snickered and wished you could share this silliness with others, but every time you go to open your mouth and say something in your little Roy Earl Pettus fatboy voice, nobody acted as if they'd heard you.

Mr. Halsey, smoke curling up to his eyes while he snipped away at Harold Hampton, Hill's daddy and the founder of Hampton Motors: "Get Sherm to put your grandbaby on first base. That'll sweat the weight right off."

"That it will." Sherm, a malevolent grin. "After Coach Wrightson's baseball boot camp, you'll walk out a new man, Roy Earl."

You liked the sound of the weight coming off. While your body hadn't caught up, your mind had already fixated on girls, but you didn't know why, nor what you'd do if you had one. That week your eye had been on Shelby Fordham, at least when it wasn't Natasha Prothro. You tingled as you pictured their faces, one angelic and blonde, the other dark complexioned and almond shaped. You throbbed with desire, even if you didn't have a clue what you ached to do with them.

Shelby, though. Flavor of the week. You tried to hold onto her imagined face. Make her corporeal. Make your simulated mental Shelby say the words:

I like you, Roy Earl. Will you go with me?

Will you GO with me?

Will you go WITH me?

Go with me. What everyone called it when a couple became boyfriend-girlfriend.

You thought about 'going with' Shelby, and it made you tingle to the point of mysterious physical discomfort. The idea of romance, however, no more real than the comics, or *Logan's Run*, or *Star Trek*, or G. I. Joe, which you had pulled out of your old toy box only the week before, thinking, how jazzed you used to feel when you played with them—these were the old style, twelve inches tall with poseable, kung-fu grip. But the dolls seemed stiff and lifeless, not comforting at all. Felt like junk. The trash of childhood. Detritus.

Shelby.

G. I. Joe.

Caught between sensations—the comfort of familiar play; the promise of damp mysterious love—you felt adrift.

You wanted to walk the pecan orchard and hear Letty Glasscock's pugs yipping.

You wanted to sit under a tree and read.

And you wanted Shelby to sit beside you. But she already had a boyfriend. Who wasn't fat.

In other words: Fat chance.

TAKE A LOAD OFF, FANNY: WHY THE WEIGHT ISSUE?

Because Mama Runelle had been the kind of mother to you, or more to the point, grandmother, who fed and stuffed and pampered. And at eleven, there'd been no growth spurt. Not yet.

In those days? You were round as a pumpkin. Plump seemed your curse.

No, you would not enjoy a growth spurt for two, almost three more years. An eternity, watching the rest get hair on their dicks. At least yours came in, finally, by the time of high school gym class in ninth grade. At least. You never did get quite as tall as you'd like. Alas.

In fact, the first day your grandmother sent you off to play baseball, you were given a packet of Reese's Cups you shoved into a back pocket. When you tried to eat them later, on the ride home from the initial practice, your snack had melted into a liquified, sticky mess all over your hands.

A new 1980 Chevrolet K-30 Crew Cab Fleetside Big Dooley with a boat hitch driven by the coach had come by to collect you. Awkward, you climbed into the back with a few older boys who lived further out on River Ridge Road. Coach Wrightson, compared to his stern but cordial demeanor at Mr. Halsey's, came off like a humorless prick, an ex-military man with the high and tight haircut, no stranger to that barbershop where this nightmare began.

"Look—Roy Earl's eating shit outta his pockets." Yep. Cecil Waugh, shouting in the back of that truck. "God-dog, beau."

Timmy Latham, lean the way all the veteran players were, and with clear blue eyes all the girls loved. "Smile, boy—show us that shit-eating grin of your'n."

Deep-voiced Marlon Ketcham, a black boy who seemed older than everyone else, added in a laconic drawl, "No wonder he fat. As a little pink pig."

Guffaws; a knee-slapper. "Little pink pig," they chanted. "*Little pink pig.*"

The practice had sucked. You'd made a near-fool out of yourself but at least hadn't been the only one, and now had to sit bumping in the coach's Big Dooley with Reese's Cups on your hands, and nothing to do but lick. You didn't want to wipe your hands on your jeans, which you should not have worn because of the heat. But because of how chubby your legs looked, squat and short, shorts had been out of the question.

The older boys almost fell out of the truck bed when you began licking your fingers, making an even bigger mess. They exploded with laughter, bouncing off one another and shouting and slapping five.

"The boy's a little shiteater," Marlon drawled. "God-dog."

"*Little shiteater! Little shiteater!*" A new chant. "Haw! Haw!"

The Coach called out from the beer window that we better calm our narrow asses down. "Way too early in the season for all this horseplay. Save it up for next practice."

After you hopped down at the end of your rural dirt-road driveway with its welcoming crepe myrtles, Timmy Latham leaned over. Didn't seem as mean.

"Hey, chubster—don't bring candy to practice."

"My grandmother—" I felt desperate to explain. "I won't."

"Candy's for babies and sissies." The rest of the boys still chortling, the truck pulled away. "But baseball's for men."

"Damn right," Marlon Ketcham called out. "Ain't no little boys out on dat field."

No wonder they taunted you so—you looked and acted like the overgrown baby you were. You had never perceived this in such an acute manner. The smell of the chocolate caked around your fingernails made you want to vomit.

◎①❉

As far as practice itself went, you'd done all right tossing a baseball to the other fat kid, Stoney Marchant, who wasn't so much corpulent as simply big all over. Square head, trunklike legs and arms protruding from a stump of a body. He couldn't throw any better than you. Winded and staggering, you were the last players to finish the laps around the field.

Your lungs felt as though they were searing in your chest. That you'd die.

When you all had started the cool-down run, you'd thought Wrightson meant running the bases. But when the leaders had sprinted along the foul line toward the back fence, you knew you were in trouble. You ran as little as possible, not even in the pecan orchard, where you were more liable to sit under a tree reading an Ian Fleming 007 novel, or maybe one of the Michael Moorcock fantasy adventures you enjoyed, Elric and his Black Blade. Your Mee-maw, always scurrying in behind you and worrying about the potential for misfortune. Her doting concern had made you want to sit still rather than move around too much, which seemed to please her.

Those orderly trees between the Pettus and Glasscock properties, how to this day they represent comfort. But the key word? Order. Compared to the gnarly hardwood copses and pine barrens all around, the pecan orchard seemed as though a sublime cosmic order had been given unto it, made it manageable and observable with clarity, describable with concision; here, you thought, was intelligent design you could get behind. It didn't take long to count how many trees there were, an odd number, thirty seven, because of the drop off in the corner of the property where the land began sloping down to the riverside glade of trees where you would camp with your pals a couple of summers later. Mr. Glasscock said they used to graze sheep back in there.

That's where you belonged—in the orchard, or the woods. Not on the diamond, forced into this awkward social construct like Cecil's brief career as a military school plebe. But you couldn't bail. Your granddaddy would never let you forget it. "A quitter never wins, and a winner never quits." One of his sayings.

Baseball seemed threatening, the first extracurricular activity you'd tried that took you away from the abandon of your lonely afternoons out on your grandparents' land, wandering and doing as you would. This Dixie Youth League represented a different structure and routine, one essentially fascistic in contrast to the prior freedom of your childhood. You didn't want to be all the way on the other side of Tillman Falls at the county rec center, dusty and hot and flat and surrounded by pine trees, near the airfield into which you'd fly one day many years later. Knowing you had to attend all these practices and appear at the games felt oppressive. Wanted nothing to do with it. If your reputation among the men at the barber shop weren't involved, you would walk in a heartbeat. Your sweet worrisome Mama Runelle would let you quit if you asked, but at hazard of forfeiting whatever maturity capital you'd accumulated by agreeing to participate. Trapped.

◎◍✳

THE NEXT DAY WHEN SHE TRIED TO GIVE YOU A SNACK BEFORE PRACTICE, YOU yelled NO and said it would get you in trouble. This time, a handful of miniature Three Musketeers, another favorite, whipped confectionary inside a delicate milk chocolate shell, the gourmet candy bar. If you weren't careful, on some afternoons you would sit on that living room rug, lost and staring at the tube, eating candy bars until you felt sick.

"Well darling! Why don't you want your candy-wandy?"

"Cause I'm gonna go play baseball. Candy's for little babies and girls."

"Oh, p'shaw." How she'd smashed them into your hands and put on her mean-mama voice, all harsh and hateful, like she sometimes would when you went against her. "You hush up with your god-durn silliness and take them candy bars."

Before the truck came you took time to shove the miniature candy bars into the ivy covering the brick mailbox, tendrils trailing up and mingling with the kudzu that'd taken over up and down that part of winding, canopy-shaded River Ridge Road. You would retrieve them afterwards. A reward, but enjoyed in privacy. You would show her the wrappers. That you had done as she wished.

Everybody in the truck bed this time sat subdued. The whole ride over to the ball fields you kept waiting for one of the older boys to say some smarty-pants crap about the Reese's Cups. But they didn't.

This time the Coach picked up two more boys, younger like you but neither one fat, and drove on the new bypass where your uncle Burnie said he heard they were thinking about putting a Kentucky Fried.

At the complex of ball fields alive with other teams already at practice, your crew exited the truck from the lowered tailgate, hopping down by twos. Pain flared in your tender ankles as you hit the ground.

Timmy Latham broached the subject. "You ain't got no Reecie-cups today?"

"Nope."

"'No, sir'."

"I ain't got to call you sir."

"Yeah you do, beau. I been playing Dixie Youth for three years now. Next year, you can make the new dudes call you sir. It's just how it works. It ain't an insult to you."

"Oh. Okay. Sir."

But you didn't like this. He was just a kid, too. Sir was for the Coach.

Timmy asked what position you thought you'd like to play. You recalled what Mr. Halsey said. "First base...?"

"Coach, guys—c'mere. You gotta hear this."

Stomach, dropping into your cleats like an overloaded freight elevator, its twisted steel cables unraveling and flaying off bits of shredded, sparking, gouging metal. Why had you said that nonsense? First base? You could barely catch or throw. Hell—you didn't have a blessed clue yet about the responsibilities of playing first base meant, not on any substantive level, only the place on the field where you'd stand. Close to the dugout. You liked that. Duck in and out before anyone could note your roly-poly body, your pink cheeks. See you as a pudgy baby compared to the lean older boys like Dickie Giuffrida, the pitcher, with his black curly hair and dark eyes and olive skin.

Dickie came from somewhere else, not Edgewater County—his family was so Italian that they seemed exotic, different. Dickie's uncle was a big engineer at the Sugeree Station, and Dickie's dad owned a heating and air company. They had blue and green vans you would see around the county. JIFFY Comfort Services. A good name.

The nuclear plant brought in families from other places, including interesting new girls like Devin's eventual girlfriend Libby Meade, who would appear at the beginning of ninth grade and capture hearts with her gamine charm and sexy intelligence—your heart, Dobbs's, Devin's. And yet you never admitted to this to anyone. Before long she and Devin had fallen in love anyway, remaining so until the day Libby died while y'all were in college, in the same car wreck that had paralyzed Dobbs. Besides, when Devin's sister Chelsea had come of coltish and freckled age—her father called her Creedence because of her initials, CCR—you'd never really wanted another woman again. That you had gained her confidence and love, ultimately, still seemed a dream come true. A fondest wish, realized.

You stood staring down at the cleats as The Coach, Timmy, Dickie, a couple of others ambled over to see about little mister first base, as you heard the gruff-voiced adult saying.

"Now you boys gather round here and settle down and shut them pie holes before you attract any more horseflies than's already out today." He wiped sweat from his brow and replaced his COACH ball cap, emerald green with a white mesh back. "I want you to look over here at Rickie Lee Pettus standing here. Now, he don't seem like much, does he?"

Somebody in the crowd of boys started singing: "*The Candyman can, oh yes the candyman can...*" Shrieks and gales of laughter.

"Hush up, shavetails." The Coach, gruff, not kidding around. Mean enough to whip some kid's ass for real. "This ain't no game."

"Since when is baseball not a—"

"SHUT YOUR FREAKING PIE HOLES. AND I MEAN FIVE SECONDS AGO."

Everyone settled. All eyes on the Coach. Arms folded. Gum popping. Someone belched. Another farted. This had turned into some war movie, the boot camp sequence. Hazing, like Cecil himself would endure later at Carolina Military Institute. Spirit-shattering.

Cecil Waugh, whose twelve-year-old body looked like that of Bluto from the old Popeye cartoons, sucked back snot and hocked it in your direction, a tumbling oblong glob of ropy mucus that landed inches from your cleats and rolled in the dust like a worm. Cecil's voice had already deepened. He seemed eighteen, not thirteen. "Whatcha want us to do with him, Coach. What'd Reecie Cup do this time."

"He didn't do nothing, Waugh. Just keep your traps shut and lemme finish my durn thought. Now, Pettus: tell the rest of these boys what you told Latham."

You don't want to. You shake your head.

"Go on—this is important. Don't be afraid, son."

You felt like peeing yourself; like an idiot standing there in your jeans with sweat trickling down your fat legs, and wearing the pastel printed tie-dye T-shirt Mama Runelle bought at the K-Mart in Dentsville. The shirt, a shade of pink, was what you would see years later in a catalog at an embroidery company as you selected fabrics and color schemes for the Spotted Banana polo shirts and visors you settled on for the chain-wide uniform, back when you were about to go to your third of three smoothie stands. Colorwash, as that style of tie-dye is designated. Simple. The pink ones looked girly. Like that old shirt. The sight of the colorwash choices in the catalog had made the humiliation come rushing back. Had made your scrotum retract.

In a high, tiny wheeze: "I told him I wanted to play first base."

The boys hooted and hollered, pelted you with gloves and hats. Someone whipped a ball that hit you in the stomach.

You fell to the ground, but soon felt the Coach's strong, leathery hands lifting you to your cleats.

"Get back, you animals."

Trying not to boo-hoo, you stood in silence at the center of their judgmental circle. Their snickering settled.

Sherm Wrightson put his hands on your shoulders. "Rickie, let me explain what's happened here today: You've made me the happiest goddurn Dixie Youth league coach in the county. You know how? By pledging that you want to shoot for first base, one of the most important positions on the field of play. Isn't that so, Timmy?"

"That it is, coach."

"In any case, that's the spirit; that's spark." He spun you around to face him. "Now boy, lemme shoot straight with you: ain't a chance in Hades of you playing first base this year, not with these veteran Dixie Youth all-stars standing here looking lean and mean and seasoned. But here's my point. You set the bar high. You showed ambition and drive. You may not know how to throw or catch or bat worth a toot yet, but today you say you want to go for first base. Today you showed gumption. You showed COURAGE, by god.

"Fellas," he continued, solemn, with tanned sinewy arms placed akimbo and the sun glinting off a stainless steel Seiko diver's watch. "I don't know what Pettus can do yet. What kind of player he'll make. Hell, he don't either. None of us do."

"I got me an idea, and it ain't pretty," Cecil had drawled to titters and threats of censure from the coach, who continued:

"But with an attitude like his—grabbing for that brass ring on his first swing-around; mercy—this young man, overweight as he may be right now, will go far in life." The coach smacked you on your pink, tie-dyed shoulder so hard it hurt. "Money. Women. You all wait and see."

The troops responded with a wave of positivity. "Hells yeah," Marlon said.

"That sound good to you, Pettus?"

"Yes, sir."

"'Yes, sir'," you heard someone mock, high like a girl. Giggles and snickers.

Coach slapped his hands together, loud like a gunshot. "Now if the rest of you little curlicues are done jerking each other off, grab your gear and go limber up. Stretch. Throw. Get them elbows and shoulders and wrists loosened up. And then? We're gonna hit baseballs for the rest of the afternoon, because without hits there's no wins. Gonna knock the cowhide off them things. So, good on you, Rickie Pettus, future first baseman—or who knows what." He clapped his hands together, breaking what had settled into a trancelike state among the team. "Anything he can imagine himself to be."

The other first-year players regarded you with suspicion, but also grudging respect. You didn't know what to think. You were still shaking. Only later would you realize what a compliment he gave you, that Coach.

On the walk to the field Cecil had whispered in your ear, "There ain't never been a first baseman alive that fat. You better lay off them valentine's chocolates your boyfriend sends you, princess."

◉①✳

SHAKING AND TERRIFIED, YOU TOOK YOUR TURN AT BATTER-UP. AS THE COACH desired, the other boys, Cecil Waugh in particular, had already pummeled the metaphorical covers off the baseballs. Launched baseballs from the tips of their aluminum and wooden bats like Apollo rockets, or perhaps ICBMs bound for hardened targets deep inside Soviet Russia. The only question? How foolish you will look.

The Coach himself pitches, and to you and the other novices he throws pretty easy. Underhand, even.

"You ready, Pettus?"

You nod, the plastic safety helmet rubbing on your shorn scalp.

"C'mon, Reecie Cup," a voice calls out. Another hollers, "Swing batter swing!"

The Coach, cussing, comes out of his stance and calls for quiet. Not only was he about to pitch, but you were ready, dang it.

"We trying to get him set for what it like on the field," Marlon said. "Ain't this practice?"

"For now, I want y'all to keep them traps shut while I pitch to this batter. If you please, ladies."

"*Oooh.*" Dickie, in a mocking falsetto. "Coach's pissed."

"Secure that crapola, Giuffrida. This boy showed pluck. Give him a chance. And you best quit calling him Reecie Cup—that makes him sound like what in the service we used to call a twinkletoes." Lowering his voice. "Y'all know what a twinkletoes is? No? You better hope you don't find out. Now—" He dropped back into his pitcher stance. "We'll give you a better nickname, boy. Frecklehead."

Everybody went haw-haw. Your face blazed scarlet and hot.

"Look at his cheeks, Coach—more like Freckle-red."

"Freckle-red. That's a first baseman's name. A first baseman that can hit, though—?"

He pitched, sudden and unexpected. Underhand, granted, but still fast.

The ball, a blur, zipped by so fast you couldn't blink; you swung anyway, but way too late.

Haw haw haw, they all laughed.

No no no, the Coach admonished them. "Not fair. Now, get yourself ready."

You did. Took a deep breath. "Yessir."

"Keep that eye on the ball."

"Yessir."

"Ready?"

"Yes-sir."

As during ninety percent of your public and social life, you now had to pee. To squeeze out that Mountain Dew Mee-maw had made you drink with your lunch.

The Coach flung the ball a touch slower. Excited, you swung early this time, stepping into the pitch with your body, which bounced off your jiggling stomach. *Whap!*

More laughter.

You stagger back. It stung. "Ow-ow-ow."

"All right now—toughen up, Rickie."

You get mad. "It's Roy Earl," but your voice breaks and they all laugh harder. "Not Rickie Lee."

"Get back up there, Freckle-red. You gonna show us how all that weight can get behind a ball and smack it."

Your stomach hurt. Your eyes burned. But this time, he tossed it easy. A sensation swept through you like warmth instead of cold humiliation, and durn if you didn't swing and connect with the ball the way you knew you could, the way you did when it was only Dobbs or Devin or Pa-paw pitching in the back yard.

Smack. Connecting witt the pitch! The shock traveling down your arms!

The ball became a dingy white comet sailing out over the shortstop's head, who did a ridiculous long-limbed leap for it despite being way too high. As everybody laughed at him instead of you, the ball bounced sharp and low into the far center left, forcing the two outfielders to scramble and bump into each other.

"Good! Good!" The Coach shouted, joyful. "Y'all didn't think this little fat turd could do nothing. And he stood right there and showed every one of you what a base hit looks like. *His first time at bat.*"

You looked to Timmy Latham. He nodded, gave you a thumb's up. Nudged Dickie, who caught on and did the same. "Good job, shavetail. Batta-up?"

"Cake batter," Cecil Waugh called out.

"Chocolate cake with peanut butter icing," Marlon drawled. "Right on."

Big laughs all around.

Crap. Your moment, stolen by fresh humiliation.

"SHUT THE FREAK UP!"

A harsh shriek that echoed across the field. Coach spat into the dirt. Walked around. Quiet. Made hard eye contact. Boy, there wasn't anybody laughing now. "So you little pukes keep on poking fun at him. By the time he's your age, mister star pitcher," thrusting a finger into Dickie Giuffrida's chest, "he'll own this team. A solid base hit. In his first five minutes. He's gonna make every one of you little smart-mouth SOBs who doubted him eat that laughter."

Dickie looked uncertain, unnerved as the Coach stalked the batter's box like one of those army sergeants in movies, frightening the humanity out of boys with their heads shorn. Like your own flattop, the cut Pa-paw always insisted you get, at least until you refused in the summer of your thirteenth year.

"Good job, Pettus. Go out to right field. Nuh-ext-uh!" he called out.

You trotted, gratefully, tossing the bat aside like Reggie Jackson after a World Series homer, everyone in the stadium cheering. As you ran by him, Timmy Latham smacked you on the bottom.

Glorious.

Fleeting; all downhill.

◉①✳

The first game came on a Friday night, hot as blazes outside compared to the earliest practices. Your Pa-paw said it felt like one of those seasons without a spring, one of those quick transitions to muggy summer weather like you get in Edgewater County: some years it seemed to go straight from the cool, clean air of late winter to Carolina swamp-soup, humid and swarming with gnats and mosquitos.

The Grape Eels, as you wish you were called, played against formidable Sykes Electronics, your Uncle Burnie's team. He'd said he didn't want you playing for him, because as Coach, someone could see it as nepotism. Since y'all were family, and all.

So far this Coach Wrightson had been good to you. What was different? With him, encouragement. Everyone else treated you like an infant. That would change by the time Uncle Burnie let you do crazy crap like drive a car back from an auction at thirteen, far from having your driver's license. At the time of the baseball debacle, though, he babied you like all the other adults.

Forget the heat-related discomfort: your team's biggest problem, besides you and two other inept and youthful members who couldn't play worth a crap, came as a frustrating development called 'delayed uniforms from the screen printer.' Your color scheme, green and yellow; the Gray-Peele logo an athletic swoosh. A real team. A few of the guys had shirts from previous seasons. But not you, nor any of the other baby-faced newcomers.

S-O-L on the jerseys, the Coach said. "Some of you guys'll have to play in your street clothes. Hate it, but ain't nothing we can do."

NO NO NO—not with *you wearing the pink shirt.*

Again.

But you knew if you went in a drawer to put on a different choice, Mee-maw would stand and ask what was wrong with the one she'd laid out, and you didn't want to defend your decision because she'd give you further grief over your defense. You had too much on your mind. And, a rad and boss team jersey awaited you, anyway.

Thanks to G. I. Joe and *Star Trek* you coveted and admired uniforms; you revered the Southeastern Redtails football colors, but sometimes you pulled for Foothills State to annoy your granddaddy; their colors were a vibrant orange and turquoise as though Howard Johnson himself coached the squad.

The Dixie Youth League uniform—you had been so filled with anticipation, couldn't wait to slip on that jersey and feel a partner in this group of athletes. You'd never been a member of a team. Or crew on a starship. Been anyone of consequence, not even expendable, red-shirt security standing tall by the turbolift on the bridge of the Enterprise. Underhanded pitch or not, though, you already had yourself a base hit. You'd earned the right to wear the uniform.

But the jerseys still hadn't arrived. Crushing. It would get worse.

◎◍❋

"Pettus—I got a surprise for you."

Maybe he had tucked away an extra uniform. "What is it?"

"I'm starting you tonight."

"You are?"

"Right smack out in center field. I know it ain't first base. But center's important."

Nodding with terror. Hoping it didn't show.

"Up to the task?"

"I can do it." But not believing you could.

"Damn straight you can."

His square jaw bulging with a thick plug of chaw and juice dribbling from the corner of his mouth, he yelled for the team all stretching and tossing balls in warm-up mode to gather round. "Take a page, ladies. Boy's got spunk —*Freckle-red's a young man to emulate.* All you turds could do was make fun of him. But now? He's a starter. And if I was him, I'd whip anybody's ass who had anything smart to say about it."

The boys, downhearted and shuffling their cleats, didn't seem to know how to take this coaching.

In a revelatory flash, Wrightson seemed to realize how mean he sounded. "Fellas—look here. I'm sorry. I got issues outside of work, so to speak. But that's above your pay-grade, as we say in the military. Now, let's go play ball."

Later, you'd hear about how the Coach and his wife split up. How he lived in an apartment, that first crappy particleboard complex they built by the Chilton freeway exit. His personal problems had been creepy, incomprehensible grownup stuff. Hazy and indistinct as the real pitches whizzing by your nose at bat. Now? You understand his pain. Big-time.

TRIAL BY FIRE: ONE OF THE FIRST BALLS HIT—OR CLOBBERED, RATHER—WAS BY AN ape-like Sykes Electronics player who, like Marlon and Cecil, looked way too old to be playing Dixie Youth ball. The hit had been driven hard, though not high, over pitcher Dickie's head. Surprised, he pirouetted in the air like a figure skater. The error showed on his stricken face. Especially when he saw the ball heading your way, angling down hard into the grass and scooting by the second baseman, who also leapt at it and missed. Bouncing, rolling into center field.

But instead of dropping down behind the glove like the Coach drilled into the team—into you, too, Ricky Lee Pettus, so you won't miss the catch—you squatted as though taking a dump rather than planting the all-important knee. The ball sneaked between your legs. It seemed to pass *through* your glove. The ghost of a scuffed baseball—there, and then not.

A collective groan—from your team, the spectators, all the guys from other teams hanging around the fence, watching and catcalling.

You weeble-wobbled after the ball, snatching it up in time to see the batter hauling ass around second and your pitcher's screaming, the ball the ball the ball, throw it Pettus, and you see the big ape rounding third by now and you go to throw to Dickie, a pitiful little boy's toss so weak it doesn't make it anywhere near him, falls short and bounces and rolls. Snatching it up and cussing at you, Dickie whirls around and flings it home, but the ape has already slid in for the run. Humiliation after humiliation. All you could do not to piss yourself. You had forgotten to make water before the game.

But at least it's the only run the team gives up that first round as Dickie, so mad at you he could spit, smokes the next three batters. As the team trots toward the dugout, he receives a huge round of applause from spectators and Coach Wrightson.

As you went jogging and jiggling right by a group of cute young girls hanging on the fence, Cecil Waugh runs up beside you and reaches into the back of your pants and grabs the hem of your panties, pulling them up hard in a wedgie, causing you to scream with pain and fall down.

Grabbing you by the shoulder, he jerked you onto your cleats. Cecil's corn-chip breath, hot on your ear and neck: "Just imagine that ball's one of them Reecie cups rolling into your mouth, fat boy. Maybe you'll catch it next time."

"Nice pink shirt, butterball," you heard a male voice call out from the stands. You could have sworn it sounded like your granddaddy.

◎◎❋

NONE OF THE GROWNUPS COULD UNDERSTAND WHY YOU WANTED TO BAIL ON baseball. But you did. You ended up boohooing to get your way, and after the next game when you made another error—first time at bat you 'struck out standing,' as in, without attempting to swing, a petrified statue with a stick of wood resting on your chubby shoulder—you were allowed to quit.

Sad. By then you had gotten the uniform, but it was too tight. Your boy-boobs stuck out. You only wore it once, during that second and final game. The pitchers flung the balls so fast they scared you with their power. You cried until you did not have to stand in front of people and have freaking hard baseballs flung at you.

Your grandfather and Burnie, shaking their heads. Sucking their teeth. Old bastards had forced you into this foolishness. "You're getting too big to cry like that," Pa-paw said, and you knew he was right.

◎◎❋

A FEW MONTHS AFTER BASEBALL WAS OVER, YOU AND PA-PAW WALKED OVER FROM The Dixiana to get your haircuts at Mr. Halsey's right as Coach Wrightson came out with his own fresh high-and-tight.

He stopped to say how much he missed you, Roy Earl, finally getting your name correct. That if you wanted to come back next year, he thought first base was possible. That you had loads of potential. How the rest of the team wasn't as strong without you.

You declined.

"Bullcrud," you said to your granddaddy after the Coach departed with his head hanging low at the failure to motivate your adolescent ass. "I wasn't worth a durn."

"Be that as it may, don't never look askance at a second chance. Don't take somebody's generosity for granted. It might not come your way again."

Meanwhile, you hoped there wouldn't be a Dixie Youth League squad sponsored by Gray-Peele anymore, to make sure Pa-paw, Uncle Burnie and Mr. Halsey didn't conspire to shame you into playing. And while a couple more teams were fielded, it wasn't long before they announced that the mill, which had been bought by an even bigger corporation than Gray-Peele, would soon close forever. As would Uncle Burnie's electronics store, in only a few more years, along with most of the other legacy businesses.

Sure enough, your fervent wish came true. Took a while, but with no sponsor, no more Grape Eels in Dixie Youth League. Yours, a powerful will. By then, you had moved on from that humiliation. You had your growth spurt, such as it was. You had your sights on Chesnee Campobello. Another disaster in the making.

❀

"THE TWO OF US HERE," YOU SAY TO CECIL, DONE REMINISCING ABOUT DIXIE Youth and getting up to go talk over the future with Button, "seem to have formed ourselves what you might call an assemblage of stakeholders."

Cecil Waugh gets a look of pleasure. "That's a good way of putting it. Man —we can really use your leadership and experience downtown, Roy Earl. I ain't kidding."

"Oh, I don't bring nothing you don't already got. Look at you. And Manny, too. He got it going on."

"Yes, he does. And I been talking to him, too, about this. Sort of a complementary organization. To the existing. Folks."

"Folks?"

"The ELMS?" He phrases it like, duh? "The Chamber of Commerce, they seem kinda hidebound and inactive, almost. But the ELMS... they can be hard to work with."

A tingle. "You were already thinking along these lines."

Cecil, frowning at your mystical reaction, explains the notion of the two of you, and a few others, starting a merchant's association there in Tillman Falls.

Great minds. Synchronicity. And such.

You get what he's saying. back in 1990s Columbia, when you were a young comer on the Downtown Business Alliance, you'd gone through a similar situation with competing interests attempting to direct the commercial energy around at their whim, beck and call rather than yours: Gasp, but a rival group of merchants comprised of longtime iconoclastic holdouts, complainers and accusers—that the DBA operated like a bush-league local mafia; true enough— attempted to form their own insurgency. The DBA, the most powerful neighborhood advocacy group in the city, you see. The upstarts, the rough trade, the mob gathered outside the gates, they got nowhere. So it all sounded too familiar; but here, like being on the wrong side of the wall.

They're getting their meathooks into you now, boy. Going into battle with the ELMS? Wait—now that he's gone, are you to live out your grandfather's life over again?

Here in Tillman Falls?

Alongside Cecil Waugh, of all people?

You tell him, sure, sure, you'll think about it. You start to say, I want to remake this town, yes, but afterwards fly out of here again, to the mountains this time, yea, and ye shall see this come to pass, but you don't say a peep. You'd sound nuts.

"Let's get over to Manny's one day soon. Slop up some down-home grease."

"I dunno—every time I eat over yonder, I got to lay down for a spell..."

You both roar and pat your solid overfed bellies, yours growing by the day from such meals as you've proposed eating yet again.

How times have changed; how nothing has changed. It's how you feel farting around in the woods down beside the Sugeree, walking with Button in the cool early morning. Like old times wandering the pecan orchard, paperback book in hand. The worst wasn't being back in Edgewater County, of course. It was the part about being lonesome Roy, with everything going for him but the love of a good and true and sweet woman.

Painful. You now find yourself wondering if it wouldn't be better to have never known the sensation of grasping that brass ring in your tenuous grip.

◎◉✳

"So look." Cecil, acting squirrelly and gripping his hands together, but keeping a big smile on his face. "I've had. Anger issues. Throughout my life."

"Welcome to my world."

"I appreciate that. I do. But part of what I've been working on, and this sounds like some 12-step alkie stuff, which I'm not—thank god."

"Word to that."

"But my journey still includes making amends to folks. Not to right wrongs, but sort of wipe my own chalkboard clean. Because stuff from the past, it weighs you down. And doesn't matter, really. But sometimes—you have to make it not matter." He seems frustrated. "Am I making sense?"

You reassure him he is; in his uncertainty, he reminds you of an earlier you, one less cocksure, less successful, and more like your old fat childhood self than your modern incarnation as the sleek and evolved modern man of commerce as here presents. "Beau? I know of what ye speak."

He nods, curt and serious. "And so: I wanna say how sorry I am. For the way I carried on. Back in the day."

"Like you said; the past is dead."

Left-field: "You know what my higher power is?"

Girding yourself. Visions of the old-timey street preachers. "What's that."

"The power of now. Right now."

How Buttonesque.

You conclude with an 'it's-all-good, brother' followed by man-hugs, but of course your mind races back through myriad instances of bullying and cruelty like the *Blues Brothers* shaming you experienced in the Palmetto Grande back in 1980, which at the time you had blamed not on the Waugh boys, but on your own family. On your granddaddy. "It's not anything I've carried with me. Everybody gets picked on. At one time or another."

"But they shouldn't. And I wish I knew what'd made me that way—hell. It was Daddy. Daddy was wicked to us, Roy Earl." He says this raw and rushed. Some awful family secret. "Me and Harlem, we were giving as good as we got. Unfortunately."

You pray he won't fully divulge. You don't need to know. Bad enough you suspect an abusive figure in Trudy's past, at least from subtext she said that only hit you much later. Best you can come up with: "At least it's all behind you."

You're in luck; he doesn't elaborate.

Instead, it's a fresh man-hug, with both praising a healthy, happy and healing morning here on the quiet green in Tillman Falls. You slap skin under the light of the sun and the moon, celestial objects hanging in the sky like symbolic cosmology governing everyone's by contrast ant-like personal realities.

You stand awed by the sight, and give thanks not to God nor the universe but Button: for teaching you to slow down and notice such everyday but amazing sights, to quiet the mind, and to experience life on terms as you suggested to Cecil, who's already learned on his own that the only time is now.

CREEDENCE

Two months of sobriety—it had turned her into a coffee fiend. But in a good way.

A professional way.

Her days now spent working at the Beanery, she rose before dawn to bake scones, make biscuit dough, frost muffins. Attending a noon meeting instead of eating lunch. Coming back to work through the afternoon, past suppertime. Since she'd begun making the kitty cat morning feeding at four-thirty thus giving her time to get the Beanery fired up by five, she paid Maggie the petsitter to continue coming to feed the brood in late afternoon. Working fourteen-hour days, she both left home and returned in darkness, darkness; Creedence rued the winter ahead. Her alcoholic blood, running thin against the cooling ocean air on her afternoon strolls behind the plaza during break time.

Besides the heavenly scent of fresh baked goods, she looked forward each dawn with keen anticipation to the smell of the first cup of the day she made for herself. Damn good coffee, as handsome and upright Special Agent Dale Cooper would declare. Keeping her mind occupied when not busy with work, she'd been Netflix binging on an iPad, the latest and thinnest and best-est model Roy had gotten for her birthday earlier in the year. She preferred revisiting TV series from her childhood rather than new content, late 80s sitcoms and other programs she remembered from more innocent times. *Twin Peaks* gave her nightmares, though, and she quit after only three episodes.

The last time she'd tried to order coffee out at a restaurant, when she'd splurged on sugar by going off-island to the IHOP in Beaufort and ordering the chocolate chip and whip cream pancakes, she had downed the entire plastic, endless pot of thin-brewed swill, like warm, acidic brine. Creedence understood, now, all of her husband's talk about third-wave coffee. Scrutinizing and identifying the flavor notes like an oenophile with wine.

The slow food movement—it now clicked in for her. She grooved on the artisan approach to food prep, imbuing with meaning the simple act of creating a beverage experience through presence and attention to detail. Every cup of coffee at the Carolina Beanery Sedge Island held its own identity, came into being and destined for a particular palette. A customer could rest easy that her four dollar cuppa joe came tailor-made. All Roy's little speeches echoed ghostly as she sipped in the quiet coffee shop, no music on yet.

The concept had been a home run in a community of means like the island where its citizens expected the finest that life offered. The well-heeled clientele here tipped out, too, if you made them feel special, a state of mind the staff of the CBSI were trained to impel in their patrons. It worked; the jar needed emptying three or four times a day. How Estes never had any money while working here, she couldn't figure.

That little dumbbell. What had she ever seen in—no, wait. She'd been sick. Her judgment screwy; her behavior self-destructive. Clear as day to her, even this soon into her sobriety. A remarkable difference in mindset and attitude.

After operating the business, seeing his fingerprints everywhere, hearing the compliments from the customers, watching every day how revenue flowed, the thought came often:

No wonder my husband Roy E. Pettus has been so successful.

And now her responsibility for this store instilled purpose in the daily routine. The record albums, old books and encyclopedias no one had wanted, cast-off props to make the place seem like a living room, or maybe a college dorm room; how the decor recalled Roy's own duplex up the hill from the Old Market, back when she first moved in with him—ten, almost eleven years ago. A happy time of dewy, golden promise and companionship and romance. How she told him she needed security to feel loved, especially with her brother's disappearance coming so soon on the heels of her mother's death. How, as Roy promised, he would provide it.

As much as she required.

Forever and ever.

She got it, now—the idea of responsibility. And loved this coffee shop for many reasons. Felt protective. Wanted to make him see how much she understood. Nothing like getting to one's early forties before finally acting like a grownup. Better late than never.

◉①✳

THE MORNING CREW ARRIVED, INCLUDING HER QUOTE-UNQUOTE BOSS SHAROLYN, who used to open in the wee hours until Creedence had proven herself and learned to bake. To organize and prioritize. To be a key-holder.

None of it came easy. Panic had been a frequent companion the first morning she had to fly solo. While drinking she'd been scatterbrained, saturated, sloshed, but the meditation tips she picked up in rehab had been helpful so far in keeping her emotions and concentration on a more stable baseline.

She kept meaning to tell Roy about her modest attempts at the practice, but they still weren't talking much. This was by her own choice, so no complaining there, sister. He kept wanting to talk through all the big stuff. And she simply wasn't ready. Where before she had been headstrong and compulsive, Creedence, taking it slow. Easy does it, as the AA bumper sticker says.

Beginning around seven-thirty and lasting until about nine, the typical morning pop comprised a set of younger regulars who worked off-island in one of several industrial parks and ports-related endeavors, or the South-eastern University extension campus closer to I-95 on the mainland. As the morning drifted into lunchtime, slower-paced retirees and tennis ladies would trickle in and out, or else linger for lengthy conversations in their cliques and flocks and groups. She had gotten to know her best afternoon customers, many of whom were garrulous, ancient and relentless in their good cheer despite the possibility of impending death staring them in their aged faces. Listening to their medical woes, stories of the old times, their non-PC jokes and entrenched political diatribes, she sweated and dripped coffee, smiling, serving.

Working. She understood, now.

Before? She'd never worked a day in her life. Answering phones behind Uncle Hill's switchboard at the dealership? Please. That'd been childish foolishness lasting a decade stuck with Dusty Wallis, followed by another ten years of cat collecting and an empty housewife existence like out of the 1950s. How squandered, her Edgewater County youth. At least she had had no beauty to lose. Not really. Despite what Roy insisted, and Estes too, and Sharolyn, for that matter.

"I don't get you at all." Sharolyn and Creedence stood tired and stooped and mopping their brows following the morning rush. "You ain't got anything to prove, girl. Not to me."

"Hell I don't." Creedence, sober but still freshly so, with many additional chores and tasks alongside this more prosaic daily toil. "I owe it to my husband and partner to do this. He's got his hands full back—*home*," in a breathy rush. "Our old home."

Sharolyn, scrutinizing her. "You just made 'home' sound sad, like the Island of Misfit Toys."

"No. It's that, my childhood dream was to get away from Edgewater County. But now, he has to be back there, or thinks he does. And that ain't gonna fly. Not for me. I'm sorry. But—I don't want to say we're done, either. I'm not sure I want it to be over. We seem stuck."

"We? Or just you?"

"He's not as certain as he thinks he is. Trust me on this. The more sure of himself Roy seems, the more insecure inside he is."

"What makes you say that?"

"Horse's mouth."

Sharolyn noted that she still doesn't see why Creedence feels the need to work as assistant GM of the Carolina Beanery. "Most people would want to cut the ties. If y'all ain't gonna be married anymore? And all?"

"Been a long time since I had to earn a living. I need to get used to it. Again."

"Girl." She lowered her voice. "Ain't y'all got plenty of money already?"

"My husband does. But I don't."

"No?"

"Not after what I did."

They had discussed no details, but Sharolyn let Creedence know she had an inkling of what went down.

Sharolyn, weary, lowered herself into the office chair. The paperwork nook sat behind the wall around from the kitchen area, where you could hang out of sight of the customers, and Roy Earl's security cameras, to rest tired GM feet. "I knew y'all had some righteous drama going on."

"You did?"

"Could feel the vibration from both of you—you and Estes. I got one of them wicked-clear third eyes, girl. Runs in my family, maternal side."

"Vibration? Hey, that's the word Roy used. Said if my vibration wasn't right with his, then he reckoned it wasn't right. But he sure didn't want to throw it all away. His words."

"Y'all have some years in. He got a point."

"It does sound right. And yet, it doesn't."

"He talking about the vibration of love. The highest vibration. And if yours ain't in sync with someone—and it ought to be in sync with everyone, by the way, all the folks here on this old earth—then it can make for a house that's not a home. And a life lived in servitude to an ideal your heart can't countenance is no life in the end."

"Sounds like dialog from one of those thick romance paperbacks my mama used to devour."

Sheepish. "It is—Nicholas Sparks."

Creedence laughed. "As Roy might put it, insight is where you find it. But really, I was blaming him for what was wrong inside me. Nobody else was pouring liquor down my throat."

"We all do stupid shit, girl. Don't be too hard on yourself."

"My third eye, if I got one, says that part of my penance is this for now. That I should finish understanding who I am, before I can be with him again, or anyone. Get a few more chips under my belt. *Help you run this business,*" dropping into a sassy imitation of Sharolyn herself. "Right?"

"If you say so." After slapping Creedence on the thigh Sharolyn added, "I should try figuring out 'me' someday, when I'm not so busy chasing a paycheck."

Creedence's cheeks flushed at the thought of how much money they—Roy—had in the bank, in stocks, in properties. Was she willing to give all that up? "Like I said, I'm planning to be one of those people myself again soon."

Sharolyn's skepticism about such an outcome manifested on her face as a side-eye and crooked fake smile. "Well. I got to finish up the food order."

Creedence went to wipe down the counters and check the bus-bin by the front door. Quiet around the Carolina Beanery Sedge Island today, tasteful and low-lit and not busy, only two ladies in tennis whites whispering to one another over pastries and lattes. She checked on them, made small talk about how hazy the sky had grown. About that time two of the regulars, retirees Chuck and Floyd, ambled in to play their daily game of chess and reminisce about the golden age when a man could smoke in coffee shops. All felt right in this corner of the world. That's what her intuition seemed to say.

On Sundays the CBSI opened two hours later, giving her time for a chilly, long walk along the winding island paths beneath the mossy cypress and water oaks like Roy. Blowing off steam, literal, her breath growing vaporous as the year drew to a close.

Later she thought about writing to Devin, but that enterprise had lost its usefulness. She'd gone to straight journaling. The conceit of writing to her long-gone and dead brother only added to her sense of isolation, now. Devin, a drunken ghost, egging her on to decry her newfound discipline and descend back into drink. She didn't owe that rascal any more letters, especially ones he'd never read. Not like he was out there waiting for an update. In any case, ceasing as many old habits as possible had been her counselor's advice to help fend off recidivism.

Still, the finality of never again writing to her brother further wounded her tender heart. Closing the door on him in this private way felt like the ultimate ending to her entire previous life, which she supposed made for an appropriate analog to her newfound sobriety. A dividing line between past and present. Embracing change in order to survive. A lesson her brother, rest his soul, should have absorbed.

If she suffered any immediate problems, they too had to do with the past, albeit a more recent one: ignoring the frequent texts and social media messages from Estes Patel. And trying to tell herself that wasn't his beater parked near the CBSI; that it wasn't him stalking her. Whatever he represented before, all had now changed. She prayed he would be mature enough to get the message intended by her continued silence. If not, one of Roy's cop buddies could deliver the message. Nobody wanted it to go that far, however. Not after all the drama already.

MANNY AND ROY PETTUS

Much happen in only a few weeks. Neecie up and decide Manny gone. Just like that. Still got to work together, but outta the durn house after all. *Buh*-bye.

Manny reckon he deserve it. When he let himself consider it all objective and shit.

So now he sit his ass out on the porch at the big house with Roy Pettus, burn with him on the vaporizer, blowing plastic bags full and suckin' 'em down at ten in the morning. The old woman, she gone off with the other one from across the pecan orchard, Jasper Glasscock sister. Hairdo day, they said. Despite being kicked out his family home, Manny dig it out here in the country. Quiet. Neighborhood where they live full of kids.

Including Manny own daughter.

Shit.

Roy Pettus earlier, he like, it too nice to sit inside, front of the durn computer or the TV the way people spend they lives doing anymore. Course, he don't watch much TV, not that Manny see. Roy Pettus say the TV always on when he was little. He not sure if that not part of his problem, so it stay off. They nothing but old 4:3 sets anyway. Flat screens at least, but square. Can't watch no HD content on them things. Might as well not have no TVs, if that's all ya got. They sit looking at shows on his iPad sometime, though. Roy always looking at that old *Star Wars* mess with Dr. Spock.

Manny don't want to know what two muh-fucks look like sitting on the porch breathing in that vapor-dope. It still seem halfway like smoke to Manny.

And the buzz take too long to come. Good when it do, though. Roy Pettus got some kind weed, y'all. God-damn. Make you feel like your hair growing.

Manny wanna fuck on that shit. Make fucking good. Gooder.

Bless him for letting Manny camp in the old house of theirs tucked over in the woods. Not too run down, dusty and musty, sitting ten years without nobody living in it. Not better than Manny crib, but Neecie put his ass out like the trash and here he be.

Turned out she wasn't playing. Course they going on at the restaurant like nothing change. Business is business. Babygirl, though—she won't talk about nothing. That hurts.

Yeah. Manny hurt and all, but taking advantage, too. Becky L, happy about them getting to wake up tangled in bed together, but also nervous. It still sneaking around, though. Still supposed to be quit, far as her relationship with Neecie go.

Roy Pettus act funky about Becky L, so Manny still meet at her little lake house in the woods. Keeping it on the DL seem for the best. He say it bother him on only one level, this sidemeat business: It complicate his whole merchant association deal, like he trying to put together the Avengers and can't have no relationship drama among the heroes.

To that Manny go, oh-well. Some shit—like pussy—more critical than downtown politics. To him, anyhow.

⊚◉❋

AFTER HUFFING OUT ANOTHER LUNGFUL OF VAPOR, COOL AND MINTY FRESH, Manny say, "Button ought to have her ass out on the green agitating to get this legal, instead of all that nuke bullshit. Like they gonna shut that rascal down. Shit."

Roy Pettus say she do got a few hemp and medical MJ pamphlets. "You don't want it legal, though," smiling and high. "They'd start selling GMO weed, full of chemicals like cigarettes."

"It would be like three-point-two beer. Don't want muh-fuhs getting all high-minded, free and easy."

"Hell no. They'd much rather you drank booze."

Manny, all vaped and ruminating. "How is it that the man can make a plant illegal. A plant that grow out the dirt from before muh-fuckas was around to make laws and shit."

That really strike Roy Pettus. "Button says the same thing. Weed, shrooms —like, humans are more wise than nature? I dunno."

Nowhere to go with that. "What about this coffee shop you got going on? Still thinking about that?"

Roy Pettus say he off that idea. He all discombobulated, still, over his old lady, his granddaddy and all. And whose ass wouldn't be?

Manny feel creeper-reefer high, now. He ought not be messing with this dope. Not with his old habits.

That all a long ass time ago. Almost forty years. Shit. Manny could've ended up a stone-junkie. But his own grandmama took care of bidness. Set him straight. Straight as she could, anyway.

While she was at it, she shoulda got him off the saxophone, too. Off that whole musician rap. Life woulda been easier just getting a damn job.

Manny try to remind himself about how good it all been. Till his dick fucked up his family, finally.

Aw, dang it. Manny always hated reefer, the part that make ya all introspective and shit.

Too much.

"So get this." Roy Pettus, holding in half a bag of vapor, and he get that look—his mouth set a certain way, hard and determined—like he gonna make a big-ass point. "My wife. I decided—I decided to forgive her. But it isn't enough, somehow. And look, I know considering your travails, you probably don't want to talk about this kinda stuff. Or maybe you do?"

Manny wave it off and say, whatever. "Go on, bossman."

"'Bossman'? Everybody else is 'champ' with you."

"What—it don't suit ya?"

"Oh, it suits, all right."

"Right on. Cause you the boss." Manny, breathing out vapor and liking that taste on the back end—Roy Pettus say this choomba called Girl Scout Cookies. They got brand names now. Like they was saying, next thing it gonna be in the stores next to the Marlboro Lights and Newports. That ain't all bad, long as his little girl not getting into that shit. It lead to fucking, if nothing worse.

Thinking about some brotherman jamming on his babygirl make cold juice squirt in Manny stomach. Manny be like, I'm-a whip ass on that mofo. Very least, shit-ass ain't gonna eat no solid food ever again. Or maybe fuck, neither. Manny liable to cut that thang off. Some jackleg get it near his babygirl.

"Manny? You gonna elaborate?"

Dang, thinking bout some dumbshit doubling down on his Lillyanne—some worthless dog like Ahmad—make Manny go and lose his train of thought.

Manny say to himself, get back on track. "Bossman, you walk in the room, you setting the pace. Your eyes sweep all around," gesturing with that half-full plastic bag full of choomba vapor, "and you get the lay of the land. You seek it on every muh-fucker's face. Searching out the eyes. I know what you doing, too."

Do-tell, he say, getting this little smile he get. Them eyes half-closed. Peaceful.

Satisfied.

Manny bump his boy's fist. "I tell you what you doing: You looking for the other bossman—for your competition. You look at me that way. That day you and Dobb ate, and we set for a spell. 'Hell, beau'." Manny try to sound like one of them redneck boys. "Your ass still do sometimes. You competing with all them other eyes. Letting them know where to look for the answers. For the agenda."

"Appreciate it, 'beau'—but I'm more interested in cooperation than competition. This other bossman, maybe I'm looking not for a rival, but a potential partner. One as powerful as me."

Manny get it. Say, yeah-yeah. "Strength in numbers."

"Somebody to have your back." Roy Pettus glance out at Rico, the old dog, laying in the shade. Big white muh-fucker, panting and whining every time he roll over. Manny don't care what no one say, he scared of the dog. That mother big as a wolf.

He attach the empty bag to the machine and mash the button. He say this called a Volcano, and it look like one, too: a little silver pyramid with a temperature readout, heat coming out the top like muh-fucken outgassing. It's some dopehead sci-fi mess going on here. Manny slap his thigh at the crazy shit muh-fuhs come up with.

The plastic bag crackle as it fill up. Manny say he had enough; and Roy say, you right, but I done vaped it, so now we got to do it.

"Pa-paw would whip my ass for sitting out here on his porch doing this," he say, holding the bag by its plastic ring, orange, that you put your lips on. "He didn't like none of that hippie mess."

"We ain't smoking—we vapin'." And man, that make Manny and Roy Pettus laugh like hell. "But, ain't no one from his generation like it."

"Yeah? Who cares—they're all gone now. Most of them..."

"And our ass go too, one day."

"True gospel."

He start reminiscing, talking about the old Pettus house Manny squatting in, for now anyway. How he got stoned one time there with this pot his friend brung him—Dobbs, he says, shrugging, but Manny don't know why it matter who. Roy Pettus say he had tried once, but nothing happen. Then Dobbs get this joint from some older cats and say, he say to Roy Pettus, you go and take this and smoke it on down. Which he did, about half of it, until he like to cough his ass to death.

"And I got so freaking high. I didn't know that's what 'high' was, though. It scared me. I went into the kitchen and pulled out a box of Neapolitan ice cream and sat there and ate the whole thing. Felt like I was gonna barf. Have a heart attack. Went into the bathroom, forgot why I was going. Went back into my room, wondered why I didn't pee in the bathroom. Staggered back outside where I had smoked to look for the other half of the joint, but forgot I had already wrapped it up to save and put it away... and then realized I had forgotten where. That half a number is still stashed somewhere in the old house. It's yours if you find it."

"You was getting all paranoid, wasn't ya?"

"Paranoid? Call it panic. Called Dobbs. He told me to quit being a wimp, and to play Pink Floyd and stretch out on the bed. I put on 'Dark Side of the Moon.' When that mad laughter comes out of the left speaker, it scared a fart out of me. At supper, Mama Runelle kept asking what was wrong with my eyes. If I had a headache. Bless her heart."

"Oh, no, dog—I heard her ask you that the other night."

"True. And I was stoned as a bat, too. Damn. Time is going in a circle."

Manny laugh his ass off. He remember his own doper days, sneaking around from his grandmama. Tell Roy Pettus it always the same for everybody with they mamas and shit.

"You friends with Dobb from back in the day."

"Since first grade."

Manny, reflective, turn down the bag, which Roy Pettus finish on his own —his ass gonna be stoned. "I ain't got no muh-fucken friends from childhood."

"C'mon. None?"

Naw, Manny say. Too many homeboys got shot or put away to rot in Angola, or got into hardcore dope, or all of the above. "And I don't much keep up with old school muh-fuckers I got left."

"It's tough."

"Yes-sir. Not unless ya still run with them."

"Well—you've got a friend in me."

Manny all touched and shit. "Neecie's my friend—much as an old lady and business partner can be. Ain't gonna work so good now, though."

"I've been spending a lot of time on such such subjects as infidelity. Conclusion? Forgiveness is the key," Roy Pettus say all slow and deliberate—he high as a mountaintop. "That's what the Grateful Dead taught me. But yeah. A few of my old friends are dead, too."

"That the way it is for everybody."

"I'm close to Dobbs, of course. And Devin, my wife's brother, back when we were little punks. He's long gone, though."

"Where his ass now?"

Roy Pettus shrug. "Dead. A drunk. He'd gotten sober, then disappeared on us again one day. After extensive searching that turned up his car, which was found in Colorado wrecked in a one-car accident, we had him declared dead. It helped clear up a probate issue on his mom's estate. My late mother-in-law was another one of those ELMS, you know."

"Small-ass town. But I hate to hear that about your bro."

Roy sigh, all wet-eyed. "And I always wanted a brother, too."

Manny remember he need to hit on Roy Pettus about Ahmad, that Neecie done told his ass to get out, too, and he see if his in-law can stay with him in Roy Pettus old farmhouse. So Manny get round-to-it. Bring it all up.

But Roy Pettus, he off in la-la land, don't give a rip. He say, the more the merrier.

"What'd Neecie get mad at him about?"

"Leaving beer cans around for my babygirl to find. Bringing home pussy like he ought to know better'n to do."

"You gonna be able to get along in that house? With your wife's brother?"

Manny shrug. "She the one who suggest it."

"A test."

"You think?"

"She's seeing your degree of loyalty. To the family."

"Loyalty? Shit. I get him to pay rent, Roy. Don't you worry."

"Nah. Forget it."

"No, his ass need to pay. Ahmad need structure and responsibility."

Roy Pettus, he ain't care. "It's like whatever, dude. Money is the last of my concerns."

Slow and stiff, Roy Pettus stand and stretch and rub his belly and walk out into the yard. He stoop and pet the dog, who roll and reach up for him. Roy Pettus baby-talk that cur like it understand him. Promise him he gonna spend more time. Go and get steak biscuits. All kinda shit.

Manny mention how that big blonde-headed crater-face turd been hanging around the green way too much. Tell Roy how Lillyanne point the brother out the other afternoon. She say he a freak who used to follow her at school before he took and dropped out.

Roy Pettus agree and say, he ain't know about that one, nor do Button, and one thing for sure: her word good as gold to the bossman. Can see it in his eyes when he say her name. "Any misbehavior out of anyone on my town green will be dealt with."

"Ain't got no doubt, bossman."

Roy gaze around behind the house, where the land slope down through the woods toward the river. "Let me ask you something."

Manny sit down on the front steps, keep his distance from the dog. "Go on with ya bad self."

"When you were a kid? When you were first—ah, hell."

"What, son?"

"You ever do a—circle jerk? With your buddies?"

Manny step back on that. *"A circle what?* Who you do that with? Dobb V? Oh, shit now."

Roy Pettus get all flustered. "Naw, naw, naw—not Dobbs. Nobody was gay."

"Y'all yanking on each other? But you know what that about. Don't ya?"

"Not like that. C'mon. A circle jerk is when you stand there jerking off to—see who can—shoot off first. Or farthest. Or both."

"Ah. See who got the money shot."

"Exactly. An adolescent ritual, like kids playing doctor."

Manny tell Roy Pettus it still sound like gay-ass shit to him. "Who idea it was—yours?"

Roy Pettus shrug. "No."

"Oh-kay."

"But look, I ask dudes sometimes."

"To have y'all-selves a circle jerk?"

"NO. Like I asked you. An anthropological survey. I read it's pretty common among adolescents, but for the longest time, I was kinda messed up. Thought it was—weird."

Manny, he wrinkle his nose. "Who it was?"

"Devin—Creedence's brother."

"I was wondering what make your ass bring that up."

"Formative experiences. Indelible."

Manny get the giggles again. "So the bro and the sis both done seen your ass shoot off."

"Yeah. Pretty perverted, all right. Thanks for pointing that out."

But he stand squinting into the distance of his memories like the circle-jerk mean even more than he give it credit. Weird or not, Roy Pettus gone back to that time, and Manny may as well let his ass talk.

Except Manny, he got to get ready to work tonight soon enough. He got to make sure lunch buffet all set; he got to soak a reed and honk on some smooth blues later. Later, though. He hook up and get it on with that woman, a lover Manny think he might also call a friend. It feel like he gonna need one. Feel lonely, when he left himself think about the consequences of what he done.

So he try not to let himself dwell on it, and listen to Roy Pettus go on about some shit from forty years ago he can't stop thinking hard on. Manny know. It cool. Everybody got some story that stick around in their head, and sometimes ya gotta let it out.

ROY EARL, DOBBS, AND DEVIN RUCKER

Manny's trying to get away but you persist, taking him on a lengthy stroll through the pecan orchard on a beautiful Carolina fall day. Several times around, all the way to the Glasscock property line, close enough to smell a blueberry pie Letty left cooling on a windowsill.

During this long walk you recount the circle jerk, which Manny thinks is queer, but that's a black dude for ya, super antsy about anything gay. Well—straight black dudes, anyway. Some of them.

Button's voice, cautioning you against generalization. Advising against the characterization or designation of The Other. A falsehood. An existential malapropism; a fallacy.

Maybe it's projection. You're squeamish about gay stuff, then as now. C'mon. You have to be, as a middle class American male. A rite of passage to use the slurs, feel threatened, that entire schtick. You and Manny are brothers. You park your cars in the same garage. You're so straight it freaking hurts. The fact that you and your buddies beat your meat together in a sacred circle out in the woods represented friendship to you, not sexuality.

AH—THE SUMMER OF YOUR THIRTEENTH YEAR, HOW YOU AND YOUR TWO BEST friends stood on the rise gazing at the rolling green hills of the land where old Mr. Glasscock kept the last of his cattle and sheep and the llama, the grassland where they grazed—their Garden of Eden.

Closer to the river lay a little valley that looked like a glen or a Glade, as you designated the area. How mysterious it seemed down in the verdant cleft of the land, seeing it from afar, from the high hill on the other side of the barbed wire. How from your house you could get to the Glade only by walking way around the rusty, sharp fencing. More fun to approach from the river. You've always wanted to go explore down in there, but you've been afraid to cut through the farmland, as though the ghosts of the animals stood guard to keep you in your place.

Dobbs is interested in seeing the beauty of the Glade, but Devin only shrugs. He didn't read the Tolkien books. "Trees in the woods. Big deal."

Devin, distracted and quick to give up on projects like long novels, building soapbox racers, or a science project for the county fair y'all started together but failed to complete. It had been your idea—a diorama of the process of the splitting of the atom, a mini-atomic bomb like the ones so often exploded above and below ground for testing, as well as the memorable pair of roman candles set off at the end of WW2. You, Roy Earl, suffer guilt if you don't finish projects. Without help, it turned out half-ass, and didn't place in the science fair. You blamed Devin. A quitter.

As for Dobbs, he never quits because he doesn't start much of anything. He'd rather listen to records and idle the time with his mother's newspapers and magazines than play outdoors. Dobbs, more Devin's friend than yours.

With that in mind, it takes cajoling to sell your crazy idea: to camp in the Glade, but get there not by cutting down through the farmland—the direct path—but by starting closer to town and hiking several miles along the river, going fishing for sustenance, and making a challenge of it all. You argue that as future scout leaders, y'all need seasoning. You emphasize this to them, neither of whom show much interest, but go along to humor you.

One must learn to lead by being on one's own—you read this somewhere; it seems wise.

You'll camp in the Glade, and come out seasoned and peppery like the broasted chicken at The Dixiana.

You'll come out men.

You propose heading upriver from the Lautenschlager Memorial bridge, through the woods and by the dried-up cascade of stones that had been the once scenic falls, and finally hooking back up with the river above where the canal shunts it out of its natural channel—the missing falls—to feed the reservoir and the nuclear plant. From there it's a narrowing channel upland to the Glade, where the next day you'll wake close to home, with only a short climb around the grazing land and the old pecan orchard to your grand-folks house where you live. Your parents died when you were a baby. It bothers you, never knowing them.

You explain how this hike emulates the dreaded desert ordeal neophyte Sandmen in *Logan's Run* must face and survive to graduate from their training.

None of this scenario Devin remembers from the movie, and you tell him how this compelling and deadly rite of passage sequence comes instead from the source novel by William F. Nolan and George Clayton Johnson.

And indeed, you blather on about all the myriad changes from page to screen, changes you don't agree with at all, not at all; and while you're at the age where you get worked up about movies and comics and sci-fi and heroes, all Devin and Dobbs can say is, movies? Yeah, uh-huh, uh-huh, what? And when you try to talk about the sci-fi or comics at home, your granddaddy reacts the same way, and Mama Runelle, too. They don't care about or relate to any of it. You know this, but talk anyway. Whom else do you have.

"The Sandmen have to endure a hundred-mile march. Have to subsist and survive mostly by their stamina and wits. We'll have it easy—it's under five miles from the bridge to the Glade."

"Who named it the Glade?" Dobbs, sour with distaste. "That's fruity."

"So you must like it," Devin said. "Figures."

Dobbs, ignoring him.

"Our ordeal won't be a death march, though."

"Or so you hope." Devin, malevolent. "Three leave, but only one comes home."

"You wish." Sounds lame, but it's the best you got.

"Five *miles*?" Dobbs folds his arms. "It does sound like a death march."

You argue until they agree; you'll let Dobbs use your old sleeping bag, which you upgraded at Christmas time in anticipation of becoming a Boy Scout, one participating in long hikes in cold weather. You wanted to prepare for any eventuality, said so and your grandfather'd been proud, real proud. Had bought you a nice-ass Slumberjock-branded sleeping bag. Orange. When stuffed into its compression sleeve it became a dense, cushiony barrel. Son of a gun rated down to ten degrees. Totally cool.

Or warm, rather. It's May in South Carolina, already muggy. You'll sleep on top.

YOU AND YOUR BUDDIES ARE BEST BUDS; YOU SIT NEAR ONE ANOTHER IN COACH Pembroke's physical science class. How you laughed your ever-loving asses off at Chesnee Campobello's project, which had been to demonstrate how static electricity from rubbing a cloth on a 48-inch tube light bulb could cause the gas inside to fluoresce. How she kept rubbing and rubbing with that certain motion you yourselves had become so practiced.

How the Coach had admonished you and the other boys who snickered. He fought not to chuckle, though, when clueless Chesnee blurted, "It's not working—should I rub it faster? Harder?"

Devin, laughing the loudest. Dobbs said, "Aw, poor Chezzie." Embarrassed for her, you laughed but your face had also grown hot.

Protective.

You liked Chesnee.

You had one godawful crush on her.

"I might ask Chesnee out this summer." A blurted admission to your two friends outside River Ridge Middle. "I think she likes me."

"That'll be the day," Dobbs said. "A small miracle."

Fuming, you sat on the rounded handrails by the breezeway with your feet hooked under the lower rail. You watched the J.V. football squad being worked on the recess field by two of the coaches from the high school along with Coach Pembroke, the men all yelling and waving their arms. In response the chubby rising ninth grade football players scurried, all too reminiscent of your miserable few weeks playing baseball.

Devin, licking his chops. "Yeah, I'd like to ask her out too. Maybe perform a few errands of mercy. Specific items on the old list. Yeah, I would."

"Stick with Shelby Fordham, son," your voice squeaking with panic. "I thought you liked her."

"Maybe I'll take both of them for myself."

Dobbs snorted, oh-ho-ho. "Listen to Casanova Jones over here."

You remember well your pithy and needling retort, and marvel, now, how it presaged all that's come to pass: "Maybe I'll ask out your redheaded little sister."

At that, Dobbs had gone oh-ho-ho again. "Chelsea Colette Rucker? Jailbait. She ain't even got her boobs yet, you perv."

Devin, sardonic: "We're all jailbait, you dork."

You popped open a can of Durkee brand potato sticks, your snack for the long bus ride home—the salty greasy whoosh, the crunch, which at the time all but sickened you, yet you kept eating them. Mama Runelle tended to feed you a lot of the same things over and over, the items to which you'd best responded, like the first time you had a canned tuna fish sandwich with mayo and mustard and fresh tomato and had freaking loved it, and so she'd fed you that for lunch every day for the entire summer of your eleventh year. To this day you can't stomach oily tunafish sandwiches, but by contrast, the adult you would swoon and weep at the sight of a salad with fried onion crisps reminding you of the blessed old Durkee sticks. Sense memories, powerful exemplars that time truly had no linear meaning. All the times you gorged on Durkee sticks the same time; all fried potatoes were one fried potato.

It occurred to you, however, that a can of Durkees could make all the difference in a survival situation. Which you said to your friends that day outside the school. "This five-mile hike will prove something to us," you said with heightened drama in mind. "That we're survivors."

Wise-guy Devin. "Sounds like a thrill a minute. Now, if you had some chicks lined up at the end to suck our dicks, that might make it worth doing."

Profane. Undignified. "Be serious."

"All right, Pettus. We'll take your little hike. And you know why?"

You waited to hear his reason.

"So you'll shut up about it."

⊚◐✳

Your squad sets out for this challenge on the first Saturday after school's out, getting dropped off by Devin's dad, a supporter of the endeavor, all the way down near the bridge over into Easton. Encumbered by dangling gear like real adventurers, you hope some cute girl like Chesnee Campobello might cruise by in time to see you all setting out.

Mr. Rucker, sitting in his Lincoln Towncar with a smoke dangling from his lip, warns to watch for snakes and sharp rocks and this'n that, sounding more like one of the doting mothers or grandmothers.

"We'll be careful, sir."

"Now, don't take a notion to go swimming. The water's too deep and fast in that channel. Am I clear about that?"

Devin, his cheeks red, mumbling 'maybe' under his breath and all-but shoving you and Dobbs down the grassy roadside embankment away from the car, your backpacks jangling and clanking. Tells his old man he'll see him tomorrow afternoon and trammels along behind.

The mighty steel bridge, looming over your heads. The reedy grasses of the highway right of way giving way to the stony clay of the river soil, cooler in its shade, a respite to do some adjusting of your packs. The South Carolina summer will be long and hot. So will your survival hike.

You begin your ordeal by sharing a cigarette, a nasty menthol Devin cadged from his mother's purse. The taste puts you off the habit because you already hate the shit out of smoking, only going along to seem as grown up as Devin does. To seem like a high school guy instead of a ginger chub they called Butterball or Freckle-red, back when you played Dixie Youth baseball.

Devin goads you into breaking empty beer bottles y'all find by throwing them against the concrete of the bridge pilings, tossing them high up and watching the glass rain back down. How entertaining and naughty it all seems, but irrelevant to the mission at hand.

⊚◐✳

Toting your packs along the river, you find the mosquitos swarming hungry in the hot sun, and all begin pouring sweat. The soft riverbank sinks underfoot, damn near impassable. You and your buddies, humping way too much gear, must fight through marshy grasses and squishy, liquified, unanticipated mud flats.

You curse yourself: idiot. You didn't reconnoiter and map out the riverbank between the bridge and the sloping farmland you call the Glade, only had a sense in your mind of what it ought to be.

Unprepared.

Your troops see none of this self doubt and pernicious inadequacy. "I figured we might get bogged down. It won't last long."

"I been stung down around my ankles." Dobbs slouches, shifting the weight of his pack. It's smaller than yours and Devin's, yours in particular because you have the tent rolled and strapped to the top, and the ten degree-rated allweather bag (that's printed on the Slumberjock box, a one-word 'all-weather' bag) weighing you down from below. Heavier, much heaver than your old bag, which you see rolled into its neat tube lying all but massless across the top of Dobb's lighter load.

Devin swats insects and says y'all ought to check for leeches and tadpoles. Squish squish squish goes the marshy water through the Keds. Your toes will become raisin-wrinkled; you curse the lack of Gold Bond talcum powder, another demerit on your private checklist of failures.

Soon your cheerful prognostication comes to pass, and you're clear of the reeds. Now, easy hoofing in your damp sneakers on hard clay and the grassy, heat-baked floodplain toward the now-nonexistent falls of Tillman Falls, South Carolina, drained dry by the hydro plant that preceded the nuclear station. In a mile you'll reconnect with the river proper, wide and muddy. Closer to home it will narrow into the swift passage paralleling the ridge that bisects the middle of the county, and out of which you are accustomed to fishing with your Pa-paw.

"Wish we could've seen the falls. The real falls."

Devin, un-slinging his pack and eyeing the weak spittle of the remaining river gurgling turbid and sluggish. "Must've been cool."

Dobbs, dry and disinterested: "Better than a bunch of ugly old rocks."

The rest of the sun-bleached, weedy riverbed lay composed of sloping, rounded boulders of innumerable shapes and sizes, ancient stones long eroded by the once endless and boundless motion of water now displaced. The forgotten, ghostly energy of the river feels like it still runs along the dry ground. Your packs resting on the bank, you sense a tingle in your lower extremities as you and your friends clamber around on the clay-baked rocks—you can swear phantom water rushes all along your ankles.

You struggle to imagine the eons of time discussed in the science class geology and geography unit, how long this river ran unimpeded before its manipulation at the hands of men. You can't. But you keep trying—not only what is infinity? But like, infinity plus one? Dizzy, trying to climb that intellectual ladder.

A pee break before setting back to the hike. Dobbs, complaining of tiny sandfly bites on his "winky-doodle."

Thinking yourself a wag: "What, you want somebody to kiss it?"

"You wish."

"Let's get going." Devin, irritated. "Or maybe I should leave you two alone."

Dobbs cracks a Dr. Pepper, one of four that dangle in their plastic six-pack binder from a carabiner. "Son, you wouldn't know what to do with it if you had it." Endless, the witty repartee of you and your pals.

THE REST OF THE HIKE, ANOTHER TWO MILES, GOES BY ON FLAT, DRY LAND LEADING to the hilly farmland that gives the Glade its distinct valley-like shape. An occasional fishing shack or other property, including a couple of nice fancy houses you've never seen, force your route away from the river and along a macadam-paved, narrow backwoods road. The metal pots hanging from a carabiner on your pack have become a clinking-clanking irritation.

When at last you arrive, it's as though you've been through several environments and ecosystems—yeah, like the Sandmen surviving the death march. The river, unperturbed by diversion canals and dams and nuclear stations, here flows in free and placid solitude. The Glade looms peaceful and welcoming.

Within, it's cool and shaded, dark and dank. As mysterious and secluded as you'd always hoped. The copse of trees in this crook of land comprise dense hardwoods instead of the spindly pines one finds throughout the middle of the county; the ground pooled swampy in spots and grassy in others around the perimeter of the dense, peaty cluster of old-grown river trees. Silent, verdant, awash in growing-season fecundity.

The Glade.

The first task? Find a good spot to relax and take a breather. Dobbs cracks open another Dr. Pepper, and with the hike already over, you have nothing but time.

The ground, muddy from recent rains, black mixing with red clay under your still-damp sneakers. You need better hiking boots. You'll ask for them for your birthday. And you'll get them, too.

"Ain't nowhere to set up." Dobbs, swatting flies and skeeters, skitters around in a near-panic. "This ain't gonna work."

But you're prepared. "I saved this for now." You distribute pocket-sized, single-use packets of Off brand insect repellant, like the handy-wipes you get with a box of extra-crispy Kentucky Fried. Next, you identify and secure a flat, grassy expanse, sunlit and baked to a level of dryness, along the edge of the trees. Plus, your tent has a dew-catcher. You'll be fine.

"After we're squared away, check yourselves for ticks." This, an order. "You don't wanna get Rocky Mountain Spotted Fever."

Having practiced so much in the back yard, you set up the tent with assured alacrity, if not outright aplomb. Even on Christmas Day itself, soon as dinner was over and fast as you could get it out of the box, you put up your new tent under the big oak tree by the fence, fumbling at first with the poles, but catching on quick. Cold as all get out that day, with Mama Runelle calling for you to get your little ass inside before you caught sinus or an ear infection, but you put your tent up with ease. Gazed at it. Ran in to grab your new allweather bag. Squirmed inside. Zipped shut the tent flap. Felt safe and warm.

You stayed there, ignoring her worried calls. Hearing your grandfather say from the porch, "Let the boy mess with his presents, woman. It's Christmas."

◉①❋

"WE SHOULD'VE DONE THIS EARLIER IN THE SPRING." DOBBS'S COMPLAINTS, endless. "Mercy, but I'm hot as blazes out here in this jungle."

While you spread out the dew catcher and pitched the tent, methodically, doing it all yourself, they traded goofball insults and fooled around. Story of your life. You went through the setup and it was good. You grabbed a couple of sci-fi movie magazines and a notebook from your pack, flopped down.

Relaxed.

You sighed, took in the silence and the sunlight. You couldn't see the river from there—not over the gentle rise beyond the copse—but you could smell it. This felt like freedom—and you'd already conquered the long walk, with most of the afternoon left to relax and play.

Play? Wait—that's what children did. You are young men. What nonsense.

Yeah. Changing into an adult. A newer and shinier you. Not a child.

Before you can issue assignments a deck of cards comes out, and your troops begin to play rummy. Devin throws a hand of diamonds, 2-3-4. "Looks like I'm gonna own you suckers. As usual."

This spirited gamesmanship feels wrong to you. "We came to camp. Not compete."

"We didn't come to lose." Dobbs, tossing down his cards. "I didn't, anyway."

You dig out your telescoping rod and reel and the lures you sneaked out of Rabbit's tackle box. "Anyway, we got to eat tonight. So it's time to fish."

Grumbling from the troops, but you bid them to follow you over the rise and down to the river, a much different spot from the red clay bluff where you always sat and fished with your granddaddy. Here the fish would not only bite, but might be unusual and exotic... yet you know in your heart that it's only upstream, and the same bream and crappie you hook and throw back when you fish with Rabbit at the bluff—you always manage to hook only the littlest ones, making you feel like a stupid fat big baby—will be biting here. If you're lucky.

⊛◉✸

YOU FELT A TUG ON THE LINE ONCE, BUT DEVIN SAID ALL YOU HAD DONE WAS SNAG the lure on a rock. It'd been true enough, but the thought of a real strike to impress your pals felt nice. You heard him. But still, you tried to convince yourself it'd been real, while knowing quite well it wasn't. That took a talent you hadn't yet mastered. Not at this tender age.

The necessary lie. To engender peace of mind. Security.

Damn your grandmother for being so frightened of the world. Maybe one day you'd understand. Once you got through undoing all the fear. At the time of the camping trip to the Glade, you couldn't have fathomed still working on these issues thirty-plus years later. Could you. Nope.

On the fish-less trudge back from the riverbank, Dobbs, an announcement. "I'm gonna run up over the hill to your house."

"You can't—that spoils the ordeal."

"I'll get Mama Runelle to fix us some baloney sandwiches. I got to go make a Hershey squirt anyway."

"That's missing the point of all this—we have to feed ourselves. And poop in a hole and cover it up!"

"Well, how is me going to get sandwiches," which Dobbs always pronounces 'samwidges' like the lunch ladies at River Ridge Middle, "not feeding ourselves? You want me to spread the mayo on them *samwidges* myself? That make you feel better?"

"Screw you."

"Ooh. Sounds like fun. Let me go make doody first."

"This feels like cheating."

"Get over it, dude." Devin, stretched out on his sleeping bag atop the lush, long grasses of the Glade. "Besides, did you really want to mess with fish guts?"

"It's something I know how to do. Do it all the time."

"All the more reason not to—ain't you sick of cleaning your granddaddy's catfish?"

Innumerable, the times you've stood hunched over that nasty sink gutting the slick silvery bodies, afterwards trying to scrub off the scales with a filthy shank of Lava soap that seemed to've sat by the faucet in the shed for the entirety of your short life. Nursing the painful wound after reeling one in and getting finned. Smelling fish guts on your hands all day. You now see the wisdom nestled within Devin's negativity. "Yeah—who the hell wants to clean fish?"

You watch Dobbs walking stiff-legged to the path that'll take him up the embarkment, through the pines and across the pecan orchard to the Pettus house. It's a half-mile. More. Maybe five football fields. A stone's throw, as you sit on the grass beside Devin trying to pretend it's farther here from the comfort of home than you truly are. How stupid it was to hike for miles when you could have strolled down here.

He rummages around in his school backpack, here devoid of texts or notebooks. With a flourish Devin produces two sandwiches wrapped in wax paper. "I plan ahead, Pettus—three moves, like a chess player. You want?"

The sandwich, superb wheat bread with fig preserves instead of grocery store grape jelly, is a miracle of flavor on your tongue. The Ruckers have a fig tree that in late summer yields ripe fruit for weeks. Devin's mother cooks so well. You always love eating there.

"You bring one for Dobbs?"

"No."

"Aw."

"I didn't bring one for you, either." Devin, mumbling through a mouthful of *samwidge*. "Get it?"

"I'm gonna save my other half," wanting to make sure Dobbs gets some.

"Yeah—that twerp might get lost and come back empty handed."

Thirsty, you gulp from the half-gallon jug of well-water, a weight you toted the whole way on your brutal survival hike. It paid off, though, the effort to bring along that sweet water from your home pipes.

◎◉✵

YOU AND DEVIN PLAY POKER UNTIL DOBBS RETURNS, WINDED AND COMPLAINING but clutching a large grocery sack your Mee-maw filled to bulging with sandwiches, fruit, cookies, chips and a carton of foil juice packets. You're irritated because it's too much, all too much—you'll have to haul back what's left.

Dobbs whips out a red-and-white checked tablecloth, snaps it open. Wiseguy Devin says: "Now we're really roughing it."

"Mama Runelle insisted we needed this to spread out and eat on. To keep the bugs and mud off. Y'all ain't never been on no picnic before? And, she sent some of them French fries out the can, too. I can't stand them things, personally. But she said her wittle Roy-roy loved them so." He smiles upon you with pity. Your mouth waters at the thought of Durkee-brand potato sticks.

"We ain't on a picnic, we're camping. We don't need no tablecloth."

"When I told her we hadn't brought any food—and that you ordered us to starve unless we caught our own fish—she said it was the silliest old thing she'd ever heard. That we didn't know our asses from a hole in the ground. That if we had sense, we'd get our butts up there and sit under the AC with her, and she'd fry us chicken and make scratch biscuits and—"

"*Mmmm,*" Devin purred. "Chicken."

"Shut up, shut up." Now you're angry for real. But it doesn't stop you from tearing into those double-stuff Oreos she also sent along. "We're camping. We came to camp."

Piteous, Dobbs shakes his head. "I'm just picking at you."

"Yeah, you big baby. I thought you were the leader."

"I am."

Devin, at his most snide: "Oh, and how's that?"

"You guys wouldn't even be here without me."

WHILE EATING YOU CONTINUE PLAYING FIVE-CARD DRAW. DOBBS SAYS, "OH YEAH, Mama Runelle said the mailman brung you a package—a tube."

"Cool."

"What is it?"

Your heart thuds. You'd ordered an *Airport 1975* 1-sheet and glossy head-shot of Karen Black, a standard publicity glamour pic, along with a couple of action stills: one of her piloting the stricken jetliner, and the other from *Five Easy Pieces*, which you'd watched one Sunday afternoon on TV but didn't get, didn't get at all. You'd ordered the poster and stills from an outfit called Jerry Ohlinger's Movie Material Store, found in an ad in the back of a tabloid news-letter called *The Golden Reel* that catered to collectors of movie ephemera. Had taken you two months of swabbing out Dixiana urinals to save up the twenty-five bucks you needed.

Airport 1975. The only aspect more laughable than Charlton Heston's plaid suit was the fact that he and Karen were a supposed couple. You may not have known much about women or relationships, but every time you saw the movie you swore the two stars displayed even less chemistry than the last viewing.

Get your paws off her, you damn dirty actor.

Oh, how you ached for your faraway angel Karen Black, abandoned at the end of *Five Easy Pieces* by Nicholson, left behind and still only wanting to hear those three little words from him in response to her own passionate assertions of love. Certainly any three words besides his response, which had been, "What do ya think?"

Cruel. Pathetic. Disgusting. Could he not see the goddess before him? How you would tell her. If only you had the chance.

Thinking, how your real Karen Black—whomever she turns out to be, that you'll one day coexist with as mate and lover and friend—will never ever have a reason to cry. Will never have to wait to hear the words from you; will not hear bullshit from some operator like this nutcase who ends up leaving her at a Gulf station. Will hear only the truth.

At the thought of love—of giving it, receiving it—your insides swell with warmth.

And if you had the words, you might have said all this to these two boys, your closest friends besides your grandparents, but you did not. At the time, they'd have thought you fruity as a nutcake, as you probably were, ordering these photos of a Hollywood actress you'd never meet. Who could not care less about a chubby kid in Edgewater County, pining for her as an ideal of femininity and grace and beauty. Foolishness.

Dobbs persists. "What is in that package?"

Again, you demur—you simply can't divulge that these are cheesecake pics of Karen Black. "Just some movie poster."

"Which one?" Devin, eyeing you with suspicion. "Please do not say *Star Wars*. I hate that goddamn fucking shit."

"No, it's—" But you stop. *Airport 1975*, not considered a cool movie, a kinda bad one. Maybe the lamest of all the disaster pics. What was more embarrassing? "You got me. *Star Wars*."

"You nerd. It's a bunch of faggoty fantasy crapola."

Dobbs, in your defense. "I like princesses and faggoty stuff, I guess."

"I just like the spaceships. That's all."

You guys go on picking apart *Star Wars* for a while, but you aren't there. You're thinking about Karen Black. Thinking about that scene in *Five Easy Pieces*—not when she's crying, but sitting up on the sink in the bathroom in her pantyhose feet, vulnerability and intimacy, so fetching and sexy and adorable that your deepest carnal desire is to lie naked against those legs—against Karen Black's legs—so you could rub your winky-doodle between her thighs and make love to her. Whatever that meant.

Imagining this scenario makes you get hard as a spike, so you roll onto your belly and try to conjure nonsexy images. Which is about to become impossible.

⚅①✸

DUSK APPROACHES. THE BUGS BITE. THE CARD GAME GETS STALE.

Devin, furtive, rummaging in his pack. "Looky-looky what I found in my dad's closet. And this is only a sample."

"Oh, mercy." Dobbs, snatching a copy of *Oui* with an enthusiasm bordering on febrile. "Let me see all them—titties."

"Let me look, too," you plead. But Devin's only sneaked two out of his Daddy's stash. Mr. Rucker seems so dumpy and doofus-y and old. You thought porno mags were for guys without girlfriends or wives. Maybe Devin's mother doesn't love his father, and he has to keep yanking it despite being married. "C'mon."

"Enough with your whining. Sit between us."

Dobbs: "You get to look at both at the same time."

"You guys suck."

"That's what I heard about you." Devin, flipping through *Hustler*, which seemed the raunchiest of the mags. "Saw it written on the bathroom wall at River Ridge."

Devin and Dobbs, perusing, pausing on certain photos—striking, glistening images. Dobbs, rapt. "Look at this crazy mess."

Sitting outside the tent looking at the porn you all get tents in your shorts, which Dobbs and Devin don't try to conceal. This gives you cover to enjoy the pictures and your thoughts. All of you are the same. You all get hard—you all play at night, too.

In an instant, you get it: all guys mess around. Not only you. Maybe you'll initiate a conversation along those lines. If you can figure out the right words.

You keep begging one or the other to slow down with their anticipatory page turning, Devin shifting and grunting and Dobbs saying, "Mercy. Look at that. Mercy."

At one full-page spread, the most detailed, closeup image of female anatomy any of you've ever seen, the sight compels you to state, "Looks like —lunchmeat."

Dobbs, a gagging sound. "Gross."

Devin, in a state of aroused grace, ignores your canny observation. "Jesus, the bodies on these women. I'm starting to feel like I'm gonna blow my stack."

Casual, almost to himself, Dobbs murmurs, "Now that I'd pay to see."

Devin begins a dreamy, speculative dialogue about the sexual desirability and availability of various River Ridge Middle ladies. Your pick, Chesnee Campobello, gets a big yawn, and this despite Chesnee having acquired breasts all the way back at the beginning of sixth grade, inaugurating in her homeroom the era of bra-strap snapping. Devin's choice, Shelby Fordham, seemed to delight Dobbs, who called her 'cute as a button,' but as for himself declines to name any particular girl.

Not at first. "Maybe Sonja Guskjolen," he finally says, tracing his finger around the closeup labial contours. "She's—different. That's what I want. Somebody different."

Devin, quick to dismiss: "Too midwestern farmer's daughter." Sonja, a transfer student from Michigan. Her accent sounds foreign. The Sugeree

Nuclear Station brings the families of engineers and other industry types to Edgewater County from faraway places. "Way down the list."

"You're blind, Mr. Magoo."

Devin pish-poshes; calls Dobbs a fuckstick. That's a new one somebody heard the high school guys using, and for the last few weeks of school everyone walking the eighth grade breezeways threw around the fresh epithet. Fuckstick. A good one.

Dobbs suggests you each describe what you'll do once you get hold of the respective fantasy girls.

Devin, saying sure. Outlines not so much what he'd do, but what she'll do for him. His recitation comes in a colorless drone while staring down at one model wearing black stockings with a black garter belt and a red rose between her glistening lips, more of a cheesecake shot than the glistening plate of pastrami in the other mag. "And after I'd told her I was ready, she'd climb on top and slide down on it. And—and sit there. Yeah. All still and quiet. Her hair would dangle down. And I'd—I'd just pump it in there. *Bam*," saying with emphasis. "Yeah, I would."

"You wouldn't like, move around and stuff?" you ponder. "Or make her move around? That's what I would do."

"If she wants. Ladies' choice."

"Well, she needs to get her thing off too." Dobbs, nodding with vigor. "Fair's fair."

"We'll take care of that. There's a secret button."

"Yeah, right." Dobbs, faking a yawn. "You don't know."

Devin points at one of the chopped-liver closeups. "Right there—see that little bundle? You pinch that and they go apeshit."

You lean in. "Are you serious?"

Dobbs pats you on the arm. "A likely story. It's Devin."

Far as you know about sex, Devin's fantasy sounds about right: you put it inside her—somehow—and start ejaculating, which goes on however long based on how sexy the girl is, and ends when you either run out (or she gets full; you aren't sure about the particulars), after which you pull out and suppose it feels like relief to be done. Then? You guess all your gunk gushes back out of the girl into the toilet.

Or—goes somewhere else?

But... where?

Sex.

Yeesh.

Plus, you couldn't help but think about tadpoles squirming out of the end of your tingling penis, tadpoles like you always see in fishing holes with Papaw. In health class last year the teacher showed a movie with microscope footage of sperm cells squiggling around? And the teacher had said, there, see

—like tadpoles? An uncomfortable association, one sometimes lodging in your mind while playing with it, and keeping you from finishing in a timely manner.

Tadpoles.

Squiggling.

You can't wait to have sex, though. As good as the brief and cathartic squirts feel, the ones you get messing around under the covers at night, on sheets your grandmother commented on being 'awfully smelly and stiff for some reason' and which you pull up over your head to better mind-focus on having your paws on Chesnee's glorious sixth-grade boobs, with your bodies lying naked and pressed together, and oh, the thought of your penis touched by the groping, tugging, tickling fingers of another! You have a hard time imagining how wonderful it will feel for your gunk to keep pumping out for as long as you stay inside her. You've read that sex can last for twenty minutes. A half hour. Longer, if you believe the stories in *Penthouse Forum*. Your mind, blown at the thought of erupting for so long. As dizzy as coming made you, it seems like you'd need to stop in the middle for a break, maybe drink some water or a soda.

Bizarre.

Confusing.

Intense.

You cannot wait to find out what's true and what isn't.

At all this thinking and staring at girl-bodies, you moan. Discreet, you reach down and thumb your tent.

"Let's take out our fucksticks," Dobbs blurts, sudden.

Devin goes *hm*. "You dick-lickers wanna see this thing in all its glory. Don't-cha."

"Yes," Dobbs says. "I mean—let's see whose is biggest."

"No prob." Devin, hopping up and unzipping. Out flops a pink polish sausage. Long. Grownup, somehow.

Dobbs, on his feet and yanking down his khakis. His dick, narrow and curved, pokes out from his briefs.

"This is weird." Devin gets up. "I'm gonna go try to take a pee."

"Hold on hold on." Dobbs, pointing at you. "Come on."

"Yeah." Devin, jerking his erection and leering. "Pettus needs to throw in."

Another stab of hot-cold panic. You don't want to—but you gotta. You look at the lunchmeat and stand up and think, this is okay. This is what friends—guys—do. It's called a circle jerk. You overheard a couple of high school swells talking about it on the bus. Scout camp, you remember them saying. That circle jerk at scout camp.

You unzip, pop it out. Next to theirs, yours looks wide and fat. But comparable in a good way.

"A fireplug," Devin says with admiration. "Righteous."

"Look how different we all are." Dobbs, trancelike and stroking. "And now, let's see—who can shoot off the farthest."

You glance askance at Devin's magazine. The model's nylon legs. The red rose in her mouth.

All three of you stand sighing and pulling at your dicks, the golden light from the setting sun elongating your shadows across the checked tablecloth. When you see that Devin has his eyes shut, you close yours as well.

A peek, however, reveals Dobbs fixing his gaze not on the magazines, but Devin's penis. In that moment you know about your friend. Don't want to believe it.

Are all three of us queer?

Devin's speed increases and he makes a sound—*waaaauuuugh*—like the groan of a lumbering *Star Wars* creature. Devin, a stagger-step backward, the spoils of his orgasm dripping off his fingers. "Whoa."

"Oh my mercy." Dobbs pops off and dribbles over his hand, down onto the grass. "MERCY."

Your friends look at each other, giggling.

"I guarantee Shelby Fordham got a hot flash just then."

"So did Sonja. You spilled it on the tablecloth, though," Dobbs says. "That's nasty."

"And the mags, too." Devin shrugs. "Now I get why some of my dad's had pages stuck together. Gross."

Now they both focus on you still rubbing away, but forget it. Nothing's gonna happen. The excitement, ebbing like when messing around late at night and hearing your grandfather come tromping in after closing down the honky-tonk. "I don't think I can."

"Think about Chesnee's big old floppy titties."

"Think about her pussy all sloppy and slippery."

Dobbs, snorting with furtive glee. "Go on, Roy Earl—choke that chicken."

Devin, zipping up his shorts and cackling with cruel intent. "Choke that chicken, boy."

"Chicken chokin' Charlie." Dobbs, stroking himself before putting it away. "A new nickname."

"I can't."

"Bro."

"C'mon," is all you can manage. "It's not gonna work."

"If you don't shoot off now," Devin, ominous, "then we'll feel weird."

Dobbs nods and watches with silent anticipation.

No way in hell, now. You start to lose your erection. "It hurts."

"You need some spit on it."

"I can't."

"Stop saying 'can't'," Dobbs finally hisses. "It's no wonder it ain't working."

You shove your sore, shamed, half-mast fireplug into your shorts and walk away, toward the river. Whippoorwills have begun trilling, but while the sun has dropped behind the hills above, the sky seems to want to hold onto the light.

"*Hey, it's cool,*" Devin's call echoes. "Buncha bullshit. Don't matter."

You wander back. "More poker? I was on a hot streak."

Devin, chucking you in the forearm. "You bet. Let's put these stroke-books away."

"Your dad won't notice them gone?"

Devin snorts. "Shit, no. That fuckstick's got a fucking footlocker full of them."

Dobbs flips over the tablecloth. "Dry on this side."

The campers rinse hands with water from your jug. And don't say anything else about the circle jerk.

Instead, y'all play poker for what feels like hours, until you must light a small Coleman lantern that soon runs out of gas. Doesn't matter. In the end you win the most matchsticks—your pile, bigger than theirs. At least you beat your friends at cards, if not sexual prowess.

◉◉✳

DEEP INTO THE EDGEWATER COUNTY NIGHT, THE CAMPERS LIE FLOPPED IN THE TENT on top of sleeping bags with scant room to spare and you in the middle, of course, despite your status as leader of the expedition. Being bullied by your best friends into drawing straws for it, you accused them of cheating because both laughed like it was a big joke when you pulled out the short one. You've all seen each other's hard wieners now. You are closer to being grownup. You can't understand why they still don't treat you like an equal.

"You're too timid," as your grandfather often says, but to that you wanted to respond it was only because of how much they baby you. How Mee-maw makes you eat Reece's Cups when you don't want them. And won't let you go on mad adventures. It's why you wanted to camp in the Glade with your friends—to get away from your grandparents, who are older than dirt and twice as scared that the world will be mean or unfair to you, for some reason.

At about three-thirty Devin awakens the whole tent with a sneezing fit, a series of explosive expulsions.

"Gracious, boy." Dobbs, groaning. "Shut up."

Devin, all stuffy and snotty. "Screw this sneezing. I was dreaming about being in Mrs. Graymont's class, and she had her titties hanging out."

Dobbs rolls over close to you. You detect additional rustling, but from outside the tent.

"Hey—y'all hear that?"

"Yeah."

"What is it?"

"Shut up," you bark before modulating to a whisper. "It's moving around nearby."

All fall silent. You hear it again. You have to pee and need to get up anyway, but hadn't wanted to venture into the midnight dark of the nighttime Glade. And now an entity unknown moves out there, unseen.

Rustle-rustle-rustle. Grunts and snorts. Nearby.

"What is it?" Dobbs, his voice trembling. "A black bear?"

"Bullcorn," Devin whispers. "Not on this side of Edgewater County."

You switch on the flashlight from the Army-Navy store. Inside the tent it now glows amber, like a warm womb. It has a red lens, perfect for foxholes to remain concealed from enemy snipers.

Devin, his face troubled and pinched, sits up. "It could be wild dogs."

Dobbs, scoffing. "There ain't wild dogs around here."

"The shit there ain't."

"It could be them fighting dogs the Macons keep upriver." An open secret in the county, the Macons and the dogfighting trade were backwoods boys as dangerous as such critters came, to hear Pa-paw and Uncle Burnie tell it. It hurts your heart to think of dogs being made to fight. Men who would facilitate and cheer such a cruel sport frighten you beyond measure.

Fear—it writhes inside your guts. You must overcome this feeling. You are the one with the army flashlight.

The leader.

Right—aren't you planning to become a real Boy Scout? Aren't you going to progress to Order of the Arrow, requiring the mastery of tests of skill and courage, like staying overnight in the woods with no tools or light or food or tent or comfortable sleeping bag? Alone, at the mercy of the night? Overcoming the helplessness of exposure to the earth and air and water elements of the dewy nighttime here in the Glade, away from your house and bed and books and toys and totems of childhood, a preview of future challenges; in an immediate sense, your captaincy at stake.

O Captain, my Captain. The voice in your head is that of Mr. Offenhauser, bespectacled eighth grade English nerd-scholar reading Whitman to the class. The recitation had seemed boring. But here, O Captain means courage, not caution, and the words of the poet resonate like a clanging gong.

"Stay here." An order, the red light shining in their wide-eyed faces. "I'll have a look-see."

"Don't worry." Dobbs, zipping himself into his bag.

Devin, however: "I'm coming with."

"Good."

Outside, you unscrew the red filter and shine the now bright-white light around, first toward the river where a light mist illuminates the sedgy grasses, and back around toward the dark innards of the Glade.

Eyes, several sets flaring. A small group of deer, more curious than frightened.

"Look at those fucksticks."

Dobbs emerges and says, "Aw, they're beautiful."

The light shines back yellow from their eyes, giving you the creeps. You turn it off. You more hear than see the deer bolt, as though the disappearance of the light frightens them more than its unnatural occurrence here in the gloomy nighttime Glade.

Giving your friend credit where due: "Man—I was worried it was wild dogs for real. Or those Macon pitbulls."

"I'm-a tell you what." Devin, sounding like one of the old men who came and played music or gambled upstairs at The Dixiana in the secret rooms you aren't supposed to know about, your Pa-paw's friends, you reckoned. "Wild dogs'll tear your ass up."

"You ever heard the legend of the skunk apes?"

Dobbs, yawning: "I swear, but you never run out of stories and mess."

"No, seriously. I saw it in a history book at the county library. A report from early settlers about some kind of Bigfoot-style dude over in the forest on the other side of Red Mound. The Indians called it Chickly Cuddly, but the settlers named it a 'skunk ape'."

You know from your own Sasquatch research that reports of the animal—if that's what it was—were rife with accounts of foul odors accompanying the sightings. "The woods are mighty thick over in the western half of the county. But I don't think we got any Bigfeet around here."

"You don't know. Anything's possible."

The thought gives you a jolt of cold terror. You flick the flashlight back on. "I forgot to use the bathroom."

You try to not think about your friends hearing you splatter onto a tree a few yards over. You squint into the dark thinking about the deer and wondering what it will be like camping for real up in the mountains, where Timmy Latham told you Scouts and other intrepid types liked to hike and camp. Peaks and hollows close to the Appalachian Trail, which he said he planned to hike one day instead of going to college. The idea made Timmy seem already grown, knowing so much about what he wanted out of life that far ahead. You couldn't yet imagine beyond the next season, much less what you would do when you came of age, whatever that meant. You haven't even lost your babyfat yet.

❁❁❁

BACK AT THE TENT, YOU FIND YOUR COMRADES BOTH STANDING OUTSIDE AGAIN, facing the river.

"Turn off that flashlight." Devin, dropping into a crouch.

You gut runs cold. You take a deep breath, scanning for foul odors. *"What's wrong?"*

Dobbs, sounding freaked out: "Look out yonder."

A fire, way off on the other side of the river. In the woods. Another campfire, you guess. Still scary as hell. "It's like that scene in *Race With the Devil*."

"Hush." Dobbs hurries into the tent. "It ain't no durn devil."

"Yeah. It's just somebody camping over there."

"Or maybe not." Devin, taking you by the arm. "Maybe we conjured something, Pettus."

"What do you mean?"

"The circle-jerk. Maybe we were doing an occult ritual. Maybe that fire is the response to our call. Maybe it's Chickly Cuddly." And laughing, malevolent, like a movie madman, before crawling into the tent.

"That's messed up, dude."

The fire across the river burns brighter, though. You slither into the tent but don't sleep another wink, listening instead for the sound of faraway satanic chanting. None comes, only the call of river birds greeting the coming dawn, as well an enormous flapping over the tent that has to be a heron or owl, so huge the sound of the animal's wings does seem.

❁❁❁

DAYLIGHT COMES AND YOU CRAWL OUT, QUIET, YOUR FELLOW CAMPERS BOTH FANS of sleeping in late. The sky, turning from peach to yellow to pale blue—another beautiful South Carolina springtime day ahead.

After camping in the Glade, you swear standing in that dewy daybreak light amidst the trees and the grasses and the river, that you'll try—no; you will—work to live this way forever. It's like heaven, here in unspoiled nature. You don't know what else you want out of life—only this feeling.

Before long your friends wake up, and before breaking down the campsite you eat more of the food your grandmother sent, suck noisily on the foil juice packets, police up all the trash. You pack out the gear over the grassy hills where sheep and cows used to graze, climbing through the rusty old barbed wire with caution, until you get to the pines, the pecan grove where you like to sit and read, and home.

Your grandparents, having their coffee and the paper, are delighted to see "their boys" back so soon. Mee-maw asks about your adventure and how hungry you all must be, which Devin reports is "right considerable, ma'am." She cooks you and your friends the biggest, best breakfast you ever tasted.

Later, after Devin and Dobbs get picked up and taken to their respective homes, an intuition seems to whisper in your ear—the three of you will get into further japes and escapades. The evening of the Glade will become a faraway, flickering firefly disappearing into the warm Carolina night compared to all to come. It's a sense you have, one escaping words. This story—yours and theirs—is only beginning.

Burning with a sense of accomplishment, you can't wait to grow up, get to college and out of Edgewater County. That's why you want to be a Scout— they go places. Camping. Hiking. Exploring. But no occult rituals, or so you hoped.

Pa-paw and Mee-maw couldn't camp with you if their lives depended on it, so crusty and old like that wall full of records they coveted, their own aging spines worn like those of the cardboard album sleeves. You have never seen either of them lie down on the ground, or take a walk in the woods except across to the Glasscock house. Your granddaddy, he can't stand the thought of wandering around amidst the trees like you do. Says he wouldn't camp if you paid him.

◉①❋

You wouldn't make new friends in the scouts, not really. Short-lived ones, including at Scout Camp two years later, but by then you weren't enjoying it like you hoped, and quit soon after. Quit before Order of the Arrow, and before you needed to get a few crucial merit badges, all of which seemed like too much trouble. Like keeping you from some other, greater work.

Not to mention the drama of the canoe trip that Runelle wouldn't let you take, even though you had been to camp, where one of the few patches you earned had been your swimming merit badge, and were by then almost fifteen years old.

You had shouted at her, "But Pa-paw wasn't much older than me when he went overseas to fight the freaking Germans."

She said was p'shaw, you're not getting in one of them damn canoes. "Son —you might drown in the river."

You've resented her over that for the rest of your life. And him, too, for not standing up to her about letting you go on the canoe trip.

Held it against them. Hard. The other scouts, how they had laughed at you.

Another sworn oath: nobody would laugh at you, ever again. They would admire you.

They would follow you.

It'd all be different in your adult life. Your mission, clear.

AS YOU PUT AWAY THE VOLCANO AND THE GRINDER AND THE WEED, AND MANNY goes off to get his rest-runt open, it occurs that if you want to chuck it all and go hike the AT, you can.

Sure—you'd hike, make camp, sleep, wake up with the dawn and do it again, day after day. And with a hot meal only at the end of a journey thousands of miles in the making, a reward best not foreseen with clarity so as to induce hunger psychosis.

Nah. That didn't sound good. Day-hiking up at Max Patch, though? Now here you got an idea cooking. Soon as you get your grandmother and The Dixiana squared away, you'll head to the mountains.

After breaking the news that the honkytonk would live on for now, Trudy, you found, managed to get over herself regarding the issue of the new smoking ban, which is nothing but aligning yourselves here in Edgewater County with the rest of the western world, finally.

Trudy. You're still hot to screw her again. Aren't you. Maybe better to have a circle jerk for one over this desire rather than see it through. But you're horny. Have halfway gotten over the fact that your boy Manny's nailing that looker LaFreniere.

What had it cost him, though? Besides everything?

What had such behavior on your spouse's part cost her?

And you?

Creedence. God, how you miss her. But it still hurts like an ice-pick daggered into your nether regions. Maybe her betrayal always would. You've a long memory for trauma, beau. That much for sure.

And yet you still want her back; want to move on from it and return to what passed for normal. Or so you keep telling yourself. Perhaps a third way will soon present itself.

CHRISTY AND BUTTON

The Asian boy who'd set up the tent on the green turned out a girl, then turned out to be a woman. A beautiful, smart one. Amazing hair, wiggling all around as she moved. So different. So unique.

Just like Christy.

Christy, smitten. All auto-magic like.

Riding into town with Newbie Harrell and hanging around all afternoon until his roommate got done cleaning the honkytonk—that's the new routine. Christy still had no interest in seeing inside, because a place like that was where his Daddy traded drugs with other losers, and no thank you to all that mess.

The man, Pettus, supposedly such a dick and an asshole, did this big turnabout and told Newbie he could come back to work at The Dixiana if he wanted, like before. Newbie was nervous about it, but reported to Christy that unlike before, and unlike the fat manager of the Applebee's with this thick glasses and walrus mustache, the Pettus guy had been super nice now. Paid Newbie in cash. A little more than what Mr. Rabbit did, which was sweet.

Christy had been watching the woman for almost a week before he got the stones to approach. To finger her brochures and to ask in his breathy whine, his stupid voice, what her name was. And when she'd told him—Button—how he thought he couldn't hear her right. That she made fun of Christy by giving him a stupid fake name.

Button. The more Christy talked to her, the name seemed to suit. Her eyes, dark and shiny, and her ropy hair unreal, like a doll. A living doll. Who smiled and talked funny. But smiled. And treated Christy like he was okay. Like he could be talked to.

As a person.

Christy, he hadn't ever been talked to like a person. Not like she did.

OMG. He freaking loved Button Sykes.

Newbie, though. That little squirt, he had been turning into a problem. Way more than the housekeeping issue. Newbie, he kept saying, "Man, I tell ya, Christy—between this and your grandmama's whorehouse? I got a whole bunch of shit on you, boy. You better remember that if you ain't straight with me, I'm-a gonna cash that check on you. Hells yeah, I will."

Christy, he whines in response: "But Newbie—I thought we was friends."

"I'll do what I got to. S'all I'm saying."

Christy didn't like the way Newbie's face looked when he said it, all shiny and glowing. Like when Christy's Daddy talked about robbing the Gas Chief.

"Or maybe you'll help me with this idea I got in my head."

"Depends," all Christy could muster, like an adult diaper full of shit—bullshit. Newbie's bullshit.

Christy, so far ahead of them all. Only playing dumb.

No way Christy would go along with some mess of Newbie's. He didn't care what favors Newbie asked, what shit he thought he had on Christy. He had given Newbie gas money, on the first day. Had took good care of his redneck ass ever since. And that would be all he was gonna get out of it.

◉◐❋

CHRISTY DIDN'T GET WHAT THE GIRL WAS DOING—SHE WANTED TO SHUT DOWN THE power plant? How would they have electricity?

Duh, she said. From the sun. And the wind. And something she called 'biomass,' which sounded like made-up science fiction crapola.

Made sense to Christy—maybe—but he didn't know how to tell her he agreed. Or about the voice he keeps hearing in his head, a woman, whispering about starting fires and how pretty they would be. He had heard it one day standing over Newbie, passed out in Christy's old bed. Only after he left the bedroom and went to straighten up the living room did he notice he clutched a lighter in his sweaty palm.

Instead, he stood silent before Button, smiling and feeling the muscles of his cheeks quivering. Being drawn to the girl. She couldn't be much older than him. Beautiful, so different. So little. Christy would hold this woman like the toy she appeared to be, cradle and possess her.

Love. That's what Christy felt from her.

And for real—at first he thought he was getting sick standing close to her, the warmth that spread from his big belly throughout his body, and not only the warmth but a sense of comfort and reassurance. The more he smiled, the more she seemed to give it to him. Christy had fallen in love, he realized, for the first time with a real woman, not some fantasy like Aisha or Lillyanne Theodore. She smiled at him too, but never wanted to talk. When he tried, she only looked scared. They all did.

Christy, smarter than everyone realized. Christy, knowing what feelings were. And that you were supposed to act upon them. When you got the chance. Before you were banned, kicked out, forbidden.

At night Christy pulled at himself while concentrating on Button Sykes, holding her image in his mind and enjoying the dizzying buildup not only in his loins but along the top of his head, a tingling, a fizzy pressure growing inside that erupted out of both ends, his mind and his dingus:

Button, came Christy. Hard.

MANNY AND AHMAD

Ahmad come down the hallway at the crack of day. "Manny, yo. You awake? Manny."

Manny roll over in his sorry twin bed in what used to be Rabbit Pettus bedroom, a basic old country house set way back in the woods away from the road and everyone else in the world, except Manny dumbass brother-in-law, who knocking on the door and waking his ass up. That shit rude.

"For real? Get on with yourself."

Ahmad keep knocking. "Yo."

"Asshole, *what*? I ain't plan to get up today till ten."

"You gotta lemme in, dog."

Manny knew having his bro-in-law stay out here in Roy Pettus extra house a bad idea. But Ahmad, he kept on drinking and toking round Lillyanne till even Neecie had it with her own brother. Couldn't blame her. Manny himself all but kick his ass out a hundred times.

Ahmad start cussing. Say, this serious, bro.

Manny get up and shuffle over in sock feet. "What, dog."

"Come in yonder. And look at this."

"Thought you said you wanted to come in here?"

Ahmad say, that was only to get your ass up to come look at this mess he found.

Manny go sleepyhead behind Ahmad down the little hallway to the back room where he crashing on this couch in there. A junk room. File cabinets, old business records of Roy Pettus granddaddy. Rabbit—or Rennie, as he introduced himself—he seemed older than shit to Manny. And he was. All this stuff make part of him come back. All this shit from the 1950s and 60s. Manny feel him there in the room with them. Creepy. Every hair stand up. Cold in here, Manny all in his tighty-whities and ribbed muscle tank.

"You rearranging, yo?" Ahmad got the couch pulled out from the wall.

"That window—a draft coming under like your ass wouldn't believe."

"Now I know you didn't wake me up to tell me that shit. What, you want me to get Roy Pettus up too, tenderfoot? So his ass can caulk it for ya?"

Naw, naw, he say. That he was messing around moving the couch, and this loose board catch, and he like to put his durn back out. "But then, it slide open. And—look."

Ahmad show Manny behind the couch. A floorboard like on a hinge, a chamber underneath. "What that?"

"I found this inside." An old leather briefcase.

"What's inside that muh-fuh." But somehow Manny already know.

Ahmad show him—cash. He don't know how much. Some of it look old.

Ahmad get excited. "I ain't know what to do. Except tell you bout it."

Manny got in his head what they call conflicted thoughts. "Why you digging and hunting in another man's house like this? That boy let you stay here, let me stay here, and you—you go and—damn your ass."

Manny can't half help himself—he see that cash, and covet it. Roy Pettus don't know about this money. If he did, he wasn't gonna let two negroes stay all up in this crib. Ain't no way. Know why? Cause neither would Manny. Nor anyone else he ain't know real good, no matter what they look like. This real money.

Manny manhandle Ahmad. Saying, now you done stirred up some kinda mess. In Manny mind, he keep thinking: Cause what nobody don't know is that his own ass could use mad cash like that.

Manny go and change his life with so much mad money.

Could go and start over.

With Becky L.

Now that he seen it? All he can think about.

Roy, he got plenty of money—Manny hear his ass say it that way. Say he lived off his coffee shop, the original durn thing he done, all them years his fruitshake company was growing. Said he just kept that money. Let it build up. And now he able to pay cash for anything he want. Said he paid cash for that Victorian house cross the way. For the truck his granddaddy drove. For his house down on Sedge Island. Cash cash cash. The boy already got it.

Hell—what the babygirl gonna cost soon? College and shit? Lord.

Manny start tingling the way he do when he think about fucking Becky L— like it a good/bad thing, ya know? Finding this headstash?

"Manny. This much lettuce get my ass outta your life for good."

"I don't give a shit about your ass one way or another. You ain't taking none of that bread. Shit is old man Rabbit's money. He want Roy Pettus to have it, and we—we gonna—"

"But Manny, shit, yo." He start doing this dance. Whispering and pleading. "If he ain't know, he ain't know. Please. Let me take some of this shit, yo. You got to. I—I found it last night. I couldn't sleep with all that cheddar sitting there."

"Your ass shoulda took it, then. Stead of waking me up. Cause you ain't going nowhere with dollar one of my nigga's money. That shit his birthright, that scratch. Who you think Rabbit hiding it for?"

"Somebody who need it. You need this shit, too. Don't you."

Manny say, naw.

"Yo. Word."

"Fuck no. Ain't no word."

"Everything you got, it all in Neecie name. I know this, yo. You think a sister keep shit from her little brother? With appetites like yours? I know your ass need a payday. Bet," snapping his fingers and going bug-eyed.

Manny go all hot all over. Think he about to pop a nut, and not all over Becky L titties but on Ahmad's thieving, skinny ass. Put his dick in the dirt.

But Manny don't. Muh-fucker speak the truth. So he got shit to decide, here.

For now he make Ahmad fix it all back like he found that shit. They pull on pants and drive over to the Waffle House to eat and get their heads together.

Manny get the scattered and smothered with patties and two fried eggs over easy. Ahmad eat like a little kid, pancakes with chocolate chips and whip cream. Flatware clinking and sizzling bacon on the grill and and mofos looking at the Columbia newspaper over coffee, which ain't half bad.

Whispering to each other: "What if he do know?"

"Roy Pettus ain't know about that money—and if he did, I wonder if his ass care."

Ahmad shake his head. "You know what Dr. Phil call that?"

"Do tell, you little Dr. Phil shit-ass."

"It's projection. Cause your ass *need* that money, yo."

And Manny think, you little sumbitch, ya done pin me to the wall. Don't do nothing but make him want to lash out, which he do, telling Ahmad, what? Was he gonna rob out from under this dude doing them both a solid, and because of what? Cause he white? Muh-fucker granddaddy stash that money, and for how he acted to Manny, they wasn't no reparations going down here. No sir. No telling what dangerous shit Rabbit Pettus done, or put up with, to skim off so much cheddar.

To this end, when they get back to the house Manny go and strong-arm Ahmad, and not saying like a figure of speech, neither, into putting that money back and forgetting about it forever. Act like none of this never happened.

Shouting, shoving, Manny pin him down on the couch and put a forearm cross Ahmad skinny chicken neck till he about die. Manny say he go and tell Roy Pettus about this money, and that be the end of it before they kill each other ass over it.

Besides, if Manny do tell him? Roy Pettus got so much scratch he might split the stash with him. That part he don't say to Ahmad. He add wishful thinking to his projection-talking self. And Manny ain't give him no opening. After this, he about done with Ahmad and his shit, before he get Manny ass in trouble worse than it already is.

ROY, SHERIFF OAKLEY, AND MAMA RUNELLE

The stiffs working the desk at the station house—rather, the 'shed' as they call the Sheriff's Department headquarters, a newer facility south of town on the bypass that'd been built back in the 80s, and had developed along with the subdivisions and bedroom community crowd justifying the Chilton commercial strip—appear unimpressed by your appearance in the reception area, nor your pleasant, neighborly demeanor.

The dispatcher and day-cop ensconced behind bullet-resistant plexiglass are robust young African-American women who fill out their brown and khaki attire adorned with symbol and flare. They regard you with cool detachment and healthy skepticism. Exchange glances like, for real?

"You say the Sheriff's expecting you?"

"Not as such."

Dry. "What that s'posed to mean?"

"He'll make time."

She leans back, folds her hands across her uniform shirt. "Is that right."

You insist to these peace officers you represent a person of character and importance in the community, how the Sheriff will no doubt receive you, unless he's unencumbered by Defcon-1 level police business. Zapping her with charisma. "C'mon. Try him. Bet a double sawbuck you won't regret it."

Without enthusiasm. "If we wasn't in the station house, I'd take you up on that."

As the dispatcher calls back to Oakley's office you realize that not only could you use a shave, but you're wearing your typical 'fuck-you, world' wardrobe of T-shirt and old cargo shorts and Keen sandals, today with little black socks because it's cool outside. To them you probably look a wastrel, like you who ought to march shiftless alongside Howdy Shull up and down dusty county roads.

But ha-ha: once they float your name back to the Sheriff's admin assistant it's revealed that (ta-da) of course he's as happy to see you as you pre-dicted, a fact you choose not to rub in while you're being led back.

"Mr. Pettus," gregarious and gentle. "You've come by at a good time."

"Not butting into anything important—?"

A handshake firm and resolute crushes the small bones of your hand. "Light schedule today. Quiet in the county."

"How I roll—always in the right place at the right time."

"Perhaps that's one of the keys to your business success," letting on he knows how you draw financial water. "A part of me would also call it luck."

"A man makes his own luck. All I can tell you." You snap your fingers, pretend to look surprised. "I should write that down. Maybe I'll write a book, one of those motivational deals like Seth Sothis," a late night get-rich infomercial huckster. "The 'Make Your Own Luck Guide'."

"If you figure it out, I'll be sure to purchase the first copy."

You and the Sheriff sigh like sated lovers. He continues, "In any case, if I were you I'd take my quiet afternoon to mean that crime here in Edgewater County simmers at a low ebb of activity. Not to toot my own horn," laughing with unctuous self-effacement.

You give the Sheriff a polite golf-clap. "Keep up the good work, and you're golden in the next election—with me, anyway. Looks like I'm a resident again, a stakeholder," just to make sure this doofus gets it. Nowadays you often have to be direct with people. Their brains are fogged by drugs and screens and invisible waves in the air, as Button has explained to you. "So I'll be keen to keep an eye on the—well. The doings and such. Elections and whatnot."

"As well you should." He slaps his thighs. "Well-sir: what else can the ECSD do for you today?"

Expansive and warm, you describe the proposed plans and intentions for the Rabbit memorial festival. How you feel that the town fathers and mothers and authorities at every level will be pleased with the tone and caliber of the event.

"Best of all, Sheriff? Plenty of overtime for you and your men—people, I mean. Traffic control alone'll generate decent coin for the department. Already discussing such matters with my folks on council, and in the mayor's office. I waited to come to you until we had some steam under us—otherwise this discussion wouldn't have been worth your time."

"You're a considerate citizen. But I consider any conversation with a man like you worthwhile."

"Back at ya. Which leads me to the real-real reason I wanted to see you today."

Leaning forward. "Go on."

"I feel a desire as regards to—ah. Okay. About making up to the town for that misunderstanding over my grandfather's funeral back in September."

Grim. "That was what we called in the service a pure-T clusterfudge."

"Epic. I get it."

"But the folks to whom I answer? No one said a peep."

"I know Hill Hampton gets hot under the collar. Hope he didn't blame you."

"All he said was, 'Well-sir, we're writing this one off.' Mr. Pettus—your grandfather—meant quite a bit to folks here in the county. And as for your memorial concert, Edgewater County could use an event for grownups like that. Decent music."

"Like old-timey country music, do you?"

"Several of the men in my unit in the war were classic country fans. I took a liking."

"I'd never have guessed."

"Got a solid collection on my iTunes, I have to say. But, one request."

"Shoot. Well—" You laugh as he reaches with a wink for his sidearm. "Go ahead."

"Think you could get Darius Rucker?"

"The guy from Hootie?"

Oakley explains how Rucker has made his mark as a crossover country singing sensation. "I enjoy his records."

"Hadn't a clue. We'll look into it. I suppose we'd consider him local talent." Speaking of local: "Sheriff, tell me about this place. This hometown of mine."

Nimoyesque, tented fingertips. "How do you mean?"

"As I said, I'm a resident now. A stakeholder. Literally, as a property owner and shopkeep of the good old Dixiana down yonder," yokeling it up. "But I'm an emotional stakeholder, too. I want to be flat-out straight with you today, about the literal character of the city, so to speak. And my part in it."

"Go on."

"Never have I desired to own a bar. Wanted no part of it. I have my reasons, which aren't germane. But wait, well, I guess they are: It's the quality of the people who invariably end up congregating in taverns, late into the night. There are shenanigans, Sheriff. I'm sure I don't have to tell you this."

He slapped his knee in a fit of fierce and mirthless assent.

"So, now I've had a bar dropped into my lap, and I want to know: where in the pantheon of homegrown vice does my old honkytonk stand?"

"From what they've told me, the only time I might have thought your grandfather's—your—hospitality establishment a player in any criminal activity would've been long ago. If I understand the mythological timeline."

Now this intrigues you. "Look here—what are these myths, exactly."

He held out his hands. "I can't imagine lending any insight you wouldn't already possess, Mr. Pettus."

"Roy, please. And, Garen—if I may?"

"Of course."

Fast thinking. "I'm toying with writing the history of the place. The Dixiana Saga."

"Funny. Jasper Glasscock told me the same thing."

"Did he, now."

"From our law enforcement perspective, the honkytonk's nothing more than a typical nightclub atmosphere, with its attendant vices. You must've seen some of that as a child."

"Well sure," but you aren't so certain. "That stuff was always—upstairs."

"Right. The center of Edgewater County's, let's call it the local gaming industry. High stakes money games." Oakley chuckles. "By South Carolina standards. And the prostitution."

In shock. "*Prostitution?*"

Shrugging. "It's only what I've been told."

"My grandmother wouldn't have allowed it."

"You're the one writing the book."

You allow the falsehood to hang in the institutional air of the sheriff's office —utilitarian, a metal desk, uncomfortable chairs—decorated only by framed photos on the cheap paneled walls of him wearing uniforms and standing alongside comrades in similar attire, whether military or LEO related. You admire the living hell out of stalwart service members and first responders like Oakley. Risking their lives to keep the world turning in an orderly fashion.

"You're a straight shooter, aren't you, Sheriff?"

"Are you asking me to shoot somebody?"

"Maybe that lizard Jez Rembert. Oops—that slipped out."

"Now there's a legendary figure."

"My way of getting around to asking about the gaming aspect. You don't think he's all in that like his father? Or connected to The Dixiana?"

Sheriff Oakley explains that as far as the authorities are concerned, Rembert's connections with the Cherokee Gaming Commission in the upstate, through casino activities on property he owns there, represent his legitimate and licensed trade and source of income. "He's got the papers," with a shrug.

It all sounds rote to you. You got it—Oakley's on the take. Anybody drawing breath with half an inkling of sense knows Rembert still runs sports betting and other gambling outside his casino interests. How the local game used to be at the honkytonk, and now occurs at Pike's, in the back.

But you're not here to talk about all that. Not anymore. "Let's cut through the gristle and on down to the bone: I'm reaching out to you today in a spirit of brothership that I hope comes across as sincere, as one community leader to another. Sure. I don't mind calling myself that. I'm planning to get super involved in stuff downtown. I can go ahead and tell you that, but it's between us." Wagging a finger. "Now, don't make me whip out an NDA."

"Terrific news. You'll be an asset."

"We'll do our best. The mayor down on Sedge Island, Chuck Benvenue—you know Chuck? No?—said much the same when I redeveloped my outparcel with the flagship Carolina Beanery location. The project set the tone for an entire commercial strip that's now prospering. They were all indebted then, I tell ya. I made many friends. I had—have—one particular cop, who's a close friend. Who I can call when I need an authoritative voice of comfort. A uniformed shoulder to cry on."

"He sits before you. Understood. You can depend on me."

An odd way of putting it, but: "Right; but what I'm asking, I guess, is who in the lower ranks. Who's your best and most trusted man?" A hot cascading flash of the modern age courses down your spine. "Or woman, yeah yeah. I don't wanna be bothering you at home late at the night over some mess at The Dixiana."

"Appreciate that. Lieutenant Truesdale's your man."

"Tommy?"

"Timmy."

"Timmy. I knew a Tommy. Older brother."

Oakley, quick-drawing a dark object from his belt—an iPhone. "If you'll give me your digits, I'll forward his. And let him know."

"Awesome." You take this moment to put Oakley's personal number in your phone. You should have gotten these cops squared away sooner.

Best part is that during this whole meeting, you are stoned as a bat. That's right, just you and the sheriff of the county, all chummy and sucking each other's powerful dicks, backslapping male camaraderie, with you all toasted like your Mee-maw's Sunbeam white bread in the morning. You remember Button's assertion about Oakley being 'down,' bro, but in no way will you spoil the fun of having blazed up before you came to visit the police by seeking that kind of validation. Maybe at a party, with him out of uniform.

He walks you out. You both lean on the truck. "So—has Mr. Rembert caused you any problems?"

"Over the mural? Some. Pretty sure his boys keep dumping trash along River Ridge Road by our turnoff. It's like I told him: if I cursed the Redtails when I rolled the mural," and you have, with the team continuing their pitiful losing streak last week against Alabama, "then bet against them every week, and you'll clean up. That's the last I've heard out of him."

"Glad to hear this." He winks, nudges you. "I'll do what I can to keep it that way."

"Now that's service. But then, you're sworn, I suppose."

"My left hand supporting the bible, and my right hand resting thereon."

You exchange a particular handshake. Discuss in euphemistic terms the activities of the lodge, about your participation. Talk about Rotary. Mention the ELMS in passing. Say you'll see each other around.

"Just one more thing," going all Columbo on the cop. "To which foundation shall I send my check?"

Oakley's grin blazes radiant. "My personal foundation? Or the officer's relief fund?" It's not a joke. He has one. Hands over a card. Nice paper stock and ink.

You answer with a bigger smile than his. Forget buying material crap—this is the way to spend money. Imagine his own pleasure, you think, when his fingertips caress the heavy linen bond of those Crown account checks. "How about both?"

"That part's—um—up to you." Oakley, whose eyes have grown narrow and red, rubs his temples. "My head's as big as a football, suddenly."

"Maybe they've got a BC powder at the front desk."

"Indeed. If you'll excuse me—?"

"You bet."

In the truck, you wonder about the Sheriff's condition, the mysterious but familiar high sweet smell, and the general corruptibility of most all individuals in positions of civic power. Only then do you notice the oily stain on the pocket of your cargo shorts where your vape pen, triggered, has been discharging THC into the air the entire duration of your visit with the county sheriff, whom you presume will spend the next hour or two with the coolest buzz he's enjoyed in some time. Maybe ever.

◉①✻

You hang out in the still of the honkytonk, daylight streaming in through the tinted front windows, dust tendrils hanging in stark relief from neon beer signs. It's like the air is smoky in here even when it isn't. Shafts of light, sharp reflections from the glass of the 8x10 glossies on the walls and the wooden posts. Your grandfather's footsteps, creaking on the old hardwoods, crunching the peanut shells. Or so you pretend to hear.

Thinking about the upstairs, you still have a sense you oughtn't go up there. Nothing but furniture and old retail fixtures crammed into the rooms, much of it from Uncle Burnie's electronics store, closed since the 80s. Run off by the big boxes. It happens.

You watch *Headline News* for a round on the flatscreen above the bar. Doom and gloom. Missing jetliners, ferry disasters, Ukraine on the brink. You develop a severe vibration of fear. Button, she only fusses at you when you tell her you've been watching the news again. She's warned you not to fall under the spell. That the media literally adjusts your brain waves and its message lowers your vibration, all by design. Feeds you fear upon which the Archons, these higher-vibrating spirits whose sustenance comes from suffering souls they keep trapped here in 3D so-called reality.

Did she tell you that? Or did you dream it?

Did you dream her telling you all that?

You get mixed up sometimes. Must be the weed.

Fear. An owl hooting last night while you sat on the porch had scared the crap out of you—his nine-noted hoot went *Who cooks for you, who cooks for you all.* Ghostly. Made you think about Big Rock over at Jenkins Pond, the corner of the stone that someone had chipped into looking like an enormous owl's head, as though enterprising teenage partiers, or ancient Native Americans, had embarked upon an epic sculpture project left abandoned and unfinished. An owl looming over the pond, its stone body covered in graffiti, stained by urine and streaked with soot from innumerable campfires built at its base.

You click and swipe your finger on the iPad, glancing at real estate. Not here; rather, in the mountains. Where you will go once you get this Edgewater County situation squared away.

You lie to yourself about not wanting to live at the beach. There'd been a time when you wanted to, for Creedence. To make her happy. Maybe because you felt her slipping away. Worried you didn't do it for her anymore like she needed. You and your lingering adolescent self-confidence issue. It haunts your every move. Still.

◎◐✲

BACK IN THE DAY, YOU AND THE SBFC GUYS, THE PARTNERS AS YOU THOUGHT OF your co-owners, had fed on the energy of those first few seasons of success, expanding the brand along the Carolina and Georgia coast, inland into the college towns and the hill country closer to the Smoky Mountains. Money, rolling in.

And you, not needing to pull out much—that's how well the original coffee shop continued to perform throughout the growth of the fruity, sweet-smelling Spotted Banana™ empire. Yep. The original Carolina Beanery in the Old Market. Any normal average human could live on what you cleared from that venture, at least after the initial capital investment got paid down. A simple life behind the counter. Making coffee. Knocking grounds into the trash. Baking scones, panini-pressing sandwiches, bantering with regulars.

Uncluttered, your days back then. In a flash you well with envy for Creedence now running the CBSI with Sharolyn. Your old routine—baking, greeting the dawn, the waves of customers and friends who'd traipse through after daybreak, answerable to no one but them, these had been less strenuous times. You've never been one for sentiment, but…

And while the SBFC largess came washing onto the shoreline of your business and personal coffers, coffee, and those emotionally undemanding times in your twenties, withdrew from your thoughts. Stashing cash, investing, hoarding, planning. Creedence, joking how she'd be surprised if you didn't have the first dollar you ever made.

You glowed with pride. Told her it came from growing up with your grandparents, depression-era children. You never knew what their finances were like in flusher times, but their savings and checking didn't retain much now. How could it? The Dixiana, unlike the Carolina Beanery, not a cash cow.

But your success? Get outta town. A reason to celebrate, especially to the partners you'd brought on board, one by one, to do the franchising while you cashed the checks. You were all buddies, tight, but not close in a human sense. Pranked each other on the phone. Watched sports together. Ogled and compared women, including your own spouses. Traded war stories, which in all of your cases involved collegiate and contemporary episodes of high spirited binge-drinking.

Guy relationships—deep as a puddle and half as muddy. Not with all dudes, maybe. But the fruitshake partners? Business. Not friendship.

Not like Devin and Dobbs. The old friends? These, the legit Partners. Those adolescent ties, they stick with you. You don't hold any such sentiment about the adult Partners. Too bad.

◉①❋

THE FRUITSHAKE GUYS, THESE CATS YOU MET THROUGH YOUR VARIOUS ASSOCIATIONS and business relationships and sorta-kinda friendships, reminded you of the jocks from the Dixie Youth league days and the high school locker room torture-era, the Cecil Waughs and Dickie Guifriddas of your adolescent nightmares.

Except now, you looked like them, too: rounded guts, short hair, T-shirts, and all way way into college ball: foot-, basket-, and base-, in particular teams fielded by the beloved Southeastern Redtails in Columbia. You faked your way through innumerable deconstructions of statistics and plays and odds of victory. Price of doing business.

But a few seasons into the partnership and the continual SBFC expansion, and after you'd gotten to know each other better, these aging frat-boy and beach bum types you more or less called friends.

Sure. Vacationing together in a magnificent beachfront mansion on

Hatteras, on a spit of land way out in the Atlantic that from the North Carolina mainland had taken two ferries to reach, you bonded with them and their spouses. A beach house, oh, what a house, one with its own sports bar: four plasma screens, regulation size pool table, an air hockey table, shuffleboard, taps for two different mini-kegs, where with tunes cranked and ballgames on the screens you'd partied harder than in the college days. After the third day, your hands would shake in the morning making the first Bloody Mary. Whoa. Too reminiscent of your brother-in-law Devin, and his ruinous alcoholism.

Because of your exalted, high status, you and Creedence took the main master bedroom in the vacation home for yourselves, and how she'd been thrilled and gratified with the elevator from the garage, the view, the luxurious bathroom fixtures. These amenities were second only to the time the year before when the Partners had all gone together to the national restaurant trade show in Vegas, and you'd slipped an extra hundred to the hotel clerk while Creedence stood dazzled by the ornate ceiling of the casino lobby to upgrade you to the high roller floor. You'd been given a palatial room with a jacuzzi tub, yeah, but also its own sauna and workout room, a marble dinner table with seating for twelve, a fireplace, plants, a bar. Damn hotel room was so spacious, over 2,000 square feet, it needed a doorbell. Bigger than most of the ranch houses back home in Edgewater County. Luxury, a taste of wealth beyond the imagination of the poor folks living in the old mill village hovels. Snoop freaking Dogg and his entourage had been staying down the hall. Top-shelf rock star living.

Hi-rollin, yo. Illin' like a villain. Chillin'. However it goes.

As in Vegas, the Hatteras master bath, with its spotless red marbled counters and glimmering, burnished gold fixtures, spoke to you not of opulence, rather of gauche and temporary wealth, only feeble construction and plating where the discerning man of means would wish to find genuine craftsmanship and the finest of precious metals. Here, all the mansions teetered with precariousness on a shoreline subject to merciless natural forces; structures built to stand not a thousand years, but only as many hurricane seasons as they could survive. But eventually, washed from foundations and splintered into matchsticks, later rebuilt flimsy and cheap but only after beach nourishment and highway repair. Again.

It had never quite been the same after that trip, the relationship between you and the Partners, who along with their wives had all been into hard-ass partying that included so much hot tub sitting and knee-bumping that you at last realized what a couple of them were suggesting.

With the rivers of alcohol flowing, Creedence had been drunk both of the first days by lunchtime, though in her defense so were at least three or four others, especially Colin, the pretty boy with the captain's license, the white teeth and the swagger and the waist smaller than yours.

Were you blind? No. But even a blind man knows when the sun is shining.

You noted how each night at dinner Colin chatted up Creedence, cornering her in the dining room over by the forest of liquor bottles arrayed along the breakfast bar while you prepared chicken marsala for eight, and watching as her drunk ass totally responded to his attention. Leaning in. Slapping him on his substantial forearm. Laughing sloe-eyed, as though he'd said something naughty.

Popped him on the forearm again.

Again.

And again.

You were waiting for the tender moment she left her soft, warm palm there —like when you were driving somewhere, and she'd rest her hand on your forearm, and it always filled you with love. Bra-ha-ha, her high laughter at some joke or funny voice you've pulled, and the slap on the forearm, one that lingers. Leads to that hand drifting southward to your thigh. And then all sorts of action.

Colin Kwoth, a sun-bleached pretty boy. Blue eyes, tan. A stupid cleft chin. A couple inches taller than her, meaning, tall. Taller than your ass, anyway, which didn't take much to accomplish. Hell, Creedence herself an inch or two above you. Forever encouraging the woman to choose flats.

Also, dude's a captain. A literal fucking licensed boat captain, with a muscular handshake like your grandfather's, rough and wide, a workingman's grip. His hands, enormous. Colin's stores, the top earners of the chain besides your crown jewels like Charleston #1. Putting his fruitshake money into fishing. His real goal, he'd explained to you, a fleet of chartered deep sea fishing boats out of the low country and Savannah and on down eventually into Florida, where he wanted to retire by fifty and fish for fun instead. The smoothies —fruitshakes—a means to an end for Colin. He got his start owning a bar in Folly Beach, one he had bought and renovated the way you did with Maxine's coffee shop. Investing proceeds into fruitshake expansion, a mini-empire of noisy, bright, high-sweet smelling purveyors of sweet sludge. Brothers in commerce.

Colin's life goals had gotten your wheels turning in another way: What was this for? In your case? All this commerce? The means to what end?

But watching him flirt with your wife, a different set of gears began to grind.

◉①✳

The next day the men had taken out Colin's fishing boat while the women sunbathed and detoxed around the pool. Colin caught a tuna, hauled it flopping onto the deck of the boat and killed it with a sharp stick, some fishing accoutrement—a gigging pole? Was that it?—he used to stab the fish to death. In triumph you motored back to the marina and brought the corpse home for cleaning and dressing to be served as dinner; in the kitchen you ate raw meat from the tuna as you all stood watching a video of the action from the boat one fisherman had captured with his Blackberry while the captain killed the fish you gnawed and which settled hard in your stomach.

That night, you saw it happening again with Colin and Creedence. For sure. And picked up on all the swingers and their little hints, because you stayed much much much less drunk than everyone, your wife included.

Forget getting that trashed. You were a long way from anywhere. You didn't want to get so wasted you couldn't deal with an unforeseen occurrence requiring quick action and right thinking. Out here, you couldn't rely on too many others to help.

Besides, you were the head Partner, weren't you? In the big main master? Children, you thought. Playing at sex games.

Sex without love had always seemed stupid to you. You never got promiscuity. What were they looking for? Perhaps swingers and thrill-seekers hadn't felt the depth of true love the way you did with your gorgeous wife.

No wonder when the opportunity arose you cashed out. Said to them all, go on, carry the torch and the banner without me. This was business. The partying was fun. But what, they want you to share your wife with them, their ordinary jock dicks and dimwitted football-driven minds?

Creedence, typically uptight. But when she drank, she let loose and fucked you for all you were worth, riding you hard and whooping it up cowgirl style. She even seemed able to come easier on your stubby dick. As the years went on and she consumed more and more booze, you assumed at some point she'd settle down and dial it back.

Here's what you kept saying: Next time we decide to get pregnant, which she kept putting off, she'll quit drinking. Maybe when it's time to have, or try for, a baby again. More to her issues than that would have solved, as you now reckon.

In any case, drinking less than the rest of the partners those last couple of days kept any swinger action from breaking out, unless it happened on a private, small scale. Fine by you. You loved your bride. WTF on the sharing bit. You are an old-fashioned country boy raised by your grandparents. Nobody was swapping any wives, not on your watch.

◎ ⓘ ✽

ANOTHER BONDING EXPERIENCE OCCURRED ON A WORK VACATION WITH ONLY THE Partners, a guy's long weekend with more fishing and golf while staying at a similar huge-ass party house on the Intracoastal Waterway in Myrtle Beach, a strong market for the brand. The redneck riviera featured the two established, highest volume SBFC locations you had first franchised to Colin, and from which he made so much his first couple of seasons that the next year he expanded into four more locations in two other resort city areas, also making bank.

Good. Good, Colin. Go go go. The checks, rolling in.

You got a part of every dollar—of dollar one. You hold the trademark.

Held. Don't forget that.

During the afternoon of golf you all drank with epic aplomb, a game at which you'd come in second out of the foursome because you had stayed a few beers behind them. Golf. Another bullshit pastime to fake your way through.

Back at the mansion overlooking the waterway, ever more golden as the sunset began and the sky turned Carolina lavender, two of the partners, Sammy Macklin and Shiggy Hamasaki, left you and Colin alone while they ran to get a stack of pizzas they'd ordered in the cab back from the golf course. Both were too drunk to be driving, but you didn't want to come off like the big boss all the time. The nanny. The nattering nabob. You want them to like you. Went back to your chubby childhood when it'd been hard, it seemed, to make friends.

"All good back at home? Eh? That leggy Creedence?"

"Who wants to know?"

Colin, perturbed. "Why the 'tude, bro?"

"All good. We're all good."

"Damn straight we are. I owe you so much for this opportunity—we're all gonna get rich."

"Work will make us free." You turned the convo toward the new markets you had in mind. Where you saw this fruitshake biz going.

Colin relaxed at the business talk—he'd sensed your vibration of mistrust, which you had never given him regarding SBFC business. You saw it on his face, a ripple of uncertainty and fear. A primal vibe, as Button Sykes would put it.

Sammy and Shiggy, son of an immigrant Japanese family of restauranteurs and who'd grown up in the hospitality trade, returned with the pies from a place called Michael's, a local joint owned by some transplanted New Yorkers who'd migrated down here in the 60s. Fantastic, some of the best pizza you could remember having since visiting NYC on trips you and Creedence took, another of her dreams coming true. Shows. Shopping. Foodie fun.

As you stood at the kitchen sink, the flash of headlamps caught your eye— a van pulling up outside into the circular drive surrounded by privacy hedges. "Looks like we got company."

"Shit yeah we do. We made some entertainment arrangements," Sammy slurred. "While we were out earlier."

"Entertainment—?"

His and Shiggy's high-five and giggles should've told you all you needed to know.

The strippers, a medium-height foxy alpha Asian, a sultry black girl, a skinny pale girl who sported a shiner covered up with heavy pancake, and a long-in-the-tooth MILF type onto whom Shiggy latched, working out some Oedipal hang-ups—put on quite a show. Lap dances for all. Licking one another all over, pressing pussies together. Pouring chocolate and caramel syrup and little dollops of whipped cream onto nipples, the paying partici-pants licking it off. Shiggy, sucking the nitrous out of the whipped cream bottle, nearly bashing his head in when he fell off his chair onto the hardwood planking of the main room's flooring; mothered by the concerned MILF stripper.

Drunk, horny as hell—bad combination. This'd been back when matters had first cooled off between you and Creedence in the bedroom. You had slurped that erect stripper nipple into your mouth, the Asian girl who'd tell you later she was half Korean. Suckled her instead of licked. A libertine.

"Ooh," the dancer purred. "That felt good."

"It did? For real?"

"You naughty boy."

Your pecker, straining at the golf shorts.

The sight of this fetching woman sent you down a naughty path indeed, masturbatory episodes from your teen years: noticing at the Pettus-Sykes Sunday cookouts as Thim Sykes hit puberty, watching her dip your grand-mother's pea salad—petite English peas, white sweet corn, diced red pepper in sugared vinegar—while you swooned with a wave of hormonal mystery both compelling and repulsing. How you had tickled your dingle-doodle while thinking about Thim, picturing her smooth skin and black hair and suspicious smile.

With such memories surging through your mind? Of course you got wound up as hell. The stripper plopped down, wiggled, bounced. Rocked back and forth. Ground into your genitals. It hurt more than seemed like sex.

The Partners had all now paired off. "We also paid for—um—private massages," Sammy announced before disappearing with his date into a bedroom. This, more than a strip show and lap dances.

Going too far, now.

But you, with a hard-on that wouldn't quit. Like stone.

Were you gonna go through with it?

You flashed on Creedence's smiling, loving face.

Changed to a vision of her having one of her moods. Her pouting and down-mouthed complaining. Depression. The hollows under her eyes. Her farts, so much fucking worse than before she'd gone vegetarian.

Liquor farts, more like it. Yeah. By then she'd started drinking hard every day. Like she'd become bored with life. With you.

You grabbed your Thim lookalike. Went hurrying into the master—the big one, the main one, as on Hatteras. You wanted to get it on, before Creedence's face turned pretty and happy and loving again.

The lights low, the so-called stripper came over and rubbed your belly. Let her hand slide right on down into your shorts. "Get undressed, honey."

Your dick harder than cement, you stammered and shook. "Oh, look—I'm married. How about just a massage."

"Just a—massage." She eyed the bulge in your cargo shorts. Tugged at it playfully. "Well then," she said. "Take off those clothes."

Shaking like a virgin you pushed down your shorts, the elastic band of your whitey tighties snapping against your erection. You watched as your stripper-angel also disrobed. She produced from her bag a tube of warming gel, one you would find tingly.

"Lie down, sweetie. We gonna give the stroke-job you been dreaming about."

"Is it—does it seem dumb? To just get a handjob?"

She touched you on the cheek. "Aw. I think it sweet. Lie down, honey."

On your back, a flagpole rocking side to side, she spilled some gel onto your belly and the pulsing head of your dick. Cold, yet warm. Running a slippery, teasing finger up and down the shaft. Spreading the gel around.

You quivered all over. Vision, doubling. Groaning, low and long.

Using only her fingertips, she smeared the lubricant onto your scrotum, which had contracted high and tight like your haircut. Squeezing the sack, gentle, erotic, thrilling. Dizzy. "Oh, I'm—getting there already."

"Settle down. Think about me taking a poo, or with my feet all stinky and dirty." She ran light fingertips back up the shaft, stopping right under the head. Her tickling, light as fluttering moth wings. "You know about edging? We gonna make this last."

Seconds later, you exploded like a fleshy firecracker.

She shielded her face from the ropy expulsions. "Ay-yi-yi, honey. You musta been backed up."

"I'm—this is—embarrassing."

The expert grabbed the shaft in what you supposed was a sex-therapist trick to forestall the remainder of your sudden orgasm, squeezing and holding tight, but two further glurts bubbled over onto her hand. She sighed and began stroking. Managed to extend the intensity of it all. Over so fast you wanted to feel humiliated, but enjoyed such physical relief you didn't care. A professional, the only one you'd ever retained for services like this.

Your cock, still hard; her hand, stroking. "I'll pay extra for the second round."

"Right on, sweetie."

She took her time letting you lick her boobs and nuzzle her neck. You stayed hard as a spike for over an hour. You don't even remember what she said her name was, which you knew was a lie, anyway.

Jasmine. Or maybe Heather.

Or Karen Black.

Thim.

Chesnee.

Trudy.

Creedence.

Creedence.

Creedence.

Something along those lines.

How when it was over the second time, you tried to put the shame and guilt of what you'd done out of your mind. Paid her a handsome tip, snapping off the crisp bill which she tucked into her bustier with a wink, and walked her downstairs to see to a cab. The other girls would stay all night.

She fingered the C-Note in her bra. "Sure you don't want me to stay?"

"Not this time. But you delivered a quality product."

You shook her hand and said thanks, cruised inside to drink more and pass out to later wake up and say, I must have had a wet dream, one starring my lovely and true wife. That's all I did. Let us never speak of this silly dream again.

◎◑❋

AS YOU GOT RICHER AND FATTER, YOU MULLED THE IDEA OF GETTING OUT OF THE fruitshake trade altogether. It happened on the showroom floor of the Las Vegas Convention Center, at the 2011 NRA show.

Yeah, ha-ha, no, not that NRA; the National Restaurant Association. You had walked through 30,000 square feet of technological innovation, handed out cards and were accosted by reps and beautiful women and beautiful men, too, receiving their cards in kind. But also seeing quite a few aging and haggard salesman types, Willie Lo-men still making it by hawking the latest automated computer-chip controlled stainless steel widget.

The keynote came courtesy a futurist named Ray Kurzweil, a loquacious genius who spoke at length not about the hospitality trade, rather this event he called the singularity, when machine learning will become sentient by merging with human consciousness to create a higher intelligence than possible from either on their own. You fretted this might start the holocaust like in the *Terminator* movies, but the speaker seemed more giddy about the prospect than fearful. As for the restauranteur crowd, in the meantime they could look forward to apps and robots and automation. Damn, you thought, if all those service jobs were going away like the manufacturing work did—hello, Grape Eel— what in the hell were Americans gonna do to earn a living?

You needed to get out. Cash out while you can. It'd taken a few years and the right connections, some of which were made at that trade show. But cash out you did.

Cash. Who was kidding who. It wasn't cash anymore, only numbers contained within computer code—fractional reserve fiat currency, only a simulation of money.

Esoteric nonsense. Robotic workers, chips in cards, wireless networks all controlled from tablets, all invisible, all in the aether. Like magic.

Like bullshit.

You felt your tenuous connection with these partners begin to slip away then, boy. You tried to talk to them about the future. About how best to capitalize on the good fortune you'd fostered for them all without you being terribly involved in any of it anymore.

All Colin, Sammy and Shiggy could think about besides these industrial blenders they'd been sold on, machines that would leave the VitaMixes in the dust, had been gambling and drinking and getting their freak on, and this with the wives along. You refused to go to the high-end Vegas strip club, even though the spouses had gone to their own version, which didn't matter to you. You played three-card poker, won a thousand bucks on one three-of-a-kind turn that provoked a cheer from the other players.

Creedence returned tipsy and horny. She fucked you for all you were worth, came hard on your stiff fireplug, which didn't always happen. It'd been a powerful experience in that extravagant Venetian suite, the two of you exploding together, and you had the thought again about getting out. As you felt energy rocketing up your spine and seeming to flood out along the crest of your skull you foresaw this future, and later? It happened more or less as you imagined.

Except the part about Creedence screwing that assistant manager of yours.

Maybe she'd been right. Maybe opening a new coffee shop had been where you went wrong. Not the hobby flying—the damned CBSI. Now it all made sense. Sorta.

A cold notion comes, one you try to shove away: how much would it cost to get Phil Webhannet, an officer of the law, to kill a feckless millennial dork nobody will miss and dispose of the body?

Fudge it. If you lose Creedence, you lose her. Long ago you ceased trying to hold on to a past, and women, unattainable, especially your mother. What else could you do?

AT SUPPER YOUR GRANDMOTHER, WITH A FRESH COIF, SITS WITH HER MOUTH SET. A talk is coming. And your intuition tells you the subject:

Mama Runelle, ready to have the big discussion. She'd been hinting for weeks. The talk about what she wants done, once her time comes. Time to figure out the details, she said. While she still can.

"You ain't going anywhere." You say this all reassuring and pish-poshy. "Not for a long time yet."

"Shit." She blows her snotty nose on the wadded tissue always clutched in one arthritic, liver-spotted hand. "Long time my skinny white ass."

But now that she's seen the death and interment of her husband, or lack thereof, she has also decided on cremation; has called the cemetery folks and sold off the four plots the Pettus's have owned for god knows how long. Didn't want burial up the hill from the god-durn Dixiana, of all places. What were they thinking, she pondered? With plots in Forest Knoll Garden cemetery at a premium, you were shocked to hear what they'd gone for, and to whom: Thurmond Pike, as the final resting place for him and his beloved Chesnee, of all people.

But death and cemeteries and cremations could but conjure sick feelings of loss, of being cheated; and, as in your youth, you cling to the scant and fading and fuzzy memories of your sweet mother like flash frames—the feel of her silky nightgown she wore as the two of you slept in the narrow bed in your father's old room, which would one day become yours.

Maybe you'd even been conceived in the house.

Nah. More likely a back seat.

No matter. The phantom smell of your mother haunts you, as does the tactile sense of that gown against your skin—the silkiness under your own smooth fingertips, the lemon yellow color. Your face, mashed up against the fabric, with her body underneath. Sleeping. The slow rise and fall of her rib cage. A whistle from her nose. You swear you can remember it all.

But soon, she hadn't been there anymore.

You had a bad dream, a nightmare about being in a car going fast and a big noise. Next thing you knew you were elsewhere, strange and bright and smelly like Clorox bleach and people all around. And your mommy, gone. One day there, next day gone.

"Mama's coming back, Mama's coming back." Runelle, holding your face in her bony hands and weeping, weeping, while your recall your Pa-paw all mad at her. Saying, don't tell him a lie like that. And in distress along with her, wringing his hands, both crying. Some of your earliest impressions of your grandparents are these images that would make little sense for so long.

You'd never see those faces again—you never saw your grandmother weep, not until losing her Rabbit. No teary old woman, Mama Runelle. Not like you, squirting salty water over your wife and the wasted years and the false front that your life's been. Boo-hooing over the father you never knew; a mother, real enough, but so faint in your memory it makes you swoon with frustration.

Weakling.

And yet continuing to stare at Claudia Ballahack Pettus's portrait you find inside an old scrapbook on the shelves of the family room, tucked away amidst yearbooks and encyclopedia volumes and book club selections. A high school senior year picture, black dress, white pearls. How plain your mother's face, but no less proud and fresh and lovely, eye makeup dark and with bangs and so achingly cute in that late 60s way. So alluring—flashing what they used to call bedroom eyes. The shape of her jaw. Almost like...

Karen Black.

How had your parents met? She wasn't from Edgewater County. Your Mee-maw has told you she doesn't know. That one night your Daddy came home on leave, with Claudia. Already pregnant with you.

Now that you've rediscovered this portrait, you won't have to look at your old Karen headshot from *Five Easy Pieces* as much—for the first time in ages, you can hold a clear and vivid image of what your mom looked like. You don't have work as hard to imagine her. But experiencing from a photo a complete human being you never got to know otherwise, except perhaps in the primal intimacy of having floated womb-borne within her slight frame, isn't possible. At least your grandmother told you the truth about the accident, and your Pa-paw's role in it.

Except for one problem: you were, and would have been, better off never knowing this little tidbit of family lore. Bless her heart. Like so much, you put it out of your mind.

She wasn't no bigger than a minute, as Mama Runelle would always say of your mother. Her being petite resulted in you turning out short. Nothing to do about it now. Never has been. It's not like you're going to put lifts in your sport sandals, now are you?

☉✆❀

YOU CLEAR AWAY THE SUPPER DISHES AND GET READY FOR THE RABBIT FESTIVAL committee, to be assembled downtown at the Fine Arts Center rather than in the more sterile confines of the conference rooms in the government complex. You debate getting stoned before the meeting, except for the fact of Sheriff Oakley's attendance and a few other muckety-mucks. After swinging by the shed with Chinese eyes, you thought about it too much and got paranoid. Pushing your luck, a voice said.

Paranoia: it'll destroy ya.

Eh. They'd never believe you were high, anyway. Except that you're still in the stage with the weed where you get ripped. It'd be obvious. The snacking alone on refreshments would give it away.

You sit with your grandmother for a spell instead of vaping in your room like a teenager. Mee-maw has taken her guitar out onto the front porch. It's almost winter, now, for real—late November, still warmish during the day, sweater weather at night, but not so much you can't sit outside. The light in the sky no longer lingers as it did all autumn—the time has changed.

You ease down on the wicker outdoor couch with a cup of Maxwell House and listen to her pluck out plaintive melodies, try to think about what to ask about your mother this time. Any fresh details. You've run out of questions about the years after the war when your grandparents farmed in North Dakota, and the opening of The Dixiana and Runelle's brief local music career, how he opened the honkytonk so she'd always have a stage from which to sing. Print the legend, as you told Gooch Wimmel after your Pa-paw passed.

But she's not into conversation. Seems she'd rather play and sing old timey songs, mostly to herself. It's the happiest you ever see her, strumming on that old guitar. Maybe you should buy her a new one for her birthday, which you're reasonably sure is in June.

◎①❋

As a kid, you had loved the sound of small aircraft buzzing overhead—you would imitate it, going HUM while wondering about the world outside Edgewater County, and The Dixiana, and the Glade down by the river. Wandering the pecan orchard in contemplation, you realize now you were already working on a meditation practice, in your own way.

Later in life you would talk with Devin about how you both felt isolated in the rural Carolina countryside; Devin, turning to drink, you to endeavor and imagination stoked by the purring of those airplane engines. Once you got the chance, i.e., the resources, it makes sense you chose flying as a hobby.

Sitting on the front porch with your Mee-maw and hearing light aircraft buzzing a few thousand feet overhead takes you back to the time when you'd first rubbed two cognitive sticks together and said, I'm going places, somewhere other than this sleepy, still countryside—they all complain about living here, don't they? And when I do, I'm not coming back to Tillman Falls. Or to my grandparents, whom I love and are my blood, but to whom, you convinced yourself, you didn't have a direct link.

Dig it: You decided you were tabula rasa or perhaps sui generis, as embraced once you twisted your mind around the concept, during that one year when you had study hall and read about forty books a term and your intellect seemed to grow more in that span than could be possible (though you kept this to yourself—to the outside world, you remained quiet, chubby doofus Roy Earl Pettus). Because you didn't have parents, or at least ones you'd known, you were orphan boy, as you called yourself. So unfair to Rabbit and Runelle, you now know. You were only trying to get it all figured out. You were dreaming of flying away, not getting closer to your roots. You were a kid.

Only time you considered staying in the country was one of the Boy Scout backpacking trips you took starting that next summer, after the time you camped with Devin and Dobbs in the Glade. It'd been up in western North Carolina, your favorite place, or at least as it would become.

After setting up camp for the night near an outcropping called Shining Rock, you were invited by two older scouts to take a short, late afternoon hike up the hillside where you found a bald carpeted by long yellowed grasses on which you'd reclined with the boys, who passed around a flask and smoked a marijuana joint they called a doobie.

"We're the Doobie Brothers now," this ruddy good old boy named Herbie Bertram said, laughing and passing you the joint, a blackening hand-rolled cigarette you barely knew how to hold, if at all, its tip soaked with the spit of the other scouts. "You're one of us, now."

No idea what to say to that. "Oh—cool."

That cracked them up. Big time.

It all shocked the hell out of you. Your first drug experience, in the Scouts? Nice. You didn't get high, not at all. But boy, did you like being in their club.

Or perhaps you did become stoned—all of you had reclined on the grasses and lay in the warm afternoon sun, the light golden beyond measure, and you felt more relaxed and at peace than ever before. Said, you could stand feeling this way forever. The minutes stretched out like taffy. Next thing you knew it was time to go eat beans and mix up Kool-aid with water from the spring, coldest and clearest you'd tasted.

Yeah. That's when you fell in love with the mountains. Maybe you'll get back soon. In the meantime, if Dobbs weren't in a wheelchair and if Devin Rucker miraculously returned, you'd make them go down into the Glade again. Heck yes, you would.

◉⊕✳

MAMA RUNELLE, STIFF AND CUSSING ABOUT HER HIPS, PUTS DOWN HER GUITAR AND decries the cool night air cutting across her sinuses. She sips and clunks down her hot tea mug on the glass-topped patio table. The wood of the rocker creaks. You switch over from the decrepit, uncomfortable couch into a camp chair you've dragged onto the porch.

"Tell me something about Mama," you hear yourself asking. The words form of their own volition. Your tongue itches and you run it under your two front teeth, wondering if it's coated. "I've been thinking about her a lot."

"Son, you was too little to remember her. You know that."

"No—the gown she wore to bed at night. It was yellow. And soft."

Mama Runelle squints at you with a wrinkled face—a crone, displeased. She bares her dentures. "You mind if I let dinner settle before you start interviewing me like Edward R. Murrow?"

Your cheeks flush warm. "An innocent request."

She sighs and tells you that, considering what's happened, it's only natural to be traipsing back into the past, wanting to make it real again. How she'd said the same at Thanksgiving, too, which had been muted and over fast, thank god. Creedence had not come to join you as you'd asked. A flat refusal. She suffered an aversion not only about seeing you, but setting foot in Edgewater County altogether.

Grieving for your marriage anew and against your judgment, you bought yourself a fifth of Crown Royal and hid it in the F-150. Soon as you heard your grandmother's snoring from down the hall, you cracked the seal and began drinking. Trying to get piss-drunk and cry your wife out of your life. Three months now. An eternity. You missed Creedence so much.

Intoxicated and weepy—you, not her. A solution to nothing.

You guys, you were best friends! That's what Dobbs keeps saying. And how y'all need to work it out. That forgiveness is the key.

You had forgiven. But it wouldn't stick. That worried you.

So maybe you hadn't forgiven with sufficient force of will—if you had, she'd be here instead of working at the Beanery for Sharolyn, on a campaign of proving herself, and of atonement. A part of you approves. How this effort could make up for the transgression of Estes, you've no clue. How your relationship recovers, you haven't the first effing inkling.

But you know this much: the hurt has ebbed, the sick sense while imagining them coupling in the ways in which people make love. Her giving herself, body and soul, to another man instilled wicked inadequacy. You were violated, on so many levels. You felt unloved.

Now? Now, you suffer horniness. And for Chelsea Colette 'Creedence' Rucker. You want to prove to her that your love is more powerful than his sex.

You believe in your heart she will let you. When she is ready.

"If I had my druthers, Roy Earl," Mee-maw snapping you out of your Creedence trance, "I'd like to discuss this here festival for your granddaddy. You been mighty durn tightlipped about what all's to happen."

"That's all squared away, or at least it will be—and besides, you'd do well to ask Becky if you're curious about the finer details. I delegate, at least when it's to a partner I can trust. That's one of my secrets, you know." You tell her you're thinking of the next phase of life not as a superstar successful business owner, but as one with a modicum of accumulated wisdom to share. "Maybe 'secrets' is a misnomer. It's about organization. Prioritization."

"If you think at my age I'm interested in learning anyone's secrets, or hearing wisdom come from out my grandbaby's mouth," sour and cranky, "you got another think coming, Mr. Roy Earl."

You smile at a familiar Mee-maw rejoinder. Tell her that, well-sir, you can't seem to figure out what to talk about, can you?

"I got a question for you, son," her voice small and pitiful. "If I could."

With immense trepidation, you wait.

"Why don't you never ask about your Daddy? About my little boy I lost?"

"Well. He wasn't little when you lost him."

"That don't matter. If you'd had your own, you'd understand."

"Sorry. That must've sounded dumb."

Shame. You don't think about him much. He got killed in the war, probably died scared, and you don't want to dwell upon it. Your mother, on the other hand, her silky gown, smell, hair and eyes, big and beautiful, remain with you. Your daddy, not at all, other than the contribution of his squiggling tadpoles. A construct. An idea, more than a human being. Not even his army portrait or high school yearbook photos could make Ronald E. Pettus any more real.

Best you can, you stammer out a version of all that. And as you do, Mama Runelle's face looks less sad and more sanguine: Smiling, she seems to understand.

Sips her tea. "I reckon that makes sense. I'm a simpleminded old Southern woman who's lived too long to put up with much more of this world. I don't know how people's minds work anymore. I truly don't."

"Nobody does. Not even the psychiatrists. Must be something they're putting in the water. Spraying in the air."

"Well, I tell you," getting some of her spunk back. "People sit there on them talk shows and sure as shit act like they do. If you ask me, it's TV that's the problem."

"Show business. Like the palm readers at the county fair. All about money."

Your Mee-maw shakes her head and rocks.

"Was the car wreck bad? That my mama was in?"

"Yes, it was," without hesitation. "Awful."

"And so: I was in there, was I?"

"Son, I hate to sound impatient, but: I want you to know that your grand-daddy and me was much about prayer and church and the Lord. But I prayed, before, in my life. I pray now, sometimes. And there's two things I have prayed for the hardest. One was that your daddy would come home from the war, but he didn't; the other?"

"Tell me, Mee-maw."

"It was that you'd have no memory of what happened in your Daddy's car. With your poor young mother dying, who'd never see the light of day again. It'd been a little miracle you'd been born whole and healthy as it was. That you came out of the wreck in one piece, and little enough you ought not to remember much, well—we always felt this was a particular blessing that you were too young to recall any of it. So please, don't ask me about the accident. I already told you all I'm willing to say. Ask me anything else."

"Like what?"

"Ask about how different you turned out from your father, because I could fill up a book."

Duly chastened, but edified. "Pretty sure I know enough about me. Maybe too much. Let's hear about somebody interesting, instead. Let's hear about you."

⊛ⓘ✳

YOU ASK HER TO TELL YOU MORE ABOUT NORTH DAKOTA, HOW DIFFERENT IT WAS there, and she gives you that sour face again. Says she's not no performing monkey onstage down at The Dixiana, prancing around for her grandson's pleasure. Besides, you know all those farming stories already—she told them when you were a boy, also sitting on a porch as she shelled peas or shucked corn, or as granddaddy bent over the homemade ice cream churn, cranking and cranking, and the Sykes's came over with their little baby grand-girls running around in the yard; reminiscing about how foolish she'd been to follow Rabbit Pettus on his durn fool scheme of becoming a cattle-and-wheat baron, all on some fellow soldier's advice. How when she'd had enough she told Pa-paw to pack up and accompany her home to South Carolina.

"The winters," she explains, relenting after an interim of silence. "Oh, me. I was a city girl, from West Columbia, you know. And so it was bad enough being out on that windy-ass prairie. But the snow…!"

You note how in your lifetime, you've never seen a real snowstorm.

"At night you could see the lights from the town four miles away—that's how flat it was—but during a blizzard, you couldn't see them at all. When the light started to glow within the storm, you knew the weather was finally letting up. Now, can you imagine two Southerners living under such trying conditions?"

"I cannot."

"So… I had to come home. Your father, once he was born? I had no other choice. The only good thing to come out of that time besides your daddy was me learning to play guitar and sing."

You remind her how Rabbit claimed to have been miserable, too. That she shouldn't feel guilty for coming back, or wanting to. You sit wondering why you needed to replay scenes like this with her now. To make living and being together seem normal to both of you, perhaps? Hearing these old stories again?

"I had to. To save my family."

This is a variant on the familiar. You ask for clarification. "You mean, from the unhappiness."

She sits shaking her head. Her rheumy old eyes become dewier than normal. She works chapped lips around her dentures.

"Obviously, I guess. But anyway, you did save us. Look—here we sit."

"But at what cost!" she barks, banging her cane and rattling the ice in her tea. "Tell me that, son."

You can only tell her you don't understand what she means. That you're confused. You want to blurt out how you're worried—that she's talking in circles, or perhaps suffering confusion. Or senility. Or whatever they now call it.

But you don't. You hold out your hands in helpless stupefaction. "At what cost, Mee-maw?"

In a voice distant and empty and weak, "Because I had done fallen in love with another man, son. And he had loved me. And if Rennie and me had not gone when we did, I might've left your granddaddy and my baby right where they sat on that durn farm. But I couldn't do that to them."

Floored. You sit flabbergasted at the intimacy of this revelation. "I'm sure sorry to hear about all that," is the best you can manage.

"It was so long ago. I don't think about it too much. Except when I get asked about North Dakota." She gets up, unsteady. "Lord, but I have a headache. I'm gonna go take me a BC powder. You want one, darling?"

"No, but let me get it. Sit down."

"Oh, p'shaw. I took care of me and your granddaddy till the last morning he was alive. And now I'll take care of myself, like you've watched for three durn months."

You try to sound like Rabbit, lowering your voice and embracing your accent suppressed and homogenized by TV, a sense as a kid you needed to sound American rather than Southern: "Honeychild, that don't carry water, not coming from some old cigarette-sucking, dried up Edgewater County piece of white trash like you."

"You old coot, I'll have you know I am from Lexington County, where my people—" Her mouth drops open. "Roy Earl. You little turd. You sounded just like him."

"It's because he's here with us now. He's inside me. In us. In a way he could never be when he was still alive."

"That sounds like hippie hooey, son. I'm sure he's in a place called heaven."

"A honkytonk called heaven?"

Playful and amused: "Lord, I hope not."

This heaven talk, it's the most spiritual remarks you've ever heard out of your grandparents' non-churchgoing, smoking, at times coarse mouths. You've had a great deal of time on your hands since coming back here, and since getting a DSL line put in, plenty of internet knowledge at hand. You've been searching, you admit to yourself. And feeling wakeful, being back home here among your people. Since you have gotten high again with Button Sykes, and have confronted the reality of marital discord and filial mortality, you have been entertaining some Big Thoughts. "That's what I'm describing. When we die, we go off as dancing beams of light. Dancing among the stars. And maybe here alongside us, still."

"I'll tell you what, if I was a beam of light? Last thing I'd be doing is hanging around this porch listening to such foolishness."

"Truth. You'd want to just 'be'," making the bunny ears. "Wouldn't you?"

"But ain't that what we doing right now? 'Being'?"

"I suppose."

You experience a warm centeredness inside, like a still body of water on a summer evening, its surface unbroken yet somehow undulating languid, comforting, and tinted purple like the twilit sky. Your marriage may have imploded, you may have inherited a honkytonk you don't want, and your hometown you've always loathed has you in its unforgiving talons, but damn if you don't feel good sitting here on this porch with your grandmother.

It occurs that you've made your life what it ought to be—you are free to live as you will, now. Walking in the pecan orchard. Reading. Left alone. To simply be. A sense of return, an echo of your old life, your childhood. A chance to live it again.

But to what end?

As well: why keep The Dixiana going? Maybe a coffee shop wasn't the answer, but you possess the power of creation.

And so, what if you not only kept The Dixiana, but also still tore it to pieces?

Wait—*what*?

Yeah. You got it. The Dixiana 2.0.

Now here, an idea with legs, with philosophical meat on its bones. Old but new; better than it was. Built to last. You get all tingly, can't wait to run it by your grandmother, who, bless her heart, seems frail. But no rush—you're now on Edgewater County time, which flows syrupy like the accents of the people born here. All the time in the world.

JASPER AND LETTY

Not knowing what Pettus had in mind long-term for that old honkytonk... damn if it didn't feel like betrayal, keeping everyone on tenterhooks. Like pissing on one of the few things about this execrable, moth-eaten town that made Jasper proud. The thought of losing his Dixiana was enough to get him into church on Sunday with Letty. Too bad it was the Methodists. If it'd been Roosevelt Nixon's church, with that fiery foot-stomping gospel, Jasper might not have strayed so far away from the house of the Lord. Hootenanny-style churching, now that he could get behind.

Letty. That sister of his. Letty, have mercy oh merciful God, giving him the grief over the drinking and his weight and the smoking, which he had all but quit, and there you had a pisser of a morning. This morning, in fact, here in the kitchen. Fox News blathered on the countertop flatscreen Jasper got her last Christmas; Letty, a politics junkie and full of opinions, but they had called a truce on such discussions.

Barbecue plates and whiskey and smokes and guitar strings. What was left to a divorced old lawyer? He'd had enough of his damn sister. Didn't care if she was right. Didn't care about much anymore.

Except the songs.

A guitar-picker without a stage? Now here was a problem. Manny Theodore might offer the answer, down the line. His room had a stage, small, but with lights and a permanent soundboard setup off to the side. Jasper had watched Manny and Roy walking in the pecan orchard one afternoon, plotting and planning, it looked like, for what must have been a half-hour or more. His curiosity burning, that's when he'd gone to eat lunch at Manny's and brought up the possibility of moving open mic. See if that shook any news loose.

Manny's would do. It'd have to. If it came to it, Roy Earl and his third-wave coffee could kiss Jasper's foot. Not before the big music festival next spring, however. Good ideas came out of the first meeting, and a scramble now to get acts and infrastructure booked. Big acts. Roy wasn't messing around.

"I read on one of those website-things that the liver's the one organ that'll regenerate itself."

Jasper, skeptical. "If you read it on the internet, I reckon it must be true."

"If you quit, that is."

"Quit what?"

"As in, a cessation of alcohol intake." Letty, quavery old schoolmarm. "For goodness sake."

Jasper swirled a glass of Diet Pepsi, washing down a generic omeprazole he'd tipped out of its bottle kept on the Lazy Susan alongside the salt, pepper, and hot vinegar for the collard greens. "Figure mine must be in fine shape. Ain't poking out my side or nothing." He felt around to make sure, resting a hand on the cloth of his polo shirt. "Nope."

A timer went off in the warm and fragrant kitchen. Too warm—for a retired caterer, his sister still made an awful lot of cookies and scones and finger foods for this and that occasion or cause. Outside football weather had arrived, finally, here in time for the playoffs. Between the bouquet from the cookies and crisp mild air, a nice season to be alive here in Carolina. In God's country.

Damn Redtails, though: they'd lost every game, 0–9, and with a power-house Foothills State squad left to face, the season threatened to make history.

As such, hotheads like Jez Rembert still pissed rhetorical blood over Roy's profane act of whitewashing the mural, still called for retribution bordering on violence. Superstition or not, the 'tails were not a strong team. Bunch of undisciplined underclassmen. The mural magic might not have helped much.

Or would it?

We'll never know. But old Roy wasn't wrong to do it.

The pugs, Letty's yapping little SOBs Chappy and Cedric, went apeshit when a big truck shifted its gears like they did to get up the hill going past the Pettus driveway. She scurried around, shushing and allaying their fears that the passing vehicle meant harm.

"Them mutts like to give me a—" Jasper cleared his throat. "A heart attack."

"I'm sure it's my dogs, and not your profligate ways, that's causing the errant fibrillation." Her dry sarcasm lay like a wilted flower draped over the lip of a dusty vase. "Boys, did you hear that? Your precious little voices have prompted Uncle Jasper to suffer himself a spell."

"I wish you'd quit with that 'uncle' mess. They ain't nothing but dogs. Lapdogs, at that. Not even good for working."

"Are you having a 'senior moment'? We don't work this farm anymore."

"Our fields lay fallow," he mused. "We work the old farm no more." Scratched down the phrases in his current lyrics and poetry notebook.

Letty, insisting Jasper consider the dogs as sacrosanct, full-fledged family members. She'd tolerate no impugning of their unique and vital addition to the life of the home, which absent their loving and delightful companionship left only human squabbling and sniping between two crusty old siblings.

More like a nuisance, Jasper said in response. "If they don't settle down I'll dump them on the other side of the river."

"Hush your mouth."

The 'other side of the river' indicated a traditional local euphemism for the Easton area where so many black folks have tended to live in Edgewater County. Other local nicknames, less diplomatic, but also increasingly archaic except among the more unreconstructed elements of society, included the wrong side of the tracks, and much worse Jasper had grown up hearing. Hard habit to break.

But Jasper Glasscock, for one, no longer suffered mistrust in his heart for black folks, not as when he'd been a boy. Deep-seated feelings against school integration festered in his inchoate consciousness, stoked by the opinions and behavior of powerful local men he thought it best to emulate. A teenage ideologue in the making, Jasper stood behind George Wallace out on the green back in '68 and wrote letters to the *Edgewater Advocate* lamenting lunch-counter integration.

But after graduating and going off to Southeastern University, getting 'turned on' in the parlance of the day, where he'd alter his worldview, march against the war, grow the hair, get high; begin to see other humans of whatever color as though a veil lifted. Letty always blamed the pot-smoking for keeping Jasper from law school until his 30s. It'd been more than that, but he preferred not to recount his youth. No point. Perfectly happy, now.

Still, the old epithets often crept into his thoughts, maybe because Jasper heard certain terms thrown around so much by young people. But no one could hear inside his head, which for the moment consisted only of Letty's nonstop prattle about Jasper's habits, like an annoying earworm.

Living here with his sister, and her dogs, a man needed his vices, his victuals. A gent required decent drink and rich grub and a smoke at the end. What the hell we here for, he wondered, if not to experience these pleasures.

Letty set her tray of her choco-chunk cookies on a cooling rack and threw stained and worn oven mitts into the basket where they lived, next to restaurant-sized storage canisters of various flours and sugars. "I suspect the organ's as shriveled up as beef jerky, if not shoe leather."

"What?"

"That liver of yours."

"Will you let that go?" But it might not be far from the truth. Last time he'd had a full workup, the doc said not only was his liver not swollen, but he couldn't feel it at all. That sometimes with heavy scarring from, say, alcohol abuse, you had shrinkage rather than bloat into fatty liver. Stages of decline either way. Of disease.

Hell, who thinks about such mess?

Jasper didn't want to consider the condition of his glandular organs. He wanted to live and pick guitar and deal with as little medical and legal crap as possible, now. At sixty, too young to quit the law practice yet, though. Didn't have squat to show for all the years of study and toil. Nicky, his ex, took her piece of pie, daughter and all. Left him with diddly-do—the old family house he shared with Letty. That was about it. Had come home to his old room, ten years ago now. Hell of a note. At least he'd kept the practice going, and stayed in touch with his kid Samantha off at college out on the west coast, Facetime and social media messaging substituting for an actual relationship.

Jasper went into the living room with his notepad, tuned his guitar, strummed. He'd written a new one called 'Hopelessly Helping,' inspired by years of fumbling attempts to assist his sister in the kitchen. It was coming together. Between this fresh ditty and 'Will My Cats Accompany Me to Heaven,' inspired by a story in the *Advocate* about an elderly woman found dead in a house of forty starving and ringworm-ridden felines, he had himself a pair of new numbers to lay on them at the next open mic.

With this output and all his prior work, plus a revised 'Better Him Than Me,' which took out a verse, way too long—a story song, but Jasper ain't no Bob Dylan—maybe he'd finally make a record. He and Button discussed it. She said with a Macbook loaded with ProTools, decent mics and a dead room, anybody could record an album. Sell it online. A wonderful time to be a musician.

Thank god The Dixiana was still alive. Whatever the Pettus heir's ultimate plans, the honkytonk survived and thrived, pretty well by its standards. Roy Earl, little smart-ass, ought to be pleased. Trudy told Jasper the numbers were up from last year. Can't ask for more than that.

A hot belch; a burning along his ribs on the left side. One day he'd tell his sister about the beautiful Indian doctor, Patel, and what she'd reported about Jasper's cardiovascular condition. Nah. Maybe not. The doc sounded far too much like Letty regarding all his beloved habits.

◉◔✳

IN SWEATPANTS, DROOPY THREADBARE T-SHIRT AND WORN CROCS, LETTY STAYED busy as ever—despite not having done professional catering work for years, still baking like mad. At her age, leaning now toward late seventies, she'd finally had to admit that her back and knees couldn't take too much stooping and lifting. From the volume of her kitchen's output, her joints seemed fine: he watched her bend and yank another heavy tray of fragrant cookies out of the big oven like it wasn't nothing.

The sickly sweet smell worried Jasper's morning stomach, a gurgling, tremulous sac with which one dared not trifle. Not this early.

His sister appeared in the doorway from the kitchen wiping her hands on a towel right as Jasper strummed the intro of 'Hopelessly Helping,' a melancholy progression of D7 to Fm to C that suited its depiction of miscommunication issues in an otherwise happy marriage. He was copping Willie's licks from 'I'd Have to Be Crazy,' but transposing the key from E to C made him feel better about his blatant thievery—call it the 'folk process.'

He rested his hands on the body of the Martin. "Yes, ma'am?"

"Don't 'ma'am' me."

"Yes-ma'am."

She made devil eyes and hurled an epithet. "I'm being serious, now. I'm concerned about Runelle. She doesn't look well. Her color's poor."

"Been through a lot recently. But for a woman her age, she looks like the old woman she is. Like the old biddy you are."

"I'll old-biddy you, boy." She went back to her baking, or rather, spraying off a cookie sheet greasy from a prior batch. "In any event, I'm concerned for her wellbeing."

"She's got Roy Earl now. Gonna be well cared for."

"I reckon so. He's planning to remain here?"

"For now, anyway."

"I'm shocked—truly."

"Marital strife drives a man back home, sometimes."

A moment pregnant with subtext and glaring stares. Lets finally broke it. "That Rucker girl, no doubt high strung like her mother."

"Eileen was a pistol. No question."

Letty and Eileen had served on the ELMS together, but had never been the best of friends. Scoffing: "One way of putting it."

Jasper slugged the last of his bitter coffee to wash down the antacid pill. And counted the minutes until the bracer he'd sneak on his way into the office. A routine. He strummed.

◉◉✹

THE CASEWORK FOR THE DAY DIDN'T AMOUNT TO MUCH: BANKRUPTCY NONSENSE, briefs to file in two minor civil cases, juggling creditors. Jez Rembert left a message reminding him about an incarcerated cousin with a hearing coming up, and making sure Jasper having a man on the parole board offered an opportunity for graft. Another exciting sojourn ahead, sitting in the upstairs office across from LaFreniere Square and its pale brick courthouse.

At least he could go casual—slacks and a polo shirt, a nice electric green soft-knit Letty got for him at the Kohl's over in Dentsville, an appealing cut and drape on the sleeves, didn't accentuate his gut too bad, a second one in navy blue still on the store hanger with its tags dangling. She had such an eye for his clothes. His ex-wife hadn't given two poops about Jasper's wardrobe, except to criticize it.

That reminded him he needed to drop off a couple of old suits and an armload of oxford shirts at The Gentleman's Affair, the consignment place over in the new plaza. Try to squeeze a few dollars out. Them fellas had been in business for years a block from the green, but moved when the developments near Chilton took off.

Hell, before long that area would be crowded as Dentsville. Subdivisions from here to Columbia, now. Bedroom communities, upscale ones around the lake. You wouldn't ever have seen a Publix, he said to the men in the clothing store, without all those lakefront neighborhoods, and all had nodded and grunted in agreement.

Jasper avoided that southernmost part of the county much as possible, taking the old state road whenever he had to drive down to Columbia. The two-lane highway sliced straight through the pines, a long gray ribbon through the hill country extending from the ridge to the fall line. Made him want to drive fast. Truth was, the troopers didn't patrol the state road like the interstate; a determined motorist could boogie.

Could have himself a nip.

Lord, but he had been remiss in his behavior. Knew wrong from right, bad from good—what lawyer or cop didn't. But an old country road straight as that one? All you needed worry about was a deer popping out of the roadside brush, and then only a busted fender and insurance to file.

He rationalized in many ways his need to drink, as well as hide it from Letty. But when he allowed himself, he felt his older sister's concern even in moments when she chose not to articulate it in a torrent of disapproving verbiage. Hell yeah, he did. Damn her.

But for now he had open mic to consider, and wasn't planning to drive into Columbia anytime soon, not unless something unforeseen came up; and so a bracer on the brief trip downtown couldn't hurt; and in any case Letty wouldn't know, or rather, wouldn't be able to stop him; and he thought all this while stepping outside to smoke, and she hollered at him about the odor drifting in the window she'd cracked in the stuffy kitchen, and how this beautiful fall morning in Edgewater County now reeked of cheap nicotine instead of her cookies.

On his way, he'd check on Runelle. Make sure she was okay, that Roy Earl was fine. And… and… maybe hint again how he desired The Dixiana to live on long-term, even if Roy didn't. Jasper would become an investor, if that's what it took, and buy the building. Somehow. He cringed and rued the thought of the neon sign never shining again—hell, it barely lit up now.

Right: He'd pop in on Runelle and her grandson, hint around. Better than heading into the office to work on filings, and a reason to put off that first bracer, too, because no time between here and the Pettus house, long driveways and all, to have a toot and chew up a breath mint.

Lord, but he didn't wish to worry anyone none. Especially his older sister, even if she was driving him to distraction. Like so many modern Americans, he suffered anxiety. He self-medicated.

After the Pettuses he'd swing by Thurmond's, check the tone of doings in the back room. Play a few axes. See what was what. Have a bracer. Get on with the day and the routine, about damn near all he had left. Welcome to Jasper, USA.

But not before swallowing another stomach-acid pill. Didn't want that first snort to tear up his gut like it sometimes did, an all-too typical aspect of his morning he could live without.

Jasper went down the highway a quarter mile to the long Pettus driveway and through the tall crepe myrtles and into the yard, which now held a variety of vehicles since Manny Theodore and his brother and who knew else lived out here. None of his business to whom Roy rented rooms.

Roy hung around on the porch for a spell yakking with Jasper while Runelle was inside taking a nap, a recent after-breakfast routine she had started.

"She doing all right?"

"Far as I can tell."

"How about near as you can tell?"

"Both polarities covered. Grieving, of course, but denying it. How you hanging?"

"Partly cloudy most of the time, but the sun peeks through." Jasper said how much he appreciated the opportunity every week to keep open mic night alive and humming. That much for sure.

"I see it's usually the strongest gross of the week," Roy said, his eyes narrow. "Can't argue with that."

"I'd take credit for that if I could. I just manage the signup list."

"Keep up that pace, and you're golden." Roy got a look. "Jasper? Question."

"I'm standing here."

Roy brought up Coy Wando, which was okay, Jasper reckoned, although why anyone would want to talk about that piece of human filth, he didn't know. Roy explained that since he'd gotten squat for stories out of his own grandfather about the formative experiences of the old man's life, might as well mine Jasper for his.

"Is what he said true? About Edgewater County? Ya-know, ya-know?"

Jasper's heart fluttered. He belched. Stood up from the porch-couch to be on this way. "I know what your granddaddy would've replied to that question."

"Yeah, I asked him one time, too."

"And what'd he say?"

"First, he cussed you up and down for making Coy Wando more famous with that book."

The author's cheeks burned. "Lord forgive me, I know it."

"But as for what Wando claimed? About secret societies? Rituals? Other missing kids through the years?"

Jasper waited.

"He said we don't talk about mess like what happened to those little girls, and what Coy Wando said about it. Not in his house."

"And what did that tell you?"

"More than I want to know."

The wisdom of the notion settled in the air around the two men. "Some questions remain better left unasked. That's how I'd put it."

"Just trying to learn everything I can about this place now. I didn't care before. But if I'm staying—well."

Here now, Jasper's opening: "How about that old honkytonk? Staying put?"

A range of emotion passed over the Pettus heir's face. "Starting to look that way."

For now, it was all Jasper needed to hear.

Realizing how his hands shook, and filings at the office awaiting, he bade Roy farewell right as Miss Runelle came shuffling out onto the porch to speak and greet. No time for that now. Not when a body's bracer had grown long overdue.

ROY AND ROOSEVELT NIXON

You're sitting at the dining room table grinding up herb for the Volcano. A large black SUV pulls into the front yard.

You almost shit a brick—it looks like cops.

Four men dressed in sharp suits of muted color pile out of the Escalade. To you the younger men's sunglasses, body language, and position—one respectful pace behind the figure who is their leader, your old friend the Reverend Roosevelt Nixon—make them look like a secret service detail.

You get an idea-r: *maybe I need an entourage.*

But you don't want bodyguards. You want a team like your guys at the hanger down on Sedge. A team of folks—if competent and committed members can be found—to go on missions, solve problems, invent solutions and implement technology to serve all mankind. Squad of Capable Bad-asses. All this flashes through your mind as you put away the weed, and gives you a different brand of hard-on than the one you wake up with every morning, a sign of good circulation.

You think on this whole idea; you envision it. Why? Because of Button's halting discourses about visualization, that all reality begins with a notion in someone's head, pretty pictures you can manifest later in meatspace through intention, attention, concentration, and diligent physical ritual. Or some such hooey—the girl exudes a boundless supply of woo-woo.

You picture your team standing at parade rest, awaiting orders. All are adorned with matching polo shirts determined by the Pantone Color of the Year® shade, with an embroidered team logo stitched onto the left breast, a symbol of your own design and charged up with all the enthusiasm and entrepreneurship available within you. Gray camping trousers. Waterproof sport sandals. Solid dude-bros you can count on, all serious, no comic relief character. Maybe addressing them with a riding crop in your hand. Boots and a helmet. Chin tipped back like George C. Scott in *Patton*.

While rinsing the sticky, stinky resin off your fingers, harsh words come from the front yard, Manny's voice: "I can't speak my mind, preach? I can't voice my own viewpoint?"

Outside on the porch you emerge upon a scene of tension—Nixon has no doubt noted Manny's remarks printed in the paper regarding the name-change campaign the new councilperson-reverend now pushes in the corridors of power and public opinion, as well on social media and the Sunday morning radio broadcast of his weekly sermon. Not that you listen or attend services, but you do agree with Roosevelt about the problematic future marketability of a name made to honor a recalcitrant, racist rascal like Ben Tillman. No skin off your nose. Ancient history. Rechristen the municipality as Saint-Royville-on-the-Sugeree, while you're at it.

"You guys know each other?"

Manny and Nixon exchange sharp glances. "Mr. Theodore and his family attend our church. Sometimes."

"What I think about changing the name of the town ain't got jack to do with listening to you preach. Besides, we put on the radio broadcast, give it a listen. We got a business to run, and Sunday brunch our biggest take of the week. My staff need me more'n the Lord does."

An uncomfortable shuffling of feet. You regard the Reverend's sons all standing behind him—his team. Decide to shatter the frost with vibes of friendship. "Rosie, hard to believe these are your kids. Last time I seen 'em, wasn't but squirts."

"Tender shoots that've sprouted into stiff-stalked, hardy young men of God. I must say." The boys' expressions don't break except for the youngest, who grunts and shuffles his polished dress shoes.

A formal moment of handshakes, as he reintroduces his sons Eusebius, Syncellus and Hammurabi, names you assume have connections to the Reverend Doctor's work as an anthropologist, ethno-mythologist, and Egyptologist. If, that is, you remember the gist, hahahaha, of his studies from the infrequent contact you had after he went off to college a few years ahead of you. You're duly curious how his academic work led him around to being an AME minister in a growing Southern megachurch, one that'd started off a clapboard country church across the bridge in Easton but now rebuilt and enormous, its asphalt parking pad second only to the Mall-wort distribution center down the road.

You noticed Nixon's new sanctuary building, with its huge parking lot and a hexagonal construction on the Easton side of the river, during the cursed flight into town that began this chapter of your life. Looked like a basketball arena. Now you know it's scaled to accommodate a congregation in the thousands, multicultural in demographic, all responding to his message of inclusive progressiveness befitting a man of his learned credentials here in the twenty-first century. A hip preacher. No fire and brimstone. Philosophy and real history mixed in. An initiate of Christianity, but also much more. A success in his field, in any case.

Of course, at the time—searching for the landing lights and a clean pair of panties—you had been preoccupied with getting wheels-down rather than cataloging unfamiliar local buildings.

Circumstances could never be worse, could they? That terrible day you flew home? Your worst day—you've had your worst day. It has been accomplished. How comforting—a bloom of satisfaction warms your cockles.

"Well-sir, this is a good-looking group, these young men." To the Reverend: "I don't think I've seen you in a geologic age, my friend."

"An epoch, at least."

Roosevelt rumbles with sad laughter and bundles you to his massive chest. Both of you slap each other's backs before concluding the hug with a squeeze from the preacher that crushes the last vestige of air from your body.

"Oof." Gasping. "*Blargh.*"

Manny, withdrawing. "Y'all seem like you got catching up to do, so..."

"I hope you'll change your mind, Mr. Theodore. And stand with us on this issue, united."

Acting like he can't hear, Manny hightails it to the old house in his tight jeans, Converse and pop culture-referencing T-shirt, today's selection a bright orange ringer with the *Soul Train* logo. Time to diplomacy the mess outta this, as well to keep the the preacher and his sons out of the kitchen where your dope sits in full view.

"You guys seem in disagreement out here."

"Roy Earl, as a stakeholder, this conversation has been overdue between us. But as for Manfred, I have to admit surprise at seeing him here. Confusion, even."

"Just a favor, letting him bunk in the house over yonder. Dude's got family problems."

"Unfortunately, we're no stranger to that."

"Amen," says Hammurabi. "A-*man*," echoes Syncellus, much softer.

The unity of this display of family loyalty and connection touches you. Makes you wish you had had a brother, or your own kids. "Sorry to hear that."

"Our mother, she left us." This, added by Syncellus.

Eusebius, angry. "Shut up. That's private."

The Rev barks at his sons: "Conduct yourselves with grace and dignity."

"So look, if you're here to discuss the naming rights issue? Or, not the naming rights, but the town name—"

"Actually? It's more about your plans for The Dixiana."

"Oh—don't tell me you got a dog in that hunt, too?"

He clears his throat, takes you by your arm. "I cannot lie to you, Roy Earl. I'd like to have seen Reynolds Pettus living a life of works that did not revolve around the sale of alcoholic beverages. I've no doubt that the community would only be stronger but for the lack of temperance, especially among today's young." He lasers hard-ass eyes at all three of his boys, who stiffen. "Who, when it comes to such indulgences, tend toward libertinism. Many young people—but not all."

"Amen," the youngest son says again. "Amen to that."

You can feel actual warmth in the Reverend's softened countenance of approbation. "Right. That's right, son."

Your friend's words cause consternation over the vacillation over the honkytonk's future, a struggle that's been bouncing around in your thoughts like one of those mixing marbles they put into spray-paint cans. If you would pivot back to your third-wave coffee plan, you'd make him a happy temperance fighter.

Alcohol. Creedence had been drinking like a goddamn lush for years. That'd been the root of her infidelity. You should stamp out alcohol. Except, The Dixiana could never go on without selling beer and liquor. Alcohol is what makes your nut in a trade like honkytonkin'.

❋

THE DAY YOU FIRST SPOKE WITH ROOSEVELT NIXON BACK IN HIGH SCHOOL, HE HAD already been a savior-figure even well before his role as a man of the cloth:

"Hey, you little faggot-ass dork. Yeah-you, Pettus. Get yer ass over here."

"You're a little homo, ain't ya? Huh? Say."

Howie Smalls slapped you on the back of your head, at the same time shoving you in the direction of the twin Waugh brothers. Cecil and Harlem had been the stars of the 1983 championship football team, the squad who had beaten Summerville so badly in the big game that the opposing coach had, in the end, cried like the pussy he was. Or so guys like the Waugh boys, seniors to your sophomore status, had said.

Harlem Waugh shoved you back toward his brother Cecil, who yanked the book bag off your shoulders so hard it ripped the neckline of your black *Star Trek II: The Wrath of Khan* heat-transfer T-shirt you'd gotten in Myrtle Beach last summer. And treasured. How you had had to hide your swollen eyes from everyone after watching Spock die.

"Don't—please don't tear my shirt."

They howled with derisive laughter. Mocked your high voice.

Cecil stepped up, his presence made worse than Harlem's owing to a stinging cloud of Frito-Lay breath filling the air around your face. "Let's tear that fucking girly shirt off him. Get a look at them titties underneath."

Cecil, twisting your flabby boob. You hollered in pain.

"Y'all, this bitch ain't no homo—he's a chick. Get a load of these jugs."

Howie whispered in your ear. "I'm-a hit this pussy, y'all."

"Go for it, brother."

"Sloppy seconds over here."

Harlem and Cecil grabbed your arms while Howie began thrusting his pelvis into your midsection. All were howling like wolves out on the plain at midnight. "Fuck on that prick. Fuck on it like you mean it."

One of the gym lobby doors to the parking lot clanged shut, an explosion that reset the energy to a resting state. A hulking shape blocked out the late afternoon sun like an unanticipated eclipse, or a back-lit avenging angel right out of the movies. A frowning, round melon of a head sat atop a letterman's jacket so big you could've made a tent from it.

Nixon's eyes blazed at his teammates, who had all frozen in their act of schoolyard violence. Cecil, not a little guy by anyone's measure, turned a whiter shade of pale at the sight of his teammate standing in the lobby with his fists clenched in anger. Howie licked his lips. Harlem grunted under his breath.

Despite his young age, Nixon moved toward them with the gait of a man for whom time itself sat willing to wait. "More bullying? To what end?"

"Stay out of it, Rosie," Harlem warned. "Punk owes us money."

"Coach'll be disappointed in you all. When he hears about this latest transgression."

"Oh, fuck him," Cecil said. "Coach can hang fire for all I care."

Roosevelt nodded to you standing behind the miscreants who only seconds before had enjoyed brutal control and total dominance, reveling in their misbegotten primacy like the mean-spirited children they were.

"What have I told y'all about the homosexual play-acting?" Roosevelt, a half-foot taller than the tallest of the other boys, moved you bodily from within their grasp. "Smalls, on the bus, after the championship game?"

Howie said yeah-yeah.

"And, what did I tell you?"

Howie gulped and said nothing, though his face betrayed that he did recall the incident in question. "Come on, Rosie. I said it's all a joke."

"Often as you make it, it's all looking less like humor than a confession."

Cecil and Harlem tittered. Howie declared 'he wasn't no fag.'

Roosevelt Nixon's face hardened with righteous indignation. "Question: do y'all homeboys wish to be thought about as homosexual?"

"We're just giving the bidness to this little freshman turd."

"I'm a sophomore."

Harlem shoved you against the brick wall by the water fountain. "Shut up."

Roosevelt snorted. "I think the coach was right about you Waugh boys. I really do. An utter lack of common sense and basic human intelligence—I think that's how he put it."

"Fuck you, Rosie."

"Yeah, go suck a dick. A big black donkey dick."

Roosevelt Nixon erupted in laughter, the mocking sort. He nudged his way into the circle and put one muscular arm contained by his red and blue letter jacket around your soft, round teenage shoulders.

"Why not take it a step further? Why don't you yokels go impregnate some livestock out in your daddy's field. Everybody needs a hobby, or so's I hear. Bestiality should suit you all." This last remark directed toward Howie, whose father did in fact own a dairy farm not far from the Pettus land on River Ridge Road. "I have to walk my man out to the bus."

Your three tormentors had hustled their way back into the gym, where the reverb from the bouncing balls and squeaking sneakers echoed in the lobby. Harlem Waugh, dumb as a box of rocks, looked back over his shoulder and whispered 'nigger' as he slammed the door behind him with a ridiculous amount of force, rattling the glass.

Outside in the parking lot where your grandfather waited in his pickup truck to pick you up—in high school! And how you couldn't wait to drive yourself!—you looked at Roosevelt Nixon feeling gratitude but also uncertainty. "Thanks, I guess."

"I rescued your chubby little butt from those bumpkins, and you say, 'I guess?'"

"No—I really appreciate it." Next to the grown man's booming baritone that issued from Roosevelt, your voice sounded tiny and squeaky like that of a preadolescent girl's. "Swear I do."

"You're welcome, I *guess*. What your name, boy?"

"Roy Earl Pettus. But most everybody calls me Roy." It wasn't true, everyone called you Roy Earl, and you hated it—like a little boy's name, one who lives out in po-dunk farm country. "Just Roy."

"Damn, boy—you look tired."

It was true. Besides being soft and flabby you always had a haggard demeanor, with purple smudges that appeared under your eyes at about age eleven and had never quite gone away. "I ain't tired. Kinda hungry, though."

"Can't argue with that, dog. You eat real food?"

"Yeah."

"You ought to have my grandmother's cooking. You'd know what food was, then. But—she ain't with us no more. She done gone home to the Lord."

"I'm sorry, man."

"Don't be. I said she's with the Lord, didn't I?"

"Oh. Right."

"Don't you know about being saved?"

You said, sure.

"*Are* you saved?"

"I reckon." In truth, you didn't know saved from Shinola.

"Well, now, good. But let me talk to you about Jesus anyway..."

On the sidewalk where the buses lined up Roosevelt Nixon had witnessed unto you faith in all things Jesus, and the ultimate fulfillment provided when one dwells within the Kingdom of Heaven. He preached for a spell. You said you'd take it all to heart.

He concluded on a more conversational and personal note. "Don't let them fellas get you down," Roosevelt said in farewell. "You come get me next time they start up, and watch them old boys shit their britches. Nothing but cowards. You know why?"

A quick shrug. "Because you're big as the side of a house?"

"Nope. Cause they ain't found Jesus, yet. In Jesus, we find our true selves, and our realest courage."

"Hey."

"Yes?"

"Why'd you help me back there? You guys are all on the team together, and all." You scratched your chin and shifted the weight of your burdensome book bag from one shoulder to the other. "Ain't that supposed to mean something?"

"I play for a different team—a more powerful one."

"Who's that?"

"The team behind the team."

After that day and throughout a friendship lasting a year or two, Roosevelt left a head full of thoughts that have lingered and informed your worldview. You might not have found Jesus, but you will forever after mull this idea of actors behind a curtain, so to speak, what Button would call a "gnostic" notion: that this reality we know is only one of many levels at which stuff happens, with some participants acting as inter-dimensional creatures including us, when you consider our sojourn here as a deliberate adventure of the spirit into flesh. Many of these all-but invisible actors may not have our best interest in mind.

How would young Nixon know whether he communed with spiritual partners benevolent and not deceptive? That's what Button has to say about religion. That we must exercise spiritual caution that the God of Abraham isn't merely the demiurge, the head Archon, having a field day feeding on energies put off by human beings in states of emotional and physical distress here in the world of shadows. That Button and her crazy raps! You couldn't just lay all that on a serious cat like Roosevelt Nixon and not be considered a flake.

Or could you? His, a diverse C-V. Intellectual. All that Egyptology and anthropology mixed in with this theological training. Still, a discussion for another time.

◉⊕❋

NIXON PRESSES YOU ON THIS WHOLE NEW FALLS CITY BUSINESS. YOU COULD GIVE two squirts, adding that the will of the people in his referendum on the matter next year should tell the definitive tale.

Also, that you couldn't speak for your grandparents, but knowing them as you did, you doubted they would be in favor. He accepts this, asks for your spiritual support, and bids you farewell following a final exhortation to join him and the congregation on Sunday mornings.

You and Manny, whose re-emergence appears timed to coincide with Nixon's departure, wave to the SUV kicking up dust in its luxury-sized wake.

Manny turns his friendly gesture into a flipped middle finger. "Forgive me, Lord, but: Nixon can kiss my black ass."

"What," you inquire, "was all that static?"

"Aw—me running my mouth too much."

"Y'all were vibrating at each other at some dangerously high frequencies."

Manny, explaining about the remarks that little shit-ass newspaper printed, and for which he has endured no small measure of retribution from Nixon and others pressing for the symbolic, inclusive name-change scheme. "Wasn't trying to piss nobody off. It just what I muh-fucken think."

"Can't fault a man for speaking his mind."

"I catch it coming and going."

You get it. "Ought to be able to tell your truth and get away with it."

"Word to that."

"Weird world anymore."

"You know how much it gonna cost to get menus and business cards changed over a new town name? Update the website?"

"Preaching to the choir, my man. Not to mention freeway signage. That's our tax dollars paying for that."

Manny mumbles 'shit' and aims to go on about his business, but not before you invite him inside for a quick vape session, the machine already warmed up from before Nixon's surprise visit.

Manny, having a hard time meeting your eyes. "Maybe not. Feeling a little paranoid."

"You okay otherwise?"

"Yeah. It nothing. Ain't slept worth a durn."

"Join the club. The weed seems to help."

"Raincheck on the choomba, brotherman."

In your room you fill up a plastic sack with vapor; your grandmother, taking her morning nap that lasts longer and longer. Maybe it's time to get her to a doctor for a checkup, which she says is unnecessary and not due for months to come.

It's hard for you to press her on such issues. In your grandmother's presence, and Roosevelt Nixon's, for that matter, you remain a little boy still, the bossman of nobody and nothing.

GOOCH, DOBBS AND MIRIAM VANDEGRIFT

As they pulled into the parking lot Dobbs said, "Are you sure you want to come visit my mother?"

"Why on earth not?"

Dobbs maneuvered his modified van into a handicapped space at the extended care facility, which offered components for those at various stages of eldercare, or decrepitude, as Bill thought of it. "She doesn't even know me anymore, much less you."

"I remember her well from dropping you off at the paper, back when you were doing your internship in high school. We spoke a few times. More than a few. Seeing me might jog her memory."

"That's awfully kind."

"Least I can do."

Bill, who had trouble, he'd realized, with remembering things, hoped his presence would indeed help. He had another agenda, but in his years of being a small-town reporter and editor and gadabout as he fancied himself, you learned to love the secret agendas you withheld and masks you wore, revel in the nonchalant ways of snooping around for information you needed, either for copy or background or out of good old-fashioned feline curiosity.

The story he wanted to break? Designating who would take care of him. He had no one. Owed it to himself to have a plan.

What did you do—throw yourself on the mercy of the system?

He'd have to take care of himself. While he could.

Dobbs would help.

Maybe Dobbs would bring Gooch to live with him—or better yet, move into the Craftsman on Whaley Way, with plenty of room once Bill took care of the paper archives, a growing problem.

But who'd want to live in such a rattrap? Bill didn't. He got lost sometimes, in the sloping stacks of magazines and books like the fabled hall of records of his life; the copies of the paper, the realest of the keepsakes, stored in one old bedroom. Hundreds and thousands of editions. Bill suspected the ones way in the back and on the bottom had dry rotted. He'd put in a humidifier to keep the rest from becoming desiccated. When the time came, he'd donate it all to Cordelia Karlaney over at the county archives.

When the time came. He still had his novel to get written. And research, ongoing. He needed to interview a few people, older folks like him.

Runelle Pettus, for one. It'd finally occurred to him she had a connection to the Sunbury School Fire at the heart of Gooch's story, two older sisters lost to the conflagration. Runelle, a toddler, had been saved while the much-older girls, one of whom had been graduating—one of those spread out farm families, long-suffering mother bearing children for the better part of her entire adult period of fertility—were at the school enjoying the play and the ceremony, but perished. Their bodies, as Gooch recalled from a fifty-year anniversary roundup he'd put together back in '83, lay buried in the mass grave alongside so many others, two-thirds of the eighty dead, interred together in a steaming, horrid clump of burned bodies.

Runelle had reasonable primary memories of the aftermath that hadn't been reported back then. A refresher on the facts—that's what he needed. Research. He'd look for his notes from the commemorative piece scrawled in one of his beloved little notebooks—an archive dive.

The whole community had suffered, as a letter-writer of the day described the pall of sorrow that hung over Edgewater County for quite some time afterwards. Hard to imagine such an awful event—the children, the community leaders, the mass grave. How living through such a tragedy must feel, particularly in the recent aftermath. But folks had persevered. Tillman Falls had gone on its way, to the present moment and beyond.

If Gooch didn't figure out the somehow part, though, he might not have what it took to write a novel—a worthwhile one, anyway. With wisdom to offer. You couldn't simply make up out of whole cloth a tragedy like the Sunbury fire, not and depict its impact with the verisimilitude and gravitas such an event deserved. To use such tragedy for dramatic ends, one ought to know what true loss felt like.

Oh, was the old reporter starting to understand loss, though. On a personal level. Most intimately. No doubt.

"Nice place," Gooch said, thinking to scribble a note to himself to CALL RUNELLE P in his current pocket-size spiral memo notebook, the piece of gear that'd formed the cornerstone of his entire career. He had several plastic bins full of old ones, and never fewer than at least one unopened three-pack—they came shrink-wrapped in threes, with primary color covers like red, green and deep navy blue—stashed in the car and the desks, both at home and at work. In earlier times he bought them from Frakes Brothers Stationary, but they'd gone out of business years ago. For a time he bought his memo notebooks by the case at the Office Depot down in Dentsville, the suburb near the lake, though the last time he'd ordered them from Amazon, a better deal even with the shipping.

He stared at the notebook, unable to recall what he'd opened it to write. "Nice and clean parking lot here. Inside the same?"

"I think it's fine."

Gooch, enthusing over the bright yellow striping of the parking spaces. "Recently touched up. Looks sharp."

"Well, it's one swanky little parking lot—sure."

Dobbs dropped open his wheelchair, unhooking his seatbelt and pulling and swinging his legs around, settling into the chair and shutting the door and chirping the lock, all smooth as silk. Bill thought, *Mercy but that's a capable crippled man.* No wonder he wished Dobbs would love and care for him.

Did he say that aloud?

Dobbs wheeled backward off the lift and clicked his remote, which caused the platform to withdrawn up and into the van. As he slid shut the door, he asked, "Why'd you really want to come today?"

Now that caught Bill off guard. "I hoped—you'd like the company."

"Normally you'd be worried about both of us being gone from the paper."

"Put to bed."

"True. That never stopped you from worrying before."

"Nope. And you know why? The news never stops."

"So—what's the reason?"

"You don't have to make everything so complicated. I just wanted the company."

Dobbs, nodding. "You'll tell me when you tell me. I feel you."

A good attitude.

Truth was, this represented Gooch's second visit here. After jerking awake in the night and having the notion come over him, one of urgency, saying, where will I need to be and how can I arrange it before I forget too much, and he'd gone out driving to look at this extended-care facility—an old folks' home, sure, but he tried not to consider it as such. It'd been five in the morning, and when he had the sense to realize that the strip of pink dawn on the horizon was dawn and not sunset, he went over to the Waffle House by the freeway and drank coffee and ate hash browns with onions and peppers and hot sauce, which he forgot made him have terrible indigestion, and he'd belched and read the *Columbia Record* and watched the sun rise, twin steam plumes from the nuclear plant's cooling towers glowing back-lit and rising dreamlike over the tree line. As scared of people used to be of atomic bombs blowing up and ending life as we knew it, the world sure tolerated putting these plants close to where folks lived. A crazy, dirty way to make steam.

Button Sykes—those were her words. The story about her protest tent. That was what Bill wanted to file today. Or had he written it already? Her crusade to point out that more reactors amounted to a bandage solution, and produced only more nuclear waste, and needed replacement by alternate ways and means of green energy generation before it was all too late, why... it was far too forward thinking. The lights were on. That's all most folks knew, and cared to know, besides how much the bills every month.

In any case, Gooch could recite Button's spiel by heart. The story would write itself. If it hadn't already.

"You ever sit there writing, and get lost in time?" Gooch's loafers crunched on the sidewalk while Dobbs wheeled himself, smiling and waving to two wizened residents taking a stroll in their yellowed pajamas and dingy robes. "After a while you look up and it's been an hour, or three hours, or five."

He referred to his latest attempts to write his epic Edgewater County historical novel, which somebody else ended up coming along and doing well, damn that Cort Beauchamp's ass, but the writer's trance applied to churning out and editing copy for the paper, too. When you got going, time—other than the deadline—didn't matter. Made all that hippie-dippy patter about time being an illusion seem to have merit. Not that hippie-dippy prattle possessed truth. Only what the facts presented could constitute a measurable reality. Facts to report. Facts that stood tall and singular and didn't have two sides, quantifiable and describable in language—

Dobbs tugged at Gooch's sport coat sleeve like a child trying to get his parent's attention. "Hey, bub. You gonna finish that thought?"

Gooch came out of his trance, which he attributed to having been thinking hard about... whatever it'd been. They had arrived at the entrance, a walk from the parking lot of twenty yards. "What was I saying?"

"Something about time. And writing."

"Oh—yes. Takes time. To write."

"To write well, certainly."

Bill, blurting: "I can't remember things anymore. I even forget that I can't remember."

Dobbs squeezed his hand, a gesture of intimacy that sent a charge through Gooch's crooked old reporter's spine. "I feel you. I hear you. And I'm ready to help."

"Ready? For what?" He had wandered from the path of the conversation again. Cursed himself. Tried to reckon on how to fake his way through. "Boy—I was born ready."

Dobbs released Gooch's hand and smoothed down his sleeve, a gentle gesture, loving and patient. "This makes me happy. I'm so happy. That book—it won't write itself. Will it."

"No. Those things. They don't write themselves. Oh—you're dwelling on Cort Beauchamp's book, aren't you? Same here. That rascal."

Dobbs, perplexed. "No—I'm talking about your book."

Bill Wimmel felt his cheeks flush. "My book? My book. Yes."

"You could get it written in one of the little apartments they have here." Dobbs, nodding at him. "Couldn't you?"

He still didn't know what they were discussing, not really, but he nodded back and said yes, yes and thanked Dobbs, beaming pleasure as they checked in and went to visit Dobbs's mother. She sat the whole time slack and inert, eyes glassy, responses rote and removed a layer or two from sentience, and only when Dobbs told her about Gooch's impending retirement to finish writing his dream novel and isn't that wonderful did Bill Wimmel fully understand that somehow, in his ongoing delusion of lucidity that the facts belied every day of his life, he'd agreed to retire and turn the paper over to Dobbs Vandegrift. His protégé.

Retirement—his life, over. Thirty years of the paper. Thirty years. The blink of an eye. Sort of like how time turned elastic when you were writing, except here, compressed, decades into moments. If only it worked the other way.

In the hallway Gooch tried to smile at a gnarled black man. His face sunken, the resident looked like a shuffling skeleton whose clothing wafted in the air conditioned institutional breeze, laundry left to rot on a forgotten clothesline.

"How's the day for ya," the resident asked Gooch with a gravel throat.

"Not bad. Good to see you," despite not knowing the man.

"S'good to be seen." And passing by with his garments rustling and the rubber tips of the walker squeaking against the waxed floor. "Can't ask for much more'n that."

"I reckon you can't."

Gooch remembered why he'd wanted to come today: a good reporter not looking for the story of what had happened, but rather what to come, and how well he could expect to live, and be treated, here at this facility. Where he'd have time, plenty of time, to explore the depths of his memories and write his novels.

Wait—dad blame it all. It was Letty Glasscock he needed to interview, not Runelle Pettus. Letty's older sisters died in the fire. Not Runelle's.

You mixed-up old fool.

He got out the notebook, scratched through RUNELLE P and wrote LETTY G. *ABOUT THE FIRE*, he added.

Wait—what fire?

What time was it? Was the paper put to bed?

Where was he? He'd ask Dobbs. Thank goodness he had an assistant like this young man in the wheelchair.

ROY EARL AND RUNELLE

Her voice croaks, weak, from inside the first-floor master bedroom, designed to be only steps from both kitchen and bathroom, glass sliding doors leading onto hardwood decking you know needs pressure-washing into pristine newness again. Check.

Roy Earl.

Roy Earl...

"What's doing this morning, Mee-maw?"

No answer.

You hum and sip coffee and shuffle down the short hallway, catching a glimpse out the small window of the bedroom deck, on the eastern side and good for enjoying sunrises and the morning paper. Has it been so long since you built this house for them that the decking's gone weathered and gray, like your own hair trends, more so with each passing day? Mercy but it never stops; you chip away at the list but it all still builds up in the corners. Tasks and nonsense and endless bullet-points endlessly renewed, the snake eating its tail, the time-is-a-flat-circle foolishness.

To.

Do.

Yea, verily, but what shall we do with ourselves, you ask the cosmos, other than whittle our lists?

A knock. "You decent?"

No answer.

"Mee-maw?"

The door's unlocked. Push it open. If she's indecent, she'll get over it.

You hesitate, call for her again.

ACT, a voice urges.

She's lying on the floor, her flimsy old nightie pushed up over spindly sticks, pale and spider-veined and twisted, skin mottled and purplish and gray in spots. Her mouth, agape. Eyes unseeing. Hands clutched at her side, stiff. The covers mussed. A glass of water, spilled nearby.

She got up to refill her water. And fell.

She's been here all night—dead.

But you heard her call out for you; she can't be gone.

And you panic, screaming and dropping to the cold, unyielding floor to try to comfort your grandmother out of unconsciousness, a moment in which you should call 9-1-1, which you run to do while cursing yourself, the universe and Edgewater County, even your own blood. "I'm getting help, Mee-maw! It'll be okay." But you know it won't.

She's gone.

All you hear is Button Sykes discoursing on how this reality we experience is the dream of our lives, that we are dreaming and we create it all, and now you can only hope and pray is that one day you'll wake up, finally, from the dream factory. And begin to live.

For now, you perform due diligence; you must get the EMTs out here. Maybe when you walk back in she'll be on her feet, yelling at you for causing a fuss. It's denial; you can't accept that your Mee-maw is gone, not this early in the day, not before finishing your morning coffee. Not yet, Lord. You're not ready to be alone.

As you watch them roll out her frail, lifeless form, you felt the Darling of the Dixiana's life energy leave along with the inert body like evaporating mist from the vape-pen you've been hitting so hard your throat burns.

When you go inside to find her strongbox of important documents, you discovered a birth certificate showing Runelle Kittery to have been born in 1924 and not 1928 as she claimed—she lived well into her nineties. You'd never have known it. Still smoked and cussed like a young woman. And took care of her family that way, too.

A long and happy life; now reunited on the far side with her great love. You'd complain, but suspect she's happier now.

❋

THE NEXT DAY WHILE MAKING THE ARRANGEMENTS—WHERE YOUR GRANDFATHER'S had been the ultimate private affair, your Mee-maw's rites would be public and lavish—you recall her admonition on the morning you were to perform Pa-paw's ceremony at the fishing bluff: your attire. You have no suit. And the one you do have, which you'd worn to the closing and the meetings at which you divested yourself of your role as bossman of the SBFC empire and took a big fat payday to do so, now hangs far too big on you.

You hustle over to see the boys at Gentleman's Affair; you wish in your heart the consignment shop were still off the main drag, but none of those old downtown businesses—except the honkytonk—survived into the modern age.

Instead, you drove from the funeral home where you paid for your grandmother's arrangement down the access road a few hundred yards to a strip mall. You reckoned you'd need about a forty-two regular, waist size thirty-two, trouser length twenty-nine. Maybe they'll have a suit on the rack close enough to ready—the funeral services will occur on Thursday. And you want to look your best. Not only for her, who watches down upon you, but for your wife. This, a chance to get her here. And perchance to keep her, again.

Only good part of this mess—all your dramas, coming at once. Getting them squared away; chippin' at the pile. You hope one day it'll all add up to make some damn sense.

You're not holding your breath.

You can roll with it. Alone or not, what other choice? Besides waiting for Creedence to call you back and give you an answer about attending the funeral —now here, an important item to check off. And maybe a signpost toward a little less loneliness than what you fear awaits.

BUTTON AND ROY

Button, visited by a version of her future-self 'Walfredo,' received a vibration beyond peaceful and fulfilling.

But also ambiguous.

Troubling, even.

Button, suspecting this the Walfredo of her future post-incarnation self, rather than an actual point in the future of her current physicalized form, in other words from her existence post-meatspace. This sojourn here in the dimensionality decoded by the five or six senses was brief, after which a return to a form of pure(r) energy in which 'we' revisit the results of our prior soul contracts to decide how best to continue through further incarnations (or not at all). Nothing complicated about it.

As the weeks passed and she traversed her lucid dreams to encounter entities like Terence McKenna's self-transforming hyperintelligent machine elves, questions directed to them went unanswered, her odd symptoms grew more niggling and persistent, and she better understood that Walfredo represented an essence of spirit transcending what incarnated souls experience as death.

Button, realizing Walfredo comes to prepare her for her own death.

Yep. Hard as it was to believe, her calls for citizens to appreciate the gravity of their impending demise from environmental degradation and other factors in fact held another layer of meaning: it represented her response to a shout from a place of farsight and wisdom out on the rim of this shared dimensionality, a call from deep in the wilderness, that her own time was ending. Soon.

Frightening.

Wait—no, it wasn't.

Walfredo, beaming back to her the brand of reassurance that all would not only be fine or simply okay, but all is forgiven, all would be perfection, for all eternity, and she got a taste every day when she meditated, and it's totes chill, dude. Clouds filling the thousand mountains. Golden flowers blooming.

Even better? All had always been thus. She needed to get back to this state. From which she, and everyone, had come.

The more she thought about it, Walfredo, seeming a wise old soul. An inner and ancient authority.

No—the more she *felt* about it. Not thought.

And through this so-called experience of 'feeling,' a principal reason for the existence of such awarenesses here in the this realm, a settling came upon her body, mind, and spirit, and a sense of an achievement of what could only be termed magical equipoise.

With all this in mind she performed her banishing ceremony, which continued to evolve, and during which she had sensed gathering entities of ill intent, but kept well at bay and shielded from her; she meditated and did a serious series of full sun salutations, best she could with the nettlesome pain in her side only becoming more pronounced. She turned the Tarot cards. Gleaned only the grimmest of outlooks. Put the deck and velvet altar cloth away in their bloodwood and cherry oak storage box in a drawer next to Button's childhood twin bed shoved in the corner of her book-and-clothing-strewn bedroom.

Stress. Concern for her charges at home. Physical duress from the leafletting, her aches and pains irritated by wrestling with the E-Z UP tent on the green. Tension from trying to remain detached about the peculiar vibes from that little group of folks, as Dubya would put it, comprising Newbie Harrell, the darkly weird giant-sized kid, and last but not least Howdy Shull, who of late gave her the sourest vibration of all.

Those worrisome cats—that's who she needed to banish.

If she could.

While hurting no one's feelings or being too aggro about it.

After completing the sacred routines, only then did she finish packing for her trip with Roy to visit Heather Ponderview. To heal his broken spirit. To help him live and learn and grow.

And to see Heather. At last. Oh, but yes. In the recent emails, the truth has become clear: Heather is not in a good place. She needs Button, this time. Not the other way around. Button—called to serve the one who had served.

Time now short. As much as time existed at all.

Not that she would let on to either of them the presumptive seriousness of her condition. That's not what this was about. This trip was for Roy. And Heather, too. The giving of oneself, of one's energy, to the needs of others, the surest method of traversing the narrow way.

◉①✳

A chore, first: Breaking up with poor Jouquoya Moulton. Not a lasting relationship. Not in Button's mind. Not like her and Heather.

Well, Jackie no doubt wanted it to become that, but the more time Button spent with her, the more the soft-voiced pharmacist had seemed far too needy, and in an egoic manner suggesting energetic vampirism. Button, feeling guilty and sorrowful, but her truest heart lay with another.

These things happen. Ships passing. And so on.

As such, too often considering Jackie as the subject in an experiment, a scientific study of the sexual response absent the element of deep love, or in a more generous frame of mind, only an abject case of convenience, of taking advantage of a willing, warm body.

Perhaps in time, a meaningful relationship might have developed. But not in Tillman Falls, it seemed, where Jackie said she'd never ever ever come out due to prejudice within a family she couldn't abide any thought of losing. Sorry, but no. Existing in a state of total truth and honesty, the only spiritual path on which Button would tread, now. No partners engaged in living lies for her.

Not with Heather so close.

Not with a door just starting to open.

She worked on a Dear Jane email for a long time before sending it.

Button suffered an immediate pang of regret and panic, and sure enough, within minutes a fusillade of wicked nasty texts and emails blew up her device. Immature, ranting, threatening, cajoling. Button, sensing Jackie's tears and confusion from all the way across town; later, experiencing them firsthand out on the sidewalk in front of the house.

"Button—don't do this."

"We had fun. It's not always. True love."

"I told you secrets."

"You can't even be out. It's not—it'll never work. I can't hide."

Shrieking and crying, she swung her arms, pacing: "I ain't give myself to nobody like that hardly ever. I'm-a fuck you up for doing this to me!" But only boo-hooing and running to get into her car, burning rubber out of the neighborhood. Faces in windows behind dingy veils.

Still caring for the girl; feeling a modest connection. As such, Button preferred not to put poor Jackie through the possible horrors of illness to come. The patient in this case would need no pharmacological advice. Not for the plan she hand in mind to handle the symptoms of her disease.

Afterward, alone and bawling it out in her room, Button lay surrounded by all the books, the copy of Steiner's *Way of Initiation* she'd been re-reading last night falling off the bed and losing her place. The book tumbled down onto the huge red volume of Shakespeare saved from a college class; she'd been perusing the sonnets, looking for one to send to Heather Ponderview. Or perhaps Rilke, as she reconsidered. You who never arrived, my love, or however that bittersweet lament went.

Button had plenty of reasons, but whether over breaking Jackie's heart or Heather's unavailability—but for how much longer?—or her own incipient mortality, either way it felt good to cry one out. Even better, then, in getting to the other side of the feeling, to examine it from the perspective of total awareness that occupied the limitless spaces beyond Button's ego and intellect. A magnetic glow. An assurance beyond troublesome, glorious emotion. A connection to source.

From this attitude of detachment yet oneness, Button, or rather the higher-consciousness version of what she considered 'self,' found all the drama and turmoil compelling and interesting. Jackie would survive. I mean, really, Button thought: any way you sliced what was coming, the GF would need to get over this brief fling they shared.

◉◑✳

THREE AND HALF HOURS FROM EDGEWATER COUNTY TO HEATHER'S PLACE, THE expansive family home set way back almost on the Tennessee border that Button visited back in the 90s, this time with Roy. Road trip buddies snacking and cranking tunes, a Dead first set from 1977 followed by prime-cut Phish, one of the Colorado sets that had been so amazing, the 'Golden Age' into 'Light' sequence the night she had her transformative mushroom experience. With light traffic, the journey north went fast, the way a drive will when you have a good friend with whom to chat, chuckle, and, continue to play getting to know you.

And to hit the vape, but also get high in ways other than from her weed. His mind, opening to the essential truths. Receptive to her talks about meditation and spirit. About connecting with higher consciousness. The emptiness of commerce, the pointlessness and unnatural nature of money, which he seemed to get. Money. It all seemed so empty, he indicated from his position of having more than he knew how to spend.

Roy took issue with her rap about 'the matrix,' that culture itself was already a form of virtual reality, with the screen-centric smartphone era ushering in a new layer on top of the already simulated state we call civilization. Her worries about fluoride—what was gonna keep the teeth from rotting? As for her power plant concerns, what would run the computers and gadgets and pizza ovens and enormous light poles for nighttime sporting events— unicorn farts? Roy could be a relentless, yeah-but devil's advocate.

But at least he was digging on mediation, and talk about third eyes, the chakras, and maybe concluding he might have root chakra issues. His, he explained, a difficult birth. Anxiety. Trouble letting go of past issues. Yeah. Root chakra. She'd explain how he could lighten his load, simply by visualizing a healing deep red light emanating from his groin while he meditated. She would get to all that, activating the chakras and so on.

Roy, receptive, the only necessary element so far as it concerned both student and master—willingness.

"Got a question."

"Sure. Shoot." Button, fidgeting with the seatbelt strap across her shoulder. Grunting in discomfort. Hiding this from him. "A kinda out-there one."

"You can't get. Too out there. For me."

"What's it all about?"

"'It'?"

He gestured with a palm, open: "What you call our shared, co-created reality."

Button mulled before offering the most succinct summation she'd ever managed. How effortless her words came, as though her vocal cords played like violin strings by one of her guardian angels:

"Our bodies, this 3-D incarnation stuff, it's an experiment in emotion: hate, jealousy, anger, despair, greed, pain; and happiness, joy, laughter, gratitude, compassion. Most of all? Love. Love is the drug."

"Love—soft as an easy chair. Fresh as the morning air."

"We're like a vessel—we fill ourselves with whatever we choose to. Pick one. Fill yourself up. But see, every moment a new reality is born, and it comes complete with total choice regarding what you wish to experience. What you wish to be. What energy you wish to fill yourself with. How much joy. How much pain. You choose your thoughts; you take your trip. And that trip is short."

"But what if it's coming from others? Giving you emotions you don't want?"

"The anchors we consciously choose to weigh ourselves down have nothing to do with others. Only ourselves, in states of the lack of greater understanding, awareness, our souls subsumed by belief systems and facts. Everything we perceive to be solid becomes, at a certain point of reduction, only space—dark matter, they now call it, for want of any more specific or meaningful term for math that doesn't quite add up. Hah. So imagine just how empty facts and beliefs are. How meaningless what other people want you to feel. So don't spend much time thinking about the why and the how. Just be."

This gave him so much to chew on that the next few miles went by without conversation, only the 'Light' bliss jam and the whirr of her Subaru Baja tires providing a soothing vibration.

Roy, soft-spoken and reflective. "I had a tough birth, or so legend has it. My grandmother always said it was so terrible, out in the waiting room waiting to hear about me. Granddaddy, Uncle Burnie, Aunt Henny, Mama Runelle, a couple other people. My daddy, he'd already shipped out by then. Never met him, as you know. And he never met me."

"I know." She watched as he took the turns as gently as he could, this winding mountain highway about to turn into a two-lane backcountry road. Roy had complained earlier of motion sickness, said he would need to drive, if she didn't mind, which she didn't. It hurt her back to drive, to shift the gears. "Can't imagine. Never meeting my own dad."

"A breech birth—I didn't turn around inside my mom. Didn't want to come out, I guess. So it was feet first, pulling me out in this dangerous way, and hurting my mom. The problem was that it would cut my air off too long, from the cord being wrapped around my neck. The doctor said it didn't look good, but he'd do his best. He had been so grim-faced, Mee-maw said. Trying to prepare them for the worst. Everybody cried. Even my granddaddy, honking his nose into one of them handkerchiefs he used to carry around. You didn't never see his ass cry. That much for sure..."

"Aw."

"I know."

"*Aw.*"

"*But it all worked out!*" he shouted, startling Button into laughter. "Mama Runelle said a big black nurse came running out hollering, he's all right, he's all right. A few minutes later they got to see me all swaddled up. I was pink and crying at the top of my lungs, which made them all happy, doctor and nurses and everyone. But they cried again later, she always said, because my dad was away. They didn't know he'd never be home again. But Pa-paw and Burnie, having been in the war... having seen what they saw. They knew the odds."

"My dad—he loved yours. Visited the gravesite often."

He nodded in acknowledgement. "And she would wrap up the tale by saying how there wouldn't be nothing but sorrow, then, for the longest time." A tear sneaked out. He flicked it away like a booger, and his next words came thin with grief. "Because Ronnie Ed Pettus never came home."

"Your mom? Was okay?"

Roy breathed, deep, shook off his sadness. "Mee-maw always described her condition afterwards as 'very tired' and that she slept all night. I never got a chance to hear my mom's version."

Button, stopping herself from going 'aw' again, a sincere display of empathy, but that might sound mocking or facile. "How mysterious. It must be."

Roy stared at the passing mountain maple and hickory trees, the Fraser firs, the sloping mountainside. "What's that?"

"Not knowing. Your parents."

"Mythical—that's what they are. To me, my folks are these legendary figures out of antiquity. Wraiths, whispering in my dreams. My mom, she has more of a realness. One of her nightgowns—a particular yellow one. That I can recall," holding out the palm of his hand. "Can remember how it felt. And the smell of her hair. I kinda lie to myself a bit. Imagine most of it, I reckon. But the nightgown. I swear I can feel it as though my hand was resting on her back right now."

"A tactile sensation of her remains, at least."

Derisive. "It's not primary experience. It's only because a yellow, silky nightgown, threadbare and petite, was in the box of her things I found in the attic of the old house this one time. When I touched the fabric, I had this electric rush, this sense memory—I remembered her. Or, I only imagined it. But it felt good. And real. All I can tell you."

"Either way it's real. She wore the nightgown. She held you. Against her bosom. You remember it, whether you remember-remember. Or not."

"Layers and levels of memory. Levels. Layers. I get it. Doesn't get me any closer to knowing my mom and dad. Does it?"

The pitying syllable slipped out one last time: "Aw."

The windows grew fogged and Button switched on the defroster, a blast of cool air streaming across their faces and making both wince. Outside in the mountains it felt like real wintertime, with a dusting of snow speckled along the roadsides. Back home, in the humid subtropical midlands of South Carolina, holiday weather meant lows in the 50s and nothing close to resembling the white stuff. Button had figured this a good time to get Roy out of town, and for Heather, too, as she discovered in hearing of the death of Heather's dad a couple months ago. All had lost loved ones in the recent past. A trio of mourners, seeking solace and comfort. A good excuse to reconnect with Heather Ponderview, right? At this point, any reason would do.

Wasn't hard to have her higher consciousness talks with Roy. As the drive had gotten underway, it'd become clear he was open to talking about anything but the fact he'd lost both his grandparents to death, and that his wife, it seemed, had somehow spurned an entreaty of his and 'wasn't ready' to get back together, the opposite of what he expected. She knew what surprise and disappointment could do to a vulnerable person's emotional state.

Roy put on a lavish affair for his grandmother, a huge funeral service at which he stood, clear-eyed and strong of voice, thundering about the Greatest Generation and country music and The Dixiana and the history of the town and the love shown him by his folks, they who reared him in a home of affection and trust and comfort and Reese's Cups and Durkee Potato Sticks; and about the necessity of honoring our forebears, the mothers and the fathers; and Button thought, mercy, but it's as though the country preacher in Roy has come out.

After the service, conducted by the Reverend Nixon, the bereaved grandson received with charisma and good humor a line of well-wishers that stretched all the way around Karlaney Funeral Home, which many regarded as a do-over for the Rabbit debacle, and which he seemed to understand presented a necessary polarity to his earlier behavior. He could have run for mayor that next day and won in a landslide.

Afterwards, though, as she stayed following the wake at the house and helped him clean up, he'd been as still and silent and cold as a robot, and not in a good way. That's when she suggested going to visit Heather, up in the mountains he said he loved so much.

"If only my wife had been with me as my partner at the funeral, I might've felt better. Some degree of comfort. But it wasn't to be, and so that's that."

Creedence came for the service and stood by her spouse, but went on back to Sedge Island with few meaningful words between them, which he said felt like a troubling reversal from an earlier warming trend on her part. Capricious. Hadn't stayed with him even for one night. Button understood only that infidelity occurred, and confusion remained, on his wife's side of the marriage, as Roy explained.

About his marital status, he still sat cagey, waving off her mild prodding to let go and discuss anything he needed to. That she was here in service to him.

Enough to say the occurrences had floored him—the deaths, the marital strife, inheriting The Dixiana. "Use your imagination."

"That's what it's all about—imagining the life we want. And living out the dream."

"So you keep telling me. I'm not sure I imagined all this foolishness, though."

But with a slight widening of the eyes, and a distinct, high-pitched, involuntary shift in his vibration, she understood that, in some form or fashion, he foresaw it all. Nobody had to tell Button. Happened to her all the time.

◉◑✳

INSTEAD OF HIM OPENING UP ABOUT PERSONAL CURRENT EVENTS, THEY CHATTED and shared college stories, in Button's case about scriptwriting and film production. Her plans included making a Phish doc that, thanks to falling too much in love with the band and going on the road and having an actual Phish experience, had never happened, along with other formative experiences like working on the Disney movies shot one fall on the Foothills State campus.

Eliding, of course, the more salacious details about having hot sex with a movie star. TMI.

Sex. There were times, still, when she could feel Roy's desire, his want, his carnal energy pulsing. Needing release. But she couldn't help with that. She had another part to play in Roy's life, was doing so by bringing him here. Not for that. Maybe he and Heather'd hit it off, though she only felt that in the most facetious of terms. He needed to redirect that kundalini energy back up into his spine, at least for now.

But wait—she was serious. If love blossomed between these two friends, wouldn't the net total of love in the world then be raised? And how could that be bad? From what Heather had said and Button has seen and heard firsthand in Roy, they both needed healing. As an enlightened spirit but who also struggled with issues of ego and desire, it was easy to feel jealous and hurt at the notion more than magnanimous. Button, still having plenty of her own work to do. But who didn't?

"So you palled around with the Durango sisters?" Roy, shaking his head and looking sour. "The tabloid twins? That's insane." He listed off several famous folks who had come through the SBFC Charleston #1 location in the heart of the tourist district, most of whom were actors making movies in the region or on vacation like Jim Carrey, Tom Hanks, Conan O'Brien; a few politicians, but nothing to match W's visit to The Dixiana, he said with disdain, only an Obama and Michelle campaign breeze-in during his brief and singular swing through South Carolina in the 2008 primary season. "Sexy gals, those Hollywood hotties."

Button's cheeks flamed. "Hey, Maddy's an actual friend. They're more than caricatures. To me, anyway." Next she walks back that attitude, proprietary and born of the jealousy instinct; more ego nonsense. "But yeah. That side of them. Is pretty true. Maddy, she was all over the place. A wild child. So was I, though."

He became distant, drumming his fingers on the leather-wrapped steering wheel. "I remember those. Didn't see them, but in the 90s I didn't catch many movies. Too busy slinging caffeine. Why do they stick out in my mind, so?"

"You tell me."

"Maybe because I saw the originals. Norrie Sortwell would show junk like that on Saturday afternoons at the Grande. *Herbie the Love Bug. Godzilla.* An old *Batman* serial from the 40s. And yeah, those Kurt Russell kid-flicks like *The Computer Wore Tennis Shoes.*" He slaps his thigh. "All that was a hot minute ago. Wasn't it."

"Time marches on."

"Who else was in the remakes?"

As Button directs Roy onto 209 at the Big Laurel Creek, she names off a couple of the other actors, but gets no reaction until the last one:

"I was Karen Black's assistant. That was part of my PA job. She was real nice. To me."

Button, realizing that Roy's face had drained of all color.

"You car sick? Road's only gonna be. More winding from here."

"I need to pull over."

Roy signaled and whipped the truck across the road, sliding into the dirt and gravel parking lot of a small general store and coffee shop at the intersection by the narrow, rushing mountain river. "Did you say Karen Black? Or, did I project that you said it?"

Button felt energy gathering at the top of her head, a warmth in her body and a tingly sense of AH along the crown of her skull, like catching a kind buzz from the sweet leaf. "Yeah. You know. From the 70s."

"Yes yes," sounding impatient. "I'm more than familiar with her. *You hung out with Karen fudging Black?*"

She shrugs—*so what*? "Sure."

"God help me. Merciful god in heaven…" When he again finds his voice, he croaks how as a kid, Karen Black was like his favorite movie star. Rattling off movie titles, most of which Button knew, even if she hadn't seen them. "More than that. I kinda, well. I loved her. It's true."

"A female ideal. Projected into your consciousness. By the flickering images."

Snide. "That's one way of putting it. To me, it seemed like love."

"Sexual attraction?"

His cheeks, shining with a revelation that needed no verbal elucidation.

"Now this? Is what. I would call—um—a synchronicity."

"A big'un. For me, anyway."

"Clearly."

He expounds upon a major title featuring Karen Black that he saw all the way through recently called *Nashville*, ironically enough, which being a country music story brings in whole 'nother crucial thread in both their lives. "I remember seeing it listed in the *TV Guide* one Sunday afternoon, this stupid-big cast list including my dream girl. And telling my grandmama about it, saying, *Nashville*, we got to watch that. Not about the Karen Black part, of course." Shaking his head, reddening. "Though I guess she had noticed the pictures of her I'd cut out of magazines at the library and scotch-taped all over my closet door."

"How did they handle? The talk?"

"The talk?"

"About sex."

Chortling. "We didn't ever talk about girls or sex or anything. Never. I suppose it was too embarrassing. Which left me to yanking it over a Karen Black pantyhose ad I'd stolen from a copy of *Cosmo*."

"How was *Nashville*?"

"Dull as dishwater. Once I got to see my favorite gal—idealized female figure, if you will—I wandered outside, and Mama Runelle turned it off and went to play her guitar on the front porch. 'It wasn't nothing going on in that durn movie'." His falsetto impression of Mama Runelle prompted a giggle from Button before he continued. "Seems awesome now—the movie. Bloody brilliant."

"*Nashville*. An American New Hollywood—um—classic."

"But the most beautiful movie star in the world, wasted. Who should've been in every frame, if only Bob Altman had asked me."

"I don't think. I've ever heard. Anyone say that. About Karen Black."

"Say what?"

"Being so beautiful."

"Maybe it's just me." Contemplative, he hooked a sudden thumb into his chest. Heaved a violent breath as though about to weep. Beating the steering wheel with the fleshy heel of his left hand. "Yeah. This redneck asshole's saying it. Still beautiful. Still my favorite."

Now Button can see, and feel, his raging tide of emotion. She doesn't quite get the meaning behind it all, but she knows there is one, and he can tell her if he wants, or not. In any case, she's bringing him here to help in his growth and healing, but a large part of that will have to come from him, at his own pace.

"But anyway. All of them. Were kind, really nice. The Hollywood folks. Truth be told? Most of the below the line crew? Were regional riggers. Union gig. Ya know."

Dreamy. "Ms. Black's a lovely soul. Isn't she."

Button shrugged. She supposed so. "For a movie star."

That seemed to satisfy him.

They took time to go inside because he said he suffered a moral obligation to check out a quaint coffee shop like this one, tucked away in the mountains by a river, and it made her happy to observe him in this mode. She watched him stand, breathe, and take it in. Watching the placid flowing water of the Big Laurel Creek.

Controlled, conscious respiration.

Leveling his emotions.

Getting centered.

Button did it too. No time for divining on the river but she wished there was, what with the light on the water dancing in a tantalizing and compelling manner. Now only minutes from seeing Heather Ponderview for the first time since their Phish reunion experience a few years ago, momentous but fleeting, it was like, get the priorities straight, girl.

"*Mochas are on me*." Roy called this out in a fit of enthusiasm and affirmation that broke his conscious breathing, put him back into his 'achiever' persona. "Special requests? We're burning daylight out here."

"Almond milk, preferably without carrageenan. If they have it."

"If they don't have any, I'll conjure it up for you." With the biggest grin in the world. As though he really could. "I'll imagine it."

His aura glowing bright, he charged through the door. Roy, calling hey-ho to the folks inside.

Button wished she'd be able to get him to relax, and it seemed to be working. If nothing else, along with a couple of liquid reductions for the vape pen she had a decent headstash of gooey, white-haired stinky vacuum sealed named strain called Sno-Cap secreted in her suitcase. If only this scratchy throat and stitch in her side would give her some peace, all would be okay.

Hell, it already was okay! Who was she kidding. Walfredo had vibed her with the idea of apotheosis. Of completion. Totes coolio.

◉◈✺

ON THE LAST LEG OF THE DRIVE, A TWISTING MOUNTAIN ROAD WITH A FEW WHITE-knuckle stretches through which Roy shifted with care, rather than fill her in on the details of his Karen Black connection—indeed, the synchronicity of it all had seemed to blow his mind in a compelling and gripping way—he spoke instead about his own personal ties to the media arts Button had studied: First through two friends, Libby and Billy, both now deceased, novice scriptwriters and good pals back in his college days.

"They lived and breathed movies. Libby was Devin's girl. There was tension over Billy. Another story. A long one."

He described his late friends with a thin-lipped sorrow that loomed fresh and immense, she could tell, and in her diagnosis exacerbated by his more recent waves of grief; and all this she read from those lips of his, pressed tight between statements as though holding back a shout, or perhaps a wicked insult leveled at the vast and spiraling untamed universe that'd so cruelly taken away his loved ones.

The next story, however, seemed to flip his attitude in polarity, from grief to mirth: by the time she reached the last turnoff to the gated entrance of the Ponderview estate called Havenhurst, he had them both streaming tears of amusement rather than sadness:

"So it's 1998, and while you're on Phish tour I've gone and bought this failing smoothie stand around the corner from the Carolina Beanery."

"I remember it. I went to SEU for a semester or two before transferring to Foothills State."

"So you remember the original place. Check. A dump. So when the guy's looking to get out, my goal becomes turning this smoothie trade into a monster. Yeah. Something about taking over somebody else's failed biz, I dunno, it charged me up. I saw with clarity and precision every detail the other guy had gotten wrong. And the more I could see his mistakes, the more I burned to wipe it all away. I said at first, hell, it'll be a turnkey thing, I won't have to change much, just do it better, supplement my income Then I said, eff that. I am gonna remake this place into my own image. I'll no longer call it Smoothie Central; I'll come up with something cooler. Catchier."

"The Spotted Banana™."

"Exactly."

"Wish we'd had one. At Foothills State." Button mentioned that while they had this breakfast and lunch counter called The Orphic Egg serving up kickass smoothies and juices, Roy's brand would have gone over well with the crunchy-granola demographic that flocked to FSU. "Spotted Banana woulda killed."

"Damn straight—don't know why we didn't hit that market. A missed opportunity."

He shrugged, troubled, while wrestling the steering wheel around hairy turns, the mountainside falling away below to reveal marvelous vistas that came and went as they wound their way through some of the highest peaks in the ancient mountain chain. "In any case, a no-BS quality product. But once I had the idea for the name—the whole 'fruitshakes' concept would come later, and that was the real catalyst, I think, more so than the Spotted Banana part—and drew my little cartoon dancing bananas, I said, I got myself a brand. But how to get the word out—that's always the rub with any business venture. And no social media engines back then to exploit, only old media! Besides the ad in the Redtail student paper, you know? And on the radio? What then?"

Seemed obvious. "A TV commercial."

He snapped his fingers. "Bingo. That's what these media arts kids said. Coffee shop regulars there at the Beanery, those hepcats. 'Run a memorable TV spot,' they pitched. And I bit."

Button, remembering various unpaid PA gigs while in the program at Foothills State. "Student labor. It's always a bargain."

Nodding with vigor. "Right. They said, we'll make the commercial, and you can get it on the cable rotation package that'll be seen by every TV customer all over the service region of the provider. It'll be a solid bit on our résumé, and you got yourself a TV spot for minimal cost. TV's the real penetration. Nobody reads newspapers, even back then."

"Images—it's easy to influence people. Mind control."

"Like a young kid being programmed to fall in love with Karen Black?"

Nodding and smiling. "The image of her. An idea she represents."

Not wishing to further deconstruct his attraction for the actress. "Eh, I don't know about that. But a catchy commercial, one that folks remember, is the ad buy you want to fund."

Button noticed how easily Roy, an otherwise strong personality and sharp mind, would still slip into programmed language he'd absorbed. "People. Sure like to watch TV. Don't they?"

More nodding. "Especially the news. And sports. And on the news, you want the commercial slot between the weather and sports, by the way. That's the time most potential consumers are watching."

He relates the crazy idea these kids came up with for his TV spot, which was to ape Eddie Murphy's 'Klump Family' multiple-role schtick: Roy would portray a chubby little kid talking to his 'grandmother'—or rather himself in old lady drag:

"'Grandmama'," Roy-as-little-Roy asked in an exaggerated voice that made him sound more like slobbering Sylvester the Cat than a little kid, "'what you gonna do with all them old spotted bananas in that bowl over yonder?' And then, cut to me in heavy makeup as the grandmama, where I said, 'Why, Roy Earl, I'm-a make a loaf of banana bread. Or maybe banana-nut muffins.' Leaned in all big in the frame. 'You want your grandmama to fix you some *muffins*, darlin'?'"

Choking back laughter, he held up a hand while he caught his breath. "And then, see, the little boy character, me, I mean, he, he says, 'Mercy, but I'm tired of banana bread. You know what I want?' And she says, 'I bet I do—you want you one of them newfangled smoothies, don't ya.' And he says, he says—"

What, Button asked him silently.

Roy, squeezing his eyes and cackling so hard again Button worried he might collapse and run them off the road to their deaths far below on the steep mountainside. "'We want FRUITSHAKES!'" he shouted, downshifting and taking an S-curve. "That was the origin of the whole fruitshake deal, that spot. New Year's Day, year zero."

"An epochal milestone."

"Truly. Lightning and thunder graphics, my voice filtered real deep and distorted. *FRUITSHAKES*—like the god-durn T-Rex roaring in *Jurassic Park*. I kid you not."

He describes how the film students had super'd dozens of Roy Earls, all screaming the FRUITSHAKES! line, and then a montage of him in various guises: in drag again, but now as a young-woman version blending the smoothie, er, FRUITSHAKE; as a dreadlocked hippie dude drinking one and flashing a peace sign; as a staid and upstanding businessman in a suit talking on his mobile phone, taking a sip and dancing a joyous jig; lastly, a veritable throng of crude, chroma'd little-kid Roy Earl's all lined up outside the smoothie stand. A mob—an army—of thirsty Roy Earls. All of which he said looked rough effects-wise, but still a riot. A water-cooler commercial.

"If you had gone the whole twenty-five seconds with it that far, the cheesy FX part didn't much matter."

Button, chiming in how that effect was called suspension of disbelief. "Sounds like you had them at 'fruitshake'."

Hell yeah, he did. Told her how that commercial ran for years, at least until he came up with the 'Fruitshake Company' trademark, which he said meant nothing except trying to make it sound like another place everyone expected to find in the food court at the mall. This idea, it'd come from a marketing firm he'd hired, consultants on building a brand. More important, he asserted, were his personal creative contributions, like hilarious pop-culture references in playful product names like the Linda Blair, a spicy-sweet green fruitshake with kale, cucumber, ginger, cilantro, pineapple, banana, lemon juice and almond milk, the self-explanatory, protein-powder enhanced Grape Ape, a vitamin rich, mango-centric Sunshine Daydream, or the baroque Bigger Boat, a thick beet and peach combo designed to resemble Chief Brody-style bloody fishing chum.

As for the product itself and its healthy ingredients, Roy had gone to a trade show in California. Saw what they were doing with smoothies out there, brought the health food angle home to Carolina. Way ahead of the curve. "I said, smoothies are gonna be big again. A millennial product. Health consciousness. After a while," sounding rueful and shamed, "it became a way to make a lot of money, of course. It always ends up dominating any other considerations."

"You did what anybody. Would've done. You wanted to grow the biz."

He shrugged at the memories, shifted, took an actual curve. "Chasing the bucks."

"A food court. It does, kinda. Make it all seem. A little less cool."

"Fruitshakes… it wasn't my idea. The marketing consultants came up with it. Hell—they recommended that we drop the Spotted Banana aspect of the name. Right? Wanted me to call it the Great Southern Fruitshake Express Company, or some such crapola. I said, forget it. But fruitshakes—yeah. Memorable. That I agreed to.

"So by the time I got around to franchising, I set up trademarks. But with that name, I didn't just own the trademark for a drawing of ripe bananas dancing around. I kinda owned smoothies themselves. In a word. *Bam*," he said, the old thigh-slapping like when he got super excited about one of his colossal successes. "Fruitshakes standing astride the mountain of blended fast food beverages, named with a nod to the idea of dessert, but steeped in health consciousness alongside extreme tastebud pleasure. Fruitshakes. Fruitshakes. Fruitshakes forever."

"One fruitshake. To rule them all."

"That's right," a harsh whisper. Roy bowed his head. A reverent moment—

Button felt the energy in the air shift. The space between them seemed to acquire mass, as though in describing the measure of his achievement the pull of gravity in the immediate vicinity around him had been magnified.

Button felt concern. Here again was ego—'owning' the idea of smoothies? Her comment about 'ruling them all' had held subtext with its seeming humor. 'Forever?' Because a marketing geek came up with a catchy euphemism? Elements of this were worth exploring, but not now.

"My grandparents—they were so mad at me over that TV spot. I came home all excited because I was sure they'd seen it, or at least my grandmother had—Pa-paw's at the bar every night at suppertime, and she would sit there and watch the news. And I tell you what, she about whipped my grown ass over it."

"*Why?*"

"Thought I was making fun of her." Imitating his grandmother again. "'But darlin', you always loved Mama Runelle's banana bread!' I told her, sure I loved her banana bread. That it was a joke, but it wasn't making fun. It's hard to get that stuff across to their generation."

"I guess. It wasn't much fun. Or joking around—"

"—during the Depression. Or the war. Yeah. I hear ya on that. Not that I'd know. They don't much cotton to yakking about the past."

"Why bother? It's dead and gone."

"Suppose so."

"Only time's. Right now."

"Sure—whatever you say."

But his eyes wouldn't meet hers, yet she knew he understood more than he might have been willing to admit. For whatever reason. The individual process of awakening unfolded in myriad and often mysterious ways.

◉◐❋

THE ELECTRONIC GPS VOICE, WHICH DIRECTED THEM ON THROUGH TWO TURNOFFS and onto a gravel road, announced in her soothing cadence: "*In one hundred feet, you will have arrived at your destination.*"

"We're here." Button, buzzing with anticipation. "We made it."

"Thank god. Those last hairpins had me ready to puke."

Roy rolled down the window and punched the intercom. Basking in the crisp air of the coming winter, Button leaned across him for a brief, excited convo with Heather—letting her oldest and dearest friend know her guests awaited outside the gates of Havenhurst.

As the ornate, heavy iron gate swung open, Button, an icy thrill sluicing into her gut. "Hah—it's Return to Ponderview Alley."

"Sounds like a soap."

In a fit of exposure and honesty—no other way to be—Button spilled the story of trying to write a novel inspired by her 'friendship' with Heather, how Button suffered the brief fantasy of writing a Nicholas Sparks-style romance and making a jillion dollars.

"Making a pile of bucks isn't all it's cracked up to be. Uncle Burnie, he used to have a ton of money. Ask him. Well—I guess you know well and good about that. But ask Mr. Ponderview," referring to Heather's late father. "Ask if he took it with him."

"That's. A good attitude. Ya know."

"It is. Isn't it."

"Totes good." She nodded. The gate made a clanking sound, as though the motor needed servicing. The estate had some years on it now, she supposed. Like they all did. She withheld from Roy what the mansion looked like. Wanted to see his reaction.

"Well dang, I wanna read that novel of yours. I could use romance in my life."

Button, saying that she never completed *The Greening of Ponderview Alley*, though in her first few years back in Edgewater County she ended up knocking off a different manuscript, which she said wasn't worth discussing. "Really only. A novella. Dusty in a drawer somewhere."

"That's still a huge achievement. At one time I thought about writing."

"Yeah, but. Only the bare minimum. Of what. A novel's supposed to be."

"Give yourself credit."

Waving him off. "Never even bothered. To send it around. Except to one person. An old mentor." This had been Brenda LaRose, still teaching poetry and fiction and scriptwriting up at Foothills.

"And?"

"Thought it had merit." LaRose, whom Button said still taught at Foothills State, had been quite complimentary, even suggesting two writing competitions. But in those days, Button had acquired no fortitude regarding rejection. Too tied to the idea of results. Wedded to outcome.

Hah. Maybe she'd let Roy read it. And send it out to some novel-writing contest. Maybe in the spring. Just for shits and giggles, as Heather Ponderview used to say when they were about to drop another dose of Molly or do one more nitrous balloon. Those were the days.

She recalled the few wrinkled pages of the Ponderview project from so long ago. She knew it well; she looked at that folder every few months, sighing and wondering what this literary seed might have grown into, a thousand-petalled lotus blossom never allowed to ripen and flourish, a reflection of the actual relationship with Heather. Flowers of the flesh, lying fetid and fallow. Enough already.

◉◐✳

As she'd tried to fertilize with her florid prose:

Earth and air.

Stardust, wafting down from a passing comet.

An abundance of nourishing elements coalescing in a place of rolling green. A dell more than a valley, one ringed by old and rounded mountains. In my time living along Ponderview Alley it seemed as though pillowy clouds rolled through constantly, in bands of wispy gray cotton that often dropped sprinkles on the farmland, with only an occasional glimpse of a puckish and ghostly white disk of a sun glaring from behind the veil. The benevolent sunlight, allowing that the plants and people below take solace knowing it warms them still from the other side of the misty vapor, like the immense and blazing iris of an even more enormous celestial, all-seeing eye atop the pyramid of the currency of my self-loathing. One peering balefully down in abject judgment of my failures.

The failures to come, however, would be far worse.

But when I first came here, it'd been mainly to heal from the first failures, which'd been grim enough on their own terms. To heal; to start over. To write someone else's book, for a change…

The plot she concocted, a potboiler and bodice-ripper: a ghostwriter drafting the memoir of a mad heiress lives alongside the subject in her high castle, one who turns out not mad at all, only lonely. A fairy-tale romance, or so Button intended. In tribute to Heather. The one she loved.

But that Heather had been long gone, it seemed, whether all the way back in San Diego, or their last visit, which had been about Phish rather than themselves; what would the contemporary version of her present? Further away? Or closer than ever? Button Sykes, unrequited hopeless romantic, about to find out.

PART THREE

Doctrine and Ritual

Every branch of knowledge which you seek only to enrich your own learning, only to accumulate treasure for yourself, leads you away from the Path; but all knowledge which you seek for working in the service of humanity and for the uplifting of the world brings you a step forward.

— RUDOLF STEINER

ROY, BUTTON, AND HEATHER
PONDERVIEW

Beau: You are thankful as *hale* to have this distraction.
You are a grief monkey.
You are alone.
But not lonely: you're with Button, but even better you're truckin' up to your happy place—a mountaintop—where your heart and soul will be at peace and open to the sky, or whatever Button-style hippie prattle you want to insert.

You've had your butt handed to you by the universe, yea, and if nothing else, you need fresh air. You must acquire distance and detachment from the vibrational energy of your dramas, as she explained.

You did not need this explained. But until Heather Ponderview, you had no clue where to run.

BEFORE, DURING AND AFTER YOUR GRANDMOTHER'S FUNERAL YOU MUST HAVE passed words with everyone in town from Kitty Berwick, your first grade teacher whom you recognized after almost forty-two years, making you realize how young she must have been, to a great aunt you didn't even remember you had, a brassy, frail nonagenarian whom the other scattered Pettuses all called Toots, to an ungodly throng of complete strangers who all knew who you were. You felt yourself a slacker and a fool, embarrassed about forgetting the great aunt. And furthermore, recognizing so few of these people who displayed such concern for your wellbeing.

But that's you, and your whole generation, culture, country and species, isn't it? Self-absorbed to a ruinous and demonstrative fault? Hey—everybody's doing it.

And yet in the overflowing funeral home chapel that afternoon you were a recipient of much love from all in attendance, unbridled affection and admiration crackling in the air like ozone. It flowed over you in waves. You tried to look every last person in the eye. Your gratitude, immense and legit. Thanking them all like your customers, but here, a different brand of energetic exchange.

Maybe not so much with Jezmund Rembert and his crew, who paid their respects by doffing fedoras and passing through the line, dutiful. Rembert gripped your hand and spoke in low and respectful tones about your grandparents and their place in the history and vitality of the county, but did so glowering and still full of ire over the mural stunt you pulled.

And how you said you'd do it again if you only could; would do it all one better, leaving your nonspecific threat of escalation dangling like bait.

Rembert, grinning, his eyes two slits. "You a real bad-ass, ain't ya?"

"I grew up watching Charles Bronson movies."

"You just need to learn to run stuff by your playmates. S'all I'm saying."

"Keep waiting."

The conflict made you steely and upright like one of those rigid George Costanza Festivus poles, a growing trend among the more secular-minded when symbolizing their holiday celebrations.

After a while, though, you desired escape from the throng gathered to bid farewell to your grandmother. Too many brought up the plane-flying bit. How amazing it was that you had your own plane. Their eyes, dancing at the thought. Not of the plane.

The money.

They imagine you've all the money in the world.

But once you finish funding Creedence so she can move on with her life, who knows how long the rest will last. As Button kept saying, however, thoughts of the future or the past only interfere with enjoying the eternal and ever-present now. She's been teaching you to meditate, but you haven't gotten 'there' yet. But you do feel your vibration calming down. Which is good and necessary.

And of course you've plenty of ConParAgCorp stock, always going up in value. You could give all the cash away, every penny, but keep the shares and play the market and continue to live like a king. Passive income from trades and dividends. It didn't get any more sweet and easy than that.

Endless economic expansion—maybe it was possible after all.

Button, no more agreeing with all that than she did a nuclear plant being able to supply unlimited power in a safe and sustainable manner. Look at Fukushima, she said. You never heard word one about it. Couldn't be a problem. All that invisible radiation. Taking its toll.

Money. You had more pressing worries occupying your mind all during the service. What Mama Runelle had told you only two weeks ago while sitting on the porch. How she'd been concerned, at one time, about your Pa-paw and Trudy Samuelson, whom you still think of as Pirkle. Trudy, and your grand-daddy. Together. "If you know what I mean."

Holy crap.

"He wouldn't do that. Maybe with one of them whores over in Red Mound —the ones your Uncle Burnie seems to think so much of. But not Trudy. Not an affair."

You could only hope not. God—your stomach, clenched. Your Pa-Paw and Trudy? God, let it not be so. But your mind, racing. If that were true, it might explain her fearful attitude after your own dalliance. The lover turned freezer queen.

Worried about your grandfather. What he'd think, and do. If he knew. His jealousy, perhaps.

Wipe thy consciousness clean of such perverse notions.

IN THE EMPTY BAR AFTER THE MEMORIAL—THIS TIME IT WOULD BE CLOSED FOR THE day and no arguments from anyone—you took a moment by yourself. Stinking and lonely and ancient, the honkytonk. Not comforting. Except that, it had been their place, and here, they still lived. Daylight glinted from the wall of 8x10 head shots, the faces like an audience of judges and icons watching you grieve.

You poured a beer, turned on the Wurlitzer and punched up a few tracks. Webb Pierce, 'A Thousand Miles Ago,' and after that Dolly and Porter singing 'Daddy Was An Old-Time Preacher Man.' The beer, a sip or two. It turned your stomach.

You cried out and flung the slender Pilsner glass, shattering it into broken shards all over the end of the bar. Trudy would shit herself over the mess. The possibility of slivers cascading down into the ice bin, a major concern for a woman like her. Lawsuits. Bloody tongues wagging at her. She wasn't wrong to worry about such occurrences. In fact, it's exactly how you would want your bar manager to think.

Someone rapped at the locked door, jangling the bells. You went over through the gloom and found Uncle Burnie, tears streaming down his face, leaning against the painted DIXIANA logo, chipped and faded, on the glass.

You let him in. "Hey, bub."

He wept, incoherent.

You saw how his hands shook. His whole body. "You need a bracer, don't you."

Pitiful, he nodded. "Does a cow tit squirt milk?"

After drawing him a cold one, you both grabbed a stool and sat in silence while he drank. You imagined it had been much the same between him and your granddaddy. After knowing each other eighty years, what remained to discuss, besides the weather, or maybe the ball game?

"You gonna cut on the TV," Burnie finally asked, "or what?" You handed him the remote.

❂①✻

LATER THAT NIGHT, HALF DRUNK, YOU TRIED KISSING BUTTON—TRUDY OFFERED A better choice for any number of reasons, but you couldn't embarrass yourself with her again, especially not after Runelle's suggestion—but found yourself put in your place.

"Whoa, whoa, whoa." Button, gentle and sweet, putting you off, and suggesting a trip to the mountains rather than her vagina. Besides, she had pointed out, it's way past due, or past time, as she corrected herself, for her to see an old college roommate named Heather. Winter weather had not broken yet. Good chance to take a hike in the crisp fall air, far from Edgewater County.

And you? You were like, what's to keep me? Manny can feed Rico. Play with him. The Dix runs itself... and your wife sure doesn't seem to need or want you.

If nothing else on this trip, you'll get to vape more of Button's heady weed with her; and who knew about Heather Ponderview, her story and connection here. Despite some weasel words Creedence had used about the future, you felt yourself a free agent; now, you suffered painful erections for Button and Trudy and even Letty Glasscock's pugs Chappy and Cedric, all in service of revenge: you wanted to have a spite fuck, a wounding glorious romp to show Chelsea Colette Rucker you knew how to rock it out too. To get your freak on. To look for fulfillment in the body of another, instead of within your own fractured marital relationship.

Which wouldn't mean JACK SQUAT to her. Or so it seemed.

❂①✻

YEAH.

After making another brief appearance the day of the funeral without staying, Creedence agreed to return and sit for a talk about the future; she would come back to Edgewater County again instead of you flying or driving down to the island. Prior attempts there had offered little comfort for either; you kept looking over your shoulder like that little prick Estes stood hiding behind every cypress tree, waiting for you to turn your back so they could have secret communications and send one another sext messages to plan their next tryst, and all this despite her continued and penitent assurances that, in sobriety, the last behavior you should expect is more adultery.

A week after the funeral you waited for her outside The Dixiana, sprawled like one of the old codgers who used to sit there, principally Uncle Burnie, whom Button wished you to banish from his favorite stool for his own good. You could not care less who drank at the honkytonk, which had been allowed to continue since you had your big realization that the idiots employed there needed the paychecks to keep food on the tables of their families. You had looked at the books. The bar, not profitable as such because of the overhead. The payroll.

You understand why your Pa-Paw kept it running. Trudy. Fridge. All of them. An honest living. His charge to keep—a job-creator.

But before Creedence arrived, Becky L swung by, a fetching vision in spandex neon exercise wear, clothing that accentuated the revelation of her shapely, long body. Sweat breaks out on your upper lip, but mercy, no messing with this lady. That'd be stepping on your new best friend's tail. Not that that married-ass black man had much right or call to a single cougar like Rebecca LaFreniere. Except that the muh-fucker had said it verged on "real feelings and shit," in Manny's parlance.

As you sit on the long wooden bench, your back sitting straight and tall against the stucco of the wall next to the picture window you notice has gone all streaky, Becky L notices you from the next block. The glass needs cleaning with spray less watered-down, a frugality measure implemented all too well; Newbie had observed your instructions to dilute the cleaner with a sedulousness that had, in its myopia, forced the results of the operation at hand straight into the ditch. You run into this all the time. People get invested, browbeat or terrorized into slavish rule-following rather than using their intuition and common sense, and the janitor ought to've known a proper dilution rate for the glass cleaner like he knows his home address. Should be rote for the little a-hole. But hell, the boy's missing a few teeth on the main sprocket. Newbie's cranium, small like a cantaloupe and almost as bumpy.

"Yo, Becky-bo!"

Becky L waved with good cheer and called from down the street. "Roy, what a delight. Hold that thought. Don't you move a muscle." She jangled keys and ducked inside the theater through the main set of doors.

Ignoring her order, you squinted down at your phone for the thousandth time and peered in the bypass's direction waiting to see the Beemer, and with it Creedence, cruising into one of the angled spaces and those still-coltish long legs popping out. You got up and did some stretching, yoga crap, that Button had shown you. Breathed. Anticipated your pretty wife's face.

Becky came trotting over with two red Solo cups and a glass bottle of some exotic herbal tea. "Share my treat with me. How are you?"

Brusque and direct, you told her that now it was time to think about real-world issues, like finalizing details regarding the music festival for your granddaddy, the only proper memorial you can give him. Becky L said it wouldn't be a problem; how Roy E. Pettus, a legacy stakeholder in the past, present and future of the town, could count on her to make sure anyone unaware of this event's importance would find themselves enlightened as to the deeper meaning and benefits of staging a bluegrass music festival.

"We might make it more inclusive than bluegrass, though. Book some jam-bands. Get in a younger crowd."

"That'd be wonderful!" she chirped. She poured the tea and handed you the cup. "If you really want to skew young, think EDM and hiphop, not jam-band."

"I guess so. I keep forgetting that jam-band isn't still the latest development."

"Not by at least a decade or two."

"Time—it gets slippery."

"Don't remind me." Her smile faltered, but by only a fraction.

You told her about your experience on the Downtown Business Alliance merchant's association in Columbia with planning street festivals, including an enormous annual St. Patrick's Day bash with its multiple music stages, all of this back in your pre-SBFC® days before you went all corporate.

"Early on I realized the importance of doing good works for your neighborhood. Of being a responsible playing piece on the chessboard of your community. Responsibility to the stakeholders besides yourself. As you put it."

"You sound like the Roy Earl Pettus I fell in love with."

Creedence's voice startles you both. She's come walking up, looking fresh and pretty with her hair pulled back by a white headband, jeans, a flower print blouse. She looks ten years younger.

"Rebecca, my wife Chelsea."

"Creedence," Becky L says. "Roy's told me all about—you."

"I can only imagine," her tone acid. "My ears were burning up just now."

A serious competitive vibe. Creedence's eyes, wide and blazing. You know this face, a villainess called Jealous Girl. You used to see it on her whenever she'd find you huddled with one of your college-girl assistant managers. There had never been anything untoward with any of them beyond flirtation, though, any more than with Becky L. Not that you wouldn't hit that stank in a New York minute, as the boys in the hanger might put it.

Becky L acts thrown off. Big time. Seems self conscious about her exotic iced tea and the cups. "We were—sharing this tea. It's all natural. Sweetened with stevia."

"And here I am right parched from my drive," all fake chipper. "Yummy."

"I'll get a cup for you."

Creedence, taking the tea out of your hand. "It's okay. I'll have a sip of his."

"Yeah," you said. "I think she can drink after her old man."

A ripple of recognition. "Married people would share. Wouldn't they."

You examined your sport sandals while the two women chatted their way out of the awkward scene. Becky, going to leave, said, "Talk to you later about stuff—y'all have a happy day!" and left you and your wife alone in front of the honkytonk.

"'Stuff'? You and her got stuff to talk about, huh?"

"Merchant's association crap. Nothing like what you're suggesting."

"Not another 'association'," with a sigh. "So you replaced me already? That's what was so important about getting together today?"

You threw up your hands. "Couldn't I ask you the same?"

"No. There ain't nobody."

"What a pleasant surprise."

"Estes wasn't nothing but a symptom of my disease. Wasn't like talking about 'stuff' with that leggy LaFreniere princess over there. Hell, she ain't even really left—look at her keeping an eye on us."

Becky L, making a cellphone call, paced in front of the Grande, gesturing and strolling in a lazy oval like a stoned picketer who'd forgotten her UNFAIR sign.

"She's a thousand miles from us. In every way."

"So you keep insisting."

"Because it's true. Did we really meet here to debate fairy tales? I say 'no'."

And it went from there, until you had called a truce and suggested that you break bread and smoke peace pipe, which she didn't think was funny and wasn't meant to be: it's your way of telling her that vaping dope has mellowed you out, this admission the first step toward suggesting you go vape and then make healing and languid love all day. But you didn't continue on with the confession because, as a fresh rehab kid, Creedence would have little to no interest in smoking or vaping cannabis.

Further, Creedence showed no interest in your suggestion of Manny's soul-food lunch buffet, in fact characterizing it that way made your wife turn her face inside out. Unhealthy or not, wasn't anything but good solid Edgewater County fare. Or so you sold it to her.

At her suggestion you'd instead gone to get a bite at the new Applebee's she noticed with wonder out by the Chilton exit, where they had been advertising new veggie burger sliders and sweet potato tots, a healthier lunch option.

"I can't half believe what it looks like out here now. Wal-mart and everything."

"Me neither. Used to be all pine trees."

"Yeah. Forty years ago."

Once orders placed, Creedence skipped the small talk and launched into her state of mind: that being apart and alone wasn't so scary or weird. That with sobriety had come clarity, and how she felt deep friendship for you. But maybe, and she didn't know yet, friendship was all she had left. And not enough on which to hang a marriage.

"So friendship's not sufficient? It's like the frozen bananas in a smoothie —the base."

"No. And it's not enough for you, either."

Your anger had bubbled over, and you had broken down and said, don't you think I could use your love and support right now? But she had only said, I know, I know.

"You have it, hon. But I can't come live here. And I don't think you should live there. I don't care about the house, about any of it. You always said when we were ready, we could sell it and make so much money that—"

"Sell it? In this economy? Are you nucking futs?"

"Please don't use that voice on me."

"WHAT VOICE?"

"Bossman."

She had you. You felt the voice's vibration lingering in your throat. A frequency not unlike that of the Blade.

As you awaited the sliders and salads, she used your prior interactions to point out, reasonably and soberly, no pun intended, that displays of anger lay at the root of her discomfort at cohabiting again—at being a couple—because, as she'd worked on so much over the last few months, she felt you, too, had much on which to work, yet; but didn't know how much work or by what mechanism because everyone is different, and her problems were hers and yours were yours. And how that's where all the 'maybe' came into the picture. That after you, too, had done this work, y'all could initiate discussion about a future. Together. Again.

"Work? You mean burying my whole family, including their dog soon, doesn't count for work? Or building that company? And buying you that motherfreaking house somewhere I didn't want to live? And looking at cat assholes with an LED flashlight? Infected anal glands, illuminated in all their glory? Putting up with all that piss. All that fecal matter. Working so hard. *It was all for you*," in a breathy rush resulting from trying not to shout. "Do you get it?"

"This," putting freckled hands flat on the table, fingers long and porcelain with frosty pink nails in need of refreshing, "is what I mean." She called the server for the check. "Let's go outside. I can't breathe in here."

"You and me neither, sister."

"Don't call me sister."

You went to take the ticket from the server and Creedence said no, this one's on me, and you turn down to-go boxes for the leftovers because of the food tasting like mushy, salty, corporate cardboard. If you didn't want the fecal matter in ground beef, god knew what chemicals where in the veggie sliders.

You allowed her to pay. Sure sure. Theatrics. It's still your money, even if she did earn it at the CBSI—sure, she takes a paycheck, a normal one, which was her decision. All of it had been.

In the parking lot your tone failed to soften, and her body language remained nervous and confined and tense, like she used to look in the afternoons before the first cocktail. Back before you realized the cocktails had flowed in earnest much earlier.

Sunlight, a cloudless sky, too brilliant and unreal for words. Asphalt. Big rigs belching black soot and shifting to go up the ramp onto the freeway. Seagulls flying around. Plastic grocery sacks blowing through like gossamer, floating creatures on a migration to the mighty garbage patches swirling in gyres upon the world's oceans.

"So, long story long—we still got a problem. I don't know what all my issues even are, yet. And yours are whatever, hon. But I don't want to live together again. And I sure as *hale*," sounding every bit her rural South Carolina roots, "don't wanna live up here ever again. So I reckon this is an official separation, now. If you want to let things lie and come back later—I don't know how long, or how to tell when—I might want to try, too. But we got a long way to go. Both of us."

Ready and calm and feeling insightful, you keep thinking about Button's advice regarding stillness and detachment. You listen to the drama unfolding. And through this detachment you acquire certainty that Creedence, for now anyway, is right about the anger, not that right and wrong factor in, only awareness; and here now your chance at leveling up to where your wife is hanging. Or your ex, rather, which you should become accustomed to saying:

"It makes me glad to hear that. Because you got to face up to having stayed a kid all this time. Instead of a grownup who's taken on real responsibilities. And cared for people. What I loved about you when I came and rescued you from Dusty and all his mess was how you seemed like a kid, still. Or again, maybe, at getting another chance. You were so excited and crazy, like the teenage Creedence I remembered. And wanted so bad I could taste it. Dreamed about it. But we grow. And sometimes when we do, yeah; we grow apart. No judgment. Respect." A power-fist, held in the air. "Work to be done. We got this. Et cetera."

Creedence, scoffing at you going all self-help on her. "I get enough of that."

Undaunted: "We grow, and it takes time." A pang of the hurt, still fresh, over the infidelity. "But I see how you're right—there are gonna be problems between us no matter what. It's too soon to know. I been through too much."

"So say we all."

"Sure; yeah. You and me—we ain't got nobody else, really. You'd think we would want to work this out. And maybe we will. The cats—it's like the vet said, they're our child substitutes. They're your dollies you're still playing with, Creedence, so you can feel like a grownup."

"Leave the babies out of this psychoanalysis, please."

But pressing on: "Feeling like a grownup is getting in touch with yourself. I see that now. It ain't money and things. I want to find out who I am too, because I don't freaking know. But one thing's true inside me, and it's that I got to be here. That I ought to be in that house—Mee-maw said I had built it for me, not for them. I kept insisting it wasn't so—that I wanted them to have it. And she went p'shaw and said, well darling, you know you want to live out here in the country and walk in that pecan orchard and—"

And you run out of steam. You lean against the passenger door of the F-150, your face only inches from Rico slobber crusted along the window jamb from all the Saturday morning rides for steak biscuits and other treats. You heave once or twice, shove the grief back down. You must appear strong and uncaring about all this, not destroyed down to your core. "Sure. We're separated now. I get it."

Creedence, her warm hand resting on the small of your back. "Honey. I'm sorry."

"*Don't touch me.*"

"Roy—"

"Go. Just go."

She said okay and climbed into the Beemer. Before shutting the door she said, "When and if you feel as though you've grown, hit me up. Maybe I'll be receptive. Or not."

"Sounds like a plan," wiping your eyes. "We'll let our pluff-mud settle. Say hi to the kitties from me."

A glimmer of soft affection. An inkling of regret. "They miss their dad."

"Well: he misses them, too."

"Are you just saying that?"

You shook your head. "You're not the only one who made mistakes. I could've stopped the cat collecting cold, if I'd've taken a mind to."

A little frown at that. She waved, sad and final, or it seemed. Your wife's taillights flashed red and she headed back to the island to pursue her continued recovery.

God, how beautiful. No freaking doubt. Imagine how this fading daylight would glint from her hair down on the island, blowing in the breeze as you strolled the beach or the boardwalks together. Surreal for her to be gone again already.

When it was good, it was glorious. But all glory is fleeting.

Alone and bereft, you could feature no solution but to call your new best pal, telling her the whole spiel and saying, let's get high, let's hang out, but Button going, wait. Um. I have a better idea—to go for a hike, she'd said. And not by the Sugeree River, either. A hike to a place you've been before, only once for real, but many other times in your dreams.

Maybe, as Button would put it, dreaming through the several lifetimes you all live until while clearing the wheel of karma, until finally proving themselves soul-worthy to forego another turn through all this meatspace crap again. As for you, anybody agreeing to suffer all this pain and grief more than once, a fool indeed and on the wrong path. A chump. In the time of judgement, you fully expected to be stamped and processed and kicked upstairs without undue rigmarole. Better be like that, anyway. Otherwise? H-E-double hockey- sticks to pay.

Arrival.

Y'all are buzzed into Havenhurst through the massive iron gate, and Button's Subaru Baja engine roars as you shift into all-wheel drive to ascend the steep grade of a hill framed by thick brambles and rhododendrons. The winding, paved driveway leads to a modest, low-slung abode, earthy and of a piece with the land; solar panels and touches of exotic landscaping and other opulence. A moneyed estate indeed.

Not to be snarky, but the house? Less impressive in scale than you expected. Would've been perfect for you and Creedence and the kitties, this split-level log cabin, maybe three-thousand square feet with a decent view. You expected much more from the house of Ponderview. At its peak the freight company had enjoyed a worldwide footprint. Now a shadow of its former success, but still a nationwide concern.

"Oh, cool—my dream house. But, only a two-bay garage? With a gate like that?"

"That's just the staff residence," Button says, directing you to proceed another quarter-mile around more turns. "The main house. Is up ahead..."

Round the last bend, however, you see another scale entirely—a Bond villain's lair. More than that, a veritable monument: A glimmering blue pyramid built into the peak of the mountain, extending down its southern face. Sunlight flashes from the glass, a strobe-like effect, blinding you.

A pyramid. Da fuh?

"Good god. What the eff is this? A temple?"

"Like, whoa. Right? The first time. Mind was blown, def. But far as I know. It's just a house. Heather's dad. Had eclectic taste. In architecture."

You go to the entrance set into the bottom of the shimmering glass pyramid, ring a bell.

A voice, gentle and feminine, crackles from the intercom: *"Hey now, guys. Come around to the front and park anywhere. Take the mosaic stone walkway to your right, down the steps and to the piazza on the other side. The way will be obvious."*

"Will do."

"See ya in a minute. Just freshening up." Heather, giggling. "Can't believe you're here."

"It's real."

"Yes."

Down the mountainside and carved out of the bedrock you find three other levels of living space facing a glorious Appalachian vista. Spread across a graded area, a recreation complex comprised infinity pool, cabanas, a yellow tennis court and the expansive piazza, with a covered outdoor kitchen and dining space featuring a regal table and chairs, looked like made of Italian marble. Reminded you of patio seating at one of the upscale Bayfront joints back home on Sedge Island.

On the table sits a half-drunk cup of tea, a Moleskine notebook with a small sticker reading 'Those Who Do Not Believe in Magic Will Never Find It,' beside which sits an aged hardcover book called *The Science and Romance of Selected Herbs Used in Medicine and Religious Ceremony.*

Feeling the breezes, scrubbed clean by the towering forests, begin to dispel the toxic emotion of the last few months, your body lightens and threatens to float away like dandelion fluff. Undulating away toward the horizon, the rolling, cloud-kissed Smokey Mountain blue-green expanse, these hazy humps of the southern end of an ancient continental mountain chain, enthrall your senses. Clouds on the ground; the earth reaching up to kiss the sky. Or kiss this guy, as you used to think Hendrix was singing, and it hits you:

The summit of good old Max Patch is near.

From a doorway in the pyramid emerges the woman named Heather, draped in a flowing Indian hippie dress and with crazy Medusa-like hair framing a round, smiling, but wearied face, and time slows down as she and Button hurl themselves at one another like Neo and Agent Smith. But it's far from a fight—the old pals hold on for something along the lines of dear life.

◉①❋

INSIDE, YOUR MIND FURTHER BLOWN BY THE TRAPPINGS OF GREAT WEALTH, BUT ALSO the clean lines and brilliant light let in by the pyramid's glass front. A living space with a view of eternity. Now this was money.

"Most impressive," taking in the billion-dollar view. "Most impressive indeed, Frau Ponderview. Oh, wait: your name. It's like—is that a synchronicity? We're pondering the view, and—and—"

"'Frau'? My family isn't German." The cadence of her voice, low and laconic, not unlike Button; her thick curly locks, quivering around her apple cheeks as she spoke. "As for Ponderview, I think it's less synchronistic than a kind of self-fulfilling prophecy, Mr. Pettus."

"Pondering. The view." Button, coughing. "I get it. Chuckle."

Heather's arms lay folded over an ample, daresay motherly bosom. "But 'Frau Ponderview'—what's up with that?"

Embarrassed, you shake your tennis-ball head. "Too literal—I didn't mean you were German. Or anything bad. I do stupid voices. I don't know, it's a modernist castle, this place. The idea of a castle made me think of *Young Frankenstein*, which made me think of Cloris Leachman—Frau Blucher, that was her character's name—and so I slipped into the whole Frau Ponderview bit. A throwaway gag."

"So—you're a comedian."

"Hardly. Just saw too many movies growing up. Iconic Hollywood moments are like this constant code running in the background." Pleading. "Moving on?"

An arched eyebrow, and the first of what you can already suspect will be a series of knowing looks between the two old buds this weekend. "The voices, eh? I work with 'the voices' too. I guess we'll have a lot to talk about."

Laughing, relieved. But subtext regarding 'the voices' lurked beneath the surface of her remarks, unseen as subtext should be, and indicating a deeper, hidden meaning you don't quite absorb.

◉◉❈

Heather Ponderview, hugging herself tight against your stranger-energy, begins the tour with a breathtaking, executive chef's kitchen.

But perhaps she's also uncertain of Button's mood, which manifests itself as anxiety-ridden hands that knot and unknot habitually, and a forced rictus oh-so different from the genuine smile of hers you know so well, that joyous, loving grin that shines onto your face like the warm and life-giving sunshine. This smile, high and tight like your haircut.

Hair—Button told she kept her hair long not for the sake of fashion, but because it offered an energetic tool, like fingernails. "Hair's like, antennae for your nerves, extensions, if you will. Helps with intuition. Getting into the flow. Picking up on the signals."

Maybe you'll let yours grow out. Become a real mountain man. See if your intuition gets sharper. One day.

Heather breezes around declaiming the futuristic unreality of this kitchen, which she says had been more rustic in decor before a renovation that'd taken most of 2001 rendered the lines and surfaces of the interior more appropriate to the coldness of the exterior. "For some reason. I wasn't here back then. None of these chilly, hard lines are quite to my taste."

"2001." A quiet remark from Button. "The San Diego sojourn."

"Ocean Beach days. I hope I did some good, while my ability to do so lasted."

"I learned a lot then."

"You were healing, sweetheart. And healing time is learning-mode."

Okay. You crash the sub-textual party. "Well-sir, alls I know is that it's one bad-ass kitchen."

An embarrassing interlude of silence. You feel fourteen again, trying to fit in with the cool kids, trying to keep up with Devin and Dobbs.

"Yeah." Button, beaming you with kindness the way she will. "Sweet kitchen."

Your face hot with self-consciousness, you ask permission to peek into the enormous walk-in pantry. Button sidles and scrutinizes the stocked shelves. Asks if she may sample a bag of gourmet dark chocolate blueberries, which you both gobble.

With rank disapproval and her own brand of embarrassment, Heather points out various junk food items, noting that all belonged to her dad. That galaxies would be born and die in the time before she would sample any of those processed foods. "The packets of chips, those are m'dad's," in a sad cadence. "Those pudding cups are also his. Not mine."

Button examines a bright orange bag of cheese puffs. "That's a sack of cancer. Right there."

"That's m'dad's," Heather says. "And look where it got him."

"Cancer?"

Shakes her ringlets. "Heart."

"Heart cancer?"

"Heart failure. No cancer. It was fast, in the end. He was lucky compared to some poor souls."

"Yeah," Button says, grim. "Totes lucky."

"Your dad, he passed away as well."

Button, nodding. "Whatever it was. It wasn't fast."

"Understood."

As you listen to them it strikes you: Creedence should see this mountain house. Walking around makes you think about your own opulent abode on the marsh, and money, and material goods, and the Piper Meridian, and the boys in the hanger, and golf courses, and Creedence.

You possess it all, still, but her.

Maybe you could sell the marsh house. After seeing this place you want more capital—not to have a hardened Bond lair like the Ponderview palace, but a sustainable home, tucked away from the rats racing each other to see who could text and crash their car in the most spectacular fashion, probably the next hit reality series now that El Trumpo will likely be president.

You don't want a mansion!

You never did.

You want freedom.

From obligation.

From conflict.

From yourself.

But these solar panels—nice. The idea of sustainability. Of independence. Now that sounds like wealth. You want your money-energy to last, not blown on exorbitant utility bills and upkeep and mortgage interest—a monster like this, oh, ho, ho, you wouldn't be paying cash, not like you did with the marsh house.

Yeah. It'd been in foreclosure—some nitwit buying into the opulence on credit alone, over their heads; idiots—and so you got the damned place in Marshside for three-quarters of a million clams, and when it was worth almost twice that? And for cash? A funds transfer? And you had plenty of bucks left? This had been before the buyout, even.

Liquidity, or rather the lack thereof, did not present a problem.

But you would not spend it on a baroque construction like this monster. No sir. A cabin. A homestead. Off the grid? Who the fudge knew. Anything possible. Hiking around for the next few days would only make this worse, as you'll find. Or better, depending on how you assessed the potentiality of your own future.

◉◉✳

At last—hiking the same stretch of Appalachian Trail as you had with Creedence, up toward your beloved Max Patch from Lemon Gap. Déjà vu time, yet all completely different. You motor a few miles on back roads in Heather's Range Rover, approaching from the opposite direction you'd driven Creedence that day long ago.

The hike underway, you find that Heather's stiff and somewhat winded— she moves like someone much older and with incipient arthritis. She talks about how her family also holds land several mountains away, way back in what the locals call a 'holler' and that she refers to as the back-land, with running streams and a spring and offering seclusion going beyond this, which isn't total; your arms stipple at the term 'back-land,' because that's what your grandparents and the Glasscocks call the area sloping down toward the river at home.

Your wheels, turning. You will suggest taking a ride to look at this tucked-away land of hers. But later.

On the hike you keep trying to make small talk about this and that—what you ought to do with The Dixiana, the festival coming up next April, Button's protest tent and its inroads, or not, as the case was, except for Newbie Harrell and Howdy Shull and that weird Beaudock kid hanging out, whom you believe to be an agent of J. W. Rembert's, what with the big fat doofus's connection to the whorehouse trade.

And Button allows this prattle, until shushing you. "No. Silence. Be still. Look around us. Listen."

"Be in the moment," Heather adds. "The only time there is."

All three of you stop your trek and experience said moment, the shafts of light filtering through the deep, old growth forest, birdsong, otherwise stillness. The wind seems to carry with it spirits, ancient and wise; their whispers brush against the tips of your ears, tickle the hairs on your neck. "Nonbeing is what we're shooting for. An empty mind. Receptive. As open as the sky—the heart, too. I feel all these trees speaking to me. And the other plants."

"Oh, sister—me, too," Heather says.

"Have you. Maintained? Your meditation practice?"

Heather, nodding, smiling. "Not much else. And you?"

"Working on it, still. With Roy, too."

Heather's smile, beatific. "Marvelous. We'll meditate together."

"Yes."

You start to make a witticism or aside, but something in the stillness stops you from speaking.

You all sit leaning against a large, mossy log—it smells musty, of its own decay—next to the trail there in the sunshine, a soft alpine breeze rippling across your faces. A small clearing bathed in sunlight and full of pendulous, tall mullein stalks amidst what Heather told you are milk thistle flowers, medicinal plants, reaching to the sky. Purple ironweed, brilliant and beautiful. Lavender asters. Jewelweed, with small orange blossoms ("Good to rub on poison ivy exposure," Heather had noted while going through the names of the various flowers and plants.) Wild Joe Pye weed, small pinkish petals. Earlier, you had passed a hillside bursting with goldenrod, with so many bees buzzing it sounded like a ceiling fan set on high speed. Butterflies flitting around the blossoms. A dance in the air, all feeding.

Magic.

Wait. Was it the right time of year for bees and blossoms and butterflies?

You think this, but don't ask it. It looks like spring to you out here on the mountainside. But it can't be. Maybe only a happy hallucination.

Is this really real?

The question and the moment both hang in temporal stasis. You are back on that scouting trip to the smaller mountain bald near Shining Rock, but also in the dream-place version as well as on Max Patch, all existing in mental simultaneity, and you realize that when Button said 'hush,' earlier?

Her lips had not moved.

You, sir, are cracking up.

"I feel like I've seen more bees this year," you finally hear your voice saying. "That's probably good."

"Well, that is good," Heather replies. "We need the bees. It's been said that if the bees disappeared, on which we depend for pollination of more than flowers? We'd all be gone in only a couple of nonproductive growing seasons."

Button agrees with but a syllable: "Duh."

Chilling. "Dang."

"Maybe it wouldn't be so bad," Heather whispers. "If we were gone."

Without people, what would be the point of this spinning rock? "C'mon. What a thought, not having people. Without traders, the markets would falter inside a single session."

The old friends shrug and laugh. "The poor markets," Button says.

As you come back down to earth from your vision, you realize with amazement that all the blossoms have vanished. It's late autumn, all but winter. You can see your breath. Heather has told you the names of patches of flowers and weeds now lying fallow. Only your imagination saw them all. Clear as looking through a window. But the flowers are not in bloom. Not for months.

You've got to let this surrealist episode go. Your head, spinning. Meditation? Sounds like you need one, champ.

Heather and Button sit back into their crossed-leg postures. Close their eyes. Breathe, deep and regular, from the belly and diaphragm up through to the top of the lungs as Button has tried to show you, what she calls the prana breath. They place their hands palms up on their knees, but not in tandem. You watch as they both come to these postures bit by bit.

Settling in.

You follow suit. Button has coached you on a few techniques, not to mention your Jimmy Buffet-themed mantra. You close your eyes and let your entire being relax, noticing points of stress you adjust to release. You allow the sounds of the environment to wash over you—as Button has advised, you decide to let all be as it is. Your thoughts as well. They come and go. You notice them, but do not hold on to them.

Realizing that Heather and Button are vibrating an AUM sound in their throats, you focus less on the breathing and more on their mantra than your own, which you are certain both would find inappropriate bordering on disrespectful.

Or maybe they'd say, whatever works.

Time loses meaning. Light dances behind your eyes—blooms of iridescent purple and blue pulse and rise and pop like champagne bubbles of loving energy. Your mantra peters out, continues in silence. When you all come out of your trances almost a half-hour has passed, and you feel better than at any moment since your troubles began, perhaps better than ever in the past. You continue your hike, the meditative interlude going unremarked.

◎①✸

"Wonder if there're any Sasquatches round here," breaking the mood with deliberate silliness, wanting to shake off the weird you felt over Button Sykes having earlier communicated with you using telepathy. "You'd think dudes hiking the AT would have all kinds of stories."

Heather and Button both seem cagey as you enter a shaded rhododendron tunnel like a cathedral, the floor of the trail moist and peaty, the limbs overhead an arched passageway. Heather answers, "If I did see one? I sure wouldn't tell anybody."

"Why the hell not?"

"Somebody'd come and try to catch it. Hurt it."

"Kill it," Button adds. "Don't you know."

"Sheesh. I only meant getting vid of it. Like that famous Patterson film from back in the day."

You stride ahead, mimicking with vigor the Bigfoot footage every kid saw in the early 70s, how the imagery and possibilities of confirmation had blown all your hungry and speculative imaginations. You swing your arm and dip your head and glance back at them as had the 'creature' in the controversial, shaky-cam shot burned into your personal and cultural memory.

"Patterson film? I've no idea what you're talking about." Heather, in her gentle voice, so soft it threatens to disappear into the steady wind racing down through the tunnel. To Button: "Do you?"

"Nah."

You're frustrated. "But my question—*have either of you ever seen Sasquatch around here?*"

But no cagey answers this time, neither with words nor telepathic thoughts.

◎①✸

As you emerge from the tunnel and the trail hooks to the left out of the woods, you realize where you are—there, the approach to your precious mountain bald. In continued silence, you ascend from the woods to the grassy slope of Max Patch, passing by posts in the ground featuring the white blazes of the Appalachian Trail. Your tendons and knees pop as the incline increases. Your heart pounds and your eyes moisten as you make the crest and spin around like Julie Andrews, mountains falling away on all sides, a light blue haze over the world; it's wintertime, but the sun blazes with celestial warmth.

This seems like home, up here in these old hills. If only you'd been able to get it across to Creedence, everything would have turned out different. If only.

◎⊙❋

AFTER A FINE INTERIM ON THE MOUNTAINTOP, YOU START TROMPING BACK THE WAY you came and before you know it, the hike's over and you're standing beside Heather's Range Rover you left parked at Lemon Gap, all of you stretching your quads and calves.

"Eleven miles, round trip." Button, wan and winded. "Haven't walked like that. Since we hiked. Back in school."

Heather, also whipped. "I should do that a couple of times of week. This weight would drop right off then, folks."

It slips out. "You look fine. Better than fine."

Blushing. "Thank you. Untrue, but appreciated."

At your insistence she drives down a winding road and into the hollow where Heather shows you the 'back-land' she owns, a beautiful, secluded property not only with its flowing, cold spring, access to nearby trails and a national forest made this a desirable, private corner of the world, in real estate language.

Heather, didactic: "Water—a source of fresh water. You want to survive what's coming? Crucial."

Button: "Plenty of nearby water. Yep yep."

"What, there ain't no city lines back in here?" Which makes them both laugh their asses off. "Septic tank?"

"Try composting toilets."

"Humanure."

You grunt. "I ain't toting around my own waste products. Besides, the economy's picking up. The world ain't gonna end anytime soon."

Heather ignores you, rambling and discursive about the problems she encountered on this land with her homesteading project, back before she'd inherited the entire Ponderview estate here in the mountains, along with the corporation, the companies, the Board of Directors, a new life with which she grapples and struggles to assimilate into her worldview. "The homestead had been in 2005, when I first came home from San Diego in no shape for such a project."

"How so?"

"I returned how Button showed up out there one time—a hot mess."

Button wishes to hear more, but Heather's like, no-way, another time. "I've had so many ups and downs. I would probably be telling you the wrong details of that one, anyway. I never got my homestead going. Never even started. All the plans stayed in my head, meanwhile I camped out in bed, stoned and re-reading books from my teenagerhood. I was lost. All my magic had left. Or so I believed."

"Your polarity. It seemed. To flip from where you were. In San Diego."

"I was nobody's den mother. However it appeared. I was play-acting the part of someone who had it all together. Who had arrived whole, and so only needed to serve. I was in no position to serve—I was still on a rich-girl ego trip."

Rueful, Heather describes how her path led to substance abuse followed by more substance abuse in the form of an ill-advised cocktail of SSRIs, for the anxiety or the depression or the ennui, or the lethal combo of all three. How the drugs legal and otherwise, no longer a factor, have left her a little fried, still, and all of this troubles Button to no end, who keeps clearing her throat and coughing, a nervous tic you notice.

"But that was the 'me' of then, and the 'me' of right now—the only me— works on cleansing my mind and spirit by being here. I'm meditating, and hiking; juicing and fasting. And trying to meet with the lawyers, and the bankers, no more than I have to. "

Button shudders. "Evil wizards."

You must chime in at this naiveté. "Evil? Wait till you need a good lawyer."

"Oh, god!" Heather, grabbing hold of Button once inside the glass pyramid. "You're the first visitors I've had in months. Rather, visitors who are true friends, and new friends. I feel alive again for the first time since m'dad passed. Thank you both—truly."

You feel her gratitude, and their love, mutual, like the heat lamps glowing amber on the serving rail at a roadside diner. "Just glad to get outta Edgewater County for a spell."

You and Button high-five it and finish the tour, leaving out what Heather calls 'the basement library,' which owing to the size of its holdings ought to be saved for a later inspection.

She stops, holds up a hand. Closes her eyes. Breathes. "Okay."

"You all right?"

"Needed to center myself after that extreme emotion. I've been studying the Confucian idea of the Doctrine of the Mean."

Button, nodding. "Mean, as in, the middle."

You get it. "A balance-thingy."

"Like the Taoist notion of occupying the center. These energetic extremes, the good and the bad, they take it out of us. Can each result in harm. I know it seems counterintuitive, perhaps, but good can also produce—unpleasantness."

"No, yeah, I hear ya. Processing it all. Button here, she's turning me onto this kinda heady jazz. I dig it."

"Wonderful." She reaches out, takes both your and Button's hand. "In fact, let's exist together in this moment. See if we can stir up a little at-one-ment."

The three of you breathe steady and measured. Hold hands. A sacred circle. It feels wonderful.

◎◉✸

WHILE HEATHER SETS TO PREPARING FOR DINNER IN THE INCREDIBLE KITCHEN, AND with a level of exhaustion like you haven't felt, well, perhaps ever, you chill and freshen up for an hour or so in private. A Jacuzzi tub soak seems the ticket, giving the old friends an interim in which to get caught up and work on a promised vegan feast.

The bathroom in the master bedroom—Heather has given you her father's old room, stunning in its appointments and view, and has been cleaned and cleared of all signs of the man—is sick in its opulence. Only that ridiculous suite at the Venetian in Vegas came close. The impressive amenity here? Besides the whole freaking deal, the sauna, the tub, the sinks, the fixtures? A stationary exercise pool like a massive granite sarcophagus, spacious enough to get a decent breast stroke or freestyle over the rushing current, the force of which came adjustable to accommodate levels of swimming skill as well as intensity of the workout.

Now, this is real wealth, here. Makes your fruitshake money into amateur hour. You feel like a novice at capitalism.

Well, shucks. You'll never have this kind of scratch. Not without busting your ass rather than waltzing around acting retired.

Instead of a swim you fill the Jacuzzi tucked into the other marbled and tiled corner, get the bubbles going, sink down into it with your tender shoulder aching and leg muscles already stiffening up, halfway doze off. Prompted by the marvelous aroma of garlic and onions wafting from a kitchen enlivened by a discordant, echoing Phish jam called 'Split Open and Melt', you dream of food and music.

◎◉✸

YOU JERK AWAKE, THE TIMER ON THE JACUZZI CUTTING OFF THE JETS AND PLUNGING the bedroom into silence. The stillness that descends feels enormous and sacred in the misty and remarkable bathroom; only the sound of a much mellower guitar jam drifting up from downstairs tells you a few minutes have elapsed.

The music in your brief dream had been bluegrass with jangling guitars and twangy fiddles, but more like a martial stomp; as you toweled off and shaved, you ruminated that this shallow dream was prompted by the traveling motion of the day-hike, the rhythm of all the footfalls, the winding path through the woodlands.

Maybe next year you'll hike the A-T. That thought keeps coming back. What would stop you?

That you aren't a hiker or camper, at least not one with any time put into the effort since your teenage years?

Such strong self-criticism has a habit of gumming up your long range planning mechanism. It always has. You reckon you could pay someone to hike the trail in your place, have them send pictures and texts and make social media posts for you to follow and like.

◉①❋

WHILE CHATTING WITH HEATHER IN THIS FABULOUS KITCHEN IT SETTLES INSIDE HOW you're lucky to enjoy a solid frame of reference with Button's friend—your mutual wealth.

But Heather's headstash, it goes way beyond yours. Money to burn, though, you have that in common. Enough to generate plenty more money simply by sitting in funds and accounts. Sits and grows. When you have enough for the process to flourish.

If, ya know. You and Heather were to hook up, you could talk about money.

But you find out it's not gonna happen, pardner; whoa, cowboy. settle your spurs:

These girls are into each other.

You know it before you hear and see it. Their gestures of familiarity, gradually creeping in the longer y'all are together.

An idiot, you've been. About Button. About everything.

◉①❋

THE CONVERSATION HAD BEEN STIFF AND AWKWARD, YOU THOUGHT, FOR MUCH OF the hike through the peaceful forest whose immense depth and beauty made the Glade back home seem what it was, a damp stand of spindly trees stuck down in a crevice. The earth here heaved and sang, had eroded and burned and experienced regrowth, settled back into itself for eons, and as Heather put it with grace and poetry, weather systems passed over with permission and dignity. Now you get it—those two had novels'-worth of history to unpack, and without your profane eavesdropping.

These had been the matters discussed as they'd hiked, while Button, quiet, kept her head down and cleared her throat and sipped water and wanted to take breaks and sit in silence, which neither you nor Heather seemed patient with, often heading on up or down and waiting for her old friend.

It was then you made your own small talk with Heather. Heard her story about her father dying and leaving her with so much responsibility she felt overwhelmed; and that she'd been overwhelmed already, with a relationship that'd fizzled, and old demons hanging around, and a loss of purpose that no inherited fortune and mountain estate could fill, because of the problems and myriad tasks and responsibilities and papers to examine and consider and sign, and all the individual actors in the company and the law firm and the accountants and, whom could she trust?

"It sounds like I'm complaining about inheriting a fortune. But it's more than money itself, it's—having to be in the world again. In a way I'm not sure I want out of life."

You blather about how you park your garages in the same car, noticing only in passing how your metaphor came inverted. "But the more I've earned, the more effort it takes in *managing* the pile. The energy you gotta expend in a physical sense, that I dig—I never shy away from a build-out or rolling paint. I like to keep busy. Always did. As a kid, I spent time alone. Had to entertain myself."

"You did? Me too. The lonely, poor little rich girl. That was me."

"I was a long way from rich then. Still am, sorta."

"Never known anything but a time of plenty. I wonder what it feels like? To not be filthy?"

"Shoot," with a wry laugh and wink. "I plumb forgot."

Heather asks if you've read any blogs by this cat named Charles Eisenstein, who was writing about issues like the next phase of money. "Shifting from the world system of usury and money as an ever-expanding source of energy to a more natural form—one that decays. He calls it demurrage currency. Money that decays."

"Decays? That's whack."

"Everything that's part of the natural order includes decay and senescence as an aspect of its cycle of manifestation. Makes money seem—"

"A little unnatural." Button caught up, winded but smiling, saying she had had a moment with the trees. A sense of presence she felt would last and expand forever, in a manner that money could only hope to in its piteous state of separation from the true natural way of reality.

At that moment you wished you had gotten high first before the hike, and right then, abracadabra, Button produced the vape and all three enjoyed a minty puff of Sno-Cap in the sunshine beside a babbling mountain brook, the same one over which you and Creedence had hiked.

Lord, but the vibe was different with these two hippie-goddess earth mothers. Heather showed you a hillside of mayapples, little knee-high trees that in their season produce a single small fruit like a persimmon. She talked of gathering ghost-pipe and other flowering herbs. Of learning to become a healer. "We need more healers in this world. And I don't mean with degrees in western medicine."

"I agree," the high coming on strong. "It's like that *Star Trek* movie? *The Voyage Home*? Where they travel back to this time, and Dr. McCoy is shrieking about how barbaric the invasive surgeries and crudely powerful drugs are?"

"Hush. That's a movie. This is reality."

You sighed, feeling present and whole and complete, but only after Button asked for you all to close your eyes and imagine staying in the moment forever —one we could share, always—and you wept at perceiving such a connection to her, to Heather, to the trees and air and sky and sun and the rushing water of the brook; the water especially, fluid and magic and coursing on its trek to the lower depths. You fixed your gaze on one set of small falls and kept your eyes there, and the moment felt suspended and broken only by the echo of a woodpecker hammering away down in the woods.

Later, a couple of A-T through-hikers came rolling on down the trail from behind you. They'd been red-eyed and determined, and as all three gathered yourselves and continued on up to Max Patch, Heather and Button discussed camping and hiking and how each of you had at one time flirted with hiking the trail, including you. But you keep to yourself the truth about this notion coming to you only in this moment. 'Hike the trail.' What a phony you can be.

◉◍❋

"HELL OF A HIKE TODAY," YOU NOTE AS HEATHER AND BUTTON DISCUSS THE WINE, which Button says she will decline and defer to your knowledge and judgement, which is far from expert. You and Creedence put away enough good wine to know the difference. That much for certain. Oy.

"The cellar's through there," Heather directs. "But it's not a cellar, it's a climate-controlled room. The code's just 1-2-3, or maybe 1-2-3-4, I can't remember. I don't think I've had so much as a glass since m'dad died—that's his wine."

"Any preferences?"

Button and Heather consult one another's eyes; on display is a brand of warmth and familiarity for which you yearn. "We're no oenophiles."

"All you, brother," Button adds with a cough. "I'll be swilling straight grape juice."

As you come bounding back in with two reds, one Napa Valley and the other Argentinian, you catch Button and Heather holding onto one another in a manner you now understand goes beyond friendship. You imagine that the sooner tonight you can drink your wine and get sleepy and out of the way, the better. This trip might have been for you, as Button kept insisting, but in that image—of long-lost lovers clutching each other and kissing and not breaking apart despite your clumsy and excited reappearance with the wine—you know coming to see Heather Ponderview has more to do with Button's own trip.

Adjusting her own reality.

Clearing her wheel of karma.

It seemed important. For whatever reason.

After y'all sit down to eat, however, and you pour wine for yourself and Heather, Button surprises you both by also downing a glass, and needing it. For the confession Heather makes would have prompted anyone to drink: she reveals how she'd once been a practitioner of magic, and not with benevolence, at least in the early days of her special relationship with a new roommate named Allyson Button Sykes.

CREEDENCE, ESTES, AND THE COP

Creedence, surprised this scene hadn't played out before now, but there he was—Estes—standing outside the coffee shop, waiting. For her. Smoking and shuffling around, deep into his phone, fingering through, making a call, totally casual in demeanor.

They hadn't talked since that night she kicked him out of bed. She ignored the texts, every social media DM. But surprise wasn't on his side: She had seen him several times sitting way back in the parking lot. As though she wouldn't remember that beater of his, a wine-red Tercel with four bald tires and covered in punk rock band stickers. Junker like that stands out here on classy Sedge Island.

This surveillance was how he knew her routine of taking a break and walking through the plaza to that short stretch of the trail winding through the trees behind the grocery store, a lovely lighted path of red-brick pavers among the low-limbed ancient oaks. She walked every day not to get up her sweat, not with another couple of work-hours to go, but for the clear air to rid her sinuses of the rich coffee shop aromas. The buzzy interactions with the people. The constant chores and tasks. Protect her energy.

She valued her solitude, whereas before she rued those long afternoons and evenings when Roy had been away, ignoring her. With him gone all the time, she saw the benefits of isolation. Not because she didn't love him or want the best. But because it was nice not having to answer to his high level of expectation. How she spent her day-by-days, one day at a time type deals, was now all her. What ought to have been fully empowering, however, often teetered on the edge of full-blown anxiety. A fragile flower.

"Don't much care for this stalking game of yours. They put assholes in jail for pestering girls now-days, don't you know."

She'd ducked out the back service entrance and crept around a luxury SUV to startle her ex-boytoy, caught staring rapt at the Twitter feed on his Android.

He cursed, his saggy earlobes wiggling—the plugs, missing. "Scared the white off my fucking teeth."

"Your ears look like they're melting."

"Fuck," fingering a dangling loop of flesh. "Bitches got knocked out last night at the gig when I surfed the crowd."

"Must've been some show."

"I guess you saw we headlined the 'flea. Sold out. Line around the building. Wild scene."

Making sure he could see how little she cared about who was headlining at The Sandflea: "Hadn't heard the first peep about it."

An attempt at self-effacement, Estes laughed like, yeah, sure you didn't. Went to hug her.

She put up her hands, pushed him back. "I need to take my break."

"Your afternoon stroll?"

"So—you *have* been stalking me."

Nah nah, he insisted. "It ain't like that, baby."

No pet names, she instructed. "Ours wasn't a love affair, honey. I mean—Estes."

Wounded and blinking as though she'd slapped him. "Please let me hang out with you."

"*Behind the building?* Shit, no."

His shock and sickness came palpable. "How could you think I'd hurt you? Dude—I did wrong in all this somewhere."

Her heart unclenched. Estes now sounded like such a wounded boy. "There's blame enough to go around. Least as far as we're concerned."

They strolled. He told her stories of the road, gesturing with his ashy-brown hands about gigging in Savannah and Macon, in Charleston and Myrtle Beach and Wrightsville Beach, even going to Charlotte and Columbia, where they opened for major label act The Fabian Socialists and which gave him a chance for his mother to catch the band. To see how far his music had come. A cardiologist by trade, and an 'uptight' one to hear her son tell it, Dr. Patel had been unimpressed with Meatbody, or so Estes reported with eyes hooded by painful disappointment.

A game effort to engage. "So where does it go from here?"

"We're gonna record the new tracks in the spring. Well—not like we got a deal. But a real recording this time."

"Not sure I agree about the 'real' part without a recording contract, but, goody for you."

"Record deals? Who gives a crap anymore. Freaks are making their tunes and dropping them—BOOM—and there ain't managers or deals or record companies."

"Famous, rich people sell a lot of records."

"You don't make the big money without records? Hell—look at the Grateful Dead, and Phish, and Pearl Jam, all those cats grinding it out on the road. None of them ever had a record that sold big-time. Not really. They're taking the music straight to the people—an art project. From the heart, yo. Feeling the love. Like I feel."

"The Dead? Excuse me?" What did this kid know about classic rock—Estes did raps and crap like that. It wasn't rock and roll. It wasn't even music, if you asked her. The proprietary and generational sense of ownership, despite never having seen the Dead thanks to her stupid husband—a long story—overwhelmed her. "Darling? Sweetheart? Whatever so-called 'music' your band plays, it's nothing like the Grateful goddurn Dead."

"Whoa, yo, hey." Estes spun Creedence to a stop there in the middle of the trail, the automobile drone from the busy traffic circle coming to her muffled by the buildings and the trees. "You got any idea what I was trying to say?"

"Other than your band is doing good? No."

"I'm telling you, we're gonna make money—some real cheddar."

"Without a record label? Good luck with that."

"Didn't you hear what I said?"

Ignoring his question. "You remember what the pops are like between four and six. I need this me-time."

"But baby. I'll have bucks, soon. Beaucoup bucks."

She whirled and shouted that she hadn't a fucking clue what money had to do with her, with them, with anything. "I might be an alkie, but I ain't shallow, boy."

Estes began to crumble. Shaking, pleading. "You saying that's not it? Isn't that why you wanted to break up?"

"No, honey—we're breaking up because what we did was wrong. I was drunk the whole time."

Not having it. "Fucking Roy Pettus. Fucking asshole. Got the money. Got the woman brainwashed, bought and paid for."

"The hell you say. My husband came by his fortune honestly. But if money's all you think matters in a relationship—money and sex—then you really are still only a child."

"Can't get over you blocking me on Insta and Facebook."

"It was a good faith gesture to Roy—he can see those accounts, although I doubt he'd want to anyway."

"Can't accept it. Nope. Hundred-percent nope."

"Well buster, if you don't accept it, I'll call my cop friend. And he'll help talk you into accepting it. Would that work better?"

Estes cursed himself blue and stomped away in his flip-flops toward the entrance to the trail. He all but shoved aside a pair of elderly prance-walkers, a new low impact craze that in practice looked like riding a little invisible hobby-horse, or skipping through the tulips. Cute.

After the blue-hairs passed, Creedence decided she couldn't finish her own stroll. The pace would keep her right behind the prance-walkers, and the vision of the women with their frosted hairdos, white sneakers and shiny, rustling wind-suits seemed too much to bear.

Satisfied she'd insulted him with sufficient force to convince him to stay away, she saw his turd-box Tercel gone from the plaza and she went back to dripping coffee, making mochas and chatting it up with well-to-do middle aged and older customers, who often told her she looked young enough to be their daughter, and thank god to feel youthful; that she had time. She had living and loving and thinking and growing to accomplish in the life left to her. And none of it had anything to do with Estes, or Roy. Not exactly.

Maybe she'd take a moment to write a Devin letter again tonight. Perhaps doing so would provide her solace and clarity while her brood of cats sat purring and mewling at her feet and in her lap and crawling around on the computer desk. Call it journaling. Call it inventory. More useful than staring at the TV, dry-mouthed and antsy, or cruising conspiracy websites and getting paranoid.

OFFICER WEBHANNET OF THE ISLAND SECURITY DETAIL ROLLED INTO THE LOT AND parked in the special CBSI spot reserved for SIPD personnel. From inside Creedence waved, noting as the expression on his face changed—what had been unrestrained longing shifted upon seeing her to forced nonchalance, a too-big smile, and a salute.

Huh, she thought. *He's got it bad for me. How sweet. Handsome boy.*

Maybe she didn't enjoy being alone after all. He'd been so kind to her.

Right. But only because of Roy.

What she knew for sure: her need to forge an identity before forging else, especially with young bucks like Webhannet and Estes. Time to step down as mayor of Cougartown.

Never say never. Maybe after she was divorced.

Maybe maybe maybe. Enough already. The word had become like one of the mantras her sponsor Russ Wetherell told her about, the meditation stuff.

One day, when she had time, she'd try it. For now, coffee to drip, next week's schedule to write, and holiday-themed pastry and other food orders to place. Her life.

BUTTON, HEATHER, AND ROY

After the shock of the confession and apology to Button—for having cast a spell of love on her back at Foothills State, an instance of magicking she regretted—Heather explained how her action had been born neither from desire nor attraction, rather in the spirit of brash and irresponsibly youthful experimentation. But Heather, also quick to point out how actual affection had flooded into her own heart. But still not in a romantic sense.

Not then, anyway.

Now? Now, a different story. Clutching Button's hand, Heather, declaring devotion to a cause she didn't even know she suffered. "I love you, angel. I've missed you so."

Button. All her dreams coming true. A decades-old transgression, Heather's spell? Forget it. Literally. Besides—Button had now returned the favor. And it had worked. Hah. What a long game, this romantic drama.

At this scene poor Roy had sprayed fine wine like a comedy spit-take. He'd been so excited about the pyramid, the hike, the bathroom, the meal, being away from Edgewater County. He'd gushed how the big table with the low-hanging, oval track lighting reminded him of the war room in *Dr. Strangelove.* "We must not allow a mine-shaft gap, Mein Fuhrer," he kept shouting and laughing. "We can't let the Russkies catch us with our pants down, Mr. President," he said in a different voice, tears running down his cheeks in mirth leaning toward grief. Living out some movie fantasy to keep from thinking about his personal losses.

As for Heather's love-spell: "I always seemed to have this power," she further explained. "To get what I wanted. A spoiled, beautiful daughter of a millionaire. No big whoop, right? But it went beyond that. I figured out how to wish things into being. And I as I got older, I would do these—magic tricks, kinda. On people. On you, Button."

"You've got nothing. To apologize for." She generated a wave of unconditional, nonspecific love, beaming it across the table at Heather.

"I had driven out my previous roommate?" Heather paused and wrinkled her nose and sipped, or rather gulped, a big swallow of the Malbec, coughing as though the admission burned her throat as much as the wine. "She was irritating and needy and weak, it annoyed me, and so I played dark tricks on her. Made her think she was going crazy. It's called gaslighting." Heather, now sounding like a speaker at the AA meeting, describing the bottoming out and the collateral damage. "And I had done it to my mother, too. But it was mostly about love—I wanted to make people love me. With you, Button, I sensed you were gay, and I said, well: let me see if I can make this girl fall in love with me the way I did with a few guys."

"Hah." It slipped out, a genuine chuckle. "Hah-hah."

"'Hah' what?" Roy, his eyes bugging. "I'm trying to parse these reactions."

The old friends both came to a fresh realization that Roy Pettus sat watching at the far end of the oval table, his face made shining and ghostly by the LED lighting. Button said to Heather, "I knew something was special about you. You were different."

Heather, giggling and singsongy. *Ev'rybody-al-ways-says-that.*"

"So what's being revealed here?" Roy, refilling his red wine almost to the rim. "What is this magic hoo-hah?"

Heather, her eyes going wide. Button also realizing that too much had been said. "Just a euphemism. For college girl head games."

Button, making hard eye contact with her old friend and lover, and the message passing between them, and Button, knowing their connection lived and thrived, because both of them now understood so much more about reality, and the way of things—yeah, of magic. But Roy Pettus, he stood far too grounded in the mundane energies like Button had heard the two of them discussing on the hike, their voices hollow and thin drifting back down the trail, talking about money-energy and other meaningless twaddle as Roy conversations tended to drift, about his smoothie business and its success and all the work, the payoff, the largesse, the power that came with money, but who was he talking to, nudging Heather in the ribs. Button, understanding Roy had to keep acting out the dramas of his life using the language-constructs he had at hand. Trying to comprehend his part in the play. It wasn't easy for anyone.

A deep knowing like that came over an aspirant only after practice and ritual and diligence and commitment to letting go of action and effort.

Happened to Button every day. All the time. Epiphanic understandings about this and that.

◎◉✸

AND SHE UNDERSTOOD, AND WHICH HEATHER HERSELF NEXT VERBALIZED AS apology to Roy and to Button for treating such intimate subject matter as dinner conversation with a guest who barely knew her. "Honestly, and all euphemisms aside, I have this sense that time's rushing river is getting away from me. That there are tasks to perform and feelings to express while we have the chance, and with Button, I felt the need—the urgency—to say those things. I don't know why time feels short. It might be true for all of us. Or just me reacting to the death of my father."

Button squeezed her hand. "Now we have all the time. In the world."

Roy, a quaver of emotion in his words, hushed and reverent. "Oh, no— don't say that. You must not know your James Bond 007 mythology."

Button did not, and neither did Heather, but they allowed Roy to direct the conversation, which eased his obvious stress about the possibility of further intimate revelations between the women.

Circumlocutory and tipsy, he expounded at a length bordering on academic about the Bond picture, its lead performance by an actor who only played the part once, and the denouement involving the machine-gun murder of the secret agent's wife at the hands of a vengeful villain. It sounded like a standard damsel-in-distress trope to Button, but why burst his bubble.

As for the reconnection with Heather, it needed to continue in a more tactile and explosive fashion, and would, later, downstairs in Heather's bed. Long time coming—no pun intended.

◎◉✸

FOR THE REST OF THE NIGHT—A NIGHT BUTTON WOULD CARRY WITH HER, FULL OF moments that would resonate in her vibration throughout the remainder of this lifetime, and probably the next, too, if one was to be—she reveled in Heather's sexual attention, her loving energy, the whispered assurances and regrets about wasted time. Button would need this to persevere through the drama to come.

Before too much longer—after done ministering to Roy Pettus and reuniting with the love of her life—Button needed to mosey on back home, get her mother and grandfather squared away. And let her dream lover in on the cellular activity inside Button Sykes's body.

Which wouldn't be easy—malignant activity.

Button herself, for all her enlightenment, had a hard time coming to grips with the latest vision from Walfredo, that Dr. Dahlonega's patient suffered not from stomach acid, rather a variety of cancerous tumors throughout the abdomen and neck.

Fear, Button's first reaction. Human and normal.

Until she realized how perfect it all was. How much it confirmed her level of understanding reached upon the hero's journey she'd undertaken. How much she had learned about the nature and fabric of reality, and how to manipulate it.

Again: Her greatest fear, besides never reconnecting with Heather, about to come true, and that meant knocking off both almost in the same gesture—personal apotheosis followed by death. How she had thought her way through increasing pain and the certainty blooming alongside it—sorta like Heather's wishing deal. Maybe the game now would be to see if she could imagine herself getting through her illness, if not out of it unscathed.

Such an outcome didn't seem likely. She could see Walfredo, shaking 'his' head in sorrow. Reminding her that, whatever came to pass, she had thought it all up herself.

Button worried most about how Roy would take the news once it became official. Not now. Not in his fragile condition. When the moment was right. And now certainly not the time to discuss the illness with Heather.

Soon, though. Soon as the patient herself knew for certain.

MANNY, NEECIE, AND BECKY L

This some heartbreaking shit, here. Ain't no doubt. But god-dog. Yo. She got to chill this junk out. Becky L act like she done lost her mind over needing to break it off.

Other times, she okay with it. She say, we all grown-ups, not that that something Manny ever aspire his ass to be. But if being one get him outta this, which he don't necessarily want... dang it. Going around in circles.

Roy getting impatient too, having to suffer all sort of mess from his old house between people he'd prefer to settle down and help him take over Edgewater County, to hear him talk about his plans. But ain't Manny starting it. Not every time.

Lord, here me speak the truth: she's the one who keep coming back for one-mo.

One-mo-time.

Please, Manny, her ass beg. Maybe I can say goodbye after one-mo-time.

You know what this shit is, he say to her? You want that big ol' hogleg. And I want to give it to you. But you got to know this deal ain't right. And never was.

After all that truthtelling? Mercy goodness. She act like she gonna cut Manny muh-fucken prick off, y'all. Worst part, though, came after Manny say how his fine fine friend on the side and Neecie been talking it out seems right civilized so far.

Wasn't no yelling then, in that old Pettus house of Roy's. Silence, except for the hum of money hidden in the floor. Her ass got so quiet Manny hear that mad cash whispering from inside its secret slot.

"'Talking it out'? What do you mean?"

Manny explain how he think it mighty big of them, negotiating over his ass.

Her pretty face go all bewilder-ness. "We haven't been 'talking it out,' your wife and I."

"You ain't?"

"Are you telling me that for months I've been sitting across that conference room table from Bernice, and she knows about—*about freaking our love affair?*"

"Problem is that she don't know we still carrying on and shit. If that gets out, hoo-boy. All bets off then, girlfriend."

Becky L pull herself together. Whiter shade of pale, now. Ain't got a lick of blood left in her face. Only hot salty water running down.

Manny try to comfort her, but she ain't having none. "How could you admit to it?"

"Now you sound like my old lady."

"How could you let us go on?"

"Cause your ass fine, girl. You about the best I ever had."

"You think this is about having sex? Good god. I'm sick to my stomach," she say.

Manny all like, whatever. "And what it about to you? Shit. I see you slinking back here for another taste."

Now she mad. "Go fuck yourself, Manny. Maybe that'll be the 'best' one of all."

Slamming that door. Going huh-huh-huh, crying hard. Spraying gravel out of the old driveway.

Manny, seeing the light in Roy Pettus room come on. Shit. Here he promise Neecie no more side-meat and break it, promise Roy E. Pettus no more yelling and squabbling with bitches on his property and she peeling out at two in the morning—Manny ain't living up to none of it. His promises don't seem worth shit.

Can't keep one to himself, even: the thought of grabbing that secret Pettus money and taking off now more muh-fucken attractive than ever. Not really. But it make a mofo think, all that folding green stuck down in the floor.

Manny; thinking. Too damn much. Mostly about lying to Becky L about it being sex and not love, just to get her to go on. It hurt about as much as any lie ever, and Manny should know—he been telling fibs for a long-ass time, now. Too long.

◉①✳

THEY HAD GOT ROUND TO PUTTING A NICE-ASS GROCERY STORE DOWN IN CHILTON, so Manny and Neecie, frosty still but getting on with it all, trying to be friends and parents to Lillyanne first before any of their stoopid shit, go and check it out. Manny saying, he can dig it. Ride down there with their babygirl to get some grub. Get a couple of roast chickens. Family night, Monday. He eat at home on Monday, when the club closed.

Maybe three birds: one for the girls, one for him, and one for Roy E. Pettus ass, who been eating that durn fast food like it fine dining. He say he do better. He got himself a crock pot black bean soup recipe from Button that gonna be healthy and good. He say she give it to him telepathically. He totally serious about it, too.

That Roy E. Pettus, he a mess, especially when he high, sitting in his big family room with all them records on the shelves built into the walls, listening on the old record player his grandfolks still used. He pull out crazy old blues records, shit like Manny ain't heard in a coon's age if he ever did. Other day Roy Pettus sitting there listening to brotherman Pee Wee Crayton, 'Phone Call from My Baby,' and the bossman was downhearted. Manny feel for Roy Pettus. He do. Manny gots too many women; his ass ain't got none. He got so much money, though, it ain't take him long to find 'the right one.' He pining, though. His miss his old lady.

And he stress eating, too. Manny boy don't eat junk food for no weird reason. He like everybody else—when you need it, there it be. Hot, cheap and now. Shit like chicken tenders and pieces at them places, though, ain't nothing but beaks and feets. That much Manny know. He had an uncle who worked in the slaughterhouse? Told him he wouldn't touch half the meat that come outta them factories. But them nuggets and shit, who know what it made of. Probably ain't no actual yardbird meat within a country mile of that mess. Come out a durn laboratory, where they squirt pink slime into it that make it taste halfway like chicken. Maybe chicken meat's third cousin by marriage.

The store, a Publix, is new, crystal and clean. Big ass deli and bakery.

"Lord have mercy but them roasted chickens smell fine."

"Ooh, they do." Manny big old stomach go URRRRRR. "I'm-a get us one."

"I'm going over to Health & Beauty," Lillyanne say in her sweet babygirl voice. She ain't turn into too much of a smartmouth, not since Manny been better about hiding his smoking. "I need cotton balls."

"Okay, sugar. You get anything you need over yond-ah."

Manny ask Neecie what the babygirl need with cotton balls.

"What you think? She wearing makeup. She got to be disciplined and take it off at night—that's our deal."

Manny pitch a snit, saying, ain't nobody ask his ass if little babygirl ready for makeup. "She need to paint herself up for homeroom?"

"You can't keep her from becoming a young woman."

"I can keep her from turning into a certain kinda woman."

"You can't even control your own impulses, much less a teenage girl's. Let church do the heavy lifting."

"Look yonder at that." He all agog before a display of these Twinkie-ass snack cakes Manny like called Zingers, which back in the day had Snoopy and Charlie Brown and the *Peanuts* gang shilling on the packages and in commercials and shit. "I used to eat hell outta them things when I was a squirt. My granny give me the yeller-vaniller ones all the time. After one of them you can't go back to no regular Twinkie. Not after that frosting on top. Can't believe they still sell 'em."

"Oh, holy hell. You can't tell me I have to put up with this."

"Yo, nobody said they was buying them Zingers. I know they ain't good—oh."

From around the end-cap come Becky L dilly-bopping along in a fine-ass yoga outfit, the bright kelly green top and purple tights and the formfitting little black jacket. With her white earbuds shoved in under the black headband holding back her short hair, she pretty as all get out and talking on the phone. It like she don't realize it Manny and Neecie. Not at first.

When she do, though? Girl draw up like she run onto that wicked ghost they say haunt the cemetery, that old Antoine of Scotsdale, or whatever that spook be. Folks say it sometimes burn the town down. Superstition, that all it is.

Maybe the next catastrophe for Manny to face, the next trial—after the great flood—is this time a fire. He sure as shit stirring the coals, it seems.

A fire like he feel for Becky L.

"Oh, Jesus—I should call you back. Bye. Bye. Bye." Fumbling with them earbuds all spastic. "Gracious. It's Bernice. And—Manny. Neecie and Manny. How—how are you both?"

Neecie, she don't mince words. "All right. Let's do this. Might as well be here."

Becky L turn a shade of pink brighter than her workout sneakers. With the worst fake smile Manny ever seen outside a mannequin: "I'm not sure I—wait. Let's do what?"

"You think I don't know about how you can't take no for an answer, sweetheart?" Neecie, extending one of them nails of her'n like she ready to smack hell out of Becky L. Looking like she could break her ass in half, and she could; and she just might. When they was young, Neecie whipped the living mud outta this one bitch she caught slobbering on Manny joint. Kicked Manny ass, too. Made it stick.

But she too cool for school to pull that now. Besides, Manny call the law on her. They ain't kids no more. After a while you ought to know better'n to beat on people. "Well, here more than a hint: he informed me he done told you, but I know y'all been hooking up, still."

Aghast, Becky L whispering all high and screechy, "I'm buying groceries. At the new Publix, I have a right to shop unmolested by my sister in the order. And my friends across the green. For whom I've caused such difficulty." Tearful, eyes dancing all around but wanting to find Manny's, which he don't let her do.

His ass keep looking at that pile of Zingers. Manny could eat fifty, he so scared right now—Neecie carry a little .25 girly gun in that purse. Hell, Becky L got one like it, too. Maybe once they initiate their asses into the ELMS they give them a teeny purse gun to carry around. Manny ain't know.

His women about to shoot each other?

Over him?

Dang. Old Dobb V write that mess up and win him one of them Pusiller Prize awards. Manny scared shit going down. But he like it, too.

Neecie keeping an eye out for the babygirl, whispering back, "I call bullshit. Manny told me how you was clinging to him."

"'Clinging?'" Becky L take umbrage. "You should have heard his assertions and promises. You might not be so eager to take him back, 'yo.'"

"'Yo?' What that shit? You trying to make this racial, 'yo'? Little skinny white bitch?"

"Look—we still have to work together. Me and you on the ELMS, and it sounds like Roy Pettus and his committee will outlive the festival event for Mr. Rabbit, forming a new downtown business alliance, and, well."

"Well what, girl?"

Sheepish. "Manny and I, we'll both serve on that, too. So we're all. Just going to have to. Get along."

Neecie, big-eyed: "Well. Let me process all this."

"In any case, Bernice, I'm penitent; I wish to atone."

Manny figure it time to chime in. "See, y'all? It all copacetic. We got to get on with shit."

Neecie steaming at that. "All right. I ain't gonna put anybody's dick in the dirt this time. Not with my babygirl three aisles over. We're going on like always. We're both ELMS, and that won't change. But Manny won't serve on committees with you, or Roy Pettus, or anybody. He got slop to serve, and a horn to honk on that stage of his, which is how we keep our lives and our business going. And feel free to shop all day at this store. You can shop till you drop, girl. But none of what you say—nothing your ass want from him—gonna come true. Not where my man concerned. You got that shit? 'Yo?'"

Becky L seem chastened. Manny allow both sets of eyes to find each other, and it's like, yowza. He love the girl, kinda. And she love him, too. Ain't no question. Anything else wasn't nothing but pretending. But that life, most of the time, one way or another. Playing the part. But this, it feel real as shit.

Manny get a tickle back in his larynx, the kind you can't stand when you trying to blow your horn clean and true, your throat wide open and your notes on pitch. He dig the idea of floating away from all this and playing way off somewhere on the road.

But he ain't. Not at his age. It like Becky L say—they all got to keep on living with each other here.

He reckoned on a third way—he suggest they chill till Neecie water quit boiling. Stick it out for a season, get back on track next year. But 'maybe' ain't enough to solve this situation. Only yes, or no. And Manny still ain't sure which it gonna be.

That the true-truth, finally. But for now, nobody need know that but him.

ROY EARL AND BURNIE;
TRUDY, TOO

Back home after the weird, wild and wooly visit to the mountains, getting out ahead of the first decent snowfall of the season—Heather had shuddered while you three stood gazing from the glass of the blue pyramid, with her complaining of how not-used to the winters she'd become in her years away in Southern California; ruing the fluffy, moist contents of a gray cloud bank building in from the west, the hunched old men's shoulders of those Smoky Mountain peaks growing hazy and indistinct with the approaching front.

You didn't give a crap about inclement weather. You wanted to stay. Like, forever. No dice.

◉ⓘ❋

After an uneventful trek home, Button quiet but happy and jamming to more Dead and Phish, you're at her house schlepping the remainder of your gear out of her truck. She's gone on inside to deal with her mother and to talk to Thim, who has been parent-sitting; you've said your farewells, for now.

You go to get into the F-150 you left parked here, your calves sore as hell from all the hiking. You try to stretch them out, hear your name being called.

"Roy Earl. *Roy.*"

"Who dat?"

Burnie, peeking from around a hedge where he's watched you drop off his granddaughter.

Creepy.

You amble over. "Taking a pee behind yonder tree?"

Looking mad enough to bite the head off a chicken, he works his rubbery old man's lips. "You—you ain't running around with my grandbaby. Are you, boy?"

"Heck no, Uncle Burnie." It's true, but still your face flames hot and shameful because of prior aspirations. "We're like cousins."

"You better be just cousins, shit-ass. She ain't nothing but a young'un. And I seen the way you come *rolling* into town, waving your big dick around and taking charge."

"Duty called. I answered."

"Oh, kiss my foot. You hurt people when you rolled the mural like you done." He chokes up. "Backstabbing like a damn yellow-assed Jap. Boy I tell you what: I ought to cut your little butt." But the threat holds little force coming from a weak old man's throat.

Burnie and that mural. Jesus. You'd like to take every rebel flag-sucking cockknocker in the county and transport them all into the nearest FEMA-administered reorientation camp. "The stupid rooster hurt plenty of other people by its very existence. And made us seem more backward than we are. What I did, Uncle Burnie, was way, way overdue. What I did was only to express the majority will, the prevailing wisdom, the way it is now."

"You deafer than I am—and you know I can't hear worth a durn from flying on them bombers in the war," in that old man's way of diverting a current thread into one of nostalgia. "I'm talking about the way you went and done it."

"I didn't have to ask anyone's permission to paint the side of a building I own. End of story, taillights flashing, not a dry eye in the house."

"That mural belonged to the whole town. I don't care whose name's on the deed of the building it was painted on. Or who it was left to. You little son of a gun. It belonged to everybody."

You implore him to lose the attitude and sentiment about that stupid old Confederate flag chicken you've obliterated to everyone's benefit, which most certainly did not 'belong' to that same everyone. "Not the paint. Nor the bricks. Nor the sentiments expressed by the image of that flag."

Deflated. Beaten. "Ain't nothing to be done now, anyway. Unless—?"

You do not trust Uncle Burnie—a shrewd operator is the way of this man. Like you've become. Your mental safeguards drop into place and your frame seeks balance and solid footing; a veil descends over your vision, like storm shutters rolled down before a big coastal blow. You wait, giving him your best ambiguous smile of nonchalance. You never let them see how far ahead you are. How many moves. How impervious to influence.

"What ya got in mind?"

Here it comes: "Look here, son: forget the damn mural."

"Done and done-er."

"I need a favor. A pretty durn big one."

"Sure you wanna owe a man like me over a favor of such magnitude?"

His eyes, already squinty, become two black slits. His chin wrinkles, or wrinkles more, and he draws his hooked nose farther into the sunken maw of his near-toothless mouth; in his elderly, sagging visage Uncle Burnie looks like a Muppet, one of the old men who catcall their pithy disdain from the upper balcony: "Owe *you*? Why the hell you think I brung up my beloved mural?"

"Couldn't say."

"You don't think you owe your Uncle Burnie over that impertinence?"

You bid him to 'settle down' and declare your willingness to help either way. "Depending on how wackadoodle it is."

Burnie nods, loses the 'tude, and now while explaining to you that he's waiting out here for the right person to ask for a ride, he becomes downright sheepish. A ride out to a place, he says, that he needs to visit. While he still can. One more time.

Your antennae, standing at attention. "And where would that be?"

"It's a particular house. Out in the country. Over near, ya know. Red Mound."

"Red Mound."

"That's right. You know where I mean?"

Holy shit—the cathouse. Mama's place, or whatever they called it. Legendary in its own way as the good old Dix, you suppose. And shocked to hear that it's still in business. Did anything change around this stupid Southern county? Would Mama Beaudock's last as long as the Indian burial ground over in the national forest? During excavation one day in the future, would archeologists find fossilized used rubbers and lingerie instead of the supposed giant skeletons once found inside the nearby mounds?

You want to say forget it; but you owe him. 'Your family owes everything to Uncle Burnie.' How many times had you heard it said by Pa-paw? And as for what Burnie asks of you—man to man—what kind of a hardhearted asswipe says no to a dude who'd been such a crucial father figure? Had been so loving and instructive? How when it came time, initiated you into the local lodge?

You tell him to hop in, meanwhile texting Button inside to say you're taking her granddad out for a ride.

YOU LINGER AT THE NEXT FOUR-WAY STOP. THEY CALL THEM SLOW & GO'S scattered throughout Whaley Way, the quiet, low traffic neighborhood of ante-bellum and antebellum-inspired homes. Bless those brave and resolute and resourceful Confederate hearts, as you always heard people say, for burning that bridge. For keeping Sherman's madmen from ravaging fair Breeleyville and its fine houses.

"You know, the signs don't change like them stoplights downtown."

"Hardy-har. Look—this is crazy."

"It sure is," he said, checking his wallet. "I ain't got as much money as I thought."

Now you must pay for his piece of ass, too. Whatever. "How much you light?"

"Depends. Been a while since I run over here. Couple hundred for the best girls. For what I want 'em to do, anyway. Maybe more."

Your skin crawls. You know that you've a thousand, twelve hundred in cash on you. Always carry at least ten or fifteen crisp Benjamins. Good solid base from which to work. "Look, I got plenty. But you gotta be careful. At your age—"

"The hell I do. I want a bottle, too. A bottle and a lay. Then I'll feel alive again. I ain't felt alive since my Henny died, and now all this mess," a broken confession that makes your heart clench. "Oh, lord help me. I ain't got nobody left."

"Shoot, Uncle Burnie. That ain't true. Button. Thim. Tinky."

He tells you, shamefaced, and not in so many words, that they don't seem like family—the grandbabies, maybe. But so far removed that something lacked.

You get it. You are touched and concerned. "Don't worry about all that. Let's have some fun. Let's get you over to this joint."

Burnie, belching and yammering, directs you to turn off the bypass, and about how this had been a dream of his for a while now, but one thing you didn't do, no sir, was ask your female granddaughter, either one, to take you to a prostitute. "Mama Beaudock's been on my mind. You doing the right thing, here."

"We try."

Beaudock. Jesus, that name again—that was the big doofusy kid that'd been hanging around with Newbie Harrell, and pestering Button on the green. Beaudock. Small world.

You recall Burnie's bomb group story, what all he and Rabbit went through during their separate and harrowing service in the war. You think about how much time's passed for Burnie, and what few like him are now left. You feel the pity and the weight of the years as though they are your own memories.

You must carry the experiences of your late grandparents, now—his friends. Your forebears. Your family.

But you have done him a disservice. His granddaughter Button would accuse you of what she'd call instantaneous manifestation, an age in which those choosing to evolve to higher consciousness here in this time of cosmic transition would soon experience such quote-unquote miracles with regularity. You have manifested pity and grief inside your dear old Burnie, who appears to you here as the last of your so-to-speak blood.

Touching.

Wait—were you responsible for this old coot now, too? Burnie and Rico?

Wait, redux: aren't you afraid of being alone? Well—which is it, buster?

◎◉❊

BEFORE THE LAST TURN OFF THE PISGETTE FOREST HIGHWAY YOU COME TO THE ghostly, lonely blinking yellow caution light that signals the crossroads known as Red Mound, its bustling downtown represented by a lone gas station and bait shop. It's a part of the county that gives you the creeps—the remains of tortured and murdered children were once found out here in the woods. The Tragedy of '77, and later Coy Wando, this was these were among many events that'd prompted your grandmother to keep you from going on canoe trips and off becoming your own person for so long.

"Last time I tried this, oh-boy." Burnie, chuckling. "You know what it was like?"

You tense up in anticipation of this TMI reveal. "Ain't got a clue."

"Like trying to slip a raw oyster into the coin slot on one of them old poker machines we had at the honkytonk." His voice, not only adopting the broken cadence of his granddaughter, but diminishing. "We used to have. In the back."

"Ah—the 'back.' I always called it 'upstairs.'"

"You know what I mean."

"I do."

An interlude, the only sound the thrumming of the truck's engine and the whirr of the tires on the macadam roadway.

"Oh, lord. Lord, lord, lord."

"What is it, Uncle Burnie?"

"I can't say."

You think he's having performance anxiety—Viagra, wherefore art thou? Grant thyself to this war hero for one last shot at carnal glory. You? You've never needed that crap. Your wife, she's always been sexy enough. Not that it matters anymore.

"You need one of those blue pills? We could go back and scare one up," thinking of calling Manny or Cecil or any of your peeps. Hill Hampton. Now there was a rascal who probably kept a stash of the V on hand. And if you couldn't call up the mayor, who could? If not you, who; if not now, when? "It'd be no prob at all."

But it's not that, and as it occurs, you ought to have known.

Because you made this reality, you little shit-ass.

"Oh—they're all gone. All but me."

"Mercy, me, Burnie. Don't I know it."

"You don't understand. It's her—she's gone, now."

A slow creeping realization crawls across the top of your skull. Compared to his wailing over Rabbit's demise, your Uncle Burnie's reaction to Runelle's sudden passing has been epic and total, on the order of bereaved catatonia.

Until now.

And, it's a breakdown, weeping and cursing and so weak and sad that he leans over, puts his head on your shoulder, and you hold him, this strong old man of the Greatest Generation. He erected his pillar of town commerce and made his presence known here, had loved and lost and now grieved like a son of a bitch for his own blood- and heart-kin taken from him, one after another, and you could see it and feel it inside him, his loss, because it was yours, too: your families, intermingled, also because, yeah: you created this scene in the truck with old Burnie Sykes. That's Button's explanation for the way of things. The mysteries. We're all making it up as we go along.

"You loved her? My grandmother?"

All he can do is suck wind. Neither nod nor wink. Only the desperate rattling inhalation of a man counting those breaths. Thinking about how many are left, now. And of loves lost. Friends.

"I know that she loved you, too."

"Oh, fuck a duck, Roy Earl. No, she god-durn didn't. What you think I'm sitting here crying in front of you for?" Snot, running out of his nose; Burnie, angry, wiping it away with a savage slashing back of the hand. "Life sure ain't afforded me much damn dignity. That's all I can tell you."

From this point you create the rest of the scene as well, which is to say you pull around in the dark middle of the country highway, the yellow beacon of the winking signal pulling you out of the national forest, empty yet full of all those night-souls among the trees—the animals, the unseen. The inter-dimensional and non-corporeal, for all you know.

The presence of those who'd passed.

Perhaps the spirits of Wando's victims. Or the mass grave that constituted the sad legacy of the Sunbury School Fire dead. All the poor folks, white and black and brown, about whom you've never heard or thought. Who've come and gone.

Maybe your own people, your own tribe, having grown beyond the firmament of their bodies and this place, now watching you and your not-blood uncle, both aggrieved and lost, only your tears silent and hidden from him who wouldn't notice, anyway. Not in his terrible condition. Shaking like a leaf. Needs a drink more than pussy.

A condition that, as you drive back to Tillman Falls, worries you—sure, easy to drink yourself to death, particularly at his age. But could an old man weep himself into heaven?

Luckily, it doesn't happen. With Button's help you get Burnie into the house and into bed, after which you have to explain it all to her, and she can only shake her head and hold up her hands and say, another wrinkle; we'll never know what all went on between and among them, our forebears.

Now you receive the lingering hug from Button that you missed before. Feel her glow from inside. Wish you could muster some of that for yourself.

◉◐❋

Wrung out, you finally head home. You turn on the radio to cut the silence of the deepening night, to the classic rock station out of Columbia you can barely pick up, but dang if it isn't that redneck Marshall Tucker Band, the flute intro to 'Can't You See' and, mercy, how you cannot stand that flute. Cannot stand it for a second.

But it strikes you that maybe you ought to say, how cool, how groovy; back in their bar days, those cats played my granddaddy's old honkytonk. Before they had hits. And how if you gave a crap, you'd see if any of the MTB boys had written a book. See if they remembered to give The Dixiana its due.

What if they wanted to come play again?

Now that it will stay open?

And you have a music festival stage to fill?

Your granddaddy's life's work. Hers, too—your Mee-maw's.

A burden to you, once, the honkytonk; now, a charge to keep.

But so lonely, this path.

Grieving, again, in solitude in the truck's cab, the green dials illuminating your hang-dog, aging visage in the rearview, you allow yourself to flood with empathy for Uncle Burnie. Allow yourself to feel the depth and breadth of his losses.

Of your own.

At home, the lights in both houses are dark—it's Manny's blues jam at his joint downtown, the buffet serving until nine. A late night. At least you have Rico, with whom you sit in the backyard and fret over his creaky hips, which you worry have caused him enormous discomfort. Maybe you'd call Dr. Kip down on the island. He owes you a consult.

You spend the short rest of the night flopping around on the wrinkled dirty sheets until drifting off not long before dawn, the pity you conjured back in the truck permeating a troubled dream sequence like oily smoke, the misty mystery of what Button said—we'll know only the barest sketch of their lives —occluding your rest. Stinging your eyes. Making your throat tickle. And waking you up, thirsty, feeling like you haven't slept a wink.

◎◉✳

SUNDAY, YOU CALL MANNY AND AHMAD OVER ACROSS THE YARD TO HAVE breakfast. You prepare pig-sausage and eggs and pancakes, and while eating both seem as quiet and troubled as you've ever known these cats—normally they sit sniping and insulting like the brothers-in-law they are. You're sure it's something to do with Becky L and the family tensions there. What else could it be?

◎◉✳

LATER, IN THE OFFICE GOING OVER THE BOOKS WITH TRUDY—A SUNDAY RITUAL you've developed, the capitalist's Sabbath, you are the Church of the Third Revelation—you're pleased that the atmosphere between you is so relaxed. You've made it clear to her that this isn't an inquisition; that with money like yours, you will not bust anyone's chops if The Dixiana isn't making a million bucks; but you'd love to see if, as a team, all of you could make it back into the profitable club of its glory days.

But it is profitable, and while you have quibbles with this and that, like needing to drop coin on upgrading Quickbooks—hell, the whole computer, which like a stone-age relic still sat running unsupported Win-doze XP—and again being fussy about minor details like, oh, inventory tracking. Overall, though, Trudy's grinning and happy and fidgety, but only because you remain rigid as rebar about the no-smoking rule.

"I'm so glad it looks good to you, hon."

"The books? Yeah. It's been overdue that I went through all this stuff. But I've been watching you over the last couple months. I knew things were going along smoothly. Big weekend while I was gone." Queen City Slim, a Charlotte-based newgrass ensemble who had gained a following opening for Gillian Welch on her previous tour, had packed the place out on Saturday. You have had your doorkeeper start asking for people's zip codes. How far away were they coming to The Dixiana? Could yet more people be drawn here for concert events? Like a music festival on the green? "Good on you."

Quiet, demure. "I been running this dump for a long time now."

"I know you have. And I appreciate it so much."

Tender. "How's your shoulder."

You tell her, mostly all better, which is a lie; it still hurts, and when you move a certain way it crackles like the popcorn you used to pop at the Grande, and later, the multiplex in college. That'd only make her feel bad. "A hundred percent. Back up to, like, twenty pushups."

"*Ooh*," a squeal of admonishment. "Don't push it, now."

"Ha-ha."

"What?"

"'Don't push the push-ups.' Clever."

"Oh—I made a funny." She sighs. "I'm gonna do something. To make that up to you. One of these days."

"Are you, now."

"I feel like I should."

"Nah. Don't sweat it. It's been a dramatic season for all of us."

Smiles, warmth, a lovely vibe. Her face when you were yelling at her, it'd been haggard, sunken, a hundred years old. Here, Trudy looked almost like her younger self.

The Trudy you'd loved.

Up those stairs. In the 'back room.'

You hadn't told her at the time, but you'd rarely been up there. And when you did? It was to lose your virginity.

To Trudy.

"Lot of history in this old barn. Who knows what all drama happened when it was the Dixie-Anna Grocery and Dry Goods."

"Lucky it didn't burn down in the fire of '26."

Tillman Falls has burned more times than you can cite, but never since The Dixiana opened. You think of the mandalas above the stage and on the Pettus houses, the hex signs. "Pa-paw always said he had arranged for some special luck to watch over us."

"Yeah, he did. I saw him do it, sometimes."

"He did teach me to make my own luck." You take a deep breath. The air feels alive between you and your first lover. "Was thinking we ought to try something new around here."

She tilted her head, scratched at an earlobe. Her blouse, unbuttoned to the middle of her chest. "Like what?"

"Something new-old."

"New-old."

"Upstairs, for example."

She blinks, swallows hard. "I know. I been thinking about going upstairs, too."

"We should, then. It's time."

"Now?"

A bloom of anticipation in your stomach—you are sixteen. Trudy. The Dixiana. Time, turning elastic. Will it go round in circles? "Just wander up there, ya know. Poke around. Get ideas for the future."

Without another word she goes out the office door into the bar, her bar. When you don't immediately follow, she calls for you. "Well, don't keep me waiting, sugar. It's been long enough."

CHRISTY, NEWBIE, THE DIXIANA,
AND ROY E. PETTUS

Another idea-r all up in that boy Newbie's pea-brain.

And Christy? He's all like, *grrrrr*. Hearing him talk makes sitting around the smelly old trailer, Christy cooking and cleaning while Newbie sprawled on the couch like an old dog, feel like impending death.

But this idea-r was different. Not like stealing from Aisha and her family. Or robbing Reverend Nixon's church. Or any of his Daddy's foolishness.

Still theft, though.

From, of all places, The Dixiana.

◉◉✳

While they ate greasy burgers served on square white bread from the Congress Street Grille he brought home after cleaning the honkytonk, Newbie laid out the grand plan of grabbing a mad-stash of cash: After the weekend take, the deposit was counted out by the tall one, Trudy, and held until late Monday afternoon, especially now that the bar didn't open for lunch like in the old days. The money would be waiting for them to take it.

"Why'd they quit with lunch?"

Newbie said the bossman told Trudy he didn't want to compete with the black man and his restaurant across the way. "They got people pulling on the door every day, still thinking it's open. Mr. Roy's leaving money laying on the table, that's what Trudy says."

Christy, whining. They'd be caught.

"Before they even figure it out, we be gone, way way gone, all the way to

Myrtle Beach if we want. Or further," sounding like *fu-tha*. "Far as we can get in my truck. On these bad tires of mine, anyway. I need tires, Christopher."

Christy shook his head. Finished drying off the last of the dishes and placing them, carefully, in the cupboard. He took his rag and wiped the dust off the cabinet door. Now he saw dust everywhere. Like it was sparkling. He had to get this mess straightened up. Newbie didn't half understand.

Christy got out a can of Pledge and sprayed the cabinet doors and wiped them off, after which they looked shiny. He felt shiny inside when he cleaned.

"Boy, you crazy with chores all the time."

"Somebody got to do it."

"You oughta go and ask Trudy for my job. If you like it so much."

Grrrr.

None of this mess sat well. But the bossman, Pettus, had made Christy extra mad.

Hadn't nobody ever paid Christy no never mind, not enough to help him get nowhere, anyway, and at first, when he was joking around with them and playing the video on his phone that day, Christy thought, he's all-right. This man was going to not only pay attention to him, listening like he was listening, and no grownup other than Button had done that before—he would take him flying. One day. In a real plane.

His plane. Christy, seeing Mr. Pettus fly away. The gold-colored Ford pickup truck. Realizing that this, the bossman, was the man he had seen fly. Driven, and flown.

Like magic.

But the whole Button problem. Pettus, keeping Christy away from her. Or her from him. Either way:

That rat bastard. Having her himself. Cock-blocking.

Newbie called it that. "They hang out all the time, Christopher. Get real. They're slappin' the ham."

"They're *what*?!"

"Getting it on, dumb-ass. You're such a kid."

That hurt. Jealousy, like sickness in his gut.

But still: "We can't pull this job. The heat's on." How Christy heard a gangster in a movie describe putting off a heist. "Not now."

"Why not."

It ain't just a movie: Christy, he tells Newbie how his Daddy always talked about The Dixiana, and how Jez Rembert's boys made sure how nobody ever pulled no shit there. One of the 'protected' places, his Daddy said. Like Christy's grandmama's place, too. Whatever 'protected' meant. Christy, he can't explain it half as good as he wants, and Newbie sits unpersuaded.

"You said you wanted to get out. Pettus sure as shit don't like us none. He don't like you no more'n he likes me. Look how he keeps running us off from around Button Sykes."

Well now! Hearing Newbie say it aloud made it hurt. That part, it made Christy furious. Like he wanted to kill the bossman. Sit on his face until he got put to sleep.

But still. The plane, the plane; he flew his own plane, Pettus. "Not yet. It's not time to leave. Not before he—he—"

Newbie, he asks, before he what?

"Takes me riding. In his plane." Christy, whining high and needy. "He's gonna take me flying. You believe that?"

Newbie could not. "Bull-corn. When did he say that?"

Christy, explaining how he hadn't yet, the bossman, but that Christy had faith it would happen. If they became friends. A decent enough man. "He unfired you, at least."

Shit, Newbie said. "All that meant was he felt sorry for me. That's what Fridge says."

Christy, concerned: "You think he feels sorry for me?"

"Shit-yes." Newbie, working his controller and shooting the bug-aliens in the game he liked, creatures and other space marines running and screaming and splattering each other. Wasn't nothing like flying, which wasn't a game. When you piloted, you had people's lives in your hands. "He thinks that way about everybody here in Edgewater County. That's what I heard Trudy Pirkle saying. And she's smart as heck, Christopher. She run that bar for thirty years. You believe that? You got to be smart to do that." He laughed. "He don't give two shits about you and me."

But wait. Christy thought the bossman was the smart one. Not Trudy. Certainly not Trudy.

He kept all that to himself. Newbie, hardheaded and slow—that's how Christy saw it. Newbie was the one who ought to've been in the Special Ed classes. Not Christy. And here the pea-brain was talking about robbing from Pettus. The bossman. Oh, boy.

"It's too dangerous." Christy, done with his cabinets and smelling the furniture polish all in his nostrils, as though stuck in his fine, blonde nose hairs.

"Christopher: it ain't gonna be like robbing nothing."

"Why's that?" He slammed shut the cabinet under the sink where he kept his cleaning products. "Stealing is stealing, bro."

Newbie, crapping out at the game. He had gotten to a level too high for his skill. But he didn't cuss. He laughed. Pushing his hips up off the couch so's he could dig around in the pocket of his greasy Wranglers that Christy wanted to run through the washer about six times to get clean, he said, "Looky here, beau. Check this out: it ain't be burglary, cuz. Not if you gots the key to the place."

Christy, examining the rusty key. "Where'd you get this?"

Newbie, explaining that it come out of the desk in the office. That he had been there the day the bossman got new keys made. And kept this one, he said, for old time's sake. "Who keeps a durn key for old time's sake?"

Christy. Handing the key back. "It don't look like it even works no more."

Oh, Newbie said, it works. "Don'tcha think I checked?"

"Well—how'm I supposed to know?"

"How dumb you think I am?"

Christy, holding his hands about a foot apart. "This much."

Slapping at the hands. "I worked this out two or even three steps ahead, Christopher."

The trailer, still so dirty, even after months of cleaning. Who wanted to sit through Christmas here? His grandmama, she hadn't even asked him what he wanted for his present. Which was flying lessons. Christy, he knew she had the money. He knew what went on, now. Thanks to Newbie. And how much scratch the girls got to do their deeds—hundreds of dollars for the prettiest of them.

His grandmother, one of those girls.

She didn't give the first crap about him.

Money.

Leaving.

The key.

◉◈✳

Sunday night. Late. The damn Dixiana ain't even open all day. The whole town silent and dark and dead.

Christy, waiting out front. In the shadows, down the block in the doorway to the old insurance office, which sat closed and had for a long time, from the looks of the faded, peeling brown paper covering the windows inside. So freaked he couldn't breathe, but nothing much new about that.

Still, this seemed different. It was like he kept having to pee, too, but all Sunday long, waiting to do this crime, when he tried? Nothing would come. Now all the pee wanted out at once.

Christy had not felt this anxious since the time back when he would have Christmas morning out at his Grandmother's. It was always bad later in the day, of course, when her guests all showed up and started drinking, but when he walked down the hallway and seen all them shiny gifts, lord, he had peed his drawers. He was back in his Granny's hallway right now, waiting for Newbie to get done with the robbery. A shiny something on the other side.

But Christmas, that was right and true.

This? This was wrong.

Christy, he whined, high and desperate. The streets, empty and spooky. The obelisk, like a miniature Washington Monument at the center of the green, piercing shadowy at the night sky. The statue of the little general on its pedestal, watching him from within its sculpted, long cloak. A dog barking, way off. Crickets. The roar of a loud glasspack muffler all the way from over on the bypass. Aware of the cemetery up the hill, but despite hearing voices and all kind of weirdness out at the mill with Howdy, Christy, he didn't believe in ghosts.

"Wake up," Christy kept saying. "You're dreaming. Ain't none of this happening." But he'd been saying that to himself ever since the night he sat on his Daddy and put him to sleep.

The dream, it went back further than that. Maybe for always.

Newbie needed to hurry. Christy, his bladder hurting.

About set to give in and take a squirt, instead he froze and drew in his breath: headlamps, flaring from across the green and backlighting the Ben Tillman statue on its red rock base. Christy, thinking: it's the po-po. Earlier a cop rolled through, but hidden, he felt certain, and he had not been seen. The deputy, rushing down Common Street. Not with his rollers on, but on his way somewhere quick.

Nope. Worse than a cop.

Roy E. Pettus's F-150 came round the curve, slowed down. Christy could hear the thumping from inside. Pettus had music turned up, guitars all going wah-wah and bass and drums. Roy E. Pettus must be the coolest grownup there ever was. He didn't give a crap. Sunday night, driving around and rockin' out. It defined cool.

◎⊕✳

"Never do what anybody tells you—do what you want." He hadn't said it that way, not exactly, Pettus, one day on the green. That made Christy feel good.

Until it had turned into, but, this is one of those times when you must do what I say, and Button, she's not sure you guys are helping her cause by hanging out.

And what had Christy done?

What the bossman said.

And now?

Going along with Newbie.

When Roy E. Pettus, with his hard handshake and inclusion of Christy while all stood together on the green chatting with Button, had explained about his big idea-r of rebuilding The Dixiana from the inside out. How he talked about taking the best of the old energy and keeping it, but sweeping out the worst of the bad vibes, and Christy had thought Pettus a wise wizard indeed.

"But keeping some bad energy handy," Button had added. "So we'll know what the good feels like. No joy without sorrow."

The bossman, he had squirmed. He didn't seem to want the sorrow part. Christy could totes dig it. Sign'd. Next thing he knew, the bossman's running him off. Away from her. And from him. That hurt. Confusing.

◎①❋

Nowhere to hide. The Ford, pulling up to the curb in front of the honkytonk. The music, silenced. Christy, trapped in the halogen glare of the headlamps. A long time. Like the truck had eyes. Staring a hole through him.

Standing still as the statue. His bladder, a stabbing pain.

The window, rolling down. Roy E. Pettus, a silhouette, the orange light of the downtown streetlights shining on his shoulders. "Beau," sounding meaner than Christy'd ever heard the bossman. "What in the holy hell you doing out here this time of night? Lurking around in front of my honkytonk?"

Christy, his piss, it let go. Running down his legs.

"Well?"

Shame.

"Get your fat ass over here."

That made the shame turn to frustration.

To anger.

Feeling outside himself, Christy went swish-swishing over to the passenger side of the truck. His wet thighs, rubbing on the rough fabric of his soaked jeans. Praying the bossman could not see the piss-pants. Trying not to glance over his shoulder at the honkytonk.

Did you hear what I asked you, son? Pettus's voice came faraway.

"Yes." He made himself look up and move his curls out of the way, to look at Roy E. Pettus's eyes, shining in the darkness like a wizard. The shadows across his face and his gruff voice made him seem like the Dark Knight confronting a villain.

"Well, look... ya need a ride? Or what?"

Maybe he could cover for Newbie, who was probably watching all this from inside! A plan!

But Christy, he couldn't get into the man's truck with pissy drawers. "No."

"I see your tongue's as untroubled by complex language as usual."

Christy, clueless. Seemed like some trick being played. Whining.

"What is your major malfunction, sport?"

Christy, panicking. Not as much as when Newbie, that idiot, coming busting out the front door of The Dixiana.

"Christopher, them deposits, they's even more than—oh."

The bossman, jerking his neck around at the sound of the jangling bells on the honkytonk door. "What in the goddamn heck do you think you're doing coming out of my business, Harrell? *On Sunday?*"

Roy E. Pettus flung open the heavy door of the F-150 and hopped out. Christy, blinking, smelling his own urine: it looked for a second, a split second, as though the bossman had a sword, a shimmering sword, strapped to his side and hanging down along his leg.

A black sword.

But then it disappeared, and it was only the bossman and his shorts and sweatshirt and sandals, despite it being kinda cold out.

"Get inside that sorry-ass roadhouse." He shoved Newbie back toward the door. "*Now.*"

Humiliation.

First: Newbie said Christy smelled like he climbed out of a pool. Pettus, also noticing the soaked jeans, but saying nothing.

"You're both gonna pay the piper for this."

Christy, shaking. "I didn't do nothing."

"The fudge you didn't. You were keeping watch."

Newbie had taken off his Redtails ball cap, the one Christy wanted to throw away or at least wash because it stunk of head funk. Only that afternoon Newbie said he would buy himself a new one at the Gas Chief on the way out of town. After the robbery.

The overhead lights were on, and it seemed brighter inside than he expected. Christy had never been to The Dixiana. In fact, he had wanted to go inside with Newbie during the burglary, since Christy would never get the chance again to see the famous honkytonk.

Now, though, it looked gray and old and kinda dirty under those bright white lights. All the 8x10 pictures along the one wall, the faces in the frames of people in cowboy hats and women with beehive hairdos, reflected the flores-cent glare.

The deposit bag, bulging, sitting on the bar; the evidence. Roy E. Pettus had been quiet, pacing around, stealing glances at Christy and Newbie, whom he had put onto a couple of the barstools. Christy's ass, wet; the bossman would get mad at him for soiling the stool, too.

Christy, he'd have to kill Roy E. Pettus to get out of this. Before he got the police on them.

He didn't know how. He remembered the awful looking sword he imag-ined, like out of *Lord of the Rings*. Christy, he must've been dreaming. Dreaming of dry panties and being somewhere else. Flying. Flying in the bossman's plane. He had had a fantasy that Roy E. Pettus would teach him to fly for real. Christy, he pictured the whole scene in great detail. A dumb stupid little kid's daydream. That's all that was.

Newbie, his head down. "You gonna send us to jail, Mr. Roy?"

Christy, whining at the thought.

"Don't call me 'Mr. Roy.' Sir is fine."

"Sir."

"And you? Shut up with that sound. What's wrong with you? Are you mentally challenged? That's your gang? The Special Eds? The Remedial Retards?"

The R word? Christy, going blind with quiet anger. "Nuh-uh."

"Coulda fooled me. Hanging around with this numb-nuts chump. And to think, I initiated you into the cult of Rip Taylor..."

The bossman cussed, which sounded weird coming out of his mouth. Slapped the bar. Seemed super-pissed. In a flash, Mr. Pettus lunged at Newbie and snatched him off the barstool by his jacket, the ball cap going flying. He dragged Newbie, hollering and begging, across the floor by his hair.

The bossman yanked him to his feet by the front of his windbreaker, which ripped at the seams. "You ungrateful son of a biscuit eating redneck piece of trash," he shouted. "There won't be any goddamn fucking police. We're going to handle this right here, right now, the way those bastards over in Saudi Arabia would—by cutting off your goddamn filthy redneck hands." Slapping Newbie's face—once, twice. "I'm gonna bury you underground."

Mr. Pettus seemed about to kick Newbie in the ribs, but thought better. Newbie, already crying like a baby.

"That's more like it. That's contrition, isn't it. You're sorry, aren't you, Newbie Harrell. A name to remember. A name to rue, eh?"

Roy E. Pettus swiveled his blazing gaze over to Christy. "And as for you..."

Christy, tensing up. Ready. This was it. He'd kill him. He'd hit Pettus so hard his head would pop off like a grape from the bunch in the crisper back home Christy had bought but which neither had eaten, the fruit shriveling and puckering into cold raisins. Christy, his stomach growled.

"Don't you know that Button told me how you made her feel? All nervous? But I said, no. He's a good kid. He's into Rip Taylor. She insisted your vibe was off. And it is, if you're too stupid to know when you've gotten mixed up with a selfish little twerp like this piece of Edgewater County white trash. Winner of the Mr. Bad Choices award for this weekend."

Christy, his entire body rigid like iron, kept silent. It was his right.

The bossman stopped a few paces away. "Your name's Beaudock, right?"

"I reckon," all breathy and quiet. "Far as you know."

Newbie, pulling himself up from the floor behind Pettus. Christy, thinking hard to his pal:

Jump him. We will sit on him until he goes to sleep. We will win.

Keeping his bossman eyes, shining and wicked and dark, trained on Christy, he said, "Harrell: take that deposit bag and put it back in the cash box."

Newbie, penitent, did so. His hands shook as he picked up the bag.

"And I know how much is supposed to be there. I was just here with Trudy, complementing her on what a good job she'd been doing. On all the money we were making."

"I'm sorry, Mister—I mean, sir. I'm gonna—gonna put it—put it back."

He finally twisted around and lasered his eyes at Newbie. "This place never needed a safe. Nah. Know why? Because The Dixiana was as important as the courthouse in this town. Yeah. All the powerful people would meet here. Upstairs, mainly, but down here too. This place is different. It belongs to everyone—even that old lizard J. W. Rembert, and his no-good son. But the money? It belongs to me."

Christy's ears perked up. The bossman hated Rembert, too, his goons with their stupid little hats! Christy's anger, abating somewhat. They could've talked about that on the flight together. How much they both despised Rembert. His thugs, a word which Christy was careful about thinking because 'thug' had a racial connotation now that Christy didn't intend, had never come back for that money Christy's Daddy owed, at least.

"But now, times's changed, I reckon." Pettus started talking like a redneck. "And beau, we gonna get a safe. I can guarantee your asses that. Times being what they are. This whole county's full of Newbies and whatever the fudge your name is, Beaudock. Ants crawling around at my feet—trying to take money off me—*argh*."

The bossman broke off from his angry speech. Staggered over, leaned on the bar. Not looking at Christy.

His chance.

Christy went to slide off the stool. Slow.

But he was stuck. His wet jeans!

Curses! Christy's chance, evaporated.

The bossman glanced sidelong, watching Newbie come back out of the office door. "We're sorry, Mr. Pettus. Please don't call the heat on us."

The bossman scowled. "Are you people deaf? I'm not tinkling any little bells to summon the LEOs. Do you nitwits not understand who you're dealing with? *I own the cops.* And because of that, I am above them. I don't need them to mete out punishment. And furthermore, the kind of penalty I'm enacting involves giving you miscreants life lessons." His voice had softened. He sounded like himself again, when he was laughing out on the green. Being friendly to Christy.

A yawning chasm opened inside his stomach: The bossman had been friendly. Christy's intuition told him the bossman was okay. But his mind, it had listened to Newbie.

Christy, certain he would not make that mistake again.

Ingratitude. That's what Roy E. Pettus was talking about!

Right?!

"Mr. Pettus." Christy, his voice so small, barely there. "I'm sorry."

"Save your apologies. I want both of you out. And don't come back. Newbie? I'm re-firing you. I hope that this makes sense, considering the circs."

Newbie, scolded and cowed. "Appreciate you not calling the law."

"Look at it like this: if there were a next time? I won't call them then, either. I'm going to slice both your heads off and put them on pikes out front."

Christy, chilled to the bone: the sword. Cutting off heads. What had he seen out there? A secret weapon only the bossman could see and use?

Magic?

Christy, terrified. The bossman's power, it was written on his face. But it was also an invisible force that felt compelling and total.

Christy, wanting this power so much. An inkling, back when he fixed all his Daddy mess for keeps.

"Is that all right with both of you? Have we forged a covenant here?"

Newbie wrinkled his nose. "That sounds like church talk."

"Well, maybe that's what it is. You need to get right with the Lord, so to speak. And right now, the Lord's me. Standing here." Hands on hips. "Now get out of here. Get out of my sight. In fact, get out of my town."

"Your town?" Newbie, little smartass. Digging a hole deeper. "Since when."

"Since right now."

"Does Jezmund Rembert know that?"

Bossman snorted. "I'm sure he's caught a whiff. If he's paying attention."

"That's what we was gonna do—leave." Christy, hot tears bubbling over like when his granny fussed and told him he was too big and loud and dumb to live over in Red Mound with her and the girls. "We was leaving anyway. We was gonna *fly*."

Bossman, super skeptical. "Fly? Sounds awesome. Earn your way out of this stupid black hole in the universe instead of stealing, and who knows what's possible That's what I did. And look at me now—I can fly whenever I feel like it, punk." Roy E. Pettus, shadows hiding his eyes. "Look at me now," he repeated, sounding dazed. "Look at all this splendor and wonder."

Newbie caught Christy's eye. "C'mon, Christopher."

Helplessness. Christy hopped off the stool. Went chafing on by the bossman, who made a salty remark about somebody needing to hit the showers.

Christy, thinking about the rabbit holes he had been down on 'teh internets,' weird pages he got led to based on Howdy Shull's crazy talking and Button's pamphlets. The circle-walking before the hooked crosses out at the old mill building—it haunted Christy. How at first he had thought Howdy a smart man, as well considering Roy E. Pettus kind and cool. And maybe he was cool, letting them go instead of calling the cops.

Christy, not so sure. Christy, remembering only that put-down. That R word. And the bossman having told them to leave Button alone, too. Christy's precious Button, an angel.

Grrrr.

◉ⓕ✽

ON THE DRIVE BACK TO THE TRAILER, SILENCE. THEIR MINDS WERE BLOWN, CHRISTY reckoned, because they were going home instead of out of town. He sighed. The windows were down despite it being cold—the smell of the urine.

"Well, *that* happened." Newbie, signaling to take the turnoff to Mayfield Acres and the unclean trailer that Christy was sick to death of living inside. "Dang."

"Now what, Newbie?"

Newbie, pissed off. "I'll be shit if I know—wait. Hold on. What about Howdy?"

Christy, going wow—I was just thinking about him! Asking what Newbie meant.

Newbie, saying how Howdy Shull lives with his sister in one of them big nice old Southern mansions over on Whaley Way. That they had money in there—rich people always had money around. Didn't they? Howdy Shull might be somebody to visit soon. Give him a ride home one day instead of watching him walk around with his two-liter bottle of gas that everybody else seems to think is Canada Dry.

"Howdy Shull likes us, Christopher. I bet if he's got money, he would let us have it. We wouldn't even have to steal. We been kind to him. Ain't we?"

Christy, reckoning they had. Feeling weird about the idea, but differently than robbing The Dixiana. They had not met Howdy's sister. She might not like them any more than Roy E. Pettus did, the thought of which made Christy feel like he might soon explode.

BUTTON AND THIM

It was time to divulge to her sister.

Back from the mountains, her days filled with happy and loving texts from Heather, when feeling anxiety over the health issues Button settled her spirit by listening through the cans to a two-hour 528Hz Whole Body Regeneration YouTube. Meditated away the pain with blinding white light called down from the stars. Did reiki upon herself. Tai-chi. Yoga, what poses she could still achieve despite the tender, decaying flesh of her body.

Prayed.

Prepared.

Upon awakening one morning Button had sketched and decoded a dream-sigil. In comparing the artwork to an anatomy slideshow, she determined the location and position of the various tumors to which she directed healing white light to stave off what felt inevitable—what *was* unavoidable. Walfredo had never been wrong yet.

The old Button would have put off such a scene with Thim, because the old Button would have imagined it in advance as a dreadful experience, and so the reality would come to pass as she had expected. Button, now—the Button of like, Right Now?—knew how dangerous it could be to believe ideas into concretized reality.

But how else did truth come into being, except through our own thoughts and dreams?

Imagination.

Attraction.

Manifestation.

Duh. Obvious. When a person thought about it.

That kind of talk, which she dispensed to Roy on their visit to Havenhurst with as much grace and subtlety as she could manage, fueled her spirit and the web of her life, now. Here in the final time before Button's vibration shifted and her ascension became complete, the realities she envisioned manifested themselves with near instantaneousness. What many or most, if they'd been privy to what unfolded, might call miracles.

◎①❋

But certain dramas, familiar as episodes of a favorite TV show binge-watched until the lines came rote, would have to play out. Button understood that her part in the play had changed, but Thim would not yet, and would continue, feral and ferocious, to stalk the boards as rehearsed.

She sat listening to Thim rant in the front seat of her BMW following a lunch at a downtown salad bar catering to the business crowd. Traffic zipped by on the busy lunchtime street; Button, watching the parking meter tick down to the last minute, and wishing she were back home walking on her path, or in the mountains with Heather.

"Might I break in?"

Thim stopped in mid-word. Waited. Furious. "I already know something's coming. You never want to get lunch."

"I'm not gonna be around much longer."

Her fury dissipated. A chuckle. "Of course. This is but one more betrayal of our family. I was waiting—sitting in that mansion, in my office, every day—for you to pull this crap on me. And here we are." Mad laughter. "Round and round we go. It had to happen."

"Inevitability is a fallacy. Reality is malleable."

Now the anger crept back in, a quiet menace: "If you start in with that new age BS, I'm gonna call in an air strike. We'll nuke the site from orbit." Thim and their dad had been good friends. Eighties action movies had been their shared passion—*Aliens, Commando, First Blood.*

Amused by her sister's hyper-aggressive hyperbole—wouldn't a powerful modern warhead kill her and everyone else, too?—Button smiled and glowed and projected love.

Her surface slick as ice, the strident sister's ill will skittered across like drops of water on a hot iron skillet. Thim carried a hard, high-buzzing frequency capable of literal physical damage to a body—in particular to the person generating the vibe. Unpleasant for all in one's sphere not trained in the ways and means of detachment, yes, but most harmful to the entity producing such a narrow, sharp wavelength. With her negative vibrational knobs cranked to eleven and wound tight as far back as Button's memories stretched, Thim, sure to one day suffer disease manifestation.

Button, too, always suffered from her mother's anxiety, passed down like dimples or a Kirk Douglas chin cleft or kinky red hair from a white Irish-blooded redneck to his Vietnamese daughter. Until the day she hadn't felt anxious, which Button traced back to the first time she'd gotten high, and in another sense to the moment in which she now found herself: a state of deep knowing and comfort, but also not-knowing, in which lay the secret.

She generated warmth, became settled and centered, and possessed a clear understanding of where and how the offending cellular activity originated. That conclusion dredged up their father's ordeal, a literal big Buddy who'd pushed both his children to excel, to learn, to accumulate knowledge, which in his mind translated into power.

Had it been any mystery, or miracle, for that matter, that her father had worked with the energy that drove all their lives, that made their existences livable in the context of the culture and civilization they'd all built and created and maintained together?

Until it killed him.

Wielding such power? Always a price to pay.

Yeah—we all make the reality of the world together. And if you believed and acted from a place of loving, glowing, heart-centered intent like she projected while sitting across from her sister in her luxury automobile, a rigid frame within which to play their malleable drama, you'd be given ultimate knowledge. But only so long as you were first willing to give everything up, at least 'everything' that you'd once thought had value, while trapped dwelling in the state of somnolence in which most people led their mind-conditioned, consumer-driven materialistic meatspace lives.

Thim, believing her politics and governor and mind control were the keys to the kingdom. Another example of misapplied energies. And oh-so ephemeral. One day the guillotines would return for the governors and other elites.

As Gustav Meyrinck once wrote:

Man is firmly convinced that he is awake; in reality, he is caught in a net of sleep and dreams, which he has woven himself. Those who are caught in its meshes are the sleepers who walk through life like cattle being led to the slaughterhouse, indifferent and without a thought in their heads. To be awake is everything.

◉◎✻

THIS THIM SCENE, DIFFICULT, BUT WHAT OF THE REST OF BUTTON'S FAMILY? HOW to break her grim news? Her mother's drift into dementia meant that it may not matter. Her grandfather, on the other hand, and against all odds and proba-bilities and typical realities of late-life alcoholism, remained sharp. At least when not grief-stricken, still, over his recent losses, that is.

Almost more than Roy himself, Burnie Sykes had grieved for Uncle Rabbit and Mama Runelle. How her granddad confessed that he'd now lived too long, if all whom he'd loved had passed on: his friends, his wife, his son. He wept, "I can't get over Runelle." Insisting through clouds of booze, "I can't, I can't, lord help me."

Button, hurting at the implication. She asked, if he'd lost 'all he loved,' where did that leave his remaining immediate family?

The still living?

For now, anyway?

"Y'all are my boy's family," he explained, bitter and cussing at having been tricked into this brutal, honest admission. "You my kin. But not my blood. Not exactly."

"That's a helluva thing to say."

"You asked, Button."

Button, feeling as though no truly kind and loving grandparent ever could have expressed such a sentiment. But then, hers had always been distant. Most of those WW2 guys were, though. Tough old birds.

She'd let it go. Loved him without conditions. And continued to care for him.

Until she couldn't anymore. One day soon.

◉①❋

So, THE TIME NIGH TO TALK IT OUT WITH THIM. THE PARKING METER'S RED FLAG popped up. "I don't want. You to feel bad. Later. But, while I am planning to leave, it's not for the reason you think."

"It's that ridiculous band. You don't have to explain. You already did. All that hoodoo a couple years back about going to Colorado and 'reclaiming your spirit.' *It was a fucking rock concert.* That's all it ever was, ever will be. It's like a movie or a play. You consume it. It doesn't change your life, except maybe to get you hooked on dope, which if the Governor ever knew that about you, it would affect the track of my freaking goddamned career. But speaking of that: Now you're leaving and abandoning your family? To go and what? Get high? Spin around barefoot? When was the last time you had a pedicure? And look at your hair, still. The governor told you to lose the dreads, Button. Don't you respect proper authority, like, ever? You listen to the same goddamn fucking music every day. It's madness." Thim cried out as though stabbed in the gut and beat the dash opened-handed, three times, *whack whack whack.* "Don't you get it? Don't you?"

"Yes." Button, her vibration steady and happy. "I think. That I do."

"I'm here to tell you, sister, that you don't. Do you realize what's coming?"

Button, saying, yeah. Pretty sure.

Her eyes, piercing. "How? How did you hear?"

"Hear what? That I've got—"

"That Sandy's running. She's throwing her hat in."

Button, smiling and shrugging. She cleared her throat and swallowed hard. Not a good day for all this talking. "But I thought. She couldn't. Run for Governor. Again."

Thim, fuming and exasperated. "Not for Governor. For. The. Open. Senate. Seat. Do you not read the *Columbia Record* anymore? Or watch WKNO? Aren't you a KNO-Nothing? I paid for the whole family to have complete website access for a year. No," she shrieked, her beautiful Asian eyes squeezed down to two dark slits, deep creases appearing in her otherwise high, creamy forehead. *"For two fucking years."*

Button hadn't looked at any mainstream news in forever. "It's not. About Phish. Or Governor Three-Rivers. Running for the Senate."

The air in the car, clearing. Thim's ire, dissipating. Her breathing dropped to a more manageable rate. She checked her device, scrolling through messages with one of her deadly mother-of-pearl fingernails. She put the iPhone down, crossed her hands, drummed those nails on the rubberized back of the cover of the ubiquitous Apple product. "Then what the fuck is this nonsense about?"

Button took a deep breath. Another. She smiled. Felt love and no fear. And told her sister the truth; told her how long until the truth became real indeed; and Thim went to pieces in a different way, which continued until a parking attendant rapped on the window and pointed to the expired meter, scaring the mud out of them both.

⊕⊕✳

ONCE BUTTON'S OLDER SISTER, BRILLIANT AND SUPERCOMPETENT AND accomplished for her age, settled into mere affectless shock at Button's grim news—she seemed to detach herself from the situation, pleasing Button to no end—Thim pulled out of the parking space and negotiated the traffic and attempted to grab the reins. After dropping Button at the Subaru parked over by the Governor's Mansion, it became clear Thim would need a further number of conversations to come to grips with the fact that her sister would pursue no course of treatment at the oncology center, a mere two minutes away from where they now stood at the first expressway exit out of downtown.

Thim, freaking out, caught up in power-tripping control delusion, still believed it possible to shape and manipulate reality through the crude and invasive and poisonous tools of the age of separation. In real terms, however, Button's illness had progressed beyond the point when any of that could help. This reality that would take time to sink in—not the truth of Button being sick.

That it was too late to fix.

That treatment would cause suffering.

Followed by death.

Which remained the least of Button Sykes's concerns.

Thim, like most people from Edgewater County, simply accepted that many of them were sick and dying instead of fully living. So used to it they didn't stop to consider, like, ever, the possibility that something might be wrong not with themselves, but with their external, shared reality. Maybe Button had time to bring Thim around. Roy Pettus, definitely—he was on his way. Her sister? A tough case. But she'd try. If there were time.

What was she saying? Of course she had time. There was Now, and vibrating at a level of cellular distress, density and disease or not, Button, like anyone able to recognize the truth, possessed all the Now she could handle or ever use.

A cornucopia of Now.

Once Thim pulled herself together, the two of them standing on a sidewalk bulging and cracked by the root beds of the towering, ancient oaks of the Governor's Mansion, she held onto her little sister and projected a glow within in a high-vibrating manner like Button had never perceived. Would the illness ordeal awaken Thim? Would love, pure and easy, bloom where now only dwelled ambition and materialism? One could only hope.

"There's something I needed to ask our father, but I never did."

"Why not?"

Thim pulled away, flicking at lint on her power suit. "I've never been scared of anything. But I was afraid of him."

Button implored Thim to reveal the question.

"Our names—Father was so domineering and driven, focused on directing every little aspect of our lives."

"Most of all wiping the Vietnamese from out of us, and her."

"Correct. So, why'd he let her choose these ridiculous names?"

"Hah—at least yours sounds Asian."

"My lucky day. But you could've been Allyson. You didn't have to stay Button-Button. Nobody would've blinked an eye."

"Too late now."

As their dying dad sat in his fetid bed, slumped and struggling to find freedom from his broken physical form, she had asked him about the names Thimble and Button. He scratched out an answer on his notepad—how he wanted to let Tinky 'have something' of her own. Thimble and Button were words she understood, and wanted to apply to her babies. *So I allowed her such power. I should have given her more.*

That had even't been the most dramatic of his notes. Those, she had ripped into a million shreds. The request about the morphine. And how she was to give it to him—all at once.

She had, ending his life and his suffering; but no one ever need know that factoid. He'd asked; she'd acted. And he'd found release from his suffering, made worse by those croakers over at the devilish oncology center.

In retrospect, helping her father leave this broken world had been the door opening in her own heart, and raised her overall vibration. No question. The warm glow of the universe's approval had spread through her in those moments as she'd watched Burton Sykes nod into blessed unconsciousness for the final time. She'd held her hands over his forehead, and as he blew his final breath against the blood beating in the veins of her wrists, she bore his spirit up and out of the shell, bidding it to merge with the All that awaited; and that matters would be fine in his physical body's absence, here on the spinning rock filled with innumerable life-forms having the 3D experience, for a limited time only, step right up, no credit check.

She described to Thim the contents of the note regarding the names. How it was an act of generosity on his part.

"Wa'n't that kind of him, beau." Thim, mocking the good-old-boy patois of their father and half of Edgewater County.

The sisters laughed; they wept.

Button, ignoring her cynicism to agree the act had been kind, and names were abstractions, and that hers seemed to suit in the way Thim's did, only not in how she may have realized. Thimble, protecting finger, in this case, herself; Button, holding it all together. Yep yep. While she still could, anyway.

For a woman like Thim, caught up in the matrix, she thought Button had lost her mind. Asked if she were being fucked with ("No," Button's answer). She said, we will revisit this. "Cancer can be beaten. It's a disease, and we have control over diseases now."

"Is that so."

"We have the tools; the talent. That type-deal."

Now Button's turn to cry bullshit. "I wish it were so."

"The drugs—all the drugging did this."

Button, amused. "None of this life. Is so reductive. Or simple. To a single reason. People want the answers. It's this; or it's that. But it's more. Always more."

Thim, aghast: "This is your life we're talking about—how can you laugh?"

"Thin line. Between laughing. And crying."

They fell into one another's arms like lovers, both of them boiling over with tears and confusion. Like never before; not after their grandmother's funeral;

not even after their father's. Good grief, at last. If it'd taken Button's own impending death to connect so deeply with her own flesh and blood, so be it.

Always a silver lining. Forever a sunny side.

And besides. Her mind had gotten her into this health trouble; it would also shepherd her out in a sane and safe fashion, normal as can be. She only needed a trusted partner for assistance in high-stepping out of this meaty, wet hologram, a task looming like one of her capable buddy Roy's checklist action items.

Now there, a candidate—the Bossman could get anything you wanted done and done, yes he could. If only she might find the enormous courage necessary in asking a friend to help a little cancer-crusty dirt surfer like her figure out a gentle way to kill herself.

GOOCH AND DOBBS

The meeting with the new owner and publisher of the *Edgewater Advocate*, Porter Bucknam, went so well that Gooch felt better than in months. Bucknam, a downsized former editor at the *Columbia Record* who'd inherited land and money in Edgewater County, seemed happy with Dobbs taking over, as well with Bill's promotion to Editor-in-Chief Emeritus, an honor and a privilege and a way to keep his toes dipped in the game.

Keeping him on the masthead; the journalistic equivalent of the gold watch.

Knowing what was coming.

Remembering what had been.

He'd been looking forward to the day, Bucknam said, that Gooch would give his blessing to a successor. When he'd been ready. "And, here we are." Bucknam, a balding, goateed man in his late 50s who looked vaguely familiar, made a theatrical flourish with his hand that seemed forced and odd.

"Wherever you go, there you are." Gooch, laughing too loud.

"Um. Right."

Bucknam, so polite. Terrible actor. Briefed as to Bill Wimmel's forgetful shenanigans, his piteous condition of mind.

But he wasn't so far gone, not today anyway, that Bill couldn't play right along with these children, yes-sir. And act like retirement was all about writing his Edgewater County book rather than his mental deterioration, which may or may not even be obvious to anyone else—he couldn't remember. He'd been talking about the issues with these men for months, years. Hadn't he?

Lord help, but you had to admire the courtesy and decorum of the Southern way of life. Southerners, Gooch knew well, could put on a good face about any mess or crisis you might hand them. When you get your ass whipped in war, and burned to the ground and put into your recalcitrant place, the survivors had to learn to persevere through a shattering and painful victimhood, though of their own making. Had had that cheerful but defeated way of thinking so ingrained it'd become genetic.

Perhaps that represented the theme of his book. The cult of the lost cause. A malingering sense of nostalgia for the 'gentler' antebellum times—a kinder and gentler era of enslaved labor in the fields. That's what some would say the industrial revolution portended on a fundamental level, with its models of production and capital and debt and wages guaranteed to foment an impoverished and exploited underclass. Endless slavery; nobody free. That was the miracle cure for what ailed those holding the reins of power.

Only the illusion of freedom.

All slaves.

All the time.

Boring. Conspiracy tripe. You found it on the internet by the ream. Gooch could not get away with printing any of it, not here in Edgewater County. They'd run him out of town just as soon as if they knew of his peccadilloes.

Or he could write about that dastardly serial killer Coy Wando. Nobody'd tackled that subject in a book. Not yet. That, or old legends Bill found surfing the new Edgewater Archives website, an account by a man named Gandee about a Salem-like incident of witchcraft accusations, as well actual cult activity a generation or two earlier one county over called the Weberite Heresy, lurid sex and seance rituals leading to murder—or rather, human sacrifice. After reading the account he had a dream such horrors still went on out in the woods nearby. Gooch awoke out of that one sweating and screaming.

"Of course I'm going to write a book," he said, thinking they'd been discussing his plans at the restaurant table. Hadn't they? Or did he simply imagine saying aloud what had been internal dialog? Ran into this all the time. Usually tried to skate on through. "Never intended not to. What wag claimed otherwise?"

"No one, no one," Bucknam said, laughing and forced. "Not a soul. But that's still a relief to hear. Sure as hell didn't expect you to retire and stop writing. Ask anyone—'Gooch Wimmel knows every story about this county worth telling'."

"Wrote those stories already," petulant and aristocratic. "In the *Advocate*. You may've heard of it."

"Well now, there's plenty more stories to tell."

Dobbs, a soothing cadence. "He knows you did, Bill. We both do."

"I know you know."

Bill, growing testy and ornery. His stomach gurgled with acid. What on earth were they doing here in this dim corner of Lucinda's, which didn't appear right to him any more than the man in the moon did winking down from the noonday sky. And yet earlier, an almost full disk sitting low on the horizon, ghostly against the blue sky, like a baleful eye watching and wagering with the other planets and stars how much Gooch might forget today.

Words, unbidden, tumbling out. "Nobody's got the pulse like me. Finger on the pulse," Gooch shouted and pounded the table, making everyone's coffee cups jump. "Finger. Pulse. Me. I know the secrets—my own, and all of yours, too. But, who's gonna report and write and edit? You two? Show me a bigger sucker bet, and an old fool like me's liable to take it."

Something about their expressions—patience; pity—calmed Gooch down. Made him wonder about what precipitated his outburst, why they made him so mad.

"Well," the man with the goatee said. "Reckon that's that."

Dobbs, eyes dewy with emotion. "Yep. No question. Gooch?"

"Huh? Oh—no question."

Wait. Gooch wondered what in the hell was happening. Nobody was going anywhere yet:

"What are you two trying to pull on me? Hold up. Let's start this little meeting over." Serious as all get-out, he sat waiting for them to tell him why this nonsense about retirement had anything to do with his life. Bill Wimmel, a young man, starting out. Journalism a mere placeholder until he got around to the GAN—the Great American Novel. He planned to spend ten years as a reporter, and not a minute more. Literature, his first love, and to this discipline and practice he would return, soon as possible.

These nitwits didn't need to hear all this. These plans were secret. Bill Wimmel, now, that rascal could keep a secret. More than anyone at this table would ever know. All right. Now he'd see what these brigands and ne'er-do-wells had to say for themselves. Find out who called this meeting.

"Well?"

"Gooch—well what?" Dobbs, trying to smile.

"If you don't know, then I sure don't."

They sat examining the crumbs on their plates in silence as the server, an overweight black girl in tight jeans and a purple Manny's on the Green T-shirt, refilled their coffees. Even though they had already eaten and the check paid, Gooch asked what specials were offered today; if Lucinda had a fresh batch of Oreo pudding coming out soon, which the girl said was right over on the buffet, and that fact alone centered Bill in a reality objective enough that, for once, he halfway felt like an actual human being. Like himself.

"Best pudding you'll find on any buffet from here to Charleston."

"Everybody says so," the server agreed with a bemused frown. "Anything else?"

"We'll let you know when we're ready to order. Now: who called this mysterious meeting," Gooch announced to the men seated across from him. Their topic of conversation had dissipated like those clouds of vapor all the young people spouted like factory smokestacks. "And remind me of its agenda."

"Gooch—?"

"Bill—?"

"You sputtering ninnies. I don't have all day for this limp-wristed folderol —I've got a damn newspaper to put to bed."

TRUDY AND ROY EARL

The soft kindness in Roy Earl's eyes—it had returned. Unlike before, in trying to shut down the Dix and being mean to everyone, it was like his whole deal had gotten dialed back a notch. That was what led to this hot emotional mess, which she could not believe now unfolded.

He wouldn't ever be the ripe and innocent boy she liked and screwed. Took his V-card. But neither was her saggy wrinkled old butt the same. Not by a damn sight.

Oh, she thought with a stab of icy panic: What will he think.

When he saw her.

Naked.

Flabby crepe for skin. The boobs, drooping. The spider veins and moles.

What was she doing? She hesitated in the parking lot of the Holiday Inn over in Chilton, which became a LaQuinta a few years back. Trudy couldn't help still calling it the Holiday Inn, which when it opened in the 80s had been real clean and nice. It had gone downhill, since. Like her body, and the damn knock-engined Taurus in which she'd putt-putted her way over to have an affair.

Happened to be one that began anew where it started the first go-round, in the honkytonk, upstairs. They finished nothing that day, only made out, hot and heavy, the most dirty part when she'd grabbed hold of his hardness through this shorts. They broke it off—their clinch, not his wiener, haha—when they heard Fridge coming in the back door to start the dinner prep.

Roy Earl's face blazed as pink as one of those Mary Kay Cadillacs. "Whoa."

"Mercy."

"To be continued?"

"Uh-huh." One more juicy slurping kiss, a smooch like she hadn't enjoyed in ages.

Roy seemed dazed. "Thirty years—it's a long time to miss someone."

Thrilling. If Fridge hadn't come in...

Buzzing with desire, she'd gone downstairs first from the musty storage area, full of junk and furniture and store fixtures from Burnie Sykes's old businesses, adjusted her knickers and pulled herself together. Felt all tingling and alive. Gave Roy Earl a moment to calm down.

He reappeared only after Fridge went out to smoke on the back porch, and without him knowing the big boss man stood upstairs with a hard-on. A tiny wet spot dotted the front of Roy's cargo shorts, a stain she thought better of pointing out—no one noticed but her.

Bless his sweet loving heart. He had gotten excited, only from kissing her. Like a teenager. She'd even blurted it out: "Oh, *honey*—you're hard for me."

Roy, looking so embarrassed. No need. What a complement to her bony, redneck ass.

⊛⊕❊

TRUDY HAD NOT BEEN AT THE CHILTON FREEWAY EXIT MOTEL IN YEARS, WHATEVER they wanted to call it. In the past she partied and fucked in its rooms, though. Stayed there with pickups from the bar. Before Samson, when she lived at home with her mama, rest her soul, and a couple of times with him after they hooked up, when he wanted to be alone with her away from his brothers and the biker buddies he rode with in those days, all of them living back in the woods in the big wreck of a farm house, sagging porches and leaking roof. Didn't matter. They had themselves a three-bay cinderblock garage out back in which to work on cars and motorbikes, and a fishing pond; and that decrepit farmhouse across from where they now lived, in what Samson's people used to call the little house. Her home for twenty years.

They made tons of improvements, back when he was healthy. It wasn't bad. Nice bathroom and kitchen, tile and granite, but from the outside still a shack, a tin roof so loud when it rained that you couldn't sleep at night. Also, every morning first thing Trudy had to endure the sight of that stupid, sagging house all gone to rot, overgrown and creepy and sad back yonder in the trees and weeds. Samson still waddled over to putter in that garage every day.

Or he did, until last year when his back went out and never quite returned. Then, his bad foot started swelling and hurting.

Shit. What a life.

While that sweet-eyed Roy Earl, off becoming rich and happy.

That son of a biscuit eater.

But, now he wanted her. Mercy, but he did. In the worst way, as he kept putting it. Driving him to distraction. Closure, continuance, he didn't know what, using smart words like a college boy would. After making out one more time in the office they decided to go through with it, but keep it super secret. Since he had Manny Theodore living out there with in the old Pettus house—where the eff was that all about?—it meant a motel.

Heck, she'd felt Roy's ardor, unmistakable, that first night she picked him up from the airfield, from having flown—flown!—in his own plane to see about poor Mr. Rabbit. She knew the whole story now about that little Rucker wench screwing around on him and breaking his poor little pea-picking heart. That c-word. Trudy liked to shit when she hugged him and could feel his sudden excitement. Weird. That's what she thought that it was—weird, and kinda perverted. Too much going on to consider the implications, though.

Then, he took his turn and had what her grandmother would've called a devil-fit, which was definitely not sexy.

Trudy's daddy had them mean spells, too. He had been in Korea, near froze to death over there fighting the Chinese. Scary. If you'd have told her decades ago that Roy Earl Pettus, with his innocent, brown eyes loving and worshipping her, was capable of what he had wrought that day at The Dixiana—raging at everyone—Trudy would've said, no-way, José. And yet it had happened. Monstrous.

A monster she was fixing to spread her legs for.

A shiver, up and down.

Her phone, buzzing in the drink holder full of grungy pennies and a cigarette cellophane wrapper pull and a shred of a straw paper. Trudy turned down the Lucinda Williams she'd been blasting. A live album, the girl all growling and half-drunk; the singer at her best. You took my joy and I want it back, she sang. Hell yeah.

His text read WHERE R U?

She finger-fumbled. ALMOST THERE.

A fast response: R U TXTING AND DRIVING??

NO IM IN THE MOTEL LOT.

A faster reply. WELL GET IN HERE ;)

Dying for a cig, instead a deep breath, some spritzer, a stick of gum. And going inside. Smelling and tasting like an ashtray—now that would have been downright dumb. But damn if she hadn't almost lit up the second she got into the car. A habit.

◐◑❋

THE AWKWARDNESS, REMARKABLE. SHE DIDN'T KNOW WHAT TO SAY. HE HADN'T come to talk. Shaking, he reached for her hands. "Please, let me hold you. Kiss you again."

"Well, sugar—are you gonna cry?"

"I thought about this. A lot. Over the years."

"About me."

"About being here. Again."

"Looks like we arrived."

"Does that mean you thought about it, too?"

"Angel—how could I not."

No more talking. Fumbling around on the bed, undressing. A major production number. Her skinny jeans, trying to peel them off. The hardest durn bra to unhook out of the whole drawer. A bunch of foolishness.

He expressed astonishment and disbelief. "Your smell. It's the same. After all this time." Roy Earl, his entire body pulsing and hot with warmth. One part more than the others. "I'm having a moment."

She said to herself, he's gonna go off like a rocket.

Speaking of that. "Do you mind? Wearing a—?"

"Oh. Really."

She tried to explain. Stammering, making it not sound too unsexy. A barrier, making it all less wrong, since they were both. You know. With others. Technically. Still. Trying not to use the word 'wrong.'

He smiled, but it seemed forced. "Sure."

Fishing around for her pocket book, and the foil wrappers. She'd snagged a couple from the medicine cabinet from back before her menopause, but not too long out of date. To save money, she had quit the pill and made him wear rubbers again. Samson acted like he didn't half care about screwing anymore, anyway. Back then she worried he was getting it at Mama Beaudock's, or elsewhere; now she knew it was because he couldn't get hard no more.

She kissed Roy Earl, deep and long. Reached down and stroked. Pulsing, leaky already. His eyes and wiener, both streaming.

Trudy handed him the condom.

He shook his head. "Put it on me."

Flustered. She fumbled trying to rip open the packet, dropped it. Bounced and rolled in a perfect little arc right off the bed, a little wheel rolling out of reach. Couldn't have done that if you tried.

She leaned way over and looked—vanished. "I swear to goodness."

He asked what was going on. She said, it's not there.

Trudy got down on her knees, peeked under the bed. The condom packet had bounced out of sight. She stretched and reached into the shadows. The thin, old carpet against her cheek stunk of sour salt from uncountable bare feet, made her want to barf.

How glad she smelled good to him. He did to her, too. She would say it was like he had when they'd been together before, but she didn't remember many details.

Back on the bed, he seemed frustrated. She finally got the rubber out of the foil packet. Gooey with lube. That was good. Trudy, with all the anxiety, hadn't been gushing with excitement.

Rolled it down. His erection, flagging from all the rigmarole. She played. It flagged more.

"Sugar—"

He cussed. Said, hold on, sat up. Ran his hand over his head. "I have wanted this moment more than I know how to say."

"You already said it. In so many ways. Will you come over here?" She tossed aside the rubber, a slimy little lizard skin. Wiped her fingers on the motel bedspread. Cold in there—her nipples, huge. She played with her own boob for him. Showed him. Got his attention.

He reclined before her. She went down. Slow. It'd been so long, but she remembered what a man liked. She did this for him back then, she figured. Didn't remember.

Took it all in. Tickled. Licked. Squeezed.

Roy Earl, groaning and sucking in his breath like he'd been stuck with a knife. "Oh. My god."

Now that thing was hard again. A railroad spike.

"Honey. Forget about that rubber. It ain't like we're strangers. To all this."

He started to sit up and protest, but she pushed him back. Slithered up his body. Put her boobs into his face, which he slurped and handled with such tenderness and awe. Now she was ready. Slick. Slid down on his hardness.

Stunning. A crackle of electricity—of magic. "Oh, honey."

If her mouth on him had been his moment of catharsis, her body melded with his struck him like a revelation. His moans and trancelike state seemed to find in her everything he must have always wanted. How flattered she felt. How excited.

He bucked underneath her.

"Slow," she begged. "It's been so long."

She sat back, balancing her hands on his chest and riding. How lovely.

"Wait," he urged. "Otherwise, it'll be over."

He meant to let him be in charge. They disentangled, rolled over, fumbled around, her hair in his mouth, bonking elbows. Not like in the movies—no mood lighting and violins playing, only the sound of the fan on the wall-unit AC kicking on and off. The stink of the feet in the carpet, and old cigarettes, and disinfectant, and Roy Earl. A man now, not a boy. Their sex.

Slipping in there.

Oh!

Going to town.

Oh! Oh!

Roy Earl's lips curled back from his teeth, his brow furrowed, a squiggly vein pulsing in his temple. Trudy held on. He jackhammered. A primal trance swept over him, and she wrapped her long legs all the way around. Pulled him close, as far inside as she could. Took him fully.

As his rhythm increased, he started hitting her special spot, and muscles, contracting and convulsing. Her back, arching. Crying out, OH.

At this peak development he also came, right along with her. Wow.

Afterwards? Roy Earl, a happy boy. Trudy, too. Not a boy, though.

Until he wasn't happy. "My head—it's killing me."

"Oh, sugar." She'd been immersed in the afterglow. Feeling confused, but in appreciation of his attention. Stroking his wet, half-hard dick.

He moaned—but not with pleasure.

"What's wrong?"

"This only complicates things. Doesn't it."

"You don't have to say that aloud."

"No?"

"I was already thinking it."

He looked at her. "You were?"

She nodded. "Let's not have that conversation. Not yet."

"Yeah. I mean—no."

"Like nothing I've had in ages."

"C'mon."

"But, it's true."

He rubbed his temples. Seemed tense and uncertain, eyes darting all around.

"Lay back, now."

He did so. She snuggled up to him. Put her head on his shoulder. So gentle next to his ear. "Believe it or not, it's not as complicated as it was way back when."

"And why not?"

She could barely get the words out. But it needed saying. She couldn't do this to Samson. All she thought about was his sweet sad face, like a big old puppy dog who knows he's growing old.

And her? At the motel getting it on with Roy Earl Pettus. Illicit then, illicit now.

But hadn't the fantasy been leaving Samson, and going with Roy? Now that he would divorce his wife? Or—would he?

"You know," he said. "I don't—I'm not."

"What, angel?"

"Not divorcing her. My wife."

That's weird; Roy, reading her mind. "I need to ask you something. Do you regret this, then?"

He sat up, gave a hard look. "No—in a way, it's been the dream of my life. More than the fruitshakes, more than the plane, more than the money."

"To be with me again?"

"An itch I could never scratch."

"I guess dreams come true."

His erection had returned. "But dreams, they're so fleeting. I want to make sure it was real."

So sweet. "Come to me, angel."

Now they took their time. And when it was over, they cuddled and dozed with their legs all tangled up.

How they would've slept together all these years.

Whatever happened besides sex, and it felt in the room like something major had occurred, Trudy thought her fantasies about leaving her husband had been foolishness and nonsense. This had been fun. It filled a sense of lack that'd been troubling for him. And for her, too.

But had to be over, or so he acted like. She tried to convince herself that it must be that way. The fantasies crept back. She wished and hoped for an outcome that made all the long-held dreams come to pass, but couldn't put her finger on how it would happen. Couldn't imagine her life changing.

Loving a man who wanted to stay married to his wife wasn't gonna lead her skinny cracker ass nowhere, cuz. That much was for sure.

◎◉✻

THEY GOT CLEANED UP AND WENT TO THE WAFFLE HOUSE, WHERE TRUDY SAID HEY to everyone and introduced Roy Earl around as the grandson of the owner of The Dixiana, but he surprised her by saying, no, more than a mere heir.

"The proud owner," he said. "With ideas about the future."

Now it was her turn to feel a weight lifted off her heart. The disposition of her beloved Dixiana, assured. What a good day. What a good day this had become.

As for what was next, she would go by the store on the way home and get beer, cigs and a few different Hamburger Helpers. Some turkey ground round, much better, less fat. Let Samson pick out his favorite flavor Helper for dinner tomorrow, when the dream would be over and she would again awaken in her old life. Seemed the safest way to think about what had happened. Safer, more realistic.

CHRISTY, NEWBIE, HOWDY, AND HOWDY'S SISTER

Since the robbery attempt, Newbie had picked up bad habits from Howdy—the huffing. Breathing in the gas. Getting gas-faced.

Christy, half ready to boot Newbie's ass out of the trailer. Wasn't bringing in no money now, anyway. Christy, able and willing to whine to his grandmother to get some, but not enough to live on. Not and live well. What-ever that's supposed to mean.

ANOTHER VISIT TO HOWDY'S SECRET PLACE, THE CREEPY BASEMENT AND MUSTARDY light and dust and trash. The circle in the floor, the hooked crosses painted on the warped and weathered old plywood pallet. Christy going along because he felt stale sitting in the trailer running his flight simulator, and Newbie had the truck and that's where he was headed, and no amount of ordering voice or threatening would change his roommate's pea-brain from its ratlike insistence on finding some cheese. Christy, not allowing Newbie to huff gas in the trailer. Too dangerous.

Howdy, marching in a circle and mumbling about Sirius B and the Dogon people of Africa and creation mythology, which best Christy knew had to do with the satellite radio service. Christy, he'd done the seven-day trial, listened to all kinds of music. But what could music and the radio have to do with anything?!

And then this blather:

"Ninety-one solar systems turn around the great central sun. The mass of this sun is 91 thousand times larger than the mass combined with all the 91 other solar systems. Moreover, the galaxy of the 91 universes of which the earth belongs is included in another larger galaxy of 91 galaxies, those all turning around a central core, of which the mass is 91 times higher. This formula is reproduced indefinitely. Gravity is the glue binding form, based on frequency compilation." Howdy, chortling and shaking his head *no, no, no.* "This is represented by fractionalized *copies* of replicated geometry."

"I ain't took no geometry, Howdy." Newbie, messed up but-good. Coming off his own gas fumes, he slumped cross-legged on the floor. Wiped his mouth and eyes, fell silent.

When at last he again spoke, he said to Christy about how they ought to think about considering the possibility of trying to rob The Dixiana again. "Ya know, after a good Saturday night. Remember all that cheddar?"

Christy, he's all like, WHAT?!! "You ain't got no key no more."

"There's win-ders in the back you can get open. Well, *you* couldn't fit through. But I can."

"I wish you'd hush up. That gas's making you stupid." Christy, he wanted to say stupider. It was true.

"It's giving me some big idears, beau. Is what it's doing."

Christy, rolling his eyes. Seriously?! More like drooling foolishness. When he was huffing Newbie's left eye would droop even more than it already did, making him look like a zombie on *The Walking Dead*. Which Newbie sat on his ass watching too much, if you asked Christy.

He knew best about most things. Still didn't quite figure on how to get it across to Newbie and everybody else, though, short of pulling a Daddy and being rid of issues as they came up. Now here was conflict resolution, to put it in the Dr. Phil way.

Christy, tired of all the zombie stuff. You couldn't get away from it! Even if you didn't watch no TV shows, and Christy didn't much—it seemed like an old or sick person's hobby—you still heard about it all the time through social media, the newsfeed. Surfing online made him tired, too. Like after watching too much TV. Or too many hours gaming. Screens screens screens. Christy, he needed new glasses. And a phone.

Christy couldn't have had his little burial at sea for his Daddy without Newbie's help, though. So who would help him if he ended up pulling a Daddy on Newbie? Or others?

Mr. Pettus? What about him?

Shut up. God, no.

Every time he came with Howdy and Newbie out here to the old mill building, Christy felt ill at ease. Like a dark, squirming coil inside him when they were in there huffing the gas and listening to Howdy's cray-cray mess. Why Christy still went along, he didn't know.

It wasn't to do the gas—Christy drank on some liquor while they did that, not enough that he drifted off to sleep. Enough to relax. Maybe he ought to be glad to have someone to hang with. So hard to chill. Christy, worrying he was going all emo.

Worth tagging along, however, because Howdy said much that was fascinating, still. Christy made notes to look up stuff later, including 'Chapel Perilous,' which Christy suspected somebody besides Howdy had painted in that creepy, dusty basement corner. He didn't know why.

The shafts of snot-yellow light streaming in. The dust and trash and fibers floated in the air, as though the mill still in an eerie half-real phase of operation.

The crooked crosses.

The light.

The stink—a place of death.

A tomb.

Where wicked spirits dwelled.

Christy, fretting about demons worming their way into his brain. Feeling impulsive. Wanting to haul off and smack people—like, even when he wasn't mad at them. No reason necessary. Hitting them just to do it.

Now, internets searches on such matters had opened Christy's mind to more questions than answers. It sounded like this one book, *Cosmic Trigger*, had some answers about 'Chapel Perilous', so Christy had searched and found a PDF he'd downloaded and planned to read. Long, hundreds of pages. It would take awhile. Daunting.

Christy, he had not read books like this. Christy was smart, yeah sure, but books with big paragraphs, those he wrangled with—once he had got to the end, it was hard to remember what the start of a long paragraph had to say. He guessed that these books and others like them, these were ways of communicating in the time before stuff like tweets and status updates. Before the computers.

His computer was getting slow, though.

When it broke for reals, how would he afford to fix it?

What if he couldn't fix it?

He'd be reading books then, boy. Just to have something to do!

Damn Newbie, looking at porn. Pop-ups. Malware. Christy, he didn't like the way those pictures and videos made him feel. The people doing the sex. The sounds—UH UH UH—like pigs grunting in slop.

He would do the sex with Button, if he only could. Out of love, though. Not like grunting nasty pigs. Would not put his mess on her face. He'd do that part by himself like always, in his hand and rinsed off clean. The right way.

Maybe not. Sex was all filth and nasty and strange. Like with his grandmama's girls—they make sex for money. Like selling stuff at the store. It didn't seem right.

But whoa, whoa, whoa: if his grandmother was doing it, it had to be okay.

And yet that seemed wrong, too. Like his inner voice saying, something ain't right in all this, and you ought to make it more right. Christy, he wanted to either stop what she and the girls were doing, or join in. Didn't know which way to turn. But Newbie's porn surfing, it remained a challenge to Christy's out-of-date virus protection software.

Took a nip on his whiskey. Calmed himself. "If we was gonna rob someone? I bet I know somebody better."

Newbie, his eyes crossed. Whispering. "Who?"

Christy, raising a finger to his lips. "Later."

Pitied Newbie but not so much Howdy, who, despite his huffing habit, still sounded way smarter than both of them put together. His brogue, so deep and distinguished despite the gas. Christy had found out Howdy's family went way back. No wonder his voice was deep. No wonder the Shull house on Whaley Way was so big and old. A mansion.

Nobody lived in one who didn't have money. Christy, wondering if Howdy might be good for more than all his high-learned talk.

◉ⓘ❋

But scrambling back to the truck through the reeds and weeds all grown up around the fencing, Howdy stayed silent. For a change. After this latest visit to the mill, he seemed weak and sick.

"Tell us about your sister." Newbie, goading Howdy, who staggered along with his Canada Dry bottle. "And that big old house y'all live in."

Right after Newbie's question, Howdy stopped to cough and retch and vomit.

"Howdy? You okay?"

"Sister? Sisters? Sisters? The seven? The seven sisters?"

"You got seven sisters!" Christy, marveling. "Thought it was only one."

Howdy retched again. Went down on his knees, soda bottle rolling away. Going *OOOOH*, clutching his stomach. "The seven sisters. The Pleiadians. The message from the Pleiadians. Earth. The earth, a living library."

"A library? I don't see no books." Newbie, kicking the dusty ground and going nyuck-nyuck like Christy couldn't stand. "Howdy ain't got no sense."

"A living library." Garbled, through more puke. Breathless. "Of all. That's possible. A living library. Of all that's possible. In this. In this. In this—" And then OOOOH again. "Physicality. Third dimension. A living library. For the whole. Of the cosmos."

Christy watched as thin, pinkish sputum streamed out of Howdy's mouth. Whining; worried. "That gas ain't no good for y'all."

Howdy, sweating, seemed to collect himself. Stood up. He sounded like he'd been gargling with pebbles. "It has been said that the sun which illuminates us is the seventh sun that circles Alcyone."

Newbie: "I always heard a seventh son was like Jesus."

Howdy's eyes locked in on Christy's. It was all eerie when he spoke, so together now, if a little wheezy. "Alcyone is, precisely, the principal sun of the Pleiades. In its orbit gravitate seven suns, ours being the seventh which circles Alcyone." Howdy described how an enormous photon belt encircled Alcyone, and that soon the earth and that seventh sun would be passing through. That the time of the great upheavals were upon us all; again. A cycle. He concluded, "Weor, quoting Hesse at the *Conferencia Sobre Alcione* in 1977."

He ran out of breath, gagged again and staggered against Christy, who shoved him over into Newbie, barely keeping his balance. The skin of Howdy's arms felt so cold and clammy and damp. Yuck.

But yo, here was gobbledygook if Christy ever heard it! Old man's nuts.

Was everyone?

Everyone but Christy?

Newbie, snapping his fingers. "We're the seventh sun. I get it. Dang, beau."

"*Newbie.*" Christy, the ordering-voice. "Howdy's sick. Ain't making no sense."

"He might be."

"No, he ain't."

"You don't know."

"Well—neither do you."

Newbie kinda shrugged like, yeah, true-that. "Ain't letting him in the truck. Not puking like he is."

Christy, noting that Newbie himself had vomited in there before, and so had he, that night they rode around after the bossman had caught them and let them go without getting the police involved. To relax, they tried getting drunk on MD 20/20 wine, which was the only booze they could get on Sunday, short of Newbie's dumb-ass idea of breaking back into The Dixiana. It come from the gas station on the other side of the bridge in Easton, where the black folks didn't care about selling alcohol to two white boys on Sunday night that late. That cheap wine burned and hurt Christy's stomach much worse than good liquor.

"Howdy probably drunk some of his gas by accident."

Newbie stuck out his tongue, coated and scaly like a lizard's. "That'd make anybody sick."

Howdy, rolling onto his side, trying to sit up. Christy, helping him. "I don't know why y'all keep on with this."

"You would if you tried it."

"Your eyes look stupid afterwards." Stupider, Christy thought.

"It's like being on another planet, beau. I keep seeing these little electric monkeys darting in and out, running up and looking at me and chattering. Damn-dest thing."

Christy whined that this place was fine. "I got whiskey. That's all a man needs."

"Bullcrud. That's outta some movie. The way people are always pouring hot liquor into a glass and knocking it back, all times of the day. That ain't the way real people live. Dang. That ain't real. None of that TV mess. This shit? This's getting high. This's getting real, boy."

Howdy moaned again. He fell forward and kneeled with his forehead on the ground, rocking back and forth. "Living library. Living sisters. The seven. Many a night I saw the Pleiads, rising through the mellow shade, glitter like a swarm of fireflies tangled in a silver braid."

"He's still in la-la land. I reckon he always is, though."

Newbie, spitting. "Gimme a sip outta that bottle."

"We can't leave him out here."

"Hell we can't."

If he didn't abide the order, Christy, he would break Newbie's head open like the cantaloupe fruit it resembled.

No—he needed Newbie. Handed him the pint of Evan Williams. "We could take him to his seven sisters. See what's inside his house."

"All right. Keep your panties on." Newbie pouted. "This is so gay."

"Shut up. That's hurtful, using gay like that. It ain't no cuss word."

They schlepped and jostled Howdy to the Toyota Tundra, parked down the road so it looked like another car from the mill village neighborhood rather than dudes messing around inside the fenced and abandoned mill.

Leaning against the dirty hood of Newbie's truck, Howdy's head lolled. He seemed pitiful.

Newbie, eyes sunken and redder than beets. "Better not puke."

"I ought to drive."

"Told you before. You ain't driving my truck. Besides, I ain't drunk."

Christy whined all high and mean, "Your eyes still look messed up, son."

Newbie cussed that they were fine. "Keep your drawers dry, pissy."

No need to bring up his pee-pants after the robbery had gone bad.

Newbie ran them out of the decrepit mill village, down the bypass and into town. He went all the way behind the courthouse complex by the Congress Street Grille to avoid seeing the neon honkytonk sign. He said he kept wishing The Dixiana would explode and burn down while the bossman sat inside counting his money.

Howdy, groggy and mumbling.

Newbie, picking his nose. Eating it. "What we gonna do with him?"

"I said, we're taking him to his house. Dummy." How was Christy gonna manage with this doofus! Lord help him.

◉◐❀

Newbie pulled up and stopped in front of the spooky Shull dump, on Brunswick Street. Big houses here, old ones. They had dropped Howdy off twice, but had never gone inside.

"Dang, Christopher. This here's a good idea-r."

"How?"

"Don't you remember? Money's here. Let's get him inside."

"Looks like a haunted house." Christy's nuts drew up inside him. His skin crawled. He already thought Howdy was Satanic. Was pretty sure, with his Chapel Perilous and walking in his sacred circle with those damn symbols, the hooked crosses. Occult. But Christy had looked up that word—he had heard it before, didn't understand—and found that 'occult' didn't mean 'bad.' Not necessarily. Just 'hidden.'

Newbie and Christy, crammed into the middle on the bench seat between them, both looked at Howdy, his head against the window. Cold outside. A plume of condensation by his mouth. This had been the longest they'd ever seen him stay quiet.

"I think he's dead," Newbie finally said.

"No, dummy. He's breathing."

"Quit calling me dummy, dummy. Not in my truck."

Christy, ordering. Harsh. "Let's get him out. Before he pukes. Now."

They slid out. Newbie slammed the door. "Stop telling me what to do. I'm older."

Cruising for a bruising. The little turd. Christy, silent, seething. "—"

They had a hard time getting Howdy up the front walk, made of red brick pavers that had gone all cattywampus from being pushed from below by the roots from the huge oak trees towering overhead, a canopy. Dimmed the light. Felt late in the day.

Up onto the wide, columned porch, a struggle with their man-sized rag doll. A yellow bug light came on despite it not being dark out yet. Its globe, full of moths and clouded by cobwebs and dust tendrils. Everything outside, all the rocking chairs and little tables on the porch with some of its planks swollen and rotten-looking, all of it covered in black yard grime. Nobody ever sat out here. Why not?! It was marvelous compared to the packed dirt and rock-hitting homeboys at Mayfield Acres.

If Howdy weren't so Satanic, Christy could get rid of Newbie and live here. Hell—room for him, too. All of them, plus Button Sykes too, if she wanted.

Newbie and Howdy could huff gas together on one side of this big house, while Christy lived on the other, playing his game-box or surfing 'teh inter-nets,' and Christy?

Yep: Training to fly the bossman's plane. Oh yeah. Newbie, still thinking about getting out of Edgewater County by robbing money? Small-time. Christy would do him one better:

They would steal Pettus's airplane. Christy, he couldn't yet work through how, exactly. Details.

◎◐✹

THE DOUBLE FRONT DOOR, ORNATE WITH STAINED GLASS AND A HUGE, TARNISHED brass knocker, cracked open to reveal Howdy's sister, frail and shaky, poking out her beak. Peering over granny glasses on a croaker around her wrinkled neck wattle, she seemed older than Howdy.

"Heavens to betsy. What's my brother done to himself this time?"

Inside, with Howdy supported between Christy and Newbie, she intro-duced herself as Dr. Everlynne Shull-Schlosser, PhD, widow of Dr. Archibald Schlosser, PhD, and Christy thought that seemed like a whole mess of doctors in da house. Her hair, long, gray, frizzy and wild. She dressed like a hippie, in a patchwork sweater and long velvety skirt with stars all over it. Music, echoing around. Syrupy strings. Classical.

BORING.

Christy said to himself, Dang! Howdy's sister's as weird as he is.

And books? Sakes alive. Books on shelves. Books on tables. Books on the floor. Pathways through all the books and magazines, too. Towers of books everywhere, like buildings in a city. Christy, thinking that to walk through them would be like Godzilla in Tokyo, these old Chinese movies they had watched on streaming video. A man in a rubber suit knocking over buildings made of cardboard. Stupid.

"It sounds like a doctor's office in here," Newbie said as they dragged Howdy, slack-jawed, into the foyer. "Or a funeral parlor. I can't stand music like that."

"I'll have you know that's Brahms, the 4th Symphony—a sublime composi-tion." Their host, peering close into Howdy's slack face, slapped him. "Its glories are not meant as Muzak in some quack's waiting room. Now if you would, please lay Howard down in the front bedroom."

Newbie, on point: "Lay him where?"

"On the bed, the downstairs guest bed."

"Right on, right on."

Through the books they dragged the loose-limbed Howdy, after which she bade them to join her in the formal living room. It didn't seem haunted, only totes ancient, more like a museum than a place folks hung out and chilled. Smelled funky. Like rotting newspapers. Mildew. Camphor. Sour. The stink made his stomach queasy.

Christy, he decided that she wasn't crazy like Howdy, because on one wall hung framed degrees with her name, a couple with Everlynne Shull and others with Shull-Schlosser, which Christy was glad he didn't have to say, because it was too many S's—when he tried saying things with too many S's, he slobbered. Was probably why they stuck him in the Special Ed classes. Christy, sounding stupider than he was.

He had decided he wanted no part of degrees and school anyway, because if he tried to go to college, when he couldn't fully explain himself right away they'd just put him in Special Ed. Why go through it all again—right?! Especially with houses like this and the library filled with books for free. And in the digital world. You could look at websites enough to never crack a book again, and most were out there anyway, like the pdf of *Cosmic Trigger* he'd downloaded. Still had to plow through all those words, though. That's the hard part.

Christy made a pact with himself that from now on, he'd read a book a month. He wasn't sure Newbie read too good, but he didn't hold it against him. His friend had come from trash no different from Christy. It was a miracle anybody in Edgewater County could read, the way them schools treated children like Christopher Beaudock.

◉◉❋

"So Howdy has made new friends, I see." The living room, cluttered not with books but bric-à-brac, doodads, vases, statues. High-backed chairs and a couch with matching floral print upholstery covered in fine white dust. She gestured for them to sit. "Guests," dry and sarcastic. "It's my lucky day."

A coffee table sat between them, huge and oval, filled with more knickknacks, statues of horses and soldiers and other animals. The Brahms in here much louder. Big drums beating, flutes playing, the strings dancing along.

Christy, unsettled. "That music's too loud."

"My apologies. My hearing, it's gotten frightful. Here—" She turned down the record player inside its large wooden cabinet. "Better."

Her voice came shaky but not nervous, more like it shook that way all the time. Once Christy brought his eyes up to hers, he could see her whole face trembling. But she didn't seem scared. It trembled to tremble, the way Christy's legs did when he diddled around while thinking of Button.

"Now, boys: Howard smells of gasoline again. That this concerns me is an apotheosis of understatement. You aren't also experimenting with inhalants, I hope. I know it's a real head trip, but the effects, they're simply too deleterious to the body and mind."

"Naw, ma'am." Newbie, his voice rising and sounding like lies. Christy had learned when his roommate was spinning stories. "We found him that way. He didn't even have his bottle with him today."

"Ah," she said, frowning. "I see. Is that what he puts in those bottles? I knew it. And that nosey Ruth DeKalb told me at the supermarket she had seen how he was drinking too much soda pop. I agreed it's not anything but carbonated antifreeze, but there's little I can do about what how much pop he drinks. Little did she know.

"But honestly—whether it's gasoline or soda pop, I'm only an old retired teacher, widowed and frail and lonely. What am I supposed to do to manage a grown man's habits? In truth, I'm thankful for the time he's out of the house. But still, I don't want him to die in a ditch somewhere like an animal."

Newbie, irritated: "We wouldn't leave him in no ditch."

The woman gaped at them through her coke-bottle glasses, eyes big as saucers. "Gentlemen?"

They sat waiting.

"I want you both to come clean. Tell me everything you've been doing with my brother."

Christy's voice, so high and thin that it froze in his throat like fog on a snowy mountaintop. Something about being in trouble with Howdy's smart sister filled him with abject terror, a distorted ringing in his ears.

He couldn't speak.

Newbie, he kept saying, naw, naw, no ma'am. "We ain't huffing gas out of that bottle with Howdy."

She seemed put out. "Now, you listen to me. My husband, he was an imminent sociologist, teacher and published author, many times over. I also taught for many years at the university level. Was on track to be an administrator, before certain problems arose. In any case, I've been halfway around the block, misters. I understand boys. Like Howard; like you. And despite never having had my own children, I know when I'm being fibbed to."

Christy didn't care for the direction this was going.

Nor did Newbie: "We ain't lying, lady. Howdy, we found him in the street. We helped his ass up."

"Don't call him that. His name is Howard. Caughman Howard Shull. You boys realize he despises being called that, don't you?" She leaned forward. "Besides, I'm the only one who gets to call him Howdy. His big sister. You imbeciles understand me?"

"Yes, ma'am."

Christy could see that Newbie had an idear, goggling his eyes all around—at all the books, the paintings, busts on pedestals. "Reckon y'all must got a lotta money."

"'Y'all?' Whom do you mean? The remnants of the Shull family?"

Newbie, sounding mean: "I mean y'all, lady."

Chortling, slapping her bony old knee. "I'm afraid to disappoint, but not unless you think social security and disability checks and an EBT card constitute a lot of money. No—my husband, he died leaving me with considerable obligations. Had had proclivities and liens that left me bereft financially as well as emotionally. Then my mother also passed away, and with my brother needing care, those pitiable handouts are the only things between me and the homeless shelter." Shaking, now, in a more direct way, a literal fist. Her face, a mask of scorn and bitter resentment. "If you must know the truth, if it were possible to sell this house I probably would. My grandfather, rest his soul, spinning in a grave over in Forest Knoll Garden right now. But not with the real estate market in such execrable condition. I suppose I'd better simply have gratitude it's still standing around my own decrepit, failing ears. Thank heavens the property taxes aren't any worse."

Newbie, scratching himself under an armpit, sat dumbfounded by her speech. Christy, remembering that mess with his Daddy needing money for taxes. Maybe it had been true, and he killed his own father for nothing. His stomach flashed ice cold.

"What's wrong with him?" He finally found the words. "With Howard."

Newbie bleated his *nyuck-nyuck* laugh. "We heard he done that acid hippies used to. Folks must be crazy to do that mess."

The old lady, tart as a lemon. "You people, you're just full of assumptions and innuendo. Aren't you. Howard's problem today, as it's always been, is one of discipline. A discipline of character, of conduct, and of ambition."

"He's a smart old dude. Talks and talks about stuff. Don't he, Christy."

Christy went uh-huh.

Howdy's sister chortled. "Smart? Perhaps in the distant past. Now, all my dear, sweet brother can do is memorize. He can't think, boys. It's all rote. He reads these books, memorizes, recites. He doesn't know what he's saying."

Christy, thinking, I dunno about that. Howdy knows a lot. He wished to argue with her about her brother, but knew neither how nor about what, exactly.

"But I'll not sit here," her voice even more tremulous and rising, "and listen to you impugn the entire idea of acid experiences in toto by dint of my brother's undisciplined abuse of mind-expanding sacraments. They are not street drugs to be trifled with like lab monkeys without a control group, which I told him then and still believe now."

"Did you really trip with monkeys?" Newbie asked. "I seen them things, too."

She laughed at him all snide and mean. "My god, you're nothing but children, ignorant boys—like Howard once was, before he got into such difficulty. But don't blame the drugs. Heavens, no. My LSD experiences, two of which I was honored and privileged to have traversed at Millbrook accompanied by no less a stellar and intellectual light than Dr. Leary himself, were the most spiritually edifying times of my life."

Newbie wrinkled his nose and scratched under his ball cap. "They was?"

"Glorious explorations, interactions with intelligences operating multi-dimensionally, multi-terrestrials in a sense, who spoke and assured me that life was, like the children's song says, but a dream. That my dear Howard found only fear and confusion in his use of those same sacraments is a testament to the low vibration he'd otherwise embraced in his intellectual predilections and associations on campus. His set and setting were improper. It's quite simple, where he went wrong. But far too late now."

Newbie yawned. "You really are Howdy's sister, with all that mess coming out of your mouth."

"Oh, you low-minded bumpkins, your organs pickled by cheap ethanol. You filthy, judgmental little nabobs. I'm trying to imagine the moral turpitude inherent in a person who would bring my brother home in this condition and then instigate a course of insulting insinuation, here in my own downstairs sitting room. I think I'd prefer that the two of you left, now. If you don't mind."

"But we was hoping you'd fix us supper." Christy had been hungry for ages, his head hurting from her blizzard of words. "We ain't eat all day."

"Yeah, lady. Howdy ain't eat nothing neither. Course, I ain't never seen him take the first bite."

"He's adequately fed. You both smell like alcohol. I want you to get out."

"There ain't no call for that. Christy's got a big stomach. He gets hungry."

"Well, apologies, semicolon, but I'm nobody's chef, not even my brother's. I feed him, but I certainly don't 'cook'. If your muddled, mottled, minuscule little minds can possibly grasp the distinction."

Christy's blood moved sluggish in his veins. Her words ran together, some of them sounding like a foreign language. They tickled his ears but made no sense. Words could be witchcraft. His skin had been crawling ever since they got in there—she was as crazy as Howdy.

But maybe more at work, here. He considered sneaking around to search for more symbols like in Chapel Perilous, for another altar with the hooked cross-question marks. Howdy—Howard—and his sister were both up to no good. That's what Christy decided. Howdy less so than her. But still. Guilt by association. Christy had heard that saying before. Now he got it.

"Why don't none of you women cook no more." Newbie's eyes had darkened. He sounded mean, mean as a short little no-neck redneck runt like him could sound. "I used to hear that out of my aunt who was raising me. With her fat butt laying on that couch not doing nothing, her nose turned up like her poots didn't stink. Christy's grandmother said the same shit to us one time. 'I ain't got to feed y'all,' sounding all high and mighty. 'I got my girls and gentlemen callers to manage'," mocking the woman's voice. "She thinks all she got to do is fuck and smoke cigarettes."

Christy snickered. Newbie, he wasn't always a dumbass. He had her pegged, that painted-up crone. Sick of his grandmother's mess. Her stinginess. That old goat. "That's the god's truth there, Newbie. Hurts to say it."

"I hate it for ya, beau." They high-fived. "Tight-fisted old bitches."

"I'm-a tell ya what."

"And who is this grandmother, young man? She certainly didn't teach you any manners or decorum."

"Mama Beaudock is his grandmama."

"Shut up," Christy barked. He made a bleat like a goat—BAA BAA BAA— that made both Newbie and Howdy's sister look at him all weird.

"Really, now. Fascinating news. Edgewater County's own veritable Whore of Babylon. That's quite a shameful background. You should aspire to better than that. Oh, my—Mama Beaudock? I swear to you both, I left this place, went many many other places—San Francisco, taught at the University of Chicago and at Purdue. Was gone almost forty years, and I come back to a place where there are still whorehouses and juke-joints right on the town green by which all may stand equally and duly offended and chagrined. Shame of the city, on display all right and proper and good. This piteous place always was about as invidiously venal as can be imagined. To hear that nothing's changed, why, you could knock me over."

This made Christy mad. This lady called his grandmother a whore. Even if that's what she was, it's nobody's business. "You shut your mouth, Howdy's sister."

"All right. That's enough. Out, both of you. Thank you for bringing Howard home. But stay away from him. And from this house. If you please. You both stink like a wagon full of leaking whiskey barrels."

Shaky, she rose gesturing with a skinny arm through the archway of the high-ceilinged living room to the looming front doors, like those of a southern castle hidden back among the old-growth magnolias and oaks of stuck-up Whaley Way. "Worse, I can smell the gasoline on you."

"I don't mess with that none," Christy whined. "That's Newbie and How— and Howard."

"Young man, I'm counting your lies." Sounding hateful as she could. "The gas is what's killing him, you little miscreants. You sad fools."

Christy, a breakthrough. "See, that's what I was saying. The gas. *No bueno.*"

Furious, her eyes flaring. "Then why have you been enabling him? You overweight, disgusting animal. Look at you. You're a beast. A literal beast. Both of you."

Now Christy changed inside from cold to hot. Blazing. Flashing on the basement back at the mill, the symbols. Howdy's mad huffing and chanting and walking in a circle. His sister's mean face, glaring at him.

He reared up to his full height. Took a step toward her instead of away.

Her eyes, already big behind thick glasses, got bigger. "Don't you loom over me, you–"

In an instant, fast as The Flash, Christy reared back and knocked Everlynne Shull-Schlosser hard as he could against the side of her stupid old head. He heard her teeth click together and a sound like GUH as her body, spindly and fragile, crashed sideways across the cluttered coffee table. Her feet bounced up and she landed on her face against the forest of sharp little statues. They scattered every which way with a clatter.

All fell silent. One last statue, of a rider on a horse, fell over and went *clink*. Howdy's sister—Howard's sister, as Christy was trying to learn—lay with her head halfway twisted around and neck all crooked.

Still as a stone.

Eyes staring.

Dead.

Newbie, sitting on the couch with his mouth hanging open. "Dang, beau."

He nudged her with his foot and heard a fart come out of the old woman. The room filled with an odor like rotten cabbage. A big wet spot had appeared on the back of her skirt, staining the stars and moons brown.

The smell brought it home. Christy, beholding the corpse and inhaling the stench of death, spewed hot liquor onto the coffee table and Newbie's pant legs.

Newbie jumped up, cussing, but got tangled in the old lady's feet covered in blue stockings. He fell across her body and rolled off the coffee table. Screaming in pain, he scrambled onto his knees and displayed a wound— sticking out of his forearm, a pointy brass statue of a man holding a deadly spear. He hollered and yanked at it. Blood ran.

Shouting at Christy. *"What'd you hit her for?"*

Christy didn't have an answer. He halfway wanted to do the same now to Newbie. A stand-off.

But again: he needed him. "After it gets dark, we get the garbage bags, the tape. We put the stones in the bags. We carry her to the river—"

"Shut up. Shut up." Newbie, panicking. "This ain't like your meth-head Daddy. She's some kind of doctor. She gets checks in the mail. And she's got Howdy."

"It's Howard."

Newbie hollered that it didn't matter no more. What mattered was that people lived around here, someone had been sure to have seen them driving through the neighborhood. It wasn't dark. The truck, sitting out front.

Christy thought hard and straight and calm as he could. They were already in trouble. Might as well poke around. "Go look for money."

"Now?"

Christy, nodding, explaining in patient sibilance that they had done the damage, and if they were in this kind of trouble, getting in more by stealing now wouldn't matter. "If there's any, snatch it up. She won't need it, yo."

"Reckon you got a point there. But you don't even know if she's dead."

"Dude." Christy pointed to Howdy's sister's broken neck. "She looks like that cat did earlier."

Newbie did his *nyuck-nyuck*. That morning he had swerved to run over a big orange tomcat scooting across the highway. Had splattered that cat. Newbie, he hated cats and other pets. Would kick a dog if he could, as he always said.

Christy thought, wait: if they got into trouble, he would blame Newbie. He even killed little kittens, officer. Newbie was Special Ed, not Christy. If it came down to it, Newbie deserved to take the rap. Christy would use Newbie if he had to. It was cold, but ya know ya know. Christy's Daddy, he had always said: the world is mean. You got to take what you can.

Howard would wake up soon. What would he say? Dang, as Newbie liked to say. They could have gone without killing the old lady. That was dumb.

CHRISTY PULLED AT THE BODY, WHICH DIDN'T WEIGH MUCH. HER HEAD LOLLED AT its bizarre angle, and Christy's stomach rolled again. More foul stink issued, this time from her gaping throat-hole with the dentures hanging loose in her mouth. It filled his nose, worse than Newbie's morning dragon-breath.

Christy, heaving clear sputum out through clenched teeth. He heaved the body back onto the sofa, where it again settled into rest upon the crackling plastic covering the floral cushions.

He could hear drawers in the other room slamming shut. "I found her purse," Newbie yelled over the classical music. "It ain't got shit in it."

Newbie came back with wadded money and coins presented in his cupped hands like the takings of a beggar. "Twelve dollars and a bunch of sticky change and two books of stamps and some cough drops."

"Money is money."

"Look—she's got some of them gold dollar coins with Sacajawea, too. Them things might be worth more."

"What about Howard?"

"Passed out, still."

The reality of another dead body weighed on him, suddenly, and Christy's mind raced; his heart, too. "Let's get outta here."

"I thought we shoulda been gone already. If you ask me."

"Shut up."

"You just gonna leave her like that?"

Christy felt hurt. "You mean 'we.' We're gonna leave."

"It ain't none of me. You done this."

"You helped me before."

"That was different. This was dumb. You ain't had no reason for it."

Seething. "Well, it's done now, and at the end of the day, it is what it is." Christy heard people talking on the TV that way. He didn't know what else to say.

"No duh. C'mon."

"They'll believe Howard done it," as the idea came to him. Christy, thinking, that's too bad, though.

"Better hope they do." Newbie snapped his fingers. "Maybe Howdy's gonna die too. That would help."

"Aw."

"Well? It *would*."

◉◉❋

LUCKILY THERE WASN'T ANYONE AROUND ON THE STREET OR IN THE OTHER YARDS, all big houses set way back behind trees standing stood tall and thick. Christy, he couldn't imagine living in these homes. How much money it took.

What had she said her husband did? A social doctor? What did they treat? Who paid for it? Christy, he should get back into school. Quit with this mess. He already pledged to read the books.

Money. How did people get it? Now they had twelve dollars, at least.

The impulsiveness that had made him chuck Everlynne Shull-Schlosser across her living room came over him in a wave. Button. Button would be impressed with his book reading. He had been practicing not thinking about her, but it hadn't been working that well. He wished he could see her. Touch her. At the thought his vibration went THRANG, a discordant frequency.

"I feel like we got out before anything too bad happened. Ain't nobody gonna care about that old lady." Newbie turned down one of the side streets of Whaley Way, which would take them to Congress Street and the bypass. "Might take Howdy a while to notice anything wrong."

Christy, buzzing with a charge from clocking the talky sister. A jolt of energy, dense and dark, low in his loins. Not like jerking off, but intense in its own way. Not a well you can visit too often, though. That's what one voice whispered. *Not unless you want to get caught.*

He tried to think sober thoughts, which the whiskey seemed to help with.

He could use more after all that drama. A drizzle of Evan Williams left. He drank it.

He hoped Howdy was okay—Howard, he meant—and wouldn't be too upset when he woke up to find his sister dead in the living room. Who knows what Howard Shull will think. Tough to know who you were talking to with Howard, as Christy often said.

He glanced over and saw a truck pulling into a driveway of another big house with a wraparound porch not unlike that of the Shulls. He nearly shit a brick, however, when he realized it was Mr. Pettus—and that the other figure in the vehicle was his beloved Button Sykes.

Everything happened all at once. Christy's blood roared in his eyes and ears and the tips of his fingers. The impulse that chucked the sister upside her head had its sights on one person and one only: the bossman.

"*Stop the truck,*" he ordered in his meanest voice. Newbie did it, screeching the tires, after which Christy, boy, he went to jump out and make good on taking what he wanted most: the romantic hand of Button Sykes.

BUTTON & ROY, TINKY & BURNIE, CHRISTY & NEWBIE

Tinky, calling from the back seat: "He your husband. He your husband, now."

"Not for lack of trying, Mrs. Sykes. Your shortsighted daughter won't have me."

Button, punching Roy in the arm. "Two words: You wish."

"He your husband now," Tinky kept insisting. "He take you home tonight."

Braking at a stoplight, Roy gripped the wheel and stared ahead. "It's kinda true—we'd make a formidable couple."

"Right on." Button, going hah-hah and trying not to cough. "Sure we would."

"Ain't kidding," but it's low under his breath, and not jokey.

Button and Roy, using his truck, were moving Tinky into the eldercare facility. She had not put up a fuss—Button made it sound as though a fun vacation at hand, and Tinky seemed taken with the surroundings. "It won't sink in for a while, if ever. Long as she. Has *The Price is Right*. The other programs. She'll be happy as a clam."

"Kinda sad. Oh, shoot—I shouldn't have said that."

"She'll be taken care of. Right?"

"Sure. We'll get Miss Tinky squared away."

Tinky, curious: "You gonna square me away?"

"You bet, girlfriend."

"Sure thing, Mom. You wait. And see."

Variations of square-away and he-your-husband-now continued on the rest of the drive, and the process of getting her settled into her room went well, and she said how much she loved the color and the window, which at first she thought was a TV, but then Button and Roy showed her the TV and the remote and she became so happy, Tinky Sykes. Button could leave her there with a smile on her own round face, too.

Like lovers, Button held hands with Roy on the walk back to the truck.

At the parking lot gate he stopped and took her other hand in his. Locking in on her eyes. *"I your husband now."*

"Not that again."

"I want to kiss you."

Button, laughing. "Dude."

But going up on her toes. They kissed, Button feeling the heat emanating from his face and body. He sneaked out his tongue. Hers responded, snakelike, but only to push his back.

Over. He stretched his arms to the sky. "God-damn."

"You not my husband now." She coughed, explosive. "But you still take me home. And make dinner for me."

"You got it, angel face." His happy vibe turned melancholic. "We were living out an alternate hyper-reality."

"But the moment ends." Her side and back aching, she climbed into the passenger side. "As they always do."

"Only to make room for more moments," Roy offered in good cheer. "I guess my real work begins now. And I don't mean making dinner."

She nodded. "Granddad?"

"I wasn't here for my granddaddy and Mama Runelle like I should've been. Houses, trucks. None of that matters. So, I need to be a friend to Burnie. This is my charge. While I'm still here, and he is, too."

"I can appreciate this. Hubby."

How long she could put off telling Roy, she didn't know. No way she'd burst his bubble. Not now. Besides, all her white-light beaming might have an effect. God knew the pain meds were helping. An excuse to pop pills again—another fondest wish come true. Button could not go wrong if she tried.

◎①❋

ROY, AT THE VICTORIAN IN THE WOODS MAKING PESTO IN THE CUISINART AND soliloquizing about his childhood crush on Thim; Button, telling him this news came as no surprise. Thim, a beautiful girl, striking and exotic, whereas Button, merely odd.

"Some upperclassmen—jockeys? They catcalled me in the hall. 'Boy, did you. Get the short end. Of the stick, compared. To that sister. Of yours.' Ouch. But like, duh. Like I didn't realize it from living. In the house. With a beauty queen."

"I went through similar trials with numbskulls like that."

"Bullying—a quaint American pastime."

"Human nature."

"Yeah, but—who's to say? What human nature is? Versus what's been put into everybody's head?"

"Never thought about it."

Uncle Burnie, whom they collected from The Dixiana, seemed fragile at being in the Pettus house. Quiet and narcotized by NFL football and maintenance drinking thanks to cold Budweiser longnecks on which he sipped, for once his inebriation gave him an air not of combativeness, but apparent resignation.

Especially, in a big surprise, as the conversation got around, via his eventual prompt, to discussing how the move of Tinky to the home had gone. How he was glad to be done with her Vietcong ass. "Quieter in the house already."

Next he display cautious curiosity about the facility, questions that made Button smile and Roy's ears perk up. Burnie, previously known for declaring how they'd never get him in one of those hellholes. But this one, he said, sounded not half-bad. All these deaths and change, a dose of reality for him, perhaps.

Or a premonition that Button, now, might be the next person to depart. She'd been sending that vibration to her grandfather. Easier than saying it aloud.

In the kitchen cleaning up, she coughed and Roy noticed. Seeing the concern on his face. Noticing that he noticed.

"What's all this hacking with you?"

"We need to talk about that."

His expression flashed terror. "What? *What is it?*"

"Not tonight. Another time."

"Too much herb. Even with the vape. That's all."

Button, nodding. "You betcha."

"Don't suppose you have any at hand."

"Sure." She dug around in her bag and produced an eighth of Blue Dream, kept sealed in one of her mother's old prescription bottles for Lexapro. "There we go. Forget all this worrying about the coughing. Nothing to do about it."

"No?"

"Not a thing. Let's get vaped."

She could see that Roy's curiosity, leaning toward worry, had been little assuaged by her nonchalance. But he respected her right to remain silent. Said, sure.

Her mindset remained one of no-worry. It's all good. It's all gonna be okay. She preheated Roy's Volcano, ground a Blue Dream nug and filled a crackling plastic sack with vapor.

❋

Back at her house on Whaley Way, right after Roy pulled into the driveway and they piled out, came a squealing of tires from down the street. She turned and noted with detachment as a muddy, beater of a Tundra came sliding into the yard.

But realizing, oh-shit: Christy Beaudock and Newbie Harrell.

Roy, seething and hissing at this turn, an opaque cloud permeating his otherwise bright aura. He had been leaning inside the extended cab F-150 to wake the snoozing Burnie, and bonked his head at the ruckus.

"What is this fudging nonsense?"

"It's the fan club."

"Not these two fuckwits." Roy's vibration? Instantaneous in its shift into the red zone. "Dead men walking."

Uh-oh. Button, worried Roy would boil over. So much stress and strain and loss; healing and growth yet to manifest.

Until she made herself stop worrying.

But Roy, having re-fired Newbie from the honkytonk. It had come up earlier, and he said he'd caught Newbie drinking a beer and not writing it down in inventory control. "Actionable offense. Double secret probation."

"Maybe. He's here to say. Sorry about that beer."

Christy, followed by a reluctant Newbie, came marching at an angle across the patchy, ill-tended lawn over which the neighborhood association forever pestered with letters of complaint and censure.

Roy stepped forward and stuck out a stiff, straight arm like Hitler saluting troops from the back of the Duesenburg. "I'll be a monkey's uncle." His words, a higher-pitched version of the day he'd upbraided the staff at The Dixiana. "So now I get to cut off both your freaking heads. Don't I, boys? We had an agreement."

Roy, she thought. *Don't. Go. Ballistic.*

But Christy, never taking his eyes off Button—creepy; intense. He shoved Roy out of the way and loomed over her, which wasn't hard considering the difference in mass. A voice she'd never heard out of Christy, like Mercedes McCambridge looping Linda Blair. *"Stop stopping me from talking to Button all the time."*

Roy, a stout fire plug, planted a sandal and lunged his body at Christy, but shouting with pain—his bad shoulder. "You don't give orders, *thief.*"

Christy changed to his normal if bizarrely whiny voice, so tiny for such an enormous human. "Button, please. I want to chill with you. I don't want to hang with Newbie. I wanna hang out with the cool kids—he's not like us. The bossman's not either. There's nobody like—you."

"You little piece of white trash. You coulda put me back in the ER with this damn shoulder."

Christy, growling like a cage-cornered animal.

"*Christy.*" Button, trying not to project fear. Not easy considering this kid's peculiar, dense vibration. A greenish-gray aura. Unsettling. Frightening. "I— can't. I don't want to. Chill with you guys. It's not personal. It's that—I don't have enough time. Sorry."

This stopped him in his tracks. Newbie, looking all freaky around the eyes. Like in shock. Both of them, scruffy and disheveled.

On some street drug, maybe?

Did it matter?

Danger, this is what Button now sensed. Danger. And Roy, a kettle about to whistle.

All her work, crumbling.

"Here, fellas. Allow me to make it personal. You smell like a brewery. Both of your sorry Edgewater County asses do. And besides, Christy—what'd I tell you about hanging around with this deplorable little creep."

Newbie, emphatic: "I ain't no creep."

"No?"

"You're the creep."

"Quite an accusation. The onus is on you to prove it."

"My onus ain't got nothing to do with none of this. You must be gay."

"Yeah, and you're gonna end up knocked three blocks over onto queer street."

Button snorted at this banter while Roy glared unbridled hatred at the boys, a wave of vibratory energy that felt hot as an oven. Kept himself positioned between the interlopers and her, a knight at arms.

Ordinarily no shrinking damsel but weakened by illness, she retreated behind him against the fender next to the engine, a comforting heat against her ribs, sore as hell after toting her mother's belongings and personal items into the home. Burnie Sykes, snoring in the back seat. Cold winter wind blowing in. Christmas lights in windows. All-American front lawn confrontation. Over what, she knew not. She placed her hands in prayerful supplication to what- ever peaceful resolution they might foster.

Christy, tears leaking out. Growling again.

Newbie, finally, breaking the spell. "C'mon, Christopher. You heard him. They don't wanna hang with trash like us."

Christy whined, high and strange. Shook his head. Wept.

Aw, Button thought.

"So beat it, then. We've had a dramatic enough day already." Roy, putting his arm around her, his hand on the small of her back, a lover's gesture. "You guys out carousing and partying, it ain't gonna fly. Not in my county."

"We ain't partying," but Newbie sounded as though they had been.

"Harrell, you better not be driving drunk. Had enough of the wet stuff to come up with another stupid little criminal conspiracy?" Brandishing his phone. Fury, bubbling over. "I can have a cop, if not the Sheriff himself, here in under a minute. Any additional second chances just departed on the 5:15 express out of town."

Maintain, Roy. Don't escalate.

"I didn't do this, Mr. Pettus. It's Christopher. I wouldn't've bothered y'all at all."

"That's more like it." Roy said this in his weird, purring voice, deep and persuasive. "That's what I wanted to hear. Now get your asses out of here before I decide to make real trouble. Unless you're both determined to go to prison after all. Or else suffer my particular brand of punishment. Which I can guarantee you both I will make stick. And stick in a painful and direct manner."

This seemed to piss Christy off anew, but no words came.

A standoff, one Roy wins: Christy, following Newbie back across the lawn. Getting into the shitty old truck, slamming doors. Puttering off into the night.

Calm, descending. But Button, seeing that Roy's anger remained off the charts. Lips, curling and twitching. Clenching fists. Rising onto the toes of his sport sandals as though he might levitate.

Beaming relaxation and resolution to him. But against an energetic wall.

With Toyota tires squealing, they departed the neighborhood toward the west side highway, and Roy finally relaxed. "I will have these twerps killed," popping his neck, "if this crap doesn't stop."

"What did you mean? 'Criminal conspiracy'?"

"A prior transgression. It's handled. This was just the encore. A coda. I vibed them with the Black Blade. Their guts are churning with fear. They won't be back."

"And how do you feel?"

The sound of Burnie snoring came from the truck cab. "Sick and exhausted. Let's call it a night."

❀

THEY HUSTLED HER GRANDFATHER, OBLIVIOUS TO THE CONFRONTATION, INSIDE AND into his room.

Burnie, pitiful. Asking for Runelle; asking for his son.

She put him to bed, made tea, and Roy stayed to discuss what to do in case something happened to Button in the near term, a conversation that made Roy so happy. He loved to plan, plan, plan. His little war on unanticipated occurrences.

Good old Roy. Button knew she'd always be able to count on him. "Are we best friends, or what?" as he'd taken to saying.

His love, genuine and present. "More than friends. But I don't mean hubby."

I know what you mean, she beamed to him. "Family."

Their hands, finding one another across the kitchen table.

It made her happy to have a best friend. You could ask them for favors, and Button, somebody who'd need a few errands and tasks completed for her. She hoped it all wouldn't be too much to ask. Nor that her corporeal absence would arrive too awfully soon.

Not that time had any meaning. Not once a soul ascended to the higher planes of consciousness and the state of ultimate anamnesis and grace, either by passing through the veil of physical death, or perhaps other means. Only problem she saw was Roy's side-eye queries whether she's feeling okay, how she simply doesn't look healthy, the coughing, and so on. She couldn't put off telling him much longer.

CREEDENCE AND DEVIN

Dearest Devin:

Life is so strange.

Every day I live with a newfound sense of myself, and with the love I feel in my heart, I think, that maybe I missed out on along the way. I don't know where I am or where I'm going, but it's better than where I was.

And that includes not being with Roy, I'm sorry to say, but it's all part of the journey. The bad with the good. And it wasn't all bad. No sir. Thinking it was all bad, that was what got me into trouble. Bad bad bad, time to do something. Get out. Go and mess around. And so that led to my poor decision-making. Which we have more than covered.

Lord, but we have. Here, and elsewhere.

Speaking of that time of misjudgment, I have finished with Estes and his nonsense. Estes has been warned to Stay Away. When I think about how I behaved, especially when I go back and revisit what we wrote to one another, I feel sick with disbelief. Like I was possessed by another person or entity.

But who needs Estes? Now that I know Phil Webhannet is interested in me, it's like having my own cop! He's hanging out more now than when Roy was giving him free coffee and danish. Well—I don't "know" it, but a woman knows kinda deal.

I enjoy his attention, what can I say. However... it's too soon for me to be dating anyone, as I have to keep reminding myself. Maybe after a year. Maybe in five years, with Phil, or no one. Some of what I've read has led me to believe I'm one of those people who cannot be alone, who cannot live without having another person. Or so I think and act. I might need to explore that some more.

In any case, I have learned to not be a doormat, to stand up and speak, and Estes has backed off. Hanging around with one of Sedge Island's finest certainly helped send a clear message, one that Phil says he will deliver with additional gusto if need be.

Estes kept on and on about how good 'it' was, and how it was the sign we ought to keep on, and how he loved me and didn't care, and that his mother, a doctor, had boo-coo money, so much she would give him some to support me, yadda yadda. Bless his heart. Trying so hard to compete with my husband.

How could he, though? Roy, his good qualities? He is bad-ass. Estes really is a punk compared to him. Roy is like a magician, almost. I have watched for ten or twelve years now, and that man touches something and it turns to money. I swear! I am a lucky girl. In a sense.

But to Estes I kept saying, if you think we were about money, or sex, or the two of us "starting over" together? Gracious. You have so much to learn. So complex, many layers and meanings beyond the surface. Which only made him mad.

People of this younger generation, I don't know. I am glad in some ways you are not around to put up with them. Working the coffee shop as I have now, supervising them, I totally understand why

Roy would want to come home and not talk to me, or go off to his plane. (It doesn't make me feel much better now about all that, but I do understand it.) These young-uns, they can't stand it when you tell them they aren't right about this or that. Like they invented the wheel. It's so irritating. Aggravating. Whatever the word.

But with Estes, I tried to explain that just because we were doing 'it' all 'good' doesn't mean we're in love. Mercy.

Roy was the one who did it to me right the first time. He made me feel like a real woman was supposed to, and all that. So don't think you got anything special going on, Mister Man. That's what I said to Estes.

Love's about so much more than all that sex mess. Sex, that's special and sacred and a part of love. Sure. How we reproduce ourselves and go on. (Not that I would know about that.) But that's not the whole story. Love and gonads are mixed up. They aren't the same. Gonads are also mixed up with how you poop and pee, too. Maybe there is some metaphor there, like in English class talking about a story or poem. In any case, my sponsor Russ tells me the more you're mixed up in your body fluids, the less you can get to what he calls the higher mind. I really should get into the meditation stuff. Maybe I will. Too busy.

Like I said, though, all that truth and honesty made Estes mad, like I was criticizing his peterpiper. Which I wasn't. It just wasn't nothing special. Not like he wants it to be. And sweet Roy, always so worried that his wasn't special enough, which of course it is. Men! (And yes, I would be embarrassed if you were actually reading all this. But who-cares. Right!?)

Again, love was what was missing. Real love. Like I have been feeling. Which if it's right, it doesn't have anything to do with gonads.

There is another level. Deeper.

And that is what I've been missing all this time —love for myself. This is one of many lessons I have learned in my treatment and meetings, listening to the stories of others and finding common threads. I have spent so much time hating myself, Devin. About forty-odd years, in fact. And a ways to go in making that love total, so I can share genuine love with another.

That is what's been so painful to get across to Roy, who says he stills feels the same as before. He also says, girl, you making it too complicated, which it is by its very nature. He doesn't understand. One day he will, I think. He's smart. But still bunched up about so much.

Poor baby. I will always love him so. Even if it isn't like he wants. He's so sweet. He says, in his all-down-in-the-dumps voice, that if we're not getting back together, he's going to just let me have the CBSI as my own place. That he'll even give me the Carolina Beanery trademark, if I want. Run with it, he said. Knock yourself out, because I've got my hands full with The Dixiana.

Boy-o-boy, never thought I'd hear him say that. He said he wants to remake it in his own image. Which is the same image it always was, only better. Weird. He went off talking about all kinda strange stuff, vibrations and all this mess like I never heard out of him. Tangents, real philosophical. Sounding like a different him. I think he had had a couple of beers. Or a couple of somethings.

Roy, I don't know. I think I blew his mind with all this talk of maybe we shouldn't rather than should.

I just feel so bad, still. I've got issues, Devin.

Guilt. It's childish, supposedly, to feel it. But I do.

What if we try again, and it's the same? He's the same?

Long story long, I must break all my habits. If I'm to stay sober. You know this. Better than anyone, but you couldn't break yours, could you.

Sweetheart. Oh, my heart, Devin. My heart. My brother.

Okay, stop this. I will wrangle this life soon.

I think I will go out Christmas shopping. Get my husband a present. The holidays are coming up.

Maybe go shopping with Phil. Not a date, but he mentioned gifts and being clueless, a big old hint if I ever heard one. Go with him after work. Even though Phil said he was off work today, and lives off-island (of course), I will bet you dollars to fresh-baked cinnamon scones he will be hanging out later at the Beanery. Pretending to read on his iPad. But instead, trying to read me. I ain't no dummy. But boy howdy, do I need to be careful as somebody crossing over a frozen stream.

A new year, soon. If there's anybody who was ever ready for the turning of the page, it's me. I'll just be glad when I've got a whole year chip in my hand. Then I will know I am getting somewhere.

My higher power, to which I have connected, and who I pray to every day with all my heart and soul, pray for my sobriety, pray for myself, and for the people I love (just as soon as I figure out who they are), it keeps me whole and sane. So far.

Ah, if only you had done more of this praying, my sweet broken brother, I'm sure you would be here now. You would be one I love for-sure. Maybe in the next life we'll be reconnected. We'll be a family again. I would wish for it in this life, and I do, but one way I'm not childish is that I know actual miracles are scarce. Wish in one hand, spit in the other. That type-deal.

Love,

Creedence

ROY AND RICO

The contractor sucks his teeth. "Well-sir—what happened to the tidal wave coffee?"

You first gave this local tradesman with a decent rep a shout back when you'd had your coffee shop vision in mind. "Third wave coffee?"

"Whatever you called it."

"Yeah; no. That plan, it's been eighty-sixed."

Rusty Neddick, uncomprehending, gape-mouths you. "Say what, now?"

"We're looking more at restoration than demo. Well—both."

"Demo *and* restoration. Check. Mr. Pettus, that's making my mind feel all empty. Like it's—I don't know the word."

"A paradox. One of those Zen things. Yeah?"

"Ain't got a clue. Talk to me like I can understand, beau."

The contractor stands outside the honkytonk listening as you describe how you're still thinking about putting in the condos on the second floor, two of them or building up another floor depending on the results of a structural survey, or else one loft-style single family dwelling and no further construction, but that in any case, you would renovate the existing business. Keep The Dixiana going. Make it new; but keep it classy and classic and authentic. Improved, but the same.

A through-line.

A connection.

A continuity.

You make a speech like the oil company engineer in an 80s movie, *Local Hero*, in which Burt Lancaster's Knox Oil & Gas plans to buy a quaint Scottish coastal town to tear down and remake into an expansive North Sea port and oil production facility, sturdy and massive enough to last for untold ages—for 'a thousand years,' the myopic, materialist capitalist said with awe in his voice. Mr. Sortwell had booked the picture at the Grande because he loved Burt Lancaster, a man's man. It seemed arty compared to most of the mainstream fare they ran. *Local Hero* didn't sell many tickets, but like so many of the movies you saw there, and at the risk of going all Walker Percy yet again about your moviegoing, you've never forgotten it.

You voice a similar sentiment. How you want The Dixiana to come roaring back better than it was, a return to former glory. Or perhaps better still, to a new peak of relevance and historicity.

"Rebuild it to last a thousand years," as you emphasize. "I'm serious."

The contractor, all belly and worn work pants and scruffy steel-toed shoes, smelling of what could charitably called fried nicotine, chuckles. Been eyeballing you like you be one crazy-ass lunatic. You both huddle against a stiff wind. At least the sun still blazed with that Carolina brilliance. "That long, huh?"

Oneupmanship. "Ten thousand years."

"Now I know you're messing with me."

You explain that while such an idea may sound like hyperbole or hubris, you're quite sincere. "All top drawer materials—we'll start by pulling it apart down to the wiring and studs, then putting her back together again. On the inside, she'll be stronger and sturdier than anyplace else around here. On the outside, though, we want her to be the same as always. If that makes sense."

"Beau—in a thousand years, ain't none of this gonna matter."

"Tell that to the signers of the Magna Carta."

Neddick held out his calloused workingman's hands: *Huh?*

Wincing at the still-sore shoulder, you gesture with your own flipper for him to follow inside the shadowy and gloomy daytime interior, to get out of this cutting winter wind that ripples the colorful foil of the municipal holiday decorations, oversized Christmastime icons like snowflakes and trees and stars hanging on all the lamp poles. Since you pulled the plug on lunch service—not forever; retooling the menu, as you have Trudy and Button researching veggie sliders and quinoa-kale salads and vegan mac & cheese, all of which made Button nod, quite pleased, and Trudy roll her eyes—this corner of daytime Tillman Falls feels much quieter.

Inside you shut the door and flip the lock, a sharp *thunk* that echoes along with the jingling bells. You lean on the sticky bar while Neddick puts down his clipboard with a clatter. A stand-off, one you break with an oration:

"Here's the news: Maybe none of this is gonna last five rhetorical minutes. But we gotta do our best to show 'em, the kids and grandkids and their kids, that we were a class act. That we subjugated nature, beat it back and bent it to our will. More over, that we could build to last, and in a way that's mad-crazy efficient but didn't drain the coffers. I don't have to say that this will be the greenest freaking construction the county's ever seen, do I? Of course not; it's self evident, I hope, in how I carry myself, in the aura I project, which I suspect doesn't seem much like Edgewater County—and listen, no insult in that, Rusty. No matter how I present to you, rest assured the muddy Sugeree runs in my blood, too."

"Mr. Pettus, I hear you. But, why don't you tell me what it is you really want. Because I almost feel like you're pulling my leg."

"Far from it: I'm sincere in my desire for those who come after to take one look and know we weren't playing some ephemeral game, not merely in that we did our best to put on a world-class development, but without discounting their future needs and concerns. The Dixiana I have in mind is a space in which the bloodline will live and die, others will come along and take their place, and this cycle will perpetuate itself down through untold generations, all of whom will revere our work. They'll view the rehabilitated Dixiana as the mark of a team of sharp operators doing it right, underscore, exclamation point. That its builders had the long game in mind. That they built not as weak, soft-handed monkeys barely out of the trees, but as gods among men."

"Sounds like them old pharaohs."

You slap the bar, scaring the crap out of the contractor. "Now you're on board. Eternal as two-hundred ton blocks of limestone."

"Hate to break it to you, but limestone—on a long enough timeline —it's gonna—"

"Don't burst my bubble."

The burly Neddick taps a pen against the legal pad on which you observe he's written few notes. "I dunno, I liked your first idea pretty good—all them yuppies putting down five dollars for a hot chocolate, them folks that come here for antiques row," three blocks away along Lafayette Street, where Uncle Burnie used to have the furniture store. "They'll plunk it down for one of them lattes like money wasn't nothing. Course, they put in a mini-Starbucks stand at that new Publix out in Chilton. You been in that thing? It's nice. They're open twenty-four-seven. Can you imagine that? Who out buying groceries at four in the morning? That beats all I ever heard of. Anyway, you can make real money off you some coffee, beau."

Who was this blathering nitwit? "Dude: we already got plenty of money. Gobs of money. Pallets of hundred-dollar bills, shrink-wrapped and ready to unload off a C-17 transport to distribute to you all. We're deciding now for other reasons. Besides money."

"What else is there besides money?"

"Money is empty energy." A Buttonism.

Neddick looks at you like you ain't got good sense. "Doing stuff for something other than money. Well-sir, I thought I'd done heard it all. Felt the same way when that shit-ass preacher come up with all that New Tillman Falls shit."

"Hey—that preacher you referenced? He happens to be my pal. As well as 'my man' on council, now."

"Call 'em like I see 'em."

You'd started to say he was your 'boy' instead of 'man,' but, in the South, and regarding a black man? No. Nuh-uh. That didn't make you much better than this possibly racist slob, if only in an inadvertent tongue-slipping manner. 'Boy' was the equivalent of a Sunni throwing a shoe at a Shite neighbor. A grave insult.

"Neddick, you seem to be getting it, also come highly recommended. But I doubt you're the only redneck around here who knows how to nail two boards together. So lose the 'tude. Nixon has a vision."

Digging a hole: "Look here: what you think about having a juke-joint over there? A minority-owned business right in the middle of New N-Word Falls— it's bound to drive down your property values, ain't it?"

"All right, now." The Black Blade, warming against your leg, an electric tickle, with its own buzzy sound effect ringing in your ears like tinnitus. "Manny T's another colleague, as well a friend of mine. Close friend. So if you don't mind, think of your opinions and epithets like a miscreant farting on a crowded elevator: only an asshole lets them sneak out."

"Hold up, hold up, now." Neddick gestures with his chewed-up Bic pen clutched in nail-bitten fingers. The man needs meditation. "You ain't wrong, and that was out of line. Sir, all I wanted to say was that I thought they served some fine barbecue, but how I didn't much cotton to all the jukin' and jivin' at night. I like country music, is all. I 'came of age' in this honkytonk too, back before I shipped off in the service."

"When was that?"

"First Gulf War, yes-sir. Served. I ain't come back all right, though, I tell you. I had that mess bad, that syndrome shit? But I got better."

"Damn. That's a helluva note."

"I didn't have it too bad. I knowed this one boy, a Corporal from Georgia? Said after he got back home, he had all kinda symptoms, but the weird one? His come burned when it squirted out. No shit. And I don't mean sting like when you pee after taking a shower. I mean, like—*it burned his old lady's woman-parts, too.* That don't make sense, does it?"

"They think it's from, what—all the vaccines. Right?"

"Hell if I know. They punched us up with all kind of shit. Keep from getting sick over there. You would walk through this gauntlet of orderlies all holding little gas-guns, them fellas shoving shots into your arm one after another, like twenty of them fuckers."

You grip your bicep. "Dad-gum."

"Them boys would come outta tent afterwards and you'd see dudes, I mean bad-ass SEALs and such, grabbing at their arms and cussing and crying cause it hurt so bad. Supposed to keep us safe, especially when them camel jocks was gonna shoot gas at us, the fuckers. Now them's some farts for you— you ain't never smelled nothing like wearing a chemical suit inside one of them tin cans with it a hundred degrees outside."

"I was worried sick back then. In college." Feeling self-conscious around this working class guy. "Thought the end-times were upon us. War in the Middle East."

"It's like we ain't had nothing-but ever since. I prayed for our boys when they went over yonder again. Mercy, I'm glad that son of a whore rolled over easy. Run him into his spider hole. Son of an effin' bitch. Crashing planes into them towers. We showed his sand n-word ass, though. Didn't we?"

"Nine-eleven? That was Osama Bin Laden."

"Who the hell you think I'm talking bout? That I-raqi sumbitch. Look here, that shit was a long time ago. That black-assed pussy we got in now ain't sending no boys anywhere, at least. That's what I hope. He ain't no American."

All your conspiracy surfing comes rushing back. "Here's something I never quite got. So out of eight pilots and thirty-odd flight attendants, nobody signaled the standard codes for the aircraft being hijacked? And all those cell phone calls. Let's roll, yadda yadda. Could they have been made from jet aircraft? In 2001? Barbara Olsen. Her call, at fifty-two minutes into the flight, that aircraft would have been screaming in its final descent toward the Pentagon, but this lady's awfully cool and collected. And about the Pentagon, why was no wreckage seen on the lawn? And why, if there were cameras all around, can't we see—"

"What, you one of them America haters?"

"I'd think somebody who didn't care about this stuff was the one who hated the country more. Not I, said he."

As you forge ahead with the matter at hand, Neddick seems relieved but cautious. "Let's talk about the demo. Tearing this old bar out. We need to include Trudy, my GM, to discuss how she wants the new one constructed— the materials, any design changes or upgrades. How it's to appear, and so on. As for the performance and soundboard areas, again, it must look the same, while being absolutely state of the art. Button Sykes will direct that area. Both of my managers will have carte blanche."

"Do what?"

"Build it however they ask. Do not question. Execute."

"Oh-kay. But I thought you wanted it the same."

"In spirit. But heck, if we're gonna go to all this trouble, might as well do it up."

"I hear that, sir. I surely do. And I'm real sorry about getting snippy on you

—my mama's took sick, and they can't find what's wrong with her. Bunch of damn croakers. I tell you," he said, patting the pack of smokes in his shirt pocket. "I'm thankful every durn day for my health. Yes, I am."

You do the walkthrough and he either nods or shakes his head at various ideas. Sucks his teeth first before saying, well, it won't be cheap, but we can 'knock it together' for you, his go-to catch phrase, and reminiscent of your staple, 'We're chippin' away at it'."

"Beautiful beams holding this place up. Structurally? Ain't no thang. Nobody builds like this anymore."

"So, ready to work up an estimate?

"It'll cost what it costs."

"I appreciate all that, but don't forget, I didn't wander out of Farmer Glasscock's turnip patch."

"I know you didn't, sir."

"I've done so many demos and build-outs for so long that I know what they should cost," grave and threatening like Daniel Plainview negotiating an oil lease. "And how they are to go."

"Yes, sir."

"If it's not done to my specs, and I find out later?" Now it's coming straight from the movie, which Neddick doubtless hasn't seen. Creedence fell asleep, but you've run it a hundred times. "I'll take back more than my money. Is that all right with you?"

The contractor's reply comes tense and chastened and small. "That's quite an agreement. For now, I'll work on these notes. With my partner. And give you a decent and true estimate. If it don't sound right to you, I reckon you'll let me know. Won't you."

You snort like a bull. Hold his eyes, unblinking, for a beat longer than any human would find comfortable. "I expect that I will."

In a flash you snatch the legal pad from his hands and scrawl your scribble across the bottom with a pen whipped out of a pocket. A signature; a deal.

"You ain't gotta sign nothing yet."

"Be that as it may. A gesture of sincerity, if you will." You hand him back the pad.

"Oh-kay, then."

He asks to do measurements and take photos with his phone, to give as thorough an estimate as professionally and humanly possible, on the price of tearing out The Dixiana's guts and rebuilding it the same; but better. And you say, by all means. Take all the time you need, but you use all you take, which makes him shake his head and laugh like, dude, you are a trip.

"You know what we're gonna do after this barn is rebuilt?"

"What's that?"

"Rebuild the rest of the damn town, too. To make it last for—" "—how long this time?"

"Forever and a day, my boy." The expanse of time suffered an inflationary effect. "For always."

The idea settles in the following silence like the stench of cigarette smoke infused in every crack and crevice of the honkytonk.

Finally Neddick grins, breaking the tension, and you both enjoy a hearty chuckle. "Reckon I'll research materials rated to last 'forever,' then."

You amble behind the bar and draw the contractor a cold PBR, which he accepts with a look of genuine surprise and pleasure. "Can't say no. Appreciate it."

While pouring yourself an iced tea: "Look: I know some of my high-toned mess sounds facetious, but the Pettus Properties developments I have in mind? That'll be when the real job security comes back to Edgewater County. We will resurface these chuck-holed streets with a concrete that won't degrade like all this asphalt. We will fund façade grants. We're gonna streetscape and bury the power lines and go with premium landscaping and a water feature or two. We'll attract new businesses while running off the ones we don't want. We're gonna market the living mess out of ourselves. Folks from all over the country and the world will plan vacations to South Carolina, and when they do, they'll discover new choices: Charleston, Myrtle Beach, and now Edgewater County. They're gonna go back to their home state thinking country music was invented here at The Dixiana."

"That'll be some trick."

"We will reshape reality. Change will come to this sleepy town." A deep breath. "Whether anyone wants it, or not."

"Like I said. The coffee shop idear sounded better."

You chortle, dismissive. "That horse has galloped."

Neddick sips his beer while he measures and makes notes, watching out of the corners of suspicious eyes for you to swoop down with more of your nonsense. Instead, you plop down with your iPad Mini to read more of the consciousness stuff Button has emailed you, PDFs of texts that blow your mind. Osho. Alan Watts. Terence McKenna. A book called *The Ascent of Humanity* by Charles Eisenstein is next on your list. He has it for free on his website. Must be more of that fifth-dimensional ascension woo-hoo Button's been on about.

The shift.

Shifting into another gear.

The high gear of your soul, as she put it. Another level of consciousness. Opening your mind to the fact that spirit is what we are, not this meat suit. Waking you up, like she has said you should do every morning with what she called your third-eye chakra. All your chakras. Little colored lights all up and down your spinal column. Twinkle, twinkle. You said, sheesh. Let me get the meditation down first before you start stringing up Christmas lights.

Out on the sidewalk you wave to Button, who hands out pamphlets to a pair of antique buyers walking off their Manny's on the Green buffet. You helped her set up her EZ-UP this morning, in that bracing wind against which she huddled and seemed miserable. Both of you still shaken up by the encounter on the lawn with the boys, you suggested it was time to pull the plug for the holiday season. She said nah; this is when many folks are out and about.

It's fine. You won't have any more trouble out of Newbie and his henchman. Not if they're wise.

Which you know they aren't.

You will keep a close watch over Button. No worries.

AFTER NEDDICK'S FINISHED WITH HIS NOTES AND PHOTOS, NEXT COMES A MEETING down the block at the Palmetto Grande of your Festival Committee, the ELMS and select town council members, all part of an executive session called by Mayor Hampton. Exec session, which you know well from your days on Columbia's Downtown Business Alliance back in the 90s and naughty-aughties, means that journalist Dobbs, excited about this music festival and what it could mean for the town, would be excluded. You would dole out the information to the press in measured dollops; controlled PR trumps the needs of truth or paper-selling headlines in tomorrow's *Advocate*—too many decisions and steps remained on the checklist.

Once the contracts with talent are executed, as Feebee Elmendorf, executive director of, and lent out from, the DBA, tells the committee, only then will the requisite press releases be prepared and issued to the *Edgewater Advocate* and other regional media announcing the festival. A carefully managed PR rollout. Everyone wants this to go well. You have charmed them into saying, well goodness, if it's a fun and safe and profitable success, we'll stage it every year in Tillman Falls: a new signature event.

Changing their reality already. Between you and Nixon rolling murals and changing names of municipalities, a fresh page on which to write future history. You get a chubby thinking about how clean it all feels.

Now time for the authority figure in attendance, your pal Garen Oakley, to chime in. "A gated event is what we have in mind, Mr. Pettus. For security reasons."

"I prefer free and open to the public."

"It can be free, if you wish. But the gated part, either way it's necessary. The times being what they are."

Yes yes, you know all about this FEAR under which everyone has lived their lives in the post-9/11 era, and make no bones about the skepticism you exude. You express displeasure that to do what the old man wanted, you find you must jump through so many gosh-darned red tape hoops. In fact, all members grouse in their own way, including the police and town officials, about the rigmarole inherent in modern life, in staging public events while maintaining standards of safety here in the terror-stricken culture of Today— putting up bollards to prevent vehicular violence, deploying god'-eye drones, armed gendarmes with combat-grade vehicles and gear, all for guarding a music concert against terror. No one would have considered such a scenario reasonable back in the day, as they say, except in the cautionary fables of dystopian science fiction.

"If you want affordable event insurance, we recommend no backpacks, bags, purses or coolers large enough for pressure cookers... only see-through backpacks and purses allowed." Sheriff Oakley, whom you note seems to have put on weight since you first met him several months ago, reads through the latest DHS regs and recs. "Like at any big public gathering."

"What?" Your hands flat on the table, you flare your eyes at the Sheriff. "No freaking TSA full body scanners? While we're all shaking in our booties? It's a music festival."

"Roy." The Reverend-Doctor Nixon, an ally, friend and councilperson you asked to sit on the committee, clears his throat from the other end of the table. "It's all about the safety of the public. The lord forbid somebody get some fool idea in their head, some racially motivated hate criminal, for instance—"

"Now, Reverend Councilperson Nixon, nothing like that has happened in Tillman Falls in fifty years." Mayor Hampton belches grease from a fried chicken lunch reeking from his wool sport coat. "Ain't no hate crimes going on here in Edgewater County, and they certainly ain't gonna be happening at this music concert. Not on my watch, beau."

Nixon: "You seem so certain, Mr. Mayor. You must have some prescient intel from the future about what may or may not happen."

"Nothing's for certain," you add, fake-cheerful. "And it can always go wrong."

"Amen," Nixon agrees. "Wisdom from Mr. Pettus's mouth to our ears."

A voice, sharp and incredulous. "Are we debating the park rules? Really? Gentlemen. We're too far along for this detail work. I'm in shock, truly."

Feebee, as the festival committee's one paid employee, had pulled all of this together, from liquor permits to talent booking to the sound reinforcement to getting a ruling from DHS on what sort of safety plan would need to be in place, had much experience with meeting facilitation, event planning, and despite the size of the check you had written her, suffered scant patience with unnecessary crosstalk.

You insist that now's the time. "We have to make the big decisions today, not the morning of the festival."

"Agreed. But, are we actually suggesting that this committee, and the town of Tillman Falls, will win a point of order with the Department of Homeland Security? All due respect," her voice echoing in the Palmetto Grande auditorium where your worldview had been shaped by Hollywood movies, "but is this worth anyone's time? As the Executive Director in charge of staging this event, I say 'no'."

"All I was doing was reading what the damn paper says." Sheriff Oakley, chastened by Feebee's forthright oration, tosses said document onto the table amidst all the legal pads and pens Feebee had provided, only to have seen no one taking any notes except Becky L, scribbling like mad in her notebook up to and including the present moment. Becky L, drawn and strained and pale. Unhealthy. Heartbroken. Another issue. She can barely look at you. Thinks, maybe, you have counseled Manny into pushing her away.

Now look: All this relationship strife needs to fade away. You need both people as colleagues and allies, not engaged in some fluid-swapping soap opera drama.

Talent, the next agenda item, with the headliner you specified, Gillian Welch and her partner David Rawlings, representing the one modern instance of 'new' pop music, so to speak, that your grandparents had enjoyed and appreciated in their later years. When told of the event and the purpose and the history, Welch, not currently on tour, accepted the offer, said it'd be a fine honor indeed. As had Marshall Chapman, a lanky Spartanburg-born Nashville singer-songwriter you remember well from her time in the 70s playing the regional circuit that included The Dixiana, as part of the country-rock wave her compatriots in the Marshall Tucker Band repped with such success following their formative years playing dives like The Dix.

Oh, the memories—a rougher crowd in those days. Late 70s. Lotta shitkickers, fights. The upstairs stuff went away about then.

The Dixiana scene calmed down in the 80s. That's when you started swabbing out those urinals for your granddaddy. Golden days. Not.

Wouldn't be long, though, before it was high times again, after Garth Brooks hit it big. Suddenly every redneck in Edgewater County went around dressed in designer jeans and a collarless button-down shirt and a wide-brim cowboy hat like their tubby, crossover singing sensation. At least by the time line dancing, another eye-roll inducing endeavor, caught on, you'd gone off to college. But another craze that kept the old girl afloat all those years. Now, it seemed the whole Americana thing that Jasper spearheaded and that had sold records and seats over the last decade, your Avett Brothers and Shovels and Rope and cats like that, had provided some steam, some grease for the economic wheels. Not bad for the cause of roots music. Not bad, too, for an old honkytonk.

By the time of the Garth Brooks's pop country, the music had changed for people like Rabbit and Burnie and Mama Runelle. At the time you had no idea. None of that country crap had been 'your' music; it was all bad. Or maybe you had some notion of the changes. The melodies of your grandparents they played from the big record collection, like her 40s swing stuff or his old blues recordings, or when you looked at the publicity picture of Runelle and the Dixiana Darlings in their little cowgirl outfits, all had seemed from an era before time itself.

Which it had been:

Before your time, little Roy Earl.

Before you.

Jasper, beside himself with delight over 'getting Gillian': He'd been the one to send her management the heartfelt email that described in loving and eloquent detail The Dixiana's role in the history of local roots music. He had booked the rest of what they were calling the Americana Stage with acts from around the state he knew through his illustrious open mic nights.

Meanwhile, Feebee's booker in Columbia had sent offers out to the latest upcoming rock stars from the music community down in Columbia to fill out the Pop Stage, as Jasper insisted on calling the rock stage. The layout of the festival, developed in a mini subcommittee of Jasper, Darren Woczinski of Glimmer Twins Sound Reinforcement and various municipal officials, improved on the typical ELMS festival footprint by having stages arrayed around downtown that pointed away from the central town green, with the area retained for food vendors, ID checking stations, and Johnny On The Spots. The DHS and police substation portable watchtower from which to view the crowd would reside at the center, offering a panopticon-like vantage point for the authorities to watch over the citizens and keep them free from peril.

As for the tribute to Rabbit Pettus and The Dixiana, the bar would be re-opened by April—surely—and would serve food and liquor all day, with additional music presented inside on the classic stage 'that started it all,' with Jasper leading a marathon all-afternoon and evening jam session of pickers, grinners and all-comers. Excepting, naturally, for during the Gillian and David slot, when he would be a part of the audience rather than leading the house band onstage.

All of which Jasper verbalized. In great detail, and in his lazy-summer-day drawl.

"Guys: that's committee work." Feebee's snappish, get-over-it mode pops for you; it's admirable. In another reality you'd be hitting on her, a strong potential partner. "Keep to the agenda items."

A checklist recitation follows of mundane bits of business like aluminum recycling and volunteers to empty garbage cans, and a last minute suggestion by Mayor Hampton to have a children's area featuring family-oriented activities like at the normal ELMS spring fest.

But this idea, shot down and with extreme prejudice—this is about old timey music, you say, along with your granddaddy and his honkytonk, and not entertaining rug-rats and yard-apes. You have no patience with the child-worshipping horse-pucky that's gotten this country in trouble in the first place, as you can barely stop yourself from announcing, but you don't have to: the Sheriff wields the thick DHS packet of regulations, which states that if certain events are designed to attract children in large numbers, a different set of protocols must come into play. "Can of worms," in his words, "to include a children's playground."

At that factoid Feebee joins into the chorus of disapproval. With your call for a show-of-hands vote, the idea's shot down like your pal The Colonel over North Vietnam.

Hampton, pooching out his lips. Used to being bossman. Wants to call for votes. "Well I think next we should—uh."

Get out of the way of the train, boy, you think hard in your most black-blade of malevolent energy vibrations, aimed right at the space between his eyes.

For an instant, damn if Hill Hampton doesn't look scared.

Like he can hear your mental threats.

"Never mind," he says.

How silly. Silly, like how you keep thinking you hear Button's voice in your head. You ain't doing telepathy.

Or are you?

◎◉✳

AT HOME ALL YOU WANT IS TO DECOMPRESS FROM THE MEETING, BUT A PROBLEM, new:

The dog. It can't get up.

It's bad this time. When you go to assist Rico, he doesn't yelp in pain.

He screams.

Panicked, you scamper around clumsy and desperate for a freaking phone book. Tearing open cabinets and drawers. Crap going everywhere. A floor lamp jostled and knocked to the hardwood; a bulb full of mercury shattered, a toxic hazmat disaster residing at number three or four on the checklist.

Nobody to help.

Alone.

Thinking: you stupid bastard. Should have taken him in before now, should have looked into this, you observed him struggle for weeks now, you stupid freaking fatboy. You watched him have more trouble getting around, but put it off and kept putting it off, Reecie Cup, because, what? Too stoned? Too busy? Pick one.

Who were you to care? Wasn't your dog.

More pet responsibility. Great. Thanks for nothing.

This freaking dog. This wasn't supposed to be your responsi—

This time, the sound of his pain freezes you in amber.

Rico, yowling. Groaning.

Suffering.

ACT!

At last you begin to think straight: *For pity's sake, beau—a supercomputer in every pocket.*

Stabbing at your iPhone to google for 'emergency vet edgewater county sc.' Cursing as your thumbs make errors and autocorrect tries to plug in ridiculous word substitutions. Supercomputer indeed.

To your dismay, you find the closest vet all the way down the freeway in Dentsville, right on this side of Columbia proper, but still twenty-five, thirty minutes.

Not the way you're gonna drive.

Not on the freeway, rather straight down the long southern run of Highway 79. Up and down those hills. You put new tires on the F-150. Had the brakes checked. Servicing; oil and filter and transmission; leaky valve covers the source of the occasional greasy puff of smoke, also fixed. In this refreshed vehicle you will own that ribbon of gray, make it your servant, make the road lay down straighter than it already is. It would know rest easy later knowing Roy E. Pettus had owned every inch of its sorry rural highway ass.

The dog yelps and howls and you shit yourself.

ACT, the voice again screams. And it ain't Button this time. This is you.

You haven't felt this freaked out in nearly twenty years, not since your first coffee shop flooded—like Manny say, you the bossman. In charge. They all look to you, and so no panic.

And now? Now, you can't panic because no one else's here.

Not your dead grandparents.

Not your estranged spouse.

No one but you.

And the dog.

◉◎✻

Your guts, churning and icy like after you bought Maxine's Koffee Klatch and re-christened it the classier Carolina Beanery Cafe there in Columbia's venerable funky Old Market neighborhood, which also happened to be both the small southern city's version of Greenwich Village as well as a basin, the lowest point in town. The streets, often flooding after gullywashers. The skies turning black that July afternoon, you watched as the air became heavy; there came the otherworldly sensation of thick air right before the clouds burst and the flash flood, a major one, rolled through and made you kneel before the forceful power of spirit as captured in a willfully and exponentially moving body of water, where before had been pavement and civilization. You and Manny, with his retreat from Katrina, why, y'all have more in common than you even knew.

You didn't let anyone see you crying. As the water from the creek in the adjacent park rose, bubbled back out of the storm drains instead of being carried away, you sprang into action, an early, more awkward version of your bossman routine, more hat than cattle but putting on a good show of being in charge: Shouting, pointing, helping lay sandbags as the rain sluiced down at an angle, falling in enormous dollops that splashed like P. T. Anderson frogs tumbling out of the opaque sky. Thunder cracked overhead and water topped the sandbags, three rows high. And the flood came under the door of your sparkling, brand new coffee shop, rushing in worse, even, from the back entrance, which in all the excitement you forgot to sandbag. At all.

Staring with the dismay and despair that only comes with seeing a foot of standing storm water in your coffee shop, you wept. And after it retreated, the mud and debris left behind on your brand-new tile floor further stunned you. The rank and filthy water had also been carrying motor oil and lawn chemicals and god knew what else in the rain itself—for all you knew, every spring shower carried Button's dreaded radiation from the Sugeree Station. But all was above your pay grade, and for the moment you thanked god you'd pulled out that cracked old vinyl of Maxine's and sprung for the unglazed porcelain tile, retro looking, durable, expensive as heck, that you would now sanitize to its glimmering, formerly pristine condition.

While you squeegeed out water, a college frat dude smelling of beer came in wanting to take pictures for his photography class. It was nighttime when it'd rained, and at the height of the flood, as you'd stood there in your sandals thigh-deep in turbid floodwaters, you cursed as drunken students frolicked laughing and splashing in the street.

Next, and despite being waved back by a fellow merchant—a desperate, etherial bohemian lady who owned a head shop down the block—a monster truck came rolling through, its enormous tires sending spumy brownish waves in its wake to slap against the windows of the Carolina Beanery Cafe, and you'd screamed and sworn death upon the thoughtless punk-ass bitches. Wanted to tear the driver's head off with your teeth, shit virulent stomach-flu diarrhea down his recalcitrant, bleeding neck-hole.

Your barista who stayed to help, a cute English major named Susie, the first of many who'd all seem younger and younger as the years piled up, noted how unlucky it seemed for this to happen to you so soon after getting the coffee shop reopened.

Then came a revelation—you remembered how calm your grandfather always seemed, even in the face of drama. How it helped keep everyone in the room calm. "Shoot, you telling me we can't mop and dry this floor and be back in business first thing tomorrow? Hell—this mess is nothing."

You told her how your Pa-paw had served in World War II, and your father, why, mortar fire had killed him in the jungles of Vietnam. Had probably died face down in dirty rice-paddy water not unlike this. A flood in the streets of the college ghetto held up to risking one's life, even dying, in an overseas war, far from hearth and home? No comparison.

◎①❋

As for the area south of the lake country to which you hurtle with the sick dog, you cannot get over how built up everything seems—bad enough back in Edgewater County around the Chilton interchange, but here, my god, the big boxes and strips and subdivisions and apartment and condo complexes and outreach medical parks and fern bars and sports bars and upscale chain restaurants and corporate gyms and grammar, middle and high schools, as well a University of Phoenix campus; sprawl; a cliché, commonplace, the fabric and rubric behind all of modern society, and silly to complain or notice. P. F. Chang's? Really? You don't even have one in the off-island suburb.

Who are you to kvetch? The SPFC® Jacksonville #2 and Knoxville #1 locations were both corner, anchor tenants in exciting new strip mall developments built near the college neighborhoods of those respective cities. You've been a purveyor of sprawl. A recipient of its largesse. A hypno-crite.

In a further wrinkle, the cop that's been chasing you for a half-mile is no doubt pissed.

Now only one block from the emergency vet, you're waving off his ass. You can see the sign. Rico's strapped down in the truck bed. He's still howling and yelping and hollering.

You made it.

Blipping the siren. The blue lights of doom.

Your response? Punch it.

"Boy, are you trying to pull over the wrong son of a biscuit eater tonight. I made it. And you're not gonna do anything to slow my ass down now. Fuck your mother. *Suck shit.* Protect and serve my cunting fucking goddamn fucking pee-hole, you simpering fuckwit. *You janitor.*" Such you've never spoken, not even when you and Dobbs and Devin were thirteen and learning how to out-cuss each other. Flipping on your turn signal, the cop right on your ass, you shriek in the cab, pounding the wheel and accelerating. "*I got a sick mother-*

fucking animal here. I hold absolute primacy over the wasteland, Mad Max." The Lord Humungous, whispering courage into your soul. *"Just walk away—just walk away, and I spare your life."*

As you whip into the parking lot of the vet, the cop's punched it and flies up right in behind, but when he hits the brakes he slides sideways like in one of those 1970s car chases your Pa-paw used to like watching at the Grande. The patrolman corrects, comes barreling back around across a grassy median dividing the parking lot from the regular doctor's offices next door, jams the brakes so hard the front end pulls toward the asphalt. Goddamned action movie.

To wit: You jump out as he's jumping out, gun drawn. Yelling for you to hit the dirt.

Shaking handheld internet video of a hundred different police shootings flash before your eyes. All these guys are weaponized with military-grade hardware. Loaded for warfare.

Oops.

You realize you're holding your iPhone clutched in your hand. You drop it, shattering the face. You howl in your own special pain, but time to upgrade anyway.

"Officer: I've got a sick dog here—!"

"I don't care what you got! Don't move, you son of a bitch!" The patrolman, a kid. As scared as you ought to be. Likely a literal soldier boy, trained to kill rather than police, or maybe a little of the latter sprinkled on top of the military seasoning. That's the problem with these cop shootings. How can you train someone to kill, only to later send them back home with a gun on their hip to maintain order in the streets?

The barrel of his service revolver, trembling. "On your knees, asshole. Or you'll taste hot holy hell."

"My dog, dude. He's in pain." Furious, you make no move to comply, gesturing instead with coiled rage at the truck bed behind you. You send a rush of blazing black-hearted energy toward the cop. You don't feel fear, only perfect courage. You think, go ahead, dipwad. Put me out of my fucking misery, soldier boy. "Do you understand? *I'm unarmed.* And I have a sick freaking dog."

Blinking, he steps back. It's as though you've poked him in the chest with a stiff finger. Shaking his head, he lowers his weapon. "Mister, I don't much care what you got going on, when the police is behind you—"

"Time is precious." You flare an additional peak of dark vibrational energy at him. This peckerhead needs to worry about the weapon he can't see—the Black Blade. "Help me."

He grabs at his chest. Says, "Shit."

"Please—help me help him." Your voice has become even and quiet. Your

employees crap their pants when they hear that tone instead of the higher-pitched, lighthearted fun-loving uncle voice, another of your useful management personas. Those who saw you get quiet after being mad knew hell simmered and awaited.

"I said—I said—get on your—on your knees." But he's got no juice. He drops the barrel of the weapon. Doesn't want to. Can't seem to help himself. "You—you son of a—"

Rico hollers and howls from behind you.

"He's in pain, pal, and I don't have time for you and your rollers and cop tires burning rubber and stinking up the joint. You're either going to shoot my fudging fat ass, or not." COMPLY, as you beam him, holding his eyes with your own blazing warrior peepers, a burst of energy crackling along the crown of your skull. COMPLY WITH ME. "Now, here's the news: I'm getting him out. And you're helping me."

"I don't give a shit. When you see them lights come on behind you—you—"

The dog yelps. Rather than deploy additional energetic blades, instead you display to him your lodge ring, and speak to the cop in a specifically coded manner that changes the tone of the encounter.

"Hey, boy. We're here. I'm getting help."

The patrolman comes over. "It's—whoa. A big dog."

"He's a Great Pyrenees. Rico."

Rico whines. His crusty eyes run with dog tears. A different energy burbles out of you. "Oh, god. Please don't let him die on me, too. *Please.*"

"Hang on, pardner."

The cop races over to the entrance, shouting for assistance.

In what seems like only seconds, the patrolman and a stout female vet tech race back out with a gurney you hope will support Rico's weight. At that moment your back twinges and your hamstring on the left leg burns like it's torn. You haven't a clue why.

"What's the clinical here?" The African-American vet tech, squat and chubby but graceful, yells and runs across the lot. She's got beautiful eyes and dreadlocks not unlike Button's, only much shorter. "Did he get hit by a car?"

"No. He can't get up. His hips have gone bad."

"Check—big dog problems. How far along is it?"

You confess, "I put off getting him checked. Nobody knows how old. He was a rescue."

"Not much I can do out here. Let's get him inside."

The three of you pull and slide him down the truck bed; you're glad you sprung for the liner. Rico stinks, needs a bath. "Soon as we get you fixed up, it's straight to the groomers for a spa day."

"Jesus," the cop grunts, but all manage to get the panting, suffering animal onto the gurney.

"That's why we call him the big dog."

On the much calmer roll inside on the gurney, you comfort Rico and tell him you'd get something figured out. "You know what, old boy? We're chippin' away at this thing. We're getting it all squared away. And after the groomer, it's steak biscuits. We'll get fifty of them, put them in the freezer, save ourselves a trip on Saturday mornings. Yes, we will," you say to Rico, smiling and stroking his fur. "We got this."

In the distance, sirens, more blue lights. "Cancel backup," the young cop says into his shoulder mic. "That's a code-four here."

●◐❋

YOU MUST MAKE THE CALL.

Rico, ten to twelve years in age, the tech says, at least from the looks of his teeth and a few other signs. "That's old. And surgery's gonna be expensive—"

Snappish. "I've got sufficient resources. Not an issue."

"—and hard on him. And you." She describes the execrable and severe condition of Rico's joints and pelvis. Dire.

This settles you down. "He won't understand what's going on with all that. The pain. The recovery."

"Don't let that part sway you. Animals, they're resilient. I'm simply saying—"

"Enough. I get it."

You take a moment alone with Rico. Make a speech, pat him on the stomach as he likes.

He groans, looking up to you. Panting. Whining.

"Goodbye, boy." Your words, but a wretched hollow screech. "Goodbye, Rico."

Do you want to remain for the procedure, you hear the vet ask? Yes, your echoing reply. An enormous syringe of the horrible blue Romulan ale, injected into a vein above his paw.

The light, going out of his eyes.

The huge chest, heaving once, twice; a third, final time, more like an enormous sigh.

Stillness. Like practicing eternity. Before your eyes.

"God help me," you hear yourself say. "Forgive me, Rico."

Afterwards the vet asked, "Do you want to stay in here with him for a few moments?"

You shouted NO and demanded to be let out of the exam room.

At the desk they handed you a card for a pet mortuary. They'll pick it up, the body; they'll be told to send two attendants. It's a business you understand from the years with Creedence and her collection of little urns, each one adorned with a picture of the kitty who'd been the ashes inside. You've always respected all that. Never thought it silly. Pets. They're family. They are her kids, the only ones she's had to raise.

You get it. Hell, you barely know Rico, but now it feels like his death has ripped out your guts.

◎◉❋

WHEN YOU COME OUT LATER, NUMB AS A STATUE, YOU CAN FEEL THE SYMPATHY IN the waiting area. The other pet owners, all sick with worry about their own, see the grim news written on your face.Outside you're irritated to see the patrolman still on site. A smart-ass, you approach with your arms raised, fingers interlaced on top of your head. You drop to your knees.

"All right, now, sir. I didn't make that situation. What's the word."

Toppling forward, you start going huh-huh-huh like you've heard Creedence weep over a dying kitty, emoting with such force it becomes nausea, and wrenching.

Sitting on the ground, you wipe your mouth and eyes. "It was down to me and him," you croak, struggling to your feet with a hand from the cop. "Now I've lost them all. My wife, my parents, my grandparents, and my dog."

Hesitant, the officer expresses his condolences. You offer thanks. He reminds you, however, that you can't not pull over for those candy-blue lights, no matter the situation.

"I would've helped you. That could've all gone another way just now."

"Don't I know it."

"Let me ask you something, though, sir: if it's you and him, how'd you get the dog in the truck? I bet an animal like that must weigh a buck and a half."

You ponder. "I guess I picked him up and carried him. Put him in the bed. I don't remember doing so. But I reckon it must be what I did."

The patrolman's mouth drops open. "Dude. This's one of them stories you hear. Like the woman able to move a whole car off her kid trapped underneath."

"My back's killing me. That's for sure."

"God wanted you to get your dog here."

This fills you with fresh grief. "I dragged him all the way here. Scared, in the back of this truck. Only to take him in there and *kill him*—" You collapse against your granddaddy's F-150. "I am a son of a bitch, aren't I."

"You gave him peace." The young cop, his nameplate reading Hertford, pats your arm. "It's a blessed miracle, though, getting him in that Ford."

"You believe in miracles?"

"Not sure. Not before this."

"I'm in good shape. That's all it is. Don't kid yourself."

"You ought to call the TV news, sir. If it was me."

"Why?"

"You ought to tell people about it. It's remarkable."

"My dog's dead," your grief turning to steam. Gun or not, if you can pick up that dog? Imagine what you'll do to this skinny fuck. You stop yourself from drawing the midnight blade from its heavy sheath and threatening, *If you say 'you ought to' one more time, I'll have your fucking badge, you insensitive little cunt-faced nincompoop, along with a limb or two. Or a necklace out of your dried, cold fingers. Your ears, cut off as trophies.*

Whence, these horrible images? Not a clue.

But then you recall his compassion, see his smile, and instead shake his hand. "Brother, that's news enough for me tonight. And look—I know you were only doing your job. Thanks for not shooting me."

He gives you a salute, goes to his prowler. Pulls out.

Now what, you think.

Home.

All the way back, this time on the interstate, you keep it below the speed limit. At the Chilton/Tillman Falls exit, you signal; it's all you can do to not keep going, though, into the indigo of the unknown Carolina night, north, out of Edgewater County and towards the mountains. Toward Max Patch.

But not tonight. Soon—someday soon. Your business in these parts, getting wrapped up bit by bit. Death by death. Losing everyone. Including your freaking iPhone. You have incentives and offers waiting, and the scratch to buy a gold-plated one, if you wish.

At least you didn't have to worry about losing Button Sykes. You couldn't wait to see her tomorrow. To tell her of the miracles you've manifested. Maybe she'd be able to further explain how it could all be so damned possible.

BUTTON AND THE PREACHERS

L eafletting the green.

For what felt like the last time.

Why?

Walfredo, proffering a fresh vibration of urgency and concern.

Of danger.

Again?

Already today?

How much more coming-to-terms with her own death was a Saigon-cinnamon, hippie-dippy dreadlocked little freak supposed to do?

Getting cold outside. Shivering all the time. From losing all the fat she'd carried around for most of her life.

Yeah—best shape of her life. Button could see every rib.

Could feel pulsing inside from the clusters of her disease. Each day, a bit more pain.

Sitting beneath the canopy in the shadow of tiny Pitchfork Ben and the looming obelisk of the CSA monument, Button enjoyed an expansive view like the imagery she'd employed in her student film *Mohammed's Radio*, shot with a vintage Bell & Howell camera through the 25mm wide lens, light bending at an angle and creating a grainy visual mood for which she'd received praise from her instructor and peers.

And while to Button college and the 1990s felt like five minutes ago, here and now stood The Dixiana and Manny's and Head Trauma and the courthouse square and the blue-silver municipal building reflecting the sky. Sitting huddled in her camp chair, shaking and distressed, the worst sin of all. Worrying about her traverse here in meatspace ending already.

But what was time?

But forget all that dying drama—her work and intention here on the green had not crumbled into ineffectual dust, instead bearing unbelievable fruit:

Only that morning, Dobbs Vandegrift had emailed her a news link that Piedmont Power was set to announce how a bankruptcy filing by the corporate parent of the company manufacturing the new reactors meant that the project was to be scuttled.

And there might not be reactor construction after all.

As with Heather last week, one of her fondest wishes made real.

Well, dang.

After reading the email and replying, she might well have pulled the plug on putting up the tent today, but hell, she could tell anyone who happened by the news about Piedmont Power.

Next she had texted Roy, with whom the walks at the park had ceased, to let him know about the reactor deal.

She knew he wouldn't think it a positive development for the county, but he wrote back in a manner more curt and sad than she could have expected. Odd how much one could read from, or maybe into, a simple text.

He had written: *Rough freaking night. Will fill you in later when I swing by the Dix.*

Rather than feel triumph, however, Button sat consumed with mortal futility. The reactors were kaput, but how many had she awakened with her pamphlets? Few. She had not needed to reprint a single one of the handouts.

As the wind cut sharp across her pinched face, she grappled with managing her hard-won detachment from emotion, begun during the time caring for her father, and continued in the years since with conscious and studious intention. Acquiring the ability to disenchant herself of the attachment to outcome, she now realized, had been her prep work for the final act of this incarnation. No comfort came from this distancing mechanism from her own feelings, however. Not today.

Dread. Waves of it. Perhaps only the normal human reaction to knowing of death's proximity.

Even the Phish she'd chosen that morning, 'Bathtub Gin' from the Murat Theater, August 13, 1993 show—a classic, venerated episode in Phishtory, the August 1993 tour—took its sudden and unsettling turn into an absurdist vocal jam which precipitated a mild panic attack, relieved only after her galloping heart had synced with the racing, melodic 'Ya Mar' to follow. Ah, even the beloved soundtrack of one's life, to trot out a useful cliché, could turn bad on a troubled listener. Panic attacks were far from the goal when jamming to her fav band.

Make that panic over still needing to break news—Button faced telling her own grandfather about the fatal illness. A miracle Thim hadn't divulged, but she'd never been close to their granddad. Not like Button. But change, waves of it, coming on strong and soon, and despite the towering Southern family tradition of never discussing any issues of dire importance in mixed company, the time drew nigh. Burnham Sykes remained too lucid about everyday life to fool much longer.

Like Thim he'd likely press on the medical details, which Button would manage by lying and saying she'd had scans and all that rigmarole. Button had needed none of it to know her time here would soon end. An assurance beyond modern medicine, beyond emotion itself. A knowing.

A giant corporation engaged in building terrifying technology like nuclear reactors verged on bankruptcy, so the day couldn't be all bad. Not even in her condition. Winning, as she tried to think as a bulwark against the pain that throbbed in her body, which the most part she merely observed rather than experienced in the fullness of its depredations. Don't ask her how.

Driving down Whaley Way earlier, the light had been bright on a cool December morning; high-altitude jet traffic hadn't yet occluded the blue, as happened on most sunny days. After those Colorado Phish shows in '12, Button had taken a no-fly pledge. Imagine the carbon footprint of even one transcontinental flight, much less going to Australia or the East the way everyone routinely did now. We haven't been jetting around long enough to know what it's doing to the atmosphere, as she said to Roy one night after he told her he'd decided to rid himself of the hobby aircraft, his Piper Meridian. He hadn't flown since the last time he came back from Sedge Island, two months now. Had mentioned offhand to Christy and Newbie one day how he'd take them flying, but this, back before all the current drama.

After she got the tent set up, however—a painful struggle; glad it was for the final time—the empty azure sky had become streaked by persistent, expanding jet contrails. While tying and smoothing the Indian mandala tapestry on top of the scarred folding table surface, she shook her head and said, what have we wrought.

Lastly and methodically, and chanting as she did so, she un-bundled the stacks of flyers and pamphlets, placing them in good order, the same every day. Held down from breezes and gusts by sparkling, colorful geodes, the materials were grouped by topic:

Health. Nutrition. GMOs and genetic mutations for profit. Fluoride. Radiation. The Georgia Guidestones. Occult imagery and messaging in mainstream media. Ancient architecture, megalithic sites. Illuminati, Freemasonry and

Secret Societies. 9/11 truth. WTC Building 7; free-fall at the speed of gravity; no plane strike? The real purpose of those persistent contrails. Consciousness. The Chakras and how to fire them up. The true age and meaning of the pyramids. Cannabis decrim. Free DVD-Rs of awareness documentaries like the *Zeitgeist* series, *Loose Change, In Plane Sight, Wake Up World, Sacred Geometry*, a few others. Whole bit. Her part to play in the truth-telling that only seemed to get easier here in the internet age, with the whole of recorded history in the palms of hands. In a place like Tillman Falls, however, she'd figured the old ways—a pamphlet; how the fires of revolution had been stoked in this country—couldn't help but connect on a basic human level.

And maybe she had connected, in a small way, with one or two of the people to whom she'd handed information. No one else had written in letters to the *Advocate* decrying the building of the reactors, though, her primary local issue of most pressing concern. A few from familiar Sierra Club and activist types submitted columns to the *Columbia Record*, which made her glad, but those had come from the usual suspects—Columbia, a small town, too. Button had wanted to reach ordinary citizens who got most of what they considered their information from the TV, still. Television didn't tell the truth about anything anymore. If it ever had. Well, not 'television'; rather, the humans who used the medium to promulgate their message of mind control. Ya know ya know.

◉◉✸

Speaking of TV, yesterday, a visit to her mother. Fun fun. Oldtimers staring at screens the same as today's kids.

"Food good here, yeah yeah," Tinky reported as she potted down the volume on her game show. "She very happy. Salisbury steak."

"Comfortable? Good TV?"

"Oh—you betcha."

Besides the thought of watching TV, Button could've also puked at the notion of eating those steak patties and the chemical horrors contained within. Commercial veggie burgers not much better, and maybe worse, depending on which agri-giant produced the product. Made her sick that Roy had sold off his fruitshake trademark to those soul suckers at ConParAgCorp. Should do positive deeds with the proceeds, which as far as she was concerned were like the spoils of black magic. A little rap to lay on him. Not now. Too heavy for her friend. His shoulder, healing, but his heart remained blood-bruised and tender.

◉◉✸

Sitting behind her table of leaflets, the corners of the brochures, otherwise weighted by the geodes, flapped in the breeze like tiny wings. She paused Murat 1993 and took out the earbuds. Quiet.

Breathed.

Counted.

Chanted.

Emptied her mind, that roomful of errant, niggling, wandering thoughts, bustling and hustling to get her attention like the stateroom sequence in *A Night at the Opera*, a hundred characters all trying to enter at once; the conscious mind beckoning them on like Groucho ordering room service. How to beat these pesky thoughts? Let the people, the ideas, the images cruise on back out the door without engaging with them.

Button, floating and painless, accessed the transcendent for a period of non-time measured only by how much shadow of the Confederate obelisk had lengthened once she again opened her eyes.

Her ear canals felt stuffed with sticky, xanthous wax; the slicing wind made her throat hurt. Worse, her back and side, hurting like mad. Sick of manhandling the E-Z Up. And how at first she'd said, this daily exertion will put some meat on me. Put some of this missing weight back on, but with muscle. Instead, only soreness every night verging on white-hot pain. She kept her discomforts to herself. Medicated with cannabinoids and now black market opioids. It was chill.

Which she needed as the day progressed, dealing with a waking nightmare that unfolded after being triangulated by two troubling personalities: first the oleaginously pious Cole Breedlove, and later the epic appearance of world-class channeler and weirdo Howdy Shull. At least Christy and Newbie had been MIA since the confrontation in the yard. Had maybe taken the bossman's advice to heart and vamoosed from the E-C.

She tooted her pocket vape and tried to project love and trust into the void of the universe, to blaze with inner light and ward off the various elementals and archonic actors she could sense vibrating just outside the frame of ordinary sensation. It wouldn't be enough.

◉◉✳

A TWELVE-PASSENGER CHURCH VAN WITH THE SHRILL SHRIEK OF A SLIPPING FAN BELT rumbled around the corner from Congress Street and slowed as it passed. Pale ovals of faces peered out at her from within the smoky window tinting. Farther up the block the vehicle maneuvered sideways into the oversized handicapped space alongside the green facing Cecil Waugh's tattoo empire. The driver, deacon Cole Breedlove, in trying to nose-in rather than parallel park provoked a slapstick comedy sequence of backing in and out; a war of inches between the chipped, royal blue curb and the tires of the van.

Button, achy and missing Heather and feeling colder, texted her great love a series of hearts and other happy emoticons while watching as the group of middle-aged men, paunches stretching taut the buttons on shirts and coats, disembarked their chariot of fire. The men, bearing Bibles and colorful soft drinks they tipped up and gurgled as they approached across the green, were all frowning.

Button, smiling, stepped out from behind her table and waited while they assembled in a tight knot on the sidewalk in front of her pop-up. Their heads bowed, the oldest of the group, the Reverend Duson Mire, lead a quiet prayer that Button, her ears still ringing from the Phish jams she'd blasted, couldn't quite discern.

At the benediction's conclusion the youngest of the group, a slender teenage boy, approached her. His countenance pale and freckled and already with thinning hair on a ginger pate, a pressed pink Oxford tucked into creased charcoal trousers and with polished brown brogans on long feet, he appeared in a stage of awkward adolescent development to which Button could relate.

In a Carolina accent thick as they come: "Will you pray with us?"

"Pray for you? Sure."

"I said with us. Not for us."

"I was praying earlier—I call it meditation."

"We ain't accepting no New Age nonsense, and we don't need you to pray none for us."

"Is that right."

"Oh, no—you shan't bother. We'll pray for ourselves."

"It all starts. With the individual's. Commitment to faith."

Suspicious. "*Ah*-men to that. Are you saved, then?"

"Sure."

"Then you won't mind that we're here to preach the Lord's gospel."

"I'd be a hypocrite. To object."

"That's right!" As though he'd hard-won a major concession. "You're durn right you would be. So—go ahead."

"Go ahead and what?"

"Object."

"But—I don't."

"But you won't pray with us."

"Depends on whom we're praying to. And about what."

The others gathered in closer, black-bound bibles held at their hips like sidearms. The breeze, dry and cool, kicked up and made their topcoats ripple. Cole winked at her. Of course—he'd put them up to this. But the oldschool preaching outside The Dixiana hadn't happened in a long time, and most of the men were elderly. "Eternal salvation. That's what we're praying to God about."

"What if you're prayers. Should be directed inward instead of outward?"

"*Heresy*," a voice from the back of the group called. "Amen," another said.

The boy continued. "You can pray with us, if you choose. But sure—always pray for yourself first. That's who I see needs praying. Whose soul needs a personal visit from Jesus Christ himself."

"You mustn't worry. About the disposition. Of my soul."

Eyes bugging, the boy lunged and stabbed a digit in her face. "I *will* pray for your soul, ma'am. And you can't stop me."

Withdrawing from his aggression, she said, "Here's where. I think. You guys are." Long pause, a pernicious tickle in her throat, coughing and choking out the words. "Wrong. To bully me like this."

They waited. The teen's eyes blazed. She got her throat cleared.

"Tell her why we ain't wrong, Enoch." Cole Breedlove, unctuous and grinning, loomed over his shoulder. "Tell the little rebel here whom the righteous serve."

"Hold that thought." Button beamed loved to them all. Felt no animosity from their vibrations of confrontation, only kinship. Emerging souls, all seeking the light. "Let me lay this on y'all: The masters teach. That a life of service. Is the key to the lock. On the doorways. To heaven. And that you should pray, all right. But to relieve the suffering of others—never for yourself."

"And why is that, young lady." Reverend Mire, squinting and puckered with displeasure.

"Because hu-man does not know. What is best for him. Or her. Only the gods know."

"Blasphemer. There's but one true God."

"It's only. An idea. I'm laying on you. Don't gotta worry. She doesn't mind. Us invoking her. This kind of—of philosophizing—badinage—" Coughing like crazy, sipping water, her throat on fire. "I'm down with it."

"*She?*" Enoch's face turned inside out. "The Hades you say."

Led by Cole Breedlove, who shot his eyes all around the perimeter of the green looking for an audience, the prayerful men spread out and began preaching en masse at her, which was the best way she could put it. Not *to* her as a person. They formed a rough semicircle around the pop-up, their voices calling across the expanse of grass, their hands and Bibles gesturing toward Head Trauma and back to The Dixiana at the far end, and the courthouse plaza to the north, the highway bypass to the south. An all-points bulletin about the good news going out to the entire sinful township. She got it. Could take a page, et cetera. Shout it from the rooftops, your truth.

Her wide-angle lens, racking out of focus. Sitting back down. Feeling exhausted.

The Reverend Mire, the ostensible leader, lingering and glaring. "See? It pains you to hear the true word of God revealed. You must repent, young lady."

"Why now, Rev? Why today?"

"Because if they let you have your say, then we shall have ours."

"Nobody said. That you couldn't. Have your say. And nobody stopped you before. Not even Rabbit Pettus."

"True; god rest his ornery, rascally old soul. But the works to be done now? At this critical time? To counter these falsehoods that you've been allowed to spread here in Tillman Falls about the world, all these things—questioning 9/11, my god, it's treasonous—call upon us to act. It's the time of year when we celebrate the birth of our savior. When we bask in the glory of his truth. This is an abomination, this literature of yours." A slashing, aggressive gesture across the colorful field of her pamphlets and DVDs in white paper sleeves. "This hooey you're spreading? It's corrupting the minds of folks old and young."

"Facts about factory farming, its consequences to our bodies and the biosphere, as well as spiritually?" Spittle flew; her mind clicked into overdrive. "About nutrition? About methane releases from underneath melting arctic ice compounding the problem of climate change, perhaps exponentially? About the 'safety' of nuclear power? Fuel rods, hot spewing rods of death, sitting in swimming pools on top of buildings in dangerous earthquake zones? Death-traps that will last a hundred thousand years, Reverend? What about Fukushima? About the radiation that's been swirling around this planet for years now? How about the dying starfish and the mottle dolphins washing up on the beaches in California? How many endangered species disappeared from the earth today, this week, this month?" Her rhetorical energy felt as though it were a column of white light emanating from her midsection. "What about all that above ground testing? *Where did the radiation go?*"

"How in the sam-hill should I know? Ain't nobody sick from it, girl."

"Where's all this cancer coming from?"

"It's the devil's work, girl—cancer is sin become manifest. That's what it is."

"Cancer is sin? That's a compelling metaphor."

The others preached on, their cacophonous explications of scripture echoing and drawing onlookers into windows and doorways. Mire said, "God don't work in no metaphors, ma'am. He works in plain truth."

In simmering anger with which she grappled to stay detached and obser-vant, Button found more breath and voice than she'd produced since the drive into the mountains with Roy. "Did you know another hundred tons of radioactive water leaked from Fukushima just this week?" She coughed, hack-ing. Dropped down into her camp chair. Sucked water from her Camelbak bottle, almost choking on it. "And look at the streaks that jet left earlier—

they've spread out. Into a gauzy scrim. Covering the whole sky. Blocking the sun. What is this particulate matter? Why are they filtering the sunlight? As far as we're concerned the sun is our god, sir. And we're blocking her out. Humanity has concealed itself within a caul of hubris, the face of humankind underneath twisted and scarred by madness in the form of civilization. Look up, sir. If you want to see what sin looks like, direct your eyes heavenward. If you please."

Squinting, Reverend Mire glanced up. Solaris glowed white, a hazy disk with a corona that looked greasy, refracting not in the full spectrum of color but an oily shimmer of red-brown-black. "Ain't nothing but ice crystals coming out the back of planes. You been watching too many YouTubes. Seen one the other day myself, where this fellow claims the sun looks whiter now than it did in our youth, when it burned yellow to gold all day. I have to admit it made me search my own memories. But it being on the internet, I know it was just made-up foolishness."

"But—how do you know that's all it is?"

"Because they'd tell us if they was spraying something up yonder. You ain't got no faith in nothing, you little communist. Yeah, I said it. You think I done forgot what y'all done to us in Vietnam? I know all about it. And aboveground testing?" He shook his head. "Here's what I know, young heathen woman: I served this country, in Korea fighting the cursed mongol huns. Everything we done in America was for you and your kind, the lessor races of the world. Every war is to preserve what we are, and who we are, and how we are, but also to make it all better for you little monkeys overseas. When we went to Vietnam, like your Daddy done, we went for you. To save all of you. And look at what you got out of the deal, all this American wealth and splendor. You don't deserve a dollar of it, I tell you." He pounded the table. Geodes leapt atop flyers. "Not dollar one. God help your thieving unpatriotic souls, every one of you foreigners taking advantage of our freedoms, and our tax dollars, and our god-given social programs."

"*I was conceived and born here in Edgewater County,*" she tried to shout, but couldn't find the breath. Her throat felt shredded, vocal fry for the ages, a harsh whisper. "I'm not Vietnamese."

"See? God has silenced you." Duson Mire leered at her. "Put that in your hippie pipe and smoke it."

Hot tears stung. She tried to smile at him and project love. It t'weren't easy. She straightened brochures where he'd unsettled them.

Cole Breedlove, flitting his gaze over every few seconds to make sure she sat watching them preach, gestured for Mire to withdraw and rejoin the good news ring. Fiery epithets and admonitions flew from lips full and pink, calls to salvation issuing from the depths of substantial diaphragms and booming back from the façades of the town's merchants and the municipal building looming over all, its sunstruck glass panels reflecting sunlight from a break in the persistent contrails.

The light reminded her of driving through downtown Atlanta on the way to a summer Phish date at Lakewood Amphitheater, a literally hot Fourth of July show featuring a wicked first set cow-funk 'Story of the Ghost.' Two-hundred micrograms of acid had kicked in before they'd even gotten to the lot to sling burritos, and the sunlight from the shimmering, blank faces of the skyscrapers along Peachtree Street had seemed a twinkling astral ballet, bright white light blazing right between her eyes, images she would recall while later raging to Page on the lawn of the massive music venue, a sacred space filled with supplicants for the most part unaware of the vibrational power inherent in the ritual to which they gave their hedonistic, primal energy.

A presence, approaching. Her entire left side, tingling. Cramping with pain. Button generated love and optimism and happiness, opened her heart chakra, pulled in white healing light from the ever-present connection to Source. Felt the ache diminish.

The presence, however, still approached, now accompanied by footsteps. Pounding, hurtling across the grassy green. A purposeful *thump thump thump thump thump.*

Sport sandals.

Roy.

Appearing at her tent, his aura, blazing in metallic amber—the color of drying blood on the blade of a warrior knight, his anger stoked and pulsing with hot febrile irritation. Leaning toward blackest rage. Cartoon steam boiling out of red ears. Seething.

Oh, no.

"Why. Are these cracker sky-pilots. Hollering like coyotes. Out here on my town green."

Button cleared her scratchy throat. "They. Have a right. To sell their schpiel."

Roy's vibration, dangerous. His fingers, dancing down at his hips and wanting to curl into fists. He had told her how both their grandfathers, and by extension Roy himself, felt about these yahoos bothering bar patrons on Friday nights.

Interfering with commerce? Not done.

DON'T, Button projected to her friend. PLEASE DON'T GO NUCLEAR.

"Ya wanna know what this is?" he shouted, waving his arms like an umpire. "It's disruptive to freaking business. *You have sinned before God today.*"

"That's what council. Worried. My tent would be."

"But it hasn't been. This, though? A public nuisance. *Against the law,*" a declaration.

"I agree to disagree."

Roy produced his iPhone with a flourish, the latest model. "Hey now, preachers," he mocked over their din. "I think I can get me some real rockin' third-party arbitration in on this. Settle it without firing a shot."

His threat made them all preach louder in a round-robin of holy admonition and penitence before the Lord thy God.

Button, a boa constrictor of worry wrapping around her midsection. Fighting it. Flurrying her freckled hands. "Wait, 'firing a shot'? Roy—you should never say an idea like that aloud. Not in a crowd. Not these days."

"True gospel. But, settle down. I have people to handle this foolishness." Roy scowled and stuck his finger in one ear, pressed the iPhone to the other, elbows aloft. "Hey yeah, Truesdale? Roy Pettus. That's right. I got some disorderly conduct action for you. Like, an active situation type-deal." Listening and uh-huhing. "Oh, fudge. Really? Damn."

Button noted a serious shift in his energy, face now a mask of disbelief and fresh concern. Something wasn't right. "What is it?"

"Well, no—ain't as important as all that." A pause. "Yeah, no, yeah, right. We'll keep our eyes peeled for that a-hole. Roger and out."

Button, hearing far-off sirens, stood reminded of the old wah-wah aural hallucinations accompanying a nitrous oxide binge. "They're coming that fast? About the preachers?"

Roy started to ring off, but told Truesdale to hold it. Squinted in distaste past the shouting men of God.

She saw what caught Roy's attention: Howdy Shull, marching toward them across the green, swinging his Canada Dry Ginger Ale bottle.

What next? This was turning into a circus.

Wait:

Roy E. Pettus.

Looking frightened.

"Timmy—dude. Howdy's coming right toward me. Like, here and now."

Button, perceiving his terror as her own, suffered a frigid wave surging through her abdomen. The cramping, returning. She hadn't felt afraid in so long, since she assisted her father with his transit out of dimensionality. She'd forgotten the juice that came with giving into the fear. The jolt of the adrenaline. No wonder the archons fed on this dark, powerful energy.

Howdy, howling and crying and approaching from the alley beside Head Trauma, onto the curb next to the church van. His hair all corkscrewed. A flapping flannel robe. Boxer briefs. Shoeless. His feet, filthy and bloodied, as though he'd walked over crushed glass to get here. Angling toward her tent.

At his lurching, shuffling appearance, the street preachers all fell silent and turned.

"It's Isis." Howdy, braying forlorn and broken like a heartsick goose. "It is she who's died this time instead of Osiris. The pieces of her body, oh, lord, they've been scattered. Scattered along the river. Please, I beg of you," to the merciless sky above, "I need the sunlight to stay so that I might search the riverbank and find her missing pieces-parts. She must be whole for the journey. Isis, she has been pro*faned*," he mewled in slobbering grief. "Pro-*faned*."

Roy, turning in a circle with palms outstretched, rotating between Button and the approaching madman. "Everybody hold their current position."

"What's going on?"

Under his breath: "Howdy's really done it this time. That's what." His energy red-lining, Roy's aura pulsed with an ugly, ochre glow not unlike the sadly unnatural, refracted sunlight leaching through the greasy scrim of the contrails. "Finally gone all the way round the bend. Surprise-me-not."

Roy moved toward the weeping Howdy Shull, went into jocular mode. "Isis, ya say? Not Captain Marvel's super-chick companion on Saturday mornings. Is that what we need? A superhero? Lucky day—you're looking at one, you butthole," yanking a thumb at his chest. "And I'm apprehending you."

Howdy, crying and hollering about Isis and pieces. The sirens, approaching.

"Howdy, yo. What's shakin'?" Button, in her most gentle and loving of voices, the one she used with her mother and Grandpa Burnie when trying to cajole or mollify. "Whatever it is, we can fix it."

"*Not this time. Now stay back.*" Roy, ordering and holding one hand out to her and another toward Howdy, pivoting to keep the approaching Tillman Falls eccentric at arm's length; also hissing like a cat to shoo the street preachers, who approached and regathered in a tight grouping.

"The devil's in that man," Enoch the young firebrand called out for all to hear. "He needs saving."

What of Howdy? Terrible, even by his standards: drool streaming from his mouth. Dark stains on his hands as well as his feet. Underpants soaked with urine. Smeary fingerprints all over the Canada Dry bottle. His fingers, covered in dried blood.

Worst of all, his weeping. Who'd ever seen Howdy Shull cry?

The madman, cradling his bottle and having a wide-eyed moment of lucidity at the sheer number of folks standing around, pulled up short of the gathering. Took the cap off the two-liter of pop to have a sip, she assumed. But instead of tipping it up, he held it and squeezed. Put his lips on the lid. Inhaled.

Howdy, acting out a bizarre ritual. The vapors of the ginger ale?

"What the hell's. He got in there?"

Roy, shaking his head. "Dunno, but we all need to stay back."

Howdy collapsed onto a bench. Repeated his breathing ritual. Moaned.

"He's huffing, y'all buncha dummies." Enoch, impatient with everyone. "Don't you unwashed heathens know nothing about today's misguided and forsaken youth? He's got nail polish remover in there. Turpentine. Or perhaps even gasoline."

"Howdy *Shull*," Roy said with judgmental disapproval. "That's raw, dude. Whatever happened to toking on reefer and kicking back to some Zeppelin or BÖC? Huh?"

"I think you mean BTO," one of the other preachers, a fellow middle-aged gent, said with considerate sincerity. "Bachman Turner Overdrive."

"No; I mean BÖC, you blithering hayseed. And listen. All due respect, but when I need to hear from you people, I'll pull the little strings dangling from the backs of your narrow necks."

The screaming sirens seemed to arrive from every direction at once, waves of tires screeching. Doors slamming. Shouting.

Button, standing next to Roy. A protective arm, draped around her. It felt good. "Something terrible is happening."

"That's a negatory, Commander Spock. Nothing but Howdy getting taken into custody. They got this."

As police cars continued to arrive from every direction, sliding into place and disgorging shouting officers brandishing drawn weapons, Howdy huffed his fumes, tipping his head back as though gargling. Gas went everywhere. He collapsed, dropping the bottle on the ground by his horrid feet, nails thickened and discolored, soles scarred and bloody.

The cops, deployed behind their cars. Lt. Truesdale, in plain clothes, called out using his car speaker. "You people over there, get back. Howard Shull, do not move. You are under arrest."

Howdy, sat up, sudden, and shouted in a stentorian oration that made him sound like the Deep South's greatest Shakespearean actor. "Isis. Isis has been killed. The soldiers, they came and ravaged her. T'was supposed to be me taken and sacrificed," he wailed, rising to unsteady feet. "Osiris. Pieces by the river. Not Isis. *Never Isis.*"

"On the ground, Shull. Hands where we can see them."

"He ain't armed, Timmy." Roy, hollering and cupping his mouth. "He's just crocked."

"Pettus," his voice echoing, "you and Button stay back. You've done enough."

Roy, irritated, gritted teeth: "Don't you tell me what to do, lad."

In the next seconds the scene wrung itself out with an awful suddenness. Howdy, who'd appeared on the verge of passing out, instead leapt from his bench, grabbing the leaking bottle and squeezing it to his body. As he lumbered toward an array of gun muzzles a spray of gas erupted, soaking through his threadbare robe and shorts.

"Stop—!"

"Back—!"

"Hands—!"

"Down—!"

He lurched back, shrieking like a madman.

Back to the tent.

Toward her and Roy.

A fusillade of shots, dozens, rang out. Everyone scattered, preachers and Roy and Button, all leaping and hitting the deck. Sparks flew from concrete. A bullet whizzed by Button's face, a hot bee. Time slowed to a crawl. Truesdale, high-voiced, called to hold-fire, hold-fire, goddammit.

She fell and rolled in time to see Howdy erupting into flames, a brilliant orange fire, head to toe. Dancing a skeletal, smoking puppet's jig until collapsing. A heap, twitching and horrible. The smell of sour meat charring too long on a Sunday afternoon grill wafted.

Button, sucking in her breath at a vision, a flash-frame: she had glimpsed in the dying flames a woman's face.

Laughing.

Beckoning.

A holy ghost—an evil one.

Agatha? For real?

Shit, dude.

Button retched and heaved up green tea from earlier, a foamy spume out of her mouth and nose.

As Howdy's body stilled, the police approached with their guns drawn and hollering in scary Batman voices for the steaming corpse not to move, to put its hands where they could see them, and so on.

"Honey, are you all right?" Roy, his own pallor gone white as death. *"Button?"*

"I'm—unhurt." He helped her up.

Roy admonished the cops. "Boy, glad no bystanders got murdered in error, you hotheads. What in the actual fudge, Timmy?"

Truesdale, only now holstering his sidearm. "A suggestion: secure that shit, Mr. Pettus."

"Howdy was unarmed."

"No one knew that."

Oh, she felt Roy think. *Am I going to put you in your place, you fucking janitor.* As clear as though he'd said it aloud. But to the cop he said, "Oakley's gonna have a fit. God have mercy on whoever has to explain this one to him."

And now Roy puked as well, heaving up his lunch while holding onto one pole of her pop-up. Everyone in the area, and all at the same moment, seemed overcome. No one there, she suspected, had ever smelled a burning human body.

◉◎✺

EMTS ARRIVED AND TOSSED A FIELD BLANKET OVER THE SMOLDERING REMAINS, investigators from State Law Enforcement Division and the FBI took about forty-five minutes to arrive. Lockdown, statements, serious faces, notes in little notebooks, whole routine.

The ambulance had roared up from over on Congress Street behind the old courthouse with its towering oaks, two of which were diseased and slated to be removed, a controversial story of late. Yellow police tape everywhere. Cops questioned onlookers who video'd the proceedings with their devices.

"You didn't have to shoot him." As he spoke to Truesdale, Roy's closed body language and piercing, accusatory eye contact with the officer depicted disgust and belittlement. "And if y'all don't start keeping those popguns put away, I—before I—I'm gonna—we're all gonna—oh, never mind."

"That's more like it. The man's covered in his sister's blood. Case closed."

"All right. But still."

Thank you, Button beamed to Roy. *Dial it back.* She went to the pop-up, eased down into the camp chair. Hid her face. Processed what happened.

"She's in shock," she heard Roy say. "Had a premonition about all this."

"No shit? Always was a little freak."

Lt. Truesdale, marching over to meet the newly arrived Sheriff Oakley, with a look on his face like Tillman Falls's next murderer—as Roy predicted, the top cop demanded answers about who had allowed this debacle to transpire, in his words, on an otherwise pleasant and normal Edgewater County afternoon.

Upon hearing the report of Everlynne Shull's alleged murder, Oakley's tone changed. "I've been waiting for that asshole to hurt somebody for years."

Button, shouting with all the air she could muster. "He wasn't armed. They didn't have to kill him."

"Allyson?" Timmy Truesdale, who had had a crush on her in eighth grade, was probably the last person alive who called her by her first name. "Leaving the policing to the po-po, hippie-chick. If you don't mind."

Something wrong here. Even if Howdy had killed his sister? Button had seen the face of the true animating spirit behind the act.

A lover of fire, and vengeance.

Agatha of Aberdeen.

No doubt in Button's mind; the notorious specter of Forest Knoll Garden cemetery turned out real. The real source of all the fires that'd haunted the town for two centuries, now. Rabbit always said she was, and how important to tend to her grave, a chore he had passed on to Button and which she had ignored for months.

Ah-ha.

To Button, an adept initiated in such esoteric matters, the ghost's meddling in earthly affairs presented no big whoop: reality existed on many levels about which most people, if they only took the time and acquired the discipline, could receive the hints and outright proofs that Button and others like her had obtained. That an apparent actual ghost 'haunted' Edgewater County and favored consumption of the flesh by fire, and represented what Duson Mire and his cadre of preachers might call a demon, surprised her not a little; not at all.

At this point, what *would* surprise a woman like Button Sykes?

Not much, anymore. Not in a universe of infinite possibilities. Not when she was about to be surfing the dirt, as Roy's grandfather would put it.

When she found she hadn't the strength to get out of her camp chair to go and make a statement about what she saw, she worried that her disease was progressing faster than she could forestall its effects, then felt wrong for worrying and admonished herself over that, broke down and took an Oxycontin prescribed to her grandfather to help with his back pain, and thanked the God to whom the preachers prayed she had Roy Pettus in her life.

As the afternoon and investigation waned, he helped her break down the information clearinghouse and stash the gear into Piper the Subaru Baja for what she already knew, or rather Walfredo had whispered this morning, would be the final time.

Howdy's remains had been taken away, Dobbs had gotten the last of his photos and interviews, all the other merchants had wandered and stood behind the yellow tape, news media from Columbia arrived in vans with satellite dishes, and Roy had finished cussing the cops—for now. Button thought that this must be as dramatic as life could get on the green in Tillman Falls. It'd all unfolded. It was still unfolding. But if reality planned to get any more nightmarish than Howdy Shull dancing into death before her eyes, it would do well to leave her out of it.

At least after she got her strength back later she could manicure the area around Agatha's grave. Rabbit always said that was the bargain. She still had not gotten to it since the previous time she remembered the cemetery duty. Button beamed 'sorry' to Howdy Shull's troubled spirit, apologizing that she had been remiss in allowing Agatha to become unsettled and angry. Had forsaken the doctrine and ritual handed down by the old honkytonk man. It wouldn't happen again.

GOOCH

Keeping an eye on the office while Dobbs went to see about the ruckus downstairs, Gooch nodded off reading the *New York Times* on his computer. He all but toppled over, spilling damnable, staining coffee everywhere—on his khakis, on his taupe colored office chair, the floor. Like piss.

Thank god his bladder infection had cleared up. Dobbs helped him remember to take the meds. Had seemed irritated at first today when Gooch showed up to work, his old assistant sighing and helping him to his workstation, giving him a link to current wire stories for him to parse for propagation on the paper's website.

Sirens.

The damn sirens had awakened him. Another meth lab probably burned a mobile home. Again.

Meth.

Meds.

Urination.

When Gooch ambled back from the restroom, he found his coffee cup on its side on the floor, but no coffee stains to be seen. But it tumbled out of his hand! The coffee, it'd gone everywhere.

Or had there been coffee at all?

Or sirens, for that matter?

He peeked out the dusty blinds. Police, everywhere.

A knot of men standing in front of Button Sykes's silly little pop-up tent. Firecrackers going off. Movement; bodies flying every which way. Howdy

Shull, it now looked like, doing a mad flaming dance on the sidewalk. Poof. Gray-black smoke from the body lying on the green. Policemen, their guns drawn, creeping forward. Shouting.

In the smoke loomed a face, a chiaroscuro image, fleeting, gone.

A laughing, vaporous woman.

An hallucination. Or else, what? A ghost?

Like Agatha of Aberdeen?

She'd been on his mind, that was all. Research he'd done for his stupid novel he wouldn't ever get around to writing, researching the Sunbury School Fire and being led to many other fires going back to Agatha's own self-immolation in the old township by the river.

Ghost stories were for children and halfwits.

Hallucination, then?

If true, the ramifications were grim. Gooch needed help. His condition, worsening. It couldn't wait. Now, instead of being mildly forgetful, where ought to be only a peaceful December afternoon before his aging, blurry eyes, he glimpsed a series of imaginary scenes.

This loss of cognition, of dignity? Damn it all, but the news coming over the wire made him think such problems were going around like a virus. Not only in Edgewater County—Gooch meant everywhere. If you could believe the news anymore. As unlikely as it seemed, Donald Trump would be president soon, the way the media were selling the guy.

The Gooches of the world couldn't afford to ignore the stories the public wanted most. They had to sell papers—or get clicks—any way they could. And Trump sold papers. Always did. Came out of nowhere in the 80s to become "America's Billionaire." Helluva story. Dereliction of duty not to report it in full detail.

Whole morning had been like this—wrestling with philosophical conundrums alongside trying to remember his own name. Earlier, before his brief nap, he imagined Dobbs saying the police reported a murder over on Whaley Way. Nonsense. Nothing like that happened in Tillman Falls. Not in Gooch's neighborhood, anyway.

Jesus, let me go back to sleep so I can hurry and wake from this silly-ass dream. Hello—reality? Anyone home? Feel free to return anytime you like.

ROY E. PETTUS AND PHIL
WEBHANNET

Only days after the incident, with Christmas approaching and stories being pushed about holiday shopping rather than distasteful tragedies, all the TV news people packed up and left Tillman Falls. Any lingering controversy over whether Howdy Shull should have been executed on the town green—the facts had been clear; guilty of murder, but unarmed—faded after a brief flurry of pro and con in the news and around dinner tables, but only in a regional sense. The poignance of this sad figure's life ending as a live-action roasting in front of God and everybody at the hands of armed authorities, why, it barely moved the needle outside South Carolina.

Another police shooting.

Another dead doper.

Yawn.

You and Creedence, on one of your infrequent calls, argued about the incident. A killer, she said. At least we don't have to pay to keep him in jail.

"It was unwarranted, excessive force," as you insisted. "I was there."

You needed the truth about your evolving relationship with your wife, but could never quite get it out of her. Only noncommittal, we-both-have-so-much-to-work-out-yet.

"Concentrate on your granddaddy's music festival," she advised. "I got the CBSI under control. And me too, for once. Trying to get used to that feeling."

"So what's to figure out? And when?"

"Oh, honey—don't. I can't. I have to go to a meeting. We'll talk again."

"But, when?"

"I don't know. Soon."

Something squirrelly happening here.

The answer? Espionage.

Best coin you've dropped in ages: The thousand a month you send Officer Phil Webhannet of the Sedge Island security forces—a little extra scratch to keep tabs on your estranged spouse—has provided you with detailed email reports, disciplined and formatted to a T and chock-full of information. Once a week he sends reports, on Sunday mornings like a liturgical sermon full of facts rather than superstition.

She's doing wonderfully, he says. Progressing. Confident. Happy. Alone most of the time. No visitors at home; no nights out in Bayfront or anywhere else. *A respectable, sober and sedate member of the community*, the last report concluded. *I'm certain you will be proud.*

Yet you still want more. What highlights she has in her hair. The extra piercings in her ears. That she's talking about getting a tattoo—um, no; okay, maybe, but only under the supervision of a professional you trust like Cecil Waugh, and boy-oh-boy how you'd never believe you could feel that way about him. Color of her toenails, two of which are thickened from the fungal infections folks get when shuffling around in a house of twelve cats, spores from their feces littering the floor alongside the gray corporate sand of their sanitation system.

His reply? No nail polish. Natural.

Her general attitude? If she says anything about you? Tone? Content? Additional remarks?

Not much, he writes back. *Sorry.*

Hungering for more, a phone call to Phil in order—like when you pick up the horn for Oakley or his man Truesdale, though your relationship with both of them has cooled. A potential problem.

No matter. If necessary, you will put your own sheriff in office in the next election cycle. Oakley isn't even an Edgewater native. He can be gone in an instant. Your intelligence has revealed any number of compromising positions you can and will exploit, if pushed to do so. Politicians like Southern sheriffs and state house representatives came cheap.

◉①✸

ONE GOOD ASPECT OF THE HOWDY SHULL INCIDENT? MEDIA COVERAGE INCLUDED tons of B-roll shots featuring The Dixiana sign, and damn if Trudy doesn't report that business since then has been extra strong. Couldn't keep the old girl down if you tried.

Unfortunately it's been weird with Trudy since the return echo of sex you enjoyed. Her husband seems sick. It's the holidays. If you need to discuss the relationship further—and you're not sure you want to; catharsis achieved—it will have to wait.

The iconic sign, due to come down for clean-up and repair. It would be costly, and take time. In the meantime, you'll pay to have a temporary banner hung to let everyone finally know that other changes are coming. Even if at first the exteriors didn't much reflect what occurred beneath the surface, inside, a rehabilitation of all that worked, re-imagining of what no longer served the common good.

And, yeah: to last until long after you are gone.

◉◔❋

WEBHANNET RETURNS YOUR CALL ON THE FIRST BOUNCE. "NOT SURE WHAT ELSE I can tell you, sir, that the emails don't already say."

"So, she's happy? My girl looks good?"

The young cop's clipped answers, no more edifying than the emails. "She's productive, talkative. Seems to enjoy her work, sir. And her cats. All I can tell you."

"But—do y'all chat about—the future? Her future?"

At first, he's as silent and inscrutable as the 2001 monolith. "Not sure what you mean, Mr. Pettus."

"Roy."

"Mr. Roy."

You hold back from a more violent tone trying to slip out. "Call me Roy, dude. We're friends. Forget the money I send you. Friends. That's a favor between friends. The money. To keep doing a swell job not only for me, or her, but everyone on the island."

"I appreciate it—Roy."

You're glad; tell him so.

"But I think I get what you're saying. And if you want an honest answer?"

Wiggling antennae: "Why wouldn't I want that?"

"You would; which is my point." Seems to gather his words. "We don't discuss personal matters. Like your marriage."

"Check. What, then?"

Small talk, he says. The coffee shop. The island. The weather. Christmas shopping. "I accompanied her to buy a few gifts. Just the other day."

"Did you, now."

"She asked."

"I see." Sounds more like fraternization than keeping an eye-on. "Snag anything nice?"

"Certainly. But I better not spoil any surprises."

"Couldn't have that."

This strikes you as positive. Super-positive. Warm inside; she got you a gift. Warm like when you meditate, which over the last couple of weeks has become interesting. Time going by different. Thirty minutes one morning had felt like ten.

Next she says she wants to talk to you—Button, that is—about the chakras, and opening them. You asked if she meant opening like cans of cat food, which she chuckled and said, um, no.

The holidays. You and Burnie and Manny T, out there in the woods in the Victorian while Button, off to the snow-dusted blue pyramid to spend Christmas with Heather, her great love. To recover from witnessing Howdy's horrific execution and immolation. Meanwhile, you along with Jasper and Letty would take care of Uncle Burnie, an impromptu family here in the backlands of Edgewater County close to the winter river; cold, but at least no snow in the forecast. Not in the midlands of South Carolina. Rare, even in the worst of winters.

Maybe you'll take your own solo hiking trip. Nothing to stop you. Search online for a cabin to rent. Get your head together. The money to Webhannet, a way of holding onto her, albeit grappling, it seems, with slippery hands.

You must consider the possibility it would never be right again, your marriage.

But with resources like your'n, what didn't constitute possibility?

The Spotted Banana™ largesse.

The marshside mansion.

The portfolio.

The Carolina Beanery Sedge Island.

The Victorian, a creampuff, sitting next to your boyhood home. Ten acres of Carolina pine- and hardwoods. River access, if you didn't mind hiking across the old grazing land down to the Glade.

The Dixiana.

But your wife, neither a business nor a property. A human being, working on herself. And if you've grown at all, you must acknowledge that forcing matters will never work; and got ya into trouble in the first place. You hope Button would be gratified by this blazing eruption of self awareness.

A Christmas tree gets put up; a fire stoked in the fireplace. Cinnamon candles burning. A bottle of Crown Royal you allowed yourself, shared with Manny and Jasper, sitting around the dining room playing cards and getting vaped on the good weed. Old records playing from in the family room, a wall of disks, so many amazing discoveries; jazz, blues, old-timey music, some on 78s from before the beginning of time like banjo-picking preacher Buell Kazee. Your Pa-paw often quoted the picker as having said that before modern psychoanalysis and other 'pseudo-science' regarding mental health, music had been humanity's therapy, a tool for adjusting and maintaining emotional equilibrium.

Roots music. Vibrations. Waves. You would discuss it all with Button.

The food, delicious, came courtesy of Manny's joint, brought over by Ahmad. He stays to eat with you, quiet and tense before heading over to the old house to do what he does—watch TV.

You never turn on the sets here, not since your Mee-maw passed. They're not HD, anyway. You never went through with upgrading them. Who the fudge cares.

◎①❋

YOU MISS BUTTON, WHO HAS WITHDRAWN INTO AN IMPENETRABLE FUNK. SHE hasn't been the same since Howdy's execution. All she can talk about now is how it's a goddamned police state. None of you need wait for the radiation from Fukushima to finish you—they'll shoot everyone down in the street like dogs. Turn their super-weapons on you all. Burn this freedom-loving American culture to the ground.

You reminded her of her own warning to you about using such destructive language.

Yeah, she said. I know. Just blowing off steam.

When you last parted the poor dear had seemed downcast, frail and anxious. Worrisome. Stress can be a killer, and you should know: between the aching scar tissue around your healing clavicle and PTSD effects from both the Rico car chase and Howdy shoot-out, you stalk the empty house with your shoulders resting somewhere up around your ears. No way to unwind; the weed only making you more paranoid and freaked.

Meditation. You would get back to it. A practice, as your pal keeps reminding. And you ain't been practicing like you should, beau. Meditation, and a soak in the garden tub you're pretty sure your grandparents never used, might not do the trick, but it's a start.

◎①❋

AFTER RINGING OFF WITH WEBHANNET YOU BUZZ CREEDENCE TO HEAR HER SWEET Southern drawl, try to get through a conversation without your own voice cracking and betraying your sorrow at being far away all the time, but she doesn't answer.

The fear nags that it can never be the same. A sense of loss. And grief.

Nothing Webhannet said makes you feel any better. No clarity. Only a terse recitation like a report from a bored Lieutenant at a stagnant front, no troop movements, few skirmishes: everyone's dug in, now.

Only for the time being. Something's major gonna shake loose. It's a feeling, but the signs seem clear: Howdy's death-scene, the end of Button's awareness campaign, The Dixiana build-out you will soon commence, and most of all, your series of personal losses. But a new year, it's dawning. It's the beginning of a new age.

Which means.

You will get this crap under control.

In a manner conclusive.

Don't tell Button Sykes, though—she'll only fuss at you for striving to achieve what she keeps telling you is impossible: nobody controls anything. You're like a fallen leaf gurgling down a wild river, at the mercy of the turbid, strangulated Sugeree. You ain't gonna control squat; the best you'll muster, and she does mean best, is going with that mysterious and desultory flow of energy.

So that's what you're gonna try to do.

Flow; go.

With your diligence and discipline, shouldn't be long now before all these nettlesome issues with your personal reality get worked out. Right? Damn straight. The world can count on you to drag yourself, and all of them, into a standing position, and on the wholesome path. You will forge ahead, making your presence known:

The lamplighter.

The master.

God's gift.

But to whom shall you turn for your guiding light? Creedence?

No. For once, an answer you already possess: Button. Your newest, best-est, and most trusted partner since those beloved childhood pals Devin and Dobbs. By far, dude.

Button Sykes forever. Yeah—a new mantra. It rolls off the tongue.

The Story Concludes

Dixiana
DARLING

CHARACTER GUIDE

POV Characters
(with supporting players)

ROY EARL PETTUS

Despite tremendous financial success, a lovely wife, and a wide-open future ahead for him, ROY EARL PETTUS (late 40s) suffers a midlife crisis of confidence and inwardly flails for purchase...but it's for good reason: When we meet him he's discovered his dream girl, Creedence, has been unfaithful. Not simply sexually—the letters he's read indicate more than a fling, rather a full-on love affair. At the same moment he gets news his grandfather has fallen ill, perhaps critically so. He flies home to Edgewater County, where he'll end up staying for some time and through quite a number of story lines, all of which revolve around his grandfather's honkytonk, The Dixiana, that Roy will find is now his to run. It's not a welcome inheritance — he blames The Dixiana for most of his childhood ills.

REYNOLDS ELDER 'RABBIT' PETTUS (also POV in *Dixiana* and *Dixiana Darling*) — 89, "father"/grandfather to Roy Earl, his presence hovers over the rest of the story, culminating as it does in a town music in his honor festival; 'Pa-Paw' to Roy

RUNELLE KITTERY PETTUS (POV in *Dixiana Darling*) — 88, "mother"/grandmother to Roy Earl, the Darling of The Dixiana, 'Mee-maw' to Roy. She calls her husband '**Rennie**'.

MERVIN PETTUS — a cousin, 40s, who attacks Roy over a dispute regarding Rabbit's estate (wife **CARLA MAE**, kids **DALE** and **DJ**). Grandson of Rabbit's brother Rutledge Pettus

RONALD EDWARD 'RONNIE ED' PETTUS — Roy Earl's father, long dead before the events of DIXIANA, a haunting presence: his father, like his grandfather in WW2, he served in war, Ronnie-Ed ends up giving his life in said service.

CLAUDIA BALLAHACK PETTUS — Roy Earl's mother, also deceased, a young waitress struggling along after the death of her equally young husband in Vietnam. Claudia, killed in what Roy Earl will find out was a car accident that also almost took his infant life.

ALLYSON BUTTON SYKES

Dreadlocked granddaughter of Burnham Sykes, this iconoclastic second principal character has already retreated to Tillman Falls well before the arrival of Roy E. Pettus, a family friend, obviously, owing to her grandfather's close friendship with Roy Earl. In her mid 30s and considering herself a failed writer, Button cares for her mother Tinky, left bereaved by the cancer-death of Button's father, as well as her grandfather. A new age devotee of the jam-band Phish, when we meet her Button has decided on a new mission in life: to protest the new nuclear reactors being built. Her plan of outreach? A good old fashioned American pamphleteering campaign on the town green. A lifelong outcast—a mix of ruddy Irish and Vietnamese, an odd physical combination—she is the story's heart, soul, and conscience.

BURNHAM 'BURNIE' SYKES (POV in *Dixiana Darling*) — 90, Rabbit Pettus's best friend for 75 years, a very important character to the overall arc of the story, and to Button and Roy personally. In the old days, Burnie's business success made much of everyone's reality possible

HENRIETTA 'HENNY' SYKES — Burnie's wife, dead for a number of years prior to present day narrative

THANH THI TRINH 'TINKY' SYKES — Vietnamese mother to Button and Thim, a nervous type, has panic, is medicated and near irrational, but as Button says, "she always was."

THIM SYKES — Button's older sister, and nothing like her boho younger sibling. An aide to Governor Sandra Three-Rivers, who has her eye on the U. S. Senate. Thim leaves the care of her mother and grandfather to Button.

BURTON 'BUDDY' SYKES (POV in *Dixiana Darling*) — father to Button, dead already prior to events of novel. The Vietnam vet who'd gone off to war with Ronnie Pettus, the one who'd returned sporting an Asian wife. He'd been a part of a unit that carried around the "backpack nuke" that could be used on short notice should President Nixon have wished to ramp up the firepower. Buddy died of cancer, possibly from his service in Vietnam, but also possibly due to his long career as an engineer at the Sugeree River Station.

CHELSEA COLETTE 'CREEDENCE' RUCKER-PETTUS

Roy's wife Creedence, 40ish (childhood initials CCR, nicknamed by her beloved late father for the 60s rock band Creedence Clearwater Revival) is in crisis as well: in love with another man but not out of love with Roy Earl, alcoholic, confused, stuck. She writes her journal in the form of endless letters to her brother Devin, missing and unheard from for 10 years—an inveterate drunk, likely long dead. Once the affair is discovered by Roy, however, reality comes crashing down, and so does her alcoholism.

> **DEVIN RUCKER** — vanished older brother to Creedence, and to whom she writes epistolary-style letters that provide exposition along with raw inner monologue
> **LIBBY MEADE** — Devin's college love, referred to in flashback only
> **EILEEN RUCKER** — mother, deceased, referred to on occasion, a former esteemed member of the Edgewater Ladies Munificence Society (ELMS)
> **DWIGHT RUCKER** — father, deceased, a town father who appears in flashback

BILL 'GOOCH' WIMMEL

Gooch Wimmel, the publisher and editor of the *Edgewater Advocate*, a once thrice-weekly paper now reduced to a weekly, is an aging, closeted gay who is lonely and unhappy about his waning influence in the town. He'd been a reporter and editor in big city newspapers for years, but found that as he aged, he longed for a more quiet and peaceful life. Working the crime beat in Atlanta left him cynical and burned out at a young age, and now in his late 60s, he suffers from severe memory issues and dementia; he keeps forgetting that he's already retired, and only helping out at the paper. Another man's the publisher now, and Gooch is supposed to be following his dream to write a great novel.

CHRISTOPHER 'CHRISTY' BEAUDOCK

Christy Beaudock has a heart filled with pain and hatred. A fat, unattractive kid with a girlie name, bullied, unhappy, and hopeless. At 15, he's now a physical giant, if emotionally stunted. Special Ed classes. But there's a secret: Christy's much smarter than that. His quiet demeanor has been mistaken for mental deficiency. His father, a meth-head, and his grandmother, the madam of

Edgewater County. Quite a troubled background, living in his trailer park and playing his flight simulator game, an obsession. When he decides he's had enough of his Daddy, then he has a new problem: what to do with the body.

> **CHRISTY'S DADDY** — Identified only in this manner, what happens with him sets this storyline in suspenseful motion.
>
> **MAMIE 'MAMA' BEAUDOCK** — The legacy madam of Edgewater County, she runs a brothel that's been around as long as The Dixiana. Mama Beaudock's is out near the bump in the road called Red Mound. Why she's still allowed to be in business—who doesn't know about Mama B's?—is something of a mystery.

JASPER ALVIN GLASSCOCK

A small-town, small-time attorney, Jasper mainly handles poor clients from "across the tracks," which in the case of Tillman Falls and Edgewater County means across the Sugeree River in recently-annexed Easton. Jasper, when we meet him, is in much worse spiritual and financial dire straits than Roy Earl: at 60, his practice is unfulfilling and barely pays the bills, he's moved back home with his sister Letty. A musician, he only wants to play guitar and sing, but how can an old Southern lawyer make a living doing that? In his younger years, Jasper had been a bail bondsman and PI, as well as a published author: he interviewed homegrown serial killer Coy Wando from death row about all the other heinous crimes the murderer committed. After Jasper finished that book, he swore he'd never want to write another.

> **LETTY GLASSCOCK (also POV in *Dixiana Darling*)**— Older sister to Jasper; they have a very close relationship, one that will be clarified by novel's end to reveal that she's actually Jasper's mother. The truth had been hidden from him because of family shame over her becoming pregnant at 14.
>
> **OLD MAN GLASSCOCK** — Letty and Jasper's widowed father, a farmer with a sordid family secret Jasper has never known

MANFRED 'MANNY' THEODORE

Manny Theodore, 50, an ex-pat New Orleans resident driven out by Hurricane Katrina, as well as his wife's desire to return to her roots in order to care for an aging set of parents. His wife Neecie thinks that, among its many possible meanings and causes, Katrina was a sign that they needed to get out. After moving to SC, money they received from an insurance payout was used to purchase Lucinda's, the dying lunch counter on the town green in Tillman Falls, which they remodel and re-christen as Manny's On The Green, a restaurant and music club that mainly features Manny himself on saxophone, as well as the occasional touring act and open blues jam night. Manny, when we meet him, is in deep trouble: he's been foolishly unfaithful with Rebecca LaFreniere, a town stakeholder and member of the venerable Edgewater Ladies' Munificence Society—as is Manny's wife Neecie.

> **LILLYANNE THEODORE, 13, daughter** — Lillyanne, a lovely, intelligent young woman who disapproves of her father's behavior
> **BERNICE 'NEECIE' (DUCKETT) THEODORE, 42, wife** — She handles the discovery of her husband's infidelity, a recurrence, with an unusual approach
> **AHMAD DUCKETT, 40, brother-in-law** — brother of Neecie, Ahmad is a troubled ex-addict from New Orleans that Manny's giving a second chance. They butt heads frequently, eventually become unwilling roommates mixed up in the discovery of a large amount of money

TRUDY (PIRKLE) SAMUELSON

Rabbit's longtime bartender and manger of The Dixiana, 51, a one time lover of Roy's, when she was twenty and he was only sixteen! A heartbreaking experience for him, she has watched through Rabbit's eyes as Roy became a millionaire. Married to an aging, sickly biker, Trudy is terribly conflicted and unhappy. The Dixiana is all she has. When Roy fires her in retribution for her rejection thirty years before, their reunion turns toxic.

> **MICKEY 'SAMSON' SAMUELSON** — Trudy's husband of twenty years, and nearly that much older than her. A former motorcycle mechanic and member of the Pagan Knights biker club, Samson has a bad toe and bad knees and a big alcohol problem.

NON-POV CHARACTERS
Note: listed in order of relevance to the plot

HEATHER PONDERVIEW — wealthy heir to the Ponderview Trucking Company fortune, owner of a magnificent estate in the Smoky Mountains of western NC. Button's one time lover and Phish fanatic on tour, Button still pines for her. She will prove crucial to Roy's development and to Button's redemption. Crucial flashback scenes with Heather take place in San Diego, at Foothills State, on Phish tour.

CAUGHMAN HOWARD 'HOWDY' SHULL — The town crazy, 60s, walking the streets with his two liter bottle of ginger ale and babbling about ancient history, secrets, esoteric knowledge, and generally being that afflicted soul that every small town seems to have. It's sad a bad acid trip did him in. He will make new friends in Christy and Newbie, with disastrous consequences for Howdy and his sister.

REBECCA LaFRENIERE — 40s, a legacy matron of Tillman Falls society; old money, the town green is named LaFreniere Square. She's having an affair with Manny Theodore. She's secretary of the ELMS, runs the Palmetto Grande Arts Center, located in the old town movie theater. She left Edgewater County to become a New York theater actress, failed, returned to her home.

DOBBS VANDEGRIFT — paraplegic reporter/writer/ad salesman for the *Edgewater Advocate* and close childhood friend of Roy Earl's. He was in a car accident with Creedence's brother Devin in college, leaving him in the wheelchair.

The REV. ROOSEVELT NIXON, PhD — a contemporary of Roy Earl, he's running for Town Council now that the formerly unincorporated and traditionally black area called Easton has been annexed into Tillman Falls. Nixon has a a mega-church, a significant force in the community, and his Sunday sermons are broadcast on WABA. He has a large family, including son and presumptive heir to the Nixon pulpit should the Rev. win election to public office. He's been agitating for more political clout from "across the river" ever since the town annexed Easton into the city limits, a move designed to capitalize on a huge project going into the impoverished county, a regional distribution center for a discount retail giant. A key plank of his platform is controversial—to remove the reference to Pitchfork Ben Tillman, Nixon wants to change the name of the town itself. A high school friend of Roy Earl's, Nixon is also an Egyptology scholar with four sons: **Denmark Vesey**, **Eusebius**, **Syncellus**, and **Hammurabi**.

NEWTON 'NEWBIE' HARRELL — a former custodian at The Dixiana, Roy's first act as new owner is to fire him. Newbie becomes fast friends with Christy Beaudock, who will get him mixed up in the disposal of the body of Christy's Daddy.

ESTES PATEL — Assistant GM of the Carolina Beanery Sedge Island, 30, Creedence's younger lover and lead singer of rap-metal band Megalith

PHIL WEBHANNET — a Sedge Island cop and Army veteran of Afghanistan whom Roy will pay to keep an eye on Creedence, which makes her think the guy has a crush on her

RICO — an enormous white dog, a Great Pyrenees, for whom Roy will take responsibility

JOUQUOYA MOULTON — a pharmacist who will become Button's friend and lover

JEZMUND 'JEZ' REMBERT — Edgewater County's chief crime kingpin, the Southern mafioso if there ever were one: his hands are filthy, into drugs, prostitution, gambling. His father and Rabbit Pettus were once partners in the underground economy. Rembert will be furious about Roy's decision regarding the mural on the side of The Dixiana, and the threat of violence from this quarter is possible throughout the story.

THURMOND PIKE — He owns Pike's Bait, Pawn, and Motorbike, whose billboards covered in dollar signs can be seen for miles on the interstate. More importantly, he has a series of 'back rooms' where organized crime figures gamble and politic among themselves, a power center to rival that of the ELMS on the legitimate side. Pike rides a motorcycle in and out of scenes but doesn't have much of a role to play in moving the story forward, but what's disturbing is that he's married now to a trophy wife, one who happens to be another unrequited childhood crush of Roy's. He's like the "tricycle man" character from Altman's *Nashville*.

AGATHA OF ABERDEEN — a pyromaniac of a spirit who stalks the town and may be the cause of a number of historical fires. Grief-stricken over the death of her handsome British captain, Agatha, who had traveled from Scotland during the Revolutionary War to be with her love, she self-immolated in the middle of then-McBreeley's Crossing, forever after haunting Edgewater County

TRAVIS 'LUCKY' LATHAM (POV in *Dixiana Darling*) — friend to Ronnie Ed Pettus and Buddy Sykes, the third friend who went off to Vietnam, who like Buddy returned safe and sound

CHESNEE CAMPOBELLO — wife of Thurmond Pike, at thirteen she broke Roy's heart: there's no way her father, a recovering alcoholic, would allow her to date the grandson of the man who owned The Dixiana.

SHAROLYN MONTINE — Roy's GM at the Carolina Beanery Sedge Island, with whom Creedence will bond as a co-worker and receive both wisdom and understanding

CECIL WAUGH — The owner of Head Trauma, a tattoo, piercing and hair salon that took the place of the old barber and beauty shop on the town green. A former football player like Roosevelt, Cecil and his brother Harlem bullied and tormented Roy Earl. Adult Roy wants to recruit Cecil (and others, like Manny, Becky L, etc) to become part of a new merchant's association to challenge the old order represented by the ELMS, especially after he finds out how much Cecil has changed.

GAREN OAKLEY — Sheriff of Edgewater County, Oakley is a tough as nails Marine and veteran of Desert Storm, an African-American authority figure, but no less corrupt than some old redneck like Whardell Truluck, the man he replaced.

TIMMY TRUESDALE — a police Lieutenant to whom Roy will be 'assigned' for special attention after bribing Oakley

YAZID OMAR JUBOURI — An Iraqi refugee family who have made their way to Tillman Falls, SC, based on Yazid's friendship with an American contractor from the area, and who have managed to become the proprietors of a convenience store called the Gas Chief. Christy Beaudock is obsessed for a time with his daughter Aisha, and a controversy over a vendor license for the Rabbit festival will cause tension. (**Fatima**, wife, **Aisha**, daughter)

MADELINE 'MADDY' DURANGO — Maddy, along with her child-star twin sister **Vangie**, are one-time America's Sweethearts: Twin actress/singer/entertainers/activists. Maddy is friends with Button Sykes, who as a student worked on a movie shoot on the campus of Button's college, a remake of Disney's *The Computer Wore Tennis Shoes,* a reboot that also starred Karen Black, for whom Button worked as a PA

COY WANDO — Edgewater County's most notorious murderer, a killer of children in the late 70s who Jasper Glasscock interviewed on death row and wrote about. Wando claimed to have killed 'hundreds' and provided gruesome detail about these other murders, including his involvement in the Tragedy of '77, the mysterious drownings of six high school seniors in the river the week before graduation

COLIN KWOTH — Roy's handsome, outdoorsy business partner in the fruit-shake empire, and a potential rival for Creedence's sexual attention while on vacation together

GOV. SANDRA 'SANDY' THREE-RIVERS — two term governor of the state and Thim Sykes's boss, she'll give some key advice to Button: cut off those dreads!

EVERLYNNE SHULL-SCHLOSSER, PhD — Howdy Shull's older sister. A confrontation between her and Christy Beaudock will turn deadly.

ARTHUR BEAUCHAMP — Roy goes looking for the writer Cort Beauchamp and finds his brother instead, who reveals an unknown corner of Edgewater County: a survivalist compound.

PASTOR DUSON MIRE — a corpulent Baptist preacher, part of a group who once used to street-preach on Friday nights outside The Dixiana.

JOSIAH 'J. W.' REMBERT — Father to Jez, Josiah will have to do prison time for a shooting he commits during a civil rights protest outside the Congress Street Grille

RON NAWALINSKI — one of Roy's buddies from down on Sedge Island at 'the hanger' where the hobby pilots hang out. He has two key roles to play in the story: he recommends a hike, and gives Roy and Button a ride

HODGES 'THE COLONEL' RINGHOLDER — A Vietnam POW war hero and former jet pilot, he's a mentor to Roy down on Sedge Island at the hanger where the other retired and hobby pilots gather for bull sessions

CAL LUCHOK — another hanger buddy of Roy's

RUSS WETHERELL — AA sponsor to Creedence, a wise figure for whom she struggles with attraction, a big no-no in recovery

KIP EPPERTON, DVM — a Sedge Island veterinarian who dispenses advice to Roy while caring for Creedence's kitties

SISSY — one of Creedence's cats on Sedge Island for which Roy holds great fondness

COLE BREEDLOVE — a deacon in Pastor Mire's church, he'll reinstate the oldschool street preaching outside The Dixiana, but against Button and her free-speech tent on the town green

NORRIE SORTWELL — the former owner of the Palmetto Grande movie theater and influential figure from Roy's childhood, to others as well

PORTER BUCKNAM — a former *Columbia Record* writer and editor, Gooch's successor and new publisher of the *Edgewater Advocate,* with Dobbs Vandegrift taking over as EIC

SHIGEHARU 'SHIGGY' HAMASAKI — another of Roy's business partners, while on a golf retreat together Shiggy will procure salacious entertainment

SAMMY MACKLIN — another of Roy's business partners, and partner in crime with Shiggy

HANK HALVORSIN — another movie theater manager, this one to Roy when he worked at the multiplex while in college

RIP SHORLEY — a dishonest usher at the multiplex where Roy works in college

MAGGIE PASSANANT — a petsitter on Sedge Island whom Roy will retain to deal with the cats

FRANKIE 'FRIDGE' WASHINGTON — longtime head line cook at The Dixiana

ETNA DIXMONT — one of the kitchen workers at The Dixiana

Dr. KADAMBARI PATEL — cardiologist to Jasper Glasscock and mother of Estes Patel

RUSTY NEDDICK — a contractor skeptical of Roy's desire to rebuild The Dixiana exactly as it is now, only with materials to insure that it will last 'a thousand years'

KALLEN SWYGERT — a stereo salesman who hooks up Roy with a turntable, amp, and speakers costing forty grand

Dr. DAHLONEGA — a d0c-in-the-box whose misdiagnosis of Button's throat condition reveals nothing about Button's true medical condition

RODNEY COWAN—Roy's financial adviser, assuring him that money will always grow, and his money in particular. He ain't wrong. Money is never an issue for Roy Pettus, so much so that it's both fraught with meaning and yet meaningless.

FELICITY BELINDA 'FEEBEE' ELMENDORF — a colleague of Roy's from his time as the president of the Downtown Business Alliance in Columbia

RUTH DeKALB — éminence grise of the ELMS, mother to a former governor and a Hollywood voice actor

MIRIAM VANDEGRIFT — Dobbs's mother, in the local nursing home where Bill Wimmel will consider placing himself

ALICE FAITH WESTMORELAND — member of the ELMS, more Edgewater County royalty

RUFUS BINDERNAGEL — the DHS rep to the Rabbit Music Festival, he expresses a number of security concerns, in particular the vendor license application from Yazid Jubouri, whose family back in Iraq has ties to terrorism

JEREMY CHIMIENTO — Button's college attempt at heterosexuality, he'll get arrested with her on a visit to Tillman Falls

DR. ABUTO OLABODE — Maddy Durango's private physician, who helps Button Sykes get through a rough patch

HERBIE BERTRAM — a fellow Boy Scout who introduces Roy to smoking weed

CARLOTTA MALDONADO — Edgewater County Memorial hospital counselor, she wrote a twice-monthly self help column for the paper and helps Gooch

JENKINS — a security agent who assists Button with the recovery of her personal items from Sancho

CHAMBLEE — with Jenkins, he accompanies Button to the New York apartment of Maddy Durango

CASSI — a barista whose tattoos—FORGIVE and FORGET—spur Roy toward action regarding his marital problems

KUMARI KANDAM — a hippie kid living in the Heather Ponderview house in San Diego

CRUNCHY CAL — a hippie kid living in the Heather Ponderview house in San Diego

JUDGE HAROLD HARTSOOK — a back room deal with Button's granddad will pull her and Jeremy's asses out of their hometown pot bust

JUDGE SHULL — Howdy's father and an old-line Edgewater County power broker

OTILYA DUCKETT — an Edgewater County civil rights pioneer

EVAN TYGH — the Roy of Independence, VA, he pulls the F-150 out of a ditch on the side of a mountain where Roy has gone for a retreat

LATRICIA THEODORE — a naughty cousin of Manny's who introduces him to sexuality

ENOCH ROYAL — a teenaged street preacher who taunts Button at her free speech tent on the town green

CORT BEAUCHAMP — Edgewater County's novelist of note, his book *The Diary of Anna Dixon* plays a role in Creedence and Roy's relationship

ANNA DIXON — protagonist of Cort Beauchamp's novel-within-the-novel *The Diary of Anna Dixon*

DURHAM DOVER — second protagonist of Cort Beauchamp's *The Diary of Anna Dixon*

TUCKER — a big box employee who assists Roy with a TV purchase

RODRIGO — a big box employee who assists Roy with a TV purchase

MR. KARLANEY — a funeral director who assists Roy

PATROLMAN HERTFORD — a highway patrolman who almost shoots Roy during Rico's crisis over failing to stop for his blue lights

CALLIOPE GILDERBLOOM — an august elder of the ELMS who presides over a tribunal of one of its members

SKEEBALL — a Dixiana kitchen employee

DICKIE GIUFRIDDA — a member of Roy's childhood baseball team

HARLEM WAUGH — Cecil's twin brother, tormentor of young Roy

SHERM WRIGHTSON — Roy's little league coach

TIMMY LATHAM — son of Lucky Latham, and a positive baseball team member to young Roy

MARLON KETCHAM — a little league player who taunts Roy

STONEY MARCHANT — another little league doofus, the only player more inept than Roy

KAITLYN — a barista at the Carolina Beanery Sedge Island

BRENDA LaROSE — college writing mentor to Button

MARGARET TUGGLE — Roy's middle school yearbook editor and crush

GREG RINKER — handsome jock and rival for Margaret's attention

GLORIA GRAYMONT — Roy's high school newspaper advisor

KITTY BERWICK — Roy's 1st Grade teacher

MRS. GARFINKLE — Roy's yearbook advisor

COACH PEMBROKE — Roy's physical science teacher

MR. HALSEY — Roy's childhood barber

MR. BATES — Christy's high school science teacher

MRS. DUNWOODY — Letty Glasscock's fifth grade teacher and fellow survivor of the Sunbury School fire

LOTTIE — a cashier at Roy's college multiplex job, a brief romantic relationship

BENJ — an usher at Roy's college multiplex job

LENZA SPINNOZI — stylist at Cecil Waugh's salon 'Head Trauma'

SCOTT 'SANCHO' McKENDRICK — the head of Button's Phish tour 'phamily'

SHARAQUE — Creedence interacts with this doorman at the Sandflea rock club

SEDGE ISLAND CABBIE — returns money Creedence left in the taxi

RAY DEKALB — Tillman Falls native and now Hollywood voice actor, a celeb who attends the festival at the (presumed) behest of his mother Ruth DeKalb.

Mr. DeKALB — a presumptive forebear of the DeKalbs, Ruth and Ray, the builder of the ill-fated Sunbury School

AVALON —a hippie chick Spotted Banana manager

SHELBY FORDHAM — Roy childhood crush

NATASHA PROTHRO — Roy childhood crush

BEV LeSAGE — Roy childhood crush and dance partner

LaVISTA TUCKER — friend of Sharolyn who bakes cakes and cookies for the CBSI

DAVIS MACON — a 1960s peer of Josiah Rembert, known as a dogfighter

IDAHLIA — kitchen worker at Manny's on the Green

OLD NEECIE — kitchen worker at Manny's on the Green

SEAN PAUL — a former coffee shop manager of Roy's to whom he sold the original Carolina Beanery

MAULDIN SAUGUS — US Representative from the district that includes Edgewater County

MOUSAM 'SAMMY' BEANHOPPER — longtime member of Tillman Falls Town Council, the first African-American member and a legacy figure

DUWAYNE DRIGGERS — an oldschool Dixiana bartender, drug dealer, and friend of Coy Wando

Lt. WETHERELL — an officer under whom Rabbit served in WW2, possibly Russ Wetherell's father or grandfather

Pvt. MAHONEY — a corpsman serving with Lucky Latham

MARTY HARRELL — Newbie Harrell's grandfather, a gas jockey at Pike's

BLANDING MacDOUGAL — a local PI for whom young Jasper Glasscock once worked as an investigator and process server

CORDELIA KARLANEY — curator of the Edgewater County archives

UNCLE WALLY KITTERY — Runelle's uncle

CHESTER — a Dixiana bartender from Roy's youth

DR. WISE — town GP

Lance Cpl. LAWRENCE LAUTENSCHLAGER — the Sugeree River Memorial Bridge is named for this fallen highway patrolman

HISTORICAL OR LIVING FIGURES
WHO APPEAR IN THE TEXT

KAREN BLACK — Roy Earl has had a crush on her since adolescence. Along with a few other celebrities, she will be in Tillman Falls for the Rabbit Festival at the end of the third book.

GILLIAN WELCH — The musician plays the Rabbit Music Festival in Book Three

DAVID RAWLINGS — The musician plays the Rabbit Music Festival in Book Three

PAGE McCONNELL — Keyboardist for the band Phish with whom Button and Heather interact, albeit indirectly

GEORGE W. BUSH — After making a photo-op stop at a nearby US Army base, the President drops in on Trudy and Rabbit for The Dixiana's famous Broasted Chicken Basket

JOHNNY CASH — in 1969, on his way to a State Fair appearance, the country music icon stopped in and did a few tunes at The Dixiana, along with his wife and a friend

JUNE CARTER CASH — accompanying Johnny Cash

BOB DYLAN — accompanying Johnny Cash

GEORGE WALLACE — the presidential candidate makes a speech outside The Dixiana

JERRY GARICA — a pre-stardom Garcia and a friend attend a bluegrass jam at The Dixiana in 1962, where they get in trouble with Mr. Rabbit over recording

SANDY ROTHMAN — Garcia's friend and fellow bluegrass traveler

ABOUT THE AUTHOR

James D. McCallister is the author of five novels, a short story collection, and numerous other shorter pieces of fiction and creative nonfiction. A lifelong South Carolinian, he lives in West Columbia with his wife and beloved brood of cats, muses all.

CONTACT JAMES D McCALLISTER:
www.jamesdmccallister.com
editor@mindharvestpress.com

RETURN TO

James D. McCallister's

"EDGEWATER COUNTY, SC"

in

King's Highway

Fellow Traveler

Let the Glory Pass Away

The Year They Canceled Christmas

Dogs of Parsons Hollow

Dixiana

and

DIXIANA DARLING (2020)

RECONSTRUCTION OF THE FABLES (2020)

MANSION OF HIGH GHOSTS (2021)

WANDO (2022)

MHP

Mind Harvest Press

C O L U M B I A , S C

www.jamesdmccallister.com